VIRAGO

AUTUMN FLEMING

This book is dedicated to
Lin-Manuel Miranda

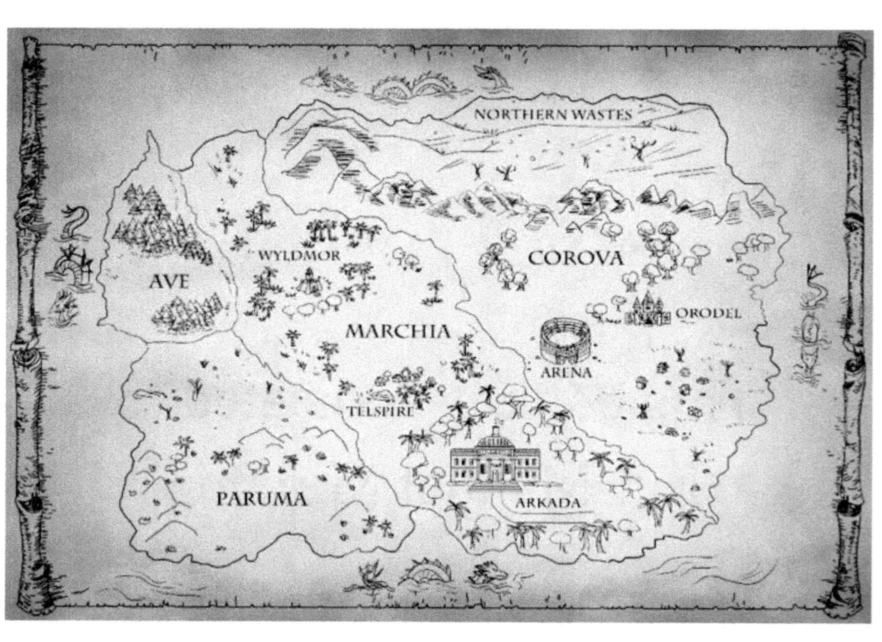

NORTHERN WASTES
AVE
WYLDMOR
COROVA
ORODEL
MARCHIA
ARENA
TELSPIRE
PARUMA
ARKADA

PROLOGUE

"Help!" shrieked the girl. Frantic, she whirled around, shouting her parents' names. The captain bellowed to his soldiers. The young girl could not discern his words amidst the endless screaming of her people, the crackling flames and the buildings that groaned with final effort before collapsing like warriors that could hold out no longer.

The night air whipped the girl's raven hair over her shoulder and into her face, determined to hinder her twisted path to escape. A man, his wife and two teenage children ran past the screaming girl.

The man reached down and grabbed her upper arm, pulling her along behind them. As she was dragged along, ash and smoke clogged her eyes until she only knew two things: darkness and flame.

She tilted her head to the sky, sucking in for air that was not soiled. The definite, stinging blackness retreated, revealing the sky above. She saw the stars far above the chaos. Far from the fire and everything that was wrong with the world. The stars remained, cold and bright. A symbol of everlasting peace so far from her reach.

The man's arm parted from hers in a jerking motion, bringing her back to this world and pulling her forward at an angle.

Her body splashed down in the mud. No, not mud. There had not been rain for a week. Blood.

The girl lifted her filthy head and before she could scream for the man to come back for her, she saw that several guards had cut him off. He drew a short sword and began swinging at the guards, shouting at his wife and children to go.

They ran. The girl watched as the man was run through with a spear. His body was thrust to the ground, the guard sliding the weapon dripping with blood out of the body like drawing a pin out of a cushion. Did these servers of the king have no conscience at all?

The man, one hand instinctively gripping his torso lifted himself up onto his knees and said something to the guards. One of them crouched beside him and grabbed a fistful of the man's hair. The guard placed the point of his dagger against the man's neck, saying something to him that the girl couldn't understand. The girl looked down into the puddle of blood seconds before the guard drove his weapon through the innocent man's neck.

Hands gripped her shoulders. She wanted to scream but the smoke made it impossible. She looked up to see a brown haired woman with a soot stained face and soft brown eyes gazing down at her. The woman was dressed in commoner's clothes. She had seen this woman before. She sold bread in the little market.

The little girl almost cringed when she saw the axe in the woman's hand. She held out her hand and the girl took it. The woman then lifted the girl over her shoulder and ran. She maneuvered quickly through the flames with no destination in mind other than safety. But escape was impossible. So many guards were there that an entire circle had been formed outside of the village. A guard swung at the woman. With a shout, she blocked the blow with her weapon and swung back, giving the guard a harsh blow in the stomach.

The bread woman backed up, brandishing her axe. The guards encircled her. She managed to hit a few with her blade but with the girl in her arms she stood no real chance against them. They knocked her to the ground, kicking the weapon away. The girl was snatched away from her. That little girl fought, kicking, clawing, punching and screaming but still she was overcome. A brawny guard carried her to a line of wagons that waited outside the village like mobile prisons. He tossed her inside.

And even though she was on the complete opposite end of the camp, the little girl heard the woman's cry as they drove her own axe into her spine.

✳✳✳✳

The sun was rising. The girl pried at the iron shackle on her bare ankle but it would not move. She wriggled and squirmed but all her attempts were fruitless.

The door suddenly creaked open, showing her the deep lines she'd gouged into the wood with her fingernails last night. The door creaked open. She tried to stand up but the chains allowed her very little freedom and she fell to the floor. One of the king's guards stood before her with a sheet of paper and a quill.

"Age," he growled.

She stared at him and gave no response.

"How old are you?" He said each word slowly so that she might understand.

"Six," she said before retracting to the corner farthest from him, curling into a ball.

"Name," he demanded.

"Aelwen."

✳✳✳✳

Pain was all she felt, all she could remember.

Orders screamed at her.

If she disobeyed, they beat her. They starved her, only giving her enough food to keep her alive. She agreed to comply.

They took her out and gave her a weapon. There was a woman standing across from her—a woman who looked like a servant of evil. She had a weapon. She ran at Aelwen, slicing. She turned and screamed. The woman cut Aelwen's arm with a blade and slapped her face. The woman told her to fight, but Aelwen did not want to fight. She wanted to be free.

That little, lonely girl slept all alone on the cold floor at night. She did not have a bed. Every morning the mean people woke her up early, walked her down long, dark halls and

6

brought her into large, shadowy rooms. They gave her pointy pieces of metal and told her to hurt them. They wanted to fight. Those mean people hit her. They made her cry and bleed. They tied her, whipped and cut her, but no matter what they did, that little girl would not retaliate.

One day, something happened. She didn't remember how it happened, all she remembered was finally snapping. After how long they had mistreated her, starved her, burnt and beat her, she had finally had enough.

That girl had been raised like glass—like a thing that was breakable and had to be nurtured and protected at all costs. Even though her family was poor, they made sure that their little doll was always safe and happy. When the girl was taken, she had no choice but to harden that glass, protecting her inner self from the harshness of their malevolence.

Somehow, something had hit that glass. Something tiny, something now forgotten, was wedged into that glass. When it was hit, a tiny crack formed. Again and again that same spot was hit and the crack widened and sprawled out like a spider's web until that glass covering completely shattered. The only thing left now was what those evil humans had been forming for all that time, the thing they had been trying to to break free—stone. Cold, hard, unfeeling stone. And flame.

Fierce flames of hot anger burst forth when Aelwen was angered and were concealed in an unbreakable case of stone when she wanted them to be. She had unbelievable control. Once she broke free, once she decided to show them what she was capable of, they did not relent. They continued to push her, to fight her until she could beat them with every weapon.

Every day the training intensified. Sometimes she was blindfolded, other times they would bind her hands, use gigantic fans to blow her unbound hair in her face, fill the room with mirrors to confuse her or even light the room on fire to force her to fight in complete chaos. They flashed lights and beat drums. She harnessed the raucous and melded it into a weapon of her own, forging the sounds into a symphony, a powerful beat to drive her onward. They made her wear all sorts of clothes ranging from fancy dresses and corsets to heavy jackets and winter boots. Sometimes they would make her fight naked. The trainers were building a killing machine they could unleash whenever they wanted.

Aelwen never went to bed until well into the night and rarely did she ever sleep. Once in a while they would take her outside so she could smell the air and feel the sun and grass. She never got to see the stars any more.

Every day and night that girl would get up and keep going. She would endure the shouts and swears, the cuts and bruises. She would go through the day, rarely making it through without a broken bone.

But she made it to the end. Every day.

In those few moments of peace she got, those moments before she fell asleep at night, she would remind herself of the reason why she kept going…because hopefully she was alive for a reason. Maybe there was a reason she was living the life she was. Maybe someday she would find her purpose and fulfill her destiny. Maybe.

CHAPTER ONE

Aelwen's arm was seized by grimy hands and she was thrust forward into the pit. She grunted, shaking her ebony hair out of her bronze face. A tall man of a solid build stood before her. His clothes were ragged with torn sleeves and frayed bottoms and he wore no shoes. Dirt covered almost every visible inch of him. There were pinkish spots on his upper wrists, marks that could only be left by manacles.

"What have we got?" shouted the man who had thrust her forward.

"Arbanon Welis," shouted a man from the other side of the arena. The man had two names; a northerner. People from the city and the south only had one, a name of their own which did not burden the people with the bearing of a second name that carried some sort of reputation.

Performing a quick deduction, Aelwen took in that Arbanon's sponsor was a royal guard, a Guildsmen as they were officially known. He was clean shaven and the sword hanging at his side was encased in an ornate scabbard, his clothes were fine yet ordinary. All of King Halmar's Guildsmenwore golden armor with fuschia markings. All of them. But beneath the armor they wore plain white tunics and brown pants, which was exactly what this man was wearing.

The guards were regularly sent out to scout the city and empty Filth Ditches— wide, barren stretches of land outside the city populated by impoverished rural Corovans. The people of the Filth Ditches often quarreled and violence arose. Homicide was just as casual as the everyday news to most people.

King Halmar sent his Guildsmen to the Filth Ditches that were becoming overrun with the scum that lived in them. The guards would capture as many people as they could, toss them in prison wagons and bring them to the king for judgement. The king would then decide if each person would become a servant of his, an Arenian—one who was forced to fight in the arena—whether he would give them a second chance to live in the city or if they would be executed. The king only had eyes for the large gatherings of filth who lived out in the sprawling countryside. He refused to recognize the horrible lives led by those who lived directly under the rule of his negligent hand.

So, this Guildsman was wanting some fun. King Halmar forbade his guards from getting sidetracked and ordered them to bring their wards to him straight to him. This one had attempted to take on the look of a commoner—except he had kept his jeweled sheath. He wanted them to know he was wealthy.

The Arena Master, Galarus, shouted across the arena, "How much?"

"Two gold," said the Guildsman, flipping a gold coin in the air. The Arenian had to keep her jaw from dropping—two gold. Two gold? The largest offer Aelwen had ever heard was sixty silver—but two—two gold?

"Alright," the Arena Master replied. Before she stalked forward, Master Galarus grabbed Aelwen's arm, pulling her back to him.

"Crush him," he snarled, pushing her out into the pit.

Aelwen shifted her feet in the sand that covered the floor of the pit. Ah, the feel of the arena. It was the best feeling she could remember, apart from those of her childhood which she would never experience again. The arena; it was where she had the most freedom.

She barely heard the Master shout, "Go!" over the sound of the blood pumping through her, the steady beat of her heart. The sounds morphed together, creating a thunderous symphony of destruction.

Arbanon barreled towards her. Usually the Master asked if the sponsor of the guest wanted weapons allowed or not. But he hadn't, so to be safe her only weapon was her hands.

Aelwen crouched, taking a defensive position as if she were going to let the man barrel into her. She shouted instructions to herself in her head. *Wait. Wait. Move! Now!*

Swiftly, she glided away from the man as if the floor of sand were ice. She brought her elbow down on his back as he passed. The point of her elbow was a weapon in and of itself—honed like a blade, hardened from years of training.

Arbanon grunted, leaning forward and nearly collapsing. Aelwen twirled, setting her hands on Arbanon's sides and preparing to throw him to the ground. One of his meaty hands reached up and closed around her leg. In a flash, Aelwen was on the ground and Arbanon was on top of her. Was he really that tall? He lifted a giant foot and brought it down on her chest. She took the weight, it barely phased her. She gasped for a dramatic effect. He wasn't wearing shoes. His mistake.

Aelwen clawed at the sand, raised a hand and dug her nails into his flesh. His skin was tough and leathery but her nails were tougher—another natural weapon. She flipped herself up onto her feet and swung at his face. He dodged and counter-punched at hers. She ducked and ran the side of her booted foot down his shin. That did it. Her opponent drew back, clenching his knees, grunting in pain.

Blood rushed from the wound and the torn skin hung limp—she tried not to focus on the gruesomeness of it. Aelwen flung herself forward, hitting a pressure point on the back of his neck, slamming into him hard. Then she crouched beside him, raised her elbow and drove it into his spine. He toppled over, tears streaming from his eyes, blood and water coating the sand.

He rolled about, yelling. Aelwen stood, raising her foot high into the air. And then she brought it down with full force on his face. He didn't scream that time—he was unconscious.

Aelwen raised a bruised brown fist into the air, hollering with victory. The guard was stricken dumb with amazement. Playing it cool, Aelwen blew the loose strands of hair from her face and walked back into the hallway that led to the Arenians chambers. Another coin earned. That was the deal; the Arenians got half of their earnings.

Aelwen sat on a bench, dabbing at her sweaty forehead with a wet cloth. Iowan took a seat next to her. "How was it?"

"I was expecting more, really," Aelwen admitted.

Iowan was Aelwen's best friend, her right hand warrior, and she was hers. Iowan was only a year older than her. She had pale skin and beautifully sleek blond hair. Her skin was covered with small brown freckles. She was easy on the eyes, even with the patch of acne on her right cheek.

Aelwen scratched the top of her head. "When are you going out?"

"I don't know," Iowan responded. "I think there are a few people before me. Business has been slow today." She sighed. "Two gold. I mean, *two gold*? Who bets that?"

"Someone who's in a tight spot at the moment and is desperate for money. Seriously, did you see his face when I beat Arbanon?"

"Yeah," laughed Iowan, the sound like honey. By some art Aelwen did not know, Iowan had managed to retain a warmth to her persona through all her years of violence. "It was priceless." She shifted in her seat uncomfortably.

"Man, you really want some action, don't you?" asked Aelwen.

"I want to get out there. Bailba comes today, remember?"

"What?" exclaimed Aelwen. "She's coming *today*?"

"Yeah, you didn't know? Galarus told us two weeks ago."

"Well, he should have reminded us again." Aelwen was sweating now. She stood abruptly, rubbing the back of her neck. She pulled her hair up above her head and tied it into a neat bun before walking away.

"Where are you going?" Iowan demanded.

"To change. If Bailba's coming, I'm not letting her see me in this." She pulled on the bottom of her dirty brown fighting tunic and entered another hall that branched off from the main chamber. Other Arenians passed by her, nudging her against the wall.

The room was a long oval with little doors around the edges. Each door was the entrance to an Arenian's room. There was another chamber of Arenian rooms on the opposite side of the main chamber. Both boys and girls shared chambers. A while ago there had been an argument that one chamber be for only boys rooms and the other for girls, but Master Galarus refused, saying they needed to get used to living amongst people of the opposite gender. He reasoned that if everyone could be civil with one another, there was no reason for concern over the issue. This was coming from a man who taught children to fight for a living.

Aelwen entered her room, which was straight across from the entrance to the chamber. Her room was small and packed with many things that were neatly arranged. Despite being a gritty person, she enjoyed finery. And being one of the Master's favorites, she got the most opportunities to earn coin, which she used to buy herself things of luxury. All useful things, of course. Mainly clothes.

She walked to her tiny closet which was home to many outfits. She wasn't even sure how she fit them all in there. What to wear, what to wear. She tried on a variety of outfits, all vastly different and extravagantly beautiful, finally settling on a black leather shirt and pants. One of her favorites.

She slid her feet into a pair of black leather boots. The only visible skin was that of her face. They said the more skin Bailba could see, the more she knew about you. Probably not true, but just in case...

Aelwen slid some daggers and two swords into the sheaths attached to the belt on her shirt. Aelwen examined herself in the full length mirror she had hanging on her wall. She swiped a bit of blood off of her sharp sepia jaw. She took a deep breath.

Bailba. Old Bailba. The old woman who came to the arena and examined every fighter. You did not speak, you stood perfectly still while she examined you. And when she was done, she would choose the best fighter and reward them. Every time the reward was different, but it was always something incredibly spectacular. But that was not what Aelwen feared.

Old Bailba was supposedly an enchantress who lived high on the summit of the Iron Peak Mountain in the Northern Wastes. That mountain was so steep and dangerous that those who dared climb it never returned. Not breathing, at least. But somehow that woman lived up there all alone, conjuring things and making potions and doing the gods knew what else.

She was a philosopher of sorts. When magic had been popular and sorcery deemed a fine art, before the mages had closed themselves off from the rest of the world to found their own country of Paruma, the magicians who had met Bailba called her the Dark Philosophess. She believed in true equality; when she chose the best she also chose the worst.

The one who was chosen as the worst fighter was taken to the butchering blocks and executed. Not openly. Secretly, in the deepest shadows, where their names would fade from all memory and no one would ever have any inclination to wonder about their fate ever again.

Aelwen didn't really expect to earn the title of the worst, but Bailba was strange and unpredictable. Even the best Arenians had that doubt in their hearts. There was a chance she could be picked as the best. After all, just today she had taken down a Snav in under two minutes and earned two gold, the highest price ever.

Aelwen exited her room, latching her door behind her. Namar, her closest friend after Iowan, was sitting on a bench near the wall. "That took long enough," he said. He was dressed for the judging in a dark blue suit with golden buttons.

"I didn't know you were waiting for me," she retorted. "I had trouble finding something to wear."

"You could have asked me. I could have helped you with the decision."

"I managed just fine on my own."

"I see that," he said with a smile, his eyes glinted like polished obsidian in the low light. "What do you think?" Namar asked, pulling his shaggy dark hair up behind his head in a ponytail. He pulled a golden ribbon out of his pocket and wrapped it around his hair.

Aelwen chortled. "No, no. You barely have enough hair to do that with."

"Alright, alright." Namar was laughing now, too. He stretched out a russet brown hand. "You wouldn't let me help choose your outfit, but can I at least escort you to the judging?"

Aelwen sighed overdramatically. "I suppose so."

She took his hand and he led her down the hall and into the main chamber which had hurriedly been cleaned up. A glance at the clock in the corner told her that Old Bailba would arrive in about five minutes. Aelwen joined the line of Arenians that stretched across the room. They were all dressed to the nines in outfits that suited them perfectly. Iowan stood on one side of Aelwen, Namar on the other. The highest earner elbowed Iowan. "Did you get to fight?" she whispered.

"Yes," Iowan muttered. "A scrawny little drunk, but I gotta tell you, that kid had a good punch." She tipped her head up to show a bruise on the bottom of her chin that was already fading. Iowan had chosen a white tunic with an embroidered skirt. White was definitely her best color.

Galarus gave a little grunt and all the Arenians straightened their backs as Old Bailba entered the chamber.

The frail old woman with a bent back and wrapped in pale blue rags stepped up to Namar. She set a long, pointed nail under Namar's dark skinned chin, tiling it upward. She moved her hand to his left shoulder, her face scanning every inch of him. Bailba's fingernail was going up and down the fabric on his upper arm.

She pressed the point of her nail into his skin and dragged it down with an awful ripping noise, tearing open the shoulder of Namar's suit which had certainly not been lightly paid for. She then pressed her nail into his flesh. Blood oozed from the little cut. Bailba squeezed Namar's skin until a drop of blood dripped onto the floor. She scowled at the drop on the stone floor.

Then, she moved to the right. To Aelwen.

Namar wiped away the blood that was beginning to trickle down his arm and stain the sleeve of his suit. He pulled the ripped fabric together in an attempt to stifle the flow.

Bailba made a hissing noise as she inspected Aelwen. Just as she had done to Namar, Old Bailba jabbed her finger nail beneath Aelwen's chin. Aelwen held her breath. Bailba pressed harder, so hard that Aelwen began wondering if the old woman would draw blood. With no blood on her fingers Bailba drew back and slid over to Iowan.

In the end, when Bailba made her selection, Aelwen was not chosen as either best or worst. Norson, one of the youngest Arenians, was taken away as the worst. And Armack, one of the older, skilled, sly Arenians was chosen as the best. Galarus decided not to release the details of Armack's prize, only saying that he would be rewarded extravagantly.'

Aelwen plopped down on the bed in her room, unstrapping her boots. "I can't believe I wasn't chosen as the best. I earned two gold today!"

Iowan began untying the fancy ribbon she had secured around her styled hair. "You earned that right before she arrived, maybe she didn't know."

"She's Old Bailba. The Dark Philosophess. She knows everything. Of course she knew." Aelwen removed her shirt in a swish of motion. "I think we should leave."

"What?"

"Seriously. Think about it." She pulled a stained shirt over her head. "We don't do a whole lot here. We fight and make money. We're only allowed to leave a couple times a month." She spat onto the floor. "If we're going to be alive, why not actually live? Why don't we leave, go far away and start over? All over, a new life and become whoever we want to be."

"I don't understand. You always said you liked it here."

"That's because I let myself believe I did."

"You're only angry because you didn't get chosen. Think it over," advised Iowan, her voice was gentle like bright sunshine, trying to shed light on Aelwen's darkness.

Aelwen sighed, "I *have* been thinking it over."

"How about we go and talk to Namar about it?" Iowan suggested. Serene, judicious Namar. Whenever there was a disagreement between them, they always turned to Namar for advice.

The girls entered Namar's room to find him lounging on his well-made bed, sipping out of a crystal flute and reading a thick tome.

"What is it this time?" he asked calmly. Namar had become used to both of them entering his room whenever they desired without knocking.

"Someone has a proposition," stated Iowan, looking hard at Aelwen who ignored her.

"Alright, let's hear it."

"You're probably going to want to sit up for this," Iowan said.

Groaning, Namar heeded Iowan's wisdom, marking his place in his book and setting his glass on his night stand. Despite being one of the most ruthless Arenians, Namar had exquisite taste in furnishing and accessories.

Once everyone was settled, Aelwen stated her case, staring at the wall. "I think we should leave."

Namar blinked. "Leave?"

"Yes. Run away from the arena."

Namar's mouth quirked up at the edges. He didn't seem completely opposed to the idea. "How did you come up with this?"

"Honestly, I've been thinking it over for months. I won't lie, when I was little, the Master was a god to me. He saved me, he made me strong, and he paid me and kept me safe. He still does, but I don't want this life anymore, I'm tired of it. I want something more…Something exciting. Tell me, honestly, that you don't."

Namar nodded slowly, satisfied that this was not a spur of the moment concept. He knew well that objectives like this took careful planning. "My life has become repetitive." He turned his stare to the wall as Aelwen had done. "I have been feeling for…a while that I have lost my sense of self. I have woken up some mornings and asked myself: who am I? and there are days I do not have much of an answer. My life is all shades, there is no color anymore."

Namar paused but the girls knew he was far from done by the yearning that shone in his polished obsidian eyes. "I would very much like to see more of the world. More than buildings, rags and dirt. To see the sky with nothing in the way, the whole sun unblocked by rooftops, fields that stretch on for miles." He laughed good heartedly. "Yes. I have thought of running, but I concluded that it was nothing but a silly dream. I didn't think anyone felt the same as I."

Iowan wondered, "Where would we run to? There is no place to go, Galarus would find us."

Aelwen answered honestly. "I have a few different plans. All of them involve us first entering the northern forests."

"We could cross the border to Marchia," Namar added. "We could experience a whole new culture, we could even visit Ave."

Iowan teased, "You don't want to go to Paruma?"

Namar scoffed. "Even *I* know better than that." The land of the mages. A realm of mystery and danger. The people who lived there painted themselves with the blood of those they slaughtered and built temples out of bones.

A new light came into Iowan's hazel eyes, something in her mind had clicked into place. "If we go to another country, we wouldn't just be saving ourselves from this life, but everyone else."

Both Aelwen and Namar looked to Iowan with interest, imploring her to explain.

"We can tell others about the state of Corova. Once they hear how bad it is, they'll want to help us. Our story could even reach people in high places if we spread it around enough. Imagine leaders of wealthy, whole countries helping us repair the lives of our people." Iowan was smiling the brightest Aelwen had ever seen. There was something new in Iowan after her small speech, something she was implanting in them all: an authentic hope. Not just for the three of them, but for their entire ragged, filthy, starving, scrappy, unscrupulous country.

Namar nodded in vigorous agreement with Iowan. "Aelwen, you said you have a few different plans. May I share one of my own?"

Aelwen, also nodding, heart pounding with exuberance, replied, "Go ahead, it's probably better than anything I've got."

"Do either of you know of the secret exit?" When both women shook their heads he went on. "It is a narrow passage, the walls are forged of steel and iron."

"Why?" questioned Iowan.

Namar held up his hand and continued. "The exit was built in case there was ever a raid on the arena. Say, if a beaten customer wanted revenge and decided to come back with a gang at their back. At the end of the passage, there's a door leading to the outside for escape purposes. The walls are fire resistant and cannot be broken by any of the weapons we have here. It's a completely safe and secret escape route."

"If it is supposedly so secret, how do you know about it?" Aelwen asked.

"Zilo and Cisli." Two of Namar's friends. "Cisli had heard rumors, Zilo and I didn't believe them. We went looking and sure enough, we found the passage."

"Did you go into it?" asked Iowan.

"Yes, the door was heavy but unlocked."

"Unlocked? Why?"

"I imagine that if there was ever an emergency, it would be a complete waste of time scrambling around to find a key. Anyway, we walked all the way down to the door at the other end. It opens to the northern training field. The woods aren't even a mile away from there. The Master has the same idea as us: if you need to make a quick escape, go into the woods."

Aelwen said, "Any idea for specifically when we should make our escape? Night, obviously, but which night?"

Silence fell as they all thought.

"Why not tonight?" asked Iowan.

Namar laughed.

Aelwen saw the sense in that suggestion. "No one is expecting it."

"Exactly," Iowan said. "That way we don't have time to risk letting something slide, we don't have time to doubt ourselves, change our minds or overthink it." Reasonable reasoning, especially coming from someone who had been opposed to the idea mere minutes ago.

"Tonight is a wonderful idea. Honestly, if we wait, I'll probably start crying as I look at everything I'm leaving behind." That was really saying something, especially for Aelwen.

Iowan, unable to keep that devious smile off her face, asked, "Are we crazy?"

Aelwen's eyes glistened as she replied, "Oh, yes."

CHAPTER TWO

Namar, Aelwen and Iowan slipped silently down the narrow halls of the Arenian chambers. All they had in their possession was a small bag each, filled with only the most necessary of items. They were fully armed and had chosen clothing that would best help them blend into the night—pale blacks, dark greys and blues.

Iowan whispered, "I bet the Master is going to regret teaching us how to move so silently."

"Shhhhh!" hissed Namar.

Aelwen just nodded in agreement with Iowan and continued along. Her legs were almost shaking and even though it was a rather cold night, sweat dripped from her brow.

Namar, leading the way, opened a door to what Aelwen had always assumed was a broom closet. The metal walls of the long corridor were unusually close together. They continued on for a long while. With each step, Aelwen's heartbeat quickened, her nerves dominated her further.

Namar stopped before a solid stone wall. He leaned against the wall, straining. The door swung open. He stepped back, giving them all a view of the night.

"And this, my friends, is the entrance to freedom." Namar declared.

They climbed out of the small door, holding their breath. Iowan whispered, "Good job," to Namar as he closed the secret door silently behind him.

Aelwen gasped as if it was her first breath of life. In a way, it was. She took in all the scents of the night air. It stunned her, like a cool drink given to someone who had been left to die under the heat of the desert sun.

Iowan gently touched her friend's shoulder, bringing her out of her thoughts.. "We'd better get going."

"You're right." Aelwen hoisted the sack of supplies in her hand up onto her shoulder. "Who knows how long it will be until the Master notices we're missing. Just… give me a second." She knelt beside the outer wall of the arena. Her friends could not see what she was doing in the dark. Out of her pocket, Aelwen drew a piece of flint and one of her most prized steel daggers. Setting her hand against the strong wood of the building Aelwen murmured, "You saved me. Thank you. Now it is time for me to save myself." She drew her blade across the flint twice, sparks sprayed and ignited the wood. Her home for the last thirteen years would burn tonight. It had to. She would not be returning.

Though she had sense enough not to scream, that did not stop Iowan from sprinting towards the building. Aelwen seized her friend's arm and yanked her back. Iowan pulled in the other direction, forcing Aelwen's grip loose. The hysterical Arenian tried to run again, half-dragging Aelwen along with her. Namar came running to Aelwen's side. Together, they restrained Iowan whose face was bright red and drenched with tears. Still sane enough to keep her voice low, Iowan sobbed, "Why?"

"They cannot find us," Aelwen explained.

"They will think we burned," Namar added soothingly, rubbing Iowan's back. "Someone will smell the smoke. Everyone will get out. They will be alright."

Iowan thrust her arm out of Aelwen's grip and punched Namar's shoulder, "How can you say that? You don't know!"

Namar winced but took the blow. Aelwen grabbed Iowan again and stared her down. "I did this for our country. We cannot go back. Get up. We cannot linger."

Pulling Iowan up and along with them, Aelwen and Namar sprinted into the woods.

It was not long before there were screams in the distance, coming from the arena. Aelwen wiped her eyes.

"I know," Namar said, "The smoke is getting to me, too." They shared a glance, knowing that it was not the smoke that caused their tears.

When they entered the forest, they slowed to a quick walk. Even though they were only a footstep inside the forest, the air was different. Everything was different. Giant trees rose up all around like pillars to the heavens. The stars twinkled between the gaps in the leaves, speckling the nightworld with faint luminescence. The air was rich with the scent of freedom. The feeling of the grass, soft and free beneath their boots, was…extraordinary.

Inside the forest, they left everything behind them. The horrors, the blood, the endurance, the screams and the flames. Those burdens would not help them now.

Aelwen looked about her to see the expressions worn by Iowan and Namar. Iowan, who had accepted the truth and realized that what Aelwen had done gave them all their best chance, was staring up into the sky, she too was thoroughly enjoying it. The bit of moonlight that cast itself upon them was caught in Iowan's hair, giving it a fascinating silver sparkle. Iowan's young face was meant for the night. All of her was.

Namar had stepped a few paces away and was slowly weaving between the trees, caressing their trunks as he walked by them. His dark curls were ruffled by a warm breeze, his deep brown skin blended with the darkness as if he too were simply a part of the night.

Roots and grasses beneath her feet sent a joyous shock through Aelwen. She had never been this far outside before, none of them had. The Master only let the Arenians into the town to buy themselves things with their earnings and before they left, the Master had to know where they were going. When out in public, the Master's spies were always watching. The only other time other anyone was allowed out was when a sponsor had paid the fee for the fight to be held at their own home or in a spot selected by the client that was not the usual arena. The Master said that there were people who would take pride in murdering an Arenian. Those whose fighters had been beaten would want revenge, especially if it had been a large bet.

Once in a while, under strict supervision, the Master allowed outdoor training in the field. His fighters had to be good on all terrains. In the winter, he would freeze a pool of ice and make them fight on that. He would bring in planks of wood and balance them on uneven surfaces and make the Arenians train atop them. Aelwen had excelled at all of the challenges he had thrown her way.

The trio traveled deep into the wood. In the dark, without an absolute sense of direction, there was only so fast they could move.

Hours later, when the world had a pale glow to it, Iowan proposed that they all sleep for a few hours.

Aelwen agreed. "We've traveled far enough."

"What if they know we're gone? We should keep going," Namar argued.

"We have been on the move for hours," Iowan said. "They must think we're dead by now."

"I don't care what you want to do, I'm sleeping right here, right now." Aelwen lowered herself to the ground. No one had brought any bed rolls so the ground would have to do.

Iowan followed Aelwen's lead and laid down herself. Namar looked down at the women with disdain, arms crossed. Iowan grabbed Namar's pant leg and tugged, causing him to stumble. "Sleep!" she ordered. "Stop worrying. We're free now."

"If a butterfly goes past at least one of us will hear it. You know that," Aelwen grumbled as she shifted about to find a comfortable position.

After waking a little past midday, hunting and cooking themselves a decent meal, the three ex-Arenians headed off again.

"You know, this is our first day of freedom," said Iowan.

"Yes it is," said Namar. "Do you have any special plans? Because I vote we keep moving before the Master finds us." His voice was tense, his dark eyes had an unusual wildness to them. It was clear he had not slept well. Namar had not been alright since they had made their break.

For the first time in a long while, Namar was scared out of his wits and without a clue how to express it. Aelwen stepped in, attempting to mitigate the crackling hostility. Contempt between themselves was the last thing any of them needed. "You want to cover more ground, Namar? Let's run."

"Run? We haven't got a clue where we're going, why would running help?" Namar snapped.

"Like Ae said, we can cover more ground. Running is fun. I think it might help us wear down our negative emotions as well." Iowan looked quickly at Aelwen, who flashed her a smile and nodded in agreement with Iowan's remark.

Aelwen ran. Her keen hearing picked up the sound of Namar and Iowan's footsteps close behind her. They ran between trees, over streams and around protruding roots. It felt like flying. As her heartbeat sped up, her feet joined its rhythm. Aelwen's long strides carried her across the ground at amazing speed, speed built from all those years of training.

Her body maneuvered its way through the forest, instinct guiding her. She focused on breathing in and out, on listening to the loud, rhythmic drum of her heart in her ears, and taking in the trees that flashed past, the whistle of the wind around her head and the strong scents of the wilderness. Her soul song was something completely untethered, totally wild, unbound by the rules of the arena or the temper of the Master. Every note was hers alone.

The company slowed after some miles without a clue where they were. Now that they'd stopped, they realized they were barely breathing. Iowan flung herself to the ground. Aelwen bent over, resting her hands on her thighs, before joining Iowan in the grass. Namar leaned against a tree, taking great, heaving gulps of air. Once Iowan had regained her breath, she began laughing hysterically. She curled into a ball, clutching her stomach. In a chain reaction, Aelwen started laughing, too. Even Namar smiled.

"What on earth is so funny?" Aelwen asked.

Iowan took several steadying breaths and sat up, her eyes wet with joyful tears. She waved her hands around her head as if she were swatting at flies. "This! All of it! We're absurd! Look at us!"

The run had affected Iowan in the same way it had Aelwen, reaching deep into her soul. Where it had cleansed Aelwen of all worry and thought, it had brought more questions into Iowan and caused her to become more aware of everything.

After the hysteria passed, Iowan and Aelwen went to find out their position while Namar took the duty of finding them a decent meal. They were free, but free did not mean safe.

The women returned within half an hour to find that Namar had captured several fish. They'd found that the king's castle, Orodel, was visible in the distance. Miles away for sure, but visible. Travelling any farther West, they would be brought deeper into the woods and bring them in the direction of Marchia. Heading East would bring them towards Orodel. South would eventually bring them to the arena. North would, in time, bring them out of the thick of the wild and onto the brutal tundra near the coast that made up the Northern Wastes. But that would take a very long time. West was their best bet. If they were being pursued, as Namar stated, the forest would at least provide some protection.

Exchanging glances, each of them saw the wild glint in the others' eyes. They ran on.

Feeling overwhelmed them all. That strange, magnificent wildness coursed through their veins, clearing their minds while also filling them with chaos.

As she ran, Aelwen sensed footsteps behind her, pattering along the ground. She figured it was just Iowan, who enjoyed trying to outrun her long legged companion— and had even succeeded a few times. Something felt off, Iowan's presence was as familiar as her very own and this one was not. Aelwen focused and listened hard. One, two, one, two…she counted the rhythm of her footsteps. Softer behind her was the same rhythm and near to that one there was another and…another. Guests.

Aelwen continued steadily, not adjusting her speed. Should she make any change, if she slowed or quickened her breathing or her pace, her pursuer would notice. She continued on, one, two, one, two…at the last moment she slowed her pace drastically, dropping behind Iowan and Namar. The pursuer, taken by complete surprise, fell back as well. Aelwen reached out, her arm wrapping around a tree trunk. Using basic physics, she swung herself behind the tree. The stranger, still behind her, did not have enough time to stop before

Aelwen stuck her arm out. The pursuer's head collided with Aelwen's arm. The Arenian wrapped her fingers around her pursuer's collar, yanking them behind the tree with her.

Her pursuer was a small female with short black hair pulled back into a small ponytail. The girl thrashed, trying to kick the Arenian off her. Aelwen already had a knife positioned at the girl's throat. She thrust the knife forward in a flash of quicksilver. Her attacker was quicker, dodging her head to the side then ramming her head back, slamming it into Aelwen's chin. Aelwen's teeth clicked together and the tang of iron filled her mouth. The next thing she felt was pain as the attacker hyperextended Aelwen's elbow, forcing her to drop the knife.

Aelwen ripped free and turned to face her pursuer. No fear shone in the woman's eyes. Before Aelwen could think to say anything, the woman attacked, bombarding Aelwen with punches. Aelwen's trained eye had her dodging blows before she could register them. Aelwen swung wide, her fist hurtling for Ponytail's head. Ponytail's size was her advantage; she was out of the way in the blink of an eye, behind Aelwen and bringing down a strike upon her shoulder.

Right on a pressure point. Aelwen doubled over for only a moment, but was back in proper combat position a second later, beating the pain from her mind with the steel rod that was her will. Ponytail whirled back in front of Aelwen, her boot meeting with the Arenian's knees. Aelwen could not stop from collapsing, grinding her teeth against the pain that surged through her legs in vicious waves.

Not broken.

She positioned her legs beneath her, prepared to stand despite the storm of pain. Ponytail threw herself upon her, one arm around her neck. No human's hands were that cold. Out of the corner of her eye, Aelwen could see the polished silver of a well cared for blade, pressed against her own scarred flesh. She kept her glare steady as she felt her own blood trickle down her neck.

"Sorry," the girl whispered into her ear. "I can't have any distractions." Aelwen felt no pain as her world went black.

Sunlight. Plentiful rays of golden sunlight greeted Aelwen as she came to. She groaned and took in her surroundings, squinting in the intense light. Her knives were at her side, as was her sword. She laid on a wooden bench. The room she was in looked simple. Plain wooden walls, dirt floor, stone fireplace contained a small fire, dark wooden rafters, a table with a clay bowl, some chairs, nothing out of the ordinary. A simple, homey cottage. Or so she thought, until her eyes hit the man standing on the other side of the room. His skin was pale like Iowan's. He was powerfully built—broad shouldered and well muscled with a sharp jaw and an intense stare. He had auburn hair that brushed his shoulders. He said, "Lysia, she's awake."

Aelwen heard a sound and turned to see a young woman, about her age by the looks of her. She was short and of a slight build, with bronze skin, narrow, angular eyes, a round face and black hair just long enough to tie back into the tiny ponytail she wore.

Anger flashed through Aelwen. Groggy, she tried to sit up, baring her teeth in a snarl and reaching for a weapon at her side. She stopped dead at a shooting pain in her side. She laid back down, exhaling heavily. She closed her eyes and concentrated on breathing as the pain spread throughout her body and slowly dissipated.

Lysia looked the same as before only calmer, gentler. She had a bruise on the right side of her jaw and her hair was messier. A bunch of hair had come loose from her ponytail and was laying across her forehead, giving her a rebellious look. She and the pale skinned man both wore plain attire, simple, functional tunics and pants of olive green and light brown.

Across the room, sitting on a plain wooden bench, were Iowan and Namar. Both appeared unharmed, satisfied to see their friend awake and alive. Surprisingly, they appeared completely calm in the home of their captors.

Regardless of the pain that coursed through her, Aelwen shoved herself into a sitting position. She knew that, in her state, physical combat was not possible. Lysia cautiously approached Aelwen, stepping lightly as if afraid that a loud step may cause Aelwen to go berserk. Neither of Aelwen's friends spoke. The captors had threatened them, no doubt. "Easy, kid. You're in no danger."

"Where am I?" Aelwen growled, her voice overflowing with barely restrained, full-fledged anger dark as endless night. One would have thought she was a wild woman rather than the urban trained fighter she was.

Her dark-haired captor shuddered and moved back a step. Aelwen's eyes were stone. "In our home in the deep forest of Corova."

"What have you done to my friends?" Aelwen's barbaric tone did not shift.

"As you can see, I have done nothing to them."

"They would not be here if that were true."

Lysia sighed. The auburn haired male, who appeared to be Lysia's companion of some sort, had not made one single action to help her answer these questions, he simply continued to lean against the doorframe, arms folded, wearing a blasé countenance.

Lysia explained, "We were saving you. We saw you running and thought you were fleeing from the Guildsmen. We both know from experience how brutal they are. Neither of us would wish for our worst enemy to end up in their clutches. We wanted to offer you sanctuary. Once I knew that you were aware of my presence, I had to stop you from warning Iowan and Namar."

Aelwen was disgusted at how nonchalantly Lysia used their names, as if they had been friends for all their lives. Lysia continued.

"After I took you out, together we convinced Namar and Iowan to come with us. We told them what we had done to you, they understood."

Aelwen's eyes had grown less dark. She stared hard past Lysia at Iowan for justification of the woodswoman's claims.

Iowan, accustomed to the many differing stares of her lifelong friend, vindicated. "They led us here unblindfolded, they haven't bound us. They've fed us and showed us around. They told us that if we feel uncomfortable we may leave. These are not bad people, Aelwen."

That was all Aelwen needed to hear. When it came down to it, Aelwen would always trust Iowan's judgement more than she trusted her own when it came to human nature.

Her head beginning to throb dully, Aelwen asked Namar, purely out of curiosity, "They told you what they did to me and you still trusted them?" Namar was the most cautious of them all, he often made poor decisions because he overthought the consequences. Based on what Aelwen had heard, Namar never would have trusted Lysia and her friend.

"I trust them," Namar stated. "They told us why they did what they did to you. If these people are, in fact, liars, they are very convincing."

He spoke as if the two owners of the house were not in the same room as he and his rebel friends. "They stopped you to save us all. If you had warned us, they feared we would attack them. If we were to be caught by the Guild, we'd be executed."

"And we never would have forgiven ourselves," Lysia added.

"They told us their stories," Namar continued. "They know the raw terror of our country just as well as we do."

Feeling much more secure than she had minutes ago, Aelwen turned her attention to Lysia once more. "Why am I in such pain?"

"Sorry, kid."

Aelwen bristled. *Kid?* "You were better than I expected. The other two didn't even notice I was running behind, couldn't have you going to warn them."

"Yeah, I guess you made the right choice. If I had beaten you, I probably would have slit your throat. What did you do to me?" Aelwen hadn't felt anything hit her over the head and she had no large wounds. She hadn't felt anything, everything had just gone black.

"Used this." Lysia walked to the table and picked up a long needle. Shiny silver, sharp point...a hair pin. Clever. "The end was poisoned. I always keep them on me in case..." she twirled the pin in her fingers and set it back down. Not a bludgeon. A weapon that would leave no mark, just sheer pain. This woman was smart. Perhaps too smart. "In case I come across a real challenge." Lysia knelt back down in front of Aelwen. "Oh, and we know your name. Your friends told us, Aelwen."

"I don't care about that. Are there more of you?"

"No, just the two of us."

"What's his name?"

Lysia did not need to follow Aelwen's gaze to know who she spoke of. "Taran."

Taran raised a hand in welcome, no grin passed over his face.

"And what are you two? Siblings? Lovers?"

Lysia huffed and rolled her eyes. "Acquaintances."

"How long have I been asleep?" Aelwen shifted a bit, pain fluttered through her body but it was weaker than before. Who the hell lived off the grid with someone who was nothing more than an acquaintance?

"Almost a day."

Aelwen grumbled but she wanted to scream. A day? That was so much time wasted. If Lysia and Taran had actually been dangerous, they could have killed them all. They could have tortured her friends and she would have been able to do nothing.

"I admit that's longer than normal. Your body must have needed the rest." Lysia stood up. "We can talk more later. You need to rest some more."

Rest? Was she insane? After sleeping for a day, Lysia thought she needed more? "No." Lysia, who had been walking away, pivoted back, astonished.

Aelwen swung her legs off of the bench, her attention again upon Namar and Iowan. "We should fight them."

Lysia's face contorted.

Iowan and Namar were both in immediate agreement with Aelwen. Iowan explained to Lysia, "We were Arenians. It's how we get to know people."

"What can a fight possibly tell you that we haven't already?"

Namar spoke up. "A fight is up close, it's personal. It's all about thinking on your feet, no time for hesitation. You might not understand it, but we do. We know how to read people by their minute actions." He paused for a second, watching Lysia with anticipation. When no answer came he said, "Well?"

Without consulting Taran, she accepted the challenge. "Weapons?"

"Yes," answered Iowan.

"We will meet you outside in five minutes." Lysia and Taran left to find weapons, leaving the three rebels alone together.

"I'm sorry," said Aelwen, staring at the floor. "I never should have let them capture me."

Namar's eyes widened. Iowan exclaimed, "What are you talking about? We're perfectly safe."

"I know, I know." Aelwen did not lift her head. "But what if they were bad people? If they had wanted to kill us all, they would have succeeded! You weren't there. Even as skilled as I am, Lysia had me out in a couple seconds. You could have both been killed and I wouldn't have been there. I should have fought harder." She took a steadying breath. "I should have been better."

Iowan hurried forward, kneeling before the bench Aelwen sat on. Her honey sweet voice was unwavering as she said, "Don't you blame yourself for this. I know you. I may not have been there when Lysia took you out, but I know you. I know how you fight. Lysia must have had many cunning maneuvers to beat you. I know she had a secret weapon and the element of surprise. Stop blaming yourself, that won't help anyone. You will fight harder next time. I know it."

Aelwen nodded, allowing Iowan's words seep into her soul. "Yesterday…that was my first time ever fighting anyone who was a real threat. Not to me or my career, to my heart. To the only two people I love. I panicked. If I had faced Lysia in the arena, things would have been different." She was speaking to herself now, not caring whether or not Iowan or Namar were listening. "I have to try harder next time. There is no other option." She rose up, making eye contact with each of her friends. She nodded in a silent command that said, 'let's go', to which they responded by standing up and following her out into the yard.

The yard of the small cottage was larger than Aelwen had expected. Rays of sunlight warmed her, streaming down from the bright blue sky above. She still savored the scent of the wilderness, so far from the crowded city that teemed with the odor of alcohol, smoke and waste.

Aelwen was suddenly struck by the realization that she felt safe. For the first time in forever. She knew, deep within herself, that Taran and Lysia possessed no bad intentions. She was about to enter a fight but felt no threat. For this was not a vicious fight, only a way of getting to know one another.

A warm breeze drifted through, the warmth of the sun wrapped around Aelwen like a blanket. There was no one coming for her, no one forcing her to do anything. There was simply her and her intentions. Intentions which she had the complete freedom to alter, to wipe away entirely if she wished to. Everything was okay.

Exiting her reverie, Aelwen watched Namar draw his own sword and give it a skillful twirl.

She did the same, relishing the confidence that came when she had her hanger blade in her hand.

"So Taran actually does talk?" she asked Iowan, who followed the lead of her friends, brandishing her gladius.

Iowan replied, "He says a few words here and there. Lysia is clearly the one in charge. My guess is Taran has had a few too many bad experiences in his life, that's why he's so aloof. My—" She said no more as Taran and Lysia approached, weapons in their grasp.

"Who's fighting who?" asked Lysia.

Iowan quickly said, "I've got Taran!"

Since everyone wanted to watch everyone else's match, Namar, Lysia and Aelwen leaned against the wall of the house while Iowan and Taran faced off.

"Who do you want to fight?" Aelwen whispered to Namar.

He simply shrugged and said, "I don't know. I'll have to see them each demonstrate their styles."

Taran was either overly confident, a marvelous warrior, obsessed with intimidation tactics or unbelievably stupid; he was wearing no shirt, displaying his large, toned chest. His pale skin gleamed in the sun. His muscles almost protruded from beneath the skin on his arms.

"Do you think looks are going to stop me?" growled Iowan, stalking up to Taran.

"We'll just have to see."

Taran swung his claymore at Iowan's gladius. Iowan whipped her sword out of the way and swung the point towards him. Taran leaned out of the way of the gladius and made to strike again, but he didn't see Iowan's foot sweeping under his ankle. Taran growled at the strike and stumbled. Aelwen smiled. Taran was stunned by the move. Iowan's strength had always been a surprise.

There was a whirlwind of blades and Iowan ended up with Taran on the ground, his claymore five feet away, the point of her gladius angled at his throat. She moved forward slowly, watching his eyes to see if he planned on reacting. Taran reached up and grabbed for Iowan's arm, the one that was not holding the sword. Iowan got out of the way and hit him in the calf with the side of the gladius, then dropped her weapon as she simultaneously dropped to her knees and pulled out a knife.

Taran fought back and somehow wound up bringing the knife down on his opponent whom he had prostrate on the ground. In a series of maneuvers, Iowan slipped past him, got to her feet and ended with his knife pressed against his spine and an arm around his throat, hand holding his chin up.

"I think I won," she muttered, backing away.

"I get Lysia," demanded Namar suddenly.

"What's the matter? You afraid to face off against him?" Aelwen teased.

"No, I want to learn Lysia's style. If she can take you down she must be good. You don't mind?"

Aelwen chuckled and shook her head, "Not at all, go ahead. I'll take Taran." Her friends always forgot that she had known them for far too long to not be able to see past their white lies. Sometimes Aelwen wished that Namar would just confess his fears instead of trying to hide everything away.

Namar and Lysia stepped out next. Namar, armed with a shamshir, against Lysia, armed with a makhaira sword. They took a moment to size each other. Once they moved, there was no stopping them. Motion occurred every instant, without ever a pause in the fluidity of the gracefulness of the combat. Each and every advance, collusion, deflection and aversion was filled with thought and purpose, the fight overflowed with a feeling of inner strength. It was what many would have called 'the match of a lifetime'.

It was Namar who emerged victorious. He probably would have been overtaken by Lysia had his life not been devoted to bloodshed.

While Lysia and Namar had been battling, the onlookers had all been too engaged to comment. When the confrontation was over, Iowan whispered to Aelwen, "If I didn't know any better, I'd think she was one of us."

"Indeed," Aelwen said, dragging her gaze from where the mesmerizing fight had just occurred to Iowan. Joy was radiating from her golden haired friend. A good, in depth fight always pleased Iowan, but Aelwen was not sure she had ever seen her companion look upon a battle with such pure elation.

Aelwen pulled out her hanger sword and marched towards her challenger. "You really should wear a shirt. It might offer you some protection."

"My skin's like steel," Taran said, grinning devilishly.

With a quick flick, Aelwen had a dagger in her hand and slashed Taran's chest. The cut wasn't deep or long, but it bled. "It looks like steel bleeds."

Taran hardly winced although pain filled his eyes. He towered over her by nearly a foot, and Aelwen was known for her height. Ludicrous men, thought Aelwen. Always so wrapped up in their outer image, how intimidating they looked that they oft forgot to look to the inside, to perfect inner image that no one saw but that everyone perceived. It was the beauty of that inner image that was the key to combat success.

"No weapons," Taran growled, watching the blood drip down his chest. "Hand to hand combat."

Did Taran think this would give him some sort of advantage? He clearly possessed no knowledge of the variety of training Arenians received, the fighting forms they worked until they were perfected.

They dropped their weapons. Taran's fist sailed at her head. Aelwen sidestepped and rammed her fist into his side. As she dodged blows and delivered them she imagined the clashing of blades. In hand to hand combat there were not such rhythmic noises. Sounds had always helped Aelwen control herself. In the arena, weaponless battles were commonly requested. No matter what sort of fighting she was performing, Aelwen made sure to keep that rhythm in the back of her mind, using it as a sort of support beam, a rope that tied her motions, her motives and her mind into one killing whirlwind.

Strike, dodge, turn, hit, no contact, strike, brace, kick, counter.

The fight was coming to an end. Both were breathing heavily and their actions were slower. Aelwen had had enough of fooling around. She was ready for this fight to end. She punched at Taran, who turned out of the way and directed her away from him. He brought a hammer strike down on her back and she took it, recoiling, rising up and ramming her fist against his chin. His jaw clacked loudly at the strike. Not wasting time, Aelwen threw her elbow into his face.

Those were the blows. The best ones. The strongest ones. Taran stumbled back, holding his face, blood gushing like a waterfall from his nose. Aelwen herself could feel many bruises forming and her nose stung from a previous blow she had failed to avoid. Taran bellowed and charged forward, landing a strike in Aelwen's stomach. His other fist came straight for her head. Aelwen grabbed the coming blow and flung it down, throwing her fist at his face.

Taran caught the blow. Time was frozen. They shared breathing space. Blood still ran from the his nose and Aelwen's body ached all over, the muscles in her jaw were trembling. She did not push against Taran and Taran did not thrust Aelwen's arm back. They just stayed there, breath mingling. Taran's eyelids sagged, he sighed. He was convinced the fight was over.

Aelwen ripped her wrist from his grip and punched him forcefully in the neck.

He recoiled, bent over himself and dropped to his knees. Aelwen grinned. Victory.

"Hey!" Lysia called to Aelwen. "Want to go?"

"In a minute. I need to breathe." Aelwen leaned over, hands on her knees, panting. She felt her nose swelling and hot liquid filling it. She didn't need to see the blood drip onto the grass to know her own nose was bleeding. Gods, she hurt. Her stomach felt like there was a cobra around it. She flopped onto the ground. Her throat was raw, her knuckles were bleeding, as was her bottom lip, and her shoulder felt like someone was driving a spike through it.

Taran was up and leaning against a tree. He had given up trying to look attractive and calm. He had both hands clamped around his nose, blood leaking between his fingers and spilling over his bare chest and onto the ground. Aelwen could hear his raspy breathing. He coughed and blood dripped out of his mouth. The cough intensified. He removed one hand from his nose and clenched his stomach. A bruise was forming on his forehead.

Meanwhile, Iowan approached Lysia. "Aelwen's going to need some time to get her strength back. Want to fight me instead?" Iowan's hazel eyes were large and filled with hope. She clearly wanted to take on this graceful, unnaturally skilled combatant as soon as possible.

Lysia smiled back. "You've all had a chance to fight us now. I think it's quite clear that Arenians will outdo us every time."

Iowan chuckled. " You're really good at fighting. Where on earth did you learn how to do that?"

A good hearted smile of appreciation bloomed on Lysia's face. She had not received a compliment in a very long time. "I used to live in the city. One of my friends set up a self-defense class. It was secret, we only did it at night, anyone was welcome. I learned a lot there."

"Do you practice with Taran?" He was good, but not nearly as good as Lysia.

"Seldom. He's not one for combat."

Iowan nodded. Awkward silence bloomed between them. To break it, she said, gesturing at the wooden cottage "You and Taran built this house?"

"Yes," Lysia replied curtly.

"Did you make all of the things inside of it? The benches, tables, windows, beds, all of it?"

"Oh, no. We stole those," Lysia said without sympathy. "Together, Taran and I went back to the city. We disguised ourselves and took from those we knew had objects to spare but were not so well off in terms of brains."

Iowan was not at all taken aback. She was, in fact, quite impressed at how much Lysia and Taran had managed to steal. "How did you manage to get entire beds and window panes?" laughed Iowan.

Humor in her voice, Lysia replied, "Night time, when the owners are out. Lots of the wealthier folks have entire rooms they set aside for guests that they don't even use, those are the easiest rooms to steal from."

"Ah," said Iowan.

Lysia cast a glance at Aelwen, who was still lying on the ground. "Should we go and see how she is?'

Iowan huffed. "No. Should we go and see how he is?" she nodded in Taran's direction.

"No."

"Why not?"

"He's in pain, bleeding everywhere and he just got beat by someone he barely knows. He's pissed as hell, I'm not going anywhere near him."

"Precisely," said Iowan. "I am in the exact same situation. Aelwen might have the thrill of victory on her side, but she's in just as much pain and, trust me, she needs alone time to recover."

"Where did Namar go?" asked Lysia.

"Probably to the bathroom?"

"I'll go look for him. I've nothing else to do."

"I'll come."

Inside of the cottage, standing in front of the fireplace, was Namar, eyes on a black pot he had hung over the fire. It was clear from the aroma that there was some sort of food in the pot.

Namar ignored the arrivals, wiped his hands on a rag, picked up a long-handled spoon and began to stir whatever was in the pot.

"Who gave you the right to cook in my kitchen?" demanded Lysia. Her voice was pointed but there was no real anger in it.

Namar balanced the spoon on the edge of the pot and turned to face her. He stammered for a moment, his face becoming an expression of panic and confusion. "I—I just thought that uh, since everyone seemed done fighting, I would, uh, make us some lunch. I mean, Aelwen and Taran are out there practically dying, you two were having a perfectly decent conversation and I had nothing else to do, so I just thought…"

"Calm down. Geez, Iowan, is he always this nervous?"

"Yeah," Iowan lied coolly.

Namar was the composed one, the wise, wordy decision maker. Iowan just said 'yes' to play along, and after she spoke she prayed that Namar knew she didn't mean anything by it.

Lysia swaggered over beside Namar. She bumped him out of the way to get a look at what he was cooking. She stirred the pot and took a taste. She winced at how hot the food was. "Good, good. I'd say add a bit more salt. You want Taran for culinary expertise, though. I don't know much about the cooking process, but I am an expert in the consuming process."

Cachinnating together, the young women went back outside.

Namar came outside with a tray of food a few minutes later. Everything was just as it had been when he had left it, Iowan and Lysia chatting as if they were schoolgirls, Aelwen and Taran both simply breathing, recovering. Namar was the extra, the one who didn't share an experience with anyone else, but he was okay with it. He enjoyed doing small, simple deeds for his friends that they appreciated. He was not an adventurous, glory seeker like Aelwen or a daring, amiable person like Iowan. He was Namar, the one who was invisible to those who did not truly know him. Those who truly knew him being Iowan and Aelwen, his two closest friends. But the ones who truly knew him could not live without him. Or so he thought.

At the sight and smell of food, Taran, who was still managing to stand, toppled over, pulled himself onto all fours, and wretched all over the ground. Namar walked over to Aelwen. "What did you do to him?"

"I put him in his place." Aelwen sat up. She had accepted her wounds a while ago and had just been lying there, drowned in her own thoughts and dreams for most of the time.

Namar asked, "Seriously, Ae, what did you do to him?"

"I don't know exactly. It was like any fight, you know? Everything else just dissolves and you go into survival mode and don't really remember anything until it's over. We both did a number on each other, though." Aelwen's lip had split again. She wiped away the blood. "If I get lucky I won't vomit up this meal."

"It wasn't supposed to be that violent."

"He asked for it."

"We don't want them to hate us," Namar said.

"They don't." She turned her attention to Iowan who was chatting with Lysia, both of them laughing and smiling.

Aelwen did in fact throw up her meal later that day. Taran never even ate. He went inside to his bedroom and they only saw him once. He left his room hurriedly and they heard him throwing up and he ended up sleeping in the bathroom.

Iowan, Aelwen, Lysia and Namar ate dinner at the table. Roasted chicken and some watery gravy with a bit of squash.

"We don't plan on staying here for a long time, you know that?" Aelwen finished her food, praying that she would not vomit later. It was time to talk business. They had been here for long enough.

"Where do you plan to go?" That loose lock of hair still lay over Lysia's forehead. The rebel look it gave her fit her well.

"We don't know," Aelwen explained.

Iowan added in, "We were thinking perhaps Marchia."

Namar immediately shot her a look. "We don't even know that for sure. It was just an idea. We weren't serious about that, were we?" He spoke quickly, trying to cover up Iowan's words.

Taran and Lysia seemed trustworthy enough, but he had no intention of them accompanying his little band of friends on their escape. He had heard their story, Lysia and Taran too had fled from the demon government, and there were few reasons for them to remain here in Corova. Why would they not wish to escape, especially with the advantage of having three fully trained Arenians to protect them along the way?

"We're not positive, but it sounds like the best idea for now." Aelwen stood up and moved to the bench she had awoken on. "We'll talk more tomorrow. Think about it tonight. By tomorrow, we'll have a plan and act on it."

CHAPTER THREE

Lysia dashed across the room, gathering together a sack of apples and bread. The morning light was just beginning to break into the cottage. "Quickly now. Quickly."

Aelwen, who had already been half awake, sat bolt upright. In a hushed voice she said, "What?"

"There are Guildsmen," Lysia said, sweeping to the other side of the room, opening a chest and digging through for some suitable clothes. "Not far from here, coming this way. They're all around, if any of them move they could come upon us. We cannot flee, if we do they may see us. Come, hurry."

Namar was already up, awakening Iowan as Aelwen shoved things into her sack. "If we cannot escape, why do you keep saying 'come'?" he asked.

"Taran will draw them off." Indeed, Taran was the only one not present.

"So then we'll be safe. We needn't run," Namar said.

"We cannot risk it. We know the guards are searching this area. They have great maps and a good sense of direction. They will remember they have not been here. They will come back to search."

Iowan was up. She tossed a cloak over her shoulder. "Even if we're not here it's not like the house can become invisible."

"No, but we can make them think it is abandoned." Lysia lifted up a chair and smashed it on the ground. "We'll make it look old, worn down." She tipped another chair over, kicked one of its legs, splintering it and then threw a clay bowl onto the floor.

As they all hurried about the house, breaking things and strewing them about, Lysia asked, "Why are the Guildsmen looking for you? The Master has no army of his own last I knew."

"He and King Halmar are friends," Namar answered quickly.

Aelwen added, frustration filling her words, "I don't understand why Guildsmen are out here. I burned it so this wouldn't happen, it doesn't make any sense."

Namar replied, "Nothing does these days," as he dropped an apple onto the floor, stomped on it and propped open the lid on the sugar jar.

They stood by the door, legs ready to run. Iowan asked, "Where's Taran?"

"He's fine," Lysia said, examining the house one last time and rushing out the door to make sure that nothing outdoors suggested recent inhabitants. Returning in a flash, she elaborated, "We had a horse tethered at the back of the house. Taran took it and is riding away, distracting the guards."

"Is he mad? There are Guildsmen all over, he'll be caught." Aelwen was already starting for the door. She had to stop him, if that man got caught and gave them away—

"Relax." Namar stepped in front of the door, pushing Aelwen back. "Taran and Lysia have lived here for years. They know paths the Guild could never find." Seeing that Aelwen had calmed, he stepped back.

Lysia, attempting to help Namar's cause, said, "He's riding to the top of a hill. He's going to light a torch and throw it. Hopefully the smoke will distract the guards and draw them off."

Staring intently through the window, Iowan announced, "He's coming back."

"Good. How far is he?" asked Lysia.

"About a half a mile."

"We still don't know where we're going," Namar pointed out.

Aelwen replied, "I've got an idea."

The thundering of hooves was heard from outside the door. They watched Taran dismount before the horse came to a stop. He gave the steed a slap on the rear and it galloped away swiftly. "They took the bait," he said. "Let's get out of here now!"

They all sprinted through the forest at full tilt, Aelwen leading them.

It wasn't until they neared the forest's edge that they stopped running. The company came to the place where there was more space between the trees and the clean, fresh air changed to the dirty, musty air of the capital city. "Where are you bringing us?" asked Lysia. "We're awfully close—"

"To Orodel, I know. That's my plan."

"Why?"

Aelwen ignored Namar's question and trudged on. He repeated himself, more authority in his voice. "Why, Ae?"

"So we can escape."

"We can't go near there. Galarus is looking for us, which means Halmar is looking for us. There is a price on our heads."

"Galarus must think we're dead by now."

Namar gave her a no-nonsense glare. "Do you think those Guildsmen would have been out there if he did not know?"

"We don't know it was us they were looking for."

"Don't play games. He knows, so Halmar knows. Those two are thick as thieves, I don't need to tell you that. We're some of Galrus' best fighters, you think he'll give up looking for us? He won't."

Aelwen quickened her pace. Namar got in front of her and grabbed her by the shoulders, halting her. "What are you doing?" he demanded, his voice shaking. "Are—are you out of your mind? If he finds us, knows we are alive and left on purpose… We. Cannot. Go. Back.”

“What can anyone do? We grew up in the arena. We know all their tricks,” Aelwen said. She tried to sidestep him, but he blocked her path.

“We might be the best, but we’re still only three.” Namar had not counted their two new companions.

“If you don’t want to come with us, then leave! No one is making you come with us!” She shoved her way past Namar and this time he didn’t stop her.

“Fine!” he shouted as the company followed Aelwen. “You can go! All of you! Be captured! I’ll go on to find freedom and none of you ever will!”

With that, he turned his back on the rest of them and ran in the opposite direction.

Aelwen shook with anger but she did not turn around. She would not.

The company of four walked without talking. There was tension between them all—an unspoken fear that Namar was right.

The city was coming into view now—uneven roads and inns and crumbling houses. Drunks, prostitutes, beggars and children wandered the streets.

“Corova,” Lysia said. “Just as I remember.” She raised her head to the sky and located Orodel not so far away. “I haven’t missed you,” she added before stepping out into the cobbled street.

Corova. The land in which they all had been raised. The kingdom ruled by a harsh king who taxed his people greatly, using the money for his own benefit and filling his castle with the finest of things. All while he sat alone on his throne and stared out over all that he owned, grinning devilishly at the effect of his great power.

As the small company wandered down the street, their faces down and covered with their hoods, Taran said quietly, “What has happened to make you all so weak? Why do you not retaliate against Halmar?”

Iowan and Aelwen exchanged glances, deciding which of them would explain.

“He took us as children,” Iowan said. “Burned our homes and killed our families. We know what he is capable of. No one could face a monster as terrible as him.”

Aelwen led them across the civilization. Calling it a city was a disgrace and calling it a town or a village was not fitting.

“Will Namar come back?” Iowan suddenly asked.

“I don’t think so, no. And I’m not sure I want him to.”

A silence fell on the group.

To break it Lysia said, “I’m surprised there aren’t many Guildsmen out. The way you all talked I thought they would be lining the street.”

“The Master is a smart man,” said Iowan. “If anyone knew where we were they would hand us over. Guildsmen would just be a waste.”

“Take a look at this,” Taran called to them. Nailed to the side of a tavern was a piece of paper billowing in the wind.

It had decent drawings of Namar, Iowan and Aelwen on it. Beneath the sketches was a reward and where to turn them in if they were found.

Lysia let out a low whistle. “That’s some serious cash.”

"We're valuable," Iowan said.

"That must be true," Taran stated bluntly. "Looks like Namar was right about one thing, the Master doesn't think you're dead. In my entire life I've only seen a quarter of this amount of gold."

Aelwen was about to rip down the notice when she glanced behind her and saw a man and his wife walking down the street. If they saw someone tearing down a wanted poster word was bound to get about and suspicion would arise. So she left it where it was and hurriedly led them down a few back alleys until they arrived at the wharf.

A large ship was tethered in the harbor and there were already men about it cleaning it and readying it to sail. Leaning against the pole of a dock was a tall, handsome man with russet brown skin and stunning deep brown eyes.

"Gavnas!" called Aelwen, still keeping her voice little more than a regular tone.

The man straightened. "Hello, missy."

Hearing that nickname, Aelwen bared her teeth in a fake growl, then approached him with a smile. "Is it ready?"

"Aye. She's almost done. I'm afraid I can't get her to the docks, water's too shallow. If I have the crew bring her around I might be able to get her closer, or I could get you a canoe to take out there."

"We'll take the canoe. Here you go." She dropped some coins into the seaman's broad hand. "Thank you, Gavnas. Really. You have no idea how much help you've been."

Iowan lightly set her hand on her best friend's shoulder, a signal that she wanted to talk in private. Aelwen wrapped up her conversation. "Ready that canoe. Namar has despaired. We have an opening on the ship if you'd like. Think about it, you've got until we return."

The three others led Aelwen around the corner of the nearest building.

"What have you done?" asked Iowan, her voice nearly shaking with excitement.

"I contacted Gavnas. He's got us a ship. We're going to take it to Marchia."

"Why didn't we just walk there? It would have been a couple days' journey but still easier than sailing." Lysia shifted slightly. She clearly wasn't fond of the notion of water travel.

"Two reasons. One: on land we have more of a chance of being caught. Halmar has the men and horses to follow us, what he doesn't have are ships. Two: the main reason, this is more of an adventure." Aelwen saw Gavnas lowering a canoe into the water. "We've got to get going." She began strutting towards the dock, then turned back to her friends. "None of you happen to know how to sail, do you?"

Iowan shook her head and chuckled at Aelwen's recklessness. Lysia sternly shook her head, clearly not finding this funny. "I do," said Taran. "Not very well, but I can manage."

Using Gavnas's hand to steady her, Aelwen stepped into the rickety boat. The others followed. "I've decided to come," said Gavnas. "My crew would also like to come, if that's alright with you. We can man the ship and at the end of the road, we will have our freedom."

Lysia muttered to Taran, "It doesn't matter what we think, only Queen Aelwen." She rolled her eyes at her last two words. Iowan had to hold back a faint smile as she overheard.

Aelwen was her best friend in the world, but even best friends had negative qualities. She had always found Aelwen a bit controlling.

Aelwen ignored the sniggering, pretending not to hear. She was a bit taken aback. Gavnas had agreed to send half or more of his crew with them and now the entirety was coming. "Of course. We can use all the man power we can get. Is the boat large enough for us all?"

"With a slight change of plans, yes. We won't take the boat I had prepared for you, we'll take my most prized ship. There will be room enough aboard her for all. And thank you. My crew are those who despise King Halmar. They will remain loyal to you, I promise."

As Aelwen nodded, an arrow flew over her head. The ex-Arenian was smart enough not to raise her head again. She rolled onto the base of the canoe, the others followed suit.

Gavnas spared a second to look over his shoulder before hurling himself into the boat as well. "Guildsmen!" he shouted, his deep voice echoing off the surrounding ships.

Sure enough, about thirty of the king's men, all dressed in fuschia and gold, were dashing to the wharfs. Many had arrows nocked to their longbows, firing rapidly while others were climbing in smaller boats and rowing out toward the escapees.

"Quickly!" panted Lysia, her throat tight, body beginning to quake. She had not been so exposed to danger in many long years.

"I'm going as fast as I can," growled Gavnas. The canoe bumped up against the side of the massive vessel. *Mist Wing* read the golden inscription on the shiny oak wood. Gavnas' crew tossed the ladder over the side of the ship. Crew members had already taken up bows and were shooting down at the attackers.

Taran lifted Iowan by the waist and pushed her up the ladder. Lysia followed and then Aelwen. A shaft whizzed past her head and stuck into the space between Aelwen's head and Lysia's feet. Above her, Lysia froze with fear.

"Move!" shouted Aelwen, swinging herself to the side to avoid another shot.

"The sails!" hollered Gavnas, pulling himself onboard. "Sails, now!"

The crew scrambled about and within moments the sails were lowered. The canoes of the Guildsmen were close now, too close.

In moments, Guildsmen were climbing up the sides of the ship and clashing with the sailors. Aelwen was one of the first to join the action. Her blood thrummed throughout her body as she cut through the people who threatened her escape. The intimate feel of using her daggers allowed her to stare right into the eyes of her prey, to watch the life leave them as they breathed their final breaths. Death was not a frequent experience in the arena, but she wasn't in the arena anymore. Those who fought in the name of the king deserved nothing. Anyone who was willing to fight and kill to contain the hopeless yearning for freedom and the starving longing for sustenance….

Aelwen hurled the body of a guard over the side of the ship, turned and plowed her dagger into the eye of an oncoming attacker. Swiftly, her blade met the chest of a brunette Guildsmen. She twisted the blade and took delight in doing so.

She pulled back from the fight for just a moment, taking in the positions of all of her friends. Taran was having no trouble cutting down his enemies and Iowan and Gavnas were faring well. Lysia flit swiftly around her opponents like a hummingbird of death.

Aelwen dove back into the raging current of the battle, her blades like a flame burning through a forest of soldiers. Someone was struggling to push down one of the soldiers. She rushed to their aid, plunging her dagger into the Guildsman's back. The body fell down, revealing a person unlike any of the others on the ship. This person was not wearing the Guild's pink and gold and they were not wearing the ordinary clothing of the sailors. This person had on a dark green fighting suit with black leather boots and a plum cloak which billowed out behind them in the wind, giving them an intimidating appearance. They had a strip of cloth wrapped around their face, leaving only their eyes exposed. But with the hood of the cloak, the shadows of the day and the face mask, Aelwen could not make out the eyes. This newcomer had been fighting one of the king's men, but did that instantly make them good?

"Help!"

The cry tore Aelwen from her wondering. She knew that voice better than any other—Iowan.

Aelwen whipped around, already sprinting in the direction of her best friend. Iowan was cornered against the edge of the ship by several Guildsmen, all of whom wielded vicious blades. As skilled a fighter as she was, Aelwen knew that no one could single handedly hold their own against so many attackers. Like a sudden gust of stormwind, the mysterious person with the plum cloak bolted past Aelwen. They dove into the group of Guildsmen gathered around Iowan and began slicing them down.

Seeing that her aid was not needed by Iowan, Aelwen ran round to the other side of the ship, killing all in her way, to see the guards leaping over the side, splashing into the harbor and swimming away as if the whips of the devil were behind them. She sprinted to the crow's nest and fastened an arrow to a bow she had stolen from a dead body. Her aim was excellent. Her arrows found their marks every time and soon the gray-blue water of the harbor was stained red. None would escape.

From her position she had a perfect view of all the happenings. Iowan was the one her eyes went to first. The crowd around her had thinned, but it was clear that her opponents were still giving her trouble.

Apparently unaware of that fact, the plum cloaked person ran their knife across their enemy's throat and bolted, breaking out of the semicircle of Guildsmen that, though diminished, still posed a threat. Aelwen did not watch where the mysterious person went next. She did not care. All she cared about was the fact that, even from high up in the crow's nest, she could see the panic growing on Iowan's face. She could see the desperate ferocity with which her best friend fought. Instinctually, Aelwen's hand went to her quiver. Her fingers clasped around nought but air. She repeated the motion. Still, nothing. Her arrows were gone. Iowan's attackers were closing in on her. For the first time in a very long time, Aelwen was powerless. She had no other weapons that could do damage from such a distance and by the time she had climbed all the way down from the crow's nest, the fate of the skirmish would be decided.

A sudden fervor seized Iowan. Her motions were swift as a coursing river, her aim as true as lightning. Aelwen's heart raced with hope. Iowan could make it out. She could. She would.

Iowan drove her blade into the gut of her final attacker. She whirled around to pitch the body overboard. The rest of the scene unfurled in slow motion before Aelwen's eyes. Just before Iowan tossed the person over the side, their hand seized Iowan's arm with an iron grip. The momentum had already begun. Gravity would not be deterred. The Guildsman fell over the side, into the scarlet water. And, with them, Iowan.

Aelwen was so enraptured by the horror she had just witnessed that she did not notice the person climbing up to the crow's nest until they were standing beside her. The need to kill engulfed the Arenian at the sight of the person's purple cloak. This person was responsible for Iowan's fate. This person had left her alone to fend for herself.

But Aelwen could not bring herself to kill them. Not until she knew who they were. Not until they knew why, exactly, she was killing them.

Aelwen slammed her elbow directly into the person's face. She felt their nose crack and their body slumped to the ground.

From her elevated position, her eyes found Taran. His wide blade clashed against his enemies'. He pushed hard and his opponent fell backwards. Taran quickly finished them and hurried to help a struggling sailor.

Guildsmen were climbing up the crow's nest now. Aelwen began to cut them down, one by one, all the while doing her best to keep her eyes on Taran to see how he was faring.

His sword was outstretched, inches away from the enemies' hip, when a blade was driven through Taran's back. It's dripping point broke through his flesh, jutting from his chest like a terrible mass of rock from the ocean. Aelwen did not scream, she knew it would do no good. She simply continued her own fight high up in the crow's nest, ignoring the blood dripping off the deck below.

The skirmish soon ended. The wounded were being brought below deck to be healed and the dead were hurled over the side. The ship was making its way out of the harbor.

As it did, Aelwen kept her eyes pinned on the water they were leaving behind them. She scanned the floating bodies and those who were swimming desperately to shore over and over again, praying she would see the familiar mess of dirty blonde hair that belonged to her best friend in the world. All she was were the gold and fuschia dressed Guildsmen and a few dead sailors.

Gavnas was leaning over the side of the ship, the wind toying with his dark hair, tossing it about. His face was set in a stern grimace, though she knew he enjoyed the sea winds. His clothes were stained with blood that was not his own.

"Dead count?" Aelwen demanded. Her heart was writhing in her chest. In her mind all she could see, over and over again, was Iowan being dragged overboard into the bloody water. She could not bring herself to mention any of that outright. She knew that if she did, she would break.

"Sixteen. Five wounded." That was half his crew. She could not help but wonder if he was counting Iowan among those numbers. She did not dare ask.

Gavnas pulled his head away from the sea breeze and looked her in the eye. She could tell what he was about to mention, and saw him think better of it as he realized how deep her grief ran. Instead, he said, "I'm surprised you are not below deck."

"Why? I have no knowledge of healing. I only know the basic herbs."

"Taran's down there."

Aelwen's eyes widened. "What? Are his injuries serious?" Of course, she had seen him be injured, but she didn't want to admit that to Gavnas. He would see her as a coward if he thought she had watched her companion be stabbed and done nothing, said nothing.

"Nasty, but not life threatening, they tell me."

"I'll go down and check on him, but first there's something I have to tell you. Come with me. Where's Lysia?"

"Down with Taran, helping clean wounds."

"Good. It's up there." Aelwen pointed up to the crow's nest. She and Gavnas climbed up. "Take a look at that." Aelwen gestured to the fallen body of the mysterious person she had knocked out.

A mass of dark curly hair had fallen out from beneath the person's cloak and was covering their face. Gavnas knelt beside the body to examine it. He did not uncover the face. "It's a male. Where did you find him?"

"I was fighting and I saw him struggling with a guard. I came over, took out the guard and saw him. He helped Iowan fight—" Aelwen's voice cracked a bit. She sealed the crack and continued, "For a bit, then he abandoned her when he realized their situation was hopeless. He came climbing up to the crow's nest after me. He wasn't one of your men and he wasn't one of the Guild's, so I knocked him out and decided I would bring up the matter later."

"Good choice." He pulled the hair away from the person's face revealing a pair of dark eyes and dark skinned cheeks. He pulled down the brown cloth. Namar.

How had she not recognized his outfit? She had seen him wear it a hundred times. Silently, Gavnas's cold stare met Aelwen's. "What do you want me to do with him?"

Aelwen said with an even, steady tone, "Take him below deck. Toss him in the dungeon. When he wakes up, don't tell him where he is. Keep him in the dark. As soon as he's awake, I want word of it, understand? Feed him, but not too generously."

Gavnas nodded. They climbed back down onto the deck. The captain signaled to some of his men that were on deck, cleaning up the mess of the battle, to follow Aelwen's orders. "I'm going to see Taran," she said to Gavnas, turning away.

It was hard to keep her legs from trembling. Her breaths got louder and shorter and her palms grew sweaty. *Stop, stop,* she told herself. *You'll figure out what to do. One of your friends is injured—you need to make sure he's alright.* Aelwen pushed open a door to the room filled with the wounded and their mourners.

Taran's cot was close to the door, making it easy to locate him. Lysia was kneeling beside him, round face wet with tears, muttering.

"We lost Iowan," Aelwen stated from the doorway.

"What?"

"One of the Guildsmen dragged her overboard."

"Did she survive?"

The asking of the very question Aelwen had not dared ask herself made her wince. "I don't know."

Aelwen approached. "Can I have a moment with him?"

Lysia turned her dark eyes and solemn face to Aelwen. "You barely know him." Aelwen noted the use of 'know' and not 'knew'.

"That means I cannot care?" she replied.

Lysia rose, "I will give you a *moment*. No more."

Aelwen's face was stone. Inside, she wanted to hug Lysia, but now was not the time. Aelwen nodded to her as she left.

Aelwen knelt beside Taran. She laid a hand on his chest; beneath the bandages she could not feel a heartbeat. She rested her head on his shoulder, breathing her words.

"I'm sorry. Don't die because of me." She had been so sure this plan would work, that this escape would be like those from the great tales of heroes. The crew slaying all of the king's men and the ship sailing, victorious, out towards the horizon, the rebels partying loudly on the deck. Why did real life have to be so different, so terrible?

Gods, Aelwen prayed, *I do not know if you hear me. I do not know if you exist. Do not let this man die because of me. I know it's my fault, I know I should have run to tell someone, I should have gone to help him...I should have come down. I don't know why I didn't. I regret it.*

Shame. That was what the gods looked for or so the masses claimed. They were often willing to take away a harsher punishment if they knew how deeply the maker of the mistake regretted their decision.

I regret it. I regret it. I regret it.

Do not let my freedom come at the price of this life.

As she finished her prayer, Aelwen wondered whether her words to the gods had only been about Taran, or if they were about Iowan, too.

Back up on deck, Aelwen found Lysia looking out at the water. "Why didn't you come get me?"

Lysia replied, "I decided it's best to let Taran rest. Rest is what will heal him, not our tears and prayers."

Hopefully Lysia was wrong. Aelwen shifted the focus of their conversation. "Did you see the fighter with the cloak and face covering?"

"Yes," answered Lysia. "Where are they? Does anyone know who they are?"

"You would have known him if you'd seen him," Aelwen stated.

It took Lysia a moment to figure it out before she gasped. "No! Namar?"

"Yes."

Lysia inhaled sharply. "What are we going to do with him?"

"Don't worry," Aelwen said calmly. "I have it figured out." She lowered herself and took a seat on the deck. She kept her eyes pinned on the horizon as Lysia took a seat beside her.

"Do you want to talk about it?"

Lysia's voice was gentle, warm tea and gentle rain. It was not the kind of comfort Aelwen needed. She needed Iowan, her right hand warrior, there beside her.

A long moment of silence passed between them.

"She was just gone. It happened so fast. I locked all over." Aelwen's voice broke. She didn't care. The person who mattered most to her in the world was gone. There was no one to stay whole for anymore. "She wasn't anywhere."

Tentatively, Lysia rested a hand on Aelwen's back. "She could have made it out. Maybe that's why you didn't see her. Maybe she'd already fled."

"If she did, they'll hunt her until they find her."

"I may not have known Iowan for long, but from what I did get to know of her, she doesn't seem to be one who would be an easy catch."

Aelwen wanted to smile at the truth of that statement, but the loss weighed too heavily upon her.

They said no more words. Aelwen shattered completely, tears streaked her cheeks. Her body shook with the strength of her sobs. Lysia wrapped her arms tightly around Aelwen, cradling her against her body, making it clear that, although Aelwen had lost one friend, she still had this one.

Later that day, when the sun had set, the sky was purple and stars began dotting the sky, Aelwen was given an update. Namar was awake and had been given a small bowl of old fish stew, bread and water.

Dressed completely in black, with a cloak for dramatic effect, Aelwen stalked into Namar's cell with her own feline grace. He was curled up in the back corner of his cell, hiding his face from her.

The room was small, the door had a slot in the top. There were cobwebs hanging loosely in the ghostly corners. Dismal was the perfect word. "Well, they really did give you the worst room, didn't they?"

Namar didn't make a noise or a motion.

"Talk to me," she demanded, her voice cold and hard as stone.

He still didn't react.

"If you expected me to come in here, kneel beside you and cry for you and thank you for coming back, you thought wrong. What you did was unforgivable. I thought I knew you, but apparently I was wrong. Now...I give you a choice. You can turn your sorry backside around and talk to me or you can say nothing and I will leave and make sure you never see the light of day again."

This time Namar moved. It was a clumsy movement for a usually graceful warrior. He rolled over to face the ceiling and pushed himself up onto his elbows. There was still dried blood around his nose, his left eye was black and swollen and his lip was bleeding, too. "What the hell do you want?"

His voice. Gods, his voice. She was so used to it being so incredibly calm, as if caramel were vocalized, but now it was raspy and cracked like the growl of a beast who hadn't had a drink in days. Aelwen tossed his own language back at him. "Why the hell did you come back?"

"I realized you were really going to get out of here and I don't want to stay here anymore than you do. Anything else?"

"Yeah. Why the hell did you leave her to die?"

Namar's face seemed to be engulfed by shadow. "I knew it was hopeless to keep fighting. We were trapped. I had two choices: stay there and die with her, or make it out while I could."

Who was this? That face. That voice. She did not know it. She'd had enough. Aelwen stomped out of the dismal room, slamming the door behind her. Back on the top deck, Lysia immediately joined her. "That was quick. What happened?"

"I'm not sure."

"Well, what did he say?"

"He said he left her because he didn't have a choice. He hasn't apologized."

"And what did you decide?" When Aelwen did not respond, Lysia added, "What's going to happen?"

"I don't know!" Aelwen tried hard to keep the snarl out of her voice, but failed. She stormed off.

Below deck, away from everything, which left her with herself and her thoughts. She had not stopped asking herself the question: *why does everything have to be so complicated? Why did Iowan have to be left behind? Why couldn't Namar say 'sorry'? Why didn't I rush to Taran's aid? I've always helped my friends before. What's happening?*

A cabin had been assigned to Aelwen earlier. Deciding that taking a look at her home for the next however-many days was a better alternative than doing nothing, she made her way there. As she walked along the planks, the ship seemed to wobble too much, trying to knock her off her feet. Thrumming filled her head, then it turned to pounding.

Many of the sailors were in their cabins, drinking and playing cards, laughing hysterically. She wanted to scream at them all to shut up. How could they all be so joyful when so much bad had happened?

Finally, Aelwen made it to her cabin. As she closed the door behind her, the ship gave a grand lurch, hurling her onto all fours. Using the bedpost, she tugged herself onto her feet. Apparently, her Arenian balance didn't stand a chance against the ocean. She slumped onto her bed and threw her sack against the wall. She'd unpack later. On the nightstand there was a bottle of wine with a note beneath it. She picked it up, swirling the liquid. It was the fine stuff. Before opening the bottle, Aelwen read the note. In pathetic, scraggly writing, it read:

For you, Aelwen. Use it as you will. You deserve a break from your troubles.

—Gavnas

She laughed mirthlessly at the note and flung it onto the floor, popping the cork out of the wine and draining a quarter of the bottle. It helped quiet the noises about her and calmed her aching heart.

Aelwen's eyes flashed open. She blinked, looking around. She hadn't even noticed she'd fallen asleep. The bottle of wine was on the nightstand, still a quarter of the way empty. She guessed the drink was stronger than she'd thought.

Waking, Aelwen found her mind muddled by the darkness around her. Slowly, the memories seeped back in. Frustration. Sorrow. Alcohol. She tried her footing and, to her immense delight, the planks didn't try to throw her off. The pain from the battle had subsided, as had the murk of questions that had nearly succeeded in suffocating her.

Above deck once more, Aelwen breathed in the exhilarating ocean air. It filled her up and, when she exhaled, it dragged the last scraps of her tiredness out with it. Innumerable stars winked at her from above, as if they were trying to tell her something.

Lysia was gone, as were most of the sailors, except for a few nightowls. Taran didn't need anyone coming to bother him, either. Just about to turn back down the steps with no one to quench her thirst for company, the rigid back of Gavnas caught her eye. His eyes were fixed on something in the distance she could not see. Perhaps he could not see it either, it was only his longing that kept his gaze locked for so long. Every time she saw him, he was staring out at the ocean. He loved it. It was his home, his freedom.

Aelwen stood next to him and leaned on the side of the ship, breathing in the sweet salt. "So," she said, but then realized she had had no reason to say it. She had nothing to say and no idea how to finish her sentence.

Gavnas looked at her out of the corner of his eye then turned his gaze back to the dark sea. "Freedom," he said.

And she knew he was right. For countless years she had dreamt of it and here she was, barely an adult and already on the road to freedom.

CHAPTER FOUR

They had been at sea for three days. Aelwen sat on her bed in her cabin, putting on her boots. Without a clock or a window, she had no way of telling what time it was. Not that it mattered very much, she supposed.

Tucking three knives into the weapons belt she wore, Aelwen exited her cabin and made her way to the top deck. Weapons really weren't necessary, but they'd become such apart of her presence over the last thirteen years that it felt wrong to be without them.

On the top deck, she found Gavnas at the wheel, just as she'd expected. He saw her before she had the chance to approach him. At the sight of her, Gavnas beckoned another sailor to take the wheel and headed in her direction.

That was one down, but where was Lysia? Aelwen scanned the ship, finding no sign of Lysia anywhere. Gavnas took up his position as her side. "Do you know where Lysia is?" she asked.

"Aye. Up there." The captain jerked his chin up at the crow's nest. Indeed, in it, was Lysia, a sailor at her side, pointing to something in the distance that made Lysia smile.

Aelwen gave a sharp whistle, drawing Lysia's attention to her. Lysia bid her sailor friend a quick goodbye and climbed down from her perch, joining Aelwen and Gavnas.

"Are we staying up here or going down?" asked Lysia.

"Down," Gavnas replied gruffly. "There's a meeting room down there. It seems appropriate for this discussion."

They followed Gavnas below deck to a circular cabin containing a table and several chairs. A large map hung on the wall, it had holes in it from where pins had been stuck. Gavnas drew out one of the chairs and seated himself. Lysia and Aelwen did the same.

Lysia took it upon herself to start the conversation. "So, what are we thinking? Who has ideas?"

"I do," Aelwen said quickly. From the moment they'd fled from the arena, she'd been pondering their exact course of action. "King Halmar must be destroyed. I've thought if over, there is no other way. To restore peace and prosperity to Corova, he has to die."

"I agree," said Gavnas. "But how do we convince the Marchian government to come and murder him?"

"We tell them the truth. If they want to help us, that's what must be done. Lying and making up grander reasons than that won't help us."

"From my knowledge, all politicians do is lie," put in Lysia. "If we want to earn their favor, a little lying of our own might not hurt."

Aelwen said, "These are Marchian politics, not Corovan. We're one of the worst examples out there. Just because our rulers get to the top by scheming and bribery doesn't mean all rulers do. From everything I know about Marchia, they're a decent, proud country with faith in their government."

"So, the polar opposite of Corova?"

"Exactly."

Gavnas said, "That's a problem in itself."

"What?" asked Lysia.

"We don't know Marchia. None of us. We've never been there, we don't know anyone from there. All we definitely know is that they're big and powerful. The rest is just speculation."

"I know that," said Aelwen. "But there's really no way for us to learn anymore until we get there, so we have to plan with what we have."

"Fine," conceded Gavnas, crossing his arms. "What's your plan to get Corova a new ruler after Halmar's dead?"

"I hadn't thought that far ahead," Aelwen admitted. "I didn't think that would be something to worry about until our first set of goals were accomplished."

"The ruler of Marchia is going to want to know," Gavnas said. "They're going to want a full plan from us, from bringing Corova from where it is now to making it wealthy and completely self-sufficient."

"The people should choose," Lysia said abruptly. "The next ruler, I mean. It's our turn to rebuild our kingdom, with rulers of our own choosing. I think that Marchia should rule over Corova for a while first. Let the city be rebuilt, stores open and lives be remade. Then, when everything's stable, the people can elect a ruler. There'll need to be supervision, trusted people on the inside to make sure there are no corrupt bargains."

Aelwen looked at Lysia skeptically. "Won't people see that as a threat? No native to one country wants to be ruled by another. People will think that Marchia is trying to get into the heart of our political system and overthrow us from within. People will be so concerned with the possible threat that they will turn their backs on what they should be doing and rebel."

Gavnas nodded. "Some would see that as a threat and it would be difficult to convince them otherwise, especially if it was Marchian soldiers who killed the king."

"Then we don't murder him. We take him prisoner," Lysia suggested. "Fake a raid, take the king."

"And do what with him?" asked Aelwen.

Lysia shrugged. "Whatever they want. He's no use to us dead, he's no use to Marchia alive." Lysia looked eagerly to the others, who traded glances.

"That seems reasonable to me," said Aelwen. She and Lysia looked to Gavnas for approval.

He stewed in thought for a moment before saying, "I agree. At least as a framework of a plan, it works." He drummed his fingers on the table before adding, "What are we asking the Marchians for, other than killing Halmar?"

"Money," Lysia and Aelwen said in unison. They smiled. Aelwen elaborated, "Even if they don't want to kill Halmar, the least we can do is get money from them."

"How much?" asked Gavnas.

"However much they're willing to spare. If they refuse to help us in any other way, with enough money, we can start making change on our own." Gavnas looked like he was preparing to say something, but before he could, Aelwen plowed on, "Money isn't the only thing we need from them, though. We need to get as many workers as we can manage from them."

"Workers?" asked Lysia, visibly confused.

"Yes. Carpenters, pavers, roofers. Government workers, too, to help stabilize Corova after Halmar is killed—er, removed. We'll need military strength as well, for the direct removal of Halmar."

Silence bubbled up in the cabin as they all thought through what Aelwen had said. After several moments, Lysia said, "Sounds like a good plan to me."

Gavnas nodded slowly. "Agreed. I feel like there are holes in it but...I can't seem to find any."

"Is that it?" Lysia laughed. "Did we really just sort out our country's problems in the span of a few minutes?"

Aelwen grinned. "New issues will probably come up along the way, but for now, I think we can work with what we have. Let's all pray to the gods that the Marchians agree to help us."

"I thought you didn't believe in the gods," said Gavnas, raising a brow.

"I don't," said Aelwen, rising. "But if I'm wrong and there's anyone out there who can help us, I want to be sure they hear us."

Aelwen examined herself in the full length mirror on the back of her cabin door. Her deep tan skin, lively, dark oak eyes, silky black hair and thin yet muscular build looked back at her.

She had never been one to obsess over appearances, but she was pleased with how well she looked now as opposed to the greenish tint she had taken on during the first few days as seasickness took her over. They had been at sea for sixteen days and had had fine sailing weather all the while. Aelwen spent most of her time below deck, training for hours on end. Freedom did not mean she would let her combat mastery deteriorate.

Lysia had become great companions with many of the sailors. Unlike Aelwen, Lysia had hardly been training at all. Apparently, this journey granted her the right to let her prowess falter. She spent their days in the sun, soaking it in, chatting with the sailors and learning their ways.

Namar still lived in his cell. He was allowed above deck under surveillance. No threats of violence had been made by him. A part of Aelwen wanted to set him free. Or, as free as one could be stuck on a ship in the middle of the ocean. When he did make an appearance, the sailors cast him withering glances. If the crew distrusted him, how could she? Not to mention, among the few words that Namar did speak, an apology was never one of them.

Taran would survive. At that news, Aelwen was sure she had never been more pleased in her life. He was on the mend. Always with a dedicated nurse at his side, he came up often for fresh air. Very used to serious injuries, Aelwen regularly visited him, giving him tips for the exercises the nurse had assigned him to increase his mobility after being bedridden for so long.

At the twenty-one day mark, Aelwen was growing tired of seeing the exact same things day after day, chief amongst them being her cabin, the kitchen and the large chamber packed with training equipment. She ventured to the top deck, where she found Lysia lounging on a woven grass mat with a group of sailors. Lysia had a wet cloth over her forehead and eyes.

"Are you okay?" Aelwen asked.

Lysia lifted up the corner of the cloth to peer at her interrogator. "Yeah, I'm fine, just really hot and the sun in my eyes is annoying."

"Ah."

Lysia grinned at her friend's sudden appearance. "You finally decided to join us."

"Yeah." Aelwen sat down on a free mat. There was no sound but the crash of waves and the creaking of the boat. Awkwardness filled Aelwen. For twenty-one days, to ward off her problems, fantasize about what would come and adjust to this new lifestyle, she had kept mostly to herself, training and eating and sleeping. Lysia had asked a few times if she was okay and Aelwen had always said she was 'fine' and brushed off the requests, wishing that Lysia would stop asking. Lysia, realizing her attempts to draw Aelwen closer to her proved futile, had spent more time with her new sailor friends who wanted her in their lives and less with the one who seemed to be pushing her away.

Such thoughts of her friendship with Lysia sparked remembrance of the greatest relationship she had ever known. Her friendship with Iowan. Aelwen's long training sessions were her way of coping with the loss of Iowan by distracting herself with physical labor rather than wallowing in her despair. But now, the floodgate had been opened and the thoughts came pouring in. No one could ever ask for a better friend than Iowan, who talked too much and had the best sense of humor in the world and gave great advice and was always there when she needed her. *Had* always been there. She was gone now. Maybe gone forever. But maybe not. Aelwen refused to forsake hope. For, if she did, what else would she have to hold onto?

Aelwen made a vow to herself. No, not only to herself. To Iowan. Someday, she would return to Corova. Stronger than she was now, she would return. She would face King Halmar. She would destroy him. Then, she would find Iowan.

Aelwen flipped over onto her stomach and watched Gavnas, captain of *Mist Wing*. She could not afford to think about Iowan any longer. It hurt too much. Namar had been a steady friend for quite a while, but now she absolutely hated him. Lysia had proved herself a worthy companion on this journey. It was Gavnas who still puzzled her.

His back was to her, but Aelwen knew that he was wearing his hard set scowl and his eyes were narrowed in focus on some distant point that only he was able to see. For a decent number of years now, Aelwen had considered Gavnas a friend. He was not the normal sort of friend, though. He was something different, like stone—steady and reliable. He wasn't someone to laugh and drink with or shop and share secrets with. He was a decent person in a crumbling kingdom who struggled to do the best he could for himself and those who confided in him, his crew. In Corova, decent people were hard to come by, so Aelwen had stuck close to the few she could find.

Even aboard *Mist Wing*, examining the sailors who sat with Lysia, Aelwen wasn't sure she trusted any of them to not pick her pocket if she were wandering down a dark alley. That was what made Gavnas so mesmerizing. He never laughed bawdily or slouched or appeared messy. Always, he stood erect and serious, his clothes were never wrinkled and he always had a shiny sword hanging at his hip. He was all hard lines and a cold disposition, he shook hands firmly but never hugged.

Aelwen enjoyed watching Gavnas move about, ordering sailors with his thunderstorm voice while keeping his gaze fixed ahead, arms firm as they hauled the steering wheel this way and that.

Gavnas loved the sea. It was no secret. It was his heart's true home, he'd told Aelwen. Sometimes, he went out on one-man boats and did nothing but sail around for hours. Last year, Gavnas had shown her some poems he had written about his admiration of the sea. He was planning to write enough for a book and, if things in Corova were ever good enough that book shops existed again, he would try to sell his work. The poems had been quite good, really, not that Aelwen had much to compare them to. She wondered if Gavnas was still working on his poetry or if he'd abandoned it.

All of his solitary ways. Wanting nothing but the sea, writing poetry, sailing alone for hours. Despite it all, Gavnas had crafted himself a family. His crew were not upstanding people with regal personas like their captain, they were street urchins and canal rats, thieves and murderers. Under Gavnas' charge, they had become a family with a chance at a better life.

Gavnas was a living contradiction. All he wanted was solitude yet he had constructed a group of people he had made it his duty to look after. Aelwen didn't understand Gavnas, which was precisely why she felt so drawn to him. He was a mystery, one she wasn't sure she would ever unravel.

"Aelwen!" someone shook Aelwen's shoulder. She turned to see Lysia. It had been sometime since Aelwen had been so lost in her thoughts that someone had to shake her out of them. Perhaps the sea was making her mad. Aelwen raised her eyebrows, imploring Lysia to continue.

"What are we going to do if the Marchians turn us away?"

"Go to Ave," Aelwen answered simply. "If they turn us away, we'll go to Paruma."

Several of the sailor's jaws dropped. One said, "You're not serious. You would dare enter that realm?"

"I will if I must. But I will force no one to make the journey with me. Let's hope it does not come to that."

Before their conversation could go any further, Taran came aboard. He was hunched over a walker that he was putting nearly all his weight on. Susa, his self-proclaimed personal nurse, walked along behind him. Her silver hair, pulled back in a tight braid, and the curve of her spine were the only things about her that gave away her true age.

Noticing that Aelwen's attention was pinned on the redhead who had just emerged, Lysia warned, "He won't want to see you."

Aelwen got up anyway. "He may not want to, but he's going to."

"His pain makes him even pricklier than usual."

"I've handled worse."

Prancing up to Taran with purposeful over-exuberance, Aelwen asked, "How are you feeling?"

He growled. "Why does everyone want to know? I'm making progress."

"I've seen lots of injuries, most of them worse than yours. I can help you." Taran's only response was a snarling noise that she was pretty sure was caused by his pain. Aelwen walked over to the short old woman and took Susa's hands in hers. "I will supervise Taran if you like. That way, you can care for the others in need of your assistance."

Susa seemed to appreciate the offer. She nodded her thanks and disappeared below deck again.

"You grew up a killing force, how are you able to be so calm and smart?" asked Taran.

With a huff, Aelwen explained, "The arena was my job, not my life. There is a distinct line between the two."

Taran appeared mildly frustrated with the response. "Well, thank you for getting rid of her. She looks like a sweet little old lady but she's been a thorn in my side."

He stood up and arched his back in a stretch. He stretched too far and bent back forward, grasping at the wound.

"Stop being so dramatic. You're lucky to be alive and you know that. You're healing incredibly quickly." Aelwen circled him, examining. "First of all, you need to ditch the walker. It's doing more harm than good."

"What am I supposed to do with it? It's not like you can hide a walker. If Susa finds it, she'll be pissed. She treats it like it's a child or something."

"Here." Aelwen picked up the walker, travelled to the side of the ship and threw it over. "You threw it over the side in a fit of rage."

"Thanks for making me sound like a good patient. And I don't have fits of rage."

Aelwen smiled. "I never said you did, but look at you. It's not hard to believe."

"Two things," Taran straightened slowly so as not to disturb his wounds. "How do you know that?"

"People reading skills, one of the few benefits of the job."

"And, second, I'm not that much of a showoff."

Aelwen cracked a smile again. "Anyone who shows up to a fight with an Arenian without a shirt thinks too highly of themselves." She began circling him again. She gave him a light tap on the back, far away from his wound. "Straighten your back. Do you want to look like Susa when you get older?"

"Ow," he snarled, straightening.

"Oh, it didn't hurt that much."

"No, it didn't," he admitted.

Now she stood in front of him, arms folded tightly. "Take off your shirt."

"What? You just complained that—"

"Don't be stupid. Take it off." He did, revealing his toned chest. "Ok, good. Now take off your bandages."

"Alright." Taran was clearly reluctant, but agreed anyway. Apparently, he knew how relentless a determined woman could be. "I can't reach the one on my back."

"Then I'll take that one off. You work on the front one." Aelwen drew a long, thin blade from her belt.

"What are you doing?"

"Cutting it off. Don't fret, you'll be fine."

"Promise?"

"Yes," she said, stepping behind him and picking at the edges of the bandage. They were brand new based on how well they adhered to his flesh. Once she had lifted up the edges, Aelwen stuck her knife under the wrapping and slit it open. She didn't bother peeling the rest off, she just wanted the cut exposed.

Taran shuddered. He had barely lifted up the corner of the bandage he was supposed to be peeling off.

"Will you hurry up? I haven't got all year."

"I'm sorry, it hurts. These ones are new so the glue is really sticky. Ah!" Taran winced.

"Get out of the way." Taran dropped his hands, seeing that Aelwen had drawn her knife again. She wedged it under the bandage and slit it open. Her knife was returned to its proper sheath with a fluid twirl.

"You aren't going to peel off the rest of the bandage? You're just going to leave it hanging there?"

"You can pull it off if you want, but I have a less painful solution." Aelwen said. "I'll be right back. Walk around a bit to loosen up your joints."

Minutes later, she reappeared with a tub of hot salt water. It took her and two sailors to carry it up from the bathing rooms below deck.

"Get in."

Taran eyed the water and gave Aelwen a questionable look. "No, not naked." She said annoyed. "Hurry up, or the water will get cold."

"Won't it sting?"

"Maybe, but salt water is good for wounds."

Testing the temperature before submerging himself, Taran dipped one of his feet into the water. Aelwen desperately wanted to shove him in, but she was afraid that might hurt him, not that he'd admit if it did. In five minutes, Taran was sitting, back arched, in the warm water. Aelwen lifted up the hem of the long olive tunic she had on and cut off the bottom, soaking it in the water. She got onto her knees and began scrubbing at the grotesque wound on Taran's back.

She scrubbed around the gaping, bloody scabs, careful to avoid ripping them open again. In time, all of the bandages dropped off and bobbed in the water. Taran objected a few times at the start, then soon shut his mouth.

"Ok," she said. "You can get out now. Don't go back down yet, the salt air will be

CHAPTER FIVE

Two and a half months passed at sea. The days became repetitive though enjoyable. Each day found Lysia becoming more and more like Gavnas. She grew to love the sea and all that it possessed. She wanted to keep sailing towards the horizon, no matter where it took her. Some days she would spend hours up in the crow's nest, enjoying the view. Gavnas taught her to sail and the sailors taught her how to navigate and tie all of the proper knots. Learning all the names for the different sections of the ship was a bit of a challenge at the start, but she had it figured out within a week. Lysia spent so much time with the seamen that she even began to talk like them. The crew dubbed her 'The Seafarer'.

Even her dress was influenced by them now. Lysia started wearing her hair up in messy topknots or high, tight ponytails. But no matter how she wore her hair, that single, rebellious lock stayed free, draped across her forehead. She wore baggy shirts with the sleeves rolled up to her elbows, loose pants with holes in them and old bandanas tied around her head. She laughed, sang and drank with all of the crew members nightly, rising with them and the sun each morning.

Taran was still on the mend, making a steady recovery. He kept to himself whenever he had the chance. Susa was constantly fussing over him, never giving him a moment's peace. Whenever he came to the top deck to walk about or lay in the sun, he was constantly being asked how he was faring and told how lucky he was to be alive. Once in a while one of his friends would walk with him around the deck and talk with him, which he did rather enjoy, although he never outwardly admitted it.

Since he couldn't do much, he started teaching himself how to navigate. Over time, he moved on to learn how to navigate without using any tools and learned to find his way using only the sun, moon and stars. To practice his skills, Taran would often spend time with whoever was steering the ship and advise them in which direction to travel.

Namar's fate still lay in Aelwen's hands. Being far out in the vast sea, there was no way to get rid of him. Although he was allowed on the top deck, most days he remained in his dark, damp, cell. A sickness was slowly creeping over him, he could feel it. He did not tell anyone, though. He felt constantly cold despite it being midsummer. Fits of shivering seized him regularly and he threw up even if there was nothing in his stomach. He spent the days sleeping, shivering and wondering. Of those, sleeping was undoubtedly the most enjoyable.

When the food was brought to him, Namar did not eat it. Acknowledging his weakening body, he began attempting simple exercises. In time, he was barely able to do those. One day, he awoke and found he could not stand. Still, he told no one. He was nothing but a shadow of a thought in the minds of some aboard, less than that in most.

Namar wondered if Iowan hated him for leaving her the way he hated himself. He had chosen self-preservation over death. It was not fear that kept Namar from telling the others how he suffered down here day after day. It was his recognition that this was justice. His suffering down here alone in the dark, that was what the universe gave him for turning his back on the greatest friend he would ever know.

Aelwen allowed Namar plentiful portions of food. She knew it was not fair to starve him. The more she thought about his crimes, the more driven she became to make a decision; a decision she had no idea what it ought to be.

Namar had damned one of his best friends to eternal hell without remorse. For some reason, the feeling had been nagging at Aelwen for some 'time that she ought to release Namar despite him not giving her an apology. Everything terrible Namar had done, he had done out of fear, an emotion she had far too much experience with. It made people do the stupidest things. Still, he had not apologized when he had had plenty of time to do so. Yet, Aelwen still felt like she needed to correct her harsh actions. Every day was a struggle in her mind. She knew she needed to do *something* regarding Namar, but at the same time, the plain truth was that it was easier to push it out of her mind and enjoy the sun on her face.

Training was the best thing to clear one's head, so that was what Aelwen devoted the majority of her time to. The training cabin became a personal school to her, where she could perfect rusty maneuvers and create her own technique without someone always at her back, screaming for her to improve posture or set her foot or lower her elbow.

She asked Taran to teach her how to navigate simply to have something more to do on this mind-numbing journey. Of all of them, besides Gavnas, who was constantly occupied with the ship and sailors, Taran possessed the most knowledge. Besides, he had to do something with his time and she thought it would do him well to have more interaction with humans who wouldn't tell him what to do as he recovered. Surprisingly, Taran accepted the proposal. He was quite a good teacher, always correcting her mistakes with an even tone even when his annoyance showed plainly in his eyes.

When Aelwen spoke with Gavnas, he asked her opinion of the ship, her crew, the journey in general. She told him honestly that she enjoyed everything apart from the fact that there was no way to train above deck. He justified by saying that most did not find it enjoyable to train in the scorching sun. To please his guest, longtime friend and liberator, Gavnas had a large sack of sand hung up in the center of the deck and convinced a few of his crew to train with her. They were good, experienced fighters, too. A good match and an even better challenge.

Aelwen noticed that the sailors used techniques she had never encountered before, maneuvers that were especially beneficial for unsteady footing upon untame seas. At first, they had been able to best her with no problem at all. After a while, she had realized that their stances gave them excellent balance but impaired their mobility. Their strikes were close and fast due to the fact that most ship battles consisted of numerous people crammed together on a single deck. Aelwen modified her technique and was able to gain the upperhand once more.

Most days, fine weather reigned supreme. The worst they ever encountered was a three hour long downpour. Never was there a grand storm at sea, as was told about in all the tales.

Overtime, bonds grew between every person on the boat, even between those who hardly ever saw one another. Tempers rose as the excitement of meeting new people wore off. The crew was generally quite skilled at learning to keep their emotions in check; however, after a month and a half, even they began to lose their sanity.

Lysia was not the only one dressing like a sailor. More and more often Aelwen found herself in loose fitting clothes that gave her a wild look while also keeping her incredibly comfortable.

Aelwen's eyes flashed open. She stared up at the dark ceiling. Tiredness gripped her. Why had she awoken? The cards of the sailors had ensnared her and kept her up well past midnight. She set her hand atop her head and covered her eyes. Her forehead wasn't hot, a pleasing sign. The ship gave a grand jerk. Booming thunder and crashing waves roiled in her ears, filling up her mind. Their first real storm.

She tried and tried, but she could not sleep. She ran her hand down to the spot on the edge of her nose. A patch of pimples had formed there and she had scratched them open more than once. Again, she dug until she bled.

Not wanting to get up, Aelwen pressed her sleeve to the tiny wound. It barely bled, and not for long. Still unable to fall asleep no matter how much she twisted and turned, Aelwen finally got up. Just for good measure, she buckled up her sword belt. The trip upstairs was not an easy one. The boat swayed and jerked about. Aelwen had eaten a lot of food that night, most of which still hadn't settled in her stomach. Being less than half awake, her legs were basically jelly and her head felt like it was made of thickened water.

Hopefully the fresh sea air would help. If she couldn't go to sleep, Gavnas would be there to talk to.

Her trembling legs took the final step onto the deck. She had worn a jacket and wished she had more on. The wind was unbelievable—ripping at the sails, shrieking in her ears, trying to knock her off her feet. The ice cold rain was like needles falling from the sky.

Gavnas and a few sailors were peering over the edge, looking intently at the water. Aelwen shoved the tiredness from her head. The voices of Gavnas and his companions were inaudible above the pounding rain and thrashing winds. A couple hundred feet in front of *Mist Wing* dark, jagged shapes jutted out of the furious sea. A forest of rocks. What a pleasure that would be to sail through in a storm like this. Gavnas, who had a soaked hood pulled over his head, turned his head to say something to his men. And when he did, a small bit of his face became visible in the moonlight. On his face was fear. The kind of fear that penetrated Aelwen's soul.

A person she had known for years, who she trusted and knew so well, was afraid. Gavnas didn't become afraid like normal people. Even the people who gloated and said they weren't afraid, when she saw fear on their face it didn't shock her because she knew they were only human and had the same emotions as anyone. But with Gavnas it was different. Gavnas, while realistically composed of blood and bone like any other human, his soul was made of the sea and sand and rocks. His inner soul was always calm no matter what chaos surrounded him.

Something, something had cracked the stone that formed his foundation. Something had disturbed his calm waters. Some great wind had blown through and disrupted his sands. And it was showing. All the fear was cascading off of him like a waterfall. And that frightened her more than anything she had seen in a very long time.

Aelwen dashed over. Terror had washed away all of the fragments of sleepiness that clung to her. She tried to clear her whirling head—to get rid of the noises, the concern—and leave room for only true intuition and thought so that she could make good calculations and not lose her head.

"Gavnas!" she shouted, "what is it?"

He whirled around at her voice but did not seem alarmed to see her.

"Do you see it?" shouted Gavnas, his voice sounding normal amidst the storm.

"No. What am I looking for?"

"There," he pointed a little ways away. "There. The dark spot, do you see it?"

She put her hand up to shield her eyes from the rain. "Yes. It's… moving." Through the dark water moved an even darker figure, gliding easily through the water. It had four thick legs, barely discernible in the darkness.

The realization struck her like a lightning bolt. Gavnas whirled around. The wind whipped the hood from his face, his unbound hair flying all around in his face. He cupped his hands over his mouth and shouted with all the force of the storm winds and the angry sea, "Dragon!"

He repeated the call over and over. Sailors dashed on deck and began preparations. Again and again, the sound echoed all around them like the call of the Gods. Aelwen had never known how much power Gavnas held within him until he screamed the alarm. Louder and louder each time the call rang until she was sure everyone on any continent could hear it.

Before she knew it, Lysia was by her side. Aelwen considered, just for a moment, allowing Namar to come up and help them fight. His expertise would be needed. No. No, he would not help them. How wrong would it be to force her prisoner to fight for her? No, she would not be like that.

Aelwen drew her sword. The adrenaline was coursing through her veins and her head was throbbing—no longer with tiredness, but with anticipation and fear. She hadn't actually fought an enemy for months.

Lysia appeared to feel the same way as Aelwen, weapons to the ready, eyes darting about in search of a threat. There they stood, two powerful young women, weapons clenched tight.

A noise like an earthquake erupted from the ocean and the fierce surface of the water was shattered by the body of a massive dragon.

The beast was enormous, double the size of the ship, crooked teeth jutting from its bottom jaw. Their eyes were adjusting to the darkness, allowing them to see that the dragon had dark navy scales with patches of lighter blue. The creature leapt up, clacked its jaws in the air and crashed back down into the water, keeping its wings tight against its body and making a large wave that nearly tipped the boat.

As the ship slanted, everyone lost their footing. Aelwen fell, scrambling on the wet deck until she was standing once more. Beside her, Lysia was struggling to rise as well. Aelwen took her friend's hand and hoisted her up.

The women ran to the side. They watched the dark shape glide along. The sea dragon was coming straight toward them. There was nothing anyone could do as the monster erupted out of the water again.

Gavnas's men did not waste their opportunity. They showered the beast with arrows. The majority of them bounced off the hard scales, but a few found their marks. By the time the dragon was splashing down again, blood was pouring from its side.

There was a moment of silence. The eye of the hurricane. People began hollering over the roaring storm, running to the sides, looking all over in the water, screaming, "Where is it? Where has it gone?"

With a boom of thunder, the dragon exploded up again, its relatively small wings lifting it a little way into the air. It snarled and gave another great roar, its mouth opening wide to reveal teeth like small swords. Its roar was not directed at the ship. Everyone turned and gazed over their shoulders. Swimming swiftly through the water, only its head visible above the surface, was another sea dragon. It was smaller than the first, but still grand.

The smaller dragon pulled itself out of the water onto a protruding island of rock. Its wings, much larger than those of the other dragon, sagged at its sides, dripping with water.

Beside her, Aelwen heard Gavnas suck in a breath.

"What is it?"

"That dragon. The small one. Ragon. I recognize him from the tales. See how he only has one horn?"

"There've got to be hundreds of dragons that are missing horns."

"No. His tail, it's bent. I know this is him."

Ragon positioned himself menacingly on the rock and snarled. The larger dragon found a separate rock to stand on, wings outstretched, long claws grinding against the stone.

Unexpectedly, Ragon lifted himself into the air with wild flaps. He soared for his opponent, claws outspread. As he flew overhead, his massive spiked tail whacked off the top of the mast.

The dragons collided in a frenzy of claws. The blackness of the night made it impossible to distinguish any definite wounds on the dragons, but when at last they broke apart, Ragon was shaking his head and favoring a foreleg while his enemy released a roar of pain and lowered itself to one of the cruel protrusions of stone, keeping one foot lifted and its head bowed in pain.

Ragon refused to back down. He hissed and slashed, darting about his opponent, the savage winds making him teeter on the slick rock face but never succeeding in knocking him off balance completely. The larger dragon would not be battered so freely;, it gave a bellowing roar and met the side of Ragon's snapping jaws with a powerful blow from its elephantine foot. Ragon emitted a dog-like yelp and staggered. He took a bad step and began rolling down the island of rock.

Near the base, his claws found purchase in the jagged stone. Before he had a chance to make any significant movements, the larger dragon flared opens its small wings. They beat over and over again through the mighty wind and rain, emitting a sound like thunder as they defied nature's strongest efforts.

There was a strange sound, barely audible above the raging storm, like cutting open a box as a new, longer flap of skin unfolded, revealing the true, gargantuan size of the massive beast's wings.

Ragon crouched in cowardice as his enemy bellowed and raised itself high into the black sky.

The sight was a magnificent one, it halted breathing and motion with sheer wonder. A monumental dragon, wings and maw open wide, ready for battle, flapping vigorously in the midst of pounding rain, gale winds and a raging sea against a tempestuous black storm sky.

"What are you doing?" Aelwen shouted at Gavnas. "Get us out of here!"

"No," he said sternly. "If we move, we'll attract both their attention."

"Does it really make a difference?" she argued. "They can see us anyway."

Gavnas mumbled something.

"What?" Aelwen shouted.

"Dragons are blind," Gavnas said, his voice cold and hard as stone. "They have incredible eyesight, yet they pay no heed to anything that does not command their immediate attention. Right now, those two dragons are focused on each other, unaware of anything else."

"When it's over, the winner will be hungry and we're some gods damned easy prey! Get us out of here, now!"

When he didn't move fast enough for her liking, Aelwen headed for the wheel. Gavnas grabbed her wrist. She tried to thrust away, but he tightened his grip. She had never known how strong Gavnas was; he'd never really touched her before.

"These are my men. I am their leader. You do not give them orders." His voice was like a lion's—deep and commanding. He threw her wrist out of his hand like a piece of trash.

Huffing, Aelwen took a step away from him and shielded her eyes as best she could against the wind and prickling rain to watch the fight.

Flapping furiously, Ragon bolted upward, the wind battering him. The larger dragon lashed out its tail in an attempt to whack Ragon, but the smaller dragon easily swept past the stroke. He continued past his enemy, heaven bound until he was swallowed by the clouds. After a tense moment, a distant, thin shape appeared high up, darker than the black of the sky. Ragon. He was dive bombing.

The larger dragon threw open its jaws and sprawled its claws, ready to impale its attacker. A great wind caught beneath Ragon's wings, sending him tumbling far off his intended path. Perhaps luck had saved him, for if he had continued his plan, he would surely be dead. Ragon skidded across the top of the fierce water, quickly regaining a safe position. He shook his head. His opponent was still flapping and roaring madly above the rock island as the wind and rain swirled about.

Ragon situated himself in the center of a steady breeze that would not toss him about. He launched himself toward his enemy. The wind propelled Ragon forward, his mouth was closed, the place where his jaws met formed an iron-strong point aimed directly at the larger dragon's exposed chest. Ragon's hard snout gouged into the belly of his opponent, who released a dragon-scream at the throbbing pain flooding through it. It thrashed to the side, dislodging Ragon who flew back, shaking his head.

Vital organs had been pierced, making the dragon's chest heave in desperation to take in enough air. It seized Ragon's neck between its front claws and drew him in close, immediately beginning to batter his head with its front feet. Ragon was too out of sorts to fight back; the other dragon, however, had all of its nimble battle wits about it still, along with territorial instincts fueled by seething rage. The larger dragon smashed one massive clawed forefoot into the top of Ragon's head. Ragon fell unconscious, he fell and crashed on the rocky island.

The sounds of the storm faded into the background, everyone's eyes were pinned on the still, bent body that lay on the rocks. The world seemed to hold its breath for a moment, enraptured by the question of whether the powerful beast would rise again. The larger dragon alighted and circled Ragon's body. For good measure, it sliced its claws across Ragon's throat then opened its wings, flapped them once, twice, then folded them in and lowered itself solemnly into the sea.

All eyes traced the movement of the reptilian shape beneath the surface. It swam along until it vanished into the black mass that was the submerged part of one of the stone islands.

Calm as an undisturbed sea, Gavnas took hold of the wheel and steered them away from the scene of the massacre.

The sailors murmured amongst themselves, then busied themselves with mundane duties about the ship. Within an hour, they had all returned to their quarters to sleep away what remained of the night. Lysia was among them.

That left Aelwen alone on the deck. She sat, back to the rail, hood pulled close about her to deflect as much of the elements as she could. The logical decision was to go back below deck to her room. Even though she couldn't sleep, at least she'd be dry. But she didn't want to do that. She wanted to stay up here, breathing free, briny air and savoring the sensation of shivering in the rain. She seemed to be the only one so shaken by the occurrence. The dragons had been so close. Everyone aboard *Mist Wing* could have died. That was why she felt it so important to stay outside, feeling, relishing, what it was to be alive.

Gavnas remained at the wheel, guiding them soundlessly through the night, not flinching or shivering in the unforgiving weather. Aelwen considered talking to him, then thought better of it. She didn't want to talk.

The whole venture could have come to an end, right then and there during the battle. Which was why Aelwen felt it so necessary to remind herself of exactly what it was she was doing, huddled on this vessel in the midst of a storm. Saving her country. Saving her friend.

All had been going so well. Everything had been so right. No one had died and there were only minor injuries, but Aelwen could not shake her horror at how suddenly events had gone from normal and safe to unpredictable and menacing. How many more trials would there be? How many shadows would appear when all seemed light?

Hours passed. The storm finally receded, the rain ceased and the clouds pulled back to reveal the stars, precious and pure, shimmering up in the sky.

What secrets did they hide, the stars? It was a question Aelwen had asked herself for a long time. What were they, exactly? Why, when she looked at the stars, did she feel so right and free, as if everything were going exactly as it should? Why did she feel such a strong sense of belonging and inspiration? Why did the sight of the stars blow the clouds of confusion from her mind like a powerful north wind and leave only clarity and the deepest, most powerful sense of intuition?

No matter the answers to her endless inquiries, Aelwen's heart swelled as she watched the stars. Surely it was only a coincidence that they had appeared in her time of despair. But she liked to think it was more than that. The stars knew her, they knew her heart. And, sensing her pain and doubt, they had shown themselves to her to remind her of her determination and reignite her hope.

CHAPTER SIX

Gray overspread the vast sky, the winds did not decrease in brutality. Chillness filled the air, nipping any exposed flesh it could reach. An occasional heavy bout of rain let loose upon *Mist Wing*, but nothing that lasted more than twenty minutes. No storm so savage as the one the night of the dragon battle.

Several days after the slaughter, when everyone was aboard despite the awful weather because they all needed to breathe free air, Gavnas called all about him and made an announcement: *Mist Wing* was only two days from her destination—the coast of Marchia.

In celebration, the crew planned a party and cleared off the top deck as much as possible, pulling out what little decorations they had to create the setting.

Lanterns were lit, tablecloths were laid, tables were set and food was prepared.

Aelwen scooped a lump of spiced seaweed onto her plate. Out in the middle of the sea, most thought food was scarce. Most people didn't have the crew of *Mist Wing* to aid them. With their knowledge and experience, the crew survived just fine.

More food found its way onto her plate: dried fish and sea plants that were roasted and tasted like peppers. Aelwen sat down at a table composed of two crates stacked and covered by a piece of linen. Lysia sat on one side of her, Taran on the other. A few crew members had gathered on the large space designated that night as the 'dance floor' and were moving vehemently to a sharp rhythm played by a band of crew members which included a lute, two drums, a trombone and a piccolo.

It was beginning to sink in now, the fact that all of what they had done was real. It was no longer a wish, no longer a daydream, no longer a goal. It was real. They had forged a new life for themselves and in two days, it was going to begin.

For all of the joy that surrounded her, Aelwen's heart stung. The food, the lights, the music. How Iowan would have loved it all. She could just imagine Iowan sitting there with them, piling her plate high with food, dragging Aelwen to the dance floor despite her protests that she didn't dance.

Never had Aelwen missed a sound as much as she missed Iowan's laughter. If Iowan had managed to make it out of the harbor alive, had she laughed since she'd watched *Mist Wing* sail away? Had she laughed since her friends had left her behind? Would she ever laugh with those friends of hers again?

A sudden movement caused Aelwen to sit bolt upright in her bed. The blankets were strewn all about her; it had been an unusually hot night.

She listened. There was no noise, not a sound. She listened harder and longer. She could hear it, the gentle splashing of the sea. No, usually the sea was louder than that. What was happening?

Aelwen climbed out of bed, pulled on a black robe and belt complete with a variety of weapons and made her way up the stairs. Groggily, she rubbed her eyes. She had been able to push sleep away for a few moments, but her tired mind was screaming, 'What are you doing? Go back to sleep!'

The wall became her support as dreariness threatened to fully engulf her. She shook her head fiercely and stood straight once more. The Arenian continued on. There were other noises now, voices murmuring. They grew louder.

Light. Faint light. Not much. A pale, pink-purple sky. Morning light with a few pale stars glimmering in the darker sections of the sky. The moon still hung up there, a faint crescent.

Aelwen tightened the belt of her robe. She pushed some messy, unbrushed hair out of her face that the wind began tossing about. Sailors were gathering all around, speaking in low tones if they dared to speak at all. Some pointed frantically into the distance. She distinguished one man as saying under his breath, "We made it."

Even in a less-than-half-awake state, Aelwen remembered her position. She and her friends were the reason for this journey. It was because they had desired freedom, because they had yearned for something so strongly that they had taken action. She was the reason for all of this; for freedom. She carried herself in a poised, graceful manner, strutting across the ship to get the best view possible.

The morning sun had risen in the east, lighting up the water like fire, igniting the sky. A passionate flame that was the joy of these people who had been slaves all their lives and were free. A burning blaze, an uncertain day filled with adventures.

There it was. Not too far in the distance, between the pastel sky and the flaming water, was a thin strip of deep green. Land. Marchia. They had made it.

Gavnas stared into the distance with absolute pride. Excitement danced in his eyes, the only place that gave way to such emotion. His body was stiff and relaxed at the same time, he stood like a war hero. An image that would make a fine statue.

Aelwen glanced around. Lysia was there, hand clapped over her wide-open mouth. She hadn't even put a robe on. She had clearly hurried up to the deck as soon as Aelwen had, based on her hair, tossed up in a sloppy topknot—except the constant rebel strand— the baggy, wrinkled pants, thin shirt and lack of shoes. Aelwen looked down quickly, noticing that she didn't have shoes on either. Lysia ran toward Aelwen, glee radiating from her. In all her wildest dreams, she'd never thought this day would come.

Lysia clapped Aelwen's shoulder. "I can't believe we made it."

Aelwen turned to her friend, who was covering her mouth to prevent screaming with excitement. For a moment, a certain ache that was becoming familiar filled her heart. She could only imagine how thrilled Iowan would be at this sight, were she here with them now.

She pushed the ache down and away. Right now, she would not mourn. She would celebrate. How far they'd come and how much closer she was to finding Iowan.

A smile spread across Aelwen's usually-solemn face. "I know!" The two girls wrapped each other in their arms, whooping with elation.

Everyone else on board was beginning to talk louder. People were gathering into clusters, laughing and gasping and talking quickly.

Nearly crying, Lysia embraced Aelwen tightly. "Thank you," she gasped, tears welling in her eyes. "Thank you so much."

They broke apart, Lysia quickly doing her best to clean the tears from her eyes. Aelwen laughed, gathering water blurring her vision. "What?" she looked around, taking in the glorious sight. The earth seemed to have accepted her as its own and revealed the grandest schemes of the universe to her. Everything fit together seamlessly, yet so much was still shrouded in mystery. Never had she felt smaller, bearing herself to the universe as she was. Never had she felt so flooded with power, reaching a goal she had never come close to accepting as possible. "What did I do?"

"You did...all of it." Lysia spread her arms, embracing this new chapter of life they had come to.

"Nonsense. I just gave us all a little nudge, that's all. Are you crying?" Aelwen was barely holding back her own joyous tears.

"No. It's the salt water, it aggravates my eyes sometimes."

They both smiled at the ridiculous excuse and hugged again.

Taran made his way on board. Susa had followed him up, not wanting her almost-completely-recovered patient moving too quickly. But when she saw what he had been so eager to see, her jaw dropped and she froze.

Taran was panting, not for physical weakness. He simply couldn't believe his eyes. For years he had longed for freedom. It had always been a hopeless dream. He hurried over to his friends, eyes brimming with more emotion than any of them had ever seen.

"I can't believe it," he said. "We're really here."

Unable to control themselves, intoxicated with ebullience, the women pulled Taran into their embrace. There was not a dry eye among them, arms wrapped around one another in promise, their throats filled with laughter at how utterly ludicrous their feat was.

Marchia was a tropical land, which meant grueling humidity that most of them had never experienced. All passengers of *Mist Wing* hurried back to their quarters, which were swiftly becoming stuffy with the heat, to change as quickly as possible into appropriate attire.

After changing into a sleeveless white shirt and pants she sliced short, Aelwen hurried about her room, shoving useful things into a drawstring bag. Knives, rope, canteens, a few sets of clothes. Still moving as fast as humanly possible, eager to stand on the deck and see the new land once again, she put on her sword belt and filled all of the sheaths so that she wouldn't have to carry as many in her sack. She stuffed in a cloak and blanket, not knowing how cold the nights might be. Bow, quiver filled with arrows. Aelwen tightened her belt, slung her bag over her shoulder and hurried out.

By the time she reached the top deck, everyone was there waiting for her. Gavnas was overlooking his crew as they lowered slender canoes into the water that would bear them to shore. Most everyone had changed into clothing without sleeves and pants with the bottoms cut off, few wore shoes and the most popular hairstyle amongst them was a tight updo. With such preparations, Aelwen hoped the climate wouldn't take too much of a toll on the Corovans, who were used to more temperate conditions.

Aelwen touched her hair line—it was wet. Even a good many miles from the coast, the humidity was getting to her. Lysia and Taran assumed their places on each side of their leader.

"Are you ready?" Lysia asked Aelwen.

"As ready as I'll ever be."

Aelwen turned to Taran. In a full-on business manner she asked, "Are you fully healed? You're sure you can travel with us?"

"Yes."

"You'd better be right. Once we get to land, we're going to be moving quickly and I'm not stopping so you can have a break. It's keep up or be left behind, understand?"

Taran nodded gravely, arms folded.

Lysia leaned in close to Aelwen and whispered, "Why are you being so hard on him? What's the rush?"

Holding herself like the queens of old, Aelwen said, voice even and commanding, "We have been at sea for three months. We've been at rest long enough, it is time to get to work and start *doing* something." She was pleased at how easily she assumed the necessary air of authority. Undoubtedly, it would be a tool she would need to wield often in the coming days.

Lysia elbowed Taran. "That's right, you'd better keep up or you'll get left behind and eaten by wolves." She followed the statement with the worst impression of yapping and growling she could manage.

Taran replied, "I don't think wolves live on the tropical coastline."

"Well, whatever's around here, it'll get you if you're too slow."

Before Aelwen could respond, Gavnas pulled her aside and lowered his voice. Was he impervious to the humidity or foolishly trying to uphold his reputation by wearing a thick, blue and gold, long-sleeved jacket and black pants with his hair unbound, waving gently in the wind?

With a curt nod, Aelwen went back to her friends. Lysia immediately asked, "What did he say?"

"Just follow me." She walked to the opposite side of the ship, heading for the entrance that led below deck. Lysia and Taran's minds were filled with questions. Each of them let out a barely noticeable sigh of relief as Aelwen paused and turned again, facing the right direction this time. The last thing anyone on that ship wanted was to have to go back below deck, to the dark and suffocating heat.

When Lysia leaned toward Aelwen to ask what was going on, Aelwen shushed her. The sailors gathered all around, clustering to the right and left until a clear, straight aisle was left down the center of them. A path that led directly to the edge of the ship where a ladder hung off the side, a ladder that led to a canoe waiting in the water.

Gavnas stood at the other end of the aisle. "Friends, this voyage has been hard for all of us. Days of heat with little to do, the same food day after day, supplies running low last week. But, here we are three months later, on the same majestic vessel that carried us from our corrupt homeland, across the vast sea, here, to final freedom."

He patted the smooth wood of the ship. "Yes, I directed you all and gave you orders. However, we would not be here today if one band of unruly Arenians had not decided it was time for rebellion. And had they not met up with two other hidden rebels in the forest while on the run. Thank you so much, Aelwen, Taran and Lysia. My people and I are forever in your debt. We owe you so much, I fear we can never repay you for what you have done. I promise, should any of you ever need anything at all, my people will be there for you, to serve you willingly. We are in your service forever. In honor of all you have done, we would like to bestow upon you all the right to board the first canoe and be the first to touch the shores of this new land; the first of us to feel and breathe real freedom."

Honored, all three inclined their heads. Heat filled Aelwen, not from the sun, but from being surrounded by so many people gazing at her with reverence in their eyes. She'd never minded attention or praise, but to be put on the spot like this was something different.

Making sure to keep her legs from shaking, Aelwen walked, head held high, down the aisle. Lysia followed behind her, Taran came down last.

As gracefully as possible, they all descended the ladder and climbed into the boat. The solid oars would have been a burden had they not all been fueled by new inspiration, to reach what they had not felt in three months. Land.

Aboard *Mist Wing*, the sailors and their captain whooped and waved to the three who had departed. A second canoe was already being put in place and followed suit after a minute or two.

As soon as the water became clear enough for her to ensure there were no strange beasts waiting to devour her, Lysia flung herself over the side of the boat. She disappeared beneath the surface, then popped back up, gasping with excitement.

"It's amazing! Come in!"

"I'll pass," Aelwen laughed.

Lysia shoved a small wave at the canoe, dousing the two other passengers. Aelwen swiped an arc of water right back at her. Lysia dove under to avoid the attacks, then burst up, showering her friends with crystalline droplets of the sea. Aelwen retaliated with a violent splash. Taran did not react to the aquatic onslaught at all, not so much as acknowledging his soaked shirt, courtesy of the Aelwen and Lysia. He had been so cheerful earlier, just like the rest of them. Now he was back to his much-too-serious demeanor, mouth always pressed in a thin line, muscles tense, eyes fixed on some far off point in space that didn't exist. It was as if he could see between worlds.

After a few minutes, the water war subsided. The sun felt different now than it had for the last three months. Aelwen tipped her chin up, soaking it in.

When the water was crystal clear and only ankle deep, the trio climbed out of the canoe and hauled it onto shore. They savored the sound of the waves against the shore, the burning sand beneath their toes and the scent of the salty breeze.

The girls sprinted along the beach, kicking up sand, screeching with delight. Soon, they were racing, then dashing to the water and tossing it into each other's faces, leaving Taran standing by himself on the shoreline without a second thought.

~~~~

Taran splashed water on his face, hoping to defeat the unbearable heat. He looked down at his chest. The wound had healed, leaving a large purple scar in its place. He bent his knees until he was chest deep in the water. Closing his eyes, he plunged his head beneath the surface. He quickly came back up, pushing his auburn hair out of his eyes.

He had felt useless for the entire journey. So many days spent in pain. Doubled over, retching whatever stomach-calming concoction he had ingested. Darkness drove him mad, sunlight made his head pound. Twelve to fourteen hours a day spent sleeping. Severe lightheadedness, numb limbs.

Why was it so hard for him? Not fine. Not fine. Two words that were impossible to say. Care for reputation had vanished after his body had been plowed through with an elongated piece of steel. There was something more to his reasoning, but he couldn't place his finger on it.

~~~~

Eight canoe trips later, the entire crew stood on land. Some stood still, soaking in their new circumstance for all it was worth. Others wept. Most danced with delight. Aelwen was among the majority until her sheer pleasure was sliced away by two sailors dragging along a man in torn clothes with wrists raw and red. The sailors shoved him to his knees before Aelwen. His shaggy black hair fell over his face.

Namar.

Her stomach dropped to her feet as she took in his condition. How could she have done this? To ignore was worse than to forget. Everytime the thought of him came, she had kicked it away, telling it to come back another day. It had and now there was no turning her back on it.

One of the sailors said, "The prisoner."

The other said, "Gods know how long until we're on board again. We didn't want to leave him to die."

"What would you like us to do with him?"

Namar jerked his head up as a sailor yanked on the rope that bound him, his dark brown eyes meeting Aelwen's.

After all she had done, there was only one answer.

"Set him free."

"What?" the sailors exclaimed in unison.

"Release him," Aelwen said, looking at the sailors. "I have held this man captive for months. He's been starved and forgotten. Release him." She knelt before him. "Namar, I know you hate me right now. I hate you, too, and I don't know that I'll ever be able to forgive you. But I am sorry. I never should have done this to you, treated you so harshly. Go now, you have your freedom. Use it as you will."

Reluctantly, the sailors undid the shackles. Namar scrambled to his feet and sprinted full-tilt into the forest, disappearing between the trees without so much as a backward glance.

Aelwen had a feeling that wasn't the last they would see of Namar.

She turned her attention to the group of rowdy sailors rejoicing on the beach and in the water. One problem was gone, leaving room for the newest one to be faced. That horrid feeling roiling in her would have to wait until she had time to deal with it.

She raised her voice, demanding the people to listen. "We own this freedom, now what are we going to do with it?" There was silence among the crowd. "Let's go!"

Many facial expressions turned stern. They had just stepped foot on new land and within less than ten minutes of reveling in their glory, they were commanded to move out. No one dared defy Aelwen with her thunderous voice and rigid, regal pose.

Unsheathing her sword like a true showman, Aelwen led the people into the forest. Gavnas, along with her other closest friends, marched by her side.

"Where are you leading us?" Gavnas asked her.

"I have no idea. Wherever we end up, that's where we're meant to be. You come from a long line of travelers, have none of them been to Marchia?"

"They must have, but I have no knowledge of this place."

"Are you sure? None of them left journal entries or anything that might tell us where we're going?"

"No."

Thick tree trunks reached high into the sky, their tops shrouded in gray mist. Their large, protruding roots were engulfed by soft mosses and broad green leaves formed a canopy high above them. Spattered rays of golden sunlight managed their way through the fog and the canopy, dappling the shadowed ground here and there. Sprawling ferns covered the cool earth in a blanket of emerald; twisted vines clung to trunks and branches alike, crawling ever upward. The forest hummed with the ambient sounds of insects, frogs and birds. A gentle stream babbled its way through the forest, over and around moss covered stones. The air was thick with warm wetness that clung to the traveler's flesh and moistened their clothes.

At first, the tedious journey was unable to extinguish the blaze of freedom that filled everyone's souls. People were chattering, skipping and singing their way through the dense jungle.

By the time the sun was sinking, the sky was purple, the shadows were long, everyone was becoming irritable. Songs sung at top volume in the morning had faded to dull hums. No one spent effort on lifting their feet all the way off the ground to continue moving forward. Thick brush, earlier a welcome change to the dull scenery of the sea, had transformed into a nuisance that had to be constantly shoved and ducked through.

"This isn't right," whispered Gavnas.

He and Aelwen were still leading the group. For a while now, Aelwen had had a tight, sick feeling in her stomach. She figured it was a stomach cramp from walking so long.

"I feel that way, too," she replied. "Let's just keep moving and hope it ends soon."

Gavnas planted a firm hand on her shoulder, halting her. The Arenian met his gaze, searching for the purpose of the contact in their mysterious depths.

"Aelwen, I know you are doing your best to lead. You have never led anyone before; I have. I know how to do this."

"Walk and talk. We need to cover as much ground as possible." Not to mention, if anyone noticed tension between the two leaders, there was a risk of division between them all.

"My crew have finally gained their freedom," Gavnas said, keeping his voice low to keep the conversation between the two of them. "But here we are again, in the middle of nowhere with almost no supplies, being led by an inexperienced girl. They blame you, Aelwen. Listen, you can hear them murmuring their disappointments."

Indeed. If one listened closely they could catch hushed phrases of disapproval.

"We're never going to get anywhere."

"That girl hasn't got a clue."

"I know. Why is Gavnas letting her lead?"

Gavnas picked up his pace and Aelwen followed suit. She had no idea the crew felt that way about her.

"I know you are doing the best you can," Gavnas continued. "But right now your best is not satisfactory. My crew will not tolerate a night of sleeping in tents on the dirt like animals."

Aelwen could not hold back the bite in her tone, not after hearing how they all felt about her. "Aren't they used to this kind of life? Ruffing it in the wilderness, days on end spent at sea, drinking and not giving a care in the world? Since when do pirates yearn for a bed, a hot meal and decent restroom?"

"I do not lead pirates." Gavnas replied, adding plenty of bite to his own tone. "My crew live by a code I have taught them. They came to me when they had nothing left. I showed them the ways of the sea and they gladly learned. We do not roam aimlessly in search of some ancient land to conquer. We are real people with real lives who have endured real hardships and are making the most of all we have left."

Another remark was forming on Aelwen's silver tongue when someone at the back of the group shouted, "Stop!"

A grizzly looking man held one of the ship's crewmen with a knife to his throat, pressing enough to cause a trickle of blood. In the dim light, it was difficult to distinguish the attacker's features.

"Who's in charge here?" shouted the grizzly man with the knife held to the sailor's neck.

The crowd parted until Aelwen and Gavnas were clearly visible to the man. The two of them swept down the aisle. Gavnas drew his sword but made no action to attack. Aelwen was quicker to anger. With a neat flick of her wrist, she had an evil blade at the ready. "Who's asking?" she snarled.

The man laughed. "Oh, missy, you don't want to do that."

"Give me a reason not to."

The man nodded to the towering trees. "Look."

"What?"

"Look closely. See them now?"

She took a cautious look around. Stock still, all lean as the branches of the trees that sheltered them, were people covered from head to toe in tight fitting moss green, brown and gray clothing. They all had nocked bows aiming squarely at the group of refugees. Aelwen could not believe they had been surrounded so easily without her noticing. Despite her continuous training, the time on the ship must have softened her senses.

"Let him go, then we'll talk," Aelwen said.

When the man laughed gruffly this time, she saw a bit of a sway in his stance. Then she realized it. He was drunk. Useless piece of trash. She angled the blade, readying to throw.

"Woah, whoa, whoa!" a man came stumbling out of the trees. He pulled down the gray cloth covering his face. "Tames!" he shouted, shoving the drunk man to the side and freeing the captive.

After watching the drunk stumble into the trees, the newcomer turned his attention to Aelwen. "I am so sorry about that. We've told him to lay off the drink, he never listens." While he talked, his hand rubbed the back of his neck, which was angled down, averting his eyes from the Arenian's.

"Are you the leader of these people?" Gavnas demanded.

"Uh, yeah. Sorry, my name's Rinly. Rinshad Ibori. Everyone calls me Rinly. I don't mean to be intrusive but, who are you and why are you in this forest?"

Again, Gavnas spoke. "We're from Corova, the Eastern Land. We have fled from the clutches of King Halmar. I am a ship captain, the majority of these people are my crew members. There are the exceptions." He gave a small nod at Aelwen.

Rinly looked at Aelwen questioningly.

"We're Arenians," she explained.

"We?" Rinly asked.

"Yes, there are more than just I." The specifics didn't matter, this man didn't need to know exactly who everyone was. Generalizations were fine. Nonetheless, the fact that that statement was a lie hit Aelwen harder than she'd expected.She made sure not to let it show on her face.

"What is an Arenian?"

"A person taken from their home and forced to fight for sport."

"She came to me with friends," Gavnas explained. "We boarded my ship and sailed all the way here, in search of freedom."

Aelwen gave Gavnas a look. He replied, "If they meant us harm, we'd be dead."

He was right, she supposed. They were completely surrounded and she had not detected any of them until the drunk had told them to stop. She mentally scolded herself for being so concerned with being able to lead that she had not realized there was danger about them.

Rinly nodded. "I see you've made it. You see, ah, my troop here are the night watch for Banyan Park."

Aelwen could barely suppress her laugh. "We're in a park?"

"Yes, ma'am. Way out on the border of it, but yes."

"How far to the nearest town?" Taran asked from the crowd of Corovans.

Rinly's eyes went to Taran. "Couple of miles and you'll be right in the capital city, Firhad." He looked back to Aelwen and Gavnas. "We know some shortcuts that'll get you there in no time."

Rinly made a motion in the air with his hand. Three of those in the trees smartly dropped to the ground. "We'll escort you there. If you're willing, of course."

Gavnas and Aelwen shared a look.

Lysia, who had been among the worst of the complainers for the past few hours, was now as sprightly as ever. She approached Aelwen and said fairly loudly, "What are you waiting for? Let's go!"

The decision made, the group followed their escort into the darkening forest.

Lysia gleefully declared, "I can't believe it! We're really here!"

"I know. A park, of all places," Aelwen said, overcome with Lysia's excitement. "A perfect example of how much better Marchia is."

Taran, who had been silently eavesdropping on their conversation, jumped in. "You don't think they're all nature people with their heads full of herbs, do you?'

"They're the most powerful country in the world, I don't think so. They just care about nature," Aelwen replied.

Lysia said, "Drugs are probably harder to get here anyway."

"Yeah, I bet they don't sell them on the street like apples," Taran agreed.

Uninterested in the rumors of the land, Aelwen directed her questions at Rinly. "Why is your troop out here? What are you looking for?"

"Oh, nothing really," Rinly replied. "Just, you know, a stray drunk or a rogue poacher. We almost never find anything, but it's good work for those of us who enjoy the night." He pushed down the brown hood that had been covering his hair, revealing a mess of blackness in a loosening coil.

Noting that Taran and Lysia were in the depths of making jokes about addicts that, should Rinly hear, would most likely lead to nothing good, Aelwen went on to ask him, "Tell me about Marchia. I've never been here before, what should I know?"

"Well, I've never been to Corova, so I don't really know the difference. People walk in the middle of the streets all the time even though you're supposed to leave room for carriages and horses. More people live here than should be possible, but somehow we remain prosperous. Firhad is overwhelming the first few times you visit, make sure you don't lose yourself." He laughed. "What about your homeland? Tell me about Corova."

"It's awful. There's garbage in the streets. The biggest business is pubs, see who has the best beer, the biggest brawls, that sort of crap. Our government is in shambles. The king just shuts himself up in the castle, barely shows his face."

"Why did he think it was a good idea to destroy his own kingdom?"

Out of the corner of her eye, Aelwen noticed Gavnas giving her a look. Unsurprisingly, he was listening to the whole conversation. How much should they tell? Exactly how trustworthy were these forest people? Aelwen heeded the stare and said, "King Vilaz was sick, he reigned before Halmar. King Vilaz had no children or anyone to take his place. He always did the best he could for the people and the country. The only problem was, once he got sick, the country had no idea how to take care of itself. They had been leaning on him for too long.

"Vilaz said that the one to take his place should be chosen by the people since he had no heirs himself. Everyone hated the idea, Corova had never held an election in history. They encouraged Vilaz to choose his successor, but he refused. When he died unexpectedly, the country was in an uproar, we had no leader.

"The government officials ransacked every room until they found a family tree of the king. It turned out that Vilaz had a distant nephew. Halmar. Corova was divided when the news came out. Half of the people wanted Halmar to be king, the other half felt there was a reason King Vilaz didn't tell anyone about his nephew. The government appointed Halmar king anyway.

"As king, Halmar made a lot of moving public speeches to gain support. He fired the council that had served Vilaz and refused to appoint his own, claiming he could make his own decisions and that any king who needed a council was not a true ruler. That was one of his first decisions that turned the people against him.

"Two months into his ruling, people started rioting and protesting. Halmar sent a sector of the army into the street to kill anyone who stood against him. Not many were killed, thankfully, but the act was enough to get them to stand down.

"Today, the only part of Corova that is strong is the military. Halmar knew it was only a matter of time before the people rose against him again. He began ordering villages to be burned and their people killed where there were suspected seeds of rebellion."

Rinly's eyes were wide from absorbing so much information. "Why doesn't anyone take a stand? To me, it sounds like about time for the people to rise up."

"We can't. Like I said, the military's too strong."

Rinly nodded gravely. "I see."

"We were raised to fear him, not to stand up to him," Aelwen explained. "Our parents were all slaughtered for defying him, that's how we ended up in the arena."

"No, no no." Rinly shook his head. "I disagree. Your parents died because they stood up to the tyrannical ruler. Look at you all, cowering beneath him like dogs. You all continue to whimper and do whatever he tells you."

Rinly did not realize how harsh his words sounded until after he had finished speaking. His mouth parted as he realized the mistake he had made.

"I'm sorry. I shou—"

Aelwen cut him off. "No, you're right. We really do need to take a stand. That's why we came here."

Gavnas, who had been lingering on the edge of the group nearly as unnoticed as the trees they wove through, said abruptly, "If there's a fire you're trying to douse, you can't put it out from inside the house."

"What's that supposed to mean?" Rinly asked.

"It means that if you want something fixed, you can't be on the inside, you've got to be on the outside so you can strike in. We can still take our land back."

A sudden chatter sprang up among them. Voices grew in volume as people contemplated the words that had so suddenly gone from being spoken between a small group to permeating the ears of everyone around.

"Yes, you're right," Aelwen's voice boomed, turning every head to her. "It sounds intriguing, but look at us. A captain and his crew, an Arenians and two hermits. No offense." She looked at Lysia and Taran who nodded, unshaken by her description of them. "We cannot overthrow an empire."

"From what I've heard, it's not the empire you're trying to overthrow," Rinly commented. "It's just one man—the king."

"And the entire military, the King's Guild, his personal defenders and the only specialized fighters who have a chance against the cleverest Arenians," Aelwen put in.

"If you need any help, you're in the right place," Rinly said. "Marchia has been prospering in every area for years. We've stayed out of foreign affairs because, as far as we knew, everything was peaceful."

"Peaceful? Really? What were you told of our land?" Lysia questioned, clearly unaware of what the king had done.

"We knew about King Vilaz dying and there were rumors about a secret relative that was going to take his place. We didn't hear anything more than that. The government made inquiries about our trade deals with Corova but never got any answers. Then, one night a man rode into the city at midnight on horseback. He was terribly sick. We took him in and did our best, but we couldn't save him. They found a note in his pocket. It was a message from the king of Corova cutting off all foreign ties. That was all we knew."

Rinly picked up his pace and trotted forward. He chuckled, a noise that felt terribly out of place. "I'd love to share more stories with you lovely people, but look where we are."

Before them, between the trees, was a sidewalk. Lit lamps lined the finely cobbled street. There were 'closed' signs in the windows of all sorts of flourishing shops. It was a type of beauty many of them had never seen, at least not since their childhoods.

A bright moon shone in the sky overhead that was speckled with dancing stars, illuminating the streets and making everything perfectly distinguishable in the warm night.

Large buildings of white stone with pillars and domes dominated the view. In the distance, one white building stood out from the rest. A golden bell sat atop it and several banners flapped in the wind.

"I'd love to show you around," Rinly said, "but I'm guessing you're all tired and ready to sleep in a real bed. I'll get you all some rooms."

Gavnas objected. "We can do that ourselves. You don't need to go to that trouble."

Rinly shook his head. "Really, it's fine. I know these people. If anyone in this town can make a bargain, it's me."

The woodsman led them to a tall building, brightly painted aqua with the name of the place in a golden scrawl. The inside was extravagant. Gold ceilings, fine dinnerware, statues…it was all so wonderful. Aelwen blinked. The sudden bright light and sweet smell of the place thrust her tiredness to the forefront of her mind.

The gray-haired woman at the desk spoke with Rinly in an undertone. Despite the ungodly hour, she seemed to be as awake as most people were in the afternoon. She was dressed just as finely, too. A black blouse with silver buttons over a purple dress, her hair wrapped tightly in a teal cloth with a jeweled butterfly clip as decoration. Her feet were not visible, hidden behind the desk, but there was a good chance she wore some type of heels.

Rinly said something. The woman held up a finger and looked on the inside of her polished desk. They exchanged a few more quick sentences. Rinly fished in his deep coat pocket, revealing a bulging sack. He dropped it on the sleek counter with a chink. Desk lady smiled. She took the bag, undid its tie and looked inside. Satisfied, she handed Rinly a ring of keys.

He tossed the ring of keys in the air, smiling triumphantly. "Follow me!" The company jogged up the nearest flight of stairs, tripping, then catching themselves on one another.

"How much money do you have?" Aelwen's words were perfectly even from years of sprinting practice.

"Enough," Rinly smiled slyly.

From behind, only able to keep up because of those pushing her on from behind, Lysia panted. "How do you…have this much energy? Are you nocturnal?"

"Half, I think. I stay up until about three in the morning, then sleep until noon the next day. The sun makes me tired after a while. It's the night, the cool air and the darkness, that wakes me up."

He led them around a corner to another flight of stairs. "Wait here awhile. I promise it'll be worth it. You two," Rinly pointed to the Arenian and Lysia, "Come with me."

Rinly asked, "Where are those two men who were here before? The captain and the red haired one?"

Lysia looked over her shoulder. "I don't know. I guess they fell back in the crowd. They're not as strong as us."

"I bought these rooms special for you four, so I suggest one of you go and find them."

"No need for that," Lysia cupped her hands around her mouth and called, "Taran, Gavnas, get your asses up here!"

"Is something wrong?" Gavnas asked, seemingly okay with how he had been summoned. Taran, on the other hand, had his mouth pressed even tighter than usual.

No one answered. They went up the final flight then all took a step back to watch Rinly fiddle with the keys. When he found one that he thought was correct, he shoved it into the keyhole.

After some fidgeting, Rinly managed to get the heavy door open. Aelwen stepped through the door and into the cool night air. There were one-room sized buildings all across the roof, about ten of them in total.

The others followed her, relishing the breathtaking view from the rooftop. They all felt immensely closer to the heavens, as if they could extend their hands and grab the stars. The moon's radiance seemed to light the way in the mysterious darkness of their future with its celestial silverness. Street lights looked like ants from so high up, all of the grandiose city buildings seemed to be as controllable as a deck of cards to a skilled player. Marchia's beauty was by no means diminished from so high up, if anything it was amplified. It was the country's intimidation was diminished. All that laid before them was suddenly much more possible than they had ever dreamt it would be.

"Gods," Aelwen breathed in the crisp air.

Everyone was smiling, awestruck by the sight.

After he had taken in the wondrous sight, Gavnas stood in front of Rinly. He towered a good foot above the younger man. His blue and gold jacket, elegant sword and impeccable posture, looking down to Rinly in his hooded umber cloak and olive green tunic made the scene resemble an experienced officer speaking down to a reckless soldier.

"Thank you. We did not expect such a greeting. Thank you, young man."

Rinly nodded with a smile. He was awkward enough around normal people, he was having a time of it not breaking down in the presence of such a grand figure. "Thank you, sir." He looked at the entire group. "Tonight I must return to my post, but I would very much like to return in the morning and give you all a proper tour."

"That would be appreciated. Farewell for now and thank you."

The night awakened Aelwen. She stood upon the roof, taking in the sights of the city for a long time. She smiled to herself as she watched a young man, eager to do his job in the world, black hair waving around his shoulders, go running into the forest.

Though she had only known him for a short time, not even a day, Rinly was one of those people who felt like a natural companion. She hoped to see him again.

When Aelwen realized she had begun drifting off, she retired to the small room that was assigned to her. Her abode was well-set with much more than she had imagined could fit into such a small space. In addition to a bed, nightstand and closet, there was a tapestry along one wall depicting a beautiful woman strolling through nature; flowers and vines were painted to be climbing up the lavender walls and there was a hand carved dresser topped with an unblemished mirror. The canopy bed was made with soft white linens and a thin sheet of fabric draped over the top. It was a type of bed that Aelwen had always dreamt of sleeping in when she was a child.

She really wanted to take a closer look at the things in her room: the potted plants, the glass statues and many more things she had never thought she would own. Yet, the desire for sleep overpowered her want, so she climbed into the soft bed, adjusted the pillows and closed her eyes. The last sight she saw behind her eyelids before sleep took her was the prosperous city they were in the midst of. She had never seen anything like it, none of them had. It was everything compared to what she had grown up with.

CHAPTER SEVEN

Unwelcome sunlight poured in through Aelwen's roof. She sat up groggily. Above her head, inserted in the ceiling, was a piece of glass. A sky window. How had she not noticed it last night? With the sun beaming through the window, heating her bed and shining in her eyes, there was no way she could fall back asleep now. She couldn't help but smile, though. There was something magical about the whole thing.

Half an hour later, she was walking down the street with Lysia, wishing that Iowan were there beside her as well. They had decided to leave everyone alone for the day and spend time together exploring the city.

Gavnas had met them on their way out. He had said, as sternly as ever, "You cannot go and play in the streets like children. We are foreign intruders. We need to find the king of this land and speak with him."

Aelwen just pushed by him, saying, "We're not children. We've been on that ship for a long time, we need a break."

Lysia intervened. "We were bored out of our wits for most of the time, there is only so much you can do to entertain yourself when you're stuck on a piece of wood floating in the middle of nowhere."

Gavnas, surprisingly, did not snap back at the insult to his beloved ship. He stepped out of the women's way and watched them go.

They opened the door that led down into the hotel, then out into the village.

"You don't think we'll miss out on anything exciting happening back there, do you?" asked Lysia

"What can they possibly do that's so exciting if we're not there?" Aelwen rebutted as she leapt off the bottom step, Lysia right behind her. She made a good point. The two young women were the fuel of the entire group.

They rushed across the welcome room of the hotel. The old lady at the counter raised a wrinkled hand in protest, but the girls were out the door before she could scold them.

In the daylight, the entire city was even more radiant. Diversity was everywhere. The sharp whiteness of the grand stone buildings, with their pillars and broad steps, accentuated the multitude of color that filled the streets. Skin tones ranged from ivory to richest black, the people wore bright skirts and shawls with dizzying patterns. In Corova, physical appearance varied extremely, but nearly everyone dressed in drab colors and worn fabrics.

Some Marchians wore necklaces of painted beads and shells, others wore metal rings in their ears and noses. Hairstyles varied extremely: braids, topknots, long, short, half-cropped, layered atop the head, adorned with feathers, beads and natural dyes. Jewelry among all was generally worn, tight or loose, made of grass and flowers or metal and jewels, anywhere they could think of putting it.

Looking around anxiously, Lysia asked, "Where should we go first?"

Aelwen shrugged, "I don't know. I've never been here before." She reached into the pocket of the trench coat she had made a mistake of wearing in this tropical city packed with people. "Wherever we go, I've got the money."

"Do they use our kind of money?" asked Lysia.

"There's only one way to find out." They began walking down the smooth sidewalks, so unlike the ones back in Corova that were all falling apart, uneven and torn up.

All the stores were lit with colorful, splendid displays in their windows. Aelwen had never seen stores as lavish as the ones that lined the streets here. In Corova, all of the stores were rundown, many had caved in on themselves and others had been converted to drug dens or brothels.

Lysia's jaw dropped when Aelwen extracted a sack of coin from her pocket. "Where did you get all that?"

"I've been saving up for years. Whatever I earned, I save seventy-five percent and spend the other twenty-five."

"Wow. I had no idea you made that much in the arena."

Aelwen looked off with a smirk. "It's not *all* from the arena. Let's just say that on my visits to town I came across a few shopkeepers with some…easily accessible money."

"You stole?" Lysia gaped in disbelief. "If the Master ever found out—"

"It's not like they were going to use it for anything useful. What else can you buy but crappy food, beer and prostitutes?"

"You don't know that."

Aelwen shrugged in response.

"I don't think they even have prostitutes here," Lysia said as she looked around the grand city.

"They have prostitutes *everywhere*," Aelwen said bitterly as she slid the coin back into her pocket. "If you have a better idea of how we're going to pay for things, I'll gladly hear it."

Lysia kept her mouth shut.

Their conversation died as they entered the closest shop. The store sold astounding hand-crafted weapons made from what looked to be some of the finest materials on earth. A weapons shop had not been what either of them were expecting to find in such a refined society.

Every weapon's detail was impossibly intricate, jewels and precious metals swirled along the hilts and engravings along the blades. Picking up a few daggers, Lysia and Aelwen determined that the appearance of these magnificent things was just as incredible as their effectiveness and durability.

A woman who worked at the shop approached the Corovans. "Can I help you?"

"Yes," said Lysia. "What are these weapons for?"

"Knife throwing, archery, all sorts of sports. There's going to be a round of games in three days at the park."

"Oh. Okay, thank you."

The worker started to leave them, then turned back. "You're…not from around here, are you?"

"No, I'm not," Lysia replied bluntly.

The woman smiled. "Well, if you have any more questions, don't hesitate to ask." She winked at Lysia and left them.

Aelwen quickly found a quiver of golden silk that she was very interested in purchasing. Not long after, she had also acquired three jeweled arrows and two daggers. When she went to the counter and inquired about the cost, she ended up leaving the shop with a meager dagger. Lysia purchased a small switch-bladed knife.

The next stop was a cloak shop. Strangely, the shop sold mostly fur cloaks, which didn't seem at all practical in the warm climate of Marchia. Lysia insisted on a thin silk cloak that caught her eye and Aelwen left with nothing.

Nearly an hour had passed by the time they finished at the two stores. Agreeing that they were hungry, they went to the first restaurant they could find. It was a little cafe called *Red Sun.* After twenty minutes of considering what to buy, the girls took their food to the shaded outdoor eating area where they sat themselves around a marble table.

Lysia mumbled something with her mouth already crammed with food.

"Eat first, talk later," Aelwen said before taking her first bite.

Taking a drink of water to clear her throat, Lysia grumbled.

"What?" asked Aelwen, who was picking through her dried and seasoned mango bits, a delicacy in the land according to the person who had taken their orders.

"Turn around."

There was someone sprinting down the middle of the street. Their clothes were not nearly as bright as everyone else's, but drab shades of green. The person leapt out of the way as a fast horse-drawn carriage straddled the corner. The driver shouted something at the running person, who ignored them and kept going, black hair bobbing with each stride. It only took a moment before the girls recognized him.

Lysia shifted in her chair. "He did say he was coming back to spend time with us today."

"Does he ever sleep?" asked Aelwen.

"What do we do? This was supposed to be our day."

"What do you mean, 'what do we do'?" Aelwen retorted. "We tell him to go away and give us some space because we just want a break from everything and everyone."

"But he was so nice," contradicted Lysia. "I don't want to send him away. We should at least give him a chance."

Rinly, a bit of his wild hair hanging in front of his eyes, stopped and leaned against the white stone wall of the cafe. He was panting so hard anyone would have thought he was trying to outrun death itself. The girls stared up at him, Aelwen still chewing, waiting for him to say something.

The ranger wiped the back of his hand across his forehead. Even though his breathing made it sound like he was about to collapse, he smiled as kindly as ever at the two women. "So, I'm back."

"We didn't think you'd be back so early," Lysia said tentatively.

Rinly said, "I didn't think you'd be awake so early."

"The light woke me up," Aelwen said. "I was so tired I didn't even notice the window in the ceiling."

"That's what got me, too," Lysia admitted.

Rinly chuckled lightly, he was still recovering his breath. "'Windows in the ceiling'? They're called skylights. They are kind of a tradition around here. Why burn oil when you can use natural light?" Based on the strange looks he was getting, Rinly asked, "You don't have them in Corova?"

"Rinly, someday we'll take you there so you can see the hell we call home," Aelwen said. "This is heaven to us, skylights and all."

Rinly changed the subject, saying, "I hope I'm not interrupting you ladies."

Aelwen took a moment to contemplate. Rinly was so kind, but she wanted this time to be just for the two of them, she and Lysia. They had been through things together that he could never understand. If she told Rinly to go away, it would seem indelicate. Ever since her capture as a child, she had been forced to suppress her thoughts, to shut her mouth and play along. No more; she could speak out now and she would.

All those thoughts had crossed her busy mind in a few seconds. Aelwen opened her mouth to turn him down, the very beginning of a word forming on her lips. She was too late. Lysia cheerily said, "No, you're fine."

Aelwne shot her friend a look, but Lysia just smiled in response. When Aelwen looked back to Rinly, she knew Lysia had made the right decision. Hope and happiness were written all over his face. How could she have thought of turning him away?

Rinly ran a hand through his hair. "Are you sure?"

This time, Aelwen spoke. "Of course! It's not like you're going to try to ruin our fun like Gavnas." She leaned back and dragged over another chair. "Take a seat."

"Okay, I'll be right out." Rinly went into the cafe, quickly emerging with a drink and food in his hand. While unwrapping his food, he avoided eye contact and kept shifting around. Before taking a bite of his sandwich, he looked at the women surrounding him, who were eating silently. "Thank you. Really, I mean it."

"Don't mention it," Aelwen said.

Lysia, nearly finished with her food, addressed Rinly. "What stores do you recommend? There's a whole lot of them and we haven't got the money or the time to go to every one."

"That's hard. Where have you been so far?"

"A cloak store, a weapon store and here."

"This is a big city. How far do you want to go?"

They discussed the issue, deciding that a radius of two miles from the hotel was a good limit. Rinly informed them of the best places to visit, which included almost every shop and tourist attraction within the given radius.

The day was spent laughing. Long into the night they stayed out. When their stomachs hungered once again, the three companions ate at the fanciest restaurant they could find beneath crystal chandeliers.

Sometime around midnight, possibly after, they sat on the rooftop of the hotel. Everyone else, even the sailors who usually stayed up late into the night, had gone to bed. Gavnas had probably demanded that they rest early to be ready for the events of tomorrow.

Lysia, Rinly and Aelwen were all out of their wits—extremely tired, with full stomachs. They leaned on each other for support and warmth. They were drinking delicious over-priced white wine out of pretty little glasses they had bought. And they were watching the stars.

"To freedom," said Lysia, raising her glass.

The group brought their glasses together. Their arms got knotted up, they had a good laugh and they drank.

"To being on land again," said Aelwen.

They clinked their glasses together and drank.

"Is it my turn?" Rinly asked.

"Yeah, go on," encouraged Aelwen.

"To…to the stars."

The women gave him strange looks. Aelwen raised her glass to his. None of them understood what that toast meant to her. That someone was toasting to the lights she had looked to all her life. To the stars that, for her, had always represented the faraway peace and goodness in the world that reminded her of the very reason she was alive.

"To spending a lot of money and not regretting it!" Lysia said. They all whooped and drank to that one as well.

It was on Aelwen now. "To us."

By the time Aelwen managed to get out of bed, get dressed and go outside, it was almost midday. Apparently she wasn't the only one who had slept in. She found Lysia and some of her sailor friends sitting at a little table eating breakfast even though it was half an hour from noon.

Aelwen ran her hands through her messy hair. She just hadn't felt like brushing it this morning. She took a seat and picked up a flaky pastry. "Where's Rinly?"

"He said he might be a little late today. Didn't say why," Lysia explained. She groaned. "I can't believe yesterday went by so quickly. I say we have another day to ourselves and deal with politics tomorrow."

Aelwen refused. "I would love to do that, but we can't keep putting this off. As of right now, no one knows we're here."

One of the sailors picked lazily at her crumbling pasty. "And obviously no one cares. There are almost forty of us here, it's not like we're invisible. Everyone staying at the hotel knows and anyone who saw us yesterday knows. These people don't have security on their borders, that's not our fault."

"Still, it needs to be done." Aelwen noticed Gavnas walking towards her with a sheaf of paper. Silently, he set them on the table. "What are these?"

"Information about Marchia's standing government. From what I've read, everything seems stable. The people like their ruler and he keeps everything running smoothly. Not 'king', *president*. These people abandoned the idea of an absolute ruler ages ago." There was a touch of satisfaction in his voice throughout the last sentence, he prided himself upon knowing this useful fact. "Oh, and in case it's of any interest, Marchia is the only country that uses an animal on its flag. All the rest of us only use colors."

"How interesting," said Lysia, taking the papers from them. She flipped through them. "How did you get this?"

"Taran got them," Gavnas explained. "He didn't really have anything to do yesterday. I sent him to the library, told him what I wanted and he returned with all this."

"Wow." Aelwen picked up the papers and began scanning the headlines, searching for something useful. "Thank him for me, will you?"

Gavnas nodded sternly and walked away.

Lysia leaned over. "What are you looking for?"

Without looking up, Aelwen replied, "Nothing really…wait—here it is!" She pulled out four sheets all bound together. She read the headline, "The President's Residence: Arkada and All Its Beauty." Not wanting to read them all on her own, she tore off the binding and handed a sheet to her friend.

"What a secretive title," remarked Lysia. "This looks like it's from a tour guide. What do you want me to do?"

"Look for any information on Arkada and on how to get there and how to behave when you get there. Look for the important stuff." Aelwen fished in her pocket for a moment. She twirled a pencil in her fingers.

One of the sailors looked at Aelwen strangely. She said to Lysia, "Does she usually carry items of sudden convenience in her pocket?"

Lysia laughed. "It would seem so."

Aelwen hardly chucked in reply. Ready to get down to business, she retrieved a notebook, then pushed the papers to Lysia and the sailors.

"Read it off to me," she ordered. "Not that fast, slow down."

While they were working, Taran appeared, receiving inaudible greetings from the women.

Once they had read off all of the valuable information, Aelwen had created a list that she assumed would be enough for them to work with.

Info on Arkada and king pres.

- Northwest
- White building, pillars
- Gold bell on top
- Fancy
- Has existed for long time/ many import. things happen
- Rebuilt 2x
- Totl 196 rms.
- Corner of westward st/ Aprals ln.

"What've you got?"

Aelwen showed her notes to Lysia. She rubbed her aching, cramped hands. She had not written very much in a long time.

"Do you know what it says?" Lysia asked the sailor sitting beside her.

"No idea. Aelwen, what does this say?"

She snatched her notes back. "Info on Arkada and President: Northwest, white building, pillars, gold bell on top, fancy, has existed for a long time/many important things happened, it's been rebuilt twice, total of 196 rooms, corner of Westward Street and Aprals Lane. Okay. We just need a map of roads and we can find our way there."

Looking at Aelwen's paper, Lysia said, "You should really learn to write better. It looks like a chicken wrote that."

"Shut up!" Aelwen said with a laugh.

"I can get you the map," said Taran. "There was a travelers section at the library, I looked at a map yesterday. I think I remember where I put it."

He left the women without waiting for their reply.

"I think he's been feeling a bit helpless of late," said Lysia. "And since when does he enjoy reading?"

Aelwen looked over her notes again. There was no telling if this was even going to work. What if the Marchians refused to help her? What if they wanted to send the Corovans back to where they had come from?

"Ae?"

Aelwen blinked and looked over at Lysia. "Hm?"

Concern creased some of her features. "Are you okay?"

"Oh, yeah. I was just…thinking about home."

"What about it?"

Aelwen looked off with a half-hearted shrug. "I was just wondering where we'll go if they say we can't stay here."

"They won't say that."

"It's a possibility," Aelwen pointed out. "We are foreigners. Foreigners can bring danger. Think about it: what if the Master finds out where we are? What do you think he'll do?"

"He can't track us across the ocean. But… if he *did*, he'd send someone after us."

"Not just someone. A batallion. The Master knows he can't capture all of us with a minimal force. He'd tell the king and have him send his best men. You saw the rangers out there the other day. Do you really think they stand a chance against Guildsmen?"

It was clear from the look on her face that Lysia now understood the reality of their situation. She let out a soft sigh through her nose.

"Foreigners bring danger," Aelwen said with finality. "And I can't blame anyone here for not wanting that danger in this paradise. If I ruled this land, I'd send us back. No question."

"It's just a possibility," said Lysia. "They could also say yes. If they turn us away, we will try Ave. And if they refuse us, we'll go to Paruma. There's got to be someone out there who will help us."

Now, it was Aelwen's turn to sigh. "I know. I'm just scared. There are so many things that can go wrong."

"There always are."

"We're not exactly safe here," Aelwen pointed out. "Marchia borders Corova on three sides, I think it was the most obvious destination. Guildsmen could be on their way right now."

"Yes, they could. I fear that Gavnas' crew already have their mind set on staying here, they're forgetting all that still haunts us. They're starting to feel safe."

"That's the worst way to feel when you're on the run."

"I know that. But, just for now, they deserve it. After everything we have been through, don't they deserve to at least feel like they're safe? Even for a little while. Have you seen them? They're so happy."

"I enjoy this freedom, too, but we can't just close our eyes and expect everything to be okay. It's naive."

"You don't have to justify yourself to me, Aelwen. Just understand that everyone isn't you. Lots of us just want to relax, to be safe, to be happy."

"And I don't?"

Lysia shook her head. "No. You'll look for another arena to master, another opponent to best. You'll always be looking for the next challenge to take up. Not everyone's like that. They want to settle."

A frustrated sigh escaped Aelwen. "So, just because I'm not ready to settle down yet means I don't want to be happy?"

"No, that's not what I mean." Lysia ran a hand through her hair. "You won't be happy until you've overcome all of the challenges. You're... a seeker."

"A seeker?"

"Yes. You seek the next challenge, the next adventure. But they don't want that. They want a normal life, without the dangers of the life they left behind. Is that so bad?"

Aelwen snorted. "It sounds boring."

"For someone like you, it would be. But for others, it's a dream."

Taran returned with a book in his hands. He held it up.

"Here it is."

Lysia and Aelwen looked at the book, then back to Taran. He handed the book to Aelwen. "This book contains all of the different roads of Marchia."

"Fantastic, thank you." Aelwen cracked the book open, Lysia watching over her shoulder. The various roads of every part of the country were color coded, giving the pages the appearance of multicolored spider webs. Overwhelmed by the jumble of lines, Aelwen shook her head.

"I have no idea how to read this," she said plainly.

"Maybe we should ask Gavnas. He knows all about navigation," Lysia suggested.

"I can read it," Taran said. His voice was still empty, perhaps he felt forgotten because none of them remembered all the time he spent studying navigation aboard *Mist Wing*.

"Well, why didn't you read it then?" Aelwen asked, thrusting the book at him.

The day turned cloudy. A few drops of rain fell from the sky every now and then. Aelwen tugged on her hood, preparing to put it up to keep her hair from becoming drenched. She decided against it. If anyone saw a group of six people with hoods over their heads heading for the government's headquarters, they were bound to become suspicious.

Gavnas, Lysia, Aelwen, Taran and two of Gavnas' most trusted crew members who he claimed were his best negotiators came to the end of Aprals Lane. The street turned, becoming Westward Street. Sure enough, right on the corner was a building. It was constructed like many of the others in the city—large and white. the entrance guarded by a row of unforgiving pillars—the only things that set it apart from them being the large golden bell that sat on its roof and the twin banners of golden elephant heads on fields of green that flapped from the corners of the building.

"Here we are," said Taran.

"It's about time," grumbled Lysia.

"I'm surprised there are no guards," one of the crew members said.

Everyone else nodded in agreement.

"There probably are, we just don't know," said Aelwen, stood before the set of steps that led to a black door encircled by gold—the door that led into Arkada— absorbing the simple beauty of the place.

"What are you waiting for? Go in," said Lysia.

"We can just walk into the royal palace without welcome?" Aelwen asked.

"I'd hardly call it a palace," Lysia muttered.

Aelwen glanced over at her friend. She obviously was not in the best of moods. Aelwen speculated the long walk in the damp weather had dampened her spirits. Still, it was not like her to be pessimistic.

Before Aelwen could respond, a man came around the corner. He was wearing long, forest green robes embroidered with gold. The same colors as the banners above them. The fabric seemed to be silk; even in the dim light it shone. He had short black hair that was wet from the rain and was carrying a leather satchel at his side. He was muttering to himself angrily. The man walked right past the group, up the pristine marble steps. past the pillars and to the front door. Before going in, he turned to them.

"What are you all doing out here? If you came to ask Tecsequaih about the bridge issue, he's working on it."

"Who is Teseqia?" Gavnas did his best to pronounce the name.

The man leaned back a bit, taking the group in again. "The President of Marchia. You're not from around here, are you?"

"How can you tell?" Aelwen said sarcastically, giving Gavnas an annoyed, sidelong glance.

"Is there something I can do for you?"

"Who are you?" Surprisingly, it was Taran who spoke.

"My name's Lin Akachi. I'm a member of the president's council, I'm his financial advisor. Can I help you?"

Aelwen spoke now. "We came to speak with the king— er, president. Please tell him we are out here."

"Alright." Lin opened the door and disappeared inside.

"Nice of him to invite us in," Lysia muttered.

The doors opened a few moments later. A tall man stood in the doorway wearing a long blue gown with dangling sleeves. Over top of the gown, draped over and around his broad shoulders, was a thick cape of woven palm fronds. Atop his head was a circlet of gold, colorful feathers and resplendent jewels intertwined with the metal.

He had chiseled cheekbones and small, focused eyes. His hair was black shot through with gray. It was long and pulled back in a silver ribbon. A beaded necklace with a large symbol of pure gold hung from the man's neck. Four swirls connected by a cross with a circle in the center. An emblem none of the Corovans understood.

He introduced himself, "I am President Tecsequaih Mayolan. I have heard I could be of service to you."

Gavnas and Aelwen exchanged a look.

"You may, sir." Aelwen took an awkward step forward and bowed. "My company and I are from Corova. We have fled—" Her words were blending together, making little more than garbled sounds.

The president held up a hand. His skin was a rich brown, the color of walnut wood. "Come inside. Be warm, relax. We will talk there."

Aelwen glanced at Gavnas who only offered a shrug.

Following Aelwen's lead, they all climbed the stairs. Aelwen locked her eyes on the president. This man was far too trusting. What kind of ruler allowed unexpected, foreign guests into their government's headquarters without even checking to see if they were armed? He was either very stupid, or very arrogant.

Or he possessed a power that none of them were aware of and they were walking right into a trap.

"Thank you very much, Your Majesty." Aelwen said.

Tecsequaih Mayolan smiled warmly. "Do not address me with such titles. I am human, as are you."

The president led them farther into Arkada. The halls were divided down the center like a road, the center line being a row of finely carved statues of the same white stone as the rest of the building. Potted plants, mainly ferns, adorned corners and otherwise empty spaces, giving the stark whiteness of the place a burst of life.

President Tecsequaih Mayolan led them to a well-decorated room with bookshelves lining the walls, a maroon sofa, a desk in one corner, two large windows, several armchairs and an unlit fireplace with a metal phoenix sculpture hanging above it. He gestured for them all to take seats on the cushioned sofa and soft chairs. The president rang a small copper bell that sat upon the desk. Minutes later, a servant brought a silver platter of tea and biscuits to the guests. The servant was dressed well, his chest was emblazoned with the Marchian sigil, a golden elephant's head on a backdrop of green. He donned a bronze belt that held up gold and green pants that matched his tunic. With an elegant bow, he left.

After all had been seated, President Tecsequaih took a seat in a velvet chair and addressed them again. "You claim that you are foreigners. Your dress and accents support that claim. So, tell me…why are you here?"

Aelwen spoke a little more clearly this time, but no less quickly. The words came flooding out of her mouth. She skipped no details, especially any that she thought might make this curious man more willing to help them.

When she finally finished, Aelwen took a sip of her tea. All eyes went to the president. There was no way to read his expression, he looked to be wrestling with everything.

President Tecsequaih Mayolan stood up, somber. He shook Aelwen's hand. "It has been a pleasure meeting with you. This information is both astounding and overwhelming. I will need some time to sort it all out and decide what is to be done." His face was hard, his eyes were focused on something beyond the walls.

Pulling himself out of the well of thought, President Tecsequaih said, "There is a dinner tomorrow night. A political dinner." He rose, went to the desk in the corner, scrawled a quick note and handed the paper to Aelwen. "This is the address. I hope to see you there tomorrow. Hopefully a decision can be made then."

Aelwen was well aware that she was smiling dumbly, but she didn't care. "Thank you, very much. That sounds like a splendid idea. What time?"

"Seven." The president showed them out.

The moment the door closed behind them, the group headed back to their residence in the heart of Firhad.

Another look was shared by Aelwen and Gavnas. Gavnas raised a brow.

"Dinner."

"It's something," Aelwen said. "Hopefully," she looked down at the paper the president had given her, "they decide to help us."

Gavnas walked past her to the stairs. "It'll be a long trip back if they don't."

CHAPTER EIGHT

A elwen looked over her shoulder, inspecting her lean, well-muscled frame in the mirror. The outfit she had chosen was a long halter dress that was tight against her upper body and fanned out at her hips. It was an eye-catching dark forest green that hugged her curves. She wore a thin necklace of golden metal woven together to form an elegant pattern. She had chosen a pair of comfortable yet formal black shoes with golden geometric shapes painted on them. Aelwen spun, the bottom of the dress flared out.

She and Lysia had gone shopping for dresses and jewelry hours after they had been invited to the dinner. The trip had only reminded her once again of the missing piece of this adventure: Iowan. Iowan would have had opinions on everything they tried on, everything they bought. Aelwen took a breath, reminding herself that this dinner was another step, bringing her closer to finding her lost friend.

As she admired herself in the glass, she realized that Marchian fashion was something she would definitely adjust to. She swayed from side to side, marveling at how the light fabric of her dress moved in even the slightest breeze.

Never in her life had Aelwen cared much for outward appearances, but she was well aware that dressed in all of this foreign fashion, she was striking. She wanted to make the perfect impression upon the president. In her mind, the fate of her country depended upon how she presented herself at the dinner.

Outside, the ground was still wet from early showers, though the sun shone brightly now. The damp cobblestone sidewalk in front of the hotel glistened in the sun. Gavnas was bringing the same sailors he had brought to Arkada. The rest of Gavnas' crew were growing restless. They were begging him to let them go so that they could start their own lives in this new land. After all, the sailors had come for freedom and now they'd found it. Gavnas was keeping all of his crew under his command until he made sure that Tecsequaih was okay with their being there. At the president's word, he would release them.

Taran, who had taken it upon himself to order them a carriage, remained as solemn as ever about the affair. He had smiled when they had received the dinner invitation, but now did not seem interested in the least. Aelwen wondered just how much Taran truly cared about the future of Corova.

Rinly wasn't there. Although he had served as their guide this far, he'd declined the Corovans' offer to accompany them to the political dinner, saying it wouldn't be right since he hadn't been directly invited and that large social gatherings were not something he was fond of. Aelwen wished he were there now, there was something about having a real Marchian as apart of their ranks that made her feel more comfortable. Since he wasn't, the Corovans would have to do their best to act proper and pray to the gods they made the right impression.

Aelwen pinpointed Lysia amongst the small throng of Corovans and made her way to her. She immediately took note of the low neckline of Lysia's dress, something that could very easily send the wrong message to those at the dinner.

Lysia smiled at the sight of Aelwen. "You look amazing!"

"You do, too," Aelwen said excitedly, her voice high with a level of hysteria that came from a combination of nerves and pure joy. Lysia wore a striking wrap of blue that started out aqua at the top and faded into a deep navy at the base. "For a woodswoman, you clean up well."

Lysia smiled even wider. "Thank you," she said, dipping into a graceful curtsy.

"How do you know how to curtsy?" Aelwen exclaimed.

"I can't give away *all* my secrets."

The two young women stood together, discussing their outfits, the pros and cons of Marchian fashion until a carriage rolled up.

It was much fancier than any of them had expected, being that Taran had ordered it for them. Four enormous, shaggy black horses pulled the carriage. The driver was wearing all black, drawing the attention of any onlookers to those he was chauffeuring and away from himself. Despite the fact that they were headed to a dinner party that would surely be packed with arrogant aristocrats to discuss political situations and the state of their deteriorating nation, they all felt, even those who did not show it outwardly, that it was a magical event.

There wasn't much room in the carriage. They were all crammed too close for comfort. Aelwen was crushed between Lysia, who was sweating with excitement, and one of Gavnas' crew members, who was avoiding human contact by looking out the window dismally.

Aelwen spoke across them to Gavnas. "We're on the same page, right?"

"That depends, which page are you on?"

"We want Marchian aid to restore righteousness and prosperity to Corova. We need to dethrone Halmar, find a new ruler and get everything under control."

With an approving nod, Gavnas continued Aelwen's train of thought. "We need to make sure that Tecsequaih knows that this will not be a quick process. We need troops and financial aid and construction workers to rebuild the city once it's all over."

Aelwen nodded her agreement, looking ahead. "Let's hope he doesn't see us as weak and desperate. We don't want them to take advantage of Corova's situation to claim it as their own."

Taran, who had been listening, spoke up when silence fell. "Based on what you said yesterday, I think that President Tecsequaih knows exactly how vulnerable and helpless we are. Maybe conquering would be a better idea. It would be like a massive assassination."

Aelwen and Gavnas exchanged skeptical looks. Aelwen said, "What are you getting at?"

"Face it: there will always be people who support the ruler no matter what that ruler is like. There will always be those who oppose the ruler, too. Even if Marchia agrees to aid us, they will not give us the aid of their full army. They will send a fraction of their full power and most likely be overpowered by the Guild and any who still support the king. Our land is in ruin. Honestly, do you think that Corovans will help to rebuild the city? Our people are born to drink and brawl, they've never really had to fight for anything in their lives except a scrap of meat on the side of the road."

"And you think a mass assassination is the answer?" Gavnas questioned.

Taran nodded solemnly. "Yes. Marchia will send their whole force to Corova. They can take over the city, expand their territory and make it whatever they desire."

"Murder every Corovan?" Aelwen questioned. She could see the reasoning in some of Taran's plan, but not that part.

"No. Not all of them. They could kill anyone who gets in their way, anyone not willing to commit to the new order."

Aelwen and Gavnas shared a look. A moment passed between them in which they allowed Taran's proposition to settle. Aelwen said, "I fear your plan makes us no better than the tyrant who sits on the throne."

Taran studied Aelwen until she looked at him. "Sometimes you have to be tyrannical to defeat a tyrant."

The carriage stopped. It was a pleasant sort of glide, not the jostling lurch that Aelwen was used to.

An orange-red glow still emanated from where the sun was sinking, lighting up the fine house of mottled gray stone.

The Corovans exited the carriage and made their way to the fine abode. It was more elegant from the outside than Arkada, with turrets and massive windows and balconies, but made of the same white stone. Flowering bushes surrounded the mansion. A fountain in the shape of a swooping dragon was the focal point of the courtyard that stretched on for acres. In the distance, there was a stable and riding arena. The woods surrounding the yard had lanterns hidden in the trees that were currently being lit by servants.

"Wow," said Lysia. "Who does this belong to?"

"President Tecsequaih never told us," said Gavnas.

They ascended the wide stairs that led to the broad front door. "Do we knock?" Aelwen whispered.

"I don't know," Lysia muttered back. They were silent for a moment, listening. Voices could be heard inside. "Sounds like there are people here. I think we should just walk in."

Aelwen pushed open the heavy door.

Tecsequaih was the first person she noticed. The President of Marchia was dressed similarly to how he had been on their first visit, with his palm frond cloak and bright dress. He donned a different necklace this time, three different sized hoops of gold inside one another, forming a target.

President Tecsequaih made his way across the room to greet the party of refugees. "Welcome, I am glad you are here. This is the grand estate of Marjia Knono, the mother of the head of my council, Silaryn." The president gestured across the room to a lithe woman with ivory skin and raven hair coiled atop her head.

A wealthy, elderly woman with too much makeup hobbled over to the newest arrivals. She shook Gavnas' hand. "Lovely to meet you."

Gavnas grinned splendidly. "The honor is mine. Your home is beautiful, Ms. Knono."

"Thank you, dear. Please, call me Madame Marjia." Marjia shook the hand of every member of the party.

"I assume you want to speak of business right away?" Tecsequaih said.

"It is very important," Gavnas said with an apologetic smile.

"We will begin soon. However, I am expecting a few more guests. If we begin our conversation now, we may be interrupted by the late arrivals. In the meantime, Madame Marjia has supplied us with a buffet and quality wine, which I highly recommend. Go, enjoy yourselves for a little while. I will come and find you as soon as I get the chance." Before leaving them to mingle, Tecsequiah waved over a man in long, shimmering robes of emerald who was in the midst of a conversation with a few people. The man quickly dismissed himself from the small group and made his way to the president's side.

"This is Lin Akachi," said Tecsequaih. "My trusted financial advisor. Lin, these are the foreign guests I told you about earlier."

"Yes, I remember," Lin replied stonily.

The president finished, "They do not know anyone here. Please introduce them. Make their presence known."

"Yes, Your Excellency," Lin Akachi said, but the president was already gone. "So, would you like to get some food first?"

Lysia spoke up. "Honestly, I'm starving."

The majority showed their agreement with Lysia, though Aelwen and Gavnas shared an annoyed glance. They were not here for a night of luxurious revelry, they were here to decide the fate of their homeland.

There were long tables set out that were covered with expanses of colorful cloth. Aelwen frowned when she saw the selection of food. Stuffed mushrooms, crackers with butter, tiny meatballs. Tecsequaih had said this was going to be a dinner party. She had forgotten that what wealthy people considered dinner and what she considered dinner were two completely different things. While these people were content to stand around eating little finger foods off of tiny plates, Aelwen preferred to be seated at a table with a full meal of meat and vegetables.

Lysia met her friend's gaze with lifted eyebrows, throwing a pitiful glance at the food. Aelwen nodded with disappointment. She leaned close to Lysia and whispered. "We can get something after."

Still, they took what they could get, sneaking extra bits of food when none of the aristocrats were looking. Servants crossed the room, refilling the glasses of the guests. Aelwen, deciding that she should take the drinking easy tonight, had her glass filled halfway with blood orange champagne.

Lin introduced them to all of the other present members of the President's Council who were present at the party. They wore long, shiny robes, each a different dazzling color. There were eleven in total and only two who were not present—the Chief General and the foreign ambassador.

After half an hour of becoming acquainted with everyone, when all of the guests had arrived, President Tecsequaih joined the refugees again, a man they had never seen before at his side. The man wore robes in the same style of the other council members, his were teal with accents of white.

"Meet Desliad Faraji, my foreign ambassador," Tecsequaih said.

Desliad bowed in greeting. "I apologize for my late arrival."

"Shall we convene there?" President Tecsequaih gestured to an empty table in the corner. Was it a coincidence that their meeting place was set apart from the majority of the socialization, giving them all the more privacy?

"You ask for Marchian aid to your crumbling homeland," Marchia's president stated in a hushed tone when they reached the table. "What exactly do you ask of my country?"

Gavnas responded, "First and foremost, we need to know that you will allow us to safely take refuge in your country."

"Undoubtedly. There is much for myself and my people to learn from you all. Immigrants have always been welcome here, hence the minimal border security you no doubt have noticed. We have nothing to fear from those who are not us."

Desliad Faraji said, "I have received reports of a suspicious boat off the coast. As far as my scouts know, there is no one on this ship. Does it belong to you?"

Gavnas answered with another question. "What is its name?'

"Mist Wing."

"Yes, that ship is mine. I am guessing that you control the guards of the border."

"Yes, myself and the Chief General are in charge of border control."

"May I bring my ship into the harbor? I would have done it myself, but I knew not how your people would react."

Desliad nodded. "I appreciate your sensitivity. I know captain and crewmen do not take kindly to anyone besides themselves commanding their ship. You and your crew have permission to bring your ship into the harbor where it can be properly looked after."

Gavnas nodded. President Tecsequaih and his aides looked to the group expectantly. It was time to discuss the serious issues now.

Aelwen spoke next, "We want to restore peace and prosperity to Corova. But we cannot liberate Corova on our own."

Tecsequaih replied, "My people hear your struggle and I am fully willing to give you whatever aid you need, please specify your needs and we shall provide to our utmost ability."

Gavnas said, "We have thoroughly pondered the following subject but have found no other way to free Corova. King Halmar must be destroyed."

Tecsequaih Mayolan and his council all looked at the Corovans, then shared a look amongst themselves. "This is what you ask of me? For me to send a battalion to your land

and kill your king?" The disgust in Tecsequaih's voice was clear. "Aelwen, you are a trained killer. Why do you need us?"

"Your Excellency, I am an Arenian, not an assassin. My work was never to kill," Aelwen corrected.

"Who would the new ruler be?" asked Lin Akachi. "Do you have anyone in mind?" He grinned with satisfaction without giving the refugees time to respond. "Precisely what I thought. You are like every other lonely soul who dreams of glory. You have an idea on how to get rid of the problem but not how to solve it. What do you know of politics? You fight in ditches of sand and live in darkness. Come back to us when you know what you're doing."

Tecsequaih stopped his financial advisor with a dark scowl. "Lin has a valid point. Who would become the next ruler?"

"The people should choose," Aelwen said. "Corova has been ruled by a hereditary monarchy for years, the fact that one of the kings proved to be a brooding tyrant is no surprise. Frankly, I'm surprised it took this long for one to appear. We think Marchia should rule over Corova for a while first. Let the country be rebuilt and lives be remade. Then, when everything is stable, the people can elect a ruler. There will need to be supervision, trusted people on the inside to make sure there are no corrupt bargains."

Tecsequaih frowned. "Some would see that as a threat and it would be difficult to convince them otherwise, especially if it was our soldiers who killed the king."

"We thought the same thing," said Aelwen. "Our solution is that you don't have to don't murder him. You can take him prisoner."

"And do what with him?" asked Desliad.

Aelwen replied, "It doesn't matter. Just get him out of power, preferably out of Corova as well."

President Tecsequaih considered. He said, "I will think about that. Aelwen, Gavnas, how do the two of you feel about serving as temporary rulers of Corova, should I agree to my country helping yours?"

Gavnas and Aelwen met each others' eyes, holding contact, having an entire conversation without saying a word. They nodded simultaneously. "We can do that," said Aelwen. "Is it possible that Gavnas and I be given places in your council? I know that Marchia is not our homeland, but, as you said, the reform of Corova will take some time, which will mean that Gavnas and I will be in power for a considerable amount of time. We have never been involved with governments or dealt with finances and I believe that a place in your council could be exactly the training we need."

Hearing her inquisition at first startled President Tecsequaih. "I do not have any posts open in my council right now…but I will see what I can do."

Murmurs arose. The president lifted a hand to silence the group. "I see this will take more thought than I expected. Let us turn our minds from that issue for now and save it for a later date. Your ideas about rebuilding your cities…"

"Everything has fallen," Aelwen explained. "No one has the patience to fix anything. Pipes have burst, roofs have fallen in. Sides of buildings have collapsed and people continue to use them because there is nothing else. I swear to you, I am not exaggerating."

"The few buildings that are in use, what are they used for?" Lin asked.

"They are mostly pubs," Gavnas replied. "A good number are brothels. Some of them are apartment buildings—or, that's what they're called. In reality they are dilapidated and filled with dark rooms that people sleep in. The people who sleep in those 'apartment buildings' are those who prefer a floor under their back to the ground outside."

"What about food? Do you have restaurants?" Desliad questioned.

Aelwen responded, "There is a market once a week downtown. There are people who live on the outskirts of Corova who lead rural lives. They come to the market and sell their homemade products at ridiculous prices, but you have to pay the price if you want to eat."

"So there are people who still have decent—"

The president was cut short as the entry doors to the mansion were pushed open and several soldiers dressed in ornate armor bearing the green and gold elephant head that was the sigil of the land came flooding in. Royal guards.

"President Mayolan!" one of them shouted.

Tecsequaih stood up and made his way across the room. His palm frond cloak swept elegantly behind him.

"There has been death at the Ave border," the guard explained.

"How many?"

"One."

"Ready me a horse." The president turned to the refugees. "I apologize for this unexpected turn of events, but I must leave. I will hold a council meeting tomorrow at one in the afternoon. Aelwen, Gavnas, please attend. With this new problem, I doubt we will discuss Marchia's involvement with Corova, but you will be made official council members and the experience will be good for you." Tecsequaih turned back to his guards and left. Aelwen gazed out of the large windows. The president mounted a large brown and white steed. He raised a hand into the air and shouted to his men. The troop galloped off toward the edge of the darkening sky.

"What's happening?" Lysia asked Lin.

The fire that had been burning in Lin's eyes went out. "Border dispute."

"Why?"

"Because two countries cannot decide where their land starts and ends." He looked like he wanted to add more but stopped short. "You should all be on your way. Without the president we can take no further action."

Aelwen glanced at Gavnas who inclined his head. "Okay. Let's go."

The party turned and headed for the still open doors, letting in the night air.

"Wait, Lady Aelwen," Desliad called.

"What?"

"Should we be expecting you at the meeting tomorrow?"

"Of course. You don't make decisions about my kingdom without giving me a say in the matter." She started for the door once more, then paused. Turning back to Desliad, she said, "Do you know what's happening with the border?"

He inclined his head. "I do."

"What?" Gavnas asked.

Desliad shifted as if he were uncomfortable. "I cannot tell you everything, but I will tell you this." He stopped his shifting. "Years ago, Marchia was a much smaller territory than it is now. It was little more than a speck of land above Paruma. Marchia was a small country with a big population and we were running out of resources. Ave held all of the land that is now ours. We went to war, reducing Ave's claim to a strip of coastline. Now, they apparently want their old land back. For a few months there have been Marchian soldiers stationed on our side of the border, ready to strike if any Aveans cross over. It seems now there has been a murder. Murder is usually the prelude to war."

CHAPTER NINE

"We fought for it! People died! We can't just give it up now!"

"Shh. I know this means a lot to you, but you didn't see it. I did. They have nothing left."

"No, you don't understand! My father *died* for that land!"

"And it was honorably done. We took too much. We can respond by owning up to our mistake and fixing it."

"He wasn't the only one. I have them, all of the letters he wrote you. I know how much you cared. And now here you are, throwing it all away! I never knew him because of you."

"It wasn't my fault. Your father made his own decision to fight."

"No, he fought for *you*. He stayed because of *you*. I know what he did, I know his story. His term ended and he could have gone home. He could have left his friends and you. He could have gone back to my mother and watched the birth of his child, he could have been safe, he could have been happy. But he stayed! He stayed and he fought! And he died."

"Please, I know you are looking for someone to blame, but please, do not lay that burden on me. My heart is still heavy with the grief of your father's departure, but I know it is not my fault. Not once did I blame myself for his death."

"Then you are a coward! You cannot face the truth. He stayed because he was worried about you. He looked into your eyes and he saw how troubled you were and he noticed how your eyes lit up when you saw him. He stayed for you, to fight by your side until the war was done, so that he could be with you until the end."

The other man tried to speak but was abruptly interrupted. "No! You don't get to speak. Do whatever you want, it's your country. But I want you to know what you're giving away, it's not just land. It's the blood of the people you loved. And every night I want you to remember him. I want you to know that he is watching you and that he will never, ever forgive you."

The great doors burst open and Lin Akachi stormed out. His gaze was on the floor, his face was covered with one hand. Tecsequaih Mayolan stood before the Corovans, a gentle, fatherly look in his eyes. It was half past one according to the tall pendulum clock in the corner. They had been waiting for half an hour. Tecsequaih's face hardened. "I am sorry to have kept you waiting. I am afraid I still have not made a decision on the border issue and it is a touchy subject for Lin. Do come in."

Tecsequaih stepped to the side, allowing them to enter. He led them up several flights of stairs white stone stairs and down a broad hall with potted ferns at every corner and a row of marble statues down the center, past many doors, a few of which were open, revealing the offices of government officials. Some were cluttered with papers everywhere, others were neat with polished wood desks with only a single inkwell and quill upon them.

Aelwen and Gavnas on his heels, Tecsequaih stopped before a pair of doors much larger than any of the others they had passed, not to mention it was not of the same sleek, brown wood as the others but of a coarser wood painted green. A great golden elephant head adorned the doors. Two armored guards flanked the doors, golden spears in their grasps.

The president pulled open the doors, saying, "Welcome to the council chamber."

A long, dark wood table draped in an emerald colored cloth with golden elephant heads sewn into it was the focal point of the room. Normally, the table was set with twelve chairs of the same dark wood as the table—one for the president and eleven for the council members. Today, the table was set with fourteen chairs, the two extra for the two young foreigners.

Silaryn Knono sat at one end of the table, President Mayolan at the other and between them, all the rest. Even Lin Akachi, who had managed to regain his composure.

Gavnas and Aelwen wore Corovan commoners clothes—study fabrics of dark, earthy tones. That alone made them stand out in the room of Marchians, all dressed in long, flowing gossamer robes. Each council member's robes were a different color. Lin, financial advisor, wore robes of emerald green; Silaryn Knono, head of the council, wore robes of royal blue; Desliad Faraji, foreign ambassador wore robes of daffodil yellow, General Fayette Ekua, defense secretary and Chief General of Marchia, wore robes of blood red, and so on.

Starting with the president and going clockwise around the table, each person stated their name and role. When it came to Gavnas, he stated his role as 'apprentice'. Unsure of what else to say, Aelwen did the same.

When everyone had made their statements, Silaryn rose. She spoke, her voice clear as water and polished steel. "On this day, we welcome to the Council of the President of Marchia two new members. Aelwen and Gavnas of Corova, please rise."

They did.

"You come to us to study and learn, to be taught in the ways of leadership and democracy. All of us who sit at this table have vowed to teach you to the best of our abilities, to guide you and teach you. Now, you must take vows of your own. Raise your left hand."

They did.

"Repeat after me: I swear, to the people of Marchia, all those there have been and are and will be, that I will serve to the utmost of my ability to protect the country of Marchia and all who inhabit it."

They repeated the words.

Silaryn continued, "I swear to serve as a guardian of the rights of these people and their land until my oath is revoked or death takes me."

They repeated the words. The council applauded.

Aelwen couldn't help but share a smile with Gavnas. Another major step on their journey had been taken. They were that much closer to reclaiming their homeland.

The Corovans seated themselves at the behest of Silaryn, who went on to read a detailed report of the most recent events.

Just as Tecsequaih had said, at this meeting, the issue of Corova was not brought up. Rather, hours passed in which the marvelously dressed council members spoke with elegance and eloquence about complicated political issues and Aelwen struggled to keep up the facade that she understood or cared about anything they were saying. All she could think of was Iowan—she could hear her screams, see her dirty blonde hair soaked with blood, feel the lifeless weight of her best friend's hand in hers, shattering into a million little pieces as she realized that everything she'd gone through to get her back had been in vain. Corova would be saved, but the person she loved most of all would not.

That was Aelwen's greatest fear. Sitting there, feigning interest in the conversations around her, Aelwen was confident she would find a way to get the council to agree to aid Corova and King Halmar would be dealt with and her homeland would see its days of glory once again. The thing she did not know, the fear that gnawed on her in the quiet dark and in times like these when her surroundings were not enough to keep her grounded, was that Iowan was already dead and that, despite all of her success, Aelwen was a failure.

She had left behind the one person she'd never thought she could go on without. Yet here she was. Without Iowan, without Namar, with only one person she really knew at all. She was still here. After having come face to face with many challenges and being beaten and bloodied too many times to count, she was still here. That had to count for something.

The council meeting came to close. Aelwen had managed to drag her attention to the matters at hand for the last ten minutes, not that she had understood more than a sentence. She was relieved to be heading home to Lysia and her soft bed, far from blabbering politicians and hardwood chairs. The council members funneled out of the chamber. Aelwen was making her way to the exit, Gavnas beside her, when President Tecsequaih beckoned them back to the table.

"I was hoping I could have a quick word with the two of you," he said.

"Of course," Gavnas replied before Aelwen had a chance to respond. "What is it?"

"Good. I was thinking about Corova last night. The issue obviously didn't come up in today's meeting, and there are other matters I must see to before we pursue aiding Corova, but still, I had some ideas. None of this is written in stone, of course, I'd like to get your opinion on my ideas is all.

Joy sparked in Aelwen. President Tecsequaih had a border dispute to deal with, yet he had spent time thinking about Corova and had a plan to help. That meant he was more committed to their cause than Aelwen had guessed.

President Tecsequaih continued. "I was considering this: Marchia will help you overthrow your king and revolutionize your country. Marchia will lend you money—realize that I say 'lend'. I intend for sixty percent of the money to be paid back within the span of six years."

"That's an awfully large time window. Thank you," said Gavnas.

"Countries take time to build. It will take a lot of money to restore your kingdom if the conditions are as bad as you say, which I do not doubt they are. As we discussed, Marchian rule would be viewed as a threat, so my thoughts are that Aelwen and Gavnas, who seem to be the rulers in this group, would become joint leaders while the city is reestablished. After that, an election can be held properly."

Aelwen spoke up, desperate to know a specific detail of his plan. "What of Halmar? Will we kill him?"

"You seem to think that is best. And while I do not agree, it is not my country. My people will take him out of power, overthrow his corrupt army and reform your government and cities. We will have him held in the dungeons. When you two become leaders, the decision will be yours. What do you think?"

Gavnas and Aelwen traded a look, satisfaction gleaming in both their eyes.

"It's a solid plan, Your Excellency," said Gavnas, speaking like a true statesman. "I see no flaws in it. Thank you for all the thought you have put into this."

Tecsequaih grinned. "We won't be able to pursue this for quite a while, unfortunately. But I'm glad my ideas are to your liking. If either of you have anything else to add or you come up with better ideas, please do let me know. Hopefully this whole Ave business clears up soon so we can help you."

Gavnas asked, "When should we return?"

President Tecsequaih sighed and looked around. "I do not exactly know. I will get word to you, though, I promise."

"Thank you, President Tecsequaih," said Aelwen. She made for the doors of the chamber, her mood significantly improved from the last time she'd been going for the exit, but she was still just as eager to get home and rest.

Aelwen and Gavnas were pushing their way out the large doors of Arkada when a deep voice stopped them in their tracks.

General Fayette Ekua, with her close shorn black hair and her mahogany eyes that matched her skin, was making her way towards them. She walked briskly, a soldier's rhythm and precision in her every movement. Her council robes were open and pulled back, revealing traditional military regalia beneath.

"Aelwen, Gavnas, may I have a word with you?"

The Corovans shared a look before nodding.

"Here, or would you like us to go somewhere more private?" asked Gavnas.

"Here is fine," said the general, voice like thunder rolling in on the mountain side. "I know that this must all be very different for the two of you and I know that you both have much experience with combat. Seeing that I also come at things from a warrior's perspective, I believe I could be of aid to you in your studies."

Gavnas replied, "That would be wonderful, thank you."

Feeling like she ought to say something, Aelwen put in, "Yes, thank you."

"I will not seek you out or force my views upon you, but if either of you need help understanding anything, especially from the pugilistic view I assume you two are acclimated to, I'm willing to help you. I've heard tell of the cause that brings you here and it is a worthy one. If I may be of any assistance, do not hesitate to contact me."

Aelwen spoke first this time. "Thank you, general. Truly. That means a lot." She extended her bronze hand, which Fayette grasped in a tight, sturdy manner. The general went on to shake Gavnas' hand, then bid them farewell.

Out in the stables, tacking up their horses, Aelwen said to Gavnas, "I think Fayette just now is the nicest any of the council members have been to us."

"Even Tecsequaih?" challenged Gavnas, buckling his saddle.

Aelwen scoffed. "I wasn't counting him."

"In that case, I agree."

Aelwen hefted Erizo's saddle onto his back. Situating it, she said, "Did you understand anything they were talking about?"

"Not at all. I stopped listening after awhile. It wasn't a conscious decision, I just couldn't focus."

"Me too."

The captain mounted. A minute later, Aelwen did the same. From here, they went their separate ways—Gavnas to the sea and Aelwen deeper into the heart of Firhad.

Before they parted, Gavnas said, "We'll be able to understand it eventually. Just not yet. Our minds are still set in their pugilistic ways." A rare smile graced his features.

Aelwen laughed. "I suppose that's true."

Honing one of her favorite blades, Aelwen stood in the parlor of her new home. Strangely, it didn't feel strange calling it that. It was a little white stone house in the middle of the city with adequate space for Aelwen and Lysia. There was an unoccupied room upstairs, void of decor but for a single bed. If Iowan ever reunited with them, the room would be hers.

Courteously, to get them on their feet, the Marchia government had given money to each Corovan refugee. All of them had moved out of the hotel. Most of Gavnas' crew, ready to enjoy their freedom, had ventured off and bought themselves small farm houses or travelled to the coast to purchase their own vessels, many of them had already headed out to begin exploring the seas of Marchia.

Lysia and Aelwen had split the bill and bought a good sized house in the heart of Firhad. Gavnas had negotiated and gotten himself a large dwelling at the wharf that overlooked the main harbor. Taran had bought a place near the southern border Ave shared with Marchia. Neither of the women had seen him since he'd moved there.

Lysia came down stairs, a shawl around her shoulders, a load of laundry in her arms. "What's the deal with these men? Why are they all so..." she trailed off, unable to figure out the right word.

"Standoffish?" Aelwen filled in.

"Yeah." Lysia dropped the clothes in a basket and carried the full basket out to the front steps. Between them, the girls had enough money to pay for the laundry to be done for them—twice a week, just before noon, a person would come around and collect laundry, wash and dry it, then bring it back later in exchange for an envelope containing twenty-three silver.

"I think that they have a harder time moving on from their past experiences. At least Rinly isn't like that," Aelwen said, not looking up from sharpening her knife.

"He hasn't come to see us for a while," said Lysia, untying her shawl. "Taran and Gavnas have both seen a lot, we all have, but we don't go and buy isolated houses next to the sea to cope with it."

"I saw Rinly in the city the other day," Aelwen said. "At least, I think it was him. I smiled at him and started to wave, but he just turned and went on his way. I hope it was him, I don't want to go around waving to strangers."

Lysia chuckled lightly, then made a show of twirling a dagger out of her belt and flinging it into the door. "Are we ready?"

Aelwen smiled deviously and put away the honing steel. "I'm ready." She darted out the door.

Lysia plucked her knife from the wood and bolted after her. They circled each other, eyes narrowed.

The girls had ensured that their house came with a large yard for training; the fight was in their blood and there was no getting it out.

Aelwen pulled out a second dagger, never taking her eyes off of her opponent. "You think you stand a chance with only one blade?" she taunted.

"Don't you know there's always more to me than meets the eye?" Lysia dropped her hunting dagger to draw a sabre from a sheath in her belt that had been hidden beneath her shirt and pants. They clashed blades and made quite a show of it.

Two weeks had passed since the council meeting. No word had yet arrived from President Tecsequaih Mayolan. He could not be blamed for not getting word to them, for a day and a half after their meeting, a hurricane had destroyed the northern coast. The land up there was rich, the air warm and the sea sweet, attracting many of those who had come to Marchia as apart of Gavnas' crew. Thankfully, neither Taran nor Gavnas himself had chosen to reside on the northern coast. Houses in the north were few and far between, with only dirt roads connecting them. Every few miles, there was a small town equipped with two to six shops that sold the bare essentials for life—food, clothing, and clean water. The people in the north were humble and quiet folk who lived with things made with their own hands. Most of them didn't have any livestock. For pleasure, they walked the wide expanse of brown sand and waded in the crisp, salty water.

Why did the gods feel the need to wreak such havoc upon people who did so little harm? Perhaps it was not to make the people suffer, but instead to test the endurance of their ruler. Tecsequaih's people who lived there made no grand contributions to Marchian society and he already had two much more pressing issues before him that involved more than his own country. Were they worth his time, in this period when everyone seemed to need him for something? Indeed, they were, for they were his people, those he had sworn to protect at all costs and would not be abandoned for the world.

Lysia's blade was thin and weak and Aelwen had broken off the end, leaving a jagged piece of metal in its place. Aelwen had one of her curved swords held at Lysia's throat. Lysia was sweating and breathing heavily. Unexpectedly, in one swift maneuver, Lysia swiped the blade out of the way with her hand, ducked, rolled to the side and popped back to her feet, suddenly up in Aelwen's face.

Aelwen spent no time on surprise. She turned her back on Lysia who took the bait, raising her arm for a strike. Just as Lysia was bringing her uplifted arms down, prepared to jam her elbows into the soft spot at the base of Aelwen's neck, the Arenian held up her arms, intercepting the blow while reeling backwards and throwing herself into Lysia. Aelwen thrust her arms back and delivered a duo of blows to Lysia's stomach. Aelwen threw her head up, preparing to ram her skull into Lysia's jawbone.

Lysia saw it coming. She got out of the way. Bewildered, Aelwen turned to see where her opponent was, but Lysia was already on the move. She hid herself in Aelwen's blind spot and in a series of moves disarmed her, sending the weapons clattering to the ground. Lysia angled her sword at Aelwen's throat and gave her the smile of a bloodthirsty killer. Lysia drove the point of her weapon straight at Aelwen's throat. And stopped.

A fraction of an inch was all that separated the point of the blade from her friend's throat. Aelwen burst out laughing. Lysia joined in, sheathing her sabre.

Aelwen plucked her daggers from the ground. It was good to be training again. Lysia's skill was unbelievable. How was this self-taught woodswoman overpowering Aelwen, who had been brutally trained for years? Lately, it seemed to be becoming easier and easier for Lysia to best her.

Since acquiring the new house, they had both been busy setting up and making sure that the payments were in order. Aelwen promised herself everyday that she would go out and train, but by the time she was done handling the necessities of life, she had no energy left.

Lysia turned, facing the front of the house. "Is there somebody at the door?"

Aelwen glanced over. "It's probably just the laundry person."

There was indeed a person at the door. A young girl, perhaps thirteen, with curly black hair wearing a dizzyingly colorful patterned skirt with a pear colored top.

"I'll go see what she wants." Aelwen dashed around and up the stairs to greet the girl.

"Yes?" Aelwen's daggers were still in her hands. The girl tossed cautious glances at them.

The girl read from a note scribbled on a torn piece of parchment. "President Tecsequaih says that he is sorry he has not been able to contact you due to the recent storm, but he is ready for your presence in his court now. There will be a ceremony held welcoming you to the President's Council at five o'clock this evening. He would like you to arrive ahead of time so that he can introduce you. He is ready for you at any time."

Finally. "Thank you. Tell him I will be there as soon as I can. I need to change into something a little more appropriate." She indicated her sage fighting suit. "I look forward to the meeting."

With a curt nod, the young girl headed off. Aelwen returned to Lysia and told her the news.

Lysia's face lit up. "He's finally ready for you!"

Aelwen gave a firm nod. The fact that she had been appointed and Lysia had not made her uncomfortable. "Yes, it's about time. Not that it's his fault, he doesn't control the weather. I'm going to take a bath, see you in a bit."

"Wait, wait, wait." Lysia stopped Aelwen from entering the house. "Can I pick out your outfit? I'm not coming, this way I can be there with you in spirit."

Aelwen sighed a laugh. Fashion sense had never been Aelwen's strong suit and here in Marchia clothing was quite obviously a valuable statement-making tool. "Alright."

"Try the purple one again."

"Again? I just had it on?" Aelwen rolled her eyes.

"I know, but I need to see it again. You want to look your best, don't you?"

"At this point, I just want to look presentable." She hated this. It wasn't that she didn't like Marchian fashion, it was how much thought had to be put into her outfit. Appearance mattered more than it ever should here in this court.

"I don't know. What do you think? Which one's better?'

Aelwen turned her back to the mirror and looked over her shoulder. She had already brushed and styled her hair. "This one. The train on the blue one is too much. I like these straps better, too. Marchian fashion is so much better than what we're used to, I love how colorful and expressive it is."

"Okay. Any jewelry?"

"No, I don't want to over do it."

"What are you doing?" asked Lysia as Aelwen swept her wallet from her dresser and started down the stairs.

"The girl said I don't need to be there until five. It's only one now. I'm going to get food, want to come?"

"That depends, where are you going?"

"I'm not sure yet. I'm going to walk around, see what catches my eye."

Lysia smiled. "Sounds good to me."

Aelwen's world felt tipped to the wrong angle. She had lived out scenes in her life a hundred times that mimicked Lysia helping her pick out an outfit and then going to get some food. But never, until the last few months, had those scenes involved Lysia. It had always been Iowan before. *It still should be.* The thought was a crack in Aelwen's foundation, her face warped for a moment with the pain of the memory. She was glad that Lysia didn't notice. If Iowan was even alive, for she was very aware that she may not be, where hell was she living? Was she under the control of the Master once more? What had he done to her? Was she hiding somewhere, forever in fear? Had she, somehow, made an escape on her own? Aelwen had to find out. She had to know. Then, once she knew who had done Iowan wrong, she would come for them.

Aelwen dismounted, her dress giving her a bit of trouble being that it was tight around her hips. She took the reins and led her horse, Erizo, to his stall. Most of the members of the President's Council took a carriage to work; however, a few did ride. Knowing that his newest member would be riding, Tecsequaih had set aside a stall for her stallion.

Her horse's stall had a piece of wood on the gate with Erizo's name painted in gold.

There was a boy at the back of the stable, pitchforking hay and divvying it up. "Can I help you, miss?" he asked.

"No, thank you." Standing there, wearing a dress and a cloak beside a rambunctious young horse, Aelwen felt powerful. An adventurous young woman who was capable of destroying worlds. Aelwen nearly laughed aloud at her own fantasy. She untacked her steed and hooked him up, giving Erizo's soft snout one last rub before leaving the stable.

Waiting for her at the end of the barn was President Tecsequaih. His long black hair hung unbound and he wore a dress of garnet and and his golden circlet and necklace, but his palm frond cloak was missing. He shook Aelwen's hand. "It's good to see you."

"It's good to see you, too." Touching Tecsequaih's hand, a strange sensation filled her. It felt like making contact with her parents again, someone to keep her in check and teach her, a feeling she had all but forgotten. A shiver ran down her spine.

Together, they entered Arkada. Aelwen was the only visitor, everyone else was in their office behind a locked door. They walked down the halls, keeping to the left of the row of statues.

"What does your necklace mean?" Aelwen asked the president, hoping it was not an inappropriate question. The one he wore now was shaped unlike any of the others she had seen him where, this one depicted an upward facing crescent with an eight pointed star in its center. She figured it had to have some significance.

Without even looking at his necklace, President Tecsequiah explained, "This one means harmony. I have many others. It is a set, passed from president to president over the years, each one means something different, a quality a president should have or should strive to achieve."

"Such as?"

"Intelligence, democracy, strength and so on."

They rounded a corner at which was placed an overflowing potted fern. Aelwen looked at it. "We don't keep plants inside in Corova."

"Why not?"

"I don't know. We just don't."

"Well, each to their own, but I highly recommend it. Plants and flowers have a way of lifting the spirit in my experience."

"I'll be sure to try it sometime."

"May I make a second suggestion?" asked the president.

Intrigued, Aelwen replied affirmatively.

"You should try wearing what you find most comfortable."

"What makes you think I find this uncomfortable?"

"Look at you. You've been shifting in your shoes all day and trying to stand up straight without ripping your dress. In the future, don't be afraid to wear whatever you want. You don't have to dress fancy to be respected."

"Okay." Aelwen was taken aback at how true his words were. Marchian fashion was something gorgeous, in her opinion and she had already come to appreciate it, but it felt unnatural to not be wearing commoners garbe—trousers, tunic, boots and jacket. The absence of the familiar, comforting weight of her weapons belt at her hips was something that had nagged at her since she'd mounted Erizo to ride here.

"Would it be inappropriate if I brought weapons here with me?"

The president gave her a confused look. "Why would you want to?"

Aelwen shook her head, feeling foolish. "I just—for the majority of my life, I've worn them almost constantly, they're a comfort, in a strange way. Being without them feels…wrong. But, if that's not what you meant by 'wear what's comfortable for you', I completely understand."

Tecsequaih was still looking at her funny. His expression, which had started as one of bafflement, was transformed into one of something Aelwen was tempted to label as admiration.

"You may wear your weapons. Even if you wished ill upon anyone here, there are enough guards present that you'd never have time to land a blow." He gestured to one of the many armored sentries standing at a corner beside yet another fern spilling out of its pot.

Aelwen couldn't believe he'd consented. For a moment, she'd been convinced she'd earned herself an expulsion from the council for even asking the question. "What about the other council members? I don't want to make them uncomfortable."

"Don't worry about them. General Ekua is always wearing some weapon or other, swords and axes most of all, and sometimes if they're coming right to work after a game, other members will have daggers or arrows on them."

"A game?"

"Oh yes, dagger throwing and archery are two of the most popular sports there are, nearly all of the council members play from time to time."

Before Aelwen could respond, a man with a ream of papers in his arms walked across the hall and entered an office. It was Lin. He didn't look at them. "What happened to Lin's father?"

"He died in battle," replied President Tecsequiah.

"And Lin blames you?"

"You overheard our conversation the other week, did you?"

Aelwen thought it best to not waste her time answering a question that did not need one. "How do you remember that far back? Haven't you been busy?"

"I may be old, but when you are a leader, you learn to remember. You have no idea how many people have come to me just to dig up problems from the past."

"So, what happened? Why does he blame you?" He would not steer his way out of this conversation so easily, an Arenian was trained to never let their opponent break their intention no matter what they tried to pull.

"Years ago, when I was a young man—hard to believe that ever happened— Marchia was little more than a few hundred miles of land."

"I find that harder to believe than your being young."

Tecsequaih smiled faintly. "Marchia was a small country packed full of people. We were overpopulating. There was another kingdom that laid claim to all of the lands that are now Marchia: Ave. Ave was a country of few people and much land. We needed more space. The rulers tried to negotiate, but never reached a peace. Our queen urged us not to fight, to wait until something happened. But we were done waiting.

"An epidemic had come and was spreading, ripping through the innocent souls of hundreds. We needed to flee, but we had nowhere to go. We needed land and we needed time to acquire that land, but we did not have either. In the night, General Toshiko rallied her rebel forces, myself included and we attacked Ave. Their forces were weak, few and unsuspecting. In just one night we won ourselves five miles of land. Not much, but something. The rebels were to be disciplined, but there was no time. The epidemic was spreading. The uninfected moved to the new land.

"More and more small raids took place. An army was forming. The queen could not say no now, for her people had already screamed yes. A full-out war was waged with Ave. Ave begged for aid from Paruma and Corova, but both kingdoms stayed neutral. Over the years, the war continued. We diminished Ave until it was nothing more than a speck on the coast. The war lasted for eight years. Then it was time for the final battle. One final skirmish to decide the final boundaries of the newly shaped countries." Tecsequaih's eyes glazed over as the ghosts of the past revisited him. "To this day, we call the final battle The Doom.

"I remember it like it was yesterday. Two armies, an ocean of tens of thousands of troops covering the ground like a blanket. Two factions staring each other straight in the eyes from across a line. A line that would be crossed. Our leader raised her sword, bellowed the war cry and we all raced forward, prepared to meet our fates.

"I don't remember anything that happened during the beginning of the battle. My survival instincts took over. I do remember bodies scattered, blood staining the ground, tattered flags flapping furiously in the wind and...the screams."

Aelwen did not press him as he took a moment to collect himself. His eyes were watery, giving way to the emotion surging within him.

"When a soldier fights, there's a moment where they don't know what they're doing. Their instincts kick in and they aren't even thinking anymore. Just...moving. Just killing. I didn't know what I was doing when it happened, but when I think back I...I can see them. The faces of those I killed. Some of them. Others are just...silhouettes. But I can always hear their death cries. There was a moment in that battle when my emotions took over again and drove away those insane fighting instincts. The flag. That is what I saw. Miles away, torn, burning, but still waving. It was not our flag, it belonged to Ave. There was silence for just a moment. It all came flooding in, everything that had happened. Thousands of people on both sides, dead, and for what? To decide where our borders would be. Was it worth it? That question did not matter anymore, I could not turn back. I was in the midst of a storm and I could not run now.

"Then I heard it. The scream that extinguished the flame of spirit from my soul. The scream of Lin's father. Soldan. I did not see where it came from, but I knew I had to get to him. I ran, my soul guiding the way until I found him, sword driven through his chest. Soldan killed his attacker and collapsed. I ran to him. I remember the last words I said to him. I said...I said..."

The shadows left Tecsequaih's face for an instant. He met Aelwen's eyes; his face was streaked with tears. "That man. He meant the world to me." Tecsequiah wiped his eye with the side of his hand. "I am sorry. I did not mean to ramble on for so long."

Aelwen placed a hand on his shoulder. "It's all right. I'm sorry for asking, I did not know it would be so painful for you."

To her surprise, he smiled. "It's a shame everyone doesn't realize that."

"I lost someone, too."

"You did?"

"Yes. It happened as we were escaping. The only thing is…she might still be alive. I have to know whether she is or not. And that's one of the reasons I'm here."

"I hope to the gods that you find her." He took a calming breath and President Tecsequaih returned. "I have to go to my office for some papers. I will see you at the meeting."

Aelwen wanted to call out to him, to tell him that she thought he was brave to shoulder all of the pressures and continue to hold his head high. But she just couldn't get herself to say anything. Instead, she waited until he went into his office, then continued down the hall.

She located the nearest clock and took a look. Seven minutes until five. She had best be on her way to the meeting chamber of the President's Council. As she passed the president's office, she heard a muffled noise from behind the door. Curiosity got the best of her. She looked around the hall. She was alone. Quietly, she walked up to the door and leaned in, listening intently.

<div style="text-align:center">~~~~</div>

Tecsequiah turned away from Aelwen. What had he done? What had he been thinking? He had written it all down. Written his feelings down over and over again, yet still he carried that grief with him. Saying it to her, pouring his heart out in the middle of the hall…someone could have seen him. He had never shared that memory with anyone, not even Lin. Why had he opened up so easily to Aelwen?

He felt tears on his cheeks and did not rub them away. By the time he reached his office, his vision was so blurry that he had to wipe his eyes to locate the lock. He did not need anything from his office. He just needed space to himself, lest someone see their president crying. Here no one could see him and that was all he needed right now.

Tecsequiah had thought of himself as stone and steel. A battle-honed warrior with a heart of solid rock and iron. When Soldan had died, his world had crumbled and fallen in upon him. Since the death, he had built himself back up, but never again would he have such a powerful wall surrounding his feelings. He was glass now. Strong, thick glass, but glass nonetheless. As he had spoken to Aelwen, the glass had cracked before he'd realized it. He had sealed it up as best he could, but there was no stopping it now. He let the glass break. He let himself shatter.

Sobs overtook him. Not weak, gasping sobs like those of a jaded lover. These were real, powerful sobs of someone who knew pain because he had stared into its stone-cold face as it snatched everything from him.

104

<div style="text-align:center">~~~~</div>

There was the sound of something heavy hitting the floor, something breaking, something snapping.

<div style="text-align:center">~~~~</div>

Papers went flying with a vigorous sweep of his hand. Tecsequaih's trembling knees gave way. He caught himself on the side of the desk, pulling himself onto his knees and into a half-standing-half-kneeling position. Tears covered the freshly polished wood, staining it dark as he felt. That covering that had held in his emotions for years exploded completely. It felt so...good to finally let them be free.

<div style="text-align:center">~~~~</div>

Aelwen's heart broke for Tecsequaih. Why did she have to ask? She wanted to knock or open the door, to console him even though she was rubbish at it. But she knew better. These were not her demons to slay.

Taking a steadying breath, she continued down the hallway.

"Aelwen!"

Lin walked up to her and they shook hands. "How are you?"

"Good, as usual." Lin avoided eye contact. "Listen, Aelwen, there is something I need to tell you and I don't want you to get upset about it, ok?"

"No promises. Go ahead." She was feeling quite bitter towards Lin for holding the death of his father over Tecsequaih's head for so long.

"Marchia will not aid you. President Tecsequiah doesn't know it yet, as of right now he plans on helping you, but the council is going to vote against him."

Anger burst forth from within her. *Don't get upset about it?* "What? Why?"

"Neutrality is safe. Marchia has always attempted to keep out of the problems of other countries. At the moment, we have no reason to help you other than that we like you. If we join your side, it will make us enemies of the state of Corova and whoever they ask for help. We cannot afford a war."

"Then why drag this out for so long? Why the charade?"

"Because Tecsequaih wanted to help you. Matters such as these are always voted upon, that was part of our new order when we conquered Ave. I'm telling you now because I didn't want you to be blindsided. I'm sorry." Lin walked past her and entered the meeting chamber. Aelwen could not believe what she had just heard. The floor swayed beneath her. She balled her fists at her sides. All her effort had been for nothing.

If she were just going to lose the vote, what was the point in even attending the meeting? Blinded by fury, Aelwen turned on her heel and marched out of Arkada.

105

CHAPTER TEN

Swinging her cloak onto the railing, Aelwen entered the home she shared with Lysia, who sat at the dining room table playing cards with Rinly, who had apparently returned to them after spending weeks helping with the hurricane cleanup.

"That was fast! How was the meeting?" Lysia called, leaning back in her chair to get a better view of her friend.

Taking a long breath, Aelwen admitted, "I didn't go."

Everyone fell silent.

"Lin told me it was all a ruse," explained Aelwen. "That Marchia would never support Corova. Rather than be humiliated in front of the council, I left."

"Why…why wouldn't they support you?" stammered Rinly.

"Apparently, the council wants to remain neutral from foreign affairs."

Lysia rested her forehead in her hand. "And you didn't stay? You didn't even *try* to change their minds?"

"I couldn't—"

"Maybe you could have. You could have persuaded them, you could have changed just one vote…"

"Aren't they going to help Ave?" questioned Rinly.

"I didn't hang around to find out."

Lysia exhaled. "They better not be. Marchia can't help one country and not the other."

Aelwen's head was throbbing. "I'm going to take a nap."

"Wait," protested Lysia. "We have to talk about this, we have to—"

"Lysia, please. I just need to sleep."

Aelwen's feet felt like lead. Somehow, she managed to make it up the stairs. She groaned when she opened the door to her bedroom. Covering the thick, warm blankets were about a dozen thick books on the laws and history of Marchia. Aelwen had got them all from the library this morning and spread them on her bed to study in preparation for the meeting.

Loading her arms with books, she stumbled to the corner and dropped them on the floor. *I'll pick them up later,* she thought.

She flopped onto her bed. Sleep took over so quickly that Aelwen didn't even remember closing her eyes.

When she opened them, she found herself staring into the narrow earth-colored eyes of Lysia.

"Lysia? What the—"

"The president's here. He wants to talk to you."

Aelwen's brain was still too sleep-addled to fully comprehend Lysia's words.

"He's downstairs. I told him you were sleeping, but he was adamant. He says it's an emergency."

More awake, Aelwen jumped out of bed. Looking in the mirror, she quickly made adjustments to her messy hair.

She jogged down the stairs and into the living room, where Tecsequaih stood, his face iron. His reason for being there was hardly a mystery. Her stomach was knotting itself up and her nerves buzzed. She hadn't had time to prepare her explanation. She bowed awkwardly.

"Sir—"

The president held up a firm hand. "Aelwen, why did you fail to attend the council meeting? I had been with you not ten minutes before the meeting began, yet when it started, you failed to appear."

"I did not attend because I was informed that my belief that your country would help mine was a ruse."

Tecsequaih withdrew a bit, his eyes searching hers. "Please do elaborate."

So she told him of her entire encounter with Lin in the hallway right before the meeting began, recounting every word they had shared as best she could remember. When she had finished, Tecsequaih's expression had changed from one of iron to one of barely contained fire.

"Lin Akachi is a man of many qualities, but I never took him for a liar." His words were low but full of meaning, like the first drops of rain before a hurricane made landfall.

"Excuse me?"

"Lin is a liar. A manipulative, scheming liar."

Aelwen could not bring herself to believe him. Lin was a liar, so that meant... "Corova won the vote?"

A bit of the fire left the president's eyes. "No. But they would have had you been present. The council was angry you did not show, they believed you to be unreliable and untrustworthy and voted against Corova. Except for Gavnas, of course."

Her heart sank to the depths of her soul. "Lin lied to me because he wanted Marchia to turn its back on Corova," she realized. "Why?"

A deep sigh escaped the president. "As you have seen, Lin is a man of passionate feeling and firm belief. He does not easily let go of the past. Years ago, in the war between Ave and Marchia, Corova refused to aid Marchia in their time of need. Lin is adamant to return the favor."

It was pointless to focus on what had been done. Everything that had happened, happened. There was no changing it. Now, they could only find ways to improve the situation Lin had created for them.

"Can there be another vote?" wondered Aelwen. "Expose Lin as the liar he is, tell your council the truth of what happened. Surely they will understand."

"The president is not kindly looked upon for spreading incriminating information about members of their council. It is only appropriate for other council members to do that, or else the president looks like a dictator trying to remove anyone who opposes them by calling them dishonest."

"I'm a member of your council, I'll do it."

Tecsequaih shook his head defeatedly. "No, no. You're too new, the council will blame you for falsely incriminating Lin just to get your way. We'll have to convince someone else on the council, someone everyone else trusts."

"Any ideas who that might be?"

Tecsequaih looked off in thought. "Let me think on it. Come to my office tomorrow morning. It has been a long day for all of us and I believe it is best if we all get some rest before we go making anymore rash decisions."

"Agreed. I'll see you tomorrow, sir."

The president gave a small nod of acknowledgement before his departure.

When she opened her eyes, Aelwen found herself blinded by the sun. Groaning, she rolled over to peer at the clock.

Nine o'clock? She flung off her covers and began dressing herself, searching frantically for something appropriate for her new job. She remembered what Tecsequaih had said about wearing what she was comfortable in. She grabbed an olive green shirt, brown leggings and black leather boots. Extremely Corovan fashion, no eye-catching designs or bright colors. Remembering that her black cloak was in desperate need of a washing, she found a red one.

She finished buckling her boots and dashed out to the stable, where she found Lysia and Rinly grooming their horses. Rinly laughed.

"Hey, hey, hey, looks who's up." How was he here so early, did he never sleep?

"I have to get to Arkada, an important meeting," Aelwen explained swiftly. She did not have time for the multitude of questions they undoubtedly had for her.

Aelwen tacked up her horse in a matter of minutes.

Rinly had his horse on the crossties. He had not asked Aelwen if he could keep his horse in her barn. What was she thinking? This barn was not hers, it was theirs. A high-class job did not place her above any of her friends.

"Look out," he said, unhooking his steed and giving it a gentle push so it would get out of Aelwen's way. "The queen's coming." He was joking, of course, but something about his words made Aelwen uneasy.

Before being on her way, Aelwen said, "I'll be back...I don't know when."

She started out trotting just for the fun of it, but then slowed Erizo to a walk so she could take in the sights around her. This city was truly amazing. Even after living here in Firhad for almost a month, she was still in awe of how magnificent it was. The simple people going about their daily routines, the tasteful set-ups in shop windows, the bright flowers, the clean white buildings. All of it. How had she lived without so much for so long?

While taking in the sights of the city and breathing in the clean, free air, thoughts began to creep into Aelwen's mind. 'The queen's coming.'

Was that really how her friends saw her now? As someone above them, with more power than them and able to control them? With this new job of hers, how could she possibly remain on the same societal tier as them?

Aelwen pushed those thoughts from her head, choosing instead to take in the types of flowers growing in the nearest shop window.

As she rode, she came to a part of town where there were no buildings in the way. The pedestrian had a full view of the rainforest and far away sea. The sea. With its storms and loneliness. Still, it was a nice place to get away. Maybe in the future, she and her friends could go on vacation by the sea or spend a few days on *Mist Wing* again.

Taran lived by the sea. Taran. She had almost forgotten about him. It was strange how easily he and Lysia had parted ways. They were never in contact anymore. What was that man doing with his life now? Maybe a visit to Taran would be an excuse to get away to the sea for a while.

With forgotten people on her mind, Aelwen began to think about Namar. Where was he, what was he doing? Was he even alive? Was he on this continent? Was he in this country? Why should she know, why should she care? He didn't matter anymore. He was out of her life now.

Aelwen found President Tecsequaih in his office, writing. His desk was covered in tall stacks of papers that nearly hid him from view. The president put down his quill and rested his forehead on his fists.

"Aelwen? Hello."

"Have you come up with any ideas?" she asked, feeling she did not need to elaborate on her reason for being there.

"I have. Though, I think it will be best if I keep you in the dark for now, until the plan is more firmly cemented. Should anyone become suspicious, it is better if only I know so that you cannot be named my accomplice."

Although the not-knowing was already gnawing at Aelwen, she understood his point.

The president took a paper from his desk and handed it to her. "Here is a schedule of future meetings. Do feel free to attend."

Aelwen nodded, taking the paper. "Thank you."

"Thank you for visiting."

As she shut his office door behind her, she decided that, to make this trip just a bit more interesting, she would take a long detour throughout the whole building.

If anyone saw her and asked what she was doing, she would say she was familiarizing herself with the building—which was not completely false. She did not have a reason for taking this detour, it just felt right.

Passing Lin's office, she noticed that the door was ajar. She snuck a look. No one was inside.

After checking the hallway several times to make sure that no one was coming, Aelwen slipped inside.

The desk was the first thing she searched. Unlike Tecsequaih's desk with two or three foot high stacks of papers, this desk was well organized. There was one paper in the middle which was half filled out. Beside it lay a quill. On either side of the middle paper was a thin stack of other papers. The stack on the left had been all filled in while the stack on the right was blank.

Aelwen found the markings on the papers overwhelming. Smooth, clean strokes, elegant numbers filling columns and rows. Those papers were of no use to her. Lin did not leave much out in the open. Aelwen started opening drawers, searching and scanning for...she didn't know what. All she could find were reams upon reams of papers filed away in perfect order, cabinets full of backup supplies: ink, quills, paper, stamps, wax seals and the like. And a single ring of keys.

After sifting through the organized papers in hope of finding something exciting, Aelwen decided it was time to leave. She took one last glance around to make sure she had not missed a thing. She had. Wedged in the corner behind the door was a stack of drawers she had failed to notice. Were they hidden behind the door for a reason? Only one way to find out.

Gingerly, Aelwen shut the door and began opening the drawers. They were all empty. Except for the middle one, which was locked. She remembered seeing the ring of keys in Lin's desk. She scrambled over and opened the desk. She snatched the key ring and hurried back to the drawers and tried every key.

Sweat trickling down her brow, Aelwen heard an unmistakable voice coming from down the hall. Lin. He was talking to someone. She finally found the key that fit. The footsteps halted for a moment. So did she.

"Lucky. See you tomorrow," Lin's voice said on the other side of the door, a ways down the hall by the sound of it. Aelwen's breath caught in her throat.

There was the sound of one set of footsteps disappearing and a door closing, his companion had left. Now one single set of footsteps was on its way, coming for her.

The sound of a thousand horse hooves thundered inside her chest. Aelwen pulled open the drawer. Papers sealed in yellow envelopes were inside. She took all of the papers out of the drawer and tucked them inside her boot. She shoved the drawer closed, locked it and put the keys back with a speed she had never used outside of a fight. She started for the door. Her hand stopped inches from the brass knob. Lin had to be close now. What would he say if he saw her coming out of his office?

"Lin!" called the voice that had been conversing with Lin moments before. "I forgot, here are the ferry records."

Lin's footsteps retracted. Aelwen turned the knob and opened the door just enough for her to peer through. Lin had his back to her, he and another person were exchanging papers. Thank the gods, neither of them were looking in her direction. Now was her chance. Aelwen fled out the door, it shut behind her with a loud click. She ceased to breathe for a second. That door had been open earlier, when Lin returned he was guaranteed to notice it was closed.

A voice said, "Hey."

Mid-step, the thief turned to see Lin staring at her, concern and confusion written all across his face. "Were you in my office?"

Struggling to keep her breathing even, Aelwen responded, "No. I noticed that your office door was open so I closed it for you."

Suspicion clouded his gaze for a moment. Aelwen went rigid. He relaxed. "Thank you. What are you doing here today?"

"Oh, the president never gave me a schedule, I didn't know if there was a meeting today." The back of her knees were sweating. "I have to get home. See you."

Once Lin had disappeared into his office, Aelwen rushed out of Arkada and released a sigh of relief. She looked down at the papers in her boot. What was Lin hiding? Why was this locked away? She straightened and went to fetch her steed. She intended to find out.

~~~~

Rinly slapped a card onto the pile.

Lysia did the same, the card she put down was her last. She grunted in defeat.

Her opponent smiled, laying out the rest of his hand on the table and sweeping all of the cards into a deck, which he promptly began to shuffle. "Another round?" he asked.

"Of course," said Lysia, tapping her fingers on the wooden surface. "You know, I thought I was good at cards until I met you."

"Everyone does."

She made sure to pay attention as Rinly shuffled. He had to be manipulating the deck somehow. No one was this good. A knock at the door broke her concentration.

"Be right back," she said to Rinly, aming her way to the door. She opened it to see the tall, broad-shouldered, red-haired man she'd spent years of her life with.

Taran's pale skin was bright red, the shade it turned after he'd spent too much time in the sun.

He shifted from foot to foot before saying, "Hi."

Lysia folded her arms. "Hi." When several beats passed and Taran said nothing, she added, "Well?"

"I came to say goodbye."

She'd had a feeling this moment was coming. In a way, it seemed long overdue. They should have had this conversation when they'd first set foot on Marchia. It would have been better to part ways then and there, to put a clean end to their old life.

"This is it, then?" Lysia said, unsure of what exactly to say.

"Yes. It's time for us both to move on with our lives."

"And we can't do that together."

"No…I don't think we can. We lived with each other because we had to to survive. We have survived. Now it's time for us to live."

Lysia couldn't have put it better herself. To continue to live with Taran in her life was to hold onto the broken dreams and old wounds. The nightmares, the constant fear, the anger and the hate. There was nothing Lysia wanted more than to let it all go— to start
~~~~

anew, the shadows of the past forgotten. While she knew it was utterly impossible to ever achieve that goal completely, severing her ties with Taran was a step in the right direction.

He was right—they'd lived together because they had to. They were two lost souls, two scraps of semi-decency, who had clung together because they were desperate and afraid and in need of company. They were no longer that. Holding onto their old companionship, forcing it to endure, would mean holding onto memories and feelings that were best relinquished so they could move on, each of them in their own way, in their own time.

"I agree," Lysia said. "You won't be helping take Corova back?"

Taran shook his head. "No. Corova was only cruel to me, it was never a home. I don't give a damn what happens to it."

Lysia wasn't surprised to hear that. What *did* surprise her was how Taran's words struck a chord within her. "Okay. I hope you find happiness. Whatever that means for you." She smiled and extended a hand to Taran.

"Same to you." They shook. It was a simple gesture that ended a years-long bond forged of mutual hatred and disgust of the world.

"Goodbye, Lysia."

"Goodbye, Taran."

Lysia shut the door. The stared at it for a moment, corralling her emotions, coming to terms with what had just taken place. Another step away from her old life. Another step towards a new one. She returned to the living room to find Rinly had divvied up the deck in preparation for a new game.

"Was that Taran?"

Lysia sat, plucking up her hand and examining it. "It was."

Rinly put down the first card. "What did he want?"

"To say goodbye." She put down a card.

Rinly stared at his cards for a moment before setting one down. "Goodbye?"

"Yes," said Lysia, not making eye contact with Rinly as she placed a second card. "I don't think I'll be seeing Taran again. At least, not for a very long time."

"Is that a good thing?"

"It doesn't quite feel like it yet…but yes. It's a good thing."

~~~~

Lysia and Rinly were there when Aelwen returned to the house. She found the two of them standing at the counter in the kitchen.

"There," Lysia said to Rinly. "Now add some ginger. Careful, not too much." By the smell of it, Lysia was teaching him how to make spice bread, a delicacy she excelled at.

Rinly spared a glance over his shoulder when he heard the door shut. He rested his hands on the counter in that relaxed way of his. "You're back sooner than I expected."

"It was a short meeting."

Aelwen could feel the folded papers crunching inside her boot. They were driving her insane, but she didn't dare take them out now. If she did, her friends would want to know what they were and why she had them hidden.
~~~~

She had endured the entire ride home with a growing sinking feeling in her stomach. She had stolen the papers in retaliation for what Lin had done to her— no, not just her. Corova. What she had done was rationalized, but not justified. To do wrong in response to another having done wrong resulted in nothing good, that she knew. Corrupt politics and behind-the-scenes bargaining were not ideals that she agreed with, it was simply what she knew based on her minimal experience with Corovan politics.

Aelwen asked Lysia, "Teaching him how to cook?"

"Yes," Lysia replied. "From years of living in the wild, he only knows how to roast meat and potatoes. I might not be the best, but I at least know how to cover up the terrible flavor with enough spices to make it acceptable. And living in the forest doesn't mean you can only cook two things."

She threw a sarcastic glance at Rinly, who chuckled lightly and said, "I'm not very good at it."

"You're a beginner, you'll get better."

"I have to look over some government papers," Aelwen not-entirely-lied.

"Have fun," said Lysia sarcastically.

"Oh, I will," replied Aelwen with just as much sarcasm.

Closing herself in her bedroom, Aelwen scrambled onto her bed and pulled all of the papers out of her boot. They were all in sealed envelopes without any addresses. Looking closer, she saw where stamps had been pulled off. What kinds of secrets were in these envelopes? Reaching for an envelope, her fingers suddenly forgot how to function.

She flexed her fingers and lifted the envelope nearest to her. Carefully, she unfolded the top and peered inside.

There was a letter inside, handwritten. It read:

Dearest Tecsequaih,

My heart aches to be away from you. Every night, I sit by the fire. As I watch the flames, all I can think of is you and your embrace. Though I know this venture is but a week, that is far too long for me to be apart from you. I miss you with every part of my being.

Aelwen stopped there. This was not useful to her. She tore open each envelope and in each one she found the same thing. Letters exchanged between Tecsequaih and Soldan, Lin's father. She spread the letters out on her bed. Each one had a neatly written date in the top right corner; she arranged them by date. The two men undoubtedly had a romantic connection and a very strong one at that.

The more Aelwen read, the worse she felt. These letters really meant something to Lin. Maybe they were all he had left of his father. What was he going to do when he discovered they were gone?

No, no. If he had not wanted anyone to find them, he shouldn't have left them lying around.

He had not left them lying around, they were locked in a secret cabinet and sealed in envelopes.

Aelwen's busy thoughts were suddenly interrupted by a deep, shattering bellow that rang across the city. She threw down the letter she was holding and bolted out of her bedroom. Breathing heavily, mind whirling with all the possibilities of what was happening,

Aelwen didn't notice Lysia and Rinly coming up the stairs until she collided with them. Lysia stabilized her mid-fall. "You alright?"

"Yeah, yeah." Aelwen rubbed her hands on her thighs. "What's happening?"

"I have no idea."

Rinly interjected. "Go up there, look out the window."

The trio scrambled to the top of the stairs and looked out of a gigantic window that overlooked Firhad. Arkada was visible, as was the massive golden bell that hung atop it that was currently echoing throughout the city streets. People were hustling out of their homes and rushing to Arkada on horseback. Aelwen shoved her friends aside and rushed down the stairs.

"Aelwen, where are you going?" called Rinly from the top of the stairs.

Halfway out the door, Aelwen shouted back, "To Arkada!"

She was out of the door and atop her horse moments later, galloping through the streets.

In no time, she was among the other riders gathered before Arkada. Erizo bumped into the rump of a palomino horse in front of her. The rider wheeled their horse around. "Watch it!"

Her heart froze when she saw the man's face. Lin Akachi.

Noticing who he was scolding, Lin softened his tone. "Aelwen! I apologize. What are you doing here?" His words were warm and normal, as if he had not sabotaged her entire plan yesterday.

Purposely avoiding eye contact with him, Aelwen busied herself with scanning her surroundings, trying to gather information of what was going on. Far up, at the head of the cavalry was President Tecsequaih. He was shouting orders she could not discern.

Aelwen registered Lin's words. "I'm not completely sure. I heard the bell, saw everyone and decided I'd come see for myself. What's happening?"

"There has been another murder."

"At Ave?"

"Yes, on the border."

"Is that all you know?"

Lin lowered his gaze, staring at the horn his white-knuckled hand was gripping. "No." He raised his head to stare at the pale grey sky. "Our soldiers were just doing their duty. The Aveans tried to provoke them, but they stood their ground. The Aveans began throwing stones. A Marchian was struck in the back of the head and her partner took action. Five were killed. That is the popular rumor, at least."

"Five?"

"Yes."

"There was only one death the first time, correct?"

"Yes."

"The first time it was only Tecsequaih and a handful of soldiers, why is the whole city going?"

"To show the strength of our country. "

Up at the head of the troop, Tecsequaih swept his arm forward and the mismatched band set off.

Aelwen watched the riders make off. She wished she could go, but this was not her arena. She smiled at the irony. In the arena, she never hesitated to go into battle. Now she was free to do it and was almost content to stand down. Almost.

She got Erizo moving.

Riding up beside Lin, still unable to look him directly in the eyes, she questioned, "The five who were killed, which country did they belong to?"

"Two Aveans, three Marchians."

Aelwen possessed minimal knowledge of Ave, but what she did know was that, with the exception of the war with Marchia, Ave had never taken a violent approach to any situation.

"Ave—what is happening there to cause such disturbance?"

"The majority of the country's water has been poisoned. There is something going on underground, tainting the water. I don't know the specifics, only Desliad and Tecsequaih do."

The Aveans were desperate, that was why they were striking out. They needed some sort of help, even if it was only a daily shipment of clean water.

The ride lasted for nearly two hours and the entire company kept to a steady gallop almost the entire time.

Closer.

Aelwen breathed in and out. The chaos was getting the better of her—the deaths, the need, the sudden, unexpected action. They were about half an hour away and in order for Aelwen to make an intellectual decision, she needed a clear mind.

Thankfully, she was good at doing that. It was a trick she had taught herself during her first months of becoming an Arenian. No matter how many weapons her opponent was armed with, no matter how brawny they appeared, she had to keep her head and look only at the facts without emotions getting in the way.

The grass was shriveled, brown and dead. The poisoned water offered no life to anything. She took a deep breath, felt the wind and focused on the synchronized pounding of the horses' hooves. She breathed to the rhythm. Closed her eyes. She felt the rhythm, she let it sink into her soul and fill her up until she and Erizo were one and the same. When she opened her eyes, blinking in the brightness of the sun, there was no distinguishing her heartbeat from the thundering of hooves. She was the horses, she was the rhythm.

Aelwen was jerked out of her spiritual world by a loud sniff from beside her.

Lin had one hand on his forehead, shielding his eyes while his other tightly held the reins.

Probably allergies. All of the horses surrounding them would aggravate any animal sensitivities.

The sky was coated with pale grey clouds, but the radiant sun refused to be blocked out. It covered the crinkled grass in yellow light and reflected off the drawn swords of the riders, blinding those who rode behind them, aggravating any headaches caused by allergies.

Lin sniffed again, a small sob escaped him.

"Are you all right?" Aelwen asked.

Lin lowered his hand to make eye contact with Aelwen. What she saw terrified her. There was so much wrath twisted into his face. Lin's face was bright red and soaking wet, tears streamed down his cheeks. He sobbed several times before harnessing the ability to form words.

"You know what happened here."

He wiped his drenched face with his sleeve and stared on ahead. Making no more attempts to hide his sadness, he let it wash over him.

How could she have been so stupid? Why had she even asked? She watched Lin for a moment and then looked away, afraid that she too might cry. There was nothing false in his pain and anger. His father had meant so incredibly much to him. And she had taken away everything he had left of him.

How could I do this?

The letters were Lin's rightful property. They were none of her business.

Guilt twisted in her gut. It had been there from the moment she had read the first letter, quelled and quashed, forced down into the dark pits of her soul so it wouldn't be a bother. Now it fully surfaced, in all its ugly power, filling her with regret and disgust at herself until she couldn't touch on the thought of the letters without feeling sick.

I hate this. I'm awful. Stupid and rash and awful. I should never have stolen the letters, if I could go back and undo it, I would.

Aelwen heard the border soldiers before she saw them. Their words were indistinguishable shouts. The closer she got, the clearer the words became.

"At least our president cares about us enough to back us up!"

"You shouldn't need back up! Stand and fight for yourselves!"

"Is that why you are begging my country for aid? Take your own advice, that's when I'll back down!"

Agreeing shouts of "Here, here" echoed around.

Close enough to see details now, Aelwen made out that there were two groups of people, distinctly separated by an invisible line—one dressed in the green and gold of Marchia, one dressed in the orange and white, which Aelwen inferred must have been the colors of Ave.

"Where is your queen? Hiding in her castle, relishing the dark quiet while the blood of her people is spilled?"

"How dare you! Queen Baric stays to help her people! She sits by the beds of the sick and cares for them herself! She trusts her guards to uphold their duties!"

"Is that why several of your companions are dead?"

The dispute ended the moment President Tecsequaih pulled his steed up beside the line of Marchian soldiers keeping to their side of the border. The silence that man struck into the souls of all around him was miraculous.

After a moment of quiet, Tecsequaih addressed the Marchian guard nearest to him. "Where are the dead?"

The guard nodded solemnly to the side. Following their gaze, Aelwen saw a roughly put together tent. She assumed the bodies were inside.

Tecsequaih inclined his head. Not meeting the gaze of the guard, he asked, "What happened?"

"Our people were holding their positions, doing nothing of offense. The Avean guards began shouting and throwing stones. One of them hit one of us, that's when we charged. Five were killed."

So the rumors were true.

Tecsequaih questioned, "How did this fall out end?"

The Marchian replied, "An Averan general heard the commotion. They rallied a small band of troops and led a neutral charge."

Aelwen's brow furrowed. She had never once heard the expression 'neutral charge'.

"The general did not wish to harm or lay blame to either side, they only wished to end the violence, which they did. Their forces drove all people back to their side of the line."

For the first time, Aelwen noticed the frailty of the Aveans. At first glance they appeared muscular and powerfully built, but on closer inspection, it was clear that that was just an illusion created by their padded armor. The Aveans were skinny and they had dark circles around their eyes.

President Tecsequaih turned his focus to an Avean. "Is the claim my warrior made true?"

The Avean avoided eye contact with the Marchian ruler. "Yes."

The president nudged his horse over the border line. "I will enter your country." It was not a question. "Where is your ruler?" No response from anyone. He repeated his question.

An Avean said, "We do not know."

"Is she missing?"

"No, sir."

Tecsequaih shook his head indignantly. "I need to be on my way. Tell me all you know."

"Queen Baric has been personally visiting all of the sick and attending regular expeditions to find water. We do not know where she is at the moment."

Tecsequaih seemed satisfied with that answer, but unsettled at the same time. He raised his hand into the air, halting his followers. "Split yourselves into groups of seven, search until the queen is found."

Aelwen joined Tecsequaih's group. He looked a bit surprised to see her. "Aelwen, when did you join this company?"

"As soon as you set out."

The president nodded and spoke to his entire group. Aelwen did not recognize anyone. "We will travel into the heart of the capital and search there. Onward!"

Not ten minutes into their venture, a voice echoed throughout the group.

"Your Excellency!" The president wheeled his horse around to see who had called his name. It was a Marchian, though not one from his group of seven. A female with wild brown hair.

"What? Have you found something?"

"Yes," panted the rider. "In the…west…West Edge Village."

President Tecsequaih obviously knew his way around the small country. He changed direction and set off at a brisk pace, the messenger loping along beside him.

"Do you have an address?" Tecsequaih wondered.

"Cypress Cottage."

Roughly fifteen minutes at a solid canter later, the horses got a rest. The company came to a stop in front of a quaint house with a painted door.

Five members of Tecsequaih's group stayed on their horses and waited outside of the house. Aelwen was not among them. She swung her leg over the saddle and tied the reins to a fence post.

Tecsequaih's horse was not bound, the reins were wrapped trustingly around the saddle horn. This man clearly had an unbelievably strong connection with his horse. The state of the president's horse was unsettling. It had been coughing at regular intervals for the last half hour, its head hung low to the ground, but it did not eat. Aelwen patted the sweaty steed. It showed its gratitude for this small comfort by resting its head on her hip. To no one in particular, Aelwen said, "Get water for the horses."

Taking note that Aelwen was following him, Tecsequaih stated, "Aelwen, I did not ask you to come with me."

"I know that. I'm coming anyway."

Whether Tecsequaih had taken the words as a threat or found them amusing, she did not know. The one freedom Aelwen had never lost was being her own person, capable of making her own decisions. This was her life and she was going to do whatever she wanted to do with it. No one else's opinion mattered.

Tecsequaih smiled the tiniest bit.

He pushed open the door to the house. It looked better on the outside than it did on the inside.

There were not any doors or walls separating the rooms from each other. There was just one large room, containing a huddled mass of people, a stove and sink and a ladder to an upstairs loft. The mass of people was really only five. One sat on a stool, two in chairs, one was kneeling and the other was standing. They were all gathered around something.

A bed.

Laying on the bed was a body. Female. Brown hair was splayed around the head of the woman. Her eyes were closed. Dead or asleep? Aelwen did not want to know. She tried to ignore how pale the woman's face was, the only visible part of her. The rest of the woman was covered with a thick, off-white blanket. No, not only her face was visible. One of the woman's hands was sticking out of the blankets, one of the people who sat around the bed clasped the unhealthy woman's hand in hers.

The other person sitting beside the bed gasped. "Mister President, you must leave. This is no place for you, you may catch the sickness."

President Tecsequaih did not let the state of the house or the words of the people in it distract him. "Where is Queen Baric?"

A woman pointed to the back door of the house. "She fled into the woods."

"No one followed her?"

"No, sir."

"For the sake of the gods." Tecsequaih exited through the back door and sprinted into the dense forest.

Aelwen stayed behind, both her heart and her mind agreeing on something for once. It was not her place to follow him. She glanced around uneasily, suddenly unsure of what she was doing.

A young man asked, "Are you a servant of the president?"

"Aide, not servant."

An old woman rose from her stool and made her way across the room to Aelwen. Despite the woman's appearance, she did not hobble like most elders did. She walked straight and proud, her body still capable of much.

"My lady, we thank you for being here, but you must go. The sickness lingers."

After a quick moment's silence in which she examined the poor condition of the house, she asked, "What happened here?"

A middle-aged woman sitting in a chair, holding the hand of the unconscious girl replied, "My daughter caught the Water Feber."

After a moment passed, Aelwen realized that the woman intended to say no more. "I am sorry. I am not familiar with that disease."

The woman ignored her, staring at the closed eyes of her dead daughter. It was the kneeling man who responded. "It comes from the poisoned water. It is extremely deadly and highly contagious. My daughter came down with it yesterday morning. There was nothing to be done. When the queen came to our home, we shut her out. But she would not be held back." She wiped her nose on her sleeve. "Queen Baric came in and stayed with Mysa until her last breath. Not an hour after the passing, the queen began coughing. She ran into the forest and has not been seen since."

"If this disease is so contagious, why do you all remain here?"

The old woman, who had returned to her stool, grumbled, but there was no ferocity in her voice, only broken pleading. "Don't you see? We are not afraid anymore. Death is a welcome friend. Have you not seen the city, have you not...Death is liberation."

Aelwen looked over the scene, unable to come up with something to say. She'd seen terrible living conditions. She'd never seen a plague.

"If you wish to live, you should leave," said the mother.

Aelwen wanted to stay with this destructed family, just to be there by their sides to let them know that someone cared. But she saw now, looking into their dark, sunken eyes and pale, sullen faces that there was nothing to be done for them. They were beyond the farthest reaches of hope. Aelwen had no intention of dying, either. Not now, not yet. She still had so much to do.

~~~~

"Baric!" cried Tecsequaih, turning in a rapid circle, his entire body tense, face frantic. Although their countries had never been on great terms and probably never would be, Tecsequaih and Baric had always both harbored a deep respect for one another. They were friends with a strained relationship due to their positions in society.
~~~~

"Baric! Baric!" He ran through the forest, doing his best to avoid roots, logs and mud. Due to his profession, he did not get to spend much time out in nature, so he was rather clumsy.

Tecsequaih stopped. The instant he had seen that dead girl he knew the cause of her death. Water Fever. The disease had been ravaging the population of Ave for nearly a month now. He guessed that Queen Baric had fled the house because she had caught the disease and did not want to infect anyone else. The disease took effect fast, festering in the lungs, turning them black while crawling up the windpipe and blocking off air supply while also working to shut down the heart. If Baric was alive, if she could hear him, she could probably hardly speak, if she was able to make any noise at all.

Tecsequaih waited for his heavy, uneven breathing to settle. The forest, which had seemed loud and chaotic while he was sprinting through it, now seemed serene and quiet.

A faint gasp interrupted the silence. Tecsequaih turned, scanning the forest for any sign of what could have created the noise. Maybe he was insane, so desperate to find something that his mind was making things up. "Baric!" he shouted.

A louder gasp, a cough. He ran, stopped and shouted her name again. "Keep making noises! I'll find you, don't give in!" After several minutes of searching and retracing his steps and listening so hard his ears felt numb, he came to a spot where two young trees grew beside each other. On her back, grasping the trunk of one of the saplings with all her might, was Baric, Queen of Ave.

Her face looked gray, as if she would turn into stone any second. Baric's usually full, silky head of tawny hair seemed thin, the ends fraying, like a vibrant tree in summer suddenly thrust into winter. She had always been a well built woman, but now she seemed pathetically frail. Tecsequaih ran to her.

His heart was thumping so loudly he thought it would explode. His legs burned and throbbed. He was determined not to stop. He ignored all of the things his body was screaming at him and pushed on.

Tecsequaih dropped to the ground beside Baric. He cradled her fragile body in his arms and let her sink into him. "Hold on, hold on," he whispered between labored breaths.

"I—" she wheezed. "Their…daughter. Water…" The queen's words faded, her eyelids drooped. The effort of forming words was enough to nudge her spirit even closer to the gate of death.

He shook Baric as lightly as he could, just enough to wake her again. "Baric. Baric." He adjusted himself, putting Baric in a more comfortable position. "Heir."

Queen Baric barely comprehended the word. In an attempt to sit up, she fell back. To steady herself, Baric grasped Tecsequaih's shirt. Her eyelids fluttered. Blinking, she made sense of the vision before her. She thought hard, trying to remember what he had just said. "What?" she breathed.

"An heir. You have no children, Baric. You must name an heir."

Sputtering, then managed, "Eiyre."

Tecsequaih held her closer to him. "What?"

"Eiyre." Queen Baric looked directly at Tecsequaih. "My cousin. Find her in… Pilyn Wind."

"Ok, Baric, I will, I'll find her. You can do this. Come on. Just, hold on. Don't leave, please."

"Find her…" murmured the queen. Her eyes fixed on a point in the mid-distance, misted with the fog of death.

"I will. I promise. Here, put your arms around my neck, I can get you to a medic—"

"She doesn't know what to do, you'll have to teach her."

"No, no. You can teach her. You can survive this, Baric, just like you've always survived."

"Find her."

"Okay," he breathed, knowing how near her end was. "I will." He laid the queen onto the soft moss. All the while he kept his face close to hers, listening to her slowing breath. With every passing second, her grip on this life was slipping.

He heard it then, the sound he had been dreading since spotting the crippled queen in the clearing. Her final breath. One last, weak exhale. Then she was gone. Just like that. It was so simple. Too simple. How could a person be wiped off the face of the earth so easily?

CHAPTER ELEVEN

The tolling of the bell stopped.

"Should we go after her?" asked Rinly.

Lysia did not meet his gaze for a moment. Finally, she said, "No. She'll be fine."

"Do you want to go finish the bread?" asked Rinly.

"No." Lysia was taken aback at how harsh her reply was. She felt even worse when she looked at Rinly's large brown eyes. "Do you mind finishing the bread yourself? I'm sorry, but I'm really tired. I'm going to take a nap."

"Okay. Do you want me to wake you up?"

"No, I'm usually good at getting myself up. Do come get me if Aelwen comes back, though."

Lysia shut the door to her bedroom, the sight of the tangerine and lapis tapestry depicting the sun and moon that hung above her bed greeting her. She straightened out the wrinkled peach blankets. She had not felt like making the bed this morning; she never did. She flopped back and closed her eyes. Sleep took her in seconds. She awoke about an hour later, her mind still fuzzy but recognizing that she wouldn't be able to fall back asleep. She sat up to put her shoes on only to realize she hadn't removed them before falling asleep.

Lysia rose, blinking the last wisps of sleep from her eyes. She wondered if Rinly was still there. Before heading downstairs to find out, she spared a look in the mirror. Her clothes were rumpled and her hair was a mess, she hadn't brushed it in two days. She reached for her hairbrush to make herself look at least a bit more respectable, but it wasn't on her dresser. Unsure of where else she would have put it, she checked her drawers and nightstand, all made of a pale wood and carved with a rose and thorn motif. She couldn't find her hairbrush anywhere.

Sighing in frustration, Lysia raked her fingers through her hair, hoping that would do the trick. It didn't.

Aelwen had a hairbrush, she knew. Surely she wouldn't mind if Lysia borrowed it.

She made her way to Aelwen's room. It was roughly the same size as hers and decorated completely differently. Aelwen's sense of style was rigid— her decor was a variety of dark colors, storm grays, rich wine reds and the like. Her furnishings were all of a matching deep brown wood with a dragon motif.

It was not Aelwen's hairbrush that laid atop her vanity that drew Lysia's attention but the many items that covered the navy blanket of her bed.

Letters. All handwritten, all a good many years old, by the looks of them.

Curiosity getting the best of her, she took a closer look. Each had a date written in the top corner, they were arranged chronologically. Lysia picked up one of the letters, which had elegant handwriting scrawled across its surface, and began to read.

Dearest Tecsequaih,

In two days time, my troop is due to return to the east camp. You know I only went on this mission for the glory of it and that I have spent everyday away from you longing to see you once more. I regret to inform you that in two days time, I will not be among the soldiers to greet you in the east camp. Last night, I received a letter. At first, I assumed it was from you, for no one else bothers to write me. But the envelope was not military issue and neither was the seal. The letter was from Mayia Akachi, the soldier I slept with the night of the spring festival. That night was one of revelry and passion. She and I enjoyed each other's company and in the morning, we went our separate ways. I never spoke to her again. Last I heard of her, she resigned from the military. Then, last night, the letter came. I nearly sent it to you so you could read it for yourself, but I somehow could not bring myself to part with it. In short, it said that Mayia is pregnant and by all accounts, I am the father. She said that I could be a part of the child's life or not, that she had no preference and would make her way in the world no matter my decision. It has all happened so suddenly. In truth, I do not know whether I want to be a father or whether I'd be any good at it. But I have decided that, if nothing else, I owe it to Mayia to see her in person so we may discuss this. She included her address in the letter. So, in two days time I will not be riding for the east camp, but for Mayia's home in the south. I do not know how long I will stay with her, though, without handing in a formal resignation from the military, I know I cannot stay for more than a few days. After that, I promise I will return to you.

Love,
Soldan

<div align="center">~~~~</div>

Aelwen wiped her brow. President Tecsequaih had returned two hours ago, emerging from the wood with Queen Baric in his arms. The royal guards were called to take her body away. There would be no funeral. No one cared overly much that the queen was dead. Thick, choking blankets of death shrouded the shoulders of every Avean, what was one more layer?

For the last hour, Tecsequaih had been leading his people on a search for Eiyre, the woman Baric had named heir. Pilyn Wind, the section of the country Baric had told Tecsequaih Eiyre would be found, was unlike the rest of the city.

The politicians had boarded themselves up in their big fancy houses. They avoided the struggles of the simple country folk—struggles which all stemmed from the issue of there being no fresh water—and continued to do their business. The fact that their people's lives were crumbling and their roofs were falling in on their heads were of no concern to the politicians.

124

Pilyn Wind was a grand section of land. Enormous, lavish buildings lined the shiny cobbled sidewalks and perfectly paved streets. All of the houses had long, wrought iron gates at their entrances and expensive doors carved from the rarest wood and decorated with golden knockers. Neatly trimmed bushes and gardens adorned with the most spectacular of plants framed the doors and polished steps that led to them.

The president pulled his horse up and addressed an Avean man who was walking hurriedly down the street. The man completely ignored the procession of foreigners heading down the road, he did not so much as look up when the easily recognizable president of Marchia began following him.

"Excuse me, sir?" said Tecsequaih.

This man strangely reminded Aelwen of Lin, or at least of her first meeting with him.

The man looked up, startled. "Oh, uh, hello." He blinked multiple times, as if trying to decide if what he was seeing was real. "Uh… can I help you?"

"Hopefully." Before stating his question, President Tecsequaih looked around as if afraid something were watching him. "Can you guide me to the residence of Eiyre?"

The man laughed. "Of course!" he said after he stopped laughing. "Down the road, take a left, fifth house on the right."

"Thank you. Hyah!" The party set off again at a steady gallop.

<center>~~~~</center>

Thoroughly intrigued, Lysia picked up the next letter.

Dearest Soldan,

I do not know whether I ought to congratulate you or apologize to you. I remember the night of the spring festival, I remember Mayia. While I was not and am not pleased to know you slept with her, I recognize that at that time you and I had not formally entered a relationship of our own and you thought of the occurrence with Ms. Akachi as nothing more than a bit of fun. I cannot imagine what you must be going through. I do not know what comforting words to offer. Just know that whatever you decide, I support you. If you must turn your back on the military for this, do it. If you need to leave me to live with your son, do. I love you. I love you so much. And whatever choices you make, I understand.

Love,
Tecsequaih

And the next.

Dearest Tecsequaih,

I am sorry I did not write sooner. Mayia and I have discussed much. She is not angry at me, for which I am relieved. She recognizes that neither of us intended this to be the outcome of our night together. She is well off and completely able to provide for herself and the child, my support is not something necessary for both of them to have a happy existence.

I have spent a lot of time thinking of what it is that I want to do with my life. That is what Mayia told me to do. She said, "I told you in my letter, I don't care what you choose. Choose what's right for you." That is something much easier said than done. After spending hours in lonesome thought and deep conversation, I have come to the conclusion that I do

125

not want to be a father. I do not want to settle. I want to be out on the battlefield, fighting. And finally, though it feels wrong to admit it, I hope you wrote truthfully in your last letter when you said, whatever I decided, you would understand, because I do not want to spend my life with Mayia. I want to spend my life with you.

My decisions are made. I now begin the journey to the east camp. I cannot wait to see you. I hope you do not think less of me than you did when I left. I love you.

Love,
Soldan

~~~~

Never before had Aelwen been so thankful to dismount. She had ridden for longer, but she was in desperate need of a new saddle. The padding of one she had just recently purchased was wearing down.

The president dismounted, followed by Desliad and Lin. His two right-hand men. Though, as Aelwen also dismounted and joined them, she could not help but wonder how much longer Lin would maintain in that privileged position.

There were no words to describe Eiyre's house. Extravagant came to mind, but even that did not fit the bill.

Aelwen stopped to admire a marble statue depicting a beautiful woman. The statue was surrounded by fire-breathers—massive red flowers, one of the deadliest, rarest and most beautiful flowers to ever exist. At the base of the statue, framed by fire-breathers, was a golden plaque. Aelwen read the words.

Eiyre Nuvo, Lady of Moonriver Mansion.

Moonriver Mansion sits among all of the high-class houses of Pilyn Wind. Eiyre owns acres of land all throughout the country. She herself has hired the caretakers of the royal palace.

Total, Eiyre owns fifty-nine acres of land throughout Ave, twelves stables, five beach resorts, two forest cottages and...

She was beginning to question this woman. What kind of a person had a golden-plated plaque on the front of a marble statue of themselves telling of everything they owned, displayed in their front lawn and circled by a fountain and fire-breathers?

At the sound of the president knocking on the broad door to the mansion, Aelwen stopped scrutinizing the statue and caught up with the three men.

A liveried butler opened the door. He stared down his crooked nose at them. He must have recognized Tecsequaih, for, without a word, he stepped smoothly to the side, allowing the visitors in. He silently showed them to an enormous parlor, where he left them.

Ebony bookshelves, books with pages lined with gold, a large white fireplace that somehow was still white even though a fire had clearly been burned in it before. Magnificent paintings depicting gorgeous people, a single diamond chandelier, two glass tables. Floral patterned furniture made from pelts, white walls painted with creamy swirls and pale flowers. Golden accents on the ceiling and golden trim.

Aelwen was not the only one examining the detailed paintings that lined the walls or touching the smooth, soft sofas and chairs.
~~~~

Eventually, after a time span in which everyone had grown a little restless and begun wondering if Eiyre was even home, a woman came down the stairs.

A flowing dress of aquamarine wrapped around her body. The dress itself was made of yards of fabric wrapped around itself over and over, overlapping in all sorts of different directions as if the dressmaker had not wanted to cut off the excess fabric but did not know what to do with it so had simply wrapped it around itself until there was nothing left. The dress was chaotic and messy if looked at closely, but on Eiyre it only made her appear more astounding.

She moved like water and wind, swift and leisurely, careful and confident and ever so beautiful.

Eiyre's golden hair was piled atop her head and covered in a silver net decorated with pale blue and silver jewels, giving her hair the appearance of a dewy spider web glistening in the sunlight. A dark purple scarf was wrapped around her neck many times over. Her eyelids were dusted with sparkling royal purple and blue.

As she gracefully reached the bottom step, she inclined her head in way of greeting to Tecsequaih. Most people who did not hold official government positions would bow, kneel or curtsy before a ruler. When Eiyre only inclined her head, she was insinuating that President Tecsequaih was her respectable equal.

"President Tecsequaih. I was not anticipating a visit from you," she said. Her voice was calm, but her words were laced with sharpness.

Tecsequaih tilted his head slightly in confusion. It was clear by his expression that he was not familiar with Eiyre. At least, not as familiar as she seemed to be with him.

"Queen Baric is dead," the president stated. "She named you as her heir. Eiyre, you are the queen of Ave."

Eiyre dropped her gaze. She reached the bottom of the stairs and ran a silver painted fingernail over the cover of a book that laid atop a glass table. She did not look sad or shocked. If anything, she looked rejected.

Tecsequiah stated bluntly, "You do not look surprised."

"No. Baric promised me she would name me as her heir and no one who makes a promise to me goes back on their word." She sighed dramatically. "I just thought that before Baric left, she would hand the kingdom over to me in a suitable state, not the mess it is now."

Tecsequaih's brow drew down. "Queen Baric did not choose to die. She died of Water Fever an hour ago."

Still, Eiyre did not seem disturbed. She picked up her head and snapped her fingers. Several servants appeared. "Pack my things. We are moving to the royal palace." The servants ascended the stairs to begin packing for their mistress. She turned her attention back to the president, whose company she seemed bored with. "Is that all?"

"No. I would like to speak with you about the state of Ave."

"Very well. There is a meeting chamber upstairs, follow me." They followed Eiyre up the polished marble stairs. Aelwen made sure to drag the muddy bottoms of her boots across each step.

The meeting chamber, like everything else in the house, was oversized. Portraits of family members and taxidermy animals decorated the room.

Eiyre poured some tea that was strangely hot and ready to serve when they arrived upstairs. "President Tecsequaih, who have you brought with you today?"

"My foreign ambassador, Desliad Faraji, my financial advisor, Lin Akachi and an apprentice, Aelwen."

"Apprentice?"

"She is from Corova. She came to Marchia to learn how to run a country."

Eiyre eyed Aelwen, who lifted her chin defiantly. "I see." Her eyes went back to Tecsequaih. "So, what is it you would like to discuss?"

Aelwen accepted a warm cup of tea. She took a small sip and had to use all of her will not to wrinkle her nose. It was awful. Spicy, almost. Sort of gritty, with a sour aftertaste.

The president took a drink and did not react at all. He cleared his throat and began, "The water supply of your kingdom. Without fresh water, your country cannot function. My council has been watching the activities of Ave."

"You are spying on us?" Eiyre took a seat in an overstuffed armchair and crossed her legs.

"No. We are watching and willing to help if things start going too badly."

"Oh, don't break your neutrality for us." After taking a luxuriously long drink of tea, Eiyre said, "What has your council seen while watching my country?"

"We see that the government has an idea to build a sort of system to gather rain. Aqueducts that run above the ground so that the water does not become infected. That will provide clean water to the people while others work to remove the source of the poison."

"Is that all you have to say for yourself?" Eiyre rose and began circling around the edges of the room like a vulture waiting for the dying animal to take its final breath. Only Eiyre was mistaken, this beast was nowhere close to dying. "Your Majesty, I too am aware of these ideas, but I am afraid they are nothing more than theories. The cost for building such things is ungodly."

"Ave has a powerful government," put in Desliad, trying to defuse the growing tension.

"Yes, and we have money. Lots of money. For now. If we spend it on these ideas that may not even work, the economy will crumble. We will have nothing left."

"I know." Tecsequaih was struggling to hold his tongue. Aelwen mentally commended the man. He was being much more patient than she would have been. "That is why I would like to give Ave a loan. A large loan to be used to gather clean water."

Eiyre stifled a snide laugh. "I thank you for your consideration, but Ave has just lost its ruler. With a new person in charge of the country, I think that Ave will be able to take care of itself."

President Tecsequaih eyed the woman. There was a silent moment wherein Aelwen was not quite sure what was happening. The two just stared at each other. In the end, Tecsequaih simply nodded.

"Very well. I will be on my way."

It was difficult not to storm down the stairs, not to slam the door behind him. It was no incident that Tecsequaih had not mentioned Baric's request for him to tutor Eiyre. After meeting the brat, there was no way she would let herself be taught and he had not the slightest intention of collaborating with her.

Outside of Moonriver Mansion, the president tapped a man on the shoulder. A trusted friend of his who was nothing more than a normal civilian. "Rally all that came. Bring them back home."

"What of you, sir?"

"Me and my council will ride with all swiftness back to Arkada. We have urgent business to attend to."

Lin, Desliad, Tecsequaih and Aelwen all mounted and rode off. Aelwen pushed Erizo up to run beside Tecsequaih. "What urgent business are we attending?"

"You'll see," he answered with a sly smile.

Throughout the entire ride, Tecsequaih did not stop grinning. At Arkada, the stablehands took the council members' horses. Aelwen's legs did not want to function after sitting for so long, but she pushed on, keeping up with the fast-paced president.

Upon entering, a servant handed Tecsequaih a letter saying, "Sir, this came for you."

Tecsequaih ripped open the envelope and read it quickly. He dropped the paper on the floor and proceeded forward.

"Sir, what did that letter say?" asked Desliad.

" It was from Gavnas, explaining why he isn't here."

"And why isn't he here?" asked Lin.

"He lives too far away. By the time he got here, we had already left."

The three council members followed their leader into his office. Although the room was an absolute mess, he had no problem finding everything he needed. Tecsequaih seized a quill, some blank legal documents and began filling them out.

"Your Excellency," Lin almost sounded afraid, as if Tecsequaih would hit him if he said the wrong thing. "What are you doing?"

"Issuing a considerable amount of money."

"To whom?"

"The country and standing government of Ave."

"Sir? The queen just refused to accept any money from you," Lin reminded his boss gently.

"Eiyre did. Lin," Tecsequaih handed him the paper. "I need this to be delivered confidentially. No one can know who sent it. I want it to be delivered immediately."

Lin looked down at the monetary amount and clapped a hand to his forehead. "Sir, this is…a *highly* substantial amount."

"How much?" asked Aelwen curiously, glancing over Lin's shoulder.

Lin pulled the paper away before she could see it, but told her anyway.

Aelwen's mouth fell open at the total. She looked to the president, wondering if he had gone mad.

Desliad spoke up. "Do you not think that Nuvo will make the connection as to who sent the money and then refuse it?"

"I am not sending it to Eiyre Nuvo. It will be sent to the financial headquarters of Ave. The unsuspecting government will reveal the loan to their queen. It will not take long for the news to spread that this money was given to Ave. Since everyone will know that Eiyre has the money, she cannot simply discard it. Otherwise, due to the state of the country, the people would riot and there would be a large price put on her head."

"Why not just deliver the money to Eiyre?" Desliad continued to question. "The process would be simpler, the country would still receive the money and the people would still know."

"Not exactly. All of the actions that take place around the selected monarch are more carefully monitored than those of the government. The only actions of the monarch that the public know are the ones that the monarch wants them to know."

President Tecsequaih dismounted. It was nearly sunset. He had not ridden the horse he had been on all day, that steed needed a break. He patted the head of the gentle roan mare he had chosen with a sigh. It had been a long day.

He approached his grand home. Despite the rumors that the overworked ruler lived in Arkada, in actuality he owned a large, highly-prized estate. A mansion, quite nearly a castle. This home alone had everything his heart desired, yet he still felt so empty. Things could not fill him up. Convenient items and pretty accessories did not make him happy. To be honest, he did not even know why he owned so much. The estate itself was a family heirloom that had been lost from his family several generations ago. In their final years, his parents had repurchased it and left it to him. He did not have the heart to get rid of it, even though he would be satisfied with a simple house in the suburbs.

Most of the things that he owned were gifts from family, from friends, from people he did not even know who revered him greatly.

Still, he wanted so much more. He wanted love. He wanted a family.

But he had loved once. It had been the single greatest time in his life. When that loved one had been taken from him, Tecsequiah's soul had been ripped open, never to be repaired.

With each step he took, he felt heavier and heavier. The day wore on him and his mind wandered. To the love he lost. To the journey he took to feeling confident enough to lead his country. And to the one who reminded him of what it was to feel again. It had been so long since he'd felt anything like that. He was still so afraid. He couldn't go through that again.

Tecsequaih looked around. His brain had been so busy thinking that he wasn't watching where he was going. He stood at the top of several flights of stairs, standing outside of his master bedroom to which he opened the door.

The first thing he set his eyes on was his massive bed. All he wanted to do was curl up and sleep, to let all of the thoughts leave him.

Instead, his feet and heart tugged him in a different direction. To the side of the room, to the corner where his desk was. The desk with a minimal amount of paper, a package of backup inkwells and three different quills in case any of them broke. This was the spot he resorted to when the best ideas came to him while he was away from his office.

He ran his fingertips over the paper on the desk. Just a single sheet. A list, with crossed out names and names with stars beside them. When was the last time he had worked on it? He glanced at the several names on the bottom of the list. Truthfully, it had not been too long since he had written that last name, but it felt like it had been ages.

The paper was weighed down with a butterfly encased in glass.

That list was of possible heirs. President Tecsequaih was no fool, he knew he was old. The choosing of an heir was one of the most important decisions for a president to make. The events with Baric brought that to the forefront of his mind. Of course, the people would vote for or against his chosen successor and there was no guarantee that his heir would become the next president, or even want to. Still, he wanted to have made a solid choice before it was too late.

He breathed a sigh and shook his head. Now was not the time. His thinking was not straight, not that it ever was anymore.

Tecsequaih curled up on his bed. His eyes began twitching. He was not even trying to hold back the tears, it was just a habit. So much sadness surrounded him that his body had become accustomed to holding back the tears.

Why? Why could he not love? Was he not meant to love? If not, then why? The relationship he had had with Baric had not been loving in any way. It had been a relationship based purely upon respect and trust. And even that had crumbled.

His eyes became so clouded with tears that he closed them since he could not see. He tried to sleep until he began to succeed. Only, instead of a dream, memories came to him.

He was sitting at a desk. Only, he was not president. He was a young officer in the Marchian military. A colonel. He had gotten stuck doing paperwork again. It was night and the camp was silent. Everyone was asleep after a day packed with training and drills.

He sighed and leaned back in his hard wooden chair. It had been repaired three times and was missing a leg.

"Bored?" asked a familiar voice. The tent flap opened and in walked the man Tecsequaih loved more than life itself. Captain Soldan.

The memory shifted.

Tecsequaih and Soldan, in their green and gold military uniforms, crouched in a thicket, bows at the ready.

The area was dappled with sunlight that snuck in through the canopy. Soldan's mahogany eyes were focused on a point in the distance, awaiting the arrival of the enemy.

Tecsequaih listened carefully, but there were no rustling leaves or sounds of footsteps, none of the noises characteristic of anyone approaching. Keeping his bow aimed should anyone appear, Tecsequaih spared Soldan a glance out of the corner of his eye. Soldan's midnight hair was pulled back in a ponytail. He hadn't shaved in a few days. His sepia hands gripped his bow tightly, his focus absorbed his whole being. He sat in that alert-yet-relaxed manner he always did when he was out on a mission, looking like he belonged out here, in the wild, fighting.

Another shift.

It was night. A small fire burned in the center of the Marchian camp. Most of the soldiers were asleep. A few stood watch, some dared not sleep, for if they did, their dreams of the horrors they had seen would plague them.

Soldan and Tecsequaih were awake. They huddled together, close to the fire. Winter was coming. Marchia was a tropical country, but winter still took its toll. Snow fell and harsh winds blew. They shared a single blanket between them.

Tecsequaih rested his head on Soldan's shoulder.

He asked, "Are you sure about this?"

Soldan shifted slightly. "Yes."

"You can go, you know. I'll be okay. We all will."

"I know." Soldan sighed. "I want to stay."

"Okay. As long as you're sure."

"I am."

Another shift.

Tecsequaih paced back and forth in his tent. The space was small, he could clear it in three strides.

Unannounced, Soldan entered. "There you are," he said, his relief evident.

Tecsequaih stopped pacing. At the sight of Soldan, a heaviness left him. "Any news on the brigade?"

Soldan shook his head, eyes clouding with sadness. "No. No one's heard anything." He stepped close to Tecsequaih and took his hands in his. "They're going to be okay, Tec."

"You don't know that."

"You're right, I don't. But I can feel it. They're going to come back. And if they don't, that doesn't mean we're going to stop fighting. It's what we do, you and me. We fight."

Tecsequaih ran his thumb over Soldan's knuckle, feeling a scar there. "Hopefully not for much longer."

"Nah. Even when the war's done, we won't stop. We'll keep on fighting. For what's right, for what's good."

"Always fighting? That sounds tiring." Tecsequaih breathed a laugh.

Soldan did the same. "Oh, it is. That's why only the strongest can do it."

Tecsequaih's worried gaze softened. For just a moment, he managed to quash down his concern about whether or not the brigade would achieve their mission and return safely. Soldan was all he cared about in that moment. Soldan, with his soft kiss and gentle touch, with words Tecsequaih always needed to hear even when he didn't know it.

The colonel rested his forehead on Soldan's. He released his hands from Soldan's and folded them around the other man's waist, drawing him closer.

"I love you." The words were a whispered breath.

Soldan looked up at Tecsequaih. "I love you, too."

Tecsequaih looked down at Soldan, savoring every detail of him. He placed his fingers under Soldan's chin. He bent forward the tiniest bit. Soldan leaned in and their lips met.

~~~~
~~~~

Aelwen shut the door behind her. She had expected to hear the chorused voices of her friends asking her what had happened. Instead, she was greeted by silence and darkness.

It was late. Rinly's horse was gone from the stable and the house was dark. *Lysia must be asleep already*, thought Aelwen, surprised that she had not stayed up until Aelwen returned to hear the news.

In a way, she was glad there was no one there to interrogate her. All she wanted to do was sleep. She had little faith in Eiyre Nuvo as a queen and feared that Marchia would become so wrapped up in whatever drama the Queen of Ave decided to start that they would never get to helping Corova.

Aelwen took off her jacket and hung it on the rack beside the door.

On the ride home, her mind had strayed to the one person she could never stop thinking about, no matter how hard she tried. A million what-ifs and terrible possibilities of the fate of Iowan had flitted through her mind, making her feel sick and guilty and frantic to find her, to know what had happened to her, even though she knew that decision lay mostly with Tecsequaih and his council now.

Making her way to the stairs, Aelwen whipped around, a dagger in her hand, at the sound of a voice.

"Some light reading?"

A candle in the adjacent room flickered to life, illuminating a round, pale brown face. Aelwen lowered her weapon in recognition of Lysia. She let out a breath of relief that it was only a prank that had caused her to have such a reaction.

Lysia held a faded piece of parchment in her hand, it was written on in ink. Aelwen's breath hitched. It was one of the letters she had stolen from Lin.

Aelwen didn't know what to do. She didn't have experience with situations like this. She was a woman of new secrets, she didn't have a lot to hide.

"How did you find them?" she asked.

"I couldn't find my hairbrush. I used yours."

The pieces fit together. Aelwen had left the letters on her bed in plain sight.

"You read them?"

"Yes."

"Why?"

"Why not?"

Aelwen couldn't blame Lysia, not really. She'd have done the same if their roles had been revered.

Lysia looked down at the letter, then up at Aelwen. "Where did you get them?"

"I stole them. From Lin's office." There was no point in lying.

"Because he lied about the vote?"

"Yeah."

Lysia's expression was unreadable at first, then a sly smile crept onto her face. "Leverage. Smart. What are you going to do with them?"

Aelwen shook her head. "I don't know. I wish I hadn't taken them."

"Feeling guilty?"

"A little," Aelwen replied sarcastically.

"Don't. Lin destroyed our first chance to save Corova. He deserves all the pain we can cause him."

"How, though? There's nothing defaming in the letters, there's just sentimental. What am I supposed to do with that?"

"Don't underestimate the value of sentimentality. You'll just have to find out what Lin's willing to do to get these back."

"No. I don't want to, I wish I'd never taken them. On the way to Ave, when we crossed the border, Lin broke down, it was horrible."

"Why did he break down?"

Of course Lysia didn't know. That wasn't in the letters, Tecsequaih had told her. "That's where his father died. He was so sad, it hurt to watch him. Knowing I stole the memories he has of someone he loved that much…I'll find a time when Lin's away and put the letters back, we can forget this ever happened."

Lysia scoffed. "After what he did, you feel *sorry* for him?"

"Yes, I do. I'm still mad about what he did, but I can understand *why* he did it. This isn't the way to get back at him, though. It's not."

Lysia crossed her arms and scowled. "You don't want to keep the letters, fine. Let me."

Aelwen's shock must have been noticeable because Lysia added, "Please?"

"You want to use them against Lin? Yourself?"

"Yes."

"I'll let you keep them, but you have to promise me one thing."

"Yes?"

"Leave me out of it. If he asks how you got them, don't tell him I stole them, don't tell him you got them from me, none of it."

"Fine. He'll never know you were involved."

"Promise?"

"Promise."

"So…what are you doing to do with them, then?"

"Use them. Not yet, though. I'll wait until he has something we need."

"And until then?"

"They'll be safely kept until it's their time to shine."

CHAPTER TWELVE

Aelwen stood on the second highest floor of Arkada. Even as she heard footsteps ascending the stairs, she did not take her eyes off of what she was staring at to see who was coming toward her.

"Here. I've got them. These records go back twelve years, if you need more I can get them."

"No, these should be enough. Thank you."

Gavnas handed Aelwen a bunch of papers wrapped tightly together. "Go back to your office. Worrying isn't going to help anything," he advised.

"I don't know why he left." Aelwen pried her eyes away from the floor-to-ceiling window, which gave her a view of most of the city. Tears threatened to spill; she held them back. "It's been two months."

Two months since Marchia had given Ave that significant loan. Ave had been building raised waterways and the people were beginning to be well again. Eiyre was officially queen of Ave but had not breathed a word about her conversation with Tecsequaih about the loan that she had rejected; she only told her people that the president had told her of Baric's passing and alerted her that she would become queen. No one knew where the loan had come from, only that it was a massive help.

Roughly twenty minutes ago, President Tecsequaih had ordered that no one follow him and was soon after seen riding a horse out of the city. Towards Ave.

Aelwen was slightly annoyed that the president had still taken no action to aid Corova, even though he had explained his reasoning to her. Tecsequaih had decided to wait two or three months after dealing with Ave. He wanted to give himself some time to get his thoughts together. Additionally, he wanted to give Aelwen and Gavnas more time to learn about government.

The papers that Gavnas had just retrieved recorded the trade of spices between Ave and Marchia. He passed them to Aelwen, who was trying to figure out the complex trade system that all of the countries used. Gavnas had no interest in such aspects of government, he'd told Aelwen. To him, the truly important thing was the connection between the government and the people. That was what he spent the majority of his time in Arkada studying.

"Thank you," Aelwen said again, ending their awkward meeting. The air felt different now that she and the captain were business partners, not just two people desperate for connection that they found in one another. Neither of them quite knew how to act around the other now.

Aelwen descended down one set of stairs while Gavnas took another. At least, she pretended to. She walked down five steps, paused, waited for the noise of Gavnas's feet to disappear and then walked back up and continued to stare out the window.

<p style="text-align:center">~~~~~</p>

The flames made the sky alive. Waving, slithering ribbons of scarlet accented with bright orange.

The girl tripped. An awful crack sounded from above. The ceiling was falling in. A large piece of flaming wood broke off and landed nearly a foot from her face.

Desperate, the girl pulled herself to her feet and started running. Suddenly, she stopped. There was nowhere to run. The fire had surrounded her, flashing strands of heat lashed down from above. It was daytime, but the black smoke had brought on sudden night.

Another sickening crack. She wasn't fast enough this time. The blazing beam landed on her leg, just below the knee, crushing her bones. She kicked at the beam with her other foot but was not strong enough to move it. The flames slithered down, closer and closer to her skin.

Smoke and ash filled her lungs, prohibiting her scream. She pulled her leg with all her might and kicked at the burning wood. It would not shift.

She tried leaning forward, fanning the smoke away from her stinging eyes and dry mouth. She reached down and pushed at the beam, searing her hands, but it would not budge. The realization hit her. There was nothing else to try. The flames were mere inches from her flesh. She closed her eyes so she didn't have to see as the fire ate her skin.

Suddenly, there was light all around her. Could this be...

A dark figure was coming towards her.

A sending of sorts, to carry her to death.

She felt muscular arms lift her. Indescribable pain in her lower leg.

Air. Real, clean air. Not contaminated with smoke and fire.

She was unable to move without pain soaring throughout her body. A strong, calloused hand touched her raw shoulder. It hurt, but just for a moment. The touch was gentle, filling her with instantaneous trust of whatever this savior of hers was. The hand moved a bit. She flinched as the fingertips touched even rawer skin. The hand retreated. She tried to open her eyes and failed.

"I'm sorry," said a smooth, strong voice. "Can you talk?"

She tried. No sound came out. She tried again. A small, scratchy noise. She took a deep breath and tried a third time. It worked. Her voice was small and quiet.

"Yes," she managed. "Did you save me?"

"I guess you could say that I did. What is your name? Do you have a family?"

The girl wheezed. "My name is..." the word was inaudible. She tried again. "Eoren."

The person repeated, "Eoren?"

136

"Yes. My family…they're all gone. I lived with my mother and father but they…" her words trailed off.

"The fire took them."

"Yes."

"Do you have any other family? Grandparents, cousins, aunts, uncles?"

"I have an aunt."

"What is her name?"

"I don't know. I just call her Aunt Mati."

Eoren could hear a faint noise, like a quill on parchment. "Are you writing?"

The man, at least it sounded like a man, hesitated. "Yes, I am. The 'saviors' as they are being called, the people who saved victims of the fire, are to get all the information that they can. We are trying to connect separated family members."

"I don't think my aunt made it."

Eoren felt the man touch her burned hands. He touched the tips of her fingers and her wrist, the two places that were burnt the least, filling her with comfort. "What makes you say that?"

" I…just have a feeling."

"You're lucky," said the strange man after a moment's pause.

"Because I survived?" Eoren had been expecting to hear this.

"Yes. And because you are a child. Do you know how many children survived?"

"How many?"

"Eight."

Eoren gave no response. She heard the man stand up and felt him pull his hands away.

"Is there anything you need? Food, water…anything?"

Eoren was a little hungry, but there was no way she could manipulate silverware. It hurt just to think about it. Thirsty, too, but she didn't think she would be able to hold a cup. "No. I'm alright."

"Okay. I am sorry, I have no medicine for you. I should be able to get some to you within the hour, though."

"Okay. Thank you very much." Eoren listened to the receding footsteps of the man. Before he left, she decided to ask one more question. "Excuse me?"

"Yes?"

"What's your name?"

"Taran."

~~~~

Tecsequaih rubbed his ash covered hands on his ash covered trousers. He pulled a large slab of broken pottery out from the remains of a house. Nothing useful. He tossed it into a bucket that was being used to collect garbage.

A town on the southern border of Ave had been burned.

The moment President Tecsequaih had received the news, he had ridden with all haste to the scene. By the time he had reached the town, the fire had been extinguished. Ever since he arrived, he'd been busy helping people. Large patrols had been sent to the nearest
~~~~

cities to gather food and medical supplies. Tecsequaih had stayed behind. He and a few others were left to search through the remains of the town for anything that might be useful—silverware, bowls, plates,cups, blankets, medical supplies—or possibly sentimental to a family.

Standing up, Tecsequaih held his hand over his forehead to block out the blinding morning sun. Was that a cart approaching? A horse drawn cart packed with supplies? Tecsequaih made his way forward. He wanted to run, but knew that his energy could be better spent later.

The surrounding land had few trees, or any other plants but grass for that matter. It was a long, sprawling grassland. The big question was how the fire had started. There had been no thunderstorms in the night. The theory everyone was settling for at the moment was that someone had fallen asleep without putting out their hearth fire. Tecsequaih, however, had a feeling that the cause of the destruction was a bit more complicated.

The president stopped mid-step, a noise alerting him. The shifting of ashes. Had that sound been caused by his own feet? He waited, holding his breath. A whimper. He headed in the direction of the slight noise. Whispering so that any onlookers would not think he was insane, he said, "Make a sound again. Please. I want to help you, but I don't know where you are. Make a noise, please, just a noise."

Another whimper. Tecsequaih flung himself towards the sound. A board shifted. The president landed on his knees and grabbed a burnt wooden plank that crumbled away at his touch. The ashes covered his hands in blackness again, but he did not mind. His entire outfit, which had initially been a silver headband with emu feathers and moonstones and a thin white silk cape along with a pale gray tunic, was now completely stained black. The president heaved the fallen pieces of ceiling and cracked roof shingles out of the way, digging deep into the pile of ash.

He flinched as something made contact with his skin. It was a hopeful flinch. His body had been frozen in fear of not finding anyone, or of finding a lifeless body. Tecsequaih reached down and touched it again. It was burnt black, the flesh was wrinkled and tough as hide. Tecsequaih took the person's hand and gently pulled them upward while brushing away the ash.

The form of a man lay before him, surrounded by debris and cinders. The man's hand had stopped moving. Thankfully, the man's warped hand seemed to be his only disabled body part. The rest of him seemed intact, though it was hard to tell because he was covered in soot.

Tecsequaih lightly dusted off the man's clothes and slowly wiped the ashes from his face. The man coughed and sputtered saliva on Tecsequaih's forearm. He wiped his eyes with his ash covered fists, then winced. The man coughed horrifically, pulling himself into a sitting position. He only stayed like that for a moment before collapsing forward. He wrapped his hands in his burnt shirt and rested his forehead on the ground.

On the back of his head was a sizable wound caked with dried blood. He must have split his head open when he had fallen. No matter. The blood was dried and the wound would heal. But there was no mistaking the irreversible damage that had been done to his hands. And to his home, to his family, to his friends.

Gently, Tecsequaih helped the man up, all the while murmuring, "Shh. Shh." He made sure never to say the words, "everything is going to be okay", because how could he possibly know? This man had lost so much. Maybe he would find his family, maybe he would be reunited with the people he loved, maybe some miracle would occur and his hands would be able to function again, maybe he would end up with a home again. Or maybe not.

President Tecsequaih led the man to one of the tents that had been set up for survivors. Medics took the man from Tecsequaih and helped him into a bed, but the man refused to stay calm. He sat up and screamed. They told him to lay down. He did. Until he began writhing, awake and sweating as the result of some monstrous nightmare.

With a sigh, Tecsequaih filled a small cup with water and sat beside a patient's bed. The wounded woman trembled as he helped her into a sitting position. She could not hold the cup herself, the fire had taken her arms and hands from her. The woman's eyelids were swollen shut, her hair was thin, burnt to a crisp by the ravenous flames. As she drained the cup, Tecsequaih moved away to fill it again and attend to the next needy patient.

Everyone was in some horrible condition. Scorched skin, missing body parts, inaudible moaning because no other sounds could escape from the ash-filled lungs of the survivors.

After giving water to a fifth patient, an elderly man who had lost everything from his hips down, Tecsequaih realized he needed a break. He had seen too much and he desperately needed to clear his head. He walked outside and closed his eyes so he did not have to see the wreckage. How could so much go wrong so quickly?

Tecsequaih let his mind stray and find his happiest memories.

Soldan.

Tecsequaih felt the tears well up and he let them out.

Why? Why was he thinking of Soldan now, when he should be in there helping the wounded? Because Soldan was his spark, his flare that showed him the light in the darkness. Yes, much had been destroyed today, but many had also survived.

Tecsequaih smiled weakly. If only Soldan were there, by his side. That would be enough.

Soldan was not there. Soldan would never be there again.

Why, in the last few months, had he found his thoughts so constantly occupied by his deceased lover? Long ago, Tecsequaih had dealt with his grief and when he could bear it no longer, he had pushed the scraps of his sorrow deep down and locked it away. It had stayed put for years. Why, now, was it coming to the surface? Because someone new had walked into his life. A young woman with a wild, fresh spirit. A woman who had been caged for so long and, against all odds, had broken her chains and flown away. Aelwen. She who carried the same energy, the same spirit, as his lost love.

Aelwen was by no means of any romantic interest to him. Besides being a third of his age, Tecsequaih was not attracted to women. In her eyes was that same spark he had seen in Soldan's, that maybe even he had when he was a younger man.

Aelwen was so like Soldan. Young and full of life, independent, rebellious, passionate, desperate to change the world. Aelwen had much to learn. And he wanted to be her teacher.

He wanted to guide her along her path in life and teach her how to lead so she might become everything Soldan might have been.

Personal thoughts were interrupted by the rolling of cart wheels over uneven ground. Three carts were being brought to the makeshift camp. Tecsequaih abandoned reason and sprinted to the carts. Slowing to a jog beside one of them, he asked the driver, "What do you have?"

"Food," the driver answered. "Easy to eat. Mashed potatoes, butter, yogurt and the like. The next two carts have got medicine."

Tecsequaih made his way to the next cart. Just as he was approaching, the driver slapped the reins and the horses galloped forward. The last cart did the same. The president turned around, heading in the direction of the camp again.

The cart drivers jumped down and, without unpacking their loot, mounted their horses and rode with great haste in the direction they had just come. Confused, yet eager to get in on the action, Tecsequaih unhitched a horse that had been tied outside of the tents and followed the cart drivers.

~~~~

Aelwen trudged down the stairs, into the library. The Great Library of Arkada was on the third floor of the building, meaning that Aelwen had to take two flights of stairs down to reach it.

"There you are. I was wondering what happened to you." Lin was sitting ready at a massive mahogany desk, economic books and papers organized around him. When President Tecsequaih had left unexpectedly, he had ordered Lin to fill in for him as Aelwen's tutor. Lin, of all people.

Tecsequaih had offered to tutor Gavnas as well, but Gavnas had respectfully declined the offer, claiming that he worked better solo. Which was true. Unfortunately, Aelwen did not. She had gotten those books about government out of the library at the start of her political career and had only perused them three times. She needed someone to push her along and encourage her to work.

"Do you have the papers?" asked Lin.

"Yes." Aelwen held up the ream. "Right here." She couldn't keep the tiredness or exhaustion from her voice.

"Don't be so sad, everything's all right." Lin advised as she sat down. He took the papers and flipped through them. "He'll be back eventually."

Lin began talking. Aelwen did not listen to a word he said.

The library had a red-gold color scheme. Red walls, fluffy red carpet, red curtains, golden trim, golden chandeliers, wooden bookshelves painted with golden swirls, golden baubles and statues.

Carefully, Aelwen slid off her shoes and flexed her toes in the soft scarlet carpeting. She heard the noise of Lin droning on about something or other, but she could not have cared less about what he had to say. She started fidgeting with a gold-plated bracelet she had bought herself yesterday. It was holding up surprisingly well considering how cheap it was.
~~~~

"Aelwen!"

"Hm?"

"I want you to complete this chart." In front of her was a page with lines and numbers and a half-filled-out, fluctuating grid on the back. She read the directions at the top of the page, but only half-comprehended them.

"I don't know how to do this."

"Give it a try."

Aelwen noticed some fine print on the bottom. *"Page 294- Worksheets for Students Studying the Basic Functions of Government, Economics and Commerce"* Lin had taken this right out of a teacher's handbook.

With a heavy sigh, Aelwen dipped her quill in the ink and began writing. She had no idea what she was doing. Sometimes she wrote the numbers quickly and sloppily, other times she took her time making them as elegant and flowy as possible. She flipped to the graph on the back. Above the graph in big, bold print it said, *Finish the Graph.* Aelwen re-inked her quill and set it on the spot where the line stopped. She drew a curvy line upwards then brought it down and around, making a swirl.

Never had Aelwen attended school nor wanted to because this was what she had always imagined it being like. With all of the work they had to fill out, Aelwen was quite sure that students had no time to themselves, to spend time with their friends and family or to have their own adventures.

Aelwen's parents had homeschooled her, teaching her to read and write, never forcing her to read chapters out of enormous, boring books or fill out worksheets.

Lin stared at the paper disappointedly as Aelwen shoved it at him. He did not bother looking closely at the paper, he knew she had scribbled in random numbers. "I know you don't know what you're doing, but if you want help, you need to ask for it."

Whenever Aelwen was around Lin, he never acted suspicious of her and she had not yet revealed to him that she knew that he had lied to her about the first council meeting. Of course, the tension was still there. He did not directly oppose her in council meetings, but both of them knew that neither was fond of the other. Aelwen had spent the first day or so after the disappearance of the letters constantly wondering where they were and feeling sorry for herself. The feelings had waned and of late Aelwen had been so busy with her work that she had put the thought of the letters out of her mind completely.

"Excuse me," she said, "I need to go to the bathroom."

Lin looked like he wanted to say something but then thought better of it. "Try not to take too long."

Her newest piece of clothing—a red tailcoat—flowed dramatically behind her as she swept out of the room.

Aelwen had no intention of actually using the bathroom. She opened the door and entered. The stalls were oversized, even for a royal bathroom. The walls were white marble with floors of shiny grey tile that were dangerously slippery when wet. At one end of the elongated bathroom hall was a window. Being that this was the third floor of Arkada, there was no way for anyone to look into the bathroom, so the window did no harm. In fact, at the moment, it would be quite useful.

After flipping the window lock, she pushed up the glass pane. Over her tailcoat she wore a black leather belt. It didn't make for the best appearance, but appearances were the least of her worries. Despite being away from the arena for quite a while, Aelwen still found it hard to function without weapons ready at her fingertips.

The fact that a foreigner who happened to be an ex-Arenian was traipsing around Arkada and having frequent meetings with government officials while fully armed was not an appealing thought, but Aelwen did not care what the people thought. As long as the president was okay with it, she was going to keep wearing what she found comfortable to wear.

Aelwen skillfully twirled a pair of twin daggers out of her belt, then proceeded to shimmy her way out of the window.

Her blade fit near perfectly into a space between two of the white stones. Unfortunately, it was unable to fit very far. Aelwen probably would have fallen if she had not still been holding onto the window sill.

Aelwen plunged her dagger deeper into the stones and let go of the window, swinging wildly on the side of the wall. Focusing on her task, she stabbed her other dagger into the wall.

Planting her feet firmly against the wall, Aelwen began to move. There was a fire escape three doors away. If she could make it there, the descent would be much easier.

Getting a grip on the wall was not as difficult as she had expected, the cracks in the walls of the stronghold of Marchia were not very efficiently sealed. It took less than ten minutes to reach the fire escape. The metal was shiny and smooth, not rusted like most of the fire escapes one would find in Corova.

Aelwen palmed her daggers and slid them back into their sheaths. She jogged down the stairs, making as little noise as possible. Luckily, there was a stable on this side of Arkada. Erizo would not get to come along this time, for she was residing in the stable on the other side. It would take even more time to reach her and Aelwen didn't want to risk being caught. Someone else's horse would be her mount today.

Trying not to overthink her reckless actions, Aelwen untied a white horse which, luckily for her, had not been untacked. Taking a quick look to make sure there was not a soul around, Aelwen led the horse out of the barn. The creature was a little reluctant at first, but then gave into Aelwen's pleas and followed willingly.

Rubbing the creature's snout, she took note that it was a gelding. "I'm sorry, I don't know your name." She mounted. "Alright. Let's get out of here." She squeezed the horse's sides with her feet, but she did not allow him to move too quickly. No one could know where she was headed.

"He's over there." The ranger pointed forward, to where the trees thinned and gave way to grass. Aelwen thanked her guide and paid him three coins.

On her way to the Ave border, Aelwen had enlisted a ranger she had found wandering the woods. Before approaching him, she had been careful to cover her face with her hood and make sure that she gave away no signs as to who she was, who she worked for, or who she was in search of. She simply showed the ranger some visible imprints of Tecsequaih's horse's hooves and the ranger did the rest. Since Aelwen refused to give her name, so did he. Nonetheless, he efficiently got her where she was wanting to go.

Aelwen tugged on her horse's reins. He really wanted to go forward, but Aelwen was not ready. She kept him still, waiting amidst the thinning trees. Roughly a quarter mile away, there was a group of people clumped together. President Tecsequaih had to be one of them.

Not giving herself a chance to change her mind again, Aelwen moved her horse forward.

~~~

The crowd parted for the horse. The President of Marchia jumped down. "What is going on?" he shouted, voice rumbling louder than the confused murmurings of the crowd. In the center of the circle of spectators, two Aveans were in a fist-fight with a person wearing a cobalt scarf wrapped all around their head, leaving only the person's eyes exposed.

There was no question about who this person was. They carried a large stick, one end blackened. One of the Aveans ripped the stick from the person's grasp while the other pinned the person to the ground. The Avean with the stick touched the end.

"Warm," she declared.

The other Avean forced the person into a sitting position. This woman obviously had years of military training. She was easily maneuvering the person's body so that the audience could see their face without once releasing one of their limbs. Grabbing the blue fabric covering the person's face, the woman pulled down, tearing the scarf away and revealing a man's face.

The man shook his head to get his grimy, snarled hair out of his face. He sat there, staring at the sky, letting the people get a good long look at him.

Eyes wild with fear. Dark eyes. A scarred face. Unkempt, wild black hair. The strip of skin around the man's eyes that had been exposed was black as night, stained with soot.

His eyes were the only thing that revealed at all how he felt. His mouth did not move. He just sat there, staring. After giving the audience a good long look, he craned his neck, turning his sharp focus to the ground. His messy hair flipped over his head, a curtain drawn upon a mysterious performance.

~~~

The clumping of her horse's hooves was enough to get the people to part for Aelwen. "What is this? What is happening?"

"Aelwen!" exclaimed the Marchian president, beside his own stolen horse a few yards away. "What are you doing here?"

Aelwen ignored him, dismounting so she could get even closer. Two women were restraining a person, a person with their back to her, head hung. The restraints were used by military members, Arenians, people who knew what they were doing.

Upon her arrival, Aelwen had taken in the scene: mangled houses, wounded people, carts of provisions, black grass, the final traces of smoke floating into the air.

There had been a fire. A massive one.

Not tearing her fierce gaze from the human's slumped back she asked, "Did they do it?"

President Tecsequaih had moved a little closer to her, slowly making his way through the crowd without his motions being too obvious. A little quieter this time, he said, "Aelwen."

"Yes, miss," replied one of the Aveans restraining the person. Grabbing a fistful of the felon's hair, forcing the man's head up so Aelwen could see his face, the Avean said, "He's the one who done it."

Aelwen did not hear the second sentence. She blocked out everything and stared at the face of the man. That face she knew. There was no forgetting those dark eyes.

Namar.

CHAPTER THIRTEEN

The expanding bubble of questions and thoughts growing inside her head burst the moment a hand tightened around her forearm. Aelwen's eyes widened as she found President Tecsequaih staring at her, unblinking and filled with rage. More people had pushed in front of them and they were now at the back of the growing crowd. How long had she been staring at Namar?

"Aelwen."

"Sir," was the only word she could manage.

"A word." The president practically dragged her into the nearest tent.

Tecsequaih stared down at Aelwen. She had never been aware of how tall he was. After the coming argument, Aelwen wondered if Tecsequaih had even attempted to restrain his anger. It certainly didn't seem like it.

"What the hell are you doing here?"

"I—"

"I ordered you to stay where you were and you disobeyed me!"

"I didn't know where you were, I was worried—"

"That doesn't matter! I gave you an order! The next time you fail to comply—"

"What?" Aelwen drew herself up to her full height and took a step forward, bringing them so close they were almost touching.

"What?" she hissed. The quietness of her voice was much more unnerving than it would have been had she yelled. "What are you going to do to me?"

Tecsequaih did not answer. He did not lower his gaze either.

"You don't own me," Aelwen continued. "My whole life, I have been told what to do. I respect you immensely, but that does not mean that I will always comply to the orders you give me. I came to this land to find freedom and I will have it."

President Tecsequaih turned his back on Aelwen. He made no move to exit the tent or to turn back around.

Aelwen's Arenian lessons kicked in. The back, the most vulnerable area of the human body and the hardest to protect. The back was the side of exposure. In a fight, if your opponent turned their back to you for more than five seconds, it was the signal that they had given up and were admitting defeat. In this way, the opponent could admit that they were losing instead of fighting their way to the inevitable end.

Tecsequaih was not an Arenian, he did not know what he was signaling to Aelwen. If he was not admitting he had lost, what was he doing by exposing his back?

That was a puzzle to solve another day. There were people dying out there and an exile she used to call her friend had just been found guilty of setting a fire and slaughtering the-gods-knew-how-many people. Aelwen stormed out of the tent, leaving Tecsequaih alone to deal with his emotions.

The crowd had grown at least a hundred people larger. Marchians and Aveans alike swarmed together.

The fire had been set in a town on the border Ave shared with Marchia. Although it was an Avean town that had been demolished, Marchians were bringing supplies and searching through the wreckage. Most of them had now joined the largest crowd: the one assembled around Namar.

Aelwen admired the people who were not taking part in staring and shouting at Namar, the people who instead were rushing into the tents that housed the wounded and doing everything in their power to save the poor souls.

She approached the mass of spectators. Her fine red tailcoat marked her as being a member of the higher class, so the people let her pass through.

There was shouting toward the center of the mass. A mild riot had begun. Aveans on one side, Marchians on the other. The Marchians were claiming that Namar was an Avean, while the Aveans accused Marchia of being the country of the culprit.

"Stop!" shouted Aelwen, her voice unheard over the raucous. She looked around for her horse. There was no sign of him. The noise had probably spooked him, causing him to flee.

The shouts increased, some people were beginning to throw things. Would this incident turn out like the one at the Avean border just two months earlier?

After being shoved about by the group of angry Marchians, Aelwen managed to spot Namar. He and the two Aveans who had captured him were standing silently at the back of the Avean crowd. Namar had his back turned, hands bound. Each of the women had one hand on either of Namar's shoulders and a dagger in the other.

Suddenly, the hollering subsided in respect for a radiant queen upon a stormy steed. She rode right in between the hollering masses and in her wake everyone fell silent.

"What is the meaning of this?" boomed the queen. Every member of the crowd spoke up, desperate for the queen to hear their side of the story. "Silence! I will choose who speaks." Queen Eiyre scanned the crowd until her eyes locked on Aelwen. "You are an apprentice of President Tecsequaih, are you not?"

Aelwen could feel everyone's eyes on her. She lifted her chin. "I am."

"I was told that the president himself is here. Where is he?"

"I do not know. I did not come here with him."

The queen searched Aelwen's face a moment before speaking. "Very well. What has happened?"

"I have only just arrived. You are better off asking them," Aelwen nodded in the direction of the two guards holding Namar.

Queen Eiyre signaled for one of them to speak.

"There was a fire. It ravaged this town this morning. A little while ago this man was caught." She shoved Namar's shoulder. "He was carrying a large stick, one end blackened and warm. The Aveans claim he is not Avean, the Marchians claim he is not Marchian. No one knows which country he is from."

Queen Eiyre examined Namar. Namar looked the queen in the eyes, not at all fazed to be under her scrutiny.

"Bring him forward," Queen Eiyre demanded the women.

They hauled Namar forward, tugging at his sleeves, although he seemed to be coming forward willingly.

"What is your name?" asked the queen.

"Sayed," replied Namar.

"He is not one of my people," grumbled a voice. President Tecsequaih made his way through the crowd, soot-stained cape sweeping behind him.

"He is not one of mine, either," stated Queen Eiyre.

How either of them knew, Aelwen had not a clue.

Tecsequiah sighed. "Then what do we do with him?"

Shouts arose.

"He is Marchian!"

"Only an Avean would do such a thing!"

"Kill him now! He doesn't deserve the luxury of prison!"

Eiyre let the people relieve their anger for a few seconds before silencing them all again with a raise of her hand. Queen Eiyre, President Tecequaih and Aelwen glanced back and forth at each other, trying to develop a solution.

Aelwen spoke up. "Marchia will claim him!"

"Aelwen, this is not your country." Tecsequiah objected. Clearly, he had gotten over his fear of arguing with her in public.

"For the moment it is. No, hear me out!" She pleaded as grumbles began to rise up. "I mean no offense to your country in any way, Queen Eiyre. Marchia has a stronger, more efficient prison system than Ave."

Queen Eiyre nodded, understanding.

President Tecsequaih seemed to comprehend this basic reasoning. "Marchia will house this villain," he concluded. "He will be interrogated and justice will be done upon him. I shall order a prison wagon from my country to be sent immediately."

The crowd dispersed, whispering their opinions amongst themselves. Soon, Aelwen, Tecsequaih, Eiyre, Namar and the two Aveans were the only ones left.

"Thank you, President Tecsequaih," said Queen Eiyre. "That was an honorable thing to do."

"It was not my decision. I believe your thanks is directed at Aelwen."

"Thank you," Eiyre said, turning her face to the youngest of the group. The face that, just two months ago, had seemed nothing more than the face of an arrogant, spoiled girl was now the face of a composed, intelligent queen.

The queen dismounted and stroked the velvet nose of her loyal steed.

President Tecsequaih withdrew a piece of paper from the folds of his cape and scribbled orders, using Queen Eiyre's saddle for a desk. The president folded the paper and handed it to Aelwen. "Take this, deliver it to Desliad. He will know what to do with it, okay?"

"Yes, sir."

Queen Eiyre interjected. "Take my horse. You will travel faster that way."

Aelwen wanted to refuse, but things were in motion now and there was no stopping them. She took the note, the reins and mounted. " Thank you. Hyah!" She barely had to touch the horse before it sprinted off in the direction of Arkada.

<div style="text-align:center">~~~~</div>

Eoren pulled the blanket up to her neck. It was hot outdoors, but a chill filled her.

Taran had come with medicine a few hours earlier. The medicine had taken effect unusually quickly, calming the swelling. Eoren's eyelids had decreased in size and she was finally able to see. Her hands were wrapped in layers of bandages so that she could lift things without them rubbing against her raw skin. She still had not attempted to stand. She knew she wouldn't be able to, being that she had only one leg. The other, the one that had been crushed during the fire, was gone from the knee down. Taran said he was going to get her a pair of crutches so she could walk when she was ready, but he hadn't made good on that promise yet.

An empty bowl sat on her bedside table. It hadn't been easy eating with the bandages, but with Taran's help, she had managed.

As she thought of him, the door to the small room she occupied was opened. Taran came in and began silently collecting the dishes. He left with them, but kept the door open behind him. Eoren could hear water, scrubbing. Clanking. Footsteps. Taran returned. He pulled up a chair and sat next to Eoren's bed. He gently took her wrapped hand, running his fingers over the bandages. She couldn't feel his touch through the wrapping but she remembered from earlier how calloused his hands had been.

"Why are your hands so rough?" she asked.

Taran couldn't help but smile at the question. "I am a fighter. I have been on many adventures in my life. Where I come from, it's a dangerous place. You have to know how to fight if you want to stay alive. So, I did lots of practicing. With fighting, it's not something you can get good at and then not practice. If you don't practice, you lose your skill. You don't forget it all at once, you forget little bits and pieces over time. I don't really think I need those skills anymore, now that I live here, but you never know."

"Did you like fighting?"

Taran hesitated, then nodded. "Fighting has an effect on me. It's calming, clears my head. It lets me focus and really feel the presence of the earth all around me. There's a strange connection to the world and the spirits."

"What do you fight?"

"Nothing, most of the time. I just stand outdoors and spin my daggers, shoot my bow, that sort of thing. Once in a while I'll ask someone to spar with me, but most of the time it's just me, practicing alone."

148

"Don't you get lonely?"

Taran released her hands from his. "Not really. Sometimes. You see, in the dangerous place where I used to live, I was hiding in the woods to avoid the danger and I lived with a girl. So, I wasn't really alone. I do like to be alone, though. It's quiet. Peaceful. I can just do what makes me happy without worrying about what anyone says."

"How long have you been living here?"

"A few months."

"Don't you think you'll start to want company?"

"Maybe. But for now I'm on my own and I'm fine with that. I can survive without anyone's help."

"Where are we, exactly?" Eoren asked, looking around the sparsely decorated room.

"In my house. In Marchia."

"Before the fire, my family was thinking about fleeing to Marchia because of the water problem. I've never actually been here, though."

To refrain from digging up too much of the past, Taran asked, "Do you like stories?"

"I guess so," said Eoren, bringing her gaze back to his .

"What kinds?"

She thought for a moment. "Adventure. Myths."

"Romance?" he asked.

Eoren's face contorted. "No!"

"Well, then, give me a moment and I shall think of a story for you."

Eoren enjoyed the silence. She turned her neck to look out the window. It was night, the stars were not visible. Today, so much had been lost, even the stars were gone.

Earlier, Eoren had cried. Whenever Taran was not in the room, which was often, because he was so busy helping all the others, she let it all out. She had cried so much that she had no tears left. She still wanted to cry. She was sure she would always be sad now.

She looked back at Taran to make sure he hadn't dozed off. He must have been able to sense her attention flick back to him, because he opened his eyes.

"Okay." Taran took a breath, like a nervous teacher preparing to give their first speech to the class. "There is a land, somewhere, no one knows where but it is far, far away."

He told her a tale of mystical creatures in a made-up world. With heroes and victory and plenty of adventure. But his tale was not like his own adventure. In the story he told to the scarred little girl, there was no pain or death or fear. Only triumph, exhilaration and joy. Because, though he had always been candid, a quality which was both a blessing and a curse, he had heard this little girl crying and even when she smiled, he saw the pain in her eyes and he could not bear it.

All he could think of were her burns and her scars. Her tears, her groans. The shrillness of her screams when her nightmares forced her awake. No child should have to suffer such a thing. Children were supposed to be beacons of light who were innocence and kindness given form. Of course, his own childhood had been quite different, but he had grown up in the city streets of Corova without a home to call his own or the surety of a meal on any given day.

Taran had lost friends and family, he had bled and cried and starved. That's why it hurts so much to see her like this, he thought. She reminded him of himself, of the broken boy he had been before he had found Lysia and fled deep into the forest to start a new life. That was why he was so determined to someday see her smile a smile that was free of anguish, to not flinch in disgust when she saw her own scars, to laugh and play and be purely happy.

Yes, he was candid. He was harsh and serious and distant. And he cared for this child. He loved her. She had seen the cruel reality of existence, it had marred her for eternity. So, instead of telling her a tale of knights with good intentions who died tragic deaths, he told her a sappy story of mystical creatures in a made-up world.

Once he was finished telling the story, Taran looked to Eoren for her opinion.

"That was good! The horse was so funny!."

Taran smiled a little. "I'm glad you liked it."

Eoren released a great yawn and nuzzled her pillow.

"I didn't bore you, did I?" Taran joked.

"Only a little," replied Eoren with a sly smile. Her eyelids were drifting closed. "Will you tell me another one tomorrow?"

"Of course." Taran let out a yawn of his own, at which Eoren giggled. "I'll see you in the morning. If you have bad dreams, you can wake me up."

"Okay," murmured the child, drifting into the realm of sleep.

Before he rose to leave Eoren to a sleep he hoped would be a peaceful one, he squeezed her hand slightly, not powerful enough to hurt, but enough that she could feel it through the many wrappings. The squeeze was reassuring, like he was silently promising he would always be there to tell her a story when the world seemed dark and the stars were invisible.

<center>~~~~</center>

Gagged and chained. Locked sixty feet underground. Below the work of the masterminds behind the function of the largest, most profitable country on the continent. All because they thought he set a fire.

<center>~~~~</center>

Aelwen set down the law book. She was nearly halfway through. She'd made it through five pages tonight and understood most of it. She wanted to keep reading. Each day the discussion of the issue of Corova became more frequent. The time was nearing when she would need to become a leader. That meant she had to be a good one, even if it was only for a short while.

Tecsequaih had taught her all about the different ways to approach different sorts of people. Foreign ambassadors were usually kind, but were determined to do the best they could for their country. To approach them, it was all right to keep your shoulders relaxed but to make sure to keep your spine straight.

Financial advisors were mostly stuck-up and over-confident, so you always wanted to dress your finest, stand your tallest and speak most eloquently when dealing with them.

150

The president had taught her the different ways to look at a situation, to put oneself in the shoes of the opposition. That strategy helped to avoid hostility and was helpful when trying to find a compromise.

He had taught her how to sort papers and books so she knew where everything was. He had shown her which charts were actually important and the ones that no one ever really used.

When Aelwen was confused, Tecsequaih never got angry at her. He just corrected her and guided her along, explaining things so she would understand.

Aelwen wanted to keep reading, but her eyes were tired and she thought that if she tried to take in anything else with a political basis, her head would explode. She was so full of information, how was she going to remember it all when the weight of actually being a leader was added?

At least she'd have Gavnas by her side. She would have preferred Iowan the most and would have settled for Lysia, but Lysia had no interest and Iowan...

Gavnas was a leader, after all. A leader to his crew. He had led rebels to freedom and kept his head in a world of insanity. Every day, Aelwen and Gavnas left Arkada at the same time. They walked down the long halls, out the great doors and down the front steps together before parting ways, Aelwen going to her city house and Gavnas to his seaside home. Every day she saw the look in his eyes, content with what he had learned, happy with what he was doing and ready for more. He always took a couple of heavy law books home and read them in a few days.

Aelwen didn't know how he did it. She certainly didn't look like that at the end of the day. By the time she left, her feet hurt from going from one place to another, her fingers were cramped from writing and her neck and back hurt from being hunched over a desk filling out papers all day.

Tecsequaih had told her at the beginning that the papers were not going to be pleasant, but they were something a leader was required to do. Charts of money increases and decreases, population censuses and the like.

Aelwen released a long, drawn out sigh. She couldn't stop thinking about politics. They were taking over her life. It wasn't as if she could get out of them, these things were important and she had to know them.

As she tried to clear her head, searching for any thoughts that didn't revolve around politics, she remembered the reason why she was involved in politics. For the civilians of Corova was the answer she projected, and it was true, but there was another reason, a personal one. There was a singular civilian of Corova she was desperate to save more than any other.

Dirty blonde hair, soft brown eyes, a face spattered with freckles.

Iowan.

What had she gone through? What *was* she going through? What did she think of her best friend for leaving her behind at the mercy of the Master? If Aelwen could even find her, would Iowan hate her the way Aelwen hated Namar? Did Iowan see Aelwen as the one to blame, not Namar?

The worst question of all writhed in Aelwen's mind.

If Iowan thought that, was she right?

President Tecsequaih set the issue:

"We gather here to discuss the matter of whether or not our recruit, Aelwen, should be granted permission to speak with the most recent Marchian prisoner: Sayed. She wishes to speak with him with no guards present and without any escort. Shall we allow her to do this?"

Fayette Ekua, defense secretary and Chief General, was the first to rise with an objection. "Absolutely not. We have all seen the destruction this man is capable of. He will not speak to us. He is dangerous and unpredictable."

"We don't know that," argued Aelwen. "For all we know, he is just traumatized. Maybe what he did was a mistake, he could have a mental disorder."

Huaji, head of the department of health, replied, "Upon his arrival, I sent two doctors in to try to perform an examination. Do you know what happened to them? He attacked them. He had a meltdown, he completely freaked out."

"That could be proof of his disorder," offered Jae, head of the department of trade.

"Why do you not want an escort, Aelwen?" questioned Seren, head of the department of infrastructure.

"I think that the guards make him nervous. They make him feel like he's being watched. If it was just he and I, he might not feel as threatened."

"Do you really believe this man is innocent?" Kumal, head of the court system, who had remained unusually quiet up until this moment, rose.

"I cannot know for sure until—"

"Did you see him when he was captured? Yes, you were there. You saw the torch in his hand. If by chance the burning of an entire village was a 'mistake', don't you think he would have tried to help? Instead he hid to the side, waited for his chance and he ran. We are glad he chose the wrong moment."

The room went strangely quiet. No objection, no agreement. Everyone seemed to be waiting for anyone else to speak. Kumal continued, "Did you see the malice in his eyes? Did he weep? Did he apologize?" He began slowly circling the elongated table. "No. He hid his eyes. He fell silent."

"Excuse me, Kumal." Aelwen was surprised when Lin stood. She had learned in her time in Arkada that Kumal and Lin were common enemies. However, since her own arrival, Aelwen had been unsure as to who Lin desired to argue with more: Kumal or herself?

Lin said, after making a hearty display of clearing his throat, "Kumal, correct me if I am wrong, but you were not there the morning of Sayed's capture, were you?"

Kumal stopped his prowling. "No, I was not."

"President Tecsequaih was the only member of the council present at that event besides Aelwen, correct?"

"You were not there either."

"I never said that I was." Lin took a seat, crossing his legs.

"Gavnas, have you any opinion on this subject?" inquired the president.

Aelwen glanced over at Ganvas. She knew he had no idea what she was doing, wanting to go down there to confront a said mad man because he had not seen the said mad man.

"I fully support Aelwen's decision." His palms were sweaty and his left eye began to twitch. He was a fabulous commander, but he was a disgrace at speaking to a room full of upper-class government folk. He could never run a country on his own.

"Why?" Silaryn, the always extravagantly dressed head of the council, wondered.

"What?" Gavnas' voice came out strange, lower than usual. He had not been expecting another question.

Silaryn repeated her question, "Why do you support Aelwen's request?"

"Sayed obviously is not fond of large crowds. If we can get her in there, one on one with him, maybe we can get some answers."

When Silaryn inclined her head a tiny bit to show her approval of his statement, Gavnas exhaled, relieved to take no more questions.

Aelwen spoke up. "Lin." She simply needed to know. "Are you supporting my decision on this matter?"

"Yes."

"Why?" Silaryn asked. She had out a sheet of paper and was quickly scribbling on it with that elegant flourish of hers.

"We need to find the root of this problem. Maybe this man is mentally ill, maybe not. All we know is that he will not respond to large groups. I do not necessarily think that Aelwen's strategy will be effective, but I do think it is worth a try." Lin maintained a slightly arrogant air, although Aelwen had the feeling that something was going on. This was the first time Lin had supported her in anything. Was it because it was the first thing they had discussed that did not somehow have a tie to Lin's dead father? Or was it because Lin wanted to send Aelwen down there alone to see if she would come back up alive, so she would possibly be out of his way forever?

"I believe the voicing of this issue has gone on long enough," Silaryn explained, rising. She never liked the argumentative discussions of the council to go on for more than twenty minutes at once. "I now ask for direct verdicts from all of you."

The voting always began with the head of the council and continued down the list of council members. Silaryn simply said, "No." She sat and, though everyone knew the order, she said, "Desliad."

Each member stood to give their verdict. "Yes."

"Kumal." Head of the court system.

"No."

"Huaji." Head of the department of health.

"Yes."

"Fayette." Secretary of defense and Chief General.

She and Aelwen agreed on most issues. "For Aelwen's safety, no."

"Wellina." Head of the department of education.

"Yes."

"Jae." Head of the department of trade.

"Yes."

"Evon." Head of the department of architecture.

"No."

"Seren." Head of the department of infrastructure.

"No."

"Ailsa." Head of the labor department.

"Yes."

"Lin."

"Yes."

"Gavnas."

"Yes."

"Aelwen."

"Yes."

The guard handed Aelwen the keys to Sayed's cell. She watched as each and every guard retreated up the stairs. Then, she slid the key into the lock and turned. It took some muscle, the lock was old and rusty. Finally, she heard a satisfying click. She removed the key and opened the black iron door. She stood in the doorway, a looming figure.

Namar, who always kept his back to the bars when he knew someone was watching, slowly revolved. His unwashed dark hair hung over his sullen face.

Slowly, he lifted his head, filthy hair falling back. His eyes were not the same. Aelwen had always marveled at them. They were his most attractive feature in her opinion, always shining. Bright and alive like newfound, polished obsidian being held in the sunlight. No longer. Now his eyes were more like empty, forever descending holes that had seen too much. That felt nothing. That were dead.

Namar stared at her. She could tell by the way his eyes passed over her that he knew she had weapons. She had done her best to hide them, but they had been taught together, the same cruel tricks that lurked in her mind had also been bred in his.

"Namar."

A cruel smile played about his dry lips. "I knew you'd come eventually." Although he was sitting on the cold floor, chained to the wall, and she was standing with arms crossed in the doorway, Namar knew he had the power here. He knew it like he knew how to strangle an opponent without making a sound. And she had come to him for answers. If he refused to give them, there was no doubt his head would not remain attached to his neck for much longer.

"What do you want?" he asked, knowing full well the answer.

"Answers." Aelwen bent her knees, lowering herself into a half-crouching position but remaining upright enough to escape if need be. Seeing the dark eyes, the tangled mess of hair and the sinking, shadowed flesh she was beginning to wonder if he would truly not harm her. She was not going to beat around the bush to find out if he would. "Why did you do it?"

Namar laughed. There was nothing positive in the rolling, almost thunderous sound. She did not remember his voice being so deep before. "You really think I did it?"

Silence.

"I thought that maybe you were different than the rest of them, maybe you believed, maybe you could see something other than what was in front of you. Clearly, I was wrong."

He wasn't lying and she knew it. But she could not prove it if he would not cooperate. "Then what really happened?"

"There is darkness. I was trying to stop it. People. Monsters. They came and I tried to stop them."

"Did your attempt fail or is your way of stopping darkness setting entire villages on fire?"

"I tried. Believe me." Although his words were pleading, his voice was not. He did not want her sympathy. "I fought. Do you see this?" He turned his face to the side, showing her what she had assumed was an awful burn running down his cheek. She realized her mistake. A mark like that was from a blade, not a flame.

"What do you mean, 'darkness'?"

"Things. I don't know. They look like people but they move differently, like water and shade."

Aelwen gave him a hungry look, asking for more.

Namar shook his head slowly. "You will have to let me out if you want to know more."

This was the truth, she could feel it in her very bones. She had no evidence. She needed proof. Or maybe she did not. She had run out of things to say. Instead of granting his wish, she exited the cell, making sure to lock the door behind her, and ascended the stairway. A cold tingle rose up her spine and spread to her bones. If her gut was right, if Namar was telling the truth, there was something to be much more worried about than him.

It was raining. Again. It seemed as if it were always raining. Aelwen rapped on the heavy door.

She nudged Erizo. The rain made him slow, but she wasn't going to leave him standing in the president's front yard. She knocked again. A familiar voice called back, "Just a minute."

Aelwen moved Erizo over. Stretching his reins, she managed to tie him to the hitching post.

The door opened.

"Hello?"

Tecsequaih was dressed unusually, for him. Instead of his usual colorful outfit, he wore traditional middle-class attire: a loose white shirt with blue embroidering, indigo pants and brown shoes with brass buckles. The only usual thing he was wearing was his large golden necklace, this one a V-shape inside of a circle and extending beyond with a line extending from the center of the V to the edge of the circle, the entire design inscribed within a square. He had either been reading or working on some important government project, for he was wearing his glasses.

"Your Excellency, I'm sorry to interrupt, but I came to speak with you regarding our prisoner."

His mouth, which had been smiling, curved downward. "Of course." He stepped to the side. "Come in."

Aelwen had never been in the president's home. She made sure to wipe her feet very well on the doormat before stepping onto the patterned carpet. She reminded herself to watch her tongue throughout the conversation.

"Well?" There was an edge to his words.

"Sayed is innocent."

"How do you know?"

"I don't."

Tecsequaih gave her a look. A look that required no words to go along with it.

"He told me he was innocent and I know he wasn't lying. Sayed didn't do it. I don't know who did, but I swear to all the gods it wasn't him. He has information, but he won't give it to us unless we free him."

"Why did you come to me now? Why not bring this up tomorrow before the council?"

"Because they won't listen. You will."

Emotion leapt to life in his eyes like a newly kindled flame. A pang of guilt rose up in Aelwen in response to her bypassing the council and breaking the rules of this land. A land that was not even hers.

"I cannot do that," Tecsequaih said. "I need proof."

"Isn't instinct enough?" Aelwen's voice was rising despite her attempt to quell the desperation surging within her.

President Tecsequaih shook his head. "I'm sorry, Aelwen. I can't."

"You're the ruler. Why can't you? Who's stopping you?"

He walked farther into his home, a signal that he was done conversing with her.

"Did you need proof that your heart was broken when Soldan died? Did you need someone to come to you and tell you how you should feel, or did you know? Was it pure instinct that shattered your heart and cracked your soul, that dragged you down into a darkness you didn't think you would ever find your way out of?"

Tecsequaih froze. Her words were a thousand daggers in his chest. They echoed in his brain, filled with truth.

Should Aelwen hold in her nerves any longer, she knew she would explode. She pulled back the iron door that kept her feelings contained, just a smidge, allowing a single tear to trickle down her cheek. Had she just demolished her relationship with her most valuable ally?

Tecsequaih came near his apprentice. He stared down at her, his face brimming with emotion. Lightly, he placed his hand on her arm. "You know him."

"Yes."

"You are sure of your claim? Absolutely positive?"

"Yes."

"If I release him, you are sure he will share his knowledge with us?"

"I do not know." Namar had become someone foreign to her, she was no longer able to predict his actions. "Hope is all we have."

She looked into Tecsequaih's eyes for a moment and saw something she had forbade herself from ever wanting again. Aelwen left the house without another word.

A man was walking down the street, a coat pulled up over his head to protect a basket of something he didn't want to get wet. The streets were practically empty, night was closing in.

Seeing a traveler astride a horse on the road, the man took an item out of his basket and began waving it frantically, making his way toward the rider. "Excuse me, excuse me!" he called, trying not to slip on the lubricious stone road. He stopped to cough violently after inhaling a water drop. The rider paused, then kept going.

"Wait, wait," cried the man, his voice hoarse. He cleared his throat. "News! News!"

The rider pulled the horse to a stop. She lowered the hood of her cloak to see the man calling to her. News? Now? The news was handed out in the morning. What this man carried was more like a flyer than a newspaper.

"Ma'am." The man held the flyer up to her. The paper was crinkled from the wind; the rain had caused the fresh ink to run. He huffed and pulled a readable paper out of his basket. "Thank you for stopping. What is a young lass like yourself doin' out in this weather?"

The young woman pulled her hood back up to block the cold rain. Instead of answering his question, she nodded to the paper. "What's this?"

"Most recent news, miss. Careful, the ink could still be wet."

The woman took the paper, shielding it with the long hem of her cloak. It read: *Hurricane Strikes Corova.*

Her earthy eyes grew twice their normal size. "When did this happen?"

"Just this morning," the newsman said. "We don't know much yet, but hopefully we will. I've heard the government is trying to help, but the Corovan king just won't have it."

She nodded. "Thank you. I will help them if I can."

Aelwen folded up the flyer, tucked it into her pocket, and snapped the reins. Erizo cantered all the way home.

A detailed report, complete with supposedly-accurate illustrations, had been published. The hurricane that had struck Marchia had made its way to Corova. Corovans had so little to live off of, the hurricane had only worsened their circumstances. It had been a quick hit, lasting only an hour before veering out into the sea.

Aelwen pressed her hand to her nose. Corova was her home, no matter how unkind it had been. The place had ripped her to shreds to rebuild her as a force of nature with a wit of quicksilver and a soul of stone and flame. Who would Aelwen be had she not been sculpted by Corova's brutality? The answer was one she never wanted to know.

Her tears speckled her shirt. Was Iowan okay? The terrible hand dealt to Iowan made Aelwen want to stare down the universe itself and demand reparations for what it had done. Had Iowan been wounded? Had she survived the hurricane? Had she survived the harbor that fateful day? Aelwen was done asking those questions. She was ready to answer them.

CHAPTER FOURTEEN

Only worry for Iowan, grief for those she had known and the land that had molded her existence occupied Aelwen's mind. Thoughts refused to form fully without exploding, sending fragments of memories that only deepened the pain soaring about her mind.

At least if she blundered she would have Gavnas to back her up.

Silaryn gave the usual speech at the start about the subject of the meeting, along with a brief outline of the basic etiquette of the gathering, as was customary. When she sat, no one immediately stood to speak. Everyone seemed uncomfortable to discuss this issue, especially with two devout Corovans in the room.

Aelwen took the opportunity. She rose so forcefully she almost knocked her chair over. "I am Corovan. For thirteen years, my country has been ruled by a cold-blooded despot. The people are not inherently wicked. The conditions of their lives have forced them to be this way. Everyone is responsible for their own wellbeing, comradery is nonexistent. Now a hurricane has struck and who is helping them?"

Kumal did not bother rising to make a snide statement. "Why should we help them when they cannot even help themselves?"

"They cannot stand if they do not have a stable foundation beneath their feet. The time is now. Marchia must stop crouching in the corner, watching lives be decimated. You must rise up and rid my homeland of the tyrant who rules them."

Averting his eyes, Lin rose. "Do they really deserve our help? When Marchia was overpopulating and desperately attempting to gain more land, when Marchia went to them for support, they turned away." His tone was smooth, almost relaxed. Aelwen knew different. The way his heels slid back and forth on the carpet, the way he held his hands together to refrain from fidgeting, the way he only briefly scanned the faces of the observers, never lifting his head to see her blazing brown eyes.

Aelwen pounded her hands on the table. "Stop living in the past!" She had not shouted in such a crowded space for so long, she had forgotten the effect it had on people. The way her voice smashed through the air like a rock thrown through a window. The way everyone fell silent, afraid that if they so much as blinked she would turn her fury upon them. She set her voice to a lower register. She knew this would do more damage than if she continued to scream. "That happened thirty-seven years ago, Lin. Countries change, people change. You must change. You cannot hold a grudge against Corova forever."

She slid back into her chair. She leaned back and stretched out her legs, tapping one boot lightly on the floor. A position that exerted calm. Not that that was what she felt. Her blood had gone from boiling to simmering; the pounding of her heart still resonated in her ears.

"Besides Lin, are there any objections to this claim?" Silaryn's voice was placid as an undisturbed lake in the northern mountains, untouched by the filth of human anger.

Fayette Ekua, defense secretary and chief general of the Marchian military, spoke up. "No. Aelwen has made her point. Anyone foolish enough to argue with her will be proven wrong." She said the word 'will' with a certain sharpness, throwing a slashing glance at Lin. "We need to begin our plans to help them. Now."

Gavnas, who usually stayed relatively silent during these meetings, stood up. "I lived among these people. There is no way to predict how they may react to any situation. Yes, action must be taken, but we also must have a clear plan on how we want to approach this event."

Evon asked, "Shall troops be sent by land or sea?"

"Land," said Desliad. "Arrival by sea could be mistaken for an invasion. Our country already borders them on one side, coming in on the other could be viewed as a siege."

"Are we going to notify them of our coming or simply show up?" Seren questioned.

"Notify them. You can't just show up on someone's property unannounced," Huaji claimed.

"No, no," broke in Ailsa. "King Halmar won't want us there. If he knows we're coming, he will send his guards to stop us."

"I agree with Ailsa," declared Kumal.

"Are we going to make any attempt to be hidden at all? Are we going to march into Corova openly?" Jae wondered.

No one was able to answer that. General Fayette said, "Aelwen, Gavnas, your opinions?"

They traded looks. Aelwen said, "Corovans are born scared, they live and breathe fear. They won't dare come near us if we're fully armed."

"We should have horses, too," commented Evon. "That would intimidate them more."

Gavnas interrupted, "That may scare them too much."

Jae nodded in agreement. "We want a respectable entrance, we don't want to scare the wits out of them."

Aelwen turned to the head of the council, "What do we have so far?"

Silaryn folded her hands. "Entrance by land. Fully armed. No declaration of our arrival. No horses."

"What other decisions are there to make?" asked Seren.

Usually-quiet Wellina said, "What are we doing once we get there? If all goes as planned, we successfully arrive in Corova. What's next?"

Seren answered, "Once we enter Corva, how much time until Halmar is notified of our arrival?"

"An hour, maybe two," said Gavnas.

Desliad let out a small gasp, a realization hitting him hard. "The Corovan border is shut down. Nothing goes in, nothing goes out."

Most of them had forgotten about that issue. A few years after the tyrant was appointed, the surplus of government money left over from the previous ruler, King Vilaz, had run out entirely. The tyrant had refused to appoint a council and would not give orders to anyone at all.

The government officials could not make any decisions, even in dire straits, without the tyrant's consent. At that moment, the country had relied fully on the profits of foreign trade. If the tyrant did not take action soon, the government would have to defy the law and beg for loans from other countries.

Newspapers slandered him. Out of anger, he shut down the border. The law was still in full effect. Not that it needed to be. No one ever wanted to go near Corova.

"That law is in effect. Not enforced," Aelwen replied coolly.

"What?"

Aelwen explained, "Yes, technically since that act has not been repealed, it is still in effect. However, the king stopped enforcing it years ago. He realized no one wanted to enter his foul country and thus brought his troops in closer to protect him."

"Entering won't be the hard part," Gavnas said. "It will be once we're in, making our way around without being attacked."

"That leaves us with one choice," Fayette Ekua said. "We march directly for the palace first. I will bring the elite of our military, we will storm Orodel and dismantle the guard system, which no doubt is precise. A smaller group will be able to enter the castle and destroy Halmar once and for all."

Jae was smiling, realizing what a reckless plan this was. They could not remember the last time the Marchian government had acted so rashly. "Once the king is gone, surely the people will accept our help to rebuild their lives and their country."

"Yes and if a flourishing life, trade system, government and financial situation are the outcome, I do not believe they would mind Marchian government ruling them for a few months," Huaji said.

Aelwen and Gavnas traded looks once again. There were a million ways this could go wrong.

Every single member of the council, including both Kumal and Lin, were smiling broadly, reveling in the fact of the great deed Marchia would soon do.

Aelwen almost intervened, destroying their happiness with one of the hundreds of "what-ifs" swirling in her mind. Then she saw Tecsequaih's face. She had seen him smile before, she had heard him laugh. She had never seen him like this. An audacious sort of look. The look he must have had on his face when he was younger, raiding Avean camps in the night with Soldan at his side.

Aelwen saw his face and knew she could not destroy that happiness.

Fog rolled in as the sun faded, blanketing the marvelous green, swadling it in gray so that it might face yet another day.

Aelwen stepped over an outcrop of stone. She could hear the faint rumbling of the waterfall and knew she was close. "Why did we have to meet here?" she called, seeing the shadowy figure waiting for her on the cliff's edge.

"Because this is where I feel comfortable. I would have liked to be on the beach, but I figured you would prefer this journey to that one."

"Damn right I would. What's the secret?"

After the council meeting, Gavnas had handed Aelwen a note asking her to meet him in this exact spot. A small clearing in the dense jungle that provided a spectacular view of a misty waterfall.

Gavnas turned his head away from her. He took a step closer to the edge, feeling the sharp spray from the waterfall on his face.

When he did not appear to be formulating an answer she said, "Gavnas, what do you want?"

He sighed heavily, a sigh too heavy for him. "I will help take back Corova." A pause, a too long pause. "I will not help govern."

Aelwen felt her face drain of color. News that Marchia would liberate Corova had spread like wildfire throughout the country as soon as the meeting had ended. Lysia and herself had wept with joy, they were to leave for a celebratory dinner in two hours.

They were going home. They were going to make it right. They were going to be heroes.

"Gavnas—this has all been for nothing?"

He smiled faintly, trying to calm Aelwen's rage before it fully surfaced. "Not for you. You have benefited greatly. You will be the queen Corova needs."

"I'm not going to be a queen. We are going to be temporary rulers—you *and* I, until everything is right again!"

"You will be a temporary ruler. Politics is not the world for me. I wish it were, I wish I had the heart of a ruler. Alas, I do not." In truth, Gavnas was scared, terrified to lead a broken country. The call of the sea inside him was growing stronger each day, he could hardly bear to resist it any longer. He had had enough of living like a plain civilian. He longed to be himself once again. "The sea calls me home."

By the look on his face as he longingly gazed at the water, Aelwen knew he was telling the truth. A heaviness grew in her chest. He was going to leave her to do his alone.

"No. I can't do this alone, Gavnas." The immobile stone that built her words was cracking.

"You're going to have to." Gavnas flipped up his hood. "I'm sorry, Aelwen. I really am. I will help you get your country back, but after that it's *your* country."

Without another word, he turned and entered the dense wood, his cloak rippling behind him.

Aelwen shouted a curse after him before she found herself alone, huffing on the cliff. This couldn't be happening. It couldn't. *He* couldn't. She looked out over the cliff, her vision becoming as watery as the river below.

A scraggly old man clad in dirty rags hobbled over to the strange visitors.

Invaders? Perhaps. What should he care? He wrapped his knobby, bony fingers around the wrist of a woman. There were none built like her around there, maybe he could grab a taste of this fleeting dish.

Aelwen was so deep in thought that she did not hear the man approaching. She leapt in surprise as gnarled phalanges entrapped her wrist.

He was barefooted. He moved with trained stealth that came from years of pickpocketing. Aelwen expected the man to beg her for money. The moment she looked into his eyes she knew what kind of person he was. One of the kind of people who, even here, had been crushed down into the lowest of classes. The kind of people who thought women were helpless and that people with skin different than their own were somehow lesser.

She shook her wrist. The gnarled, clawed hand held on. "What are you doing here, young lady?" His voice was like gravel, his teeth were chipped and yellow. "A woman's place is in the bedroom, don't you know—"

Aelwen shook her arm so fiercely that the deranged man fell to a heap on the ground. Grumbling, he began to rise. He didn't make it far before her foot collided with his ribs. There was a sickening crack as her boot met his body once again. She slammed her foot into him again and again, grinding her teeth together so she did not scream. His blood stained the filthy cobbled street.

At last, Aelwen relented, breathing heavily. Her eyes, full of fury, stayed on the broken man. His chest rose faintly, then fell. He opened one eye, the flesh around which was bruised black from the beating. Keeping her flaming gaze pinned on him, she spat, "A woman's place is where *she* says it is."

Sparing the wretch no more words, Aelwen rejoined the troop. The Marchians' eyes were wide in astonishment, but Lysia and Gavnas were undisturbed by the occurrence. Anyone who'd ever lived in Corova under Halmar's rule had experienced far worse.

Aelwen re-assumed her position at the front of the group, beside President Tecsequaih Mayolan.

"Are you alright?" he asked.

"I'm fine. Trust me, I've handled worse. We all have."

Tecsequaih was visibly unnerved by that, but he did his best not to let it show. With a sweep of his arm, the troop was in motion once more, green and gold banners bearing the Marchian elephant head sigil held high, flapping in the breeze, marching through the wretched streets of Corova.

Before Aelwen knew it, Orodel, the castle of the monarch, was looming before her, a shadowy mass that reeked of darkness. It's dark stone walls did not glisten or shine. No bells or banners hung from the structure; all that adorned it was a single flag of fuschia and gold, the nation's colors, waving lazily in the wind from the topmost spire.

The hairs on the back of Aelwen's neck rose. Her fingers fluttered toward the hilt of her sword. An old habit.

The Guildsmen had seen them long ago. They had hoped with all of their being that the strange party was only passing through. But they knew. They knew by the way the trespassers walked, the way their knuckles whitened around the hilts of their blades. They knew that if they failed to stop these rebels, they would be executed.

The trespassers approached the front gate of Orodel. The doors were guarded by a row of Guildsmen, all dressed in the customary gold and fuschia, jeweled swords hanging at their sides.

The lead Guildsman said something to his followers in a harsh tone and they ordered themselves into pairs, crossing their weapons to create a barrier.

President Tecsequaih, who held his sword at his side, revealed its great length in a regal flourish, the sun reflecting on the blade, blinding everyone for a second.

At that moment, the Guild knew what they faced and that they could not conquer it.

Aelwen stepped in front of Tecsequaih, brandishing her own weapons, a pair of twin daggers. "This is my country and I will have it back. Step aside or you shall not see the light of a new day."

The leader huffed. The guards solidified their line, weapons vertical.

"Out of our way. Now," growled the ex-Arenian.

No reaction whatsoever.

"You have chosen death." Aelwen's voice was as cold as it had ever been. In a flash, she was within a mass of guards.

Aelwen flung herself at the Guildsmen in front of her. The guard held up their iron axe handle, blocking her strike. Other guards amassed around her. This was nothing she couldn't handle.

Her killer instincts took over. She had seen the Guildsmen all her life, had taken time to learn how their armor was assembled. She knew exactly where the weak spots were.

The chest plate covered all of their torsos, up to their collarbones. Their necks were covered by another steel plate attached by chain mail which also connected to the helmet.

The Guildsmen rarely ever fought any more, they were mostly just for show. Their armor was old, no matter how consistently they shined it. Metal wore with age, especially their type of mail.

Aelwen wedged her dagger in between the chest plate and the gorget. Her strong blade sliced through the mail and all of the tendons, flesh and bone beneath.

The armor was so tight fitting that the guard's severed head could not fall off. Blood poured from the slice she had made, drenching that guard's armor.

The first slaughter had been almost too easy, she had expected more interference from the other guards. When she turned to take another enemy's life, Aelwen saw what had made her first kill so simple. She had been so set in her murderous ways that she had not realized her allies had broken through the circle of guards and begun fighting their own battles.

Aelwen killed two more Guildsmen in the blink of an eye. She swept her dagger in a circle, slitting a guard's ankles, which were not padded nearly as much as they needed to be. She brought her dagger up in a flashy arc and prepared to stab it into the neck of another guard.

Just as she jabbed, a hand clasped around her other wrist. Not an enemy hand, the warm hand of a familiar friend. Lysia was staring at her. She didn't have to say a word.

There was an opening in the ranks of the Guildsmen, they had been pushed back far enough to create an aisle leading directly to Orodel's doors. At that exact moment, every Guildsmen was too preoccupied to notice.

Aelwen wanted to plunge her dagger forward, but even more strongly she wanted her kingdom to rise again. She lowered her hand. With Lysia at her side, she dashed into the castle.

Orodel's doors were heavy but unlocked. Everyone knew where the king's throne room was: right behind the balcony the king stood on while making speeches— not that Halmar had ever made a speech. Both Aelwen and Lysia were decent with directions. They entered the large welcome room.

The area was enormous, the entire welcome room larger than the entirety of the arena Aelwen used to fight in. Gold trim, smooth white marble floor, stone walls with tiny details carved into them. Shiny wooden stands held porcelain vases decorated with floral designs holding the largest, brightest, sweetest smelling flowers in the land. A massive glass chandelier with diamonds hanging from pale silver chains hung in the exact center of the room. Perfect, all of it. Beautiful. Not gaudy. This one room represented what most people only dreamed of. What so many people lived without. What so many people were deprived of.

To the left was a spiraling obsidian staircase. They raced up. Lysia took the lead. About halfway up, Lysia paused suddenly, hand in the air, eyes flashing bright with alertness.

Aelwen could not hear anything beside her footsteps as she caught up. She stopped abruptly. "What?" she whispered as quietly as she could.

"Footsteps."

After Aelwen adjusted her ears to the pounding of her own heart, she heard them too. Soft, but quick. The long black stairwell spiraled, Aelwen moved to the railing and looked over.

She couldn't have been more relieved at what she saw. General Fayette, Gavnas, three Marchian military members and President Tecsequaih.

Lysia was just as glad to see who it was.

When the six caught up with the two, they exchanged no words, just nodded to show their trust in one another and continued up the stairs.

As they made their way down the long hallway that led to the king's chamber, the hall grew darker. A long horizontal window ran across the entire wall, providing the king and his family a glorious view of their country. Heavy, dark, wine colored curtains were drawn across them, blocking out the light. Blocking out the view of this king's failure of a kingdom.

The doors to the balcony that allowed a view into Halmar's throne room were shut and locked tight. Separating the balcony and the room was the hallway they were traveling down. Surprisingly, the door to the king's room was open.

In most countries, the ruler had two separate rooms: a throne room and a bedroom. A throne room for being a formal ruler and a bedroom for being a real human being, living their own life. In Orodel, the rooms were one and the same. Corovans believed that while in a position of leadership, their ruler should live and breathe their title always.

Aelwen had been expecting the chamber to be flooding with the light of a thousand jewels, lit by extravagant lamps and chandeliers. Instead, there was only darkness and gloom.

Lysia pushed through the group, trying to see into the room. Gavnas held her back. "No."

"We can't kill him if we're just standing out here," she explained. "We have to look in to see what's happening."

Aelwen peered around the corner, into the chamber. What she saw she wouldn't have imagined in a million years. She pinned her body against the wall, using all of her might to silence her panicked breaths.

Lysia's eyes filled with concern. "What is it?"

Aelwen shook her head. One of the Marchian warriors came up to Aelwen and said near silently, "Is it worse than anticipated?"

Finally managing to be sensible she said, "You decide for yourself."

Costively, each of them took a turn peeking into the room. The people in the room were too intent on their task to notice the stalkers.

A figure wearing a cloak of tyrian stood over a middle-aged man on a throne of carven stone. The figure pulled out a knife and proceeded to drag it down the man's wrist, making a long, shallow cut. The blood of the king leaked out. The cloaked figure pressed a hand to the king's arm, just below the cut. Inky, spidery swirls and tangles seemed to seep into his flesh around the cut, creating a sort of sick tattoo. The strange markings were visible for only a moment, then disappeared as if they had never been there at all.

An arrow whizzed past Aelwen's ear. She could not hold back a gasp. The shaft spun through the air, sailing straight for the back of the purple figure. It whipped around in an instant, hand up. A swirling, multicolored void formed in front of the mysterious person, shattering the arrow. The figure was now facing them, but the shadow of the room and the mass of fabric it clothed itself in hid all distinguishing features.

The swift second of stunned silence ended. A massive silvery blue dragon erupted from the floor before the figure, sending shattered pieces of tiled floor scattering into the air with such force that some of them impaled the solid wooden walls.

Aelwen hardly felt as a piece dug itself into her shoulder.

The figure turned in a circle, sweeping its cloak around itself. It appeared on the back of the dragon, perched atop a brown leather saddle. The figure held onto thick chains that served as reins. The dragon burst through the ceiling, shrieking furiously as it ascended.

All of the Marchians cowered to avoid being injured by the falling roof. The moment the shattering noises stopped, one of the Marchian guards, quickly followed by the rest of the group, raced to the balcony. They stared into the blue sky. Nothing. Nothing at all.

"Who in hell fired that?" growled Tecsequaih.

"I did," admitted Gavnas, not showing the slightest twinge of remorse.

A horn's call bellowed throughout the twisting halls of the castle. Running footsteps. Clanking armor. More Guildsmen were coming.

"We have to get out of here. Now." Fayette ordered.

In the instant Aelwen turned to run, a voice sounded. The shell of a voice she had known so well.

Everyone was racing down the stairs.

Aelwen froze at the top, drowning out all noise but the one she sought.

"Wait."

It was a hushed sound, holding within it an echo of strength.

A hand closed around Aelwen's arm. General Fayette. "Aelwen, we have to go."

Aelwen clapped her hand on Fayette's armored shoulder. "You go. Make sure everyone makes it out."

Fayette inclined her head, her steely eyes searching Aelwen's. "What of you?"

When the Corovan gave no answer, Fayette did not press for one. She squeezed Aelwen's shoulder reassuringly and sprinted down the staircase.

Aelwen stared into the wrecked throne room. There was a huge hole in the floor where the dragon had burst through. On the other side of that hole was the king's throne.

"Is someone in here?" hollered Aelwen.

Her mind began to fill with doubt as no answer came.

Then, a faint, desperate, "Yes! Over here!"

The voice was raspier than it had been the last time she'd heard it, but the cadence of the words was the same.

"Help, I can't move!"

As the dust of destruction began to settle, Aelwen was able to see across the gaping hole. Upon the throne sat Halmar, slumped over, blood oozing from a wound on his head caused by the falling roof. Wrapped around the arm rest of his throne was a chain. Aelwen followed the chain with her eyes. A large chunk of the roof pinned the chain to the ground. At the end of the chain was a shackle and within the shackle was a leg, rubbed raw by the metal. The woman whom the leg belonged to had dark circles under her eyes and wore clothes that were too large. Her hair was stringy with grease and her nails were chipped and dirty.

"Iowan!"

Aelwen dashed around the hole in the floor to where Iowan crouched, covered in dust from the ceiling and floor. She drew her sword and hacked at the chain that bound her friend. After several hard whacks, the chain broke.

Iowan's eyes grew twice their normal size as she made out the face of her savior. Hands trembling, she reached for Aelwen.

"I can't believe it's you," she murmured. Aelwen hated how cracked Iowan's voice sounded. She fell to her knees, putting her on the same level as her friend.

"I know, I know." She flung her arms around Iowan, wrapping her in an embrace tight as the bond they shared. She withdrew, staring into Iowan's eyes that had been the color of the summer sky last time she'd seen them and were now more like a misty lake. "We have to get out of here, okay?"

Iowan nodded furiously. Aelwen stood and outstretched an arm to Iowan, who graciously accepted the help to stand. She wobbled as she stood on her own two feet, free of the chain.

Aelwen steadied her. "Can you run?"

Iowan did not hesitate before answering, "Yes."

Within a minute, they were through the great doors, sprinting across the courtyard. The rest of the troop Aelwen had come with were all outside, continuing to fight. They had nearly vanquished the opponents. General Fayette shouted, "More are coming!

"Charok!"

"Mailin!"

Names were hollered until everyone knew they had to go. They had to run, run for their lives.

The first troop of Guildsmen came sprinting through Orodel's doors. A bold soldier ran forward and grabbed one of the injured Marchians around the waist. Both of them fell to the ground. The Marchian flailed and kicked wildly at his attacker. The guard wrapped her arm around the Marchian's throat and squeezed. She finagled her other hand around to her back where a small knife was hidden.

Fayette wasn't about to leave one of her own to be slaughtered. She ran up to the soldier and slammed the sole of her boot in the Guildsmen's face. "Don't touch him!" she shouted. The moment the Corovan fell back, Fayette grabbed her warrior under the arms, helped him to his feet and ran with him by her side, not letting go of his hand while they fled.

Everyone went their own way. Some ran by themselves, taking independent paths, while others stuck in groups. Aelwen fell into a group with Iowan, Gavnas and two Marchian soldiers. The winter was slow approaching, but the air had already turned thick with cold. Every time she gulped in a new breath, her lungs wheezed and her throat stung.

<center>~~~~~</center>

The girl heard the noises. She knew the call of the horn, the horn that called for the swiftest of the king's men to come to the hunt. There was yelling. She was accustomed to yelling. Someone was always yelling about something around these parts. This yelling was different. It had more heart to it, the voices had strong meaning in their rich tones.

A heavily armored, dark skinned woman with short hair ran past. Her armor bore the Marchian crest, the head of a golden elephant on a field of green.

The girl pinned herself against the wall of her shack-house as she saw who was running after the woman. A Corovan soldier, furious, fire burning in his dark eyes.

The girl smiled slightly to herself. Some burden was lifted from her shoulders. She felt lighter, as if life could be better someday. Maybe not for her, but for her children, her grandchildren. She felt near to happy, a sensation she had not felt for as long as she could remember. She smiled to herself. She knew freedom was coming.

<center>~~~~~</center>

168

Aelwen didn't know how long she had been running. She only knew that she could not stop. A realization whizzed through her head. Something about this thought was electric, important. She let it in.

She couldn't keep running with this group. She was the center of this uprising. Aelwen knew that she was most wanted and if she were killed, this rebellion would not continue. None of her friends quite had the influence that she possessed. By staying with this group, she was putting all of them in danger, not just herself. Plus, she alone would be less noticeable.

Aelwen broke off, sprinting immediately behind a building. She ran down one side of it until she came to the back of it. She dashed down an alley and took several turns. If someone *was* following her, she would be harder to target snaking through the more concealed parts of the city.

She ran out onto a street that was occupied by two Marchianswho were fighting against six Guildsmen. Not the place she wanted to be in. At the sight, she quickly hid herself behind a stack of crates that happened to be stacked against the wall beside her. The stench of the crates almost made her retch. Gods knew what was in them.

Backtracking would do no good, but she was not willing to risk entering the street that lay before her. Aelwen took a closer look at the crates. They were stacked quite high and there were enough footholds on the side of the building she could use for footing. There was a good possibility that she could scale the wall and reach the roof of the building completely unnoticed.

Using the crates as a ladder, Aelwen climbed up the side of the building, placing her feet on uneven siding, pipes and window sills. She ran along rooftops for what felt like half a mile; she had never been good at measuring distance and had no idea how long she had been up there.

Her head felt too empty. Her legs were starting to feel like they were not attached to her at all. It was time to get down. She had run for so long that she had entered the part of Corova where all of the buildings were built in a similar fashion, each had smooth sides that offered no aid to one who wished to climb down them.

She found a building that was made in a foreign fashion, made of large round stones rather than wood, which was the most common construction material in Corova. The building had a roof that was horizontal on the front side of the house but slanted down at a dangerous angle at the rear. The house was not very tall. The shingles that decorated the roof might be an issue, they had no doubt been there for too long and were no longer attached properly.

The jump was long, but nothing she couldn't handle.

She leapt across to the flat side of the roof. She had too little momentum behind her, causing her to skid on the shingles. Her prediction had been completely correct. The moment her feet touched them, the shingles started sliding and poking up in different directions as they rammed into one another.

Aelwen fell forward as the shingles moved beneath her feet. She held out her hands to catch herself. The sharp edges of the slate slats dug into her skin. Pulling herself into a sitting position, she wiped her bloody hands on her shirt. Her desperation to keep going was the only thing that kept her from falling again.

She waited for the shingles to settle. She could not hurry across them, that much she had learned. She had to move slowly, placing her feet in logical places. Aelwen stood on the beam of wood that separated the two vastly different sides of the roof. She stared down the drop. It was farther than she had thought. From her years of forced-risk-taking, Aelwen knew that no thought was always better than too much thought. She jumped. Her eyes snapped shut with fear.

The chill wind battered her face. She felt a shingle cut her ankle as her feet found them, but she kept moving down, sliding down. Slate jabbed at her. She had not jumped out far enough and had met the roof again.

A shingle cut through her pants, slicing from the underside of her rear all the way to the bend at her right knee. Her eyes flashed open at the searing pain.

A total reflex, Aelwen's legs bent, her feet found purchase that had not been there moments ago and propelled her out into the air. She closed her eyes again, she had never been able to stand watching herself fall. She folded herself into a ball as she hurtled into the air, forgetting to brace, and rolled across the frozen ground.

Aelwen swept out her uninjured leg and pulled herself up. When the foot of the wounded leg touched the ground, she cringed. Once the shock of the jump and the impact cleared away, she heard yelling again. Knew she had to get away. Knew she had to make it to Noclen, the place they had all decided they would meet should things take a sour turn.

She ran again, fear shoving the pain of her injury from her mind. She concentrated on the rhythm of her breathing, the rhythm of her steps, how they blended together to make her soul song. Ignoring the storm of pain and fear. Embracing the arms of the cold around her as the wind blew at her back as though nature were pushing her onward, saying, "keep going."

A cloud of darkness swarmed about her head. She did not stop running. The darkness disappeared, then returned again, thicker this time. It formed a mass around her, blocking all of her senses from working.

High-pitched ringing filled Aelwen's ears. She flung her arms wildly to clear away the blackness. She could no longer feel her feet on the ground. Dread filled her heart.

A sliver of light flashed in the dark. Followed by another. It was as if a knife was slicing through black curtains, letting in the long-banished light. More and more cuts in the cloud. The ringing remained, but it had lessened significantly. Aelwen could feel her feet thumping along the frozen ground. The darkness swirled more slowly until it all dissipated into thin air.

All of Aelwen's senses came flooding back to her much too quickly. She did not have time to process everything or to stop herself before she tumbled into a freezing river.

Everything slowed down. Her body sank and sank. Bubbles formed in the dark water and ascended towards the rippling surface. She reached out to touch them, but they swerved away from her groping hands. Beneath her was dark, beside her was dark, above her was dark. She stuck her arms out and propelled herself outwards and upwards. Her head broke the surface for a single moment before she dropped down once more.

There was no chance here, the current was too strong. She closed her eyes and let the force of nature drag her downstream, farther from her goal.

Aelwen's frozen eyelids fluttered open painfully. She knew she was alive. It was not her breathing that told her she was alive. It was not that she could feel the river rolling over her ankles or see the trees around her with their falling orange leaves. It was not the smell of the crisp cold air, either. It was the inner knowing that her work was not yet done, that people depended on her, the world depended on her.

Aelwen ran her fingers over her shirt. The parts that were not frozen stiff were soaked with ice cold river water. Her wounds where the piece of the floor had embedded itself into her shoulder and where the roof had cut her leg open were beginning to scab.

She pressed her hands into the cold gravel of the bank and stood. Night had nearly fallen, the sun had sunk below where she could see.

Aelwen grabbed the neckline of her shirt and pulled. Her hands were too weak from the cold. She fumbled with her weapon belt until her frozen fingers managed to remove a blade. She gingerly slid the knife between her shirt and skin, slitting it down the middle.

Were the Guildsmen still out there? What would they do if they came upon a half-naked woman wandering through the forest? Based on how ragged she appeared, she could pass herself off as Corovan.

Using the small bit of light that remained in the sky from the sunken sun, Aelwen headed off in a northeastern direction, north to get nearer to the meeting place, east to locate any town so she could form an idea of exactly where she was.

She knew who she was. She knew where she had to go. And so, she kept going.

CHAPTER FIFTEEN

Iowan rolled onto her side, eyes fluttering open, clutching her stomach.

She'd collapsed seconds after she'd arrived at Noclen. When her head had started to swim while she was racing through the streets with them, desperate to put as much distance between herself and Orodel as possible, the people who'd come to kill Halmar had told her to go to Noclen. They'd told her she'd be safe there and, so far, they had proven correct.

A hand squeezed her shoulder. "Hey, Iowan." The voice came from above and behind her. It was not Aelwen's.

Iowan turned to look. Lysia sat beside her head, dressed in fighting leathers, a smear of blood on her round bronze face. That rebel lock of raven hair lay askew across her forehead. "Hi," murmured Iowan. She took in the rest of those around her. Soldiers milled about, their armor emblazoned with an elephant head sigil. The mark of Marchia, if the map in King Halmar's throne room illustrating each country and its flag was correct. So her friends had made it. They'd gone to Marchia and convinced the government to help them. And they had just raided Orodel and freed her.

They'd come back.

They'd freed her.

After all those days of worry and hours of fear that *Mist Wing* hadn't made it or the Marchians refused her friends or killed them or they had made sufficient lives for themselves in Marchia and had changed their mind about reclaiming Corova, they had come back. They had saved her.

Lysia rubbed soothing circles on Iowan's back and said nothing.

Pain coursed through Iowan, though she was thankful for Lysia's poor attempt at comfort. After so long without it, any scrap was welcome.

Iowan had not moved in such a way as she had during her escape in months and the toll on her body was a large one. Her body no longer possessed its Arenian skill. She clenched her teeth against the pain, letting it run its course. She listened to the nearest soldiers talking.

"She's still not back."

"Where is she?"

"Did they get her?"

"We should send out a search party."

Lysia followed Iowan's gaze and said, "They speak of Aelwen. She's the only one who hasn't arrived." A pause, then she added, "I'm sure she'll show up eventually."

Iowan hoped that was true. She wasn't prepared to face the consequences if it wasn't.

One of the soldiers—a tall, dark-skinned man with long graying hair—glanced in Iowan's direction several times, then waved at her to join him. She was about to ask Lysia who the man was and what he wanted with her when Lysia said, "I'll be right back." She rose from her spot beside Iowan and went to the man. Iowan let out a breath of relief that she was mistaken and it was Lysia, not her, the man was summoning. She watched the two of them converse and tried to hear, but their voices were too hushed for her to hear anything more than mutters.

The hushed conversation was short. Mere minutes later, Lysia returned.

"What was that about?" asked Iowan.

"Tecsequaih wanted my opinion on whether we should send out a search party."

"What did you say?"

"I told him I don't know. I don't. I have no experience with these sorts of things. I told him that his judgement as president was worth more than mine."

Iowan started. "President?"

"Yes," Lysia laughed lightheartedly. "I forget how much you don't know." She nodded at the soldier she had just spoken with. He was dressed like all the others, nothing marking him apart from the others save for the sword at his hip which was fancier than the rest. "That's President Tecsequaih Mayolan. Ruler of Marchia. And that," she pointed to another soldier dressed like all the rest. The soldier was a woman who wore a menacing scowl. Her black hair was cropped close to her scalp and her skin was darker than the president's.

Lysia continued. "Is General Fayette Ekua. Chief General of the Marchian military."

Iowan asked, "Anyone else I ought to know?"

"I don't think so." A second later she added, "Oh, Gavnas is over there."

Iowan followed Lysia's gaze to a spot where a still body lay, two soldiers crouched beside it tending to wounds. She never would have noticed if Lysia hadn't pointed it out, but it was clear that the still form was Gavnas.

"Is he okay?"

"He will be," replied Lysia. "One of the Guildsmen stabbed him on the way here. The wound isn't too bad, from what I've heard. He just needs rest."

"Don't we all," grumbled Iowan, rolling onto her back. The pain was relenting, but it was still very much present. She wished for sleep to take her so she could stop feeling so awful. Trying to make her wish come true, she closed her eyes. It felt good to do so, but sleep felt no nearer.

"Iowan?" Lysia said from above.

"Yes?" answered Iowan without opening her eyes.

"Are you okay?"

Iowan let out a deep sigh, contemplating. "No."

Realizing Iowan planned to say no more, Lysia asked, "Is there anything I can do for you?"

Iowan let the silence build as she thought it over. "No. Just...don't leave me. You're all I have."

"Okay…" said Lysia, Iowan's request was clearly unexpected. "I won't go anywhere."

Iowan flitted on the edge of sleep. She remained aware of the ambient sounds of the soldiers talking and the feeling of Lysia's presence beside her, for which she was truly grateful. She was finally free and her best friend was missing and Gavnas was unconscious. She had heard nothing of Namar or Taran. She nearly asked Lysia about them, but decided against it. Her questions could wait until her safety was something more definite and she wasn't in so much pain that she doubted her ability to stand.

She had one friend at her side. That was more than what she'd feared in her darkest moments during the past months. Lysia was there beside her, alive and able. They may not have known each other well, but Iowan trusted that Lysia would be there for her. Not only here in Noclen, but in the future as well, standing with her no matter what happened.

Nothing was certain—Iowan knew that better than anyone—yet she couldn't help feeling that she was right about this one thing. There was no logic to it, only blind intuition and a tie she felt for the woman at her side that she had not felt before.

~~~~

Aelwen had absolutely no sense of self left. She knew only one thing: the location she had to reach. It did not matter that she could barely breathe, it did not matter that she was in the beginning stages of hypothermia, it did not matter that she was hungrier than she had ever been in her life. The only thing that mattered was that she reach that place.

After walking for many hours, she finally stumbled into the camp. Her people had risked no fire. No tents, only small cots. Most of the Marchians and rebel Corovans were curled up on the ground with their cloaks wrapped around their knees. All of them were resting, but none of them slept.

Aelwen could not hold on any longer. She fell to the ground.

The last thing she heard was Iowan gasping her name.

Light. Bright, warm light. Aelwen moaned and rubbed her head. Her body did not hurt, she only felt tired. Why, then, was she lying in a bed in a healer's ward?

"You're up."

"Yes." Aelwen sat up to see the healer who had spoken, leaning on her down pillows. "Why am I here?"

"Iowan carried you. She found you laying on the ground and carried you all the way back across the border. She said you were breathing when she found you, but your eyes were closed. You were unconscious when you got here."

Aelwen rolled out of bed. "I need to go."

The healer chuckled. "They told me you'd say that."

Aelwen threw back the covers and was suddenly aware that she was stark naked. "Could I borrow some clothes?"
~~~~

"Of course. In the closet at the back, to the far left. They should fit you. If you can't find anything, let me know. We seem to be about the same size, I could dig through my own dresser." As Aelwen searched, the healer commented, "Nothing in there is very stylish. I don't think anything matches either."

"It's fine." Aelwen emerged from the walk-in closet, dressing quickly. Before she left, the healer stopped her, "Aelwen."

"Yeah?" Her breathing was already quickening with stress and excitement at what was coming next.

"Your body's been through a lot. Take it easy."

"Right."

Aelwen was barely noticed when she arrived at Arkada. President Tecsequaih stormed across the hall, Nayre Nowak, captain of the guard, on his heels. "You let him go?"

With the inkling that this was a conversation she'd want to hear the whole of, Aelwen slid around the corner where, thankfully, one of the many large potted ferns happened to be positioned. She sank to her knees and peered through the leaves, watching and listening intently.

The president nodded sternly. "Yes."

Captain Nayre crossed her arms, anger rolling off her in waves. Though she was not officially apart of the president's council, Aelwen had heard tell of Nayre, how headstrong she was. Aelwen looked upon Nayre Nowak now, she was a muscular and heavily built woman with keen eyes and blonde hair cropped close to her skull, just like Fayette. She stood a good five inches over Tecsequaih.

Keeping his voice level, though it was evidently a struggle, President Tecsequaih explained. "He told us he could help us. We saw things in Orodel that led us to believe that what he said was true. He said that if we let him go, he would track the evil forces and gain knowledge of their operations and bring that knowledge back to us, we have to hope he was telling the truth."

Her voice less well-contained than the president's, Nayre said, "He was a prisoner. He burnt a village, took many lives and ruined many others."

"I know that. After what we saw, we're losing hope and we need any shred of light he can offer."

"That means forgiving him for murder?"

"No. It means taking a leap of faith out of necessity."

Captain Nayre sighed deeply. "You'd better be right about this."

"I saw no lie in his eyes."

She rolled her eyes. "Maybe he's a good liar."

Tecequaih sighed this time. "Sayed is gone, there is no getting him back until he returns."

"*If* he returns."

Her anger dull but still very much present, Captain Nayre shot the ruler one last look of rage and walked briskly down the hall. Tecsequaih closed his eyes, breathing rhythmically.

Aelwen watched the captain until she was out of sight. Then, she made her own appearance.

"You set Namar free?"

The president flinched in fright at the sound of her voice, his eyes flying open.

The moment his gaze fell on Aelwen, all of the frustration disappeared from his eyes. He seemed suddenly lighter, as if a great burden had just been removed from his shoulders. Shoulders that would soon have greater, heavier burdens placed upon them.

He barely had time to say her name before he had her in his arms. "You're okay…"

Aelwen returned the favor as President Tecsequaih hugged her with all his might. "It's going to take more than that to get rid of me."

After a moment of warmth and comfort both of them cherished, they split apart. "What have I missed?" Aelwen asked.

"As you have heard, Sayed has been released."

"You believed me?" She could hear the joy in her words. For all his argument, he had known she had spoken the truth.

"I did. And I'm scared and disturbd by what we saw in Orodel and I hope beyond hope that by releasing Namar I made a choice that will give us a considerable advantage, but that all depends upon whether he was serious about getting us information in return for his freedom or whether he was playing those cards because he had no other choice."

"Thank you, nonetheless," said Aelwen. "Why didn't you discuss it with Captain Nayre, though?"

"I knew she would never consent and I didn't want to waste valuable time arguing, so I made an executive decision." He paused for breath before continuing. "General Ekua has called for any and all Marchians to join her forces now and has set up various training facilities. A war is coming."

Aelwen tensed. She had known this was coming as soon as that purple-garbed figure and their dragon had flown out of Orodel, but hearing it made it all the worse. Hearing it made it real.

"The Marchian military is the greatest on the continent. What's the point in recruiting new soldiers now, with war so close?" Aelwen asked.

Tecsequaih sighed. "There is only one type of human I know of capable of doing what that person was doing to the king."

Aelwen feared she knew the answer.

"A mage."

Her heart sank. That was the answer she'd feared.

"Why," she shook her head in disbelief, "Why would a mage be dealing with Halmar?"

"If only we knew."

"Where is the nearest facility?" Aelwen asked, doing all she could to focus on what she could do to save as many lives as possible rather then being distracted by the impossibility of their situation.

Tecsequaih's brow furrowed. "What?"

Aelwen met his eyes. "The nearest training facility, where is it? I can help train the new recruits."

President Tecsequaih had obviously not been expecting this response. "Aelwen—we—you're a politician now. You—you're one of the most valuable assets in this entire movement. We can't risk you. You need to stay here, plan from the inside and stay safe. You need to prepare as much as you can for when you become Corova's leader. Leave the war to my forces and when we win, your people will call upon you."

"I'm only going to train them, not fight on the front lines." Though, as she said the words, Aelwen doubted their truth. Based on the look on Tecsequaih's face, he did as well.

He offered no response.

If he was not going to tell her where the nearest facility was, she would find out for herself. She strode to the door.

Tecsequaih followed her, his long legs clearing the space. "Aelwen, wait."

Who's going to stop me? Aelwen did not speak.

Tecsequaih halted as the large doors to the building clattered shut behind her. His guards were still standing where they had been before. Without looking at them, he growled, "Leave."

Once he heard the final pair of rhythmic footsteps fade away, he approached the large doors. He put his hands on the thick, smooth wood. The door had been there for centuries. Still so stable and strong. This door had seen so much and yet it just stood there, proud and solid, watching all the world pass by.

<p style="text-align:center">~~~~</p>

It felt wrong. Lysia shouldn't be the one showing Iowan their home in Marchia, she shouldn't have been the one telling Iowan everything that had happened since they'd set sail from Corova while they travelled from Noclen back to Firhad.

Aelwen should have done it all. Iowan and Aelwen were best friends, not Lysia and Iowan. They hardly knew each other.

But Aelwen was unconscious in a healer's ward and someone had to be there for Iowan.

Iowan beside her, Lysia opened the door to the little white stone house in Firhad that she shared with Aelwen. The parlor welcomed them with its gossamer curtains and slender coat rack.

Neither of them had stepped over the threshold before they heard rapid footsteps from within the house, coming in their direction. Iowan flinched, a look of panic on her freckled face.

Lysia knew better. She recognized the pattern of the erratic footfalls and was proven correct when Rinly burst into the parlor from the hall that led to the living room.

"You're back!" he cried, embracing Lysia. Drawing back, his dark eyes fell on Iowan. "Are you—"

Glancing at Iowan, but seeing that she was nothing more than confused, Lysia replied, "Yes, that's her."

Rinly extended a hand to Iowan. "Iowan. It's so good to finally meet you."

Looking at Lysia with wide hazel eyes that begged for an explanation, Iowan shook Rinly's hand.

"Iowan, this is Rinshad Ibori. He's called Rinly for short," Lysia explained. "He was the first Marchian we met and he's remained a friend ever since."

"Oh," said Iowan, awkwardly shifting her eyes between her companions. "Nice to meet you."

Rinly stepped to the side, ushering them in. Together, he and Lysia gave Iowan a tour of the house. Iowan showed no enthusiasm at anything they had to show her, all she did was nod and half heartedly agree when the others shared their opinions of the furnishings. The tour ended with a room upstairs that was empty except for a bed.

"This will be your bedroom," Lysia said. "I can take you shopping tomorrow to pick out decorations if you want."

Iowan smiled, but her heart wasn't in it. "Okay. Thanks."

The tour ended, the trio made their way downstairs. At the bottom of the stairwell, Rinly said, "You two haven't eaten since last night, right? You've gotta be hungry. I know I am and I had breakfast two hours ago. I'll go make something and meet you in the living room."

Before either of the women could confirm that they were hungry, Rinly walked off to the kitchen. Whether it was because he was genuinely being kind or because he felt just as awkward around Iowan as she did, Lysia did not know. All she knew was that she was alone with Iowan once more without a clue what to say.

She led Iowan to the living room where they sat next to each other on the sofa. An uncomfortable silence expanded between them. The first thing Lysia could think of to say was 'are you alright', but Iowan had already answered that question back in Noclen. Instead, she tried, "How are you doing?"

"Better than I have been for a long time," said Iowan.

Lysia expected her to say more, but when she didn't, she said, "What do you think of the house?"

Iowan raised her brows, then they fell and disappointment overtook her. "I like it. I do. Sorry I wasn't more interested."

At least the disappointment was in her own shortcomings, not in the house.

Iowan continued. "The house is amazing, Marchia's amazing, it's all amazing and wonderful and I love all of it. It's just...hard."

"Hard?"

"Yeah. To adjust to everything. I was chained to King Halmar's throne, then I wasn't, then I was on a horse surrounded by a bunch of strangers. Well, mostly strangers," she corrected. "Now I'm here, in a city I barely know. I haven't seen Aelwen since she rescued me, Namar's evil and Gavnas hardly said two words to me on the way here and I haven't seen him once since we arrived. Rinly seems nice, but I don't know him. You say Taran doesn't want anything to do with us anymore. On top of all that, I have to learn not to be afraid and how to be strong again, and normal. I want to learn all of that, I really do, more than anything, and I'm trying. But it's hard. It's all really hard."

Iowan's eyes were rimmed with red, tears streaked her cheeks. Lysia expected Iowan to wipe them away, but she didn't.

Just as she had many times in the difficult, uncomfortable, usually forced conversations she'd had with Iowan lately, Lysia was at a loss for words. Iowan hadn't said so much for many days, sticking to nods and curt words. Lysia had seen the signs of tears on her pale face often as well, but she never said anything. She didn't know if Iowan would want to talk about why she'd been crying, especially since the answer was so obvious. But now the tears were right in front of Lysia and there was no sidestepping them.

Lysia sidled up to Iowan. Iowan wasn't trying to hide her tears. She was looking right at Lysia, letting them fall. Lysia wanted to look away and hide from the grief Iowan bore. It wasn't hers to bear, it was Iowan's; this was Iowan's struggle, not hers. She tried to convince herself of that, but she failed to believe it. Yes, the grief belonged to Iowan. As did the pain and the struggle and the fear. But Lysia knew those things too. Not for many years; they were pieces of her past in Corova before she had fled into the forest and made a new life for herself, but still, they had been her constant companions once as they were Iowan's now. She remembered the anguish of sleepless nights and the long stretches when the days bled together and all she knew was fear. She would have given anything for someone by her side back then, a friend. No one deserved to feel so utterly alone as she had, in rags, begging on the Corovan streets.

Lysia reached up, cupping Iowan's red, tear-streaked face in her hand. "I don't know what you've been through. You don't have to tell me about any of it if you don't want to. Or you can tell me all of it. Whatever you want to say, I'll be here to listen. You've lost so much. So many people you used to know are gone. But I'm not. I'm still here. Whenever you need to talk or cry or just be with someone, tell me and I'll be there. Whatever healing you have to do, it will take a long time and it won't be easy. But I'll be here through it all, I promise you. Okay? You may not have much, but you have me. I'm here, okay? I'm here."

Through the tears, a smile broke upon Iowan's face. She nodded. "Okay."

They leaned close, pressing their foreheads together. Two souls suddenly bound, promising to face together whatever the world had to offer.

~~~~

Aelwen wanted to find the farthest facility from Arkada that she possibly could. She trekked all the way to the other end of the city until the buildings were few and the flora were many. She found a forest ranger and asked her for directions to the nearest training facility.

When Aelwen walked into the camp, she was satisfied to find that the instructor was none other than General Fayette Ekua herself. The general exclaimed when she saw the newest arrival, who stood a good distance away from her. Her senses were even sharper than the Arenian's. "I figured you would show."

Aelwen smiled, a tad bit weakly. "Tecsequaih didn't want me to come."

"I know. That's the main reason I figured you would." They both grinned at that.

Behind Fayette, there were crates of weapons and about thirty students, young and old, before Fayette, looking all a mixture of confused, anxious and excited.

"Most of them have no training in any form of combat," Fayette explained. "We're starting with basic stances."
~~~~

Aelwen nodded, ready to begin.

Fayette turned to the group. "Line up!" She gave a shrill whistle. What the students formed was not the straightest, tightest line, but it was a line nonetheless. "I'm going to count off, remember your number!"

Aelwen had never seen Fayette like this. She liked it. It set the tone for training. Fayette's eyes turned darker and more focused than usual, she stepped with a certain deadly elegance, poised and ready. A killer who demanded to be obeyed if Aelwen had ever seen one.

General Fayette counted off down the row by two's. She took the ones, Aelwen got the twos. The groups separated.

To her group, Aelwen called out, "Rule one: do not turn your back to your enemy. Your back is your weakest point. It's a blindspot and one of the deadliest places to be hit." Aelwen swept her eyes over her people. Not one remotely resembled the other. Despite that, none of them looked like warriors. They were shopkeepers, tinkerers, everyday folk. They did not belong on the battlefield.

Aelwen continued. "Basics: stances, strikes and kicks. Let's start with stances. The most basic fighting stance is this." She positioned herself. "Don't put your feet too close together. Depending on your size, there should be about a foot length between them. Don't put your back leg directly behind the front one. Then, when you try to kick, your front leg will be in the way. Rest on the balls of your feet. Good, all of you. Now, hands. In front of your face. Keep your fists relaxed except for when you are ready to attack, then tighten them. Keep your thumbs on the outside. Good. Now hold that position, I am going to come around and check each of you individually."

After they had all gotten the hang of that stance, she decided to mention a few kicks since this was the common kicking position. "We're going to start with the basic snapping kick. Think of it as four easy steps. One." She lifted her leg up, bent at the knee. "Two." She snapped her leg out and held it there. "Three." She pulled her leg back into position one. "Four." She set her foot back on the ground, in the fighting stance once again.

"Got it? Here we go. One. Two. Three. Four." She ran through the format three times, making her way down the line to make sure they all understood.

"Very good. Now we are going to do it faster as one quick movement. Before you bring your kicking leg forward, tilt your opposite foot at an angle." She noted their confusion. "Like this." Aelwen got into the fighting position. "I'm going to kick with this leg." She tapped her right leg, which was back. "I'll do this slowly. Watch my left foot." As she drew her right leg forward in slow motion, she turned her left foot a couple inches outward, opening her hips, giving her more freedom of movement. "Think of it as if you were on a tightrope over a pit. You've all seen performers before— when they walk the rope do they keep their feet straight or at an angle?"

No one responded. They all knew the answer, but Aelwen's very presence was intimidating. Aelwen answered her own question. "At an angle. Once you finish your kick and bring your kicking foot back in, make sure you also reset your angled foot because you need stability and your next move might not be a kick."

Hours passed. Aelwen watched with pride as her trainees grew in confidence. She taught them a variety of kicks, stances and strikes. All just the basics. She did not point out the small errors each of her students made. This class was not for them to become lethal weapons, it was to train them how to save their souls.

As the sun dropped lower and lower and the bright purple strokes in the sky turned dark, a sharp whistle cut through the air. Fayette shouted from across the camp, "Wrap it up!"

Aelwen nodded obediently. "Circle around me." They all did. Respect and fear tinged their eyes. "Listen," she turned in a slow circle as she talked, looking them in the eye individually. "I am proud of all of you. You have all shown your skill today. Thank you all for respecting me and for putting forth all the effort you possess." She completed one full turn.

Each time her glassy mahogany gaze landed on someone, they would give away their nervousness. Some blinked, others flinched, a couple clenched their hands into fists and most of them began fidgeting with one thing or another whether it was their own fingers, something in their pockets or a loose string on their shirt. None of them looked away from her solid eyes, though it was clear they all wanted to.

"I see it in you. Fear. Of me. You know what I am. I know what I am and I am not afraid of it. Why are you? I am not a reckless monster. I have a capable mind. If you fear me forever and can never learn to trust me, you will never reach your full potential. I ask you all now not to forget what I am nor to ignore it. I ask you to accept it and look past it. Try to see who I really am. For then, you can find who you really are and once you do, the power you release will be incredible."

Fayette departed from her group. Aelwen followed the general's lead. They met in the middle of the clearing and turned to face the sweaty mass of students.

Fayette explained to them, "Tomorrow we'll switch groups. I want you all to get good rest. Meet here at noon. Tomorrow will not be so kind as today and soon the real work will begin. Go now. Rest."

As the students headed off, the Arenian and the general organized the clearing, hiding away the crates of weapons and picking up little things the students had left behind. "We ought to start a lost-and-found pile," Fayette stated.

"I agree," said Aelwen.

"How far did you get with your group?"

"We practiced basic strikes and stances."

"Kicks?"

"Yes. Tomorrow I plan on showing them how to blend their moves together to fight fluidly and maybe teach them a couple little tricks."

"Good. I did the same thing. At the end, I started showing them different ways to wield weapons. My plan was to work with weapons tomorrow, but I think your idea is better. We can work weapons the day after tomorrow." Fayette closed a box of knives and shoved it under a bush. "I'm going to meet with all the other instructors tomorrow morning to make sure we're all on the same page."

"Sounds good," Aelwen said.

Fayette slid another box of weapons into hiding, then stood up, adjusting the collar of her shirt. "You never took me up on my offer?"

Aelwen racked her brain, trying to think of what the general was talking about. "What?"

Fayette smiled, unoffended that Aelwen had forgotten whatever it was she was talking about. "My offer to help teach you after your first council meeting. I offered you and Gavnas both, neither of you took me up on it."

Oh, *that* offer. Aelwen had completely forgotten about it until Fayette had just described it to her. Now that she recalled it, she regretted never taking advantage of it. "There was just so much going on, I totally forgot about it. Sorry. I would've taken you up on it if I remembered."

The general shook her head, indicating that it wasn't a big deal. "That's fine. I was only wondering. I expected you at my office the day of the next meeting, but you never showed. It's more than reasonable that you forgot about the offer, given all you've had to deal with."

A misting rain began to fall as Fayette and Aelwen entered the city.

"I am surprised it is not snow," Fayette remarked.

The weather was nothing compared to what Aelwen had suffered in Corova. However, for Marchia, it was a cold front indeed.

"Fayette! Aelwen! What are you doing out here?" demanded Lin.

Aelwen rolled her eyes. Why was it that anytime Aelwen ran into anyone, it was always the person she would least like to see?

"I could ask you the same question," Fayette countered strongly.

"I had to stay late at work. There was an emergency meeting, so I'm out doing my shopping now. Where were you two?"

Fayette replied, "We were training. The president knew that."

"Where?" Lin sounded mildly frantic.

"In the forest. What happened?"

Lin wiped the moisture gathering on his forehead. "Ever since he became king, Halmar has only given one order."

Everyone knew that. "To close every Corovan border," Fayette stated.

"Until today. Today, he released his second command." He swallowed. "A formal declaration of war upon the country of Marchia."

There was a moment of pause, then the general sprinted into the darkness.

Aelwen did not know if she should move. She didn't want to. She wanted to freeze the world, never to see the horrors that were sure to come.

Lin watched Aelwen's unresponsive expression for a while and then turned his gaze out to the darkness.

"I never thought I would see war," he said. Aelwen looked at him. "I thought my job was to heal the broken world my father died for. I guess I was wrong. Maybe the time for reparations will never come, perhaps the world will be swallowed up in an endless, churning cycle of war."

He looked different than she was used to seeing him. He looked... scared.

"Aelwen," he started. "We've been at odds plenty of times, but I want you to know that I don't want you to be my enemy."

He finally looked at her. She looked back at him. Really, truly looked. An alone, broken man standing in a dark, rainy night. A man assumed to be aloof because no one cared to scrape away the outer shell to see what was beneath.

Aelwen took a tentative step forward. The first step that she hoped would break all barriers between them forever. She hugged Lin.

Iowan had cried herself to sleep, head resting on Aelwen's shoulder. The two of them had still not had a proper conversation about what hell Iowan had suffered back in Corova. She had only just escaped, but already violence seemed to be ready to find her again. She and Aelwen had all fallen asleep in a bundle on the sofa.

President Tecsequaih would want Aelwen to be at Arkada that morning. Her students needed her.

She dressed simply when she got up. Then she gathered all of her weapons she could find and left the little white house on horseback.

Aelwen checked the position of the sun as she came upon the wide clearing. She was early. As she dismounted, she was surprised to see that General Fayette was already there. The students were paired together, practicing hand to hand combat.

"Fayette!" Aelwen called, jogging to meet the general. "What's going on? Why is everyone here so early?"

"War is coming. We don't know when they will strike. We need to be ready. We don't have time to teach them individually. They need to know how to fight right now."

Aelwen nodded. "Okay."

"Walk around. Advise them. We are going to give them weapons in the next hour."

"Fay—General," Aelwen corrected herself smoothly, "They've had no instruction with weapons yet."

"I plan to give a short course." Fayette departed, strolling around and in between the groups, judgement filling her deep, dark eyes.

How had everyone known to meet here earlier than they had decided yesterday? Why had Aelwen not been notified of the time change? It was not worth the effort of asking. In a time of war, one needed to be able to filter out what was truly worth saying since any word spoken could be your last.

Aelwen began her journey of many, many circles around the clearing. "Straighten your back. Don't look away. Never turn your back. Ever! Don't extend your arm all the way. Move your leg to the right. Duck lower. Bend your knees."

As Fayette had said, there was a short lesson on how to use basic weapons.

"The weapon is an extension of your arm. Once you hold it, it becomes a part of you. Without armor, I don't want any of you practicing on each other, so last night I dug out some old trainers."

"What's a trainer?" asked one student.

"A human-sized figure made of straw and fastened with twine used for fighting practice of any kind, but mainly when weapons are involved. Aelwen, you have used trainers?" Fayette inquired.

"Yes."

"Could you show them how to set one up while I go get the rest?"

"Of course."

Fayette dragged out of the brush a long crate that resembled a coffin but was long enough to hold about eight bodies. Aelwen opened the crate full of trainers. There were foldable wooden stands at the head of the crate. "This is a trainer and this is a trainer stand," Aelwen explained. She showed the students how to assemble the trainer and the stand before instructing them on how she wanted them to go about practicing with the trainers.

After passing out the equipment, Aelwen scanned the group for those who needed help. She located herself beside a teenage girl who was having trouble with the basic dagger spin. "Hold your knife. Tighter. Now relax your wrist, I'll move it for you." Aelwen put her hand on the girl's wrist and moved it. She repeated the motion a couple of times, loosening her grip with each twirl. "Now you try."

The girl moved her wrist, spinning the dagger. Successfully, but not quite confidently. Aelwen said as much, "There. You've got it. Now believe in yourself."

She had taken one step towards the next student to help him with his posture when a boom like the splitting of the earth ricocheted through the air. Everyone in the camp froze, ears ringing from the noise. The sound had come from far away. To the north.

Hooves pounded behind her. Motion flashed by her; Fayette, astride a dark horse.

"Coming?" General Fayette's voice was harsh as ever. Aelwen practically jumped onto the horse. Fayette snapped the reins, squeezing the steed's sides with her feet. The horse bolted.

That horse was, by far, the fastest horse Aelwen had ever ridden. It seemed to glide above the earth rather than run on it. The world flashed by so quickly that Aelwen had to stare at the saddle to keep from being sick. She had not had any time to position herself correctly before the horse ran, so she wrapped her arms around Fayette's waist, trying not to squeeze too hard.

What awaited them? Aelwen knew of nothing capable of producing such a sound. All she could see in her mind's eye was the figure cloaked in purple that had stood before King Halmar. It was the only thing she could imagine that had caused whatever destruction awaited them.

Fayette must have known quite a few shortcuts through the country because, although Aelwen had not been watching her surroundings or really paying attention to the ride at all, the journey seemed far too short.

As the horse trotted to a stop, Aelwen raised her head. They were at one of the many training camps, it was larger than the one they had come from, with tents and firepits and many more people. Not that anyone from this camp, skilled instructor or able beginner, would be of any use. The training camp was littered with corpses. There were bodies everywhere. Still, lifeless.

Everything was whole. The tents, the bodies. Nothing was broken, nothing was bleeding. But everything was dead.

CHAPTER SIXTEEN

It was strange for Aelwen, operating with Gavnas in Arkada, at her side as if all was well between them.

After an hours-long council meeting and a session with some of the other council members in the Great Library going over battle strategies and how to draw them, as mapping out possible ways to defeat their magic-wielding enemies in war was the paramount business of the council at the moment, Aelwen was alone in the library with Gavnas.

He sat at a different table than her, poring over some tome, not looking at her. She'd been forcing herself to do the same, but the itch to look at Gavnas, to say something to him, finally became too strong. "Why did you fire the arrow?"

Gavnas froze, then slowly raised his head to look at her. "You were all wasting time, watching when you should have been taking action. I knew that if that thing saw us, we wouldn't get another chance. So I took mine." The words were level, easy, calculated, void of emotion. The captain lowered his head, all of his attention on his book once more.

Aelwen looked back down at the book she was poring over without a response. She'd only half-expected him to answer her and certainly not so simply as that. She knew perfectly well that she was angry at him, though her wrath was dampened by the war. But how did *he* feel about her? Gavnas hadn't spoken to her outside of asking her to pass him a pen or saying 'excuse me' when he needed to get by. He didn't shoot her dagger glares or offer smiles of reconciliation.

Before she had a chance to decide whether or not she wanted to ask Gavnas outright his opinion of her, he said, "Are you familiar with the history of the mages?"

"No," replied Aelwen. "Are you?" The question was laced with sarcasm. Gavnas wasn't an intellectual. Beyond what he was doing here in Arkada, he didn't spend his time reading or studying or learning. That was Namar. He was Gavnas, rugged, serious, confident Gavnas who sailed the wild seas with his crew of misfits. Not Gavnas who read books and knew ancient history.

"I am."

Aelwen started. "How?"

Gavnas rose. He skimmed the shelves packed with leather bound books, their titles etched in gold. "I read…this." He pulled a narrow book from a shelf he had to stand on his toes to reach.

"Since when do you read?" she scoffed.

"Since I realized it would be to my benefit to do so," said Gavnas, making his way to her. He set the book on the table in front of Aelwen, who picked it up.

The binding was brown leather, not overly worn. There was no title or author to be found anywhere. The spine was bare, as was the back cover. On the front, there was an etching of a slender branch bearing three orchid flowers and several buds.

"What's the orchid got to do with mages?" asked Aelwen.

"Read it."

"I *really* don't have time for that," she said, a mixture of annoyance and anger in her voice. It was true. When she wasn't out training the new soldiers or studying at Arkada, there were barely enough hours in the day for Aelwen to eat three meals and sleep for a decent amount of time. She didn't have spare time to read a book about mages. She didn't care very much, either. All that mattered was that an army of mages was trying to kill her and everyone she cared about. She flipped the book open, expecting to find the inner pages thin and worn, the ink barely readable, based on how far back the history of the mages went. However, the pages were in near perfect shape—thick, white and crisp. The smell of new ink still clung thickly to the pages. The writing was large and legible, a slight swirl at the end of the letters. The book was handwritten.

"Is there anything in here on how to defeat mages without using magic?"

"No."

"Then why the hell should I waste my time reading it?"

"It won't help you defeat the mages, but it will help you understand them," said Gavnas. "Why they're doing what they're doing."

Aelwen sighed, flipping the book closed. She ran her fingers over the orchid engraving. "Can't you just give me a synopsis?"

Gavnas shook his head. Perhaps she was reading him wrong, but Aelwen thought he looked almost amused. "It's not that long." He glanced at the large pendulum clock in the far corner of the library. "There's another two hours before we leave. You can have it read by then."

She took a moment to consider. She'd been sketching battle plans and reading books on combat strategies for hours now, they were all starting to blur in her mind. This book *was* a welcome respite, though she wouldn't admit that to Gavnas.

"Fine," she grumbled, cracking open the thin book once more. She had it read within an hour.

The book told of another era of the world; an age when mages had roamed freely, sharing their gifts with the world. An age when a mage could be hired and make good money as a performer, an architect, a smith or any other profession where they could use their powers. In that ancient age there had been three main bloodlines: the Orchid Line, the Anthurium Line and the Hibiscus Line. Those three lines had practically been worshipped as gods; they had been given seats in the courts of monarchs and presidents, known to be on a first-name basis with the rulers of the world.

Until people began to grow weary of magic. Magic had somehow become meaningless to the majority of the population, they had become blind to beauty. Hate groups formed, protestors raged in the streets, mages were fired from their jobs.

"Malhelas" was the name designated by the mages to those who despised magic. The name meant 'darks', for the mages believed that without magic the world would become ugly and dark.

Then came The Great Burning.

All mages who had not yet fled society, including the Lines of the Orchid, Anthurium and Hibiscus, formed communities in tents and wagons, putting on shows of magic for the public. Since magic was no longer respected, only the lower classes attended and donations were few and far between. One fateful night, a mob of Malhelas gathered. They had managed to locate every community of mages and that night they traveled throughout the continent and burned every single one.

Those few who survived had no choice but to flee. To remain would only result in death.

The mages took over the desolate southern end of the continent and named their land Paruma. They sowed seeds and used their combined power to call to the spirits and to the earth itself and beg for their new country to become a place of life and plenty. Over time, the land was transformed from the harsh, dry climate into one of thick foliage and abundant life.

Ever there they dwelled, in their own corner of the world where they could use and enjoy the magnificence of their powers. The mages of Paruma shut out the world the way the world had shut them out.

That was the gist of it.

The final pieces of the puzzle, those not in this book, were easy to put into place. The mages had had enough of their foul treatment, so they had banded together and risen from seclusion to get revenge on those who had wronged them centuries ago.

Aelwen clapped the book shut. She found the spot Gavnas had taken it from and put it back.

"What did you think?" asked Gavnas, not looking up from the battle plan he was sketching.

Aelwen shrugged, returning to her seat. "I've never been a lover of history. But, as far as history goes, it's interesting, I guess."

"Interesting? That's all?"

"Yeah. Why, what did you think of it?"

"I think that book makes sense of everything the mages have done."

Aelwen hoped she didn't know where he was going with this. "Go on."

"The book justifies everything they've done, all of it. It all makes sense," said Gavnas. "The mages have come to take everything they deserve. For all the hate dished out to them, for all the hurt, for all the blame, for all the world that has been taken from them. Now they've come to take it all back. They've been sitting in silence, keeping to themselves in

Paruma, for hundreds of years. They've finally stepped into their power, they've come to reclaim everything we've taken from them."

Aelwen's mouth was dry. She must have misunderstood him. There was no way Gavnas was justifying everything the mages had done and would do because of a book on ancient history.

"Gavnas, I—"

"Don't you see?" he implored. "We're going about this all wrong. Fighting the mages when we should be talking to them, apologizing and trying to make things right."

"They have made it abundantly clear that they don't want to talk to us. They want to kill us," said Aelwen, her anger burning brighter with every word.

Gavnas opened his mouth to say more, then closed it. It seemed he'd realized that she would not be swayed from her opinion. He dropped his gaze back to his sketch and for a moment Aelwen thought he was going to go back to his studies. Then he started to shake his head slowly.

"I thought you would agree with me. I really did."

Aelwen scoffed. "Agree that we should have sympathy for people who want to murder all of us? No. No, I don't agree with that."

Gavnas exhaled, long and deep. Abandoning his sketch, he rose from the table. "I'll be off then. You were my only hope."

Hating his cryptic ways, Aelwen said through gritted teeth, still struggling to process the fact that he was on the side of the enemy, "For what?"

Gavnas was shaking his head again, as if whatever he was going off to do wasn't something he wanted to do. "I thought I could convince the council if I convinced you. My plan was that after you read the book, you'd agree with me and together we could convince the council to stop the war."

Aelwen stood, the rage within her growing with every passing second. She addressed the final point of his statement first. "The council never *chose* to go to war, the mages attacked us! Then Corova declared war! What did you want us to do, say, 'thanks for the offer but we'd rather not fight'? They declared war on *us!*" She paused for breath, all of the yelling draining the air from her lungs. "Why can't you convince the council yourself? Go talk to them, make them read the stupid book!"

Gavnas responded with a level, concise tone tinged only slightly with irritation. "They don't like me the way they like you. The council, I mean. President Tecsequaih included. I'm the blot on the side, no one pays much attention to me. But you? You've always been the star of the show."

There was denying that Gavnas was right. Aelwen was the favorite to an absurd degree. "Well, if you're not going to try convincing the others yourself, where is it you're off to? To join the mages?"

"No." The word was flat. Succinct.

"Why not? I thought they were your new favorite."

"I considered it. But I could not bring myself to do it, knowing that if I did, I risked coming face to face with people I care about in battle."

"Meaning me?"

"Not just you. Iowan. Lysia. Tecsequaih, Rinly, anyone from the council. Maybe even some of my former crew members. But I also cannot fight with you, knowing that I do about the mages' past, knowing they are in the right."

Aelwen kept her expression unreadable as he spoke. She would not give him the satisfaction of a dramatized reaction.

Gavnas went on. "So I will go to the sea."

Aelwen rolled her eyes. "Of course. Where else?"

Gavnas continued, ignoring her snide remark. "I've maintained contact with some of my crew since we arrived here. I'll take them with me and together we'll sail away towards the horizon, never looking back."

"Why not just keep out of the war? Or you could start a cult of non-magic mage supporters. That might catch on."

"I don't want to live on a continent that is torn in two. I'll sail until I find a place where there is true equality. No corrupt kings or beggars on the streets, where no one is oppressed or hated. A place with only peace and harmony."

First, Gavnas told her to read a book and now he was talking like one of Namar's poetry books. Aelwen wished she had spoken to him more often of late. Perhaps she could have stopped this dreadful transition he'd made. "That's very idealistic of you. I don't think such a land exists."

"If it doesn't, I'll sail on forever. I'll never stop searching."

"Have fun with that. Why not try to fix the continent you live on instead of trying to find a perfect one?"

"I don't want to fix things anymore. I've been trying to fix things for forever. I'm done. The sea is my true home, you know that, so it is where I shall wander, in search of everything I desire."

"And you're going to leave? Now?"

"As soon as I'm done speaking with you, yes."

"Shouldn't you hand in a formal resignation to the council? Or at least tell them you're leaving?"

Gavnas shrugged. "What difference would it make?"

Aelwen found it in her to steady herself. If this was her goodbye to Gavnas—which it thoroughly seemed to be—she didn't want to spend it yelling. He may have turned into a fanatic, but he was more to her than what he was in this moment. He had been a steady friend for many years, someone she dared confide in outside of her fellow Arenians. Without him, there was a chance she might never have made it to Marchia at all. She didn't know who Gavnas was anymore, all she knew was that she didn't know what her life would have been like without him.

"I don't understand this plan of yours. I really don't. I think it's completely ridiculous. But I hope you find what it is you're looking for, Gavnas. And if you don't, I hope you find a way to be happy."

Gavnas inclined his head in thanks and extended a russet brown hand to her. "I wish you luck in all your endeavors."

Aelwen didn't take his hand. She spread her arms and beckoned him to her. Gavnas was not a hugger. He obliged nonetheless. Aelwen wrapped her arms around him. She'd never touched him like this before. She was afraid the motion would feel forced, false. It didn't. It felt perfectly correct. She rested her head on his firm shoulder.

Gavnas was stiff in her embrace at first, but after a moment he softened.

"Thank you for everything," Aelwen whispered against his shoulder.

They drew apart slowly, neither quite ready to acknowledge that this was the end of them, for a long while if not for forever.

"Thank *you* for everything," said Gavnas.

Aelwen wasn't quite sure what he meant by that, but she nodded in gratitude nonetheless.

Gavnas made his way to the doors of the library.

Their time wasn't up for the day, though it didn't much matter since Gavnas wasn't planning on returning.

Without so much as a final glance at Aelwen, he walked out.

From the library windows, she watched Gavnas ride away towards the sea.

~~~~

Iowan sat up rapidly at the sound of a knock on her bedroom door. She'd been laying on her bed, staring at the ceiling, until the knock had jerked her from her mind. Fear sparked through her, her heart raced at the sound. Bracing herself on the bed, Iowan took a breath to steady herself. *I'm safe now*, she reminded herself. "Come in."

The door opened, in walked Aelwen. Intense, beautiful, built for combat, with a confidence in her stride and a proud tilt to her chin. Iowan had always admired Aelwen, but whenever she used to start glorifying her friend a little too much, she was able to remind herself of just how similar the two of them were. Their backstories were nearly identical, as most Arenians' were; they had overcome the same challenges and both grown into strength because of it. Such thoughts were not a comfort anymore. Iowan had become bony and weak, her body was in poor condition, from her muscles to her hair. She practiced with weapons in the backyard, sometimes alone, sometimes sparring with Lysia and Rinly. Those training sessions helped her to uncover her talents that had become buried while she'd been chained up. She was glad to find that her natural poise and graceful speed were still there, hidden within. Progress was being made, there was no denying that, but it still hurt to see Aelwen, a specimen of pride and physique, in comparison to her meek self with bags under her eyes, straw-like hair, wavering gaze and arms that couldn't lift the heavier weapons.

"Hi," said Iowan, tapping the space on the bed next to her. It wasn't like Aelwen to come knocking on the door to spend leisure time with Iowan. She was too busy with her studies at Arkada and training the new soldiers with General Fayette Ekua. Based on the way Aelwen's jaw was set, Iowan had the feeling she wasn't here for a friendly chat. She hadn't come for one yet. She was too busy to have a real, in-depth conversation with her best friend. Whatever she was here for, it didn't look to be something good.
~~~~

Aelwen sat heavily, causing the bed to creak beneath them. She stared at the opposite wall a long moment before looking at Iowan. "Gavnas isn't with us," she said flatly.

"What?"

"He's a mage sympathizer, apparently. He's not going to join them, though, because he doesn't want to fight against his 'friends'."

"What's he doing, then?"

Aelwen rolled her eyes. "He's going to sail on *Mist Wing* in search of a perfect world."

Iowan frowned. "Since when does he do something like that?"

"I have no idea. He's made his choice and by all I could tell, he doesn't plan on changing it. That's not why I'm here, though." Her deep brown eyes bore into Iowan. "I need you to tell me what happened. I haven't talked to you about it once. Whatever inner battles you're fighting, they're your own, and I know I don't have the right to barge in and demand anything until you're ready to tell me. If you turn me away right now, I won't blame you for it. But there's a war out there, Iowan. Lots of people have died and, trust me, lots more are going to before this is over. I don't know if anything you have to say can help us or not, but I know I'll never know if I don't try asking you. That's why I need you to tell me what happened to you. From the moment we left to the moment we came and got you."

The air was swept from Iowan's lungs. She inhaled deeply, filling herself up. Whatever she'd been expecting Aelwen to ask or say, this wasn't it. Aelwen was right, Iowan hadn't told anyone yet because she didn't want to. The grief was still too near.

Aelwen was giving her a choice, Iowan reminded herself. She didn't have to do this. On the other hand, keeping her mouth shut could cost lives, if there really was something of use in what she had to tell. Iowan had had the same thoughts as Aelwen, that her experience could somehow provide insight into the inner workings of the mages, and, as far as she could see, it didn't. Aelwen was a trained stateswoman, though. Surely she would be able to spot details Iowan had dismissed.

Aelwen was right, Iowan was working through a process to heal herself not only physically, but emotionally, from what she had suffered. Telling Aelwen everything now, when she wasn't ready, risked crumbling all of the progress Iowan had made.

No. She was an Arenian. A fighter, a warrior. Blood, fire, stone, steel. Iowan had managed to retain more softness than most through her time at the arena, but at her heart, that was what she was. She had fought against plenty of enemies, physical opponents in the arena and the dark demons of depression. None of them had bested her. This one would not either.

She said, "I ran for three weeks. I camped in the woods and hunted my own food, I walked in rivers so they couldn't' track me. But they found me."

"Who's 'they'? Guildsmen?"

"Yeah. Galarus was with them when they found me. He told me he wanted to kill me, he wanted to kill all of us." The words Galarus had spoken down at her from atop his horse still burned in her brain. "I remember, he said, 'I wanted to kill your wretched friends, too. We could've sent ships after them and brought them back alive so I could have slit their throats one by one. I would have liked that. But Halmar turned me down, saying he doesn't want to waste the resources pursuit would take. He told me I could keep hunting only you since you were on home turf. He said, if I stopped badgering him about going after the rest and caught you and brought you to him, he would make me rich. Give me one of those mansions out in the country and all that. So, if you're wondering why I'm not running you through or dragging you back to the arena, that's why.'"

Iowan cleared her throat, relieving it of the strain of her half-hearted impression of the Master. This wasn't quite as hard as she'd thought, but it was far from easy. "They brought me to Halmar. They chained me to his throne. I expected them to interrogate me, but no one did. Halmar talked to himself more than he talked to me. He would drone on and on for hours about his childhood, about how no one had ever appreciated him and he was so glad that someone did, talking in circles, the same things over and over again. I thought he meant me, about the person appreciating him, because I had to rely on him for everything. But then I found out that he meant her. The mage woman. She always wore something purple. And that iron mask."

"What mask?" asked Aelwen, her interest piqued.

"The metal one. I think it's iron. I never saw her without it. She had her hood up the day you came, that's why you never saw it. It fits her face perfectly, it has flower carvings in it. Anyway, she would show up at Orodel at random times and tell Halmar about how unfair her life had been, how she and him were the same because no one had ever appreciated either of them. She'd cut his arms and pour her magic into him. She'd blindfold him and make him drink strange things. She'd tell him not to eat anything but bread and water once every twelve hours, that fasting like that was a way of proving himself to the gods. She told him that the gods had led her to him, that they must bind themselves together to save the world from destruction."

"What sort of destruction?"

Anger was rising in Iowan. She was trying to tell her story. Trying and succeeding. With every word she spoke, the harder it became to say the next one. She wanted to get this over with, to plow through to the end, and just when she seemed to have good momentum going, Aelwen would butt in with a question. Iowan leashed her growing rage and continued. "She would never specify. Just that the union of her power and his was the only way to stop the world from succumbing to evil. She told him that the gods sent orders through her to him and that he had to follow them all or else he would die without ever getting the respect he deserved.

"I made a friend at Orodel. Jornik was his name. He was a servant. He would come to clean out the bucket I used as a toilet. He would try to come when Halmar was sleeping. The day after I arrived at Orodel was the first time I met him, he told me his name and that he was sorry for what had happened to me."

Iowan paused to swallow. Anguish was creeping its way up her throat. "Jornik found out what Rhea was making Halmar drink. It was a sort of poison that causes muscle atrophy and dizzy spells. I think she gave it to him to keep him weak and under her control. I think that's why she did everything she did to him."

Aelwen nodded, understanding seeping into her. "She fed Halmar lies and made him weak so he had no choice but to do anything but what she said. So she could control Corova."

"I don't think she cared about Corova at all, Ae. I think she just cared about one part of Corova."

Aelwen raised her brows. "The military. She needed to be able to put her mage warriors in as part of the Corovan army so she could force Halmar to declare war on Corova and, when he did, that would be how she started war between mages and non mages. By making her arrival as part of a nonmage country, not from Paruma." Aelwen leaned back a bit, nodding in approval of her own deductions. "How long has she been controlling him?"

"I don't know. A long time, though, that's for sure. I hardly saw him make any decisions on his own. Other than getting me, though. The mage never talked to me, always acted like I wasn't there. Sometimes she would glare daggers at me. I think, and I could be wrong about this, but I think that me being there represented Halmar's ability to make his own choices and that made her feel like she was failing."

"Well, that makes sense, except, why did Halmar have you chained to his throne in the first place? Why would he choose to do that? Why not throw you in the dungeons? Why let you see so much?"

Iowan shook her head. Dark feelings bubbled up inside her. It was starting to feel like too much. "I have no idea. Maybe what he said was true—maybe he really just wanted someone to talk to. He doesn't have any advisors or friends. The mage would go missing for long periods of time, leaving him all alone and barely strong enough to take care of himself. He wanted someone to listen to him. Galarus was out hunting for me, that way he didn't have to take a random person off the street and chain them up for no reason. It being me could justify it, in Halmar's mind. That's just what I think."

"If he really wanted you to talk to, why chain you up? He didn't want you to like him, he just wanted to talk to you. It doesn't make sense."

"He's crazy, okay? That's all there is to it," Iowan ground out. Her heart was thundering, sweat was dripping down her neck.

Aelwen started at Iowan's sudden shift in tone. She laid a hand atop Iowan's thigh. "At least we know that not all who serve Halmar support him. Would you be willing to try to contact Jornik? I can talk to Tecsequaih, we'll figure out a way."

"Don't bother. I can't contact Jornik. No one can. He's dead. Halmar or, the mage more likely, found out that Jornik was disloyal and he was executed." Iowan gulped. She had managed to hold back tears this far, but she couldn't hold out much longer. She squeezed her eyes shut, quelling the sadness and the pain. Then, she said, "That's all. Everyday was pretty much the same until you came. I was never let off the chain, Halmar would babble senselessly, sometimes the mage would come and cut him and make him drink."

Aelwen stared into space, deep in thought. Iowan looked to her, hoping to see some flash of realization, a clue hidden in her story that could help save the Vatre-darah. "Anything?" she asked hopefully.

Aelwen thought for a few more moments, then shook her head. "No, nothing. It explains why the mage woman was in Corova and what she was doing with Halmar. That's good knowledge to have, but it doesn't help us beat them." Aelwen patted Iowan's thigh where her hand still rested and rose to her feet.

Iowan's heart sank. "That's it? There's nothing useful?"

"I don't think so," said Aelwen. "Thank you for telling me, though. I know it wasn't easy. Thanks."

Iowan didn't get a chance to say 'you're welcome' before Aelwen was gone from her room, the door shut behind her. Iowan flopped back onto her bed. Now that Aelwen was gone, the tears had retreated for the most part. A scant few ran down her cheeks and onto the blankets.

Aelwen had never been a comforter. Consolation was one of the few gifts she did not possess. Still, Iowan had seen her try harder to comfort wounded Arenians back in Corova than she had tried to be there for Iowan while she stumbled her way through her history of agony. She'd hardly tried to comfort Iowan at all. She'd asked questions, gotten answers and when those answers had failed to provide the solutions she sought, she'd left. It was the longest conversation Iowan and Aelwen had shared since Iowan's return and, throughout it, Aelwen had been exactly as she had been since Iowan's return. Stoic, calculating, distant. While, in a way, those were crucial factors of the Aelwen she had always known, they made up too much of Aelwen now. Aelwen used to spend time with Iowan because she genuinely enjoyed it, she would come knocking on Iowan's door to share a meal or a drink or some new gossip and they'd stay together, talking and laughing, for hours. Their relationship wasn't one of usefulness, it was one of enjoyment of each other's company. Did Aelwen not enjoy Iowan's company anymore? Had she moved past that friendship?

Iowan revered their names and asked herself the same questions. She didn't know the answers. Everyday on the run, everyday chained to that throne, Iowan had daydreamed of nothing but Aelwen returning to save her. That had happened. Her dream had come true. Iowan hadn't thought past that one goal, though. Never entertained how they progressed after she was saved. How *did* they progress? Iowan entertained a love of Aelwen that she was not willing to relinquish just yet. A lot had happened. Their lives, which had been near mirror images of each other for years, were completely different now. They barely spoke and were rarely in the same place together. Of course there was a rift between them. A rift they would mend, together, in time, Iowan promised herself.

All the fear of speaking too soon, the chance that talking to Aelwen could destroy the progress she'd made, and what had come of it? Nothing. Absolutely nothing.

Alone in the quiet of her bedroom, the darkness started to creep into Iowan, weighing her down, making her feel worthless. She clenched her jaw at the now-familiar feeling of the sorrows she'd suffered pushing their way past her flimsy barriers when she was vulnerable in moments like this. She wouldn't let the darkness take hold. No. It would not overcome her, she would fight it.

Iowan scrambled through her thoughts, searching for something good that had come of her encounter with Aelwen. She found something and clutched it close, a shimmering light to hold back the pain of the dark.

She'd done it. She'd really done it, opened up about what had happened before she had deemed herself ready, and completed her story without breaking. It was a challenge she'd doubted her ability to overcome and she had overcome it. It was a victory. One more step towards becoming her whole self once more.

~~~~

The training camp attack had occurred nearly a month ago. Since then, there had been no signs of the enemy.

The new training ground of the Marchian warriors was a massive field. All of the small training camps had been combined into one. No more would there be death because others were too far away to help.

General Fayette had ordered the hours of training extended and for all instructors to train their students harder. It had been so, so stupid of her to place the training areas so far apart. If only they had been closer, she could have gotten there in time…

War was coming. For certain. No one knew when the monster of death would next spread its wings nor who it would take away with it.

Aelwen was practically going out of her mind. With the help of her friends, she had set up a training arena in the backyard. They trained whenever they could. Attempting new techniques and perfecting old ones. Aelwen knew well that sleep was crucial to a successful warrior, but it never came easily to her. Not when she knew an attack could come at any moment. She had taken to attending night patrols at the Banyan Reserve with Rinly just to keep herself busy. She seemed to be the only one so perturbed by the threat that loomed over them. Lysia and Iowan were undoubtedly scared, but they had no difficulty sleeping the way she did, at least not that she knew of.

Perhaps after all she had endured, Marchia was a paradise to Iowan as it had been to the others when they had first arrived, despite the declaration of war. Good meals, a real bed and the love of her friends had all been missed greatly by Iowan, Aelwen was sure, though she had not yet brought herself to ask outright what Iowan had suffered at the hands of King Halmar. It never felt right to ask and she figured that Iowan would rather not relive that portion of her life anytime soon. Aelwen could not help but wonder if King Halmar was the only one at fault for Iowan's abuse. Or if the purple cloaked figure, the mage, had been a part of it as well.

She had not forgotten that cloud of darkness that had swirled around her head the day of the attempted murder of the Corovan king. Nor the dragon that had burst through the floor and shattered the ceiling. Nor the dead would-be defenders of Marchia.

Aelwen's legs ached. She had never been a good runner. Just to take her mind off of everything but her breathing and physical pain, she had decided to join a group of trainees in their daily laps around the border of the training area. There were obstacles at some points, tough terrain at others and long stretches of nothing but flat land.

While Aelwen wasn't the fondest of running, she loved how close it brought her to experiencing her inner self. She harbored the rhythm of her feet and her breathing and her heart and the wind racing past her. The pounding, the whistling, the breath of life all came together to make her soul song. In the times when everything just felt too overwhelming, Aelwen would lay outside and watch the stars and hear her soul song in her mind.
~~~~

Clearing a section of hurdles, Aelwen stopped in her tracks as her soul song was interrupted.

A horn. Bright and clear as daylight, blasting through the camp and miles beyond. The horn blew a second time, quicker, sharper than the first.

Aelwen veered off course and accelerated. To the heart of the camp she ran.

"Fayette!" she screamed. again and again. Aelwen froze as she saw the justification of the blowing of the horn. A great dragon swooped through the air, observing the forest below.

"To arms! To arms!" shouted one of the senior soldiers. Anyone who had not been training with a weapon was given one. "Form ranks: pikes, swords, axes, form lines! Archers: run back to the crest, await a volley!"

The swooping beast progressed toward the field with every circle it made.

Aelwen had been running weaponless, in no armor or protective gear, only a plain leather combat suit. With the evil approaching, who knew how much time she would have to change into proper fighting garments? She would just have to make do.

Aelwen ran to one of the guards passing out swords from a barrel. She took a look at all of the weapons the warrior carried. Varieties of swords from every corner of the world: falchion, pulwar, nimcha, kilij, talwar, shamshir, longsword, cutlass, katana, khopesh and zweihander. With careful consideration, Aelwen selected a talwar. "Have you seen Fayette?"

"No," the warrior replied. "Would you like a second weapon or a shield?"

"Shield."

"Shield over here!" The warrior called over her shoulder.

Another soldier appeared, hauling a rack of shields with her. The rack, like the barrel of swords, contained variety. Parma, pavise, kite and heater. She decided on a painted steel parma. She asked the warrior passing out shields the same question she had asked the other. The warrior said she had seen Fayette not too long ago but did not know her exact location at the moment.

Aelwen sent a silent prayer up to the watchful gods that Fayette would be there when they needed her most.

The dragon was so close now that Aelwen could easily make out that there was a figure astride it, wrapped in a violet cloak, as well as the fact that the massive creature was indefinitely a silvery blue color. The dragon bent its head downward, watching things in the trees. No doubt the sly army of its rider.

Everyone was armed. The lines began to assemble.

"Mounts!" shouted someone. Aelwen barely had time to register the word because she had to jump out of the way to avoid being trampled. Astride a white and black appaloosa, General Fayette galloped up to her small army. The hope of Marchia rested upon the shoulders of them all. If the army broke through this first barrier, they could proceed to destroy the realm.

Aelwen grappled for the reins of one of the stampeding horses, released from the stables on the far side of camp in case something like this did happen. She had never fought astride before. The loop of the reins caught on her wrist, yanking on her as the horse tossed its head. Aelwen pulled the reins down. The enemy was so close, there was no time to be gentle. Aelwen slipped one foot into the stirrup, swinging her other leg over and shifting in her saddle. The horse still had its head down, rubbing it against its legs. "Up!" she ordered, pulling roughly.

General Fayette was covered completely in mail and armor. The only visible part of her body was her eyes and that was only because the visor of her helmet was up.

"Form ranks!" she shouted. "Pikes, leave space enough for two rows! Cavalry, anyone else behind!" Fayette appeared to be satisfied that the archers were already positioned on the crest. One of her most trusted captains was in command of the archers, they would be fine.

Ranks were formed in minutes, people panicking, trying to figure out where they should be.

In position, armed, mounted. Nothing left to do but wait. Stand, breathe, watch and wait.

The waiting. It nearly killed her. Aelwen's blood was pumping through her at a speed she did not know was possible. Her first war. She hadn't thought about it until now. She had always thought it would be just like fighting in the arena. Had she ever been more wrong in her life?

Aelwen found herself praying that the opposition would arrive just so she could let her instincts take over and forget her fear.

The dragon flapped in place over the edge of the forest, staring down the awaiting army. The rider, leader of the enemy forces, clad in a cloak of violet, spoke. The voice was deep, amplified by some paranormal power and of some indiscernible sex.

"I am Rhea. Descendant of the great Bloodline of the Orchid. I have come to reclaim what is rightfully mine." In an overly dramatic maneuver, Rhea unbuckled her violet cloak, tossing it into the air in a swirling motion, revealing her fully. A mask of shining silver metal covered her entire face. She was dressed in a flowy lavender dress, something most would have expected a dainty young princess to wear, not a rebel mage determined to conquer the world.

Excess pieces of the lavender fabric billowed all around her. Rhea looked over her shoulder, into the forest. Her dragon, anxious for battle and perhaps a good-sized meal, attempted to dart forward and down. Rhea turned back forward, jerking the dragon's head back with a rough wrench of the chain reins.

"The world belonged to my blood once. Your kind destroyed us, set fire to us until we were naught but ashes. We have risen like phoenixes from the ashes. We will have our revenge."

Rhea wheeled her dragon backwards. The sky-colored beast alighted in the jungle, the tops of the trees swayed at its landing.

The Marchian warriors held their breath.

Through the emerald canopy broke the giant reptile, its purple-clad rider upon its back. Only, this time, Rhea was not its only rider. Behind her was a second person, a bag over their head, their hands bound. A tangle of ropes and chains bound them to the saddle so they would not plummet to their death. They thrashed as much as their bonds would allow and screamed desperately.

The dragon pumped itself high into the blue sky with grand flaps that shook the trees below. Rhea slapped her mount and it stopped moving upward, instead hovering where it was, keeping itself aloft with leisurely waves of its leathery wings. From the moment they'd set off, the mage hadn't cast a single glance at the rider behind her.

Rhea spoke, her voice amplified by her terrible power. "He was lucky I let him see me and my people once. It was a game and we won. Then I heard he wanted another round. At the order of the Marchian government, if I'm not mistaken. So I let him find us again. I nearly killed him right there and left his body for the beasts, but I changed my mind. If I killed him then, you'd never know what happened to him. And I need you to know. I need you to know that this man—who you made promises to in exchange for information you so desperately need—never obtained *anything* I didn't want him to. He thought he was clever and so did you, so you put faith in him and bargained with him, hoping his cleverness would save you all.

"It didn't. It won't. He and I were playing a game of hide and seek and I was *always* in control. I still am."

The mage whipped around, facing the second rider for the first time. She seized the hood over his head and wretched it off.

Namar stared down at the sea of soldiers below, their green banners bearing the golden elephant head of Marchia waving lazily in the wind. He stopped thrashing and screaming. There was nothing for him to do but sit frozen in fear.

"I need you to know that this man died because you underestimated me. I strongly advise against making the same mistake in the future."

Rhea held out one slender hand, a stiletto materializing in her palm. In a flash, she was gone. Namar was the only one upon the ugly dragon's back. His senses seemed to flood back to him as his eyes came alive with the fire of fear. He reached down to undo a chain across his waist.

The mage appeared as suddenly as she had vanished. Rather than sitting in front of him as she had been seconds ago, she was behind him now, her stiletto pressed to his throat.

Slowly, she undid the multitude of ropes and chains that secured Namar to the dragon's back. When the last tether was undone, Rhea leaned close to Namar and whispered something in his ear. She drew the dagger across his brown throat, spattering him with blood. Then she shoved him off.

Namar was still alive as he fell. He screamed as he plummeted downward, the sound garbled and wet because of his injury. He tried to right himself, the same way all Arenians were taught to if they took a bad fall. He succeeded. Maybe he could survive this. Maybe…

The dragon was too high. The ground was too low.

A sickening crack as, still-alive, his body shattered upon the earth.

No one survived a fall like that. Not even Namar.

Aelwen's heart stopped. The world froze. All there was was Namar's body, broken, lifeless, bloody, laying in a contorted head upon the green earth. All there was were all the words she'd never said to him.

Under some command of Rhea's, the dragon spewed that same horrid call it had expelled when it had rescued Rhea from Orodel. On that mark, Rhea's own armed forces burst out of the jungle, clearing the space that separated them from the Marchians.

Rhea's warriors were dressed in shades of the forest, like elves of ancient lore, clad in leather breastplates and leggings, silver armor adorned with lotus etchings, thick shin guards and dark green cloaks. They were armed with fine, thin blades and light, powerful bows with metal shafts and white feather fletching. All of the Rhea's army wore head coverings, making it impossible to determine their genders.

Aelwen, a member of the cavalry, watched as Rhea's warriors were impaled by the first line of defense: the pikes. The pike wielders fought well, slicing away a considerable number of Rhea's forces.

General Fayette, also a member of the cavalry, shouted an order, lowering her helmet visor. "Forward!"

Aelwen held her sword hand down beside her, slicing at Rhea's army.

She knocked an opponent down, hitting them in the neck with her blade. She was going for another swing when there was a sudden, sharp pull on the neck of her shirt. Aelwen whipped around, almost dropping her talwar.

An opponent had climbed onto the back of her horse, crouching on its back end. The enemy had a dagger in their belt, but no weapons currently in their grasp. Aelwen did not want to keep her eyes off the ground for much longer. Lifting her sword up to her level and angling it, she jabbed. The opponent leaned, but they only had so much room. Aelwen's weapon sliced their shoulder. Aelwen spun forward again. She turned too quickly and at an odd angle. Pain spiked in her hip and shot down her leg. She forced herself to ignore it. She took a moment to steer her horse, avoiding the points of enemy blades. As her horse trampled through the mass of humans, Aelwen, sword lowered at her side, swung it behind her. It hit nothing. Her surprise attack had failed. If her opponent wasn't back there, where were they?

Aelwen looked over her shoulder. She saw the silhouette of a body on the rear of her horse in one moment and in the next it was gone. A dark figure suddenly appeared in front of her face. The reins were ripped out of her hand. The opponent had leapt from behind her to in front and had snatched the reins. The opponent slammed an elbow into Aelwen's face, while simultaneously jerking the horse into a quicker canter. Head reeling, Aelwen fell off the horse. She skillfully managed a complicated tumble as she hit the ground, saving herself from any broken body parts.

A body of one of her fellow warriors fell to the ground, its killer turning their attention on her. Aelwen had been forced to drop her sword as she had fallen, for if she had not, it would have impaled her. The killer brought down their sword. Aelwen held up her shield, her only method of defense. The contact of blade and shield never came. Convinced her attacker had been sidetracked, Aelwen lowered her shield, peering over the top edge of it. Her attacker lay dead on the ground, an arrow sticking out of their chest.

Aelwen immediately ducked beneath her shield again, protecting herself as a storm of arrows fell upon them from the far off crest. Their archers had not failed them.

Once the arrow rain ceased, Aelwen retrieved the sword of her would-be-attacker and fought her way with it. Cutting down enemies using her sheer cunning and years of training, Aelwen fought.

This battle called for more awareness and speed than an arena skirmish did. There was absolutely no chance to stop to think of her next attack. She just kept fighting. No fear, no questions, no considerations. She just fought, cutting down her enemies. Fate would do the rest.

Rhea, seated atop her splendorous mount, watched from high in the sky. She pulled a knife out from deep within the folds of her elegant gown. She ran the knife the wrong way across the scales of her dragon's neck. The motion drew no blood. The dragon knew that signal. It released one of its shrieks, one loud enough for even the most engaged warriors, caught in the midst of the loudest brawls, to hear. Everyone heard the cry, but no one headed it. Just an attempt at intimidation, they thought.

Aelwen went in for a killing blow. She had taken on an opponent that was more skilled than herself. Nothing new. This opponent was a cunning one, but their fight had endured for long enough. Aelwen had landed many blows on her opponent's leather armor; she had worn it thin. Foolish of Rhea, Aelwen thought, to have her warriors wear naught but thick leather into battle.

Her opponent dropped one of their weapons and raised a hand, a strange teal light emanated from it. A blast of light erupted from the enemy's hand, shattering Aelwen's blade.

Aelwen froze in disbelief. Her eyes darted about. Rhea's warriors had all discarded their weapons, multicolored bursts of power surged from their hands, decimating the Marchians. Rhea wasn't the only mage. They were all mages.

The mage who had destroyed Aelwen's blade took a single step forward, bringing them within Aelwen's guard. Before she could make any move to harm the mage or move away from them, the mage raised their hand. Light burst forth, knocking Aelwen to the ground. Her vision blurred for a moment, then returned. She watched helplessly as her opponent sauntered away.

And then came the pain. Pain that shot thought every fiber of her being and made her want to scream. She tried to coil up, but it hurt too much. She closed her eyes. If she could not move, it was better to pretend she was dead than to reveal that she was alive and completely powerless.

Every couple of minutes, Aelwen would flick her eyes open just enough to get a sense of what was going on. Others, like herself, had fallen. Dead or in too much pain and pretending like her, she did not know.

There was no question left about who would win this battle. Rhea's warriors, mages, with their hidden powers, were crushing the Marchians. The mages had somehow stopped all of the archers. Only two lines of Marchian warriors stood, blocking Rhea's forces from entering Marchia.

What was the sense in watching the last lines of defense be slaughtered? As she lay there, destitute, Aelwen closed her eyes once again. How could she have ever thought that war would be anything like the arena?

War was so much worse. Rarely in the arena did the battles ever come to death. Serious injuries, occasional paralysis, unconsciousness, yes. But almost never death. Aelwen had not beheld the sight of so much death since her childhood. Her memories of that horrifying night began to bang against that wall of steel and stone she had built up around them, concealing them from the rest of her mind so that she would never have to remember again.

Aelwen had convinced herself she had forgotten that night. What a fool she was. Those memories were still there and they wanted to be let out of their eternal prison. It took all of her determination to keep the walls up as she heard the screams and felt the blood of others soaking into her own clothes.

The last screams died away. Aelwen felt vibrations in the ground near her. A large company was coming towards her. She fluttered her eyelids just enough to get a fuzzy picture of her surroundings. The boots of mages were all around her. They were retreating. No, not retreating. Leaving. Walking back, exhausted, into the woods and back to whence they had come from.

Aelwen fainted. Her body, mind and spirit needed rest. When she awoke, she felt no stronger. At least the mages were gone.

She flexed her legs. Pain lanced through her, but not nearly so terrible as before. The muscles quivered, she could feel the ache of gashes she had received. At least she could move without wanting to shriek. She tried to pull herself into a crouching position and failed miserably, tipping over onto the blood soaked earth. Barely catching herself, Aelwen coughed horridly. Her throat was dry with thirst.

"Aelwen! You're alive!" A Marchian soldier covered in bent armor, blood and dirt fell to the ground beside her on her knees. The soldier dragged herself onto her haunches, taking Aelwen by the arm. "Come on. Let's get you up."

Legs shaking, pain shooting through her, Aelwen pushed herself upward, trying with all her might to stand. *Stand, damn you,* Aelwen commanded her body, but for once in her life, it did not listen.

"Easy. Easy." The soldier said. Aelwen grunted in pain and swayed forward. "I've got you." The soldier spoke softly and lifted Aelwen into her bloody arms.

CHAPTER SEVENTEEN

"What the hell happened?" Aelwen ground out, blinking away exhaustion. She was still filled with significant pain, but that was nothing she did not know how to deal with. She was lying on a cot in the council room of Arkada. She would have been startled had there not been other, more pressing matters at hand.

President Tecsequaih and the rest of those occupying the room shared looks of relief at the sound of Aelwen's voice.

Desliad answered her, "Rhea's army attacked and left."

Lin elaborated, anger lining his voice, "They did not make any attempt to conquer."

"It was obviously a show of power," the president said.

"Yes," said Jae, head of trade. "What we don't know is why."

Aelwen suddenly realized that General Fayette was not present. Tecsequaih had not been at the battle. That made her the only one in the room who knew Rhea's motive. "Rhea seeks revenge."

"On us?" asked Jae.

"Yes."

"Why?" more questions rose, similar to that one.

"She and her people are mages. She claims our kind have oppressed them. They want revenge."

Intent on getting them back to the point, Aelwen said, "Do we have any idea of when and where the next attack may occur?"

"No," the president answered.

"Where is General Fayette?"

The court exchanged glances.

"Is she alive?"

Uncomfortable silence was the only answer.

Still, Aelwen persisted and she intended to continue to do so until she got an answer. "When was she last seen?"

Seren answered shakily, "There are reports of her running into the jungle, but we know nothing for sure. She was not found among the dead or the injured."

"Why have troops not been sent out to search for her?"

President Tecsequaih answered, "We do not know where our enemies are, sending anyone out would be a suicide mission."

"Besides," added Evon, "there are only vague reports of her departure. Nobody has the slightest clue where she is."

"What kinds of reports?" asked Aelwen.

Silaryn flipped a sheet of paper and read. "'There was a very, very brief moment when I had my opponent down for an instant, I thought I saw her sprinting towards the forest.'" She flipped the page again and recited, "'I saw her slice her way past me. I took on two enemies and when they were down I took a second— a second, no more— to look around me and I swear I saw the general running away, toward the wood.'"

"How many people have given reports like those?"

"Five."

Five. Only five people, out of the sea of hundreds, even suspected that they had seen Fayette.

"I suppose we just wait for her to come back, then," Aelwen said, although it did not please her to do so. "In the meantime, President Tecsequaih, you should do everything possible to inform your people of the situation and to fortify Marchia and its major cities against new attacks. Our enemies are mages, so we must find a way other than brute strength to overpower them."

Everyone in the room seemed slightly taken aback at how forthrightly Aelwen had spoken to their ruler.

"War is here," she declared, "There is no time to be wasted upon formalities, we must all speak our minds. Action must be taken now."

Silence swelled in the room as everyone took time to process and accept the truth that Aelwen had just dispatched.

In the midst of the silence, one of the grand doors to the council room was opened and a servant walked in. He was a fine looking young man who was well dressed, as all of the president's servants were. He walked straight to Tecsequaih, pulled a decorated envelope out of his back pocket and handed it to him. Tecsequaih nodded in acceptance and the servant exited the room.

There was no sound but the ripping of paper as the president opened the envelope and extracted the letter inside, which he promptly unfolded and began intently reading.

Aelwen noticed the envelope lying on the table. It was lilac with golden swirls, she had never seen anything like it.

President Tecsequaih stopped reading and stared off blankly.

Impatient, Aelwen asked, "Well, what does it say?"

The president read, "'Vatre-darah, I have realized since our most recent conflict that it is nothing less than utterly unfair for my people to use magic against you. With our magic against your nothingness, the war would be won much too quickly. You could be wiped out in a matter of days with no pain at all. That is not the way we wish to see things done. You must suffer long and hard against our hatred of you, as we mages did for years. I wonder if you've yet realized that the problems that have plagued you of late were all caused by us. It was I who weakened Halmar of Corova and my people who poisoned the waters of Ave.

It was all one elaborate scheme to strike Marchia without having to worry about interference from your neighbors. It seems our hard work has paid off. We eagerly await the next time we meet you on the battlefield, this time in full equality." Tecsequaih added, "It's signed Rhea of the Orchid, Leader of the Hakmarres."

"What does that mean? Hakmarres?" asked Lin.

Tecsequaih turned to his servants who stood at the door. He scribbled down two words and handed a piece of paper to one of them. "Find the meanings of these words," he ordered.

It was swiftly discovered that Hakmarres translated to "vengeful" and that Vatre-darah meant "fire-blood".

Aelwen entered the kitchen, an empty cup in her hand. Iowan sat alone at the table, picking at a roll of bread without butter. It was the first time they'd found themselves together in a room void of the presence of Rinly or Lysia since Iowan had told Aelwen everything that had happened to her. That encounter had been a strange one. It had held almost none of the warm familiarity Aelwen was used to when she spoke with Iowan. Aelwen knew that the awkwardness of it was partly her fault—she had purposely stuck to being cold and direct, hoping to avoid causing Iowan to dredge up negative emotions from their time apart that she didn't want to share. That was why Aelwen had left as soon as Iowan was done telling her what she needed to know; she hadn't wanted to linger and by doing so force emotional memories from her best friend. She knew how necessary alone time could be after doing something difficult, so she had left Iowan for that reason as well. Since Aelwen had closed the door to Iowan's room behind her after that talk, she hadn't been able to shake that she had gone about it all wrong. She wished she had asked if Iowan wanted her to stay or go, to be comforting or distant in that moment. She hadn't given Iowan the choice, she had made it herself when it was not hers to make, and she had regretted it ever since. Now she found herself alone with Iowan once more. With all that was going on in the world, who knew when they would find such a quiet moment of togetherness again? Aelwen could try to amend her mistakes now, or leave the loose ends dangling forever.

"Hi," Aelwen said, and proceeded to begin rinsing her cup.

"Hi." The word was flat, almost toneless.

"I saw you out training today. You look good." She set her cup on the counter and joined her friend at the table.

Iowan didn't look up from her crumbling bread. Strands of her blonde hair hung in her face. "No, I don't.

"What do you mean? I saw you out there—"

"Stop it, Ae!" Iowan slammed her hands against the table. "Look at me! I'm thin and pale and I'm always tired. You said you saw me training today?" Her eyes, full of hurt and anger, locked on Aelwen's. "Did you see me using a claymore because I couldn't lift an axe? That's right, I'm too weak to lift an axe."

Aelwen dropped her gaze. "I'm sorry. Just keep training, keep trying. Don't give into whatever sadness you're feeling, fight it."

"That's a lot easier said than done." Iowan looked back down at the table. "You know I always feel like someone's watching me? Like someone's going to jump out and grab me and bring me back to him? Tie me back up and make me watch all the sick things she does to him?"

"No," Aelwen said honestly. "No, I didn't know that."

The room went quiet. Iowan looked up at the ceiling. "I was thinking about Jornik earlier. Why is it that all of the good people always end up dead?"

"We're still here, aren't we?"

They exchanged weak smiles.

Aelwen added, "And you know I'll be here for you? I know I'm away a lot, but, whenever you need me, it's okay to reach out. I've been your right hand warrior for years." A smile flickered on her face at the term. "I don't plan to stop now."

Iowan's expression was one of relief and happiness. "I know."

Aelwen wrapped her arms around her best friend. "I'm so glad you're back. I missed you so, so much."

Iowan rested her head on Aelwen's shoulder. "I did too, Ae. I did too."

Aelwen had hugged Iowan many times throughout her life in many different circumstances. This didn't feel like any of them. It was as if Iowan was distant, separate. The sensation disturbed Aelwen, she didn't know how to make it stop.

They split apart.

"Is there anything I can do to help you?" asked Aelwen, hating how paltry the words seemed.

Iowan considered for a moment, then shook her head. "No. I don't think there's anything anyone can do." She offered a small, sad smile that Aelwen did not reciprocate. "I think the thing I need right now is to go to bed."

"Okay."

Iowan rose and headed up the staircase. Aelwen watched, her gut coiling with emotions she didn't understand. Iowan had regained much of her strength, but she was too thin. Her shoulders slouched like they never had before. She was changed. For worse or better, Aelwen did not yet know.

"Iowan," she said, pausing her friend mid-step.

Iowan turned, looking down at Aelwen. The circles beneath her eyes were even more pronounced in the dimness of the stairwell. "Yeah?"

"Sleep well."

She smiled, but it was not the broad, careless smile Aelwen loved. Instead, it was small and haunted, and it only made Aelwen's stomach tighter. "Goodnight, Ae."

And so the house slept, except for Aelwen, who occupied herself in the kitchen, cleaning up the last of the day's dishes. The hour was not late, the sky had only just grown dark. Lysia had never been one to stay up late and, though Iowan used to, her ways had changed since Aelwen had found her again.

To keep from wrestling with the tangled mess of emotions that were her feelings for Iowan, both the old and the new, Aelwen focused wholly on the clatter of the dishes and the sloshing of the water in the basin until her soul song had drive all uncomfortable thoughts from her mind and they were locked deep down behind an iron door with a myriad of others.

The gentle rhythm of her soul song was shattered by a knock at the door. Ensuring she had a dagger at the ready, she answered it.

Gavnas stood before her. Aelwen out a tight leash on her emotions.

"What?" The word was sharp and she was glad to hear it.

He withdrew an envelope from his waistcoat.

Aelwen's heart skipped a beat. Fear washed over her, and vanished quickly as it had come. These were not Lin's missing letters, the envelope and seal were different.

"I think you'll want to read it," said Gavnas, extending it to her.

Aelwen did not reach out to take it. "Why?" She didn't want to hear anything he had to say. He had made his choice, and though she could accept it, she did not like it.

"Please."

That sparked Aelwen's interest, though she did her best not to let it show. Gavnas didn't say please. He was a commander who was respected and his orders followed. He didn't ask twice and he didn't say please.

She snatched it from him. "Come in," she said coldly, stepping to the side. He hadn't asked to come in, she didn't know if he wanted to. But if this letter was important enough to make Gavnas say 'please', then he deserved to see her read it.

Aelwen led him to the parlor where she sat herself on the sofa before a tea table. Gavnas did not sit. She did not invite him to.

She peeled open the envelope and flattened the single piece of paper on the dark wood table. The first place her eyes darted to was the bottom of the page, to see who had written this.

Namar

Her breath caught. A lump was rising rapidly in her throat. Once, she'd known that elegant scrawl so well. Now, she'd nearly forgotten it. She swallowed hard and read from the beginning.

When we got here, I ran into the jungle. I had no idea where I was going, I just ran. I got lost and I couldn't find civilization anywhere. I know how many cities and villages there are in Marchia, I never realized how much wilderness there is too.

Eventually, I gave up looking for civilization. I made myself a permanent shelter. I was good at hunting by then. I figured if Taran and Lysia could do it, why couldn't I? I settled down, adapted to a new life. I was able to enjoy the beauty of nature. I made a life for myself. It wasn't bad at all, I'll even say I liked it. But then that all changed. I was out for a hunt like I did everyday. It was a normal day. Just another day. I heard what I thought was an animal. I stalked it. I moved so it was in my sights. But it wasn't an animal. It was a person. They were wearing a lilac dress and a metal mask.

I lowered my bow and I followed them for a long time. All the way to a valley filled with all sorts of people. There were stone buildings and little fires, it was a whole community.

None of the other people were dressed like the one in the mask, the rest of them were all wearing normal clothes. I almost showed myself to them, but something in me said not to. I felt strange and unsafe. The person with the mask talked to some of the other people. After they talked, the people—but not the one in the dress and mask— went to the side of the valley, and demonstrated a new battle technique for the masked one. I was an Arenian, you know that—I know how to recognize combat demos. But this wasn't just a normal training display. The people used magic. Magic.

Of course, I'd never seen magic before that, but I'd heard stories and seen pictures in books, so I knew what it was. I went running. I still can't believe it, but no one came after me. I ran all the way back to my house and I—I broke down. I was hysterical, I cried so hard. Mages. Real live mages. Here. In Marchia.

I've read enough books to know what mages are. Evil. Destructive. Clever. Wicked. Everything that's bad, that's what makes a mage. I'd read in some book somewhere that mages hate fire. It's their one weakness, it destroys them, they're terrified of it. I knew I had to set fire to their camp. I went back the next day, but nothing there. No mages. Even the buildings were gone. I tried to track them—I'm not a very good tracker, you know that— but there was no trail. I looked all around, thinking maybe I was in the wrong place. I looked for hours, then days. I couldn't find anything.

I tried to go back to living as I had before. Alone, feeling peaceful, safe. I couldn't do it. I had nightmares about the horrors of what the mages could do. I had no idea what they were doing in Marchia, but I knew it couldn't be good. I couldn't stop thinking about what I'd seen, even though I was starting to doubt if I'd seen anything at all. I thought I was hallucinating or something. Still, I couldn't let it go. I left and went back to living as I had when I first got here, making makeshift shelters and sleeping in caves, catching meals day by day. I never stopped looking for the mages, but I never found anything.

Finally, I stumbled out of the jungle and into a town. I visited it. People looked at me strangely—I can only imagine what I looked like after living in the wild for so long. It was a small town, there wasn't much to see. I had no money to buy anything and I was still desperate to find the mages. I was on my way to leave and go back into the jungle when I saw someone. At first, I didn't recognize them, but after a few minutes I realized that they were one of the mages I had seen performing the demonstration. I followed the mage, waiting until I could corner them alone. They went behind a building, I ran around behind the building and I used my flint and steel to light a branch. I threw it at the mage without any hesitation. Somehow, they knew I was coming and as soon as they saw me, they got out of the way. The torch hit the side of the building.

Before any serious damage could be done, I grabbed the torch and smothered the flames. A few boards were burned black, that was all. I was so relieved that I'd prevented the fire that I forgot about the mage until they had me pinned on the ground. They stole my flint and steel and set the building on fire. They shot me in the chest with their magic and ran away. The magic didn't kill me, but it did enough damage that I couldn't move for quite a while. That is, until almost the whole town was on fire.

It all happened so fast. The flames... they were so tall so fast. They were everywhere. So many buildings were on fire, it was complete chaos. There were people screaming and a part of me wanted to help them, but all I could think of was saving myself. As soon as I could manage it, I ran. I think you know the rest.

I don't know if you believe any of this and I guess, since I'm dead, it doesn't matter. I just had to write down the truth so someone knew. I left this for you, not Aelwen, because I knew she wouldn't want to hear from me and that she probably won't even bother reading this. But, if you could, can you bring it to her, ask her to read it? Thank you.

Namar

Aelwen breathed out sharply. "Where did you find this?" she asked without looking at Gavnas.

"On *Mist Wing*, pinned to the wheel with a dagger. I have no idea how he got it there."

"When did you find it?"

"Today."

Aelwen braced herself on the table. The letter was so characteristic of everything Namar had been. To-the-point, detailed, reliable, logical. He had loved to read flowery poetry, but not write that way. He never wasted ink on frilly language. Aelwen hated him for it. As soon as she'd seen who had written this letter, she'd hoped that it would have something to do with his relationship with her. Whether he hated her or respected her or still cared about her, even, a little, Aelwen was desperate to know.

Now she knew she would never know. She had not realized that, somewhere deep within her, buried under dust and ash, she still cared about Namar, until she had watched his body break upon the earth. Since that moment, questions that would never be answered had battered at her walls, wondering if he had cared at all for her. If, had she had the opportunity to speak with him and hear his truth from his own lips, not from dried ink on crusty paper, she might have forgiven him and he her.

Could their relationship have been mended? Could they have become some semblance of friends, or even distant acquaintances? There were no answers. There never would be. Because Namar was dead. And, if Aelwen hadn't been so cruel to him, if she had talked to him instead of leaving him locked in the dark, and forced him off to fend for himself in a land he did not know, Namar would not be dead and she would have those answers. She would have the second best friend she had ever known, who loved fashion and literature, who was the voice of reason yet had made choices she did not understand, here with her in the parlor instead of a salty smelling seamen and a crinkled piece of paper.

Gavnas left and took the letter with him at Aelwen's bidding. She left the rest of the dishes unwashed and went to bed. She cried herself to sleep.

Time passed. Everyone felt like an invisible snake was coiling around them, slowly choking the life out of them. Aelwen, just as aware of the sickening pressure as everyone else, took advantage of every moment. Death and destruction were coming and she was going to be ready to face it with everything she had.

She spent all of her time pouring over books on war strategies, making sketches of battle plans and training intensely. The major difference between a fight in the arena and a full on war was that all battles in the arena were completely spontaneous. On the battlefield, after getting to know their enemy, the Marchians needed a clean-cut plan in order to win. Aelwen spent much time drawing up different battle plans, something she had learned to do while studying what it took to rule a country. Each plan accomodated a specific idea whether it be one army outnumbering the other or a variety of possible terrains.

Hundreds of footsteps thundered through Firhad.

Rhea led her armed forces upon the back of her ice-blue dragon, as always, symbolizing her power over them. The army marched mechanically, weapons held vertically in white-knuckled grasps. Streets emptied as the Hakmarres passed, onlookers bolted their doors and fell silent. The invaders made no move of aggression, they only marched through the wide streets of the city.

President Tecsequaih's council members urged him to make the first attack, giving the Marchians the first chance of the war to direct a battle. The president refused. He rallied his forces but kept them hidden from view. He would not unleash them until the Hakmarres made the first move; he did not want to give the Hakmarres an excuse to label him as a bloodthirsty, rash decision maker.

The Hakmarres launched their attack. They fought without mercy but refrained from using magic, as they had promised. No one understood the benefit of the location the enemy had chosen to attack from. They were in the middle of the capital city, trapped on both sides by tall buildings and crushed into streets without a direct route of escape. Not an ideal location for either army.

President Tecsequaih Mayolan and his council stood within Arkada, protected by the thick stone walls and many experienced royal guards. They all stared silently out a massive window, watching the battle raging below. Many council members were itching to arm themselves and join the battle, but Tecsequaih forbade it. He said that if everyone participated in every battle, there would be no Marchians or rebel Corovans left by the end of the war. Aelwen had protested, but the president quickly told her off, reminding her that he knew too well the ways of a great war.

Aelwen stared coldly out of the window, the same one out of which she had watched the president ride away to the Marchia-Ave border not so long ago. That day felt a hundred years away. How she wished they could go back to a time when the biggest problem in the Marchian government was a border dispute with their neighbor.

The battle churned like an angry sea far below them. Neither side seemed to be winning. For how much longer would the senseless battle rage on?

Her thoughts and those of all the others were abruptly halted as a royal guard hollered up the stairs to the council. "Get out, now!" Guards flooded down the hallway, forming a circle surrounding the council members, brandishing their weapons.

"What's happening?" demanded the president.

Nayre Nowak, the captain of the guard, shouted back, "Hakmarres troops are breaking in! You all need to leave! Now!"

Aelwen drew her sword. With the war upon them, she and all of her companions were constantly armed.

With the royal soldiers encircling them, the president's council moved as quickly as they could, continuously bumping into each other.

Cries of combat and clashing metal echoed down the halls. Aelwen twisted her neck to look back. Over the heads of the numerous green-and-gold armored guards protecting them, she managed to catch several quick glances of many mage warriors overtaking the soldiers of Arkada.

Still encircled by the guards, the council burst through the massive back doors of Arkada, gasping with relief as their feet made contact with the sidewalk. They only had a brief moment to gaze up at the white majesty of Arkada, wondering if this was the last time they would see it in its splendid entirety.

Horses were brought to the council members who all swiftly mounted despite their billowing robes. Each horse held at least two council members, it would be easier to keep track of fewer horses and safer to travel with a partner.

Led by Nayre, who assumed what would usually be the still-missing Fayette Ekua's place, the cavalry of the council galloped through the winding city streets, taking a complicated route of narrow streets and back alleys to avoid drawing the attention of the Hakmarres.

What would happen to all of the ordinary folk, those who did not sit on the president's council? The Hakmarres had not harmed them yet. Did that mean they would?

The home Aelwen shared with Iowan and Lysia was just a block away. If she rode fast enough, she could go get her friends and rejoin the council within minutes. That was, if the Hakmarres didn't kill her in the process. But the circle of Marchian warriors surrounding the council was too compact for Aelwen to have any hope of escape. All she could do was send silent pleas to any Gods that would hear her and beg that the lives of her friends be spared.

Within an hour, the council was completely evacuated from the city. All of them sat astride austere horses which stood proudly upon the crest of a high, green mountain far within the jungle of Marchia.

The grand heights offered a breathtaking view of much of the vast country. It was almost unsettling to see so much of the greatest country in the world from atop one monumental slope.

Arkada was the easiest structure to locate, defined from the rest of Firhad's buildings by a thick covering of raging flames. Smoke the color of a starless midnight swirled up into the air, giving the previously crystalline sky an inky film.

The boisterous tolling of the great golden bell atop Arkada was barely decipherable from their position, the faint sound was the only sign that it still stood, for the bell itself was blocked by fierce flames and choking smoke.

"Where do we go now?" breathed Lin.

The president replied, "To Telspire." The second largest city in Marchia, less than half the size of Firhad.

"And if they take that?" Lin challenged.

"They won't."

That voice did not belong to Tecsequaih. It was so easily distinguishable that everyone gave a gasp of relief before they turned to see who it was. The secretary of defense, chief general of the military, still clad in the heavy armor she had last been seen wearing weeks ago, a defiant, ready blaze in her eyes, stood at the edge of the forest.

"General Ekua!" The president dismounted and embraced his most loyal follower. That did not halt him from asking the most pressing of questions. "Where have you been, general?"

"Wyldmor,"

"No," the president answered harshly.

"Why not? They have magic, we cannot win against them. Not here, out in the open. We need to go somewhere that is built for war."

Tecsequaih answered calmly, "They have vowed not to use their magic against us any longer. They want a fair fight just as much as we do."

"You trust them?"

President Tecsequaih paused, then sighed deeply. "I do not know," he answered coldly. "I do have an idea to win Firhad back. If that plan fails, we will all evacuate to Wyldmor, but let us not leave without trying first."

Frustration still flickered in General Fayette's eyes, but she accepted the deal. Nayre was still among them. The president ordered her to rally all Marchian survivors and spread the news of the move to Telspire.

Aelwen looked between all of the council members. "What's Wyldmor?"

Aelwen and Fayette shared a horse. The road to Telspire was long and tiresome. Each of them was thankful for the other's company.

"What is Wyldmor?" Aelwen questioned the general since no one had answered her earlier. She knew she had read of it before, but with all of her avid war studies and combat practice of late, much of the politics and geography she had learned had been cleared from her mind.

"An ancient fortress deep within the jungle," Fayette explained. "It has not been used for a century, it is completely overgrown. Almost the entire structure still stands, though there have been a few collapses."

"Why did you go there?"

"Once I realized just how much of an advantage the mages had on us, I knew that we could not fight from a modern city."

"They are called the Hakmarres."

Fayette shifted. "Revenge."

"Yes."

Not ready for unsettling silence that would allow all of the worst thoughts into her head, Aelwen went on, "You really believe that, within Wyldmor, we will be safe? Do you think that we can win from there?"

"Now is not the time to question whether or not we will win the war. We must focus on each battle. Wars are long lasting, we must not be hasty about anything. That is how we will all wind up dead."

The sky grew gradually darker as they traveled. The air cooled and the road became narrower. Aelwen's body felt limp. She wanted to curl up into a ball and fall asleep, leaving all of her dark thoughts of the possible fates of her friends behind for just a bit. But she knew she would not sleep. None of them could, though they all wanted to. The war kept them awake, fear kept their eyes pried open.

"How do you keep your head?" Aelwen asked without looking over her shoulder at her companion.

Fayette lifted her head. Had Aelwen awoken the general, who no doubt needed much rest?

"The stars," Fayette answered without any drowsiness in her voice.

"How? They are so far away, they can't help you."

"No, but they do symbolize everything I need to remain sane. They are still and distant, yet always there. They are calm and everlasting. Peaceful and far away. I believe that all of civilization should aim to function like the stars—stable, bright, peaceful, forever."

Aelwen didn't respond. Her mind was dragged back in time, to a black night of evil and flame. A night when her only hope had been the stars.

That's foolish. The stars cannot save me now. We must save ourselves and not get lost in stupid fantasies. A motto drilled into all of the Arenians by Galarus crept into her head. *Dream, but dream a real dream that you can make come true using all of the power you have in your soul. Otherwise, if you dream too much, you will get trapped in your head and miss out on your entire life.*

By the time they reached Telspire, it was noon the next day. Not one of them was fully awake. Soldiers had ridden ahead and gotten an entire mansion for the president's council. Aelwen drowsily dismounted and handed the reins to a stable hand. The dark thought of Erizo flickered through her mind. Where was her horse? Was he alive? Would the Hakmarres take him or harm him?

The horrifying thoughts only lasted for a moment before dissipating away into the endless abyss of floating nothingness that was her mind at the moment. Nothing made sense, everything was vaguely hazy and tilted. She truly did not understand how she was upright when her legs felt like gelatin.

Aelwen dragged herself up a flight of stairs that seemed endless. She was so tired that she did not take in any of the details of the mansion around her.

She only slept for four hours, her mind and body forever trained to function like an Arenian. She was well aware that she needed much more rest than that, but the horrifying thoughts of all to come, along with the uncertainty of Tecsequaih's plan, forced her awake.

Restless and unsatisfied with herself as she lay awake but motionless in her bed, Aelwen decided to get up. It was no easy task, she shared the room with four Marchian soldiers. Every council member had their own room to spend the night in and each council member was protected by four to six soldiers. Despite Aelwen's great value to the cause, due to her exquisite fighting skills she was guarded by only four. One of them shared the bed with her while the other three occupied the corners of the room.

Once again, the former Arenian's mastery of stealth showed its usefulness. Taking all the time she needed, Aelwen managed to slink out of bed and creep out of the room without waking any of the noise-sensitive soldiers.

Stepping into the hallway of the mansion, Aelwen was baffled to find that it was still light outside. Her mind was still a bit fuzzy, but she had enough wit to figure out that it was about six in the evening.

Without anything else to do and not wanting to venture far, Aelwen decided to explore the mansion. Life seemed to burst from every tile, stone and floorboard. The floor itself was made of colorful glass tiles that formed a mosaic of wild creatures. The walls were painted with swirling designs. Hidden within the rainbow swirls were the forms of flowers and birds that seemed to look upon her and, instead of gazing unsettlingly, instilled her with a certain self-confidence that was nearly indescribable.

The stunning, untamed wall designs only showed up so often as most of the walls were obstructed by thick panes of crystal clear glass that allowed for an alluring view of the city outside.

A few doors down, Aelwen noticed an engraved wooden door that was wide open. Once again, her Arenian stealth proved useful as she prowled closer to the open door. She peered inside, risking only a second-long glance lest the inhabitants not wish to be looked upon.

The room was as marvelous as the rest of the mansion. Wild plants grew in through the open windows and potted plants filled much of the room. Upon the walls, an intricate jungle scene was painted, complete with dazzling insects and radiant beasts.

In the center of the room was a polished stone desk with flowery potted plants set upon each corner. President Tecsequaih sat at the desk. He pored over a thin pile of papers. His head was down, staring intently at the top sheet. The president dipped his quill into a colorful ink jar and began scrawling all over the paper. His hand moved nimbly, without hesitation, yet the ligaments in his wrist stood out and the skin on his arms seemed to be stretched tight over his muscles.

Seeing who it was, all apprehension washed from Aelwen. She peered in again. She kept watching, hoping that the president would notice her so that she did not have to enter herself. Tecsequaih was so entranced in his work that he took no note of her.

Fed up with waiting, Aelwen walked in. "You're lucky I'm not a murderer."

President Tecequaih jumped in fright so horribly that he almost fell out of his chair. "Aelwen!" he gasped.

"That's me," she said sarcastically.

The president's face seemed to have gathered more wrinkles since yesterday. The flesh around his eyes was looser. The war seemed to be slowly killing him already, and it had only just begun.

The president gave the smallest of smiles. It was not in response to Aelwen's minor joke. It was because he had barely seen her since they had left, he had hardly been able to talk to her. He did not know how she was doing and not knowing was another great weight set within his soul.

Aelwen looked over Tecsequaih's shoulder to see what he was writing. His handwriting was so elegant and miniscule that it was unreadable even from the distance Aelwen stood at. "What are you working on?" she asked.

Tecsequaih seemed mildly taken aback by the question. He had become submerged in thoughts of…everything. He truly needed to learn to pay attention, even to small conversations like this one, if his country was going to win this war.

"Working on my plan," he replied.

"What exactly is your plan? You mentioned it before we came here and I've been curious to know ever since."

He gestured for Aelwen to look at his paper as he explained, "This may not be the most ingenious idea out there, but I have heard of it being used before," he paused for a short breath before adding, "and succeeding."

The president's explanation was halted as a crimson and sunflower bird with a marvelous tail swooped in through the open window, landed on Tecsequaih's paper, and began preening itself.

"I guess there's someone out there who doesn't respect the President of Marchia," Aelwen snorted in amusement. It was absurd and never would have been as amusing in other circumstances, but with a war of the ages brewing, the president planning an attack, rebels escaping their homeland, tyrannical kings and vengeful mages, a carefree bird shamelessly intruding on the president sharing his battle tactics was one of the most humorous things to occur.

After watching the fan-tailed bird for a few moments, Tecsequaih went on, "We will use the Hakmarres' strategy against them. Engage them in the front. I am thinking that we should build a barricade before the entrance of Arkada and position many archers there to fire up into the building. While they fight, we will send troops through the back and reclaim our city."

Aelwen gaped at the simplicity of it. Using the enemy's strategy against them. The plan was so straightforward that it just might work.

The president's council sat in the mansion. There was nothing for any of them to do but wait. Tecsequaih would not have allowed them to fight even if any of them wished to. All of them, even the most stubborn of them, realized that this was a battle that none of them should attend. It could cause major changes if the Marchians won, but still, the war was young and there were still much grander, more crucial battles to come that would require the entire strength of the militaries of both sides.

Aelwen looked down, unsure of what to do with herself. *Where do I look? Should I slouch? Should I fidget? Should I disappear into my thoughts and forget that people are out there dying and I can't even see it?*

She glanced at the table beside her. Upon it there was a sheet of parchment written upon with General Fayette's messy yet professional handwriting. There was a rough sketch of Arkada with shapes to represent warriors and arrows illustrating their movement. The short of it was that one Vatre-darah troop was going to engage the Hakmarres at the front entrance while a smaller one snuck around through the back and did serious damage.

The Marchians had adopted the phrase the Hakmarres had coined for them. The Hakmarres had clearly meant for the term to have no pleasant meaning, for it to be something destructive and terrible. Their attempt to shame the non-mages with the phrase had failed miserably and the Marchians and rebel Corovans had accepted the phrase, changing its intended meaning to one of determination and pure strength. Not to mention, they liked what it meant. Fire blood. They all liked the thought that they had fire crackling within them.

Aelwen shuddered inwardly. She remembered the fire that had started it all. Not the real one that had decimated her home village and so many others. The figurative one that had ignited within the veins of herself, Iowan and Namar. The one that had spread to Gavnas, Lysia and Taran. They had all shared that fire. Now what did they share? Aelwen hardly ever saw any of them anymore. Before the war, she had seen Lysia everyday and Gavnas nearly as much. Iowan had just reentered her life, they were just getting to know one another again . Now…now she couldn't remember the last time she'd seen them. It had been even longer since she had seen Taran.

She shoved the thoughts away. None of her friends or personal issues mattered right now. The war was all that mattered, everything else could wait. It had to, or else they would all parish and never see one another again.

CHAPTER EIGHTEEN

At the moment, there was nothing to do but watch. Lysia's vantage point was not one near to the battle, but the blood that spattered the white walls of Arkada and the corpses of the fallen and the screams of the dying were too easily discernible for comfort.

For all its gruesomeness, Lysia could not peel her eyes away from the battle. In her heart, she felt she had a duty to watch this until its end, no matter the outcome. Iowan stood beside her, watching as well. The two of them held hands, each in need of a tether to their reality when the horror they were watching seemed too real.

The Vatre-darah let loose a storm of arrows that shattered the windows of Arkada. Glass still falling, they carried out volley after volley, arrows sailing through windows. Fully armored Hakmarres rushed to the window spaces and took shot after shot of their own, gravity driving their arrows into the Vatre-darah with lethal force. The plan seemed to be working based on the number of Hakmarres firing at the crowd of soldiers below. The only question was how many Hakmarres were in Arkada that were *not* engaged in the attack? In other words, how many Hakmarres were there to face off against the cadre of Vatre-darah whose job it was to strike through the back entrance of Arkada, demolish all in their way and reclaim the building?

Rhea's dragon emitted a shrill roar that shook the walls of the house. The sky-colored beast perched menacingly upon the roof of Arkada, in a divet where the great bell had stood. After burning anything of value in the capitol, Rhea's dragon had bowled the bell from its position, knocking it into the streets below where it shattered into lots of little pieces.

Looking down at a terribly bloody battle and sitting astride a dragon, in a halter dress of orchid, Rhea looked as marvelous as the queens of yore. Surely she had a power not unlike theirs. Though, in all of the tales, the queens fought side by side with their warriors. By all accounts Lysia had heard, Rhea hadn't fought in a single battle, she just sat up in the sky and watched her people slaughter. Was she saving her strength or was she a hypocrite? Only time would tell.

Lysia shuddered as the Hakmarres launched a rain of arrows from a balcony, impaling a good number of the Vatre-darah below. Iowan's grip on her hand tightened. The Hakmarres were capable of so much without their magic. If they hadn't made that bizarre bargain, if they had their magic now, what would they be capable of? Would any of the Vatre-darah trying to take back Arkada still be alive? Would any of them?

Thankful as she was for the Hakmarres' promise to abstain from using magic, Lysia did not understand why they would make such an oath, and she didn't trust anything she didn't understand. All she knew was that they were fighting an entire people who had endured too many years of oppression, a people with unfathomable power and hatred for the world that had built up within its cage for generations and was finally bursting through the bars and attacking without remorse.

~~~~

A heavy set woman jumped off of a sweat-drenched horse. She gave her steed a quick pat on the snout as an apology for forcing it to go so fast for so long. She did not bother to tether the horse before she went sprinting up the steps of a magnificent mansion with a mosaic mural covering one wall. The woman was young with straight black hair that had not been washed in some time. Her clothing was made of plain brown material, her shoes had holes and her cross-body bag for carrying letters was stained beyond belief. As a messenger, she was on the mission of a lifetime, one she had never expected to receive. She was a mix of emotions, mainly horror and sorrow whirling around with excitement and disbelief. She raced up to the third floor of the mansion and found the president of her country standing before her.

President Tecsequaih, so close she could touch him. He was wearing his usual robes, as were the many council members standing around him. They had all been watching the city out of a large window until she had arrived, and now everyone's eyes, the eyes of all of the most renown people in the country, were on her.

"I come with a message," she said, voice trembling in awe and nervousness. If she screwed this up, her one chance to ever talk to the president… "The Vatre-darah have lost. The battalions were intercepted and the archers were burned to death. There is no one left."

Aelwen suppressed a shiver. She had feared this whole time, deep down, that President Tecsequaih's retaliation attack was naught but a fool's hope. The Hakmarres had a fortress now, they had confidence and inspiration and a dragon.

General Fayette placed a hand upon the Tecsequaih's shoulder. "We must leave. Now."

Aelwen corralled her feelings and shoved them deep down. There would be no time to deal with emotions until she was done. Done living, done fighting, done suffering.

Would it all ever truly end? She pushed that thought down even deeper than her feelings. Questioning would do no good now, nor would doubt. Action was the only option.

In no time at all, they were all back upon horses, encircled by several rings of soldiers in armor of green and gold. Always in motion. Would a break ever come? A foolish question, of course.

Aelwen kept towards the center of the group, she needed a break from being valuable to the cause. Just for a little while she wanted to be normal. She listened to the hushed whispers of the other council members that sounded here and there, like ripples in a mostly
~~~~

still pond of silence. Instead of thinking, which was something she really did not want to do at the moment, Aelwen turned her attention to her surroundings.

For a city, there was nothing spectacular about Telspire. It looked almost like Firhad except emptier, as if all the life and color had been sucked out of it. Word of the war had spread and no one was brainless enough to keep pretending that things were normal now that enemy forces controlled the capital.

A warm gust of wind passed through the streets of Telspire, a green Marchian banner fluttered by in the wind. There seemed to be a cloud of gray over the city even though the sky was a cheery shade of blue. While a chilly, gray day with spotty showers would have fit perfectly, the world seemed to be challenging them to see it all differently. The sun shone bright and warm, a blanket of hope wrapping up their shadowed souls.

When Telspire was out of view and the sight of the dense jungle was no longer entertaining, Aelwen took a pencil and a stack of parchment from her bag. Resting the papers against her saddle, she started to sketch out a battle plan. She'd read enough books to have a general idea of what she was doing and she couldn't think of a better way to pass the time. An hour later, she had something she was mildly proud of. She folded up the plan and started another.

Hours of sketching and scribbling and detailing passed before Aelwen ran out of parchment. Just as she folded up her final drawing and tucked it away, General Fayette, astride a massive dark bay mare, rode through the crowd of muttering council members.

She approached Aelwen, who was riding a chestnut stallion. And so Aelwen's short time of being slightly normal ended, not that she wanted it to last for too long. She enjoyed being valued as something other than a fighting machine.

"Aelwen." The general's voice was stern, as always.

The former Arenian twitched at the sound of her name, not because it startled her but because, for the first time since she had met Fayette Ekua, she noticed something achingly familiar in her deep, commanding voice. That tone, she had heard it a million times. The same tone that Galarus used when he was training with his Arenians, giving them advice, whacking them in an area they had not realized they had left open to attack.

Aelwen hoped that the general had not seen her twitch. "Yes, general?"

"Come to the front. The president and I would like to have a word with you."

Gods. Fayette's dark brown face was so incredibly serious, as if she had never smiled, never seen a day without suffering.

The way she had said that sounded to Aelwen like she was about to receive some sort of scolding. She moved her horse forward, weaving between the other council members in their marvelous robes.

Either President Tecsequaih did not hear Aelwen's approach over the sound of the many hooves or he did not care to look at her. Once her horse was beside his, he spoke without turning to face her. She guessed it was the second option.

"We cannot win this war." The words were spoken stoically, emotionless.

"It has hardly begun," Aelwen replied just as stoically.

"There is no way for us to win without magic."

"There is so long as they agree to not use any."

"How long can we trust them to keep to their word?"

"They have kept to it so far."

"The war has hardly begun."

Aelwen glowered as he threw her words back at her.

The president asked, "In the arena, how much did you rely on trusting your opponent not to hurt you?"

It took effort to keep her shoulders from slouching with defeat. "Never," she admitted.

"We need magic. We need you."

Fayette, who had sat quietly beside them until now, explained the plan outright. As a general, she did not care for those who beat around the bush. "Aelwen, you must go to Paruma to learn magic. We have received a letter from a mage, one of the few who opposes Rhea and the Hakmarres. They have offered to teach you magic to give the Vatre-darah a fighting chance. You must go."

Aelwen hated the way Fayette used the word "must". None of this was a choice and she knew that, but it still made her feel like a subservient fighter in the arena who did exactly as the Master bid. Not that the general's no-nonsense words were the first of her worries.

"I'm not a mage. How would I—"

"The author of the letter says they know that one of your ancestors was a mage," explained Tecsequaih. "There is magic in you and they can help you awaken it."

"That's absurd. How do we know this isn't some kind of trick?"

"I'm asking you to trust me, Aelwen," Tecsequaih said steadily. "If you have never trusted me before, please, do so now. Go to Paruma. Let them teach you."

Aelwen scoffed. "I can't be the only one with magical ancestry. Maybe you're part mage, maybe you're both part mage. Why just send me?"

"We can't deplete our forces. We send you because you're one of the few we can spare. Besides, the letter asked for you directly, no one else was mentioned."

"Spare me?" Aelwen asked incredulously. "And no one else? Because I'm useless or something? I can fight just as well as any of the others—"

Tecsequaih cut in before she could finish. "You're not useless. You're valuable and that's exactly why we have to send you away. You are a centerpiece of the Vatre-darah, one of the driving forces, we can't risk losing you in battle. Sending you to Paruma will keep you safe and make you stronger so that when you come back, you won't have to keep off the front lines anymore. Hopefully, you'll be able to put an end to the entire gods damned war."

"I still don't understand—how can I be the hope of an entire people?"

"If all goes as planned, you will have something greater than their magic."

"What are you not telling me?"

"Nothing I know the answer to. So, will you go to Paruma?"

Fully aware that she didn't really have a choice, Aelwen said, "Yes. When do I leave?" This was going to be a great ordeal, there was no question about it, and she was going to need time to prepare for the journey, emotionally and physically.

It was General Fayette who spoke this time. "That will be a bit of a problem, but I've already got it nearly figured out. We need a way to get you safely to Paruma while also remaining as unnoticed as possible, which means no soldiers will escort you, you'll be on your own. You will not depart until we get to Wyldmor."

"Why not? I could go right now. That would save us all time. You should know better than anyone how precious time is when it comes to war."

"Do not lecture me."

The president took over explaining. "The refugees of Firhad are being brought to Wyldmor. If all goes as planned, they will meet us in the evening. Tomorrow, we will split into three groups and lead them to Wyldmor."

"How are they getting out of Firhad?" asked Aelwen.

"Soldiers have gone to the houses and led away anyone who wants to get out, which happens to be most of the city's residents. The Hakmarres have made no move to stop the evacuation."

"Why would they let their enemies go?"

"Even I cannot say for sure, but I do have an idea," said Tecsequaih. "I do not think that the ordinary citizens are the target. The Hakmarres want the most important Vatredarah. They see our society as one of leaders and followers, not individual free will like they believe theirs is. They think that if we fall and they take over, the people will not rebel."

Aelwen snorted with contempt. "They think their society is one of free will? All of those who parade around behind Rhea and do her bidding and killing exactly as she wishes?"

Tecsequaih nodded. "Rhea is smart. Incredibly, terrifyingly smart. She has a way with words, she knows how to manipulate the mind."

"You sound like you admire her."

"I do. Not for her brutality, but for her unmatched cleverness. Brains are deadlier than any weapon, do not ever forget that."

Fayette nodded in agreement.

Aelwen could not deny Rhea's wittiness, yet she did not believe that was the only thing Rhea had going for her. "She is probably just using strong magic to control her followers."

"I do not doubt that, but I do know that any spell can be broken if you resist it hard enough. Intriguing words and marvelous promises cannot be pulled away from so easily."

"And after we get to Wyldmor? What then?" asked Aelwen, drawing the focus of the conversation back to her mission.

"I'm still working out the details," said General Fayette. "Give me a little longer and I should have it all worked out."

"Okay," said Aelwen, turning her horse so she could rejoin the heart of the crowd.

"And Aelwen?" said Fayette.

Aelwen tugged on the reins, halting her horse. "Yes?"

"Don't tell anyone about this."

"Okay. I won't."

The horses clomped along the overgrown, unmarked path for hours. Aelwen allowed her vision to blur. The low noises all around her gradually faded away, submerged and eventually completely drowned out by her thoughts.

Magic.

I am no longer a valuable pawn in this twisted game. I am everything. The fate of the world is upon me.

What should I be thinking about? What do mages think about while they're training? Do they even think at all?

Calmness is a must. In the arena, before a fight, you have to look as menacing as possible and if the opponent is too terrifying for you to keep that mask of bloodlust on, then you must appear neutral, even though you're raging and shaking on the inside. This is completely different. I remember those mages out on the fields, they breathed and they fought. I never saw fear in them. If I'm going to learn magic, I must be calm on the inside as well as the out. I'm going to have to control my emotions, channel them. Is there a way to change your emotions, to transform fear into confidence? There must be, no one could face down the greatest army in the world without a glimmer of fright.

All of those mages have undoubtedly been training their entire lives. What will I have to endure to become a full fledged mage so quickly? How much will I have to sacrifice? How long will I have? No more than a couple months at most, I guess. What if I cannot learn magic? What if, for some reason, I just can't? What will happen to us then? What will happen to the war?

What should I be expecting? I'm not ready. The road to Wyldmor is long yet. There is still more time to sort all of this out. How will I find my way to Paruma all by myself? How am I supposed to find the mage to train me? Are they already waiting for me?

"If all goes as planned we will have something greater than their magic."

What will the Parumans give me?

Aelwen lay flat on her back, fiddling with a twig. They had stopped to make camp a while ago.

She snapped the thin piece of wood in two and picked at the bark of one piece with the tip of the other. No fire was allowed in the wide valley they had declared as their camp for the night and she was not quite hungry enough to eat the tasteless dried meats that had been brought along. She would have slept had she not been waiting for the people of Firhad to arrive. She prayed to any listening deities that Iowan, Lysia and Rinly would be among them.

Iowan could fight just as well as Aelwen, even better in some areas, but her time under the authority of Halamr had undoubtedly weakened her substantially, how capable a warrior was she still? Aelwen was not sure she wanted to know the answer.

Lysia had trained frequently with Aelwen, she would probably be fine.

She had never seen Rinly fight, but she figured that rangers were taught all sorts of combat techniques. Hopefully the skills of Lysia and Rinly combined would be enough to keep Iowan safe.

Aelwen snapped her body up into a sitting position at a loud thud nearby. Every part of her awakened. She released a small sigh and leapt to her feet as the powerful, thundering noise she had heard turned out to be the galloping hooves of the fully armed military escort of the ex-inhabitants of Firhad.

Everyone was on their feet in a matter of seconds. People hollered in excitement and shouted the names of those they sought in the massive crowd. There were so many people. The city streets had always been bubbling with life but somehow, with all of the Firhadians clumped so tightly together, there seemed to be more of them than imaginable.

The sea of rejoicing people spread throughout the valley they were spending the night in, wave after wave of terrified yet excited Firhadians washing in.

Aelwen wove through the people, searching and scanning every cluster for the familiar freckled face and dirty-blonde hair. Her ears tingled with all of the voices buzzing around her.

Where was she? Where was she? Where was she?

She was on the verge of franticness when she heard a voice she knew, like honey and sunshine, shouting, "Ae! Ae!"

She whirled in the direction of the voice. Sure enough, in the midst of all the jostling bodies was Iowan, and beside her, Lysia.

Aelwen shoved her way through the crowd and threw her arms around her best friend. She pulled back, hands on Iowan's shoulders.

"Are you okay?" she asked, voice serious. She examined Iowan. Her face seemed to have gained more color than when Aelwen had last seen her. Her eyes seemed brighter, too, even in the darkness.

"Yeah, yeah, I'm okay. Are you?"

"I'm fine." Aelwen turned her attention to Lysia for the first time. "And you?"

"I'm alright," Lysia replied, her words flat and dry. The shock of the Hakmarres seizing Firhad had evidently had a lasting effect on her, she wasn't acclimated to violence the way the ex-Arenians were.

"Is Rinly with you?" Aelwen asked, hoping he was somewhere amidst the crowd.

"No," said Lysia, sounding even drearier than before. "We haven't seen him since they took the city."

"Oh. I hope he turns up soon. I'd like to see him before—" *I leave*. Aelwen remembered Fayette's sword-sharp words just in time. *Don't tell anyone.* Disobeying that command could lead to the death of them all. Something in her gut twisted at not being allowed to reveal her new secret to her longest friend and proven comrade. *Don't tell anyone.* The words rattled her. Iowan and Lysia were anyones and so they must not be told. It should not be so hard to follow an order as simple as that.

"Before what?" asked Iowan, gazing at Aelwen with that peculiar fondness of hers. Her eyes roamed Aelwen's face in a soft, caring way. Iowan always had to know that Aelwen was okay and, though she had never realized it until they were dragged apart, Aelwen felt the exact same way about Iowan. What would Iowan do when she was gone, disappearing without a trace?

"Nothing. Before the end, is all."

Iowan gulped. Lysia shifted uncomfortably and Aelwen didn't miss the way her angular eyes widened at Aelwen's statement.

Aelwen stumbled over her words, desperate to correct herself. "I don't mean—I—we *could* die and we have to recognize that. I want to see everyone I care about before the war gets any worse so *in case* I don't make it out alive, at least I've seen everyone one last time."

Whatever joy and levity there had been between them was completely gone by the time Aelwen stopped talking. To keep that fact from being the focal point of their conversation, Aelwen continued on, as if her previous words were nothing more than idle conversation. "Come with me, I'll show you the sleeping area. You might have to sleep on the ground if there's not enough bed rolls."

There weren't. Aelwen yawned and settled down onto her own bed roll. Iowan laid down beside her on the grass and Lysia curled up next to Iowan, drawing her cloak around her knees to block out the chill of the night.

Iowan watched Lysia for a few moments until she closed her eyes and tucked her face down to her chest. Then, she turned to look at Aelwen, whose eyelids seemed to be gaining weight with every passing second.

"Ae?"

"Hm?" mumbled Aelwen, sleep closing in on her. She was afraid Iowan was going to ask something along the lines of 'we're going to be okay, right', a question which Aelwen would feel awful answering either way. Many words had passed between her and Iowan throughout their years together and from all that she could recall, not one of them had ever been a lie. Aelwen was relieved when the only thing Iowan said was, "I don't ever want to lose you."

"I don't want to lose you, either. Not again." Her words weak with fatigue, Aelwen let her eyelids drift shut. With that single action, sleep consumed her, and she was glad for it. As happy as she was to see Iowan, there was a pain that lanced through her at the sight of her best friend, her right hand warrior, all due to her upcoming journey. As long as she saw Iowan's face the ideas of her anguish when Aelwen left swam through her mind and, although she had survived the arena for thirteen years, those thoughts were almost too much to bear.

Lin sidled his horse up beside Aelwen's. The mass of ex-Firhadians had been split into three groups, increasing the chances of more of them making it to Wyldmor. The groups had to be large enough to defend themselves and there was an unspoken agreement that no families be split. The president led one group, the general led another and the former Arenian led the last. Due to the high probability of being attacked, a second and third in command had also been designated to each group. Lin was Aelwen's second, her third was Geno, a revered soldier and spy of the Marchian army.

She had led a revolution but never had she done anything so major so solitarily before. Her friends had always been at her side through everything. Now it was just her, on a mission to lead about a thousand people across the wilderness to an ancient fortress that could possibly save them all. It was crazy, absolutely crazy. But the craziest part of it all was the one man whose father's last correspondence she had stolen and managed to lose was her right hand man. They had agreed not to bicker during the war, but there were some tensions and buried feelings that ran too deep, cutting into bone and muscle.

Tecsequaih had been getting on her nerves, too. Ever since he had told her that she was leaving, Tecsequaih had been acting strangely. Whatever was going on, Aelwen did not like the position she was in. It was as if her future was being decided by someone other than her.

The day was relatively warm without any major obstacles to overcome. All of the travelers were surprisingly quiet, giving the trip an eerie essence. Aelwen had expected raucous gossip and stories of Firhad's condition, a few arguments, possibly a couple of protests about the route she was leading them. Instead, though the group was large, the only noise was the dull hum of low voices. Everyone seemed to fear that if they spoke an octave too loudly the Hakmarres would descend upon them. That was by no means an irrational fear, Aelwen just wished for a conversation to distract her from dwelling on the what-ifs of her upcoming adventure.

There were still so many details she yearned to know. Fayette and Tecsequaih had promised to tell her more once everyone was safe at Wyldmor. Why did they demand that she wait? How much were they going to tell her and how much would she be left to discover on her own? The general's words still thumped around in her mind. *Don't tell anyone.* The harshness, the pleading in those words. Fayette had never spoken to her like that before.

A gasp nearly escaped her as several pieces clicked together. There was a spy amongst them. *Anyone.* It could be any of the thousands of people moving to Wyldmor, everyone was a possible enemy.

Aelwen closed her eyes, calming herself. Now she knew. All of the details would be figured out in time and not by her. She had her own mountain of problems to deal with.

To halt her worrying, she closed her eyes and listened to her soul song, composed of all the gentle noises that surrounded her. She focused on the rippling muscles of her horse beneath her.

She had never ridden this horse before, yet it instantly seemed to trust her. Back in Corova, she hardly ever got the chance to ride and was by no means an experienced rider. She had always loved horses but had never been very good at getting them to trust her. Erizo had been a trustworthy companion, but they had had a lot of time to adjust to one another. This massive dark bay gelding obeyed her every command. There was some deep understanding between them that Aelwen had never felt before. This steed was an army horse as well, so it's obedience definitely had something to do with that fact.

Aelwen turned to her third in command. "Does he have a name?" She gestured to her horse.

"No. Military horses are not given names, only titles like captains or commanders," Geno explained.

Aelwen thought that was genuinely stupid. How could a warrior form a true relationship with their horse if it did not have a name?

Her skepticism must have shown because Geno added, "Horses die often in war. Connections are severed too often in battles, we needn't add horses into the mix of those to grieve for."

She nodded with understanding. "While I am riding him he will have a name. Which military rank involves the most trust?"

Geno considered. "Every one. If one must be chosen I would say messengers. If a messenger lies, it all falls apart."

Another piece of the puzzle snapped into place. Their attempt to reclaim Arkada. Every Vatre-darah warrior there had been slain. The operation had crumbled. Not because Rhea could predict their every move, because a spy had given the plan away.

"I'll call him Sahe. It means messenger," Aelwen said, recalling the word from one of the books on foregin languages she had read in her studies. She patted Sahe's sleek neck.

"In what language?" inquired Geno.

"Old Narik, I believe,"

His eyes widened. "You know Old Narik?"

"I'm a practicing politician, I know all sorts of useless stuff."

He cracked a smile. "Do you enjoy politics? Must be different from what you're used to." She wanted to slap him. Why was it so hard for some people to believe she was more than a bloodthirsty barbarian?

She shrugged. "Some days are more exciting than others. Your security really is terrible." She spoke nonchalantly, finding much satisfaction in the way his jaw dropped a few inches. "You have plenty on the outside. It is the inside where you are seriously lacking. There are guards at every doorway, I know, I've seen them. And I can tell you that maybe half of them are usually alert and ready for a fight. I come from the arena, I know how to hide a weapon. By now, I could have killed Tecsequaih and most of the council twenty times." She changed her calm yet vaguely condescending tone to a sappier one as she finished. "Of course, I wouldn't want to tell you how to do your job."

Aelwen had planned for their conversation to stop there, but when she noticed that Lin seemed closer than earlier, she struck up a conversation with Geno once again to avoid talking to her second. "How is it being a soldier? It seems to me like you do a lot of standing around."

Geno tensed at the insult, then chuckled. She had never seen a soldier laugh so easily. It probably had to do with the growing threat. Without a clear indication of when his end would come, he probably wanted to laugh as much as possible before he met it. "I'm a trainer, so no, I don't do a lot of standing around. I teach all of the new soldiers complex techniques and secret signals."

"There are secret signals?" Aelwen wondered if they were anything like the secret code used among the Arenians, different hand gestures to communicate opponent information such as "all brawn, no brains" and "she never keeps her right side covered".

"Of course there are. How do you think we keep track of every official all day? Soldiers are always stationed in pairs and every pair can see another. There are signals indicating which direction an official is heading. For example, you are walking out of the library to the president's office. When you walk out of the library, I signal to another guard that you are heading toward him. He watches for you and if you do not show up there is a search party sent for you."

Geno regaled her with such tales until all hell broke loose.

CHAPTER NINETEEN

Iowan and Lysia's horses were side by side, close for comfort. The two young women refused to be separated in the sea of travelers now that the storm clouds could burst any moment. Especially now as the group was making their way through a segment of the magnificent, dense rainforest—a place far too easy to get separated in.

They had been forbidden by the president to be a part of Aelwen's group. He claimed that the Vatre-darah could not afford to lose every rebel Corovan thoroughly devoted to the war. He had managed to split them from Aelwen, but when he attempted to send Lysia to General Fayette's group, the pair of women had strongly refused. Upon Iowan's return to the group, she felt as if she had been slowly sliding away from Aelwen and towards Lysia. There was some unspoken, indescribable connection between them that they both felt but were unable to put into words.

Lysia reached across the foot of space separating her from Iowan. Feeling Lysia's cool fingers, Iowan wrapped her own around them. They both had calloused skin and visage's less than unblemished.

They hardly spoke. Neither of them knew what to say and they both feared that if they parted their lips in an attempt to make a sound their tears would choke them. They had to be strong. Every single one of them, every person, mage or not, on each side of the war.

Why was strength so difficult for an Arenian who had harmed people for thirteen years as a profession? Why couldn't a woodswoman be strong in the face of war?

Both of them rode most of the way with their eyes closed, breathing in the fascinating earthly scents, processing all that they had been through and all they still had to face.

Iowan yelped.

Lysia snapped her eyes open, her nerves crackling with adrenaline. Iowan was unharmed, her eyes were wide and trained on an area of the ground not five feet away where a metal arrow was deeply embedded in the rich soil.

A second arrow whirred into the crowd. Skillfully, Iowan tumbled off of her horse's back and onto the ground. Following Iowan's lead, Lysia dismounted and dashed behind her horse.

~~~
~~~

In no time at all, the group was completely surrounded by Vatre-darah soldiers armed to the teeth. Aelwen drew her sword, it whispered as it was drawn. The Hakmarres were here.

Already clad in armor, a more than necessary precaution to take on this trip, Aelwen flipped down her helmet visor and issued the most powerful rallying cry she could muster.

The Vatre-darah formed a target shape— ring upon ring of warriors with non-warriors safely clustered in the center. This could very well be Aelwen's last battle before she left for Paruma. There was no way she was sitting it out.

~~~~

Lysia brandished her broadsword, Iowan drew her battle axe. It was still a bit difficult to wield, she was still recovering from her time tethered to the throne of the king, but the damage it inflicted was well worth the difficulty. They nodded solemnly to each other and sliced their way into the fray.

The Hakmares were smarter than before. They wore real armor now, not just leather. Without their magic, they either had the choice to wear armor or give up before the war really began.

~~~~

A sword slashed up at Aelwen's shoulder. She leaned in the opposite direction and kicked her opponent over. That strange familiar calm flooded through her blood. She swiped her sword in a wide arc, slicing open multiple Hakmarres. She veered Sahe to the left, avoiding an attack from behind, and spun her steed, sword at arm's length, cutting mercilessly through anything in its path.

She had not felt so alive in a very long time. The battlefield felt like the arena now. Her body had adjusted, so had her mind. Armed with those two weapons and the one gripped tightly in her hand, she was an unstoppable force.

~~~~

Iowan brought her axe down in an arc. The muscled Hakmarres warrior before her stepped back. A fiendish grin spread over their face as the battle axe struck the earth, burying itself deep, leaving Iowan without a weapon. The Hakmarres released a cackle and drew a long, slender blade perfect for carving up meat.

Iowan released the axe and vaulted into the air, landing on the handle of her weapon, kicking the Hakmarres in the face with a swift roundhouse, then leaping down from her perch and bashing the Hakmarres in the face with her shield.

~~~~

The stench of blood wafted through the air, filling her nostrils. The clang of metal became the steady background rhythm, the grunts and shouts of the clashing warriors were the main theme.

The shriek of a falling horse filled her ears and sent them ringing. Was there a worse sound in the world than an animal dying? She could not let the noise distract her, she jabbed with her sword, ducked and brought her weapon up in a killing swoop.

Her sword collided with the neck of a Hakmarres, blood sprayed all over her face, dripping into her eyes.

She wiped a splash of blood from her hand and nimbly whirled through a circle of Hakmarres forming around two Marchian soldiers.

It was all a dance to a melody and harmony of turmoil.

~~~~

Everything was whirling, there was so much noise. She had never faced so many opponents at once.

Lysia slit through the dented breastplate of a Hakmarres and watched them fall, blood pooling all around them, soaking the woodland moss, so fresh and green just minutes ago.

Blood obscured her vision completely in the same moment as a pain greater than anything she had ever felt crashed through her abdomen. Blindly, she swung her sword. The gods must have been helping her, for she felt her blade make contact with something. She picked up her arm to wipe the blood from her eyes but even that movement caused too much pain. She had not slept in a hundred years, a deep slumber was calling to her from across a void. The pain pounded through her like a dutiful drumbeat. Consistent, overpowering. Her knees gave out, she crumpled to the ground in a helpless mess of flesh and blood. She could not feel anything but pain.

~~~~

Aelwen allowed none of her horror to show as she caught sight of the mountain side rising up behind her, so tall it brushed the clouds. It was far too close for comfort. If the Hakmarres trapped the Vatre-darah against the stone, they were done for. None of the Vatre-darah would ever make it to Wyldmor and to safety, none of them would ever live in peace again other than in the endless halls of the gods. She would never make it to Paruma.

She turned Sahe in a half-circle, riding back behind the outer lines of soldiers. Once she was safe, at least a bit, in the center with the so-far-unscathed civilians, she leaned forward and rested her forehead upon Sahe's neck. She quieted her soul song. She let the world fall away. It was only her and Sahe. She breathed in and out, slowly, over and over until all of her anxiety had been exhaled. She rotated her neck, making it pop in a most satisfying way.

She sat up and opened her eyes. All of the overwhelming noise flooded her senses. Immediately, without hardly any thought at all, the shouts, clangs and screams became an anthem, urging her onward. She gripped Sahe's reins in one hand, sword in the other. As her steed dashed forward, straight for the danger without a flicker of fear in his heart, she screamed. Her voice was full of freedom and recklessness. In no time at all, warriors were assembled behind her and she led a charge straight into the ranks of the Hakmarres. The move was completely unexpected by the enemy and she knew well that sometimes all it took to beat the greatest opponent was a surprise.

Iowan twisted her head this way and that. There were so many bodies. Where was Lysia's?

The battle had ended minutes ago and the blood of the wounded and the dead stained the green forest a terrible shade of red. The survivors had been counted, only a portion remained definitely alive with a significant amount severely wounded. She had searched the groups of the wounded without stopping. Lysia had not been among them. She had roamed throughout the groups of those alive, crying despite being victorious. Lysia was not among them either.

Where was...

Her thought was cut short as the sight of blood leaked into her periphery. It was not the blood that attracted her panicked gaze, but the face down body covered in it, completely motionless. It was incomprehensible how Iowan's eyes focused on that single drenched, red body amidst a sea of them and knew in a moment's glance who it was. She screamed as she hurled herself to the earth, not caring as moisture seeped through her pants, staining her flesh. She hefted the body into her arms, hugging it to her chest.

Tears clouded her vision, she wiped them away with her shoulder. She pulled Lysia's scarlet-drenched hair away from her motionless face, which was only speckled with blood, the rest of her body was thoroughly doused in it. Iowan didn't understand why Lysia's magnificent face remained almost untainted, the same pale brown it had always been. Those lovely angular eyes and that single lock of rebellious black hair.

Lysia seemed to be sleeping peacefully. Her face still looked so very alive, so purely calm. Iowan had seen the dead before, the way the color flushed from their faces, how their jowls drooped into a depressing frown. Lysia did not look like them.

Desperate, Iowan ran her hand over Lysia's chest. There was no beat there. She ran her hand over the scarlet clothes and flesh, praying that she would feel a heartbeat somewhere. Anywhere.

Her breath hitched as one of her fingers hit a divot. No, not a divot, a hole. Iowan was a frequent friend of repulsive, oozing holes, bleeding tears and gushing gashes, but the sight of this deep red hole in the gut of this person made bile rise in her throat. Iowan swallowed hard and turned her head away from the horrific sight. The image was still there, burned into her mind like a farmer's mark branded onto a bull's hide. Iowan hardly had time to pivot before she hurled all over the forest floor, adding her vomit to the repulsive mixture of blood, bile and innards on the ground.

As she turned to the side to steady herself, she placed a hand on Lysia's body and planted the other firmly in the wet earth. Iowan gasped as she felt movement beneath her hand, the one on Lysia's chest. She did not bother to wipe away the strand of drool hanging from her chin before she had both hands pressing up and down rhythmically on Lysia's chest.

In a few moments that felt like years, she felt a faint flutter beneath her palms. It was not much, but it was hope and that was all she needed.

Iowan scooped Lysia into her arms and sprinted in search of the nearest healer, shouting at the top of her lungs for someone to help Lysia before it was too late and if no one did then she would personally dig out the throats of all of the healers with her own fingernails.

<div align="center">~~~~</div>

Aelwen stared blankly at the barren field that stretched before the vertical, sheer rise of the gray mountainside. Bodies of every shade and size dotted the view, pools of their blood bright red flowers on the brown ground. Lin, drenched in his own sweat, a splash of blood not his own covering his lower torso and a long slice over his shoulder and down his back, approached Aelwen.

"More than half remain, but only just."

The words grabbed ahold of her bones and shook them. She had lost nearly half her group.

Aelwen turned away from Lin. President Tecsequaih had trusted her. General Fayette had trusted her. She had ruined everything. So many lives were gone because of her. She was not a general, they never should have put her in charge. She had led her people to freedom, of course she could be trusted. What had she done so wrong? Hundreds of lives. Gone forever. Because of her.

She inhaled. It was one of the deepest breaths she had ever taken. She seized ahold of all of those wild feelings, choked them, and dragged them down, down, down, burying them with all of the other feelings she had felt too strongly of late.

Aelwen raised a bloody, gauntleted fist into the air. "Let's go!" She had not meant to holler. Her voice should not have sounded like the ice covered, brutal dark gray cliffs that arched over the angry black northern sea. But it did. She hated it. All of it. This entire Gods damned war. Lives should not be lost so easily. A slice of a sword that hit the right artery, that was all it took. People should have more of a chance. The Gods were supposed to sit upon pristine thrones in the Great Hall, an endless land of light and happiness. If the souls of the dead really went to a land that was so much better than this one, why did it hurt so much when they left?

The backs of the travelling horses were loaded with two or three riders each since so many of the animals had been slain in the skirmish. It had not been a full out battle, only a single attack without any complicated weaponry or grand plans in place. Rhea's dragon had not been there, very few of the Hakmarres had ridden horses. They had appeared so suddenly and walked to meet their enemies. It had been nothing special at all, nothing that would be written down in history books and discussed around an open fire or in a classroom. How many lives had been torn apart? How many people would never be the same? All because of a small, bloody skirmish.

A Vatre-darah soldier marched up to Lin, she had to tilt her head backwards to look up at the councilman who sat upon the tall horse in his flowing robes of green. "The horse ridden by an elderly woman travelling with her eight year old daughter has just stumbled and broken its ankle. Would you be so kind as to lend them your horse? I know it is a rude question for such a high ranking man, but no other horses remain."

Lin nodded without hesitation and dismounted.

He walked along beside Aelwen's horse. Lost as she was in her own thoughts, Aelwen's Arenian instincts picked up on Lin's labored breathing, the hurried, uneasy rhythm of his steps. His efforts to keep up would not hold out for much longer.

She slowed Sahe and looked down at Lin. She was well aware she was glowering and probably looked like she had not slept for the better part of a year. "Want to join me?" Her voice was still too gravelly.

Lin's only response was a quick nod. He slid a foot into a stirrup and settled behind Aelwen. A few quiet minutes passed. Aelwen could not see him, but somehow she sensed when Lin's lips parted. She stopped him before he could begin, jabbing him in the side with her elbow. She wanted to talk to Lin. She needed to if this tension between them were ever to ease. Now was not the time.

Once they got to Wyldmor, they would each be too submerged in their individual duties to have time to talk. Then Aelwen would leave for Paruma. Who knew how long she would be gone? Who knew if she would come back?

Aelwen waited an hour. Maybe more, maybe less. No one had a watch on hand, which seemed to give time the opportunity to shake off the tethers humans had created for it and move at its very own pace.

Without looking at Lin, Aelwen said to him, "What?"

"Hmm?"

"What were you going to say? Earlier, you started to talk." Her voice had a sharp edge to it, but was less cruel than before.

"Nothing."

She felt him shake his head without looking.

"Just…this is not your fault. None of it. Not the blood or the death or the endless sorrow. Do not blame yourself for any of it. You didn't make it happen."

Aelwen scoffed. "Nice try, but I'm the leader. The lives of everyone in this group are my responsibility. I lost far too many."

"Do you think Fayette would have done anything differently?"

Honestly, she had not thought about that. The answer was obvious enough. "Yes," the word was rigid steel. "She would have saved people. All I did was kill so I didn't get killed. I never ran to the aid of anyone but myself."

"Yes, but if you had not killed the Hakmarres who attacked you, they would have gone on and murdered many more of us. You are an Arenian, you are used to protecting only yourself. By doing that, you saved lives today. All people save other people in their own way."

The horses lumbered along, dragging their hooves in the dirt. Their heads drooped and their coats were soaked with sweat. The forest was so dense it was nearly impossible to see anything but bunches of broad, deep green leaves.

All of the people were travel-weary and many were still mourning the dead. Would their suffering ever end? Everyone longed for a decent meal, cold water, a moment of peace.

Aelwen was not among them. The forest fueled her, the incredible natural sights sent newfound energy coursing through her veins. She desperately wanted to lead her horse off the beaten path and go charging through the wild terrain to climb mountains and feel the wind in her hair.

Is this what Gavnas feels like when he is with the sea? I understand why he wants to go back to it now. How can he ever stand to be away?

For a vague moment, Aelwen cut all the tethers of responsibility and let her soul fly.

Freedom filled her body, mind and soul. There were no more worries or responsibilities. No duties. Nothing but pure carelessness and independence.

Aelwen blinked. That was enough time spent on fantasizing. She could spend all her days having adventures like those after she mastered magic, won the war and took back her country.

Before she knew it, an enormous fortress of black stone, five times the size of Arkada, loomed before her.

It seemed to grow out of the jungle, a palace of the Gods of the earth. Across its outer walls was strung red fabric, put there by General Fayette on her first visit there so that they would all be able to find it. Aelwen looked around. They were the first ones to arrive.

The outside of Wyldmor was so much more than she had ever imagined, even draped with foliage that covered much of the outer walls. She could only imagine what wonders lay waiting on the inside.

Lin and a few soldiers followed her as she dismounted. Working together, two soldiers started a small fire. Aelwen and Lin picked up long sticks and lit the ends using the fire. Aelwen held her flaming stick, a too-long torch. As the first leader to reach Wyldmor, it was her honor to begin the burning. It felt almost cruel to destroy all of the nature that wrapped around Wyldmor, cradling it as if it was its child. She breathed. *Would you rather save a couple age-old trees that have seen more of this world than you ever will or give every Vatre-darah a real chance at winning this?*

She stretched out her arm, the tip of her torch made contact with a bunch of intertwining vines that seemed to be all huddled together in an effort to receive the most sunlight. With barely a touch, the flames crawled off the stick and began devouring the vines. There had been worry that the burning would not work, that the plants would be too wet. They had been wrong.

Aelwen took a step back, the sudden flash of heat pushing her away. She watched in awe as fire swallowed up the true beauty of the world in order to provide a safe haven to those losing a world-altering war.

~~~

Tecsequaih's horse cantered into the clearing, shadowed by the great green canopy above. He took a deep breath. The scent of smoke clung to the air. His group was not the first to arrive. Tecsequaih steered in a circle to break the beast's momentum. He stared up at Wyldmor and it stared back, dark, stoic and full of promise. Wyldmor was sculpted to look like a temple from those old days, all linear with straight edges, steep sides that reached high, culminating in a sharp point. The stone fortress was a relic of a bygone age from the
~~~

days when blind faith in the gods, not trust in chosen rulers, dominated the hearts and minds of the people.

The president hadn't laid eyes on the fortress since his time in the war. The Marchians had not resorted to using Wyldmor then. Tecsequaih and his troop had passed by it on the way to a battle, marvelling at its size and moving on. Back then, the whole thing had been completely overgrown, nearly invisible behind the mess of vines that had claimed it as their own.

His group was the second to arrive, judging on the amount of people that milled about. He inspected them, trying to decipher which group had beat his. He didn't see General Fayette or Aelwen anywhere.

Lin came running out of Wyldmor, heading in Tecsequaih's direction. It was Aelwen's group that had arrived, then. But where was Aelwen?

Arriving at the foot of Tecsequaih's mount, Lin swept a bow. "Mr. President, welcome."

Tecsequaih nodded and dismounted. "Apologies for the delay. We were ambushed on the road."

"So were we," said Lin.

Tecsequaih clenched his jaw. "Then perhaps the attack was not an act of chance."

Lin gaped. "You think the Hakmarres coordinated attacks against us?"

"I know nothing for certain, but I would put nothing past them. We face a clever enemy, that's all that can be said for certain." His eyes travelled from Lin to the depths of the sprawling jungle. Realizing his thoughts had begun to consume him, Tecsequaih forced his attention back to his financial advisor. "The burning has been done, then?"

Lin gestured over his shoulder at Wyldmor, massive, dark and not draped in vines and leaves. "Indeed it has. I wonder if that was the wisest course of act, though. Surely all of the smoke gave away our position."

"I should think it has." Tecsequaih clapped Lin's shoulder. "Don't worry. Everything is going according to plan, for the most part." The president left Lin standing there and headed for the entrance to Wyldmor, weaving through the crowd. This building would be the Vatre-darah stronghold for the foreseeable future. That was, if the Hakmarres kept their bizarre promise to refrain from using magic.

Before he reached the main entrance, someone else appeared in it. A great weight was lifted from him at the sight of that raven haired young woman he loved as a daughter, who had eased the pain of that gaping hole in his heart.

"Tecsequaih!" Aelwen exclaimed, hurrying to him and tossing her arms around him. He leaned into her embrace, gratitude that she lived on overflowing within him. Gratitude was not the only thing he felt. Remorse surged up as well. Any day now, he would have to let her go. Had he not been president, he would have fought against her leaving, but as president, he could not put the safety of one person over the possible salvation of his people by something greater than magic, whatever that meant.

Reining in his emotions, the embrace ended. Tecsequaih was preparing to say something to Aelwen when the thunder of hooves dragged both their attention to the head of the clearing, where General Fayette Ekua's group came galloping in. The third group had arrived. That meant it was time to get down to business.

~~~~~

While the other two people in the small, round, dark stone room sat, Aelwen remained standing. The thought of sitting again after a three day, non-stop journey on horseback was not appealing in the least and the fact that all of the possible seats were carved out of hard rock did not appeal to her either.

"You must leave as soon as possible," declared Fayette. She was still clad in heavy armor from the journey, her dark eyes as unforgiving as the walls of the room.

"I do not know the way to Paruma. I'll never make it on my own," Aelwen protested.

"Go south. That's all you have to do. Go south. Do not fret on that point. The Hakmarres know where we are, we all know that. If their coordinated attacks on the travelling parties didn't explain that, the smoke from the burning surely gave us away. It is only a matter of time before they make their move, which is why it is necessary that you are completely sure of what you are supposed to do. Once the battle commences, you will slip away. You will not fight for any longer than you must. You will sneak off and you will make all haste. I do not care if there are seven Hakmarres following you, you will not turn back. Your fear is insignificant. You have to be on the move, always."

President Tecsequaih, the third person in the room, nodded gravely when Aelwen cast him a quick glance. She didn't want to do this. Personally, she still wasn't sure this wasn't some elaborate trap. Though, why the Hakmarres would spend so much effort to get only her was an explanation that evaded her. It was selfish and wrong to want to get out of this scheme, really. The majority of the hope of the Vatre-darah lay with Aelwen, with this scheme, with her learning magic and 'something greater than magic'. She knew that, yet the idea of leaving everyone and everything behind to flee to the home country of the enemy—a journey that was bound to be time consuming—to train in magic with someone she didn't know for the gods knew how long with just wasn't something she wanted to do. She would do it, for the greater good, but she could not bring herself to like it.

~~~~~

Lysia's bloodsoaked clothes had been peeled away and replaced with white linens. White seemed like a lousy color choice for someone with open wounds, but the white was so that the healers would be able to see if the patient was bleeding out.

Iowan flinched internally whenever she thought of Lysia as a patient. Lysia had never not held her own, at least not that she had seen.

Iowan had never seen Lysia be weak. No matter the challenge presented, Lysia had always risen and to face it. It was sickening to see such a powerful person lying half-dead before her. What if Lysia never rose again? What if this challenge was the one she would not overcome? Iowan swallowed at the thought of it.

She allowed herself to ask the question, but to delve no deeper on the subject. She knew that sometimes, when there was nothing else, hope was everything.

Iowan gave Lysia's limp hand a gentle squeeze, then left the healer's quarters for the first time since they had arrived. She could not stand to leave Lysia alone, but she needed to distract herself from all of the horrific *what ifs*.

There was a balcony a little way down that hall. She leaned against the banister as she looked down from it. Two floors below, on the ground level, people rejoiced. There were more tears than she had ever seen shed in one place. Friends and family who had been separated during the journey clung to one another, never wanting to let go again. She had been in such hysterics upon arrival, so concerned with getting Lysia properly taken care of, that she had not noticed that another group had beat them here. She spotted Lin in the crowd, murmuring with President Tecsequaih. It was Aelwen's group. Aelwen was down there somewhere and they had not even seen each other. Though Iowan has been reunited with Aelwen for some time, she could still feel there was space between them. Space she wondered how long it would take to breach.

Iowan left the balcony and wound her way through the fortress, getting to know its cold stone walls and sheer storm gray corners. The whole place had such a serious, militaristic demeanor that she was surprised to find a library on the top floor, a level so high that looking down made one abruptly nauseas. She had thought this to be a place of blood and steel, not paper and ink. She hadn't guessed it could be both.

Before her was the library, a massive ring of rooms with thick chains over the doors, large, impossible-looking locks and fireproof coverings. The Wyldmorians clearly valued knowledge more than anything else in the universe.

A hundred years earlier the fortifications upon the gargantuan library would have been impenetrable. Now that the chains were worn and rusted and the locks were eroded, entry was as easy as slicing through the chains and locks with her axe. The fireproof covering was the only barrier left and they simply slid over the door and could be pushed into a slot in the wall when one wished to enter.

The sight made Iowan's head throb. This was not the average ancient library. All of the books looked to be mint condition, their covers bright, the pages a crystalline white, not the expected yellowish color. There were no cobwebs lining the shelves and there was not a speck of dust on the polished marble floor, which Iowan found quite curious since this was the first place in Wyldmor she had seen that was not made of stormcloud stone. The shelves were carved out of the white rock walls and had been cut with special care, sculpted like all variety of beings of the earth.

There was so much in the room, Iowan almost turned on her heel and left. But with the choice of staying a while in this overwhelming room or going to her own room with no pleasant thoughts to accompany her, she endured the sensory overload and scanned the shelves. She located the nonfiction section, which occupied two of the rooms that made the circular library. Iowan narrowed her search to history, then to Marchia, and eventually found books on Wyldmor itself. Quite possibly, whatever she found in this book could help the Vatre-darah in some way.

After three hours of reading from the books, Iowan stopped. Her butt ached from sitting on the rigid chairs of white stone, the only seating to be found in the library, and her eyes were bleary with tiredness. But neither of those factors caused her to halt her reading.

She had just read a section on a series of tunnels built beneath the fortress. Until now, she had not considered that those tunnels could still exist, she had thought of them as something out of a folktale, long gone from the world they lived in now. But that could just as well describe Wyldmor itself and here she was, sitting in it. Iowan found a servant in the hall and told him to fetch the president immediately.

~~~~

The general drew over a chair and gestured to it. Aelwen sat. She closed her eyes as she heard the shears chop away her hair. She had had long hair her entire life. As Fayette sliced it away, for the Vatre-darah, for the world they had always known, it felt like a small part of Aelwen was being cut away too, though she knew it was ridiculous to feel that way.

"Done," the general said. She nodded and smiled a tiny bit as Aelwen grinned falsely at her. Fayette did not understand why, to so many people, getting a haircut was such a big deal. Hair was naught but an item, one that could be lost and regained at that. That was more than she could say for all of the lives that would be lost in this war.

Aelwen picked up the mirror they had acquired and examined herself in it. As she did so, it hit her how long it had been since she had actually looked at herself. Her house in Marchia had a mirror in the bathroom, but she never did more than glance at herself for a moment or two. Now, she was really looking at herself.

She noted the lines of her face, still prominent and sharp, yet not so sharp as they had been when she had been on a strict Arenian diet. Her cheeks were fuller, but not plump. Her jawline was still lean and angular, just how she liked it to be. Her hair, although it was hacked treacherously short, was more plentiful than it had been back during her Arenian days.

Aelwen tilted the mirror and focused on her hair. Perhaps the cut was not so terrible. Her ears stuck out and seemed much larger than they ever had when they were covered by her ebony locks. She thought that the haircut made her look tougher, more rugged. Her eyes appeared wider than before, but there were distinct circles of darkness around them. Probably a result of always being on the lookout for trouble and constantly worrying about the war. Her brows and lashes were longer and thicker since they were no longer constantly being shoved into sand and blood in the arena. The only thing that seemed unchanged to her was her fleshtone. It was still the fabulous brown it had always been, a shade right in the middle of light and dark, alluring and gorgeous.

Aelwen nearly dropped the mirror when a guard hollered to the general from down the hall. Fayette bolted out. Unsure, Aelwen decided to wait for a Fayette to return rather than snooping around military business. There was no sense in getting into any of it since she would be far, far away from it all much too soon.

The information could not have been too drastic, for the general returned in a matter of minutes. To Aelwen's bewilderment, she was grinning devilishly.

"Our plan is set. The Hakmarres are coming. We will beat them."

"What? How?"

"They have been spotted by our scouts. They are moving this way at a steady rate. If they continue, they will be here by late afternoon tomorrow."
~~~~

"But how are we going to beat them?"

Fayette chuckled briefly. "It is all thanks to your friend, Iowan. She was researching Wyldmor up in the library," she gestured to the floors above them. "And came across a passage about a bunch of tunnels, an entire network beneath us."

Aelwen shook her head, utterly baffled. "Iowan was researching?"

"Yes, she was reading a book called *Stone Temple* all about this place."

It was unbelievable. Iowan never read. Of all times to pick up reading as a hobby, why would she choose now?

Fayette's usually hard set mouth quirked upward in a smile. "Don't you see? These tunnels are our path to victory and your path to saving us all."

Yes. Sometimes all it took to beat the greatest opponent was a surprise. The tunnels were their surprise. The Hakmarres would never see it coming and their blindness would be their downfall.

Aelwen strapped on the strange armor. She had never seen such a thing before. It was like the thick wool clothing people wore in the Northern Wastes, except it had plates of metal sewn into it. The outfit was impossibly heavy. There was no other word but torturous to describe what being on the run while wearing this would be like.

When she moved to step towards the countertop to retrieve her helmet, the dense fabric wrapped around her leg tightened and the force of it nearly tipped her over. Grunting, Aelwen regained her balance, seized a dagger out of her weapons belt and sliced open the backside of her leg armor, allowing her to move more freely.

She placed her helmet on her head and fumbled with the straps. This was yet another odd contraption. The top was pointed, the sides came down in direct points that, were they extended, would slice into her ears. A piece of crimson fabric had been twisted tightly and wrapped around the base of the helmet for a reason she did not know. On the front rim of the helmet was a thin, folded sheet of chain mail that could be let down to protect her face without obscuring her vision. Normally, the top peak of the helmet had exotic bird feathers sticking out of it, but to avoid suspicion they had been removed.

This was her escape uniform. A costume that would disguise her from the Hakmarres while she ran. They would not be looking for a short haired woman in centuries-old battle attire. She hoped.

Truthfully, in the span of less than twenty-four hours, Aelwen had already begun to appreciate her new haircut. Having short hair was more freeing than she expected, although she was still not over the habit of reaching back to flip her hair over her shoulder or run her fingers through the full length of it. However, if it helped her avoid the Hakmarres, it just might help her save the world.

Save the world. What a thought. Aelwen had been audacious enough to attempt to save her own country nearly single handedly. But the world was so much more, especially now that an entirely new player, magic, was now in the game. A force that took time and patience to harness that had once dominated the world and, were they all not careful, may destroy it.

She checked the straps that secured her weapons to her. Ensuring they were all secure, Aelwen headed for the door. She was expected at the tunnels in no more than a few minutes. Before she opened the door, a small stack of papers beside her bed caught her eye. They were the only belongings she'd brought with her to Wyldmor other than her weapons—the battle plans she'd scribbled out of boredom during the trip. She picked them up to examine them. It seemed her last bit of time at Arkada had packed full of studies of battle strategies and how to draw plans had paid off. The plans she'd drawn were really quite impressive.

Aelwen scoffed. She was being arrogant. Her battle plans were good, especially for someone who had learned so quickly, but surely they were nothing compared to the genius of the minds of people like General Fayette who had devoted their lives to honing such skills. Aelwen folded the papers up. They were good enough that she didn't want to see them fall into enemy hands. She scanned her room for somewhere safe she could hide them. A crevice between two blocks of storm gray stone proved the perfect spot. She shoved the papers into the hole and dashed out of her room and down to the lowest levels of Wyldmor.

The stone walls of the tunnels dripped with water. The air was hot and moist, an extreme version of the humid air of the jungle above. Aelwen held her sword vertical before her face, a common pose held by warrior leaders. The troop she was leading out of the tunnels waited at her back, fully armored, standing in neat rows. It was time to leave. She would slip away during the battle, a drop of water escaped from the raging sea. She moved to brush her hair over her shoulder and then stopped, remembering that it was not there.

She heard the blow of a horn echo all around, the sound bouncing off the stone walls. She let down the piece of chain mail that hung off of her helmet, an old sort of facial protection. Aelwen began the march through the wide, winding tunnels. Her path was marked by slim white slashes in the charcoal walls.

The way vibrated with the rhythmic *thud, thud, thud* of Vatre-darah warriors marching to battle. As they travelled, Aelwen drowned out the thunderous marching and focused on the noise above. She could hear the sounds of bloodshed: the all too familiar clang of metal on metal, shrieks, screams and hollers of corporals and the wounded, the raucous amount of noise made by all of the feet scrambling around up there.

There were five units making their way through the tunnels, all composed of over a hundred Vatre-darah, armed to the teeth and ready to do whatever was necessary to win this. Each unit was led by an established military officer, except for hers.

Aelwen was sweating in all of her layers. She wore the thin, mobile armor of Marchia over her ancient battle suit. In this battle, one with far too many prying eyes, someone was bound to take note of a warrior dressed unlike any of the others. Aelwen's unit would emerge third. Not near the beginning, not near the end, right in the middle. The least noticeable spot.

General Fayette Ekua was fighting somewhere up above. Aelwen could see her in her mind's eye, that forever flame burning in her dark eyes. She could almost hear the determined grunts of the general as she drove her sword through the gut of a Hakmarres. Aelwen could remember the way the general's muscles shifted in training, the force behind every motion. There was a power in General Fayette Aelwen had never seen in anyone else.

Aelwen was an Arenian, an extremely skilled one at that, but she would never be able to carry herself in a battle the way that Fayette did.

Aelwen hardly had time to finish admiring General Fayette in her mind before it was time for her to emerge from the tunnels and break upon the battle, the third wave of a tsunami that would drown the Hakmarres. Hopefully.

She let loose a blood curdling battle cry and fought her way past only three Hakmarres before flinging herself to the ground in what she could only pray was a convincing portrayal of collapsing mortally wounded. She dragged herself along for a bit, moaning dreadfully.

Once she was close enough to the sidelines and had cast about enough quick glances to make sure that no one's eyes were on her, she scrambled to her feet and darted into the dense jungle.

She had noticed that Rhea was not there, unless she was fighting alongside her people like any valiant ruler would, but she highly doubted that would ever happen. Rhea had not been there when the Hakmarres had raided her Vatre-darah group either, but Aelwen had heard that all three travelling groups had been attacked. Rhea did not need to be present to do damage.

Deep into the discombobulating jungle, Aelwen stripped off her Vatre-darah armor and scaled a broad tree in her bizarre outfit. She positioned herself in the crotch of two branches and leaned back, angling her body into an area of shadow to hide her from the sight of any searching hunters. She remained there in the tree just long enough to see the lines of Hakmarres begin to recede and once she heard the victorious cries of the Vatre-darah, which could very well be the most glorious thing she had ever heard, she shuffled back down the tree and continued on her way, breathing a bit easier than she had when she'd set out.

CHAPTER TWENTY

The road was long and winding. Aelwen had to avoid being seen at all costs, which made her trip even longer, bringing her many miles off the beaten path so she could pass through long stretches of harsh nature. Swamps with mud the color of dung that made awful sucking noises when stepped in. A wide, flat, barren area with tall grasses, and sharp, dry winds that sliced at her exposed flesh. The forests were so cruelly dense that it was impossible to move without being stabbed by branches.

Her soul song was a thunderous beat of dread. The pounding of her feet against the solid ground mixed with the frantic pounding of her heart and the sly, sharp whispers of the wind.

She splashed through streams and shoved her way through thorny tangled branches, all the while feeling that the shadow of death was keen on her heels. Everytime she glanced over her shoulder or turned her eyes to the sky, fearing she would see the great shadow of a dragon above her, there was never anything there.

At night, sleep never came easily, no matter how much her body ached and her mind blurred. Even exhausted and hidden by the dark, the threat of being found was still too prominent to allow her to sleep soundly.

In the back of her mind were the determined grunts of warriors she'd fought beside, caught in a sea of terror and desperation in the middle of a plain soaked in blood. Although she knew that she had left all of those warriors so she could save them, still she could not stop her heart from clenching in shame that she had abandoned them. They would be slaughtered at the hands of monsters while she hid.

She was too far to turn back now, so she pushed on with the fist of doubt clenched firmly about her heart.

Aelwen stepped over the threshold, into the kingdom of Paruma.

Everything was different. Everything was so alive. It felt like there were thousands of eyes upon her. Not enemy eyes, but so many that they unsettled her nonetheless. Aelwen did not know whether or not she should draw her sword.

She was no stranger to the stories of the Parumans. Savages with a code of morals only deemed moral by them. They dressed like the tribal warriors of old, painted their bodies with the blood of their enemies, pierced their bodies with rings for every life they took and built temples of human bone. They had a dislike for modest clothing and spoke in grunts and squawks. They fought with simple weapons, handcrafted spears and knives of broken stone. But their true weapon was not any they held in their hands. They fought with magic. No one knew how they harnessed such wild power or how they controlled it. But they did. And she would be one of them the next time she saw anyone she had known before this moment.

"Finally," cackled a throaty voice that could only belong to someone of great age. There was something eerily familiar about it. "I thought you'd never show."

Aelwen flinched and drew her sword. To her right, where she would have sworn a bunch of spindly trees had grown five seconds ago, was a tiny stone hut. One side was completely open, as if the walls had been hacked off with a blade of deadly precision, giving a full view into the gut of the home.

Sure enough, a hag stood before a hand carved countertop while stirring some sort of liquid that filled a handcrafted clay bowl. This woman did not remotely resemble the barbarians told of in every tale Aelwen had ever heard. The woman's clothes were made of natural fabrics, most likely hand sewn. A one-shouldered dress of gray covered the woman's body. She seemed to be challenging the deadly humidity by also having a thin, brightly painted shawl draped over her bony shoulders. The woman's posture seemed all too familiar. The fluid way her hands moved triggered something in Aelwen's memory. She took a step which allowed her a full view of the crone's countenance.

"B—Bailba!"

Old Bailba. The Dark Philosophess.

"That would be me." Bailba's tone was cheerier than Aelwen had ever heard it. She almost sounded like grandmother material. However, her voice still maintained its uniquely honed edge.

"But you're—"

"Really, girl?" Bailba left the spoon in whatever it was she was stirring and waddled over to Aelwen, leaning heavily on a carved cane. "I expected you to be smarter than that by now. You'll never learn magic with a brain like that." She wacked Aelwen in the shoulder with her cane.

"All this time? All these years?" Her voice quaked. The last word came out almost as a shout. She did not know whether she had intended the effect or not.

"Forever, dear."

'Dear' was the last word Aelwen would have ever expected to come out of Old Bailba's mouth.

"I couldn't shut myself out completely. I needed some connection. Being alone is only enjoyable until you start feeling lonely. I came up with that story that you all believed and it spread like wildfire. When people don't understand, they will grapple for any thread of understanding, even if it is as far from the truth as possible."

"You're…you're a mage? But what about Iron Peak Mountain? All the Arenians you took away?" It didn't make sense. Yes, Bailba could have easily lied about who she was, but what about all of Galarus' trainees she had plucked as the best and worst and whisked away with her to some unknown fate?

Bailba cackled. "I never lived on Iron Peak Mountain. No one ever has. That was all part of my story."

"But—"

The crone plowed on, seemingly oblivious to Aelwen's attempted interjection. "As for the Arenians I chose, they were the ones who had family that had managed to escape Corova when Halmar was on his tirade, burning villages and whatnot."

Aelwen bristled at the destruction of her village, her parents, her childhood friends, being minimized to 'whatnot'.

Bailba went on. "I located their family members, saved them from the arena life by way of the Judging and delivered them to their families."

It was nearly too much to take in. Another falsehood, another lie, another ruse she had taken at face value because she hadn't considered it to be the product of deceit.

Nearly at a loss for words, all Aelwen managed to stammer out was, "You're...you're going to...train me?" Everything sounded wrong. It *was* wrong.

"Oh yes. Very much. It won't be easy. I may not be who you thought I was, but that doesn't mean I'll start being kind all of a sudden."

Aelwen straightened a bit, shifting into the beginnings of a fighting stance, the true meaning of why she was here seeping into her soul. "What do I do?"

"Come. You must know where you are to know where you are going."

The Arenian did not move.

"Come, girl. Here." Bailba pointed beside her. Cautiously, Aelwen stepped to the spot. Color flashed before her eyes. There was not enough air. Where had the ground beneath her gone? Then everything was steady and clear again.

Aelwen hardly had time to part her lips before Bailba was waving a hand carelessly in the air and saying, "Magic. Get used to it."

As if that would be easy.

Aelwen turned in a slow circle, examining the place. The hut she had stood in a second ago was gone, now they were in a much larger dwelling. The walls were smooth wood covered in snaking vines.

"Where are we?" She walked to a window without glass and peered down. The ground was a hundred feet below.

"In my house."

The outer walls of the abode were dark brown. They looked coarse. Vines crawled up them.

Old Bailba did not live in any mountain, she lived in a tree like some mythic sprite.

Aelwen was about to ask another question when a ferocious grunt followed by a blast shook the tree.

"What the—"

The sound came from above. She tipped her head upwards and saw that the ceiling above them was glass. And though it was a ceiling to this level, it was a floor to the next. Standing on the glass floor of the next level of this strange abode were two young women. One resembled Aelwen a bit too much, except for a mass of curly black hair, and the other was lithe with pale skin and long, fiery hair. They threw blasts of magic at each other, deflecting with multicolored shields and striking again .

"Who are they?" asked Aelwen.

"My other trainees," explained Bailba with a wicked little grin. The old woman reached a hand above her head and a bolt of magic flashed from her palm. It split right through the glass ceiling-floor and flashed between the two girls, so focused on flinging magic at each other they did not see it coming.

The redhead leapt back, taking on a defensive posture. The brown skinned, raven-haired girl with steely eyes stiffened where she stood. She glared at where the bolt had struck with all the anger of a thousand summer storms, her teeth gritted in ferocity.

"Down here, now!" As Rhea did astride her dragon high above the battlefield, Bailba made her voice float up to the warring young women who turned their backs on each other with flames burning in their eyes. In a moment, both of them stood beside Bailba and Aelwen. The girl whose hair was a blend of fiery colors planted one hand firmly on her hip, the other dangled loosley at her side. Although, based on the way she twirled her fingers, sparks of colored magic flicking between them, Aelwen assumed that the position was anything but relaxed. The darker girl had her arms crossed, not even attempting to look civil like the redhead. Her coffee-colored eyes glinted as she sized up this new, inexperienced opponent.

Bailba looked purely annoyed as the three females shot dagger glares at each other. "Outside, let's go." Aelwen was mildly surprised that Bailba hadn't just magicked them out the door.

Standing on the vibrant rainforest floor, Aelwen flexed her hands, praying for some sign of the magic within them. Not a glimmer appeared. The two girls leaned menacingly against the trunks of two trees a good distance away from each other. Both of them stared at Aelwen with too much expectation. Bailba waddled over and took up a position about ten feet away from the newest arrival. She raised a hand and the beginnings of a spell began to form.

"Wait!" hollered Aelwen in a much too desperate voice. "I don't know what I'm doing!"

"That's how you learn!" crowed the hag and then she tossed a ball of whirling red and gold magic at Aelwen who tumbled out of the way and then dodged and rolled to avoid a whoosh of cerulean power.

A dart of swirling green and purple whizzed past her ear and a stream of alternating color flew up in front of her face, causing her to backflip and slide along the grass. Aelwen tried many times to shout at Old Bailba to stop this, that she had no idea how to fight back, but every time she started to speak up, another attack would be launched at her.

A whirlwind of color formed around her, buzzing in her ears and clouding her vision. In a whoosh of motion, she was out of the trap and back on her feet, leaning and dropping and flipping to stay alive in the mess of color. Magic was an ethereal sight, but that did not make it any less deadly. If anything, it made it more so, because while one was entranced by the beauty of it, it could be slowly murdering them.

Aelwen rolled onto the ground as a whirl of orange flashed over her head. She was just preparing to draw herself back to her feet when Bailba unexpectedly lowered her hands and stepped forward, the countenance of an old warrior faded and was replaced by the comforting old woman demeanor. She offered a hand that Aelwen refused, shoving herself up and wiping at the grass stains on her armored pants. She was still wearing the absurd travelling armor. It was a miracle she had been able to move like that in it.

"What the hell was that?" Aelwen growled through gritted teeth.

"Calm down, dear. That was not to test your magical abilities. It was to make sure you had the skills you need to become a powerful mage. I had to make sure all that living in Marchia had not made you soft."

Aelwen turned her head until her neck gave a satisfying crack. "I never stopped practicing."

"Thank the gods for that. Your body moved in perfect response to my attacks. Your movements were fluid and confident. You did not flee from the fight either. You protested, but you did not run. You accepted the challenge and gave everything you had to offer. That demonstrates the two things that a mage needs more than anything to be powerful and successful: physical and mental strength and stamina."

That sounded like four things to Aelwen, but she did not argue. A sheet of ice covered her gut when she saw how the other two trainees were glaring at her. The fire in their eyes was gone, replaced by frozen stone.

Bailba released a shrill whistle and, like trained sport hounds, the other trainees swaggered forward.

"Aelwen, this is Marliza and Valiran, my two other trainees. You will be practicing with them once you harness your abilities, which I do not think will take long to do."

Marliza and Valiran rolled their eyes. Valiran was the menacing redhead and Marliza was the ruthless curly haired girl.

Aelwen straightened a bit. These women were intimidating, but they were not her enemies, only her practice dummies, which made them take a backseat in her mind. Aelwen was a warrior and she would not cringe before anyone.

"You did well," said Bailba, that warrior-ness creeping over her features again. Aelwen wanted to snort at the old woman for saying that what she had just described as 'absolutely perfect' was merely 'well'. "But now I need to know you can function just as well with multiple opponents." As if that was some kind of cue, Valiran and Marliza began circling Aelwen, hands up, ready to attack.

As Bailba took up the position too, she explained, "My girls do not think twice and they do not forgive."

Then the storm clouds burst. Silent whirls and spikes of magic flew around her, skimming over her shoulder and barely missing her eyes. Marliza and Valiran did not think twice and neither did Aelwen. Her panic level rose, but she kept it in check, channeling the waves of energy into each and every move. Her feet twisted in a complicated form as the first chords of her soul song were struck and her body began a dance that would perplex even the most talented performers.

The mages relaxed and dropped their hands. The magic stopped. The song faded away. Aelwen had not even broken a sweat. A light smile played about Old Bailba's crinkled lips.

Marliza's stance was one of bubbling jealousy covered by an impressive mask of barely restrained anger.

Valiran's jaw was clenched and set at an angle to keep it from dropping in amazement.

Aelwen swept a hand through her short hair. "What, you can't do that?" She made sure to sound arrogant, sure of herself, she had to in order to gain the respect of the mages. But on the inside, she was amazed at how efficiently she had managed to dodge all of their attacks after just struggling to avoid those of Bailba.

"Not when we started," snarled Marliza.

"Well, some of us are more skilled than others." Back in Corova, being an Arenian with a home and a semi-honest job that paid decently had seemed like a privilege. Out there in Marchia, that feeling had disappeared. Now that old feeling of privilege was back and she felt a few pounds lift off her shoulders.

"You have amazing prowess. That will give you a head start which, in your case, will be most beneficial." Bailba said to Aelwen, diffusing the tension a bit. "We can get straight into the heart of the training, teaching you how to access and control your powers."

Aelwen asked a question she had been pondering throughout her entire journey. "How do you know I have magic?"

"Magic calls to magic. One mage can sense another."

"Even though I've never used my powers before? I didn't even know I had them."

"Yes."

"I'm not a mage, so that means one of my ancestors was, right?"

"That is most certain."

"Who? And how can you be sure, after all this time, that their magic lives within me?"

Bailba stepped close to Aelwen and stared directly into her deep brown eyes. "You do have magic inside of you. You must be willing to dig deep enough to uncover it. Once you set it free, it will dazzle the world."

The crone laid a brown hand upon Aelwen's shoulder. Aelwen almost shuddered as the nerves around the area became electrified, buzzing with energy.

"You feel that?" Bailba said, not really needing an answer at all. "When you came here, did you think it was pure, exceptional fortune that kept you from being attacked by the enemy? No, dearie, that was my magic, reaching out and connecting to yours, forming a shield that would keep you safe from them. It took much effort to maintain the protection for your entire journey, you should learn to travel faster." Her lips quirked upwards in a quick grin. "I used every bit of power I had because you are worth all I can give." She removed her hand from Aelwen's shoulder and took a small breath Aelwen probably would never have noticed if she had not been watching Bailba's face so intently. "Magic connects to magic. My magic could not protect you if there was no magic in you."

A moment of silence deep as the sea flowed throughout the space of forest between them all, finally broken by a low growl. Aelwen clenched her stomach, a new wave crashing over her, one of horrid hunger, the beginnings of a savage need for food.

Marliza snorted. "We wore all her energy off, she needs to refuel."

Bailba waddled over and slapped Marliza in the shin with her walking stick. "You take a week-long journey with minimal supplies, the constant worry that you could die any second and wearing that thing, then arrive and be forced to train with all of your might and let us see how hungry you are."

Aelwen almost audibly chuckled at Bailba's retort, then remembered how well Marliza wielded magic and kept her laughter to herself.

Without being asked, Valiran waved her hand and a polished marble table and chairs appeared. The practicing mages disappeared simultaneously in a flash of blue, leaving Aelwen standing awkwardly beside Bailba.

"Where did they go?"

"To get us food."

"Why don't you just magic some up?"

Bailba snickered. "I suggest you stop talking about magic that way as soon as possible. You sound like a canal rat when you talk like that. Use the words 'conjure', 'create' or 'procure' instead. We do not conjure," she stressed the word so much it was almost annoying, "meals. Keeping up a steady diet is a large part of becoming a good mage, as you will soon learn."

"When will I start learning how to use magic, Bailba?"

Bailba stared out into the trees, a look of consideration on her face. "Hmm.... how about tomorrow? I want you to be somewhat settled in and comfortable around us all," That was never going to happen. "You need time to replenish your strength as well."

Truly? After the amount of expertise and stamina I just demonstrated, Bailba wants to give me time to recharge? Doesn't she know how crucial it is that I return to the war as soon as possible? Doesn't she realize the severity of the war, what could happen to thousands of innocent people if it drags on for too long?

Aelwen's instincts were hollering at her to say what she was thinking, but she could not so much as part her lips before Valiran and Marliza were back in a flash of red, arms full of an assortment of food. *Where did they get all that? Did it come from the tree house? Where was it stored?*

Surrounded by three powerful mages, Aelwen did not feel as uncomfortable as when she had arrived in this country of witchcraft and death, but the fear of what lay watching still made her spine tingle.

She took a seat at the table and forked a hunk of well cooked meat onto her plate. She was about to ask what it was, then decided better of it in case she did not want to know the answer. It had a spiciness to it that was almost unsettling. Aelwen scooped some berries from a bowl of carven stone. They were small and round with dark purple skin. She tried one. It was tart and full of gritty seeds. Not bad, though.

While they ate, most of them kept their eyes on their plates, except for Marliza, who kept her eyes, full of steel, straight ahead and trained on Aelwen's every move. In an attempt to ignore Marliza's unwavering glare, Aelwen spoke to Valiran, whose hair had burnt red shimmer in the evening light.

"How long have you been training?"

"This is my seventh year," answered Valiran, her voice was tinged with mild surprise, as if she never would have expected Aelwen to pick her as her fellow conversationalist.

Compared to an old woman and the living combination of ice and fire, Marliza, Valiran was indefinitely the best choice.

"Oh. You are really good, I saw you training. I don't think I'll ever be able to fight like that."

Valiran finished chewing and said darkly, "And I think you had best drop that attitude right now or all of your hopes of saving the world are about as dead as this hog we're eating."

Aelwen stuffed her mouth as she concocted a reasonable response. Valiran beat her to it, though and thankfully completely changed the subject. "What exactly are your goals magic-wise?"

"Everything, I guess," Aelwen said with a shrug. It had never occurred to her there was more to magic than using it to demolish enemies on the battlefield.

Valiran snorted. "That would take more than a hundred years. If you are really sure you want to do this, you need to be really sure about what your goals are."

"Honestly, I don't know much about different sorts of magic, so I can't say for sure what I want to achieve. The basics of fighting, I guess. How to throw all of those energy blasts you were attacking me with earlier and how to protect myself and, if possible, a good number of my people, with a shield of magic "

"'My people'?" Marliza sneered, jumping suddenly into the conversation. "You will be their savior, so you think they are yours? People are unpredictable. People do not comply. People cannot see beyond themselves, no matter how badly they want to. People have limits that they refuse to see."

"I didn't mean it like that," was all Aelwen could think of to mumble. What was happening to her? She was considering people that she hardly knew, that were not from the same country as her, to be her own?

~~~~

Lysia opened her eyes at the sound of the door to her room opening. Joy tinted her features at the sight of her blonde haired, freckled visitor.

"Iowan." Normally, she would have exclaimed her friend's name, but she had just awoken a few hours ago and her head was swimming and her body ached.

Iowan gasped, rushing to Lysia's bedside and clenching her hand so tight it hurt. Lysia didn't tell her that. Instead, she inspected Iowan, the crease of her pale brow, the wideness of her hazel eyes, sensing the relief radiating from her in waves.

The pieces were easy enough to put together. She'd awoken a few hours ago, giving her time to regain her senses and memories. There had been an attack, which she recalled little of and nothing after. That fact, along with the gauze stuck to her and the way they stung when she poked them, indicated that she had been wounded in the attack. She laid in a dark stone room that was not familiar in the slightest, making her think it was Wyldmor, the place she and Iowan had been heading for before they were attacked.

"How are you feeling?" asked Iowan.
~~~~

"Sore, but alive." Lysia poked at her bandages. "They got me?"

"Yeah," said Iowan, settling onto the side of the bed beside Lysia. "The healers said it wasn't the stab that knocked you out, though."

"Oh. What was it?"

"A blow to the head, they think. When I found you after the battle, you were covered in blood, but apparently most of it wasn't your own and the wound isn't even that bad."

"Ah. And how long was I out?"

"Three days. Good news, though," said Iowan, smiling that bright smile of hers. "The Hakmarres attacked us and we won."

Lysia's jaw dropped. Could it be true? "We beat them?"

Iowan giggled at Lysia's astonishment. "Yeah. Ae's group got here first and did the burning. All the smoke led them right to us. It turns out there's a network of tunnels underneath us. We used them to surprise the Hakmarres and we won. We probably would've won without the tunnels, knowing how much this place has been through. I'm glad they came in useful, though. That way I can take some of the credit for the win."

"What?"

"I found out about the tunnels. After we got here, I sat by you for a while and then I went for a walk around and found the library where I found a book about this place and the book told about the tunnels. I told Tecsequaih about them, and now here we are."

"Amazing! I can't believe I missed it. I'll be sure not to get knocked out again." While Lysia had been talking, Iowan's face had fallen, the usual softness of her features becoming hard. "What is it?" asked Lysia.

"There's bad news, too," said Iowan.

Lysia was silent, awaiting further explanation.

Iowan continued. "In the battle—the one with the tunnels—Aelwen disappeared. I looked for her body, so did other people. No one found her anywhere."

"That's good," Lysia said quickly, seizing that single scrap of how. She knew how much Iowan had already gone through. To lose Aelwen could very well be the final straw for her.

Iowan went on, "General Fayette sent out a few search parties, but nobody found anything, other than some battle plans hidden in her room. They showed me, thinking it was some kind of trick, but I told them I knew it was Ae's handwriting. I don't know why she had the plans hidden. General Fayette took them.

"Honestly, I don't think Ae's dead. Maybe that's just me refusing the truth, though. Nothing else I can think of makes sense. She had no reason to desert. I talked to Tecsequaih about it and he said he has a feeling she's out there somewhere, alive. He sounded really confident, but I think he was just trying to make me feel better."

Lysia stretched out her arm, gently taking Iowan's hand in hers. Iowan's hand was dotted with scabs and her fingers were calloused. Despite those marks of hardness, when Iowan entwined her fingers with Lysia's, there was a softness in her touch. How any part of Iowan could be so tender after all she had endured was something Lysia could not comprehend, but that did not keep her from admiring it.

"There's more," said Iowan dismally.

"More bad news?"

"Yeah." Iowan dropped her eyes, fidgeting with a wrinkle in her tunic with her hand that did not hold Lysia's. She swallowed. "A report arrived this morning listing everyone who died in the attempt to retake Firhad."

"And?" prompted Lysia when Iowan said no more.

Iowan swallowed again. "Rinshad Ibori was on the list. Rinly's dead."

All went silent. Lysia and her sorrow were all there was.

Rinly was dead. She hadn't said goodbye. She had never told him how much he meant to her. The one who had become a source of light for her, who had been a more than wonderful friend, was gone. No more jokes. No more shared meals. No more card games. His smile and his kind eyes and his shaggy black hair blazed in her mind. She would never see any of those things again.

Would there be a funeral for him? It didn't matter if there was. She was stuck in a fortress of stone in the middle of the jungle, she couldn't attend the funeral even if there was one, which she doubted there was.

Rinly. Rinshad Ibori. He'd gone from being a stranger to one of her favorite people so quickly. He was the kind of person one immediately liked without pretense. More than that, he was a kind person. Genuinely kind, someone who wanted to make other people smile. People like that weren't the easiest to come by.

He'd loved nature so much, spoken so fondly of the trees and the wind. Lysia hoped he would feel comfortable being laid to rest in the earth. Perhaps for him it would be like coming home.

Lysia's hands twitched in a spasm of grief. One hand moved freely, the other could only move so far because it was still holding onto Iowan. The sensation of her hand, clasped tight in those gentle, calloused fingers, was the tether that pulled her from the well of despair that threatened to swallow her and return her to the world of all that was. Rinly was dead. Aelwen was missing. The Vatre-darah had won against the Hakmarres for the first time. Iowan was alive and well and safe. So was she.

The world was full of terrors, more of which were sure to come. But there was more than just the bad things. There was good as well. The death of Rinly was a pit in her chest, but she would not let that pit consume her. She was shocked and sad to an extent she had not been for quite a while. But she would not let those feelings take over. She would recognize her pain, accept it and feel it, and she would get out of this bed, find reasons to smile and go on living her life. The darkness would not become her, it would drive her further towards the light.

Lysia blinked the tears from her eyes. She tightened her grip on Iowan's hand.

"I'm sorry," murmured Iowan, her words like a tightrope walker above a chasm. "He was a friend to you, I know. I didn't know him very well, but from what I did get to know of him, he seemed very nice."

Lysia exhaled, long and steady, clearing a path for sensible dialogue through the tangle of her grief. "He was," she said. "He was." She closed her eyes, making peace with the sadness, squeezing out the last of her tears. She opened them, feeling the best she had since Iowan had delivered the news. "Okay," she said. "I think I'm ready to get out of this bed."

<div align="center">~~~~</div>

"Will you teach me to fight?"

Taran stiffened at the voice, then relaxed. He turned away from the table to face Eoren, who stood in the doorway, perfectly balanced between her two wooden crutches. She'd taken to using them quickly. She was able to move about nearly as efficiently as if she had two whole legs. The room Taran inhabited had been the parlor, initially, but he had converted it to a workshop. A large piece of sanded wood sat on the table before him, along with some shavings and scraps and a few different saws.

"Shouldn't you be in bed?"

"I'm not tired," she said with a shrug.

"It's dark out, Eoren. Go to bed."

"It's winter. If it were summer, it'd still be light out. I've always liked summer much more than winter."

"Oh, really?" He said, silently cursing the child for being so smart.

"Yeah. What are you making?" Eoren peered onto the counter, examining the hunk of wood.

"Something."

"Now? Shouldn't you be in bed?"

Taran scowled playfully at Eoren. He gestured to the wood. "I'm going to make it into a leg for you. That way you can walk without those," he said, pointing to her crutches.

Eoren's eyes grew wide. "Will I be able to run?"

"Not right away. But, in time, yes."

"Yay!" she exclaimed. She stepped closer, inspecting the project. Taran expected her to ask something else about the leg he was building for her, but instead she repeated her initial question. "Taran, will you teach me how to fight?"

"Why would you want to do that?"

"There *is* a war going on."

Taran lifted a saw and went to work on the wood. "I'm well aware."

"So, I ought to be able to fight so I can protect myself. And you."

Taran's immediate response was to point out the obvious detail of her crutches and how she couldn't fight with them. He held his tongue. Degrading her ability to function was something he'd been careful to avoid doing. This question did get on his nerves a bit, but he had enough sense not to take his counterargument that far. "You think I need you to protect me?"

Eoren shrugged again. "You never know."

Taran shook his head. "You don't need to worry about the war. We're safe here."

"Why?"

"Because the Hakmarres are focused on other areas. Cities, important places. They don't care about tiny farm towns out in the middle of nowhere."

"What will they do when they've taken all of the cities and important places? Then will the mages come for us?"

"The Vatre-darah will have wiped them out long before we come to that."

253

Eoren watched intently as Taran sawed apart the wood. "The Vatre-darah will win?"

"Of course they will. Marchia is the greatest country in the world."

"But…they're fighting against mages. With *magic*."

He swept the newest scrap of wood into a pile on the corner of the table so they were out of his way. "The mages agreed to keep the fight fair."

"You believe them?"

"I don't know."

"So, can I fight?"

"No."

"Why not?"

"Eoren…you've already been through so much." He didn't miss the way her eyes darted quickly to her missing limb. "You don't need to go through anything else. You're safe here. Don't worry about the war. You and I, we'll just go on living our lives. We're not going to fight or even take sides. We're just going to keep living. Okay?"

Eoren considered for a moment before responding. "Okay."

She adjusted her crutches beneath her arms and exited the room.

"Where are you going?"

"To bed. I'm tired now."

Taran finished the woodwork by himself, feeling like a failure and trying to find out why.

<p style="text-align:center">~~~~</p>

"Someone in my family must have been a mage. Who?" Aelwen asked.

"I do not know," Bailba replied sourly.

The two of them sat alone at a table in Bailba's tree dwelling. Valiran and Marliza had long since retired to bed, but Aelwen was too full of questions to sleep yet, even though her body longed for it.

"But, if I have magic, then that means that someone in my bloodline also had magic and it was passed on to me."

"Yes, that is correct."

"Who was it?"

Glass orbs filled with flame were the only source of light in the darkness, casting the women's faces in ghostly, dancing shadows.

"I've told you: I don't know. I'm not withholding an answer from you because I want to, I'm not telling you because I don't know."

Aelwen's shoulders slouched in disappointment. "There's not some way you can trace my family using magic? Magic calls to magic, you said."

"That doesn't work for dead people."

Aelwen watched the floating lights that illuminated the tree. She took a drink. "If I have magic and one of my ancestors had magic, does that mean that everyone in between also had magic?"

Bailba nodded, her eyes narrow. "Yes. Though whether they all chose to uncover it as you have, or were even aware of it, is another question."

Aelwen bobbed her head in understanding. She watched one of the small spheres of whiteness glistening purely in the dark, casting an eerie shadow on the crone's face. "Bailba...if I have magic within me, but I didn't know...Then surely I'm not the only one like that, like this." She stared at her battle-scarred hands in the pale light. Hands that somewhere, deep within them, help a power she did not understand.

"That is more than likely."

"Then why am I the only one here training? Why not bring everyone who has magic and train them all?"

The creases of Bailba's face deepened. "First of all, you were undoubtedly terrified of being found out on your journey here, correct?"

She had to remind herself that fear was not something to be ashamed of. "Yes."

"We all thank the Gods that you made it here safely. Imagine how dangerous it would have been to send not one, but hundreds, of Vatre-darah here. The risk of discovery would have been too great and then all hope would have been lost."

"Is it not already?" asked Aelwen, her voice low and her eyes still on her hands.

"Not quite. You will find your magic."

"Can you be so sure?"

"Yes, I can."

Aelwen spread her hands so they were palm-up on the table. "I don't even understand what magic *is*. How can I expect to harness it?"

"Perhaps it would help if I explained it to you?" The old mage raised a brow.

"I think it would, yes."

Bailba blew out a breath, preparing for whatever speech she was about to give. "Magic is the earth's power. The very fiber of what it is to exist— to live, to feel, to connect. To be a mage is to have a shred of the power of the earth within you and to become a magic is to learn to take that power in your own hands and wield it to do as you wish."

"So, a mage is capable of doing anything? There's no limit to the power?"

"No, there are rules. But the borders of magic are blurry and uncertain, unable to be defined simply."

"Will you try to explain them to me?"

Bailba nodded slowly. "I will." She settled back in her chair. "There are different levels of magic. The simplest is to draw the earth power, the magic, from oneself and use it as a weapon of sorts."

"Combat."

"Yes, combat. That is what you are here to learn. The easiest form of magic, and one of the most important. After that comes amplification of sound. A mage can use the earth's power to expand upon a sound that has already been created by themselves or something near to them. Mages cannot create sounds other than their own voices, but they can amplify existing sounds, and only sounds within a certain distance of themselves. That can be useful in battle, for giving speeches to large audiences, to distract, to overwhelm and so on."

"I've seen Rhea do that. When she was in the sky on her dragon, we could hear her perfectly clear on the ground. That must have been what she was doing."

"Indeed it must have."

A thought occurred to Aelwen then. "And the boom that we heard before we found the training camp massacre—I bet Rhea manipulated some sound to make it that loud. But why? She must've known we'd hear it."

"Perhaps she wanted you to hear it," said Bailba. "She wanted to get your attention." Before Aelwen could interrupt with any more revelations, the old mage continued, "After sound amplification is the conjuring of physical objects. We cannot create anything living—no plants, animals or humans, or anything that was once alive, so nothing made of wood or bone or hide. What we can create is everything else. Anything made of stone, metal or clay or so on can be made."

"How does the earth power help you do that?"

"We use the power of the earth to call to substances of the earth and meld them into what we desire."

"Aren't blood and bone substances of the earth?"

"We cannot work with those substances."

"Why?"

"Because they originate from living things."

Aelwen exhaled. "The first time I saw Rhea, I watched her cut open King Halmar. She touched him and there were marks on his skin. I thought it was the blood from the wound making the marks. But if mages can't control blood, then what was making those marks?"

"Probably just her magic. By creating an open wound, it's easier to get magic into someone, especially if your intent is not to kill."

"Not to kill? Based on what you've told me, why would a mage touch a non mage if they didn't want to kill them? I don't know if mages can heal, but if they can, it doesn't make sense. Why cut him open just to heal him—"

"Mages cannot heal. The answer to your question is simple: to weaken them. Rhea didn't want to kill King Halmar, she wanted to manipulate him. She needed him weak to do so."

Aelwen was silent, letting the information seep into her.

The crone waited a moment before continuing. "Teleportation comes next. Mages can only transport other mages and the items they have directly on them, such as clothes and weapons. Mages cannot transport those without magic, or animals, plants or extra objects. The highest number of mages to have ever teleported together at once was five. No more than that has ever been achieved. Mages can only transport themselves to places they know and have seen, as well. We do it by using the earth's power to connect to the earth beneath our feet and stretching it in our minds between where we are and where we wish to go. The mage must have a crystal clear image of the place they want to go in mind, or else it doesn't work.

"Then there is shapeshifting. One of the most difficult forms of magic that few have ever managed to master is the ability to use the earth's power to change their physical form. I know of plenty of mages who attempted this without proper education and I will spare you the details, but let me tell you that it was never a pleasing sight."

"You said that Rhea has immense power. Can she shapeshift?" Aelwen asked, partially fearing the answer. If Rhea could turn herself into any sort of massive beast of destruction, then the Vatre-darah were in even more trouble.

"To my knowledge, no. The farthest her powers reach are to teleportation, which is an impressive skill for someone so young as her to have a firm grasp on."

"What about you? Can you shapeshift?"

"I can, but I prefer not to," Bailba explained with a shrug. "I've taken on multiple forms, but I never feel comfortable in the skin of anything other than myself."

"Is that it? Is shapeshifting the highest form of magic?"

"There is one more. A mage can use the earth's power to stretch the cloth of time."

"What does that mean?"

"Time manipulation. Mages can slow time, but only by so much, and they can never accelerate time."

"Are you capable of doing that?"

"Indeed I am. As a matter of fact, time is slowed right now as we speak."

Aelwen couldn't help her jaw from falling open.

Bailba barked a laugh. "That's why I haven't been rushing you. This way, you have all the time you need."

Aelwen closed her mouth. "You did say that you can only slow time to a certain extent, though. How much?"

"For every day that passes out there, four pass here."

Aelwen leaned back in her chair, a sigh of relief escaping her.

Bailba allowed Aelwen to process the information before asking, "Does all of it make sense? I know it is a lot to take in and that it can be awfully overwhelming." For a fraction of a second, the crone's eyes darted off to the side and a hurt seemed to overshadow her features. Then, a moment later, she was back to her normal mysterious yet kind self.

"It does, it's just a lot. I'll sleep on it to let everything gel together. That's all, right? Everything to know about magic?"

Another laugh leapt from the crone. "If I were to tell you everything there was to know about magic, all of its intricacies and mysteries, by the time you'd gone from here the war would be won and a century passed. Have I told you everything you must know to have a basic comprehension of magic? Yes. Go to bed now, lass. You'll need strength for tomorrow and all the days to come."

"Okay." Aelwen rose from her chair. "Thank you. For teaching me."

A soft smile formed on Bailba's features. "It was my pleasure."

Aelwen nodded her thanks and made her way to her room, her curiosity satiated. At least for now.

~~~~

Winter in Marchia was a strange thing. The sky was gray and the earth was cold, snow fell from the clouds, the waters froze. Despite all of that, the grass stayed green, as did the bushes and the trees. The winds howled and the earth was blanketed in white, but life held onto its color.
~~~~

"Ready?"

The general's voice snapped Iowan out of her reverie. She turned to see General Fayette Ekua, fully armored, standing behind her. Iowan took her helmet out from beneath her arm and put it on. Flipping the visor down, she replied, "Ready."

She rejoined the rest of the troop in the clearing that had become the main Vatre-darah camp. About half of the soldiers were armored and ready for battle, the others—those who would not be participating in this battle—were sharpening weapons and readying horses for those who were going to fight.

Iowan acquired a steed from one of the warriors who was sitting this one out, mounting it in one fluid motion. Situating herself, checking that her sword, axes and shield were all secure, Iowan got her mount moving toward the head of the camp where the soldiers were congregating.

Amidst the throng of armored warriors, Iowan caught sight of a soldier with twin katanas crossed on their back. With the helmet and full armor, it was impossible to tell, but being that she had shown a preference for katanas during their last few training sessions, Iowan was willing to bet that the warrior was Lysia. Her suspicion was confirmed when the soldier pushed up her visor and ran a hand across her brow.

Iowan brought her horse up beside Lysia's.

Without looking at Iowan, Lysia said, "Remind me why we have to be in full armor when the battle site is two hours away?" She shook her head, the rebel lock of raven hair falling across her forehead in the direction opposite all the others.

"So in case the Hakmarres raid us, we'll be ready," Iowan replied, though she knew Lysia's question had been rhetorical.

Lysia huffed and donned her helmet once more. She kept the visor up. "I don't know how anyone can see with that gods' damned thing blocking their view."

"It just takes some getting used to. If you'd actually wear your helmet during training, that might help."

"Would it?" Lysia asked sardonically.

General Fayette, taking up her position as leader of the troop, whisted sharply and hollered to her warriors. "Vatre-darah! Move out!"

Nudging their horses to get them moving, Iowan and Lysia shared a look. Their admiration for Fayette was undeniable—she was a crucial factor in how well the Vatre-darah were faring—but that didn't always make her dominating aloofness any easier to bear. Over the last few days, Fayette had been particularly hard on her soldiers which, while it definitely made them stronger and better, also strained their relationship with the general.

"This one shouldn't be too bad," Lysia said out of the blue.

Iowan, who had started to get lost in her own head, said, "What?"

"This battle. If all the reports Fayette got are correct and she's not leaving anything out, then this battle won't be that big a deal."

"I know. It's just...I'm still getting used to the whole 'war' thing. It's not like fighting in the arena, you know?"

"I don't. Obviously, I've never fought in the arena." Lysia looked down to adjust her vambrace. "But I know that every battle is terrifying and everytime I'm afraid I'm going to die. I hate how I can't wash all the blood out of my clothes and I stay awake all night sometimes because I know that if I fall asleep I'll have nightmares." Lysia looked up, her eyes meeting Iowan's. "And I don't think that's what it's like in the arena."

Iowan swallowed. "No, it's not." She drew her eyes away from Lysia's, then wished she hadn't and looked back. "I'm glad I have you. It'd be so much worse if I was alone."

The beginnings of a smile played about the corners of Lysia's mouth. "I'm glad you're here, too. You've been a real light for me."

"A light?"

"Yeah. This probably sounds stupid, but you've made a lot of hard days easier. Some days, when the sadness is really getting to me, you show up and smile and then I feel better."

Iowan's cheeks heated. No one had said anything remotely like that to her before. "Thanks," she stammered. She didn't tell Lysia that she had the exact same effect on her.

<center>~~~~</center>

The area around them reminded her of the drawings of nervous tissue from all the books on human anatomy used to teach the Arenians the best places to land an attack, except it was glowing an array of pulsing blue and purple light. Marliza and Valiran were training by themselves deeper in the forest, leaving Bailba's abode and a few miles of land around it to the trainer and the trainee. The old woman cast the bubble of spider web magic around them.

Harder than diamond, was how Bailba had described the magical cage. Impossible to break through, a trick commonly used in combat to seal one's opponent in, the only downside was that it trapped the conjurer in as well.

Bailba flexed her fingers, the one part of her body that seemed to have maintained the same abilities they had during her younger days. "This is about focus. Avoid the attacks, obviously, but focus on your inner self, find the magic. Break all of the barriers you must. Grab ahold of your powers and drag them to the surface. Force them out." She left the last bit unspoken but no less understood, *I will not stop until you do.*

The mask of a warrior fell over her face, so creased, concentrated and disturbed that it made one wonder which was the facade: the warrior or the caring woman.

The assault broke like a wild storm, breaking loose and showing no mercy. Aelwen spun out of the way, dodging every cursed bit of deadliness that came flying at her. Her soul song began, her instincts took over, she disappeared within herself.

How deep the soul was. She did not venture there very often, for she knew how hard it was to escape once entering. It was so much easier to push everything down here and forget about it than to face it. At least, that was the case until the next time she decided to dive down into the cavernous area, swirling with old grudges, surprising ideas, stupid thoughts, age old wishes and memories that would never fade no matter how badly she wanted them to.

Sometimes, she forgot just how complex and horrifying she really was. If someone were to split her soul open and all of this chaos came pouring out, what would they think? Would they hate her? Would they abandon her? There was no way someone could still think the same of her after they saw all of this, for even she did not.

259

The worst thing someone could do to themself was to forget who they truly were.

Bailba knew Aelwen too well. Or perhaps she knew the same elements of soul that all humans shared, for it was not long before Aelwen broke through the first barrier. It was a thin one, easy enough to destroy. She traveled a bit, then shattered the next, more shoved down feelings exploding into the open. Aelwen continued down, down, down through the darkness that only she could navigate.

There it was. The final barrier. Thicker than the layers of the earth. A dark, impenetrable thing. She hit it. Not a crack. She punched it. Not a splinter. She pounded upon the barrier, but it never so much as shook beneath her force. It was the first thing that refused to break before her in a very long time. She had forgotten how menacing that feeling was.

Then Aelwen realized. She did not know whether it was some message Bailba was sending through her magic or if her mind had made the breakthrough of its own volition. No matter how it came, Aelwen suddenly understood. In order to break this final, opaque blockade, she had to *want* to. With all of her existence, she had to want to ruin this obstruction and see, with everything she had within her, what lay in the deepest parts of her.

She closed off all thoughts and noise, she even silenced her soul song. She breathed down there in the depths of everything she was. She yearned and let the full weight of it seep into her and she wanted it, not only because she needed it but because she *wanted* it. And when there was no force in the universe so powerful as to destroy the wild desire within her, she let loose upon the barrier and it shattered into a thousand pieces before her eyes.

Unlike the fracturing of the other blockades, nothing exploded out of this one. Down there, on the floor of her soul, was a globe of pulsing light. After everything else was swept away and cleared for good, one thing was left, one sphere of brightness that had the potential to save everything she cared about and, by extension, the world as she knew it.

Aelwen positioned herself before the magic. She did not reach out to it. She neared it until its power, neither hot nor cold, comforting nor unsettling, had filled every crevice of everything she was. Then she returned to the surface, let everything that was fill up her senses and then she opened her hands and roared.

Bailba paused for the slightest moment and then her assault upon Aelwen continued, unhindered.

It made no sense at all. Why had Aelwen's attack not worked? She could feel it within her, alive and quaking and yearning for freedom as she had once done. Yet it would not come. As she twirled and ducked, she tried to force it out. She screamed, she focused, she gritted her teeth so hard it hurt. It never came. Not a spark of color came from her. All of it was right there and yet there was nothing.

Once she was bleeding and bruised in too many places and her lungs felt nearly raw, Aelwen dropped to her knees and shrieked, "Stop!"

Immediately, Bailba dropped her arms.

Aelwen leaned forward, bile and blood dripped from her bottom lip. "Stop," she barely had the strength to pant it. All of her energy had been used to issue that one terrible shout.

"Stop. I can't. It's…it's there…I can feel it. But—I can't." She shook her head. She had forgotten how awful defeat felt. "I just can't."

Wrapping her arm around Aelwen's shoulders, with no words, Bailba lifted Aelwen to her feet and transported them into the tree. Aelwen took a seat on a woven grass bench, forehead resting on her knuckles. Bailba brought her a bowl of vegetable soup.

~~~~

The Hakmarres had broken their promise. Tecsequaih had watched in awe and horror as their magic had brought the looming majesty of Wyldmor crumbling to the ground, that mighty fortress reduced to rubble. Some had been killed and injured, but the majority of the Vatre-darah had made it out safely. If the Hakmarres continued to use magic to destroy any advantage the Vatre-darah had, then Tecsequaih's forces needed Aelwen to return soon or else she would return to find only their bodies and bones scattered across the earth. The strange thing was that since the destruction of Wyldmor, two battles had occurred, and the Hakmarres had not resorted to magic in either.

With their stronghold destroyed, the Vatre-darah had set up a camp in a sprawling field. It offered little protection, but it had enough room for everyone and lookouts were always on duty. The Hakmarres had made no move to attack the new Vatre-darah base, whether they knew where it was or not was a mystery.

Tents were pitched, fire pits and training areas were made. Being there, Tecsequaih felt like he was back in the Marchia-Ave war all those years ago, when Marchia was a sliver of land fighting for more, not the great power it was now. The last time he'd been in such an establishment, he'd been wired with adrenaline, a mix of anticipation, fear, excitement and hunger for glory coursing through his veins. Now, he only felt afraid. Sometimes when he saw a group of his soldiers clustered around the fire at night, laughing, that old sensation would return. He would try to snatch it, but always it was gone before he could fully recall it, and he was left feeling tired and old and slightly hopeless. A leader was never supposed to give up on a cause, no matter how hopeless it seemed, he knew that. Knowing that didn't make it easier to keep the floodgates of despair barred when the Hakmarres had toppled Wyldmor simply by raising their hands, or when General Fayette or any of the other military leaders returned from battle drenched in blood, heads bent, obviously about to relay their defeat.

Tecsequaih would have preferred to be in a different camp than Fayette to increase their chances of survival, but he needed to be able to be in near constant contact with the Chief General. Being apart from her at the moment would be even harder, given that winter was arriving. All was dusted with a single layer of cold white flakes. Soon, more snow would come, drifts would form, making travel difficult, especially for anyone who wished to go unnoticed. Most thought snow was for the forests of Corova and the Northern Wastes, not the lush rainforests of Marchia. Tecsequaih knew better. In his more-than-half century of life, he had seen all manner of weather in Marchia during the winter months, from treacherous thunderstorms that lasted for days on end to blistering heat waves to exactly what they were stuck with now—snow and ice that obscured the green of life but did not harm to it. The winter months would end and with them, the earth would thaw, snow and
~~~~

ice would melt, revealing the luscious plantlife to be as plentiful as it had been before the winter came.

Tecsequaih inhaled, enjoying the crisp cleanliness of the cold air. He cast his gaze about, taking in his many soldiers. For the most part, they were healthy and strong. As of yet, the war had claimed but a fraction of his forces.

His warriors did not look the way he secretly felt. Some sat together talking, others sparred. Their motions were fluid, their expressions were fierce. They were anything but hopeless. Perhaps the future was not as dark as he'd feared.

~~~~

Marliza and Valiran were Aelwen's only companions as she traipsed through the forest. Bailba told her to walk and breathe, to relax and maybe, hopefully, come in contact with her magic. The two snarky mages were for protection, Bailba had claimed when Aelwen had protested to their coming along, but Aelwen had a feeling that the crone had some deeper motives.

"You both know your way around here, right? You're not going to get me lost?" The joke was pathetic, but to Aelwen a sad attempt at a joke was better than the uneasy silence between them.

Marliza's face twisted into a sick grin. "We'll see about that. We could tell you we wouldn't, but words don't mean anything. Especially not to mages. Language is empty and full of holes. Magic is not so false."

Was speaking in mystic proverbs apart of becoming a mage? Or was that how Parumans were raised to talk?

Aelwen replied, "Does that mean that everything you just said was a lie?"

Marliza rolled her eyes and flipped a strand of curly hair over her shoulder. Apparently mages didn't have an answer for everything.

"How did you access your magic? When you first started learning, how did you get it to come to you?" Aelwen asked instead.

The question was not addressed to either of the mages. It was simply a matter of who would answer first.

To the surprise of everyone on the hike, Marliza was the first to explain. "It took me forever. I couldn't tap into it and it was the worst feeling in the world."

The expression on Marliza's face did not match her words at all. She still had that slightly crooked smile, the natural swagger in her step, her voice was as normal as ever. Her words did not sound broken or even bent. A strong woman stood beside Aelwen, a woman who had invisible armor ten feet thick on the inside and out.

"I finally got it when I was being attacked by six mages. Not people helping me train, real mages with real power and real intent. I wasn't able to think. It just happened. For me, it was focusing too hard. I had to let go of everything and let my instincts do it all. My mind was what got in the way."

How did this walking, talking piece of iron and ice talk about her feelings so freely, without the slightest change in her tone or posture? Was that apart of being a mage, too? If it was, it was something Aelwen could certainly look forward to.
~~~~

"For me, it was completely the opposite," Valiran said. "I spent hours sitting by myself, meditating, clearing my mind. It took me four months and it didn't happen until I was so incredibly busy and my mind was muddled."

"Gods, I don't have that much time," Aelwen said. "Isn't there some way you two could use your magic to, I don't know, extract mine?"

Valiran snorted. "That's ridiculous. No. It's all you."

"She's right," Marliza added. "Every single one of my people has a different story for how they discovered their magic. They're like snowflakes, not one is the same as the other."

Aelwen started. "Your *people*?" This was the same young woman who had just torn her to shreds for calling the Vatre-darah her people when, in a manner of speaking, they *were*. Hers to lead. Hers to save. Who did Marliza consider herself to rule?

"Yes, *my people*. I am an heir, I have thousands of people whose lives will all be by responsibility someday. Why do you think I am here training with Bailba, for the fun of it? I have a real future. I need to be a powerful leader, especially when the wave of this new world finally breaks. Whichever side wins this war, I must be prepared to lead my people through it."

"And whose side are you on?"

"Neither. Rhea is right."

Marliza's mouth quirked up when Aelwen cringed.

"It is time for the mages to rise. We deserve the world. Death is not the solution, though. She is wrong to go about it the way she chose to. War and bloodshed are not condoned by Parumans. If Rhea had at least tried to negotiate with your leaders, then I may be on her side. I cannot blame you—what do you call yourselves?"

"Vatre-darah."

"I cannot blame the Vatre-darah for how they have reacted. I would do the same if my people were so suddenly threatened. I am not on a side, but I am ready to survive no matter who wins."

"Wait, you said that Parumans do not support murder. Why does Rhea have so many followers, then?"

"I believe the answer is simple," Marliza explained. "I believe Rhea is simply making a promise to her followers. Whether she can keep that promise or not, no one knows. But it is enough."

"And what promise would that be?" asked Aelwen.

"A world of their own, where they do not have to hide anymore. That is such a glorious prize that her followers are willing to do anything for it."

"That's it? Promise and manipulation? No magical brainwashing or anything like that?"

Marliza barked a dark laugh. "You can't use magic to control anyone's mind. I thought Bailba had explained it all to you."

Aelwen went quiet, embarrassment seeping through her walls.

Valiran chimed in, "Honestly, I wouldn't be surprised if Rhea is the first mage to learn how to brainwash people. She's already accomplished so much so quickly. She's so young, that amount of mastery in that amount of time…it's unheard of. Who knows what she'll be capable of in ten years or twenty."

Aelwen scowled. "Assuming she lives that long."

"Right," Valiran said. "Though, I fear it will take the combined force of many master mages, a force we do not have. Bailba is one of the only master mages left."

"And what is a master mage?"

"A mage with full control and knowledge of all areas of magic."

"Oh. Bailba didn't mention that to me." Aelwen's heart sank. If Valiran, a true and trained mage who fully understood how magic actually worked, thought it would take a coalition of the best mages that existed to destroy Rhea, how could anyone expect Aelwen to be able to defeat Rhea after she had merely managed to harness her magic and demonstrate the barest control over it?

In an attempt to raise her spirits, Aelwen asked, "Exactly how many mages are there who have not joined the Hakmarres?"

"Twenty-three city-states out of the fifty-seven total." Marliza rattled the numbers off like a true stateswoman.

The number was less than what she'd hoped, but it was not a complete letdown. "Have any of these twenty-three attempted to stop her yet?"

"No," Valiran said. "Most have views like Marliza. All of them are afraid for their lives, for their world. If Rhea wins, they will have free reign of the world. If she loses, life goes back to the way it was. If they oppose her and she wins, death will find them and it will not be quick. I knew Rhea before she turned. When she was still just beginning to form this wretched plan of hers, she told me bits of it. She told me how she would punish the prisoners of war. Those thoughts still make me sick to this day."

Marliza swallowed. "It's wrong for us to use our powers like that against you. She is trying to terrify you into submission instead of making you understand the beauty of what we are. Rhea does not realize it, but she is feeding your hatred of us, making it harder for mages to be accepted back into the world, not easier."

Aelwen sighed. "When all of this is over, when Corova is restored to what it once was, I will do all in my power to make it a safe country for mages, for them to live amongst the non-mages without fear. I left my country to rebuild it as a place of equality and equality includes everyone."

CHAPTER TWENTY-ONE

The lands surrounding the cottage, once so green and vibrant, were gray and cold. The air had lost its humidity, the warm breezes were replaced by sharp, bitter winds.

When he'd first arrived in Marchia, Taran had thought it was a place of eternal paradise. Sparkling white sands and marvelous aquamarine waters that stretched on as far as the eye could see. Stunning beaches, vast, dense tropical forests and sprawling green valleys that he'd never considered would be the prey of winter winds and snowstorms. Yet there he stood, in the front door of his home, watching thick flakes falling from the slate colored sky and blanketing that breathtaking green in a layer of soft white.

There was a beauty to it, but he had known the stark, unforgiving beauty of winter for every year of his life. Upon leaving Corova, Taran had recognized that there would be few things he missed about his homeland, and winter would certainly not be one of them. He'd enjoyed thinking of the nights he'd spent huddled with Lysia in the freezing cold and the days he spent smashing ice for water and the hours long he'd spent shivering, tracking animals through the forest for so long he couldn't feel his limbs, as something of the past.

About a month ago, Taran had caught the scent of winter on the wind. He had dismissed it, thinking that it was just a smell borne from Corova by the winds. But as time went on, the scent became stronger, as did the winds, and then the snow began to fall.

He looked around at the village he was a part of. In a way, it felt strange to be part of a community again. In another way, it didn't. What *was* strange was the fact that he was one of the only able bodied people left in this village. The place could have been called a ghost town were it not for the disabled and the children and the elderly who could not fight in the war. They were the only ones left here now, other than Taran and a scant few other cowards.

While the war raged in every direction, this small, nameless village endured. Everyday, the people could see smoke rising from one direction or the other. Everyday, the people made their bread and did their laundry.

Yesterday, Eoren had asked Taran, "Why don't you fight in the war? Everyone else who can has gone to battle."

Taran had answered without a moment's hesitation. "I stay for you. If I left, who would look after you?"

Eoren did not seem to understand. She had listed the names of their neighbors and the old women down the street and the young lady in a wheelchair on the other side of the town. All townspeople Eoren had made friends with. Simple folk who loved simple things, none of whom were capable of fighting in the war.

"Go and fight, if you'd like," Eoren had said to him. "I won't mind. You like fighting, I know. Go on, it's okay, they can take care of me while you're away."

In response, Taran had only shaken his head. "I'll stay here with you," was all he'd said before the subject changed and they'd played in the yard and pretended they were the mythical creatures from Taran's stories.

Only now, as the conversation replayed in his mind, did Taran realize that he did not like fighting. He had, for a long time. But not anymore. He had no desire to harm or destroy, to relieve his own pain and anger. His only desire was to look after Eoren, to see her smile and grow and be safe. That was all he wanted from life.

~~~~

The three mages had hidden themselves somewhere among the trees. They waited, watching her, waiting for her to open and strike.

Aelwen reached out with her senses, trying to cast out a web of the magic she could feel tingling beneath her skin to detect who was where. But it would not come, so all she could do was wait and listen. She had fought all kinds of people in the arena but had never faced a camouflaging mage, let alone three of them. Bailba had decided it would be good to see if Aelwen's powers might reveal themselves under pressure.

A burst of power exploded behind Aelwen. With a stifled yelp, she rolled. Several blasts of color dropped from the sky, a whirlwind of magic swept towards her. Wits sharp as ever, Aelwen nimbly dodged the blasts and twisted away from the tornado of magic, letting the two devour each other. A wave of roaring magic rose and crashed down, suffocating Aelwen for the briefest moment.

Another wave crashed down upon her, then another. Unlike the others, this wave did not wash away. It remained, swirling around her as a treacherous multicolored whirlpool. Though the magic blurred her sight terribly, she could still see. It was becoming harder and harder to breathe trapped within the magic. There had to be a way out somewhere.

Magic, if you are really there, now would be a more than perfect time for you to show yourself.

Aelwen gave her magic a mere second to come out. When it did not, she took action herself. She had never relied on miracles before, now was not the time to start.

Her lungs stung. Running through magic was by no means an easy task, but when her life was on the line, her muscles came upon some unusual new strength.

When her body broke through the magic around her, Aelwen had all she could do not to drop the ground as a blessed woosh of oxygen poured into her lungs. She managed to cough just once before she was on the move again, weaving and bobbing as magic lashed out of nowhere, occasionally striking her flesh. She had no weapons, but her body knew, nevertheless, it was time to hunt down the mages and finish this. Her magic did not come
~~~~

when she was minutes away from death, it would not come today, not this way. It was time to put this to an end.

Two bolts of power flashed up from the ground at the same moment as several other soared at her, all from different directions. One of the blasts hit her clavicle. The only attention she gave the wound was a minor snort of pain. By now, it was clear which directions the attacks were coming from.

Aelwen let the attacks drive her to the left until she was directly between a triangle of trees. As she bowed under a purple streak of deadly power, she whirled around the farthest tree that formed the triangle and swung her fist.

Connection. The familiar snap of bones beneath her knuckles. The spectacular disguise of brown and green, all perfectly shaded, melted away, revealing the pale flesh of Valiran. Valiran's punched eye was already swelling and the new cut below it, made by the sheer impact of Aelwen's fist, was dripping blood that matched the color of her hair.

Aelwen hardly had time to see the miniature tornado of magic rising up behind her before it was digging into her skin like freshly sharpened knives. While Aelwen was caught in the storm, Valiran somehow managed to tolerate the pain and plant a firm driving kick in the small of Aelwen's back.

She felt her spine crack but not break. She gave the pain two seconds, no more, then, squinting through the whiteness of the power that surrounded her, she swung. She hit nothing. Valiran had struck from right there not moments before and now she was gone. The whirlwind fell away, melted and gone, replaced by a shimmering, opalesque wall. The wall expanded upwards. Before it was large enough to obscure her view, Aelwen sailed forward and launched her arm into an uppercut. *That was possibly one of the best chances I have ever taken,* Aelwen thought as Valiran's jaw popped and she spit a wad of blood and saliva onto the ground.

Six slices of magic flew at Aelwen, all hailing from the same direction. Aelwen crouched behind Valiran, who tossed up her own emerald shield to keep her safe from the attack. The magic hit the conjured shield and burst into multicolored sparks. Valiran took a step back, tripping over the Arenian who had been using her for protection the entire time. She lifted a foot to roundhouse Aelwen in the face, but the Arenian was too fast, on her feet in a flash with her arm wrapped around Valiran's airborne boot in the next. With a twist, Valiran was on the ground, more body parts throbbing at once than ever before.

Aelwen threw herself at the place where all of the slices had come from. Before she made contact, Marliza flickered into view with both hands raised, color swirling before her palms, ready to be released. The magic flew. It was a careless attack, Marliza's intent was to frighten, not actually harm and she was most definitely not prepared for a counter attack. Aelwen arched her back, lowering herself in a limbo position. As soon as the attack passed by her, she sprang upward and wrapped her arms tightly around Marliza, locking her in. She drove her chin into a sensitive pressure point just above Marliza's shoulder blade, instantly crippling her.

One remained. A deafening howl erupted from the sky, as if the heavens themselves had been split open. A cloud of magic dark as the night sky gathered over Aelwen. Purple and golden streaks of magic struck down all around her, forming a cage. This was a prison she could not break out of. Aelwen touched one of the cracking bars and a severe jolt raced through her. She could have sworn that her heart stopped for a split second. There was no escape. The cloud gave a deep rumble and it's center began swirling, blue and violet light blending together. A final, ending strike was coming and there was no getting away this time. In her last desperate moments, Aelwen considered throwing herself out through the bars of magic, but she knew that they would kill her just as this final attack would.

Death is here.

A light brighter than any possible afterlife she had ever imagined stung her retinas. Then there was blackness. No feeling, no scent, no emotion. Emptiness. Blurbs of quick moving light flickered in the darkness. They seemed surreal. A vision, perhaps the cloak of death was sliding away and the gods were there to take her.

Everything came back into focus, though the colors were vaguely distorted. Bailba stood there, cane in hand, an unreadable expression on her sagging face. Valiran and Marliza were both on their feet, each without a single scratch or bruise. The forest looked perfectly normal, not a sign of the chaos that had just happened. Bailba's cloud was gone, so was the magical prison she had created. Everything was normal.

Confused, with only one question in her that mattered, Aelwen asked, "Did I—"

"No," Bailba snapped. "All of those final theatrics were my work. I had to make you believe that it was your end. I thought for sure that it would work. Fighters like you are so good that they learn to forget the threat, combat is almost fun for them. They always have something on their minds while they're fighting because the motions are so natural that they don't need to concentrate. I thought if I could make you remember how real death was, if I could make you let it all go, empty yourself and accept that, your magic might show itself. I am wrong, and so the world will pay."

Bailba stomped off, disappearing into the shadows of the wood. Marliza and Valiran cast glances at Aelwen.

"You were fantastic," Valiran said as Aelwen took a seat in the fresh, pure grass, untainted by war.

"I hardly think so," breathed Aelwen.

"Old women can be just as angsty as teenagers. Bailba has her moments. She will be over it tomorrow with a new perspective. It will be like this never happened. Try to forget it did."

Aelwen offered no response. Bailba's admonishment had dug in deeper than any remark Galarus had abused her with. The pain was dreadful, but what really bothered her was why it hurt so very much when she had endured so many scathing reprimands in her time .

"Stop being soft," Marliza scolded Valiran. She turned her attention to Aelwen, "You need to try harder if you really want to save the world. Or anyone at all."

~~~

Iowan stomped on the frozen stream, cracking the thin layer of ice so she had access to the water below. Crouching, she cupped her hands and splashed water on her face,
~~~

clearing away the blood and grime from the latest battle. One of the Hakmarres had nicked her cheek, but other than that, she had emerged virtually unscathed.

Behind her, the war camp bustled with life. Supper was being assembled around the fire, the just-returned warriors saw to their wounds, General Ekua discussed battle strategies with Captain Nayre and President Tecsequaih and those who had not participated in the battle spent their time practicing so that they would be ready for the next confrontation.

Scrubbing away the dirt caked beneath her fingernails, Iowan rose and made her way to the heart of the camp, getting as close to the fire as she could. The water from the stream may not have been frozen, but it carried the intensity of the ice in every droplet.

Soon, the food was fully cooked and ready to serve. Accepting her bowl of mush that tasted much better than it looked, Iowan took a seat on the cold ground and began eating. As usual, after getting her own dinner, Lysia joined her. She had a bandage wrapped around her bronze forearm, already bloodstained.

With her spoon, Iowan gestured to Lysia's wound from the day's battle. "How's your arm?"

"Not too bad. It stings, but it looks worse than it feels. I can still hold a sword, that's all that matters."

"True," said Iowan, shoveling another spoonful into her mouth.

"I still can't believe it, you know?"

"Being stabbed in the arm?"

Lysia huffed a laugh. "Being part of a war. An actual war. When I was little I would play war with my friends. We'd use sticks as swords and each side would wear different color bandanas. I always thought it would be so amazing to be a real warrior, with armor and swords, the whole lot."

"I thought the same thing." She paused to swallow. "I'm not sure I've ever been more wrong about anything in my life."

"Me neither," Lysia confessed quietly, staring into her bowl. A quiet that was not uncomfortable formed between them. It was the sort of quiet that could only be shared by two people sharing the same trying experience, both constantly suffering, neither able to put their pain into words.

The quiet went on until the scrapping of their spoons against the bottoms of their bowls was the only sound. Scooping up the dregs of her supper, Lysia broke the quiet.

"Listen, Iowan, I know it's been hard for you. You've been through so much, I can't even imagine. You are *so* strong. I know that no one can be strong all the time, so, if you ever need to just let your guard down and talk to someone, I'm here, okay?"

Iowan stilled. She had not been expecting Lysia to speak, especially not to say something like that. "Okay," she said, because she didn't know what else to say. She figured the usual appropriate response would be to say something along the lines of 'and I'll always be here for you, too' but she couldn't make a promise like that. Not right now. Lysia was right, she was fighting with a lot of demons. Until her own were slain, she would not be taking on those of another.

Through her years in the arena, Iowan had learned that, in order to survive, she had to put herself first, always. When it had been decided that she, Aelwen and Namar would flee

Corova, she had planned to put others before herself for the first time in her adult life. She would be safe in Marchia, so she could focus on helping the people of Corova. But then that Guildsman had dragged her off the side of *Mist Wing* and she'd watched, a bloody mess, from the Corovan harbor as the vessel sailed out to sea and from then on her only concern had been herself.

Iowan had never looked out for anyone but herself and she wasn't sure she knew how. She certainly wasn't ready to, so she kept her mouth shut and watched as Lysia nodded, an inscrutable expression on her fine face, and walked away to rinse out her bowl in the stream.

~~~~

The morning light didn't wake Aelwen until almost noon, which was not something she had a problem with. She was still rattled by the harsh words the mages had thrown at her yesterday afternoon. That had been her second bout of training, most mages had to practice for years before they gained their powers, let alone learned how to control them. But she didn't have years, or even months. If this war turned suddenly, if the Hakmarres decided to use their powers in battle again, everyone could be dead before she so much as tapped into her abilities.

What if this was all for naught? What would she do if the Hakmarres won and took over and everyone she had ever known was dead and gone, buried not in a grave but in a field of blood?

The sunlight soaking into her feather-stuffed blanket was plenty warm enough, yet she wrapped herself still tighter in her soft cocoon. Perhaps this political life had softened her more than she had realized. She was an Arenian, she indulged in pain and cruelty, she showed mercy to none and never let that curtain of steel that covered her true self be lifted. When had she gone from having that as her creed to hiding in blankets, afraid to face the day because an old woman and a mage-heir had spit knives at her?

Aelwen travelled down two floors, connected by unnecessary spiral staircases that would have saved time and work had they been straight like normal stairs. This entire fortress was truly unnecessary, as a matter of fact. No one needed to live in a hollowed out tree decorated with floating lights and spiral stairs with flowers and vines growing in through the windows. Let alone a grouchy old woman who lived by herself, except for a few young people, who she spent all of her time bossing around and criticizing.

Aelwen scanned the room. Everything about it was normal, in the same place it had been since the day she had arrived, except there was only one person in it: herself. There was not the slightest trace of any of the other mages. For once, she actually wanted them to be there. Valiran, at least. She was the only one who had shown Aelwen a bit of kindness yesterday.

"No need to look so frightened."

Aelwen whirled, fists up, taking on an immediate fighting stance. She loosened immediately as she saw it was only Bailba, standing at the doorway she had not been in a moment ago. She sighed with relief. "Where are Valiran and Marliza?"

"Away."

"How very specific."
~~~~

"They are training in Havon, Marliza's town. She went to visit her family and took Valiran with her."

"Of her own accord?"

Bailba huffed. "No."

Aelwen waited for a few moments to see if Bailba would offer a further explanation. The hag began searching through the marble and jade cupboards for some ingredient or another and stopped paying any ounce of attention to her trainee who, in Aelwen's opinion, deserved all of the attention Bailba had to give.

"Why did you send them away?"

Though her crooked back was to Aelwen, it was clear by the way her silver hair moved that Bailba was nodding. "Good lass. If you want answers in times like these, you must not be afraid to ask outright. Don't waste whatever life you have left dancing around the tough questions." She took down a glass bowl of white powder and continued. "You were not accessing your magic with them here. I thought you might if they were not."

"Ah."

Due to Bailba's arched back, it was easy for Aelwen to look right over her shoulder. "What are you making?"

Bailba took two spoonfuls of the powder and put it into a separate dish. She set two things that looked like aquamarine pearls into a bit of the white powder. After adding two droplets of a blue liquid, she said, "Things of destruction."

Why were all of her answers so annoyingly simple? There were plenty of people in Aelwen's life who she wished would learn to talk less, but the one person who she wanted to give her detailed explanations only ever responded in a few words.

"Why?" The question made her feel like a child.

"I saw the war last night. It has worsened, both sides are struggling. Let's say that your beloved Vatre-darah have lost much of their darah."

The crude joke made Aelwen shiver. "How bad is it? Is there any way I can see?"

Bailba scooped some of the strange concoction out of the bowl and packed it into an empty nut shell. "You will see once you have mastered everything you came here to do."

Images of terror filled Aelwen's mind. A mashup of blood and fire and darkness without any clear objects, only horror and loss. She gasped suddenly, pushing down something that she had locked within her strongest vault. She let herself remember that certain thing in bits and pieces, here and there, when she needed it, but never since her old self had been murdered had she ever fully opened that catacomb.

Choking on her words as she forced them back to whence they had come, Aelwen said, pointing to the nut shells, "What will this do?"

The mage had filled both halves of the nut shell. She squished them together, holding them like that for a few moments before letting go. The two halves of the nut stuck together like a whole. Bailba whacked the nut with her spoon to test its endurance. It did not split.

"It will explode," she explained.

"Couldn't that do more harm than good? On the field, both sides are all crammed together, you will harm one side just as bad as the other, it will do nothing to stop the war."

"It will do great harm if not placed correctly."

The crone packed and put together three mcre nut shells. "These are called Kula nuts. They grow only in the heart of summer. Very hearty and, as you can see," she banged the third nut on the counter. Just like the other two, it did not crack. "Very durable." She put the nuts in a dish with a lid, and slipped it to the back of a cabinet where it was surely safe from any prying eyes, nothing but a tiny dish of sugar or salt.

"Come," Bailba ordered, picking up her cane. "Let's get some fresh air."

Out in the forest, Bailba took a seat on the vibrant forest floor, getting down with more ease than anyone would have expected from such an old woman. Unsure what else to do, Aelwen joined her.

Bailba propped her walking stick at the base of a nearby tree and explained, "A big part of harnessing magic for most is learning to let go. In order to let go, you must first accept."

What is she talking about? Is she going to acknowledge what happened yesterday?

"Your past haunts you because you turn away from it. For all of your strength, you turn your back on the part of your life that is so essential to who you are. You must accept all of who you are, even the ugly parts, if you ever want to reach your full potential."

Bailba crossed her legs like a hill-dwelling monk. With her long, flowing garb and wise, old face, it was not hard to imagine her being a yogi. She crossed her arms tranquilly in her lap. "I will tell you my story first. When you open up, it should be because you want to, not because I am forcing you to."

Like I would ever want to do this, thought Aelwen. Before she could think anymore, color exploded in her mind as her vision of her instructor's face was wiped away and replaced with a vivid image of a time long ago. As Bailba spoke, the image moved, like some strange animation that Bailba was narrating.

"I was a young mage. Full of myself, full of life."

A girl who could not have been any older than Aelwen herself stood in the center of her gaze. She was short and lean, with mature features, blowing dark hair and a determined look on her face.

"I had a teacher, just like I am yours. Back then, we were all taught that magic and duty came before our own personal emotions. I spent much of my free time flying over other countries, watching people."

That was definitely not one of the most bizarre things Aelwen had ever heard.

Sure enough, right before her, the young mage drifted into the air and began sailing along, blown on her own course by an invisible breeze.

"My favorite place to be was Corova."

Hovering in the sky, the young woman looked down upon a land that Aelwen hardly remembered. It was Corova, but not like she had known for more than a decade. It was buzzing with life, people of all trades filled the streets, laughing and bantering. There was an array of color more mesmerizing than that which filled the streets of Marchia.

"My trainer knew, of course. Trainers always find out some way or another. He told me I had to stop spying."

Back in the dense green woodland of Paruma, the young woman stood before a tall brunette man who, although whatever words he yelled were silent, was clearly furious with his student.

"If I fought with my teacher, he would know exactly how angry I was and would ensure there was no way for me to escape again, so I took the punishment without retort. Not an easy thing for me to do."

While the man yelled, the young woman hung her head, her lips did not move. The scene shifted, growing suddenly dark. The girl rose up into the air, wrapped in a blanket of blackness and starlight. As she began to drift along, her body melted out of sight and became one with the night all around her.

"I flew to Corova in the night under the protection of a powerful cloaking spell. Once I was there, I pretended to be without magic and got to know the people I had been stalking. One of them in particular I became very close with."

The black night and the cloaking spell drifted away, revealing the same girl with a rebel smile stretching across her face standing in the lively streets of Corova, the morning sun making her grin all the more radiant. A series of images flashed before Aelwen's eyes. The young woman and a young man. Them together, sitting on a city roof, in a restaurant, in a field. The images sped up so that she could not tell one from another.

"We got married and had a child."

Try as she might to focus, the scenes were simply too quick for Aelwen to understand any more than Bailba had just told her. Why could she not see this part of her mentor's life? Was it because Bailba could not show it to her or because she did not want to?

"When my instructor found out, he made me come back to Paruma. As punishment, he filled me with all the knowledge of the elders. At such a young age, all of that information was dangerous because it was so impossibly overwhelming and difficult to sort out. I was constantly confused and I had severe headaches that lasted too long. They felt like burning knives cutting into my brain. I tried with everything I had to conjure a time slowing spell, but the information was too jumbled. I had a harder and harder time controlling my magic. I was so afraid of hurting someone. Anyone. Myself. What friends I had left. I had my instructor finish off the spell. I was able to take as much time as I needed to make sense of all of the information. I lived in a world that was slower than anyone else's. It was my very own world, with me alone as its inhabitant. Over time, too many years to count, I processed all of the information and mastered all of the different sorts of magic. That is why I am so old even though I only ran away from my people about twenty years ago."

None of the images made sense anymore, they were no more than whorls of color that were making her sick. The colors faded and the real world came back into view. There sat Bailba, just like before, watching Aelwen calmly, waiting for her to open up.

Aelwen took a breath that quaked more than she meant it to. It was talking, just talking. Nothing to be afraid of.

She knew what Bailba was asking for. When someone asked, she gave. When Galarus asked for more grit, more energy, she gave it to him. When the evil look in her opponent's eyes begged her to beat them, she did. When she even tried to get the words into her throat, her gut tightened. Her body was shouting 'no!' at her, the same thing she had yelled at it so many times within those first treacherous years when the memories tried to be stronger than her will to keep them down. They had never succeeded, not once. Now it was time to release what she had left to rot in the dark for so long.

"I—" her breath hitched. One word was out. That was something.

"I was walking with my parents." She shoved the words out in a rush. They had become so accustomed to their gloomy, lonely hole that they did not want to come out.

"Ma was holding my hand. Her fingers were thin. They had soot on them. She had just come home from helping our neighbor, a blacksmith."

Aelwen felt a brush of warmth on her knuckles, serene yet filled with power. Her mind whirled back in time at the sensation. She was young again, with a mind of purity and a tall, dark-skinned mother standing right beside her. Hand in hand they walked. She squeezed her eyes shut and forced herself out of the memory. To speak it was painful enough, to relive it was unbearable.

"Da was on Ma's other side. He had had a haircut two days earlier. Ma's scissors slipped when she was doing it so he had a funny cut in the front."

A steady stream of snot ran down her lips. With an unsuspected sob, the gateway opened and her tears ran freely. They were a river of sorrow, the only thing left in a world that had been stripped of goodness.

"We were all going to the farmer's market to look around. When we were a block away, Da handed me two copper coins. He told me, 'those are yours to spend on whatever you like.'"

Aelwen fell back into her mind again and there she was, so small and weak, a little thing with still-round cheeks and smooth flesh that had never felt a stab or punch. Her mother was wearing a close fitting, one-shouldered shirt and a skirt. Together the two clothing items made her mother look like a walking sunrise, which was not at all a poor comparison to the way Aelwen saw her. Then there was her father, short for a man, with dusty hair and a teal jacket. Da had always loved color, especially blues and greens. He said they reminded him of the seas he had sailed with his family as a child. She felt the roundness and coolness as Da set the coins in her hand.

No, I have to get out of here.

When she wretched herself out this time, she was sure that she had wretched her heart out, too. Aelwen did not cover her face as she sobbed into the warm air. All these years, she had been nothing but a vessel for a massive creature of sorrow that she had kept locked in an impenetrable cage. She had not seen it, so she pretended it was not there. She was paying for that mistake now and she had hardly begun. There was still so much more old grief that had to be set free.

"The market was so busy. I loved it. There were people from all over the world who spoke with accents I could barely understand. Ma held one of my hands, Da held the other. They couldn't bear the thought of losing me." *I never really thought about how horrid it would be if I lost them.*

"We looked at all sorts of things. Things I'd never seen before." *And I remember them all perfectly to this day.* "Everything my parents wanted to buy was too expensive and we didn't really need anything anyway. I got a wooden toy sword."

Aelwen paused and sucked in a breath. Through the rains of sadness and its choking winds, she went on. "Ma loved physical exercise. She was always telling me how important it was to stay healthy. Da was a good storyteller, my favorite ones were always about the heroes and demons. With the sword, I thought I could learn to move like Ma to be just like my favorite heroes from Da's stories."

She coughed and spit onto the ground. With a sigh like that of a god who may have breathed to produce the clouds, Aelwen began again. She let the tears take their course but kept her voice as firm as possible as she finished.

"At the end of the day, my parents felt, since we had walked all the way to the market and would have to go all the way back, that it was foolish to take such a long trip and have nothing to show for it but a wooden play sword. They decided we should get a family portrait done.

"The artist was kind. She was really short and kept making jokes about her own height." Aelwen ran an arm across her nose. "I thought that was really brave, to have such confidence in yourself that you could talk badly about your own body and still not let it bother you. I got bored very quickly, so she was nice and painted me first. I went into her back room and practiced with my new sword. I only did that for a little while, I didn't like being without Ma or Da. So, I went back and danced around them while the nice artist lady painted. I made weird noises and silly faces to try to make them laugh. The painter didn't mind at all, or if she did, she was so nice that she never yelled at me once." A choked giggle escaped Aelwen, to her surprise. "I must have been being an absolute pain in her rear.

"She finished, though. I was tired from the day full of walking, but we still had to wait for the paint to dry. She let us come up and have dinner with her while we waited. She gave us the food for free. It was… it was really good food. She used spices I'd never had before.

"She told us how she lived alone to focus on her work and how she loved the life she lived, even though she was freezing every winter and had ended up living on the streets twice after leaving her family to follow her passion. I wish I had known her name. Da and Ma liked her too, but I think they thought that she was strange for living how she did. I bet, if they had more time to get to know each other, she and Ma would have gotten to be friends.

"We got the painting. Before we left, the artist invited my family to come and visit whenever we were around. I wonder if we would have if we ever had the chance.

"The painting was great. It was like the family portraits the royal families had done. I wasn't excited about it until I saw the end result. I'll never understand how artists do what they do. It was like looking in a mirror, but better. I had on a purple shirt with white embroidery and white pants. You could barely see my pants in the painting, though. I always wondered if that was on purpose. I was a child, I know my pants were no longer pristine white by the time we were getting the portrait done."

Aelwen could not believe her own ears as she heard herself laugh again. It was not bawdy, it was a small noise, hardly a chuckle, but it was natural in every way.

"By the time we were back at home, I was full of energy. It was one of those times when you are so tired that your body goes hyper and gives you way too much energy. Da was exhausted, so he went off to bed. Ma said she wasn't tired either, but I think she was, she just didn't want to deal with me bouncing around while she tried to sleep.

"She took the handle off the broomstick and I used my new sword. We dueled in the living room. It wasn't long before my excess energy was all worn off. I bet we weren't playing for more than twenty minutes, but that is my favorite memory. Of anyone, anytime. I finally got to be that hero, and when I did, the one who watched me, so full of pride and newfound strength and silly childish excitement, was my mother, the woman who was my everything. I loved Da, he was my best friend in the world, but Ma, she was more than a friend and more than a mother. She was anything I had ever learned or loved."

Anyone who knew a smidge about Aelwen knew the rest. There was nothing left to say, only despair.

Aelwen dissolved. The gods seemed to be replenishing her tears and pulling every last bit of sadness she had ever felt out of her soul. She was doing so much more than crying. She was feeling. Feeling every pain she had ever pushed away as it left her. The pain sliced her heart open with a serrated blade of misery and ripped open every wall she had built up. The melancholy swelled in her throat and eyes, obscuring her senses with no more than keen memory and agony whose force had only multiplied over time.

Aelwen's body had been a temple of resilience that was now shaking and crumbling in on itself as it's base fractured from the earthquake of innumerable sadness.

CHAPTER TWENTY- TWO

"**W**ill you keep me safe?" Eoren sobbed, clutching herself to Taran. She didn't want to fight anymore because now, the war was real and she was afraid.

The former woodsman sat on the child's bed, the child beside him, holding tight to him while she cried.

In the distance, the sky was stained black with smoke. The Hakmarres had broken their promise. They used magic ruthlessly. The latest victim of the mages was a village a few miles north of where Taran and Eoren lived. If the fast-spreading news was to be believed, the Hakmarres had used magic to destroy the village and then proceeded to burn it to the ground.

We're safe here.

That's what he'd told Eoren.

We're safe here.

Now, she was crying and shaking, her face buried into the crook of his arm.

We're safe, he'd told her, and now the danger was mere miles away. How long until it reached them?

Taran had lied to the child once. He refused to do so again. He also refused to make a promise he could not guarantee he would keep.

"I'll try."

No child should lose their family. No child should watch their home burn. No child should be trapped in the midst of a war they were powerless to fight. Whatever scraps of hope and goodness remained in Eoren, Taran vowed in that moment that he would not let them be destroyed.

~~~

The Weeper. That was what Aelwen had decided to call herself. For days, she had done nothing but wander the forest by herself, lost in thought and memories, each new one that she accepted caused a brand new wave of anguish. She was sure that her tear ducts had access to the well of depression within her, where they drew out the sorrow and transformed it into tear drops.
~~~

Aelwen did not walk alone because no one would come with her, all of the mages were back and every one of them had offered more than once to accompany her. Once, the first time Valiran asked, she accepted. Perhaps company, the reminder that life and power still existed, would prevent every thought that fluttered in her head from being one of loss. She had been wrong. Valiran's presence did not help at all, it added shame to all of the horrifying things she was feeling. In front of Bailba, ripping herself open had felt natural. In front of Valiran, if felt anything but. No way was she ever going to let the ice cold Marliza accompany her any day. So, she was alone. Strolling, standing, breathing, sobbing.

Bailba said that by accepting her past, by realizing it and letting go of it, Aelwen would feel some great weight removed from her life. The only thing that Aelwen felt was pain and heartache deeper than any sea she had sailed.

After the torment, frustration began to swell. Frustration at herself. She had spent much too long weeping over what was done and over. Aelwen had let all of it out, she had felt all of those torturous feelings, she had submerged herself in them, spent time with them, gotten to know them better than she had known some of her fellow Arenians. She should be able to move on, to begin whatever the next step of this bizarre process was. Yet, all she wanted to do was walk around aimlessly, ignoring everything and keeping to herself.

After several days of longing to be out of the gloom, Aelwen knew that since she was ready to move on, this stage was over. The only problem was how to move on. She had found that it was more than arduous to pull out all of the terrible emotions, but once they were released and were all that occupied her mind, it was just as strenuous to get back out of her own mind.

Aelwen lived in her mind for one more day. She sat by a babbling brook she had discovered in her travels, dipping her fingertips into the chilly water. She closed her eyes and entered her soul again. Despair was all there was, a jagged maze of darkness that she could not find a way out of.

Once an Arenian, always an Arenian. An Arenian never stopped fighting. Aelwen would do what she had always done. Keep fighting. She opened her eyes and gazed at a leaf twirling in the breeze. She focused on its beauty, its simplicity. Then, in her mind's eye, she saw the leaf begin to crumble to ashes. She shifted her vision to the stream with its small gray pebbles, each from a different source. Was one of those from the northern mountains, was one from a cliff on the coast of Ave? What stories could those pebbles tell? Aelwen had played in a brook just like this one with her father when she was little. They would splash around together, chasing after fish. She'd had a rock collection, a bunch of the prettiest pebbles from the creek bottom.

It was impossible. Everything she would ever see for the rest of her life would remind her of the grand life she had lived with the divine parents she had once had.

Aelwen watched Bailba give tips to Valiran and Marliza who were about to begin practicing a new exercise. The crone finished talking, the girls faced each other. In the blink of an eye, Bailba was beside Aelwen again. Without a word from either of them, Aelwen followed Bailba into the woods. Bailba was the first to break the easy silence.

"I am proud of you. More proud than you can ever know. To do what you have done and not lose yourself completely… it is phenomenal. You may not think it right now, but you have strength that rivals that of Rhea and her army."

"Thank you. Now, I need to know… what is the next step?"

"For you to fully understand what I have just told you."

Aelwen blinked once and then Bailba was gone. What an ever-so-helpful old mage she was.

Fighting was her first instinct. She could not see a reason why fighting this would not work. This cocoon of bitterness was her enemy and it was up to her and her alone to vanquish it. If her body refused to move on of its own volition, then she would make it.

Aelwen awoke the next morning with a wide grin. She hummed as she prepared for whatever the day held and savored the food that Bailba had cooked for breakfast. She would not get another lesson or tip until she had solved this puzzle. Recalling her first days of freedom, as she had sprinted through the wild woodland with Iowan and Namar, she decided to try running.

The muscles within every inch of her burned. Throwing herself to the ground, Aelwen hacked up a wad of bile. She dragged herself to the riverside and tossed herself into the water. The coolness was a blessing upon her blazing skin. The icy water continued on, flowing over her sweat-soaked body, adding another layer of water to her sweat-soaked clothes. The water babbled on, its mellow tune uninterrupted by the obstacle that had just splashed down into it.

Aelwen counted as she lay there, sucking in waves of crisp air and relishing every drop of freezing liquid that drifted onto her body. Twenty-three minutes. Then, sopping and still tired, Aelwen scaled a nearby tree. The tree was not a terribly easy climb, but it was all worth it once her head broke through the canopy. A new wave of fridigness washed over her face. She felt her hairs stand on end at the blast of unexpected cold. To the north, in a world that had not seen magic for so long, winter was beginning. There in Paruma, the sun still kept them all wrapped in its warm embrace, not a single tree had dropped its leaves. Paruma and the other countries were so very different, maybe their time was different too.

Her eyes could only see so far, but it was enough. She spotted the mountains she had crossed to come to Paruma, tiny gray specks smaller than her fingernails from this distance. There was a clear divide between the countries that, although they shared a continent, were almost like separate worlds. A distinct line seemed to run between Paruma and southern Marchia, bright green on one side, brown and gray on the other.

How were the Vatre-darah fairing? Which of her friends were still alive? What in the world was happening with Namar, the forgotten traitor-prisoner? Was Lin okay? That man had so much to him, locked away within himself, that she yearned to know. Were Iowan and Lysia both still as alive and determined as when she had last seen them? President Tecsequaih, how was his army doing? When had General Fayette led the last attack? Was the courageous warrior even still alive? Were any of them?

Aelwen enjoyed the breeze and the tremendous view for a few more minutes, then descended the tree and began the trek home.

By the time Aelwen entered the clearing and saw the gargantuan tree rising up before her that was her temporary dwelling, night was casting its sheet over the world. That did not at all seem to bother Valiran, Marliza, or Bailba who were working together to conjure a series of floating glimmering lights. A table and benches, a fire pit complete with a roaring fire and bowls and plates that they bustled about to fill with food.

Aelwen's mouth extended into a foolishly large smile. She could feel how ridiculous it was to force this happiness, but it was her best shot. Actually, if she really thought about it, some of the horrors that had swam around in her brain this morning as she had faked her way joyously through breakfast seemed to have diminished, maybe even vanished.

"What is all of this?" she asked Valiran as the mage set down a bowl full of greens.

"Food," smirked the mage.

Aelwen grinned, it was not as phony as the other ones had been, but it was by no means an easy thing to do.

"We decided to make dinner a little more exciting tonight. We've all been here for weeks, doing the same things day after day. Bailba said that it was time to change things up a bit, even if it's only for one night."

Bailba came out of the tree and placed a hunk of meat on the table so large that it occupied two plates.

Aelwen gazed at it in wonder, her stomach immediately grumbling. "What is that?"

"Racken thigh," explained the crone before she hurried back into the treehouse to grab another dish.

Aelwen hadn't the slightest clue what a Racken was, but it looked like it gave off a serious portion of deliciousness.

The food was beyond anything she had ever tasted in her life. Every scrap of fat and stalk was more delectable than any food she had eaten, even at the political dinners concocted by some of the world's most highly esteemed cooks.

As she chewed, savoring every drop of juice from the meat, Aelwen said, "You magicked this food, don't lie." bailba had told her that food couldn't be conjured, but this food tasted so unlike anything she'd ever tasted that she failed to believe it.

Marliza's already hard glare turned to freezing flame as Aelwen used that insulting word.

"No," Bailba chuckled, letting Aelwen's slip of the tongue slide. "We hunted and grew it all."

"Where? I've been here for weeks and have never seen a garden."

"I have a place of my own to the west. I go there to gather food once every several months."

"Spill your secrets," Aelwen demanded, relishing a bite of a pink flower dipped in a creamy orange sauce.

"Only the old ones get this knowledge," Bailba's face quirked up a bit, a gesture that Aelwen, the only one there who really knew Bailba's story, would understand.

Eager to keep talking, to stay standing on this cloud of bliss she had suddenly found, Aelwen refused to let the conversation drop. She struck it up again, gearing her question at Valiran. The steel flesh Marliza had made for herself still shone on her cheeks and it was not something Aelwen wanted to look at while she was consuming the greatest meal of her life.

"Marliza is an heir, I know, but why are you here?"

Valiran smiled and shrugged. The way she smiled, the way her mouth tilted up just a little and she showed her teeth, reminded Aelwen of Iowan. "I needed training."

Aelwen threw her a look that needed no words. *Only the most skilled, best of the best, important mages get sent to Bailba.*

Valiran added with another easy shrug, "I was talented. Mages aren't like humans, we don't require money and status to get the attention we deserve. Here, raw talent is enough."

The words stung, although by Valiran's even tone it was clear that she had not meant to cause any harm.

To keep the words from biting her anymore, Aelwen immediately followed up, "What are you here training for specifically?"

"Originally, I was here for performance purposes. I want to learn how to put on amazing magic shows. Ever since Rhea's turn and the start of the war, I've been spending all of my time on combat training."

"From what I've seen, you're doing really good." It felt good to compliment someone.

Out of the blue, Marliza piped up. "Do any of you mind if I get some music going? The quietness isn't working for me."

No one protested, but Aelwen could not help herself from bursting out stupidly, "You can conjure music?" No one had mentioned that.

Marliza gave a devious smile and pursed her lips at Aelwen's ridiculous question. "Yes." The mage's word was drier than Aelwen's throat after that day's sprint.

Sure enough, a rhythm filled the air. It was disconnected at first, the notes took their time weaving themselves together, becoming an inspiring symphony. How the mages molded the earth power within them to create magic, she hadn't the slightest idea.

As the music grew in volume, the old legends crept into Aelwen's mind, she recalled all of the strange things that she had convinced herself were only rumors about the Parumans.

"I was told that an eerie music filled the air of Paruma, that it was unnatural and hypnotizing, the Parumans would entrance you with it and then murder you."

Bailba ignored the sentence entirely, thoroughly focused on devouring a round, blue fruit. Valiran and Marliza, on the other hand, both had distinct reactions. Marliza's countenance was even tighter and angrier than usual and Valiran was shaking her head.

The fiery haired mage laughed without humor. "Not all of what you heard was false then."

While Valiran thought that the notion was utterly stupid, Marliza appeared deeply offended.

"All art forms are treasured by us. We worship the earth and the land that has been so generous as to provide us a home. Our music is a way of connecting us with it. Tell me, Arenian, what other rumors have you heard?"

Aelwen shook her head and said no more. Things were just beginning to get a little bit better and then she had gone and ruined them all over again.

"I may have never left Paruma in my lifetime, but I know enough about the crude lies spread by your people. You are still so new here, let us correct and inform the error of your people. Indulge us."

With a heavy sigh and every eye at the table on her, Aelwen explained. "My people say that you put rings in your body for every life you take and paint yourselves with the blood of those you have murdered. I've heard that your temples are made of bones and that your language is uncivilized, all grunts and screeches. They say that you wear little clothing because you have a strange obsession with bodies."

"Is that all?" Marliza's entire face had turned to glimmering silver steel.

"Yes, those are the things that everyone believes about you."

"Do you?"

The words came like arrows that Aelwen easily dodged. "Not anymore."

Marliza emitted a noise that was a mixture of an exasperated sigh and a growl. "Since I *am* an heir, I suppose it would make the most sense for me to correct all of those idiotic misconceptions. The shama who are the priests and worshippers who live by themselves and spend their lives trying to interact with the spirits do have piercings, 'body rings' as you called them. Each ring represents a spiritual encounter. The shama with the most rings is the Shalo, the high shama, even more revered than a priest. The rings are mined from a Garnre, a sacred pool that the spirits are said to have ascended from.

"The body paint is worn on nights of celebration and yes, it is red, the color of passion, strength, radiance and determination. The paint comes from the Ekunu, a tree that was the first species ever to grow that gave birth to the first mages, hence the reason our blood too is red.

"The temples of bones are no more than lies. Even the temple of the Shalo is simple, made of natural resources, decorated with plants. Fortune is not the way to connect with the spirits, as your people think it is, and neither is death. The language, as you have no doubt learned, is also just another lie. We all speak the same language, the exact same one as you. Clothing and bodies probably came about because in the dead heat of summer we do indeed wear very little clothing and that is because with it many of us would constantly be fainting. I also might add that we are not ashamed of our bodies, nor do we think of them as items of humor and sexuality. Our bodies are works of art, sculpted with care by the spirits, each for its own purpose, and by showing our bodies openly, we are showing the spirits that we are proud of what they have created."

Aelwen nodded. It all made complete sense. Her people were morons. Her people. Their people. Weren't they all just people? "It is so deranged. The only thing that separates our people is magic. Not even that, anymore, once I have harnessed my power. If I have magic in my blood because of my heritage, surely others must too. We are all humans. I will never understand how the hatred arose in the first place. The ordinary people did not fear you, they simply grew to hate you."

Valiran shook her head solemnly as she stared into her lap. Marliza continued to explain, her voice ground like stone on stone. "It was overexposure. Mages were very popular, so many people hired them for events, for work. Ordinary people had enough of magic after a few decades. It didn't entertain them anymore and since there was no more money to be made, mages had to be gotten rid of to bring in the next big trend. The governments slandered us and the people followed suit, believing every lie that was spoon-fed to them. Our banishment was not anything like the reason you left your country, so don't try to compare them. This was not one corrupt administration, it was all of them. All of the people, too. Soon, it was all of the world against us, and there was no way for us to win without paying a terrible price. If we'd wanted to keep our power so badly, we could have fought against the people and started the war that is happening as we speak right now. But we had respect, we did not want to kill. So here is where we are, trapped in our own world."

Aelwen set down her glass and pushed her plate to the side. She raised her voice the way she would to address a training unit of the Vatre-darah. She stood up and put one foot on her chair.

"Hatred, prejudice and separation have gone on for too long in this world. When this war is over and the world is restored with the Hakmarres nothing more than a memory, the mages shall be welcomed back into the world!" Aelwen thrust her fist into the air and stepped onto the table, nudging the dishes out of the way and taking up a defiant stance in the center. "The borderline will be shattered and every human in this world will recognize the beauty of every other person they share this world with!"

All of the mages clapped. Even Marliza smiled a tiny bit. The dream was outrageous, but didn't all of the most amazing feats of history start out as outrageous ideas?

A brilliant melody of hope and power filled the air all around them. Blood filled their bodies, flesh covered them, they were all human.

Aelwen outstretched her arm to Valiran, who took her friend's hand and joined her on the table. Valiran clapped to the music and spun Aelwen around. Within the next four measures, everyone present was on the table, swaying her body, swinging her hips and waving her arms to the music. Not one of them had touched a drop of alcohol, they were all drunk on something better than any beverage—hope.

<div align="center">~~~</div>

Queen Eiyre sat on a stump, poring over battle plans. Her blonde hair was greasy, it had been some time since she had last bathed.

Her haughty air remained, but the treasure trove of snark and superiority had been stripped away, leaving a confident ruler who demanded respect. When she had pledged the Avean forces to the cause of the Vatre-darah, she had abandoned her lavish gowns for shining armor and joined her people on the battlefield. At the moment, she had set aside her heavy armor and donned only basic fighting leathers, her only accessories the khopesh at her side and the leather satchel she had slung across her chest.

President Tecsequaih approached her. He peered down at the plan she was scrutinizing. Keenly aware of his presence, Eiyre raised her eyes to him.

"Yes?"

"It's okay to take a break, you know," said the president.

"When my people are being slaughtered? I don't think so."

283

"All I'm saying is do not tire yourself. Your people need you at your strongest." Tecsequaih let out a long breath and sat himself on a rock beside her. "You were such a lady," he mused.

"Just because I wore silks and jewels doesn't mean I never relished the feel of a blade in my hand."

"Fair enough."

"I used to train with the stablehands. I never dreamt that one day I would be here."

"Nor did I think I would see one war in my lifetime, let alone two." Tecsequaih let out a second long breath. "You have proven yourself beyond a doubt."

Eiyre cast him a sharp look. "I know. You weren't the only one who thought me unworthy of the throne."

"And am I not the only one who believes in you now?"

It was Eiyre's turn to sigh. "I do not know that lies in the hearts of my people other than dread. All I know is that I can fight beside them until the end, and I will." She rolled up the battle plan and stuck it in her satchel. "Do you have any advice for me? This being my first war and all."

Tecsequaih was silent for a moment as he considered. "Keep the faith. Don't let them see the doubt behind your eyes."

After a moment of silence, Eiyre asked, "Is that all?"

"Yes. You're doing very well. Do not let the words of an old man change your course of action, which has proven successful so far."

The queen breathed a laugh. "You shouldn't be so hard on yourself. If I'd thought the Vatre-darah a lost cause, I never would have pledged my country to it."

"Understandable, though I fear your gratitude is misplaced. The credit is not wholly mine to take."

"I'm well aware. I doubt you would have made it this long without General Ekua."

"We most certainly would not have. I have never known a better commander." The president clapped his hands together and looked at the soldiers that milled about the camp. "There is much I must see to. I do not know when we will speak again. If this is our last meeting, know that you are a ruler equal to Queen Baric and that you have made your country proud." He extended his hand to her.

Eiyre rose and shook it. Her grip was steady and sure. Her sapphire eyes locked onto his deep brown ones. A silent sort of reverence only rulers understood.

The handshake ended. Before he left Queen Eiyre, he said, "Do me a favor and take my advice."

"I will. I promise to keep the faith."

"I meant about resting."

She smiled. "I will."

~~~~~

The heat was worse than any Aelwen had ever felt. Of all the days she had been in Paruma, the morning sun had never felt so oppressive. The rays themselves seemed alive and content to worm their way through the down blanket and into Aelwen's bones.
~~~~~

Before the morning sun had risen, a few tears had squeezed their way out. Shadows still flitted through her mind, but they were lesser than they had been before. The party last night, although it had only been the four of them, a table and mystical music, had ignited a flame that had burned away the fog of shadow.

Now, a different flame was slinking through behind her eyelids and warming her eyes, a sensation she had never felt before and was more than happy to never feel again.

Aelwen's head still throbbed with tiredness, but the heat would not withdraw. If the light was warming her eyes when they were closed, what would it do when she opened them? Her eyelids peeled open, the dried, crusty moisture from her leftover tears cracked away. As her vision cleared, the room dimmed. Marliza was leaning against the wall, a ball of white and gold magic flickering above her open palm.

"What the hell are you doing?"

"I was trying to wake you up."

"Why?"

"Today we are going to go on an adventure of our own."

"Yay."

"Shut up. You'll like it more than you think. We'll never make it back before dark if you don't haul ass."

Aelwen rubbed her temple. "I thought you were the all powerful heir. You can't handle yourself at night in a dark forest?"

"You don't know these lands like I do. Let's go."

Aelwen crawled out of bed and slunk to her closet full of various outfits Bailba had created for her. She looked over her shoulder to see Marliza still there.

"Are you going to watch me change?"

"A warrior shouldn't be so insecure about her own body."

"I'm not."

"Then why do you care?"

"Because it's weird."

"All women are built the same."

Deciding that the argument really wasn't worth it and that by talking back Aelwen was giving the snarky mage exactly what she wanted, she told Marliza, "Fine, but don't get too excited." She pulled her nightgown off in one fell swoop, leaving her entire body completely exposed. As she searched naked through her rack of clothing, she snuck a glance at Marliza who stood with her arms crossed, waiting impatiently and looking unfazed by Aelwen's nakedness.

Dressed in leather pants, combat boots and a leather jacket with metal plates, Aelwen nodded to Marliza who took her hand and they magicked out of the tree house together, touching down on the forest floor.

"Can't you just magic us to wherever we're going?" Aelwen made sure to use the word Marliza hated and took delight in the way the mage bristled.

"I could, but that would take all the fun out of it."

"You're not going to tell me where we're going, are you?"

"No."

Marliza took the lead and Aelwen followed a few steps behind. A brown leather pack was strapped on Marliza's shoulders and rested against her back. Aelwen almost inquired about the contents of the pack, then decided it was wiser to keep her mouth shut. Marliza never appreciated anything Aelwen had to say, anyway.

Aelwen was fine walking in silence, following Marliza's lead, until the mage started changing her brown skin to hard metal for no apparent reason. From all of the training sessions Aelwen had looked in on, changing her flesh to steel was one of Marliza's favorite defensive moves. Was she on defense now?

"Why are you doing that?"

"What?"

"Making your skin metal."

"It's fun."

"Are we in danger?"

Marliza huffed. "As an *Arenian*, I thought that you wouldn't need to ask that question." Aelwen bristled.

The mage rolled her eyes. "No, we're fine."

"Then can you stop it?"

"Why?"

"It makes me uncomfortable."

"I thought a blood and bone warrior would have more guts." The metal dissolved, leaving the natural formation of real skin in its place.

Aelwen hated how Marliza kept ragging on her for not being an expected Arenian. While Marliza despised her for being so opinionated about mages, she was just as opinionated about arena fighters. While an Arenian, Aelwen had always taken special care to keep from letting the lifestyle swallow her up. It would have been all too easy to lose all sense of feeling, let go of emotion completely and look at the world as a place of death and destruction. Yes, her job had been to wound and overcome, to draw blood and give her all to hurt other people who she had no reason to other than the fortune waiting on the other side of their defeat, but that was her job. When the day was over and she could be herself again, she spent her time doing normal human things. Talking with her friends, shopping, doing her laundry, reorganizing her quarters. She had never spent her spare time brawling or heavily drinking. Throughout the storm of her life, she had kept a thin bit of morals with her always.

"How do you do that anyway?" Aelwen asked, hoping that if she continued to converse with Marliza, the mage would soften towards her.

"The metal skin thing?"

"Yes. I know you can conjure metal, but I didn't think you can make it part of you."

"You can't. Unless you perform surgery on yourself, that is. The metal isn't actually in my skin, it's just so close that it looks like it's part of me."

"Oh."

"Maybe you'll learn how to do it one day."

"Maybe I will." The words were husks, empty and hopeless. Some of that deep sorrow still ate at her.

Marliza stopped walking. "We're almost there." She looked up, examining the obstacle before them.

A craggy, grey, natural monstrosity rose before the two women. A gargantuan mountain with ragged sides, an impossibly steep slope and a snow covered, broken tip that was shrouded in mist stood before them. There was not only one mountain either, a whole range of them that seemed to grow out of the ground, a wicked gate yanked from the earth by the gods, stretched on for miles, far beyond what any eye could see.

"Please don't tell me we have to climb those." Was this the 'fun' Marliza had implied at the start of this foolish trek?

"Yes. Stop whining and get a move on," Marliza twiddled her fingers, two curved knives appeared in her hands. She dug them into the rock face and hoisted herself up, jamming her feet into space between one spike of rock and the next. "Or else we'll be making the journey back in the dark." She climbed up another several feet. "If this scares you now, just wait until you can't see and you haven't got a clue what's waiting right next to you with its maw dripping."

Aelwen kept herself from shuddering. "Mind giving me a pair of those?" She gestured to Marliza's climbing knives.

"For an Arenian, you're awfully poorly equipped."

"Being magic, I thought you would be able to get me whatever I need."

The mage rolled her eyes again. "Don't assume that people are going to be willing to help you. Not every friend is what they say they are." She arched her neck backwards, a pair of daggers just like the ones she had wedged into the rock dropped to the ground inches from Aelwen's toes, their evil tips digging into the ground.

She forced the daggers in and began to climb. Halfway up, refusing to look down, Aelwen said, "What the hell? The rest of Paruma is all forest, what is a range of snowy mountains doing here? They don't fit in at all, there aren't even trees on them."

Maliza grunted as she pulled herself up, she was only about a foot away from her followee. "You don't know a thing about my country. You'll understand when we get there."

"Why is it all riddles with you people? Do you ever say anything straight out?"

"Shut up and trust me. Talking now is a waste of your breath, we're not even halfway to the top."

The mountain blocked the sun, but they had to have been climbing for almost an hour.

It would have been mildly kind for Marliza to tell Aelwen how much worse the downward journey was than the upward one. Shimmying down with their knives was too much of a risk since they could not see where they were going. Marliza took two thick ropes from the pack strapped to her shoulders and they lowered themselves down, bit by bit. The knots they had to tie around themselves as they made the descent took a good five minutes to tie before they began their way down.

Marliza coated her hands in metal for the lowering. The rope was thick enough that after a few lowerings, both of them trusted it to hold them. It was the texture that was the true torture. Aelwen had not felt pain like that in a very long time. By the time she reached the bottom, her hands were rubbed raw from the rope hairs. Anything she touched set the wounds on fire. At the arena, she had endured worse pain, but Galarus had always had plenty of medication available. He needed his best warriors to know pain and endure it.

Aelwen's legs shook as she continued on behind Marliza, on even, moss covered ground once again. It was like the day she had gotten off of *Mist Wing* after the months' long journey. Marliza held herself with too much poise. The trick may have worked on an ordinary person, the mage was incredible at disguising her pain, but Aelwen had learned how to spot injury in an opponent, even when they were doing their very best to hide it. Marliza was hurting just as badly as she was. The only difference between them was that Marliza was doing everything in her power to cover up the agony that swirled wildly through her limbs and muscles while Aelwen accepted the pain and let it run through her. Pain was a part of her, she had learned that lesson more than well within the last week or so, and it would not be one she forgot for a very long time.

"Be strong," the words from Marliza sounded like a warning when they should have sounded reassuring.

For once, Aelwen did not question. She straightened her back which had slumped from the ache in her body after dragging herself up a mountain. The way Marliza walked, with an angle to her head and one hand out, indigo magic whirling around it, Aelwen got the sense that the fear she had felt on the whole trip, of being attacked by a crouching beast, was very real right here. Where was *here*, anyway? It looked like any other place in Paruma. There were no people, not a sign of civilization. For all of the words she had heard about the communities of Paruma, Aelwen had yet to see one with her own eyes, excluding Bailba's tree.

The air whooshed around them, but neither of them felt the slightest breeze. It was as if a windstorm were making its way through the area but they were trapped in their own personal bubble, safe from the storm. Maybe Marliza had cast a protection spell around them to keep out the wind. A new noise joined the whistling wind, a purr-growl, like the one that might come from a wild cat. Numerous purr-growls blended together into one, creating a mysterious symphony of fear. Slowly, the noises drifted away. The women stood in silence again.

"What was that?" Aelwen hissed.

Marliza threw up a hand that almost collided with Aelwen's face. The Arenian fell silent. Marliza stared at a tree with focus sharper than any blade Aelwen had handled. The tree the mage was watching was different from the others. Aelwen never would have noticed if her attention was not so pointedly drawn to it. The tree was curved, its trunk was thick and twisted, the bark was sleek and scaly. Its branches were thin and stretched like reaching fingers. Dark green leaves shaped like cats' eyes covered the branches' fingertips. There were not many branches, but the leaves were plentiful. There was a large cluster of them towards the top of the tree. The plant looked more like it had once been water turned to wood than a natural tree. The leaf cluster shook and moved apart from the rest of the tree, as did a section of the trunk. The tree that was not the tree shifted slowly, its color pattern changed. First to violet and turquoise, then to silvery blue and sea green and finally to a magnificent iridescent color.

The color changing beast slunk down the tree's gnarled trunk and stuck its snout toward the females. It's shiny, scaly snout contracted as it took in their scent.

Marliza stood like a statue as the creature inspected her. Aelwen, on the other hand, could not keep her eyes from darting, absorbing every detail of the brute judging them. It was covered in iridescent scales that scattered the sunlight throughout the clearing. The beast had a long tail that split in two at the end, each tip glistened with a golden spike. A double row of platinum spikes ran up its tail and the entire length of its lizard-like body up to its head, which was crowned with a magnificent pair of silver antlers, grander than the rack of any stag she had seen. The creature had alert, golden eyes. The monster's most disturbing feature was not any of what Aelwen had just seen, it was the wings on its back. There were not one pair of wings like other winged things that she had been, but two. One was stretched to its full length, each wing a good forty feet at least. The second pair was still tightly folded to the brute's back. It's wings were the same moonstone color as the rest of its body, its many curved claws the exact platinum of its back spines.

While the wings were a surprise, the monster's teeth were just as disturbing. The rest of its body was an array of shimmering, beautiful colors. It's teeth were a glistening white, but the color was not what was strange about them. It was the way that they stuck at all angles, wrongly shaped to fit into the beast's mouth, sharp points that jabbed out here and there, each one could easily impale a person with a simple shake of the monster's head.

This was not just a monster. It was a dragon.

Aelwen's first instinct was to scream, but she forced her jaw shut as the dragon sniffed her out. After an agonizing few minutes, the dragon drew back into a sitting position and stared at them both.

"What does it want?" Aelwen whispered.

Marliza stopped her statue imitation, her voice took on a normal volume once more. "She's judging you."

"Why?" Aelwen could not bring herself to raise her voice above a whisper.

"To see if you are worthy."

She wanted to scream in frustration. "Of what?" she forced through gritted teeth.

"Her."

Both mages fell dead silent as the dragon suddenly darted forward. Inches from them, the dragon lifted herself into the air with a grace the most talented performers never mastered. The dragon disappeared into the forest.

Just as Aelwen was about to ask if that was a definitive no, the dragon came swooping back, her claws soared just above their heads. She turned again, flying back towards them, this time rising higher with each rapid wing beat. She began flapping in perfect circles, each complete round bringing her a couple feet higher. As she neared the canopy, the wind from her wings moved the branches. The dragon flew up in her entrancing spiral until she was a spec in the blue sky. Then began her descent. Still spiraling, this time downward, the dragon came closer and closer to the women with each round. Aelwen did not understand what the dragon was doing. She was not sure Marliza did either, based on the way the mage watched the creature with shocked amazement.

The beast landed, the canopy closed up again. The dragon put one platinum clawed foot toward Aelwen, whose breath caught in her throat at the motion. She could handle any normal human, but a monster was another story. One swish of its tail, a flick of its claw, a shake of its head…The dragon bowed her head with closed eyes. An unmistakable gesture of surrender.

Aelwen reached out a hand. Her immediate instinct was to touch the beast. With a second thought, she pulled her arm back. Needing confirmation, she looked to Marliza, whose mouth hung agape at the sight. Marliza nodded swiftly, practically begging Aelwen to make the move.

She did.

A power she had never felt awoke. Parts of her soul she had never known existed snapped to life. The energy of a storm swelled in her, the ferocity of fire filled her. Never had she known what it truly felt like to be alive. The power was better than any material thrill, it was an otherworldly sensation that zapped her again and again with the realization of exactly how much power she held within herself.

The dragon nuzzled her head against Aelwen's thigh, she rubbed its pearlescent scales, which were smoother than she ever could have anticipated. They were like pure ice made even slicker by a rainstorm. Still, Aelwen bet that the scales were harder than diamond. She reached up and felt the dragon's silver antlers. Firmer than any bough.

"She is yours," Marliza said, softer than anything she'd ever said to Aelwen. Her sarcastic, acidic edge was completely gone. "Give her a name."

Aelwen rested her forehead against the dragon's. The creature was magnificent, except for her crooked teeth. Rhea's mount had teeth like that, too. Perhaps it was a trait of all dragons. Although, Rhea's did not have protruding antlers, two pairs of wings or a forked tail. Or scales like moonstone.

"Who are you?" she whispered onto the scales. She drew back. The power still coursed between them, but there was not enough known for her to give a name to a creature so splendid. Turning to Marliza, she explained, "I cannot name her yet. I must know her first."

The only other person she had ever seen with a dragon was Rhea, and she was always astride it. Without any other ideas of what to do, Aelwen raised one leg to swing over the dragon's back. Before her pant leg even had the chance to brush against the dragon's scales, the beast had drawn back and flapped away in a flash, vanishing into the thick foliage once again.

With the majestic dragon gone, Marliza's demeanor returned to its normal stoniness. She rotated one shoulder and said, "We'd better head back."

"We only just got here." Aelwen was by no means the best judge of time, but they surely could not have been with the dragon for more than an hour.

"I told you to haul your ass this morning. Tomorrow it won't take so long, I promise. That is, if she really trusts you."

"She? As in, the dragon?"

"What other shes do you see around here?"

"She bowed to me. I may not know much about Paruma, but I know that when a dragon bows to someone, it means they are going to be loyal."

Marliza did one of her annoying huffs. "And I know that dragons can lie just as easily as humans can."

The trek back to Bailba's home felt no shorter than the one to meet the dragon. It was no easier, either. The only thing that made it better than the first was that Aelwen no longer had to keep wondering where they were going. She knew every natural obstacle that they came to face. However, this time they never had the chance to slow their pace for fear of being stuck in the pitch dark.

Back inside the sure safety of the marvelous tree, Aelwen lay on a conjured velvet cushioned loveseat. On her way down the mountain on the trip back, she had lost her footing and dislocated her ankle. Marliza had set the bones back into their proper places. When they had reached the tree home, Bailba had rubbed a thick, sour smelling gel all over Aelwen's ankle. The pain was significantly less now, but it was still very real. Even the lonesome walk to reach this foreign place had not been so painful. She hadn't had an angsty, sneering old mage nagging her on that trip, either.

Aelwen yawned, reaching her arms as far above her head as she could.

"I think I'd better go to sleep now," she announced to the room that was empty except for herself and Bailba, who was hunched over the countertop while concocting some recipe beyond her reckoning. Valiran and Marliza had gone off to do whatever it was mages did together.

"I think that would be a good idea," Bailba answered, and Aelwen could hear the smile in her voice.

Aelwen kept laying there.

"Did you fall asleep?" Bailba wondered after a few minutes flitted by.

"No," Aelwen answered. She set her bad foot flat on the ground and put a bit of pressure on it. She suddenly guessed what Bailba was thinking: the crone thought that Aelwen was waiting for the old woman to offer her a hand to stand up. And she was right. But mages stood on their own no matter the pain. Once upon a time, Aelwen would have done the same.

The ex-Arenian stood. The pain in her ankle was the weakest it had been since the injury. It was barely there at all, a faint throbbing was all that remained. It felt good to stand without help. A feeling she had not felt in a while that she was pleased to feel again. Before Aelwen headed towards her room, she said, "Thank you for sending me to the dragon. The journey wasn't easy, but it was worth it."

The old woman turned from her recipe book and looked Aelwen directly in the eyes. "That was none of my doing. Today was all Marliza's idea."

"You didn't do a thing?"

"Not one."

Smiling for a reason she did not fully comprehend, Aelwen went to her bedroom. Curled up in her fuzzy down-stuffed blanket, Aelwen nuzzled her pillow and shut her eyes. Before her eyelids fully closed, she realized with a tiny smile that she had hardly felt any sadness today. It was creeping away bit by bit, and she knew that in time she would be free. Once she was free, she would be unstoppable.

CHAPTER TWENTY-THREE

The Vatre-darah thundered into the camp on horseback. The clearing was bathed in the warm golden light of the just-rising sun. The warriors whooped and cheered, waving tattered banners and bloody weapons in the air. The battle had lasted through the night, but they had won. It had been a defensive battle to maintain their current holdings. The price they'd paid had not been a small one, but in the end, they had emerged victorious.

The warriors dismounted, hurrying to the basins of warm water prepared by those who had stayed behind in their absence, eager to wash the filth of the battle from them.

In her tent, Iowan shucked off her blood covered armor, hurling it to the ground in a heap, soon followed by her sweat drenched tunic. She stuck her hands into the basin that had been given to her and tossed handfuls of water on herself, using her fingernails to scrape away the worst of the grime. The water had been warmed over the fire, but already the heat was nearly gone from it.

She made quick work of her washing, pulled on a fresh tunic and hustled back to the center of camp. The soldiers hugged one another and cried out in victory. Iowan flung her arms around the nearest soldier she could find. He wrapped his arms around her and together they jumped up and down, shouting with glee.

After she split from him, Iowan hugged another soldier and another, dizzy with euphoria by the time the celebration was dwindling. She had enough of her wits left to realize there was one soldier she hadn't seen yet. She made her way to Lysia's tent, pulling back the flap and entering without announcing herself.

Inside the tent, the sounds of celebration outside faded to a dull and distant hum in Iowan's mind as she laid eyes on Lysia.

Lysia sat on her bed, tending to a stab wound on her left shoulder. The water in her basin was stained red. She had her neck turned to an uncomfortable angle, trying to apply a bandage. At Iowan's appearance, she looked up.

"Need some help?" asked Iowan with a grin.

"Yeah." Lysia handed her the bandage and leaned forward, allowing Iowan access to the wounded area. It gaped up at her, red and oozing. She knelt on the bed, angling the bandage to best cover the whole wound. She pressed it down, smoothing it with her hands. Lysia winced.

"Sorry," Iowan apologized, standing up. "Going to come join the party?"

"I'd love to," Lysia said dryly. She'd never been one for post-victory revels. "But I don't think my shoulder would. I'll just stay here and rest, I think."

Iowan frowned. The celebrations were few and far between, so she didn't want to miss it, but they were never as much fun without Lysia. "Want me to stay here with you?" she asked.

Lysia shook her head. "No, you don't have to do that. Go, enjoy yourself."

"Okay." Iowan offered a small smile and ducked out of the tent.

She *did* enjoy herself. She drank and sang bawdy songs at the top of her lungs with the other warriors for hours, until the early night of winter settled it. They all would have stayed to celebrate for even longer in the dark had General Fayette not shown up and told them all, in her rumbling, not-open-for-debate way, "You've had your fun, now go get some sleep. I can't have you drunk on the battlefield."

Not needing to be told twice, they'd all finished their drinks, said their goodnights and retired to their tents. Despite the general's command, Iowan knew she was far too awake to dream of sleep. She did not head in the direction of her tent. Instead, she went to Lysia's. It was more than likely that Lysia was asleep, but if she didn't check, she wouldn't know, and then she wouldn't have a choice but to lay awake in her tent, staring into the darkness while equally dark thoughts swam in her head.

Iowan walked into Lysia's tent unannounced. No lantern was lit, it was pitch dark.

"Lysia," she whispered quietly, not really expecting a response. She waited a moment. Nothing.

Iowan had parted the tent flap to make her exit when Lysia mumbled, "Hi."

Iowan turned around. "Hi." She neared Lysia's cot. "Did I wake you?"

Lysia's blankets rustled as she sat up. Her form was barely distinguishable in the dark. "No. I was awake." She rolled over and lit a lantern, casting a pale orange glow and long shadows about the tent.

Her sleep mussed hair and the circles around her eyes made Iowan question if she was telling the truth. "Are you sure? If you were, I can go. I just wanted to check on you—"

"Iowan," Lysia said, halting her mid-sentence. "It's fine. Stay." She patted the strip of unoccupied cot beside her.

Iowan obliged, taking a seat. "How's your shoulder?"

"Hurts like hell," said Lysia, giving the bandage a tap and grimacing. "I can't believe we won today. I really didn't think we would."

"Me neither. All thanks to General Fayette once again."

"Honestly," Lysia said, flopping back against her pillows. "I don't know what we'd do without her."

"Not stand a chance against the Hakmarres, that's for sure. I've never seen anyone who fights like her, she's incredible."

"Agreed."

Silence swelled, but it was not of the uncomfortable sort. In the lamplight, Iowan took in Lysia's features. They hadn't been this close in such calm circumstances for a long time. They would touch foreheads before a battle and spar together, which often brought them in close proximity to one another, but to be so close in the quiet, with all the time in the world before them, was a strange and welcome thing.

They shared a bond that grew stronger with every passing day. It was Lysia who had been the first to comfort Iowan after her escape from Corova. It was Lysia who fought with her in every battle of this gods forsaken war. Lysia had become something different to her than Aelwen had ever been. Lysia was not a mere companion or a trusted confidant. She was the one who had proven she would be there for Iowan through all the terror to come. Lysia would be there through the good and the bad, the easy and the hard, the angry and the joyful.

Iowan leaned back, resting against the pillows. She reached across the small space separating her and Lysia to rest her hand against Lysia's light brown cheek. Lysia leaned into the touch, dispelling Iowan's slight fear that she would pull away.

Lysia leaned forward, resting her forehead against Iowan's the way they did before every battle.

The air crackled with possibility and Iowan wondered if Lysia felt it too or if the hours of revelry had tainted her mind. Iowan knew what she wanted in that moment they shared in the dark quiet in that tent. She prepared to say something, then stopped before she opened her mouth. What if what she was about to say ruined the relationship she and Lysia had built together? What if Lysia didn't want what she wanted?

Moments like these were rare, she knew that. Any battle they walked into could be their last. Death loomed around every corner, it could strike anywhere, anytime. Nothing was promised. For all either of them knew, they might never share such a moment again. Shouldn't they make the most of this one, then? Say all they wanted to say?

Iowan steadied her breathing. She didn't want to die without Lysia knowing what she meant to her. She slid her hand from Lysia's cheek down so it was cradling her neck.

"Lysia," she said, her voice little more than a whisper. "Can I kiss you?"

She felt Lysia stiffen and feared she had made the wrong choice. She should've kept her mouth shut.

"Yeah," breathed Lysia. "Yes, you can."

The pent of tension bundled in Iowan dispelled, leaving her feeling light and nothing but happy.

Iowan kissed Lysia.

Lysia kissed her back.

They kissed over and over. The lantern guttered and went out and still they continued, savoring the warmth and rightness of their closeness, the flame of their passion, the delight of their pleasure. When at long last they fell asleep, it was together on that cot, wrapped in each other's arms, the worries of the world of no concern to them.

~~~~

The wind atop the mountain was worse than it had been the previous day. It seemed intent on whipping Aelwen's hair into her face no matter how many different ways she tried to tuck it away.
~~~~

Before they had set out for the day, Marliza had advised her that the mountain would not be pleasant this morning. So there Aelwen stood, wrapped in several layers of various furs, a winter outfit complete with a fluffy hood that covered her ears and a pair of fur-lined hiking boots. The winter in Corova was always a harsh time, but Master Galarus had always kept a massive fireplace well stocked during the frigid time to keep the Arenians in their best possible health. In his mind, it was perfectly fine to torture the Arenians in every possible way as long as they were not in a real match. Once they were in, he wanted every bit of their physical being to be at its highest possible point.

"Are you sure she's coming?" Aelwen hollered over the roaring wind, scanning the clouds for any sign of her dragon.

Marliza stood before her, dressed similarly in layers of fur and thick fabric. The wind tore her hood down, sending her curly black hair bouncing freely in the wind. "She will."

Both women intently watched the gray sky. Not so much as the shadow of a dragon.

"Why are these mountains here?" Aelwen asked. "I've never seen them on any map." She feared that with the howling of the wind Marliza could take a bad step and Aelwen would not hear Marlzia's cries for help, so she did her best to keep her talking so she would know where she was. "I've never seen them on any map."

"You haven't figured that out yet? I thought politicians were supposed to be smart."

To think that Aelwen had been grateful for Marliza's kindness the day before.

Marliza went on, "They are the separations. The mountains were made by the gods when tension began to arise between the dragons and humans. The mountains are the sure border. Exploration is allowed, but if one crosses into the territory of the other, they cannot claim that it was a mistake. Perhaps if those without magic focused more upon education than ignorance, they would have visited Paruma in the last century and seen these mountains. "

Aelwen felt the shame of stupidity begin to seep into her. It was by no means as bad as the omen of dread that had been following her for the last week, so that was a plus.

As if the dragon could sense her new companion's sudden sinking, the creature appeared out of the clouds just as suddenly as she had yesterday out of the tree.

Looking the dragon in the eye, Aelwen said, "I am sorry for what I did to you yesterday, trying to ride you. I didn't know what I was doing. I still don't. Tell me what to do and I will do it."

Marliza unexpectedly said, "There is a well known proverb among the Parumans. 'You must trust yourself before you can trust someone else with yourself.' I have never seen a better chance for that saying to be brought to life than right now."

Aelwen still could not make sense of it all. She had spent much time around politicians, yet rhetoric still made her brain stumble sometimes.

"Does your magic let you talk to animals, too?" Aelwen asked.

"No, but the bond between animal and human is strengthened when magic is gained."

"Bailba didn't mention that, either."

"She probably didn't think it was important for you to know. It's true, though. As a mage, you are able to feel the intentions of animals. That probably doesn't make any sense, but once you learn, it will."

Aelwen took the mage's word. She had gotten her this far. In this case, the trust involved was flight. At least, that was how she interpreted it. She repeated the phrase to herself and edited it a bit, 'you must fly yourself before you can trust someone else to fly you'. It sounded stupid, but it made sense. She didn't know much about dragons, but she knew from the legends how proud they were. They would not associate with cowards or weaklings. She had to prove herself to the dragon.

By flying.

Impossible.

They stood at the apex of a mountain. What better chance would she have?

Aelwen rested a gloved hand lightly upon Marliza's shoulder. "I am trusting you just as much as I am trusting her," she whispered and somehow knew that the words were not blown away by the wind even though Marliza's expression did not change.

Aelwen held out her arms, imagining they were her very own dragon wings, something she had done as a child. A child that had been shoved down and held and forced her way back up because she did not stop. She would not stop now. She leaned forward unflinchingly. Her feet parted from the rough stone. She fell.

The wind roared like all of the beasts she had imagined in the forests. Her heart thundered like the hooves of the army out there, fighting against the darkness. She closed her eyes and enjoyed the symphony.

The thoughts of terror and death tried to break their way into her head. She kept her walls up. She refused to consider it.

A firmness was suddenly beneath her, so sudden that it knocked the wind from her. The howling of the wind was not the same as when she had been falling. Aelwen opened her eyes. They watered as the wind stung them, her vision was distorted as the unstoppable tears welled, but the image was unmistakable. The carriage-sized, glistening moonstone head of the dragon, complete with shining, pointed antlers, a rack that any hunter would desire.

Aelwen shifted cautiously. The dragon's back was wide, but the fear of falling was still there. Her dragon had saved her once, she would not rely on the favor again. As the beast flew steadily, Aelwen got herself into a more comfortable position, sitting between two of the dragon's back spines and leaning forward, groping the spine in front of her with all of her might.

Marliza used magic to amplify her voice. "Not quite the fearless Arenian you thought you were."

The remark was not as snide as usual, Marliza actually laughed after she said it.

"Really?" Aelwen shouted back. She pulled her hands off of the spike and threw them above her head. She yowled into the frigid wind, the animal in her taking over. Never had she felt so purely powerful, she could bring down worlds if she wished. The yearning for adventure surged within her: what other worlds were there? What lay beyond the sea? Visions of herself fully armored with a sword and shield in hand filled her mind, she saw herself slashing effortlessly through countless enemies on a field that ran with blood.

The dragon would not allow her rider to be so cocky. She snaked to the side and dove.

Aelwen shrieked as her mount's body lurched, she hardly had time to take a new breath before the dragon was diving, her armored nose aimed at the jagged rocks that lined the base of the mountain. Her mind was nothing more than a puddle of confusion, excitement and terror until all of the reckless motion was over with and they flew unwaveringly upward again.

The dragon's pristine claws touched down on the mountaintop. She lowered herself and her rider dismounted. Despite the moments of raw fear, Aelwen longed to climb back on and ride again.

"What did she do?" Aelwen shouted to Marliza, who had a real smile on her face. Not a sight she ever would have expected to see the day she met the mage.

Marliza did not stop smiling. "I've never seen anyone ride a dragon before, other than Rhea. She used a great deal of force to gain her dragon, their relationship is one of servant and master. You and her… you're something else entirely."

"Like what?"

"Bonded, meant to be. It's amazing." She looked between rider and dragon, her expression one of pure marvel. "Go with her," she nodded to the dragon. "She has a lot to show you. I'll meet you back at Bailba's."

Aelwen trusted Marliza's connection to the animal, so she complied and mounted the dragon once again.

"Okay," she said softly, patting the dragon's neck.

The wind still blasted all around them, but the dragon seemed to receive the message without difficulty. She took off the moment the words were spoken.

Aelwen sighed with relief as the hazardous mountain climate was left behind them, replaced by mild weather and a land of green. The dragon touched down in a clearing and folded her wings in tight after Aelwen dismounted. The forest was too dense for her to have her magnificence extended.

"Where are we going?" Aelwen asked, she truthfully did half-expect the dragon to reply. She was so full of surprises, maybe speaking the language of humans was one of them.

The dragon snorted and began walking. It was not a complete answer, but Aelwen was sure that the dragon had at least comprehended her question.

Aelwen had forgotten how alive the forest was. In her long days of sorrow, all she had known was her own sadness. She had never noticed the birds or the wind or even the creak of the branches as they swayed in the easy afternoon breeze. All of those things had always been there, but perhaps it had not been only her anguish obscuring the music of life all around her. Her magic seemed to be a little more awake, close to the surface and very much alive. Once it was released in all of its glory and she could control it, with this dragon beside her and a loyal army at her back, what would she be able to do?

The dragon stopped suddenly, facing Aelwen. The creature inclined her head but did not break eye contact, as if she were bowing to Aelwen again. Then the dragon began to disappear. The exact pattern of the surrounding forest began to swallow her up, like a napkin soaking up water. Then the pattern retracted, the same process backwards. Aelwen reached out her hand. Beneath her palm she felt the slick scales of the dragon. It was not the dragon leaving completely. It was her changing her scales.

"You're like me?" Aelwen breathed.

The dragon made her head a pale turquoise and her antlers lime green. She tilted her sea colored head.

"Magical."

The dragon blinked once, still not understanding.

"You can't tell yet, I haven't harnessed my magic, but I can feel it. It's right under my skin but it won't come out. I promise it's there. You'll see someday. The whole world will."

The dragon set her already crooked jaw. She lowered herself, belly almost touching the ground, like a cat preparing to pounce. Her tail lashed. Her scales changed from shade to shade, becoming every color of the spectrum. The dragon was a dizzying mess of color.

Aelwen stomach somersaulted. She averted her eyes. "Okay, okay, stop, you're going to make me sick."

The dragon sat up like a massive mastiff, giving the Arenian a look that she thought was a dragon's version of a smile.

"You're amazing, now let's go," Aelwen said. The dragon did not move; she did not have to. She was in the heart of her territory, she could summon whomever she needed. The dragon threw her head back, looking as free as Aelwen had on her dragon ride. She let out a noise that had Aelwen cupping her ears in seconds.

The dragon's scales finished changing, settling on a regal appearance, royal purple scales with flawless blue features. The dragon seemed to sit with practiced elegance, her front feet slightly angled outwards to showcase her curved claws, highlighting the immense power that was mingled with her breathtaking beauty.

Aelwen flinched as what felt like a piece of cool leather brushed her arm. Her Arenian instincts snapping to life, she balled her other hand into a fist and plowed it into whatever had just touched her.

Sometimes it paid to look before she reacted. Aelwen gasped as her fist collided with the side of a leathery green beast. Another dragon. The beast reared and roared, its jaws snapped shut where Aelwen's body would have been if she had not tumbled out of the way the moment she saw what she had hit. The green dragon reeled and prepared to attack again. It froze as a royal purple clawed foot came down in front of its snout. The green dragon looked up and cowered before the forceful glare of Aelwen's partner.

Aelwen rose, feeling no threat as the green dragon slithered away. She turned in a slow circle, taking in the unbelievable sights all around her. Dragons were coming. All colors, all sizes. Beasts of legend, crawling and alighting, gathering all around Aelwen's dragon who stood in the center of it all. Then she realized. Her dragon was not a normal dragon. Her dragon was something that even Rhea's merciless monster would grovel before. Her dragon was the Queen of Dragons and the queen had an army. An army of dragons. Something greater than magic indeed.

Never had any human, not even the most committed researchers, seen as many dragons as Aelwen had that day. Her whole walk home was occupied with thoughts of everything she had seen. Dragons with features she had never imagined, dragons smaller than her fingernails and more dangerous than any assassin. All of those creatures for her to control. Her dragon was their queen. The one who swayed the queen swayed her kingdom, and this queen's kingdom was an entire race. Something greater than magic.

The prospect of what they could do to the Hakmarres, untethered on the battlefield, made Aelwen shiver with excitement. Once she had her magic, too...The Hakmarres had better surrender before she was ready to take the reins of the Vatre-darah again or she was going to make them wish they had never started the damned war in the first place.

The dinner that night with the other mages was the first one where Aelwen didn't feel inferior to them.

"Did you know?" she asked Marliza, who seemed to have recovered from her laughing fit completely and returned to her normal, unfeeling air.

The mage chewed, her lips revealing the beginnings of a smile.

"You did!"

Marliza swallowed. "I didn't drag you all the way out there for nothing."

Valiran's eyes darted between the two women while Bailba kept quiet, eyes on her food. "Know what?"

"Nothing," Marliza snapped. She shook her head the tiniest bit. Aelwen took the hint and shut her mouth.

~~~~

Lysia and Iowan had been drawn together since the start of the war. It made sense. Neither of them had anyone else. As far as Lysia knew, she and Iowan were the only Corovans fighting alongside the Vatre-darah since Aelwen had disappeared. The other soldiers were comrades, but not friends. She would laugh and train with them, but she didn't actively seek them out because their presence was a balm on her wounded soul the way she did with Iowan. When it came down to it, what was there for she or Iowan to be in love with but each other?

Was it even love they felt, or did they seek comfort in one another because to each the other was a familiar face in a sea of strangers?

Lysia sighed deeply and dragged herself out of bed, Her shoulder throbbed, but the pain was nowhere near as bad as it had been yesterday. As she got dressed, she came to realize that her relationship with Iowan was nothing like her relationship with Taran. Her bond with him had been forged of mutual loneliness, loss and hatred of the world. They'd come together because they didn't have anyone else and they both needed someone, anyone. With Iowan, the shared experience and mutual craving for connection was definitely part of it, but only part. The rest was...affection. Genuine care. Trust, comfort, confidence. Lysia didn't know much of it, but given what she did, all of those feelings mixed together into a single blazing feeling was love. Of course, there were different kinds of love. She might have questioned the type of love she felt for Iowan before last night. Now, there was no doubt about it. Friends didn't kiss until the light burned out. Friends didn't kiss at all, in her experience.
~~~~

Sliding a sword into the sheath of her belt, Lysia exited her tent. She scanned the camp for Iowan, and found her chatting with one of the soldiers who was finishing their breakfast. It felt awkward to barge into their conversation, but Lysia had questions she needed answered.

At Lysia's behest, Iowan excused herself from her conversation, not looking surprised to see Lysia, but not looking happy either. Lysia led Iowan to a copse of trees on the edge of camp. Privacy was hard to come by in these times. She would have brought Iowan to her tent, but at this hour, all soldiers were supposed to be out and about. The only reason that had left Lysia alone was because of her wound.

Iowan shifted from foot to foot, her hazel eyes darted around, looking everywhere but at Lysia. She clearly knew a conversation about their interaction last night was coming and was not looking forward to it.

A part of Lysia felt bad for putting Iowan on the spot like this. Maybe she shouldn't force this talk. Maybe she should let the words be spoken in their own time. No. With a steadying breath, Lysia crossed her arms. The need for these answers was clawing at her, so she would get them and know the truth, whatever it was.

"What do you want to be?" asked Lysia.

"I want to be together. With you," Iowan replied, her eyes meeting Lysia's for a second before flitting away again.

"But?"

"I'm scared." This time, her eyes locked on Lysia and did not waver. "I lost everything once already. Now Ae is gone and Namar's dead, you're all I have. And we're stuck in the middle of a war. I could lose everything all over again at any moment."

"Isn't that all the more reason to hang on to everything you have, tight as you can? Cherish it because it could be gone at any moment?"

Iowan scoffed. "I don't even know what I have." She looked down at her scarred hands. "I have blood on my hands. A history of violence. I hardly think I'm worthy of cherishing anything."

"Don't you say that," said Lysia, the force of her words making Iowan look directly at her. "You are worthy of everything this world has to offer you. You have lived a life of blood and violence because you had no other choice. You took the life the gods dealt you and made something out of it. That makes you worthy of everything, Iowan. Love included."

Iowan shook her head. "You don't love me, you just think you do because there's no one else to love. If we weren't in this war, if life was normal, you'd find yourself someone much more impressive than me."

"That is not true and you know it. I've known plenty of women in my life and none of them, *none* of them make me feel the way you do. Sure, they're pretty and clever and some of them are dangerous, just like you, but none of them have lifted me out of despair the way the very sight of you does. None of them make me want to keep fighting for the future so I can keep seeing their smile."

A smile danced across Iowan's face, her eyes sparked with joy. "You're sure this is what you want?"

Lysia clenched Iowan's hand in hers. "I want to be with you. I want to fight by your side and cry with you when the weight of the world becomes too much to bear. I want to stare death in the face with you and say 'You will not take her from me. Our love is stronger than you.' I will have you, Iowan. Will you have me?"

Iowan cupped Lysia's golden brown face in her pale, scarred hand. "I will have you."

~~~~~

The perfect name.

A simple name, full of power.

Aelwen threw off her blankets and got dressed faster than she ever had. She did not bother to brush her hair before she flew up the stairs and raced into Marliza's bed chamber. The mage drearily looked up at the raucous.

"What the hell are you doing?" she snarled.

"We have to go see my dragon."

Marliza flopped back down and closed her eyes. "She's a dragon. You really think you own her?" Apparently she wasn't too tired to make a snarky remark.

"I know I don't actually own her, I just call her mine. But I won't have to call her that anymore because I came up with the perfect name. She's never going to get to know it if you don't hurry up."

Marliza stuck an arm out of the blankets and waved Aelwen away. "Go by yourself, you know the way by now."

Aelwen wasn't about to argue. She hustled down the rest of the stairs. She wrote a quick note and left it on a table, explaining where she was going. She was the only one up at this ungodly hour, the sun had hardly risen.

Just as yesterday, Aelwen met the wonderful dragon atop the mountain. She pressed her hand to the beast's snout. The dragon shook her head rambunctiously, eager to take a flight.

"Zarah," Aelwen said, looking the dragon in the eyes.

Just as the day they had met, the dragon bent her neck and lowered her eyes, accepting the term.

The two of them, dragon and human, Aelwen and Zarah, spent day after day together, only parting when the night forced them to.

Everytime she was with Zarah the magic sitting beneath her skin fizzed with life and that incredible feeling of raw power filled her up.

Together, she and Zarah mastered all sorts of flying tricks, dives and spins of every sort. Zarah refused the saddle that Aelwen had spent a day making her. Of course she did, Aelwen realized. It was stupid of her to think that a queen would accept a saddle.

Whilst she was with Zarah, she ignored the mages and practically everything about magic. She'd decided to give up on controlling her magic for a while, hoping that maybe if she didn't focus on it, it would just happen.

The bond between human and dragon strengthened with time until even their minds were connected. Aelwen found herself able to detect Zarah's intentions and sense her
~~~~~

thoughts. At first, the impressions were bleary and sometimes indecipherable, but with time they became distinct.

Knowing how Zarah felt and what she was feeling was something Aelwen had to adjust to. She had her own feelings to deal with, she didn't need any excess. Thankfully, most of what Zarah felt came to her rider as inspiring sensations of power and surety, her thoughts as segments of observation and command and confidence, so she wasn't burdening Aelwen with negativity, but nonetheless it was no easy thing balancing two sets of conflicting emotions. Aelwen learned to recognize Zarah's feelings, process them, and let them go. They weren't her emotions to keep.

That new ability, though it presented its challenges, was also something quite helpful. Being able to sense when Zarah was about to dive or spin gave Aelwen the time to prepare for the motion, enabling her to balance better and ride with increased confidence. Likewise, after a while, all Aelwen had to do was think of a command and Zarah would comply without Aelwen saying a word.

The bond they shared was something profound. Strange and familiar at the same time, crafted of power and vigor.

Aelwen met Zarah, Queen of Dragons, on the mountain peak everyday at the exact same time. She had long since adapted to the climb, the harsh climate did not bother her anymore.

Today, Aelwen gave a new order when she mounted Zarah. "Take me to Marchia."

She had made up her mind on the trek to the mountain that morning. She had to see the war for herself. It was the only way she could know what was happening, truly.

The flight was long and the winds were the coldest they had been in a very long time. Aelwen's power still sparked beneath her skin, but it felt deeper than usual, heavier. Zarah's spines lay flat against her pigeon color scales, sensations of her wariness made their way to Aelwen. She wondered whether Zarah feared something herself or if those feelings were her response to Aelwen's own apprehension.

When the country that had been her savior came into clear view, Aelwen's heart dropped in her chest.

Barren flatland of green dusted with snow welcomed her, what ruins remained still smoldered. The scent of the destruction travelled all the way up into the sky, filling Aelwen's nostrils with an acrid smell she had forced herself to remember so recently, a smell that would always yank her back to that night of horror.

Where had everyone gone? No bodies littered the ash-riddled ground. All was gone.

Something stirred within her, magic or instinct, she could not tell. It was a sense, an inkling with no proof, yet it felt truer than all the lies she had lived through. The Vatre-darah were battered and weak, but they would not give up. They fought with hope in their hearts. Aelwen was that hope. She would not allow any more to die without seeing that hope come to life before their eyes.

Aelwen tapped Zarah's neck.

"Go back."

The cool air made her throat and lungs feel raw as she sprinted through the forest, she ignored it. She did not think twice about the burning in her calves. The anger within her drove all of the pain away.

Aelwen thrust open the door to Bailba's tree. The old woman stood in the main parlor, gazing out of a window. Aelwen had no idea what the crone was watching. All there was to see was a bunch of trees. There was not a sign of Marliza or Valiran, which worked in her favor. This was an argument between she and Bailba, no one else.

Bailba examined the sight before her, a young woman dressed like a mage, sweat soaking through her clothes, hair sticking out at unnatural angles, a rage blazing in her eyes.

"I have had enough of your idiotic games!" Aelwen took a long step forward, a step that would have put her nose to nose with Bailba if the mage were as tall as she was.

She wasn't about to stop there. Her wrath burst forth in a torment mightier than the sea, each word breaking upon the unforgiving cliffs. "Your riddles are getting me nowhere! Why can't you talk? Just tell me what I need to do! People are dying out there, thousands of them! This is not a game, not for me! I am done with your tricks! Either you explain it all to me, right here, right now, or I'm leaving! I might not have magic, but I'll be able to fight alongside my people! How can you stand to let them die?"

Bailba stood there, looking as unfazed as she had when Aelwen had made her entrance. She was the rugged cliff face that refused to be moved by even the strongest storm.

Aelwen looked into the crone's eyes, less than an inch separated them. "You have seen it and yet you have done nothing! What is wrong with you?"

Even the final explosion did not shake the mountain. Bailba shook her head, but not with disappointment. "There is much sorrow in the world. Much grief and little hope. This is a journey you alone must make. There are no shortcuts or secrets. I cannot force your magic to show itself and neither can you. It will come when it is ready."

"I am done waiting! I will die beside the Vatre-darah, as one of them, rather than stay here waiting for a day that will never come!"

"You may leave, if you like. Go and die in the war. Just know that if that is your choice, the one true hope your people have dies with you and with your death you doom the rest of the Vatre-darah to death."

Aelwen huffed and stormed out of the tree, not bothering to slam the door behind her.

The next morning, Aelwen did not rise from her bed for many hours. She had spent hours wandering the forest last night until at last the cold became too much to bear and she had snuck back to Bailba's tree. Careful to avoid the eyes of the mage, she had crept upstairs to her bedroom. Despite her late-night wanderings, Aelwen had slept well. She did not stay in her bed because she was tired.

In her heart, Aelwen knew Bailba had spoken the truth yesterday. To die with the Vatre-darah without her magic was to throw away their one chance at victory. Yet, the desperation, the desperate need for her magic, the hatred that she was lying in a real bed and was not constantly plagued by the dread of her own death while all the people she loved—if any of them were still alive—were living in a world completely different than the time-altered one she inhabited, it all made her stomach ache and her head throb.

She pulled the covers over her head to keep from looking at the clock on her nightstand. Knowing what time it was and precisely how many long hours she had slept would only make her feel worse. Aelwen curled beneath the covers, feeling sorry for herself, when a raspy voice she had feared for more than ten years of her life sounded out of the blue.

"You're alive?" said the creaky voice, poking Aelwen in the side.

Aelwen grunted and tossed the blanket off of her head. "Yes, leave me alone."

"It's almost two."

"I don't care."

Silence stretched between them until it was too much to bear.

"How long has it been?" asked Aelwen.

"For us or for them?"

"Both."

"Today is four months and twelve days for us. For them, a month and three days," replied Bailba.

"And all of that happened?"

"Your eyes did not lie. Once you were gone, the Hakmarres broke their promise. They have been demolishing your Vatre-darah ever since. Laying around will wear down your muscular endurance, now would not be a good time to lose that."

Aelwen flipped onto her back.

"Don't you think Zarah will be missing you?" Bailba asked.

"She knows I won't be there."

"How do you know?"

"I just know. Do you have an animal? Some fearsome beast you share a connection with?"

Bailba ran a finger along the wall of Aelwen's room. "I don't know if that is the best way to describe him. If you get up and come with me, you can see for yourself."

Intrigued, Aelwen forced herself to her feet. After dressing and shoving food into her mouth, she headed out the door with Bailba in the lead. She was thankful that the old mage did not seem to hold a grudge of any sort. She wasn't sure she herself would have been able to forgive someone who had admonished her the way she had Bailba last night and definitely not so quickly.

"Where are the others?" she asked. There had been no sign of either of the other mages since yesterday.

"They went to Marliza's village. Her father called her back. With you being gone all the time, Valiran did not wish to stay here by herself. She somehow doesn't realize how much Marliza dislikes her."

"Does Marliza like anyone?"

Bailba smiled. "She is quite fond of you."

"I know that she led me to Zarah, but other than that she hasn't shown me any direct affection."

"If she did I'd think she were sick. Marliza does not express herself easily, she is a woman with a wall. Her people call her 'Woman of Steel' for her personality and her signature battle move."

Aelwen grunted. "It's a good one. Do you think she would ever consider joining the Vatre-darah? She would be a mighty asset."

"I doubt it. Marliza's first priority will always be her people. By staying neutral she is keeping them safe, no matter the outcome. If she were to join the war, the Hakmarres would attack her people. I do not believe she could live with that."

Aelwen shook her head. "I'll never understand that level of patriotism."

"Not everyone does. It is a rare feeling. Many people claim it but do not truly own it."

A chill wind whooshed past them, one she hadn't felt since being in the mountains.

"If time is changed here, why do the seasons still change?"

"That is something that would take much too long for me to explain."

"Can I ask where we are going then, or will that take too long to explain?"

Bailba laughed. "It's just another place in the forest. Not too far."

"You know, I fought with you last night because of what you said."

"I say many things, you will have to be more specific than that."

"About saying what I want to outright without dodging around the point."

"I'm glad you did."

"Aren't you mad that I screamed in your face? At all?"

"No. I am old, girl. I have taught many students, had too many fights to count, verbal and physical. You needed to say it, so I let you."

Aelwen fell silent. The sounds of the forest mixed together, she listened to her soul song in the back of her mind. It was not the type of song she was used to, it was the most different version of it she had ever heard. There was no powerful downbeat, no forceful melody or pounding harmony. It was a concoction of wild sounds, nothing but tranquility. The noises were barely noticeable, an ordinary person without warrior trained ears would never have picked up on half of them. They floated in her mind, swaying gently to their own soft rhythm. Each sound made its own melody, there was not one theme but a combination of many different ones, each coming in at different moments, all at their own speeds with their own time signatures. They came together to create something that was more than beauty and unadulterated serenity.

A streak of red flew from Aelwen's fingertips. Both women gasped in unison. Aelwen glanced from Bailba to her hand, then back again. "You saw that?"

"Oh, yes."

She took a deep breath and held out her hand. A flash of blue erupted, hitting a tree trunk. That feeling she had had buzzing under her skin did not feel the same anymore, it felt satisfied and prepared, no longer eager to be set free. Because it had been.

Barely breathing, body quavering, Aelwen stuttered, "Did I—"

Bailba grinned wide. "You did indeed."

Aelwen waved her hand, a swath of multicolored energy appeared out of thin air, then disappeared. She swooshed her other arm in a great arc, a swirl of green power filled the air. She laughed. It was the greatest fit of laughter she had ever had. Her stomach squeezed in on itself, she could not breathe properly. Tears wormed their way out of her eyes and poured onto the ground, splattering the grass. Her body rocked back and forth, shoulders heaving. Her whole face was soaked with tears in no time, her gut felt like it had been punched twenty times over. She lifted her head towards the sky and screamed from the deepest parts of her existence, "Yes!"

The rest of the walk, Aelwen spent marvelling at the energy blasting from her hands. She never knew what color would come. Each flick of her wrist was a surprise. The magic sent a shockwave of power through her each time she used it, it was a feeling more fulfilling than any drug.

"You'd better stop that now, you might scare him."

Aelwen looked over at Bailba. "Him who?"

"You'll see."

Aelwen rolled her eyes. For once the ancient mage did not make her wait too long. A thick clump of bushes rattled, out crawled a creature half the size of Zarah, almost as tall as a several year old tree. It was adorable and unsettling all at once.

The creature's face was pointed, it had a brown, twitching nose the size of an adult's hand on the end of its snout. Fur that reminded her of a snowstorm covered the strange thing's underside. It had beady eyes that were set far from its nose and rounded ears that poked up from its furry head. The thing had no tail, she had been expecting something like that of a rat. It's legs were only a foot or so shorter than Aelwen stood, they were twiglike with claws the color of mud on the end. The part of the creature that was the most undeniably noticeable was its back. Its back was not covered in the same white fur as its belly and face, or the pale brown of its skinny legs. Its back was coated in layers of spines that resembled branches, a couple even had buds on their tips.

"What in the name of the gods is that?"

Bailba chuckled. "His name is Tezani. He is a bosvark. It translates to bushpig."

"Paruman pigs must look a hell of a lot different than ours do."

The old lady laughed again. "I haven't the slightest idea why anyone thought these animals looked like pigs."

"He's your...pet?"

"I don't know if 'pet' is the right word. Tezani and I have a relationship like you and Zarah. We collaborate, but we do not own one another."

"What does he do? He doesn't look very fearsome."

"He can hold his own on the battlefield. When we get closer to leaving to join the war, you will learn more about his abilities."

Aelwen reached out slowly, just like she had done when she had first met Zarah. The bosvark stuck its snout forward and sniffed her fingers, he bent his head, leaning into her hand. Tezani snapped his pointed teeth shut on Aelwen's fingers then drew back into the brush, only his snout poking out.

"Damn!" cursed Aelwen, shaking her bloody fingers. "What the hell, bushpig!"

"Sorry," Bailba said, though she did not sound it. "He can be a bit of a difficult one sometimes."

"I'd say." She wiped the blood on her trousers.

"I don't want to have brought you all the way out here and to go back with nothing but a bosvark bite to show for it." The crone whistled, out crept Tezani, his nostrils flicking open and closed. Before Tezani was all the way out of his hiding place, Bailba tapped Aelwen's shoulder and in the blink of an eye they were both sitting atop Tezani, looking down at the green earth below.

Aelwen wrapped her arms around Bailba's shoulders. "He just bit me, I don't think he wants me on his back!"

"He'll have to deal with it. Tezani's all show, he doesn't really mind you that much."

To Aelwen's surprise, the branch-like spines she was sitting on did not poke into her at all. The feeling was definitely different than riding Zarah, but nowhere near as uncomfortable as she had expected.

Bailba whacked Tezani in the side with her foot. "Let's go." She felt Aelwen wince behind her and explained, "That doesn't hurt him. With all of those spikes, he can hardly feel it."

Tezani had an awkward gait, his steps were slow and bouncy, joggling the riders up and down with every wobbly step.

"Where is he taking us?" Aelwen asked after a good twenty minutes of riding in silence.

"What do you think I am going to say?"

"You'll see?"

"You've got it. Do people really tell you everything you want to know in the other countries? If they do, then how boring your lives must be."

"Not everyone loves surprises. Besides, in politics, everyone is always looking for a straight answer. Everything is direct."

"Why would anyone want to be in that business, then? It sounds absolutely dreadful."

"It isn't the most fun, that's for sure, but it is interesting. Most people do it for the money, too. Plus, in my case, it's not because I like it, although I have grown fonder of it than when I began."

Bailba nodded. She said in a voice that was not much louder than a whisper, "Be quiet now. We don't want to have taken this bumpy ride for naught."

Tezani broke through a barrier of foliage. Aelwen could not believe her eyes. What she saw could not be real, it was too perfect. A broad clearing dotted with young trees, a landscape of the most luscious green. A small waterfall that flowed like molten silver into a pool of cerulean that lay so calm one would think it were glass. The setting was the very definition of magnificence.

"The finest training area I could offer," said the old mage.

"Bailba..." Aelwen had known what she was going to say but the words had fled as quickly as they had appeared. "It's—I..."

Bailba shifted atop Tezani and offered a small shrug, acting like this was one of the ordinary things she might give to any student. Aelwen had been with the mages long enough, she knew Bailba's ways well enough, she had seen how she treated Marliza and Valiran. This was not normal.

Dryly, the crone said, "Will you be able to find your way back here?"

Aelwen opened her mouth to reply, but the words got stuck in her throat. It was as if speaking would shatter the inconceivable sight before her.

"I'm taking that as a 'yes'. I have to get back to work on my projects. You shall return here tomorrow, I don't want you out learning by yourself for the first time. You can practice back at the house for today."

The bosvark waddled back through the wall of foliage that separated the normal forest from the utopia, so close to any who passed by but seen by so few.

CHAPTER TWENTY-FOUR

Taran could only run so fast with Eoren in his arms. The hard wood of her fake leg dug into him. His body ached but he did not slow. They had been travelling for days, avoiding main roads to avoid attention, cutting their way through the wild, heading ever eastward. Taran doubted he would ever have been able to find his way so well were it not for all the time he'd spent studying navigation aboard *Mist Wing*.

The air of Corova was sharper than that of Marchia, the land itself had a harshness to it that he'd nearly forgotten while living peacefully in his country home bordered by the jungle.

He bounded across a frozen stream, veered left and continued up a snow covered slope. Stumbling down the slope, hoping to keep his footing lest he go tumbling and drop Eoren, Taran caught sight of a familiar pond in the distance. They were close.

At the base, Taran stopped and let out a breath of relief that he'd made it down without falling. He shifted, settling Eoren into a more comfortable position on his hip.

"It's not much farther," he said. "Think you can walk it?"

"Yeah."

The word had barely left her lips before Taran was setting her down, incredibly grateful that his body was relieved of the burden of her weight.

"I can't keep up with you running," Eoren said, although they hadn't begun travelling again.

"We can walk now, we're close enough."

"Okay."

So they walked. Over earth and under trees they walked until at last they came to it: an abandoned cottage alone in the forest. The place Taran had called home for many years of his life.

It had been a sanctuary to him, once. He prayed that now it would be again.

Inside the cottage, spiders had made themselves at home. Cobwebs draped from every piece of furniture and dust clung to every surface. Taran used to care about such petty things as a clean home. Now, all he could think of was whether Eoren would feel comfortable here, whether she would feel safe. Whether she would *be* safe.

This was the last step in his journey with the child. No more running with her in his arms, no more sleeping in caves or forcing Eoren awake at the first light so they could cover as much ground as possible. From the edge of Marchia, across miles and miles or wild terrain, they'd made it.

"You used to live here?" Eoren asked, her young voice full of that childish innocence, so much of which he knew she had been robbed.

"Yes."

"It's dirty."

Taran was surprised to find a smile tugging at the corners of his mouth. "Yeah. There hasn't been anyone living here in a long time. We'll get it cleaned up and then it'll feel much more like home, I promise." His eyes strayed to the dinner table. Big enough for two. An unexpected pang of loneliness caught him off guard. Of course he'd known that Lysia wouldn't be here—she was in Marchia, fighting. If she was alive, he thought darkly. And he was here, hiding.

No, not hiding, he told himself. Protecting.

Eoren released a long, drawn-out yawn. "Are there beds here?"

"Yes," said Taran. "This way."

He led her through the dining room and the kitchen and down a short hallway, at the end of which were two doors directly across from one another. The handle took some jiggling, but after a moment Taran managed to open the door to Lysia's old room.

It was the definition of plain. She'd never been one for excessive decoration, or any decoration at all. The sight of it caused another shock of loneliness to course through him.

Taran gestured to Lysia's old bed. She'd made the frame herself, he remembered the hours she'd spent carving it. He'd offered to help but she'd refused, saying she wanted to do it on her own. She'd done quite a good job, too.

"There you go. I'm going to sleep too, I'll be in the room across the hall."

Already climbing into the bed Taran had assigned to her, Eoren nodded. "Okay."

Taran watched with foolish admiration as she laid down and nestled her head into the pillow. She was only a child, a type of human he'd never been particularly fond of, yet everything she did filled him up with pride and giddy joy, as if, with this tawny haired child lay the hope for the future.

"Come get me if you need anything."

She hummed an affirmative. Her eyes drifted closed. Her chest rose and fell with the gentleness of sleep.

Eoren's body, covered in pink scars from the fire that had nearly consumed her, was at once fragile and strong. She'd cried in his arms for many hours on many days, yet she still smiled and laughed with him. The world had been so cruel to her yet she remained as a speck of light that refused to be dimmed no matter how the darkness gnawed at her. With her in it, Taran's world was a better place.

Now that he no longer felt the need to be on the constant lookout for danger, sleep began to blur Taran's vision.

Whether it was an illusion he'd crafted out of desperation or a true haven, Taran felt safe in this house.

He swayed on his feet. Sleep was clawing at him, forcing itself upon him and he could no longer deny it. Taran slipped soundlessly out of what was now Eoren's room and entered his own.

Plopping onto the edge of his bed, Taran shucked off his shoes, which were worn and caked with grime from weeks of travel. Next, he removed the leather bandolier he wore that was full of a variety of knives. A protective precaution he had taken and thankfully never needed to use, other than to carve up meat for their meals.

He crawled into his bed, at once something comfortingly familiar and too foreign, and closed his eyes. Before sleep fully took him, Taran couldn't help but think of Lysia. With the dirt floor beneath him and that familiar wooden roof over his head, at the sight of the table and her bed, Taran was as aware as he had ever been that he had never lived in this house without Lysia.

He had never gotten along perfectly well with Lysia. When they'd shared this home, the two of them had fought regularly and sometimes avoided talking to each other at all beyond what was absolutely necessary. They'd never shared the details of their pasts, at least not all the details, with each other. Both of their pasts were clouded with so much sorrow, the same sort of sorrow that anyone who was a child during the beginning of Halmar's reign had suffered, that it was easier to avoid speaking of it. Their own burdens were enough, they didn't need someone else's.

The two of them had found each other when they needed each other and had lived together because neither of them could bear to live alone. They were both broken pieces with jagged edges who instinctively knew to respect one another's borders. There had been conflict between them—spats and disagreements and thunderous arguments. Such things were unavoidable when two people chose to inhabit the same space together for years on end. They'd done more than argue and avoid each other, though. They'd built this place together along with everything in it. Well, everything except what they had stolen. They'd shared meals and stories of their old lives and fragments of their pasts. Sometimes, they'd even laughed together. Not just exhaled chuckles or mirthless chortles, but real, bellyaching, chaotic, joyful laughter.

Living in this house without Lysia would be no easy thing. Living without her at all had been strange at first and he'd already grown mostly accustomed to that. Surely it wouldn't be long until this house became his and Eoren's and not his and Lysia's.

Just as sleep seemed determined to pull him under its soothing waves, Taran felt flesh brush against his arm. His eyes flew open, his hand shot to his chest for a blade that was not there.

Seeing only Eoren's round face before him, Taran eased.

"I thought you were asleep," whispered Eoren, settling in the bed next to him. The cold wood of her fake foot made contact with his skin, making him flinch at the chill.

"I almost was," grumbled Taran, his words foggy with sleep. "I didn't hear you come in."

"I was being quiet so I wouldn't wake you. I thought it was working."

"It almost did," he said. He shifted over, making room for her beside him. "Couldn't sleep?"

"No. I started having bad dreams. I never had bad dreams on the way here when we slept in the caves and I was next to you."

Taran nodded groggily. "Okay. Just don't snore."

Eoren's giggle was the last thing Taran heard before he succumbed to the wondrous serenity of sleep.

~~~~

The seasons were changing. Even in this realm of altered time, nature took its course, albeit slower than the rest of the world. The night came on quicker and the darkness was the coldest it had been since Aelwen's arrival. In time, the whole country would be as frigid as the mountain curtain that separated the dragons and the humans.

Aelwen roared in frustration as a bolt of power shot from her hand and struck the canopy above her, disintegrating the leaves in a flash. She had intended to shoot her magic at a rock in front of her.

Her magic was showing itself now. Its unsuspected reveal had been a surprise in itself, a surprise better than anything Aelwen had ever felt. That extravagant feeling was already ebbing away, replaced by waves of anger and frustration. Yes, she had the magic, but it was no less than impossible to control it.

The mage swung her arm in a broad arc, palm open. *Magic,* she thought, *Magic, hit that rock right there, magic, make contact with the chipped grey rock sticking out of the dirt.*

A whorl of energy whoosed out of her hand, shaking the branches. Apparently, a mage was not safe from the effects of their own magic, Aelwen learned as her smoke-like magic filled her lungs and throat. She collapsed to her hands and knees, pounding her chest with her fist until she was confident in her ability to breathe once again.

"You have done well."

Aelwen did not look up at Bailba who had suddenly appeared at the door of the tree house. "Don't lie to me," she snarled.

"Perhaps you should take a break. Do not exhaust yourself. Losing your power is much worse than being unable to control it."

"Can a mage truly use their power so vigorously that it runs out?"

Bailba explained, "It is called enervation. An extreme fatigue, the inability to draw out any more power. A burnout."

"How does one tell when they are nearing a state of enervation?" She had hardly had her magic for eight hours yet and she was already speaking more eloquently.

"That's the hard thing about it, one almost never knows. When you are at the height of your abilities with power coursing through you like you've never felt before, you feel like you can conquer the world and all of your dreams will come true. You're in absolute ecstasy, and then you fall. Imagine that the buildup of your power is your ascent into the sky, the enervation is the fall. It is hard and fast. You are left utterly helpless, your chest seizes, you will have trouble moving, you will collapse and faint."

"Gods," breathed Aelwen. "Have you ever experienced enervation?"

Bailba raised a brow. "How do you think I know so much about it?" The crone tapped her cane on the mossy forest floor. "Help me carry the food out, lass. Let us talk of magic
~~~~

as much as we wish with our bellies full. Hunger has the ability to make one do terribly stupid things.”

The young mage almost laughed. It was perplexing how easily Bailba was able to let go of one thing—a conversation, a dispute, an event—and move on to the next without ever glancing over her shoulder to see how that past occurrence had turned out.

With Bailba stacking her own arms with dishes and the strength of Aelwen’s durable arms, they had the whole meal outside and the table set in a matter of minutes. Normally, the elongated table seemed relatively appropriately sized, but without the other two mages it felt too big for just the two of them. Despite this, Bailba had cooked the same amount of food. Bowls of salad ingredients, three different dinner plates, each with a different type of meat on them, smaller bowls with seasonings and sauces and extra bowls for the bones.

Aelwen filled her plate. The eatingware used by the Parumans was significantly larger than any she had ever seen before. Tonight was the first time that she had ever covered the whole thing in food and at the same time had no doubts about her ability to consume it all.

The elder mage said, “Magic uses a lot more of your energy than you are aware of. You will develop a much larger appetite.”

Aelwen shoveled a forkful of juicy fish covered with exotic spices into her mouth. Through the food she got out, “My magic, why did it show itself when it did?” She swallowed a bit of her mouthful. “You told me that magic comes when you are in a state you are not normally in. I was just walking through the forest with you. I’ve done that a hundred times before with you, Marliza, my friends, myself.”

Bailba took a small bite of a salad she had made for herself. How a mage, one with as much power as her specifically, was able to eat so slowly and such a small amount was beyond Aelwen’s comprehensions. The apprentice listened intently as Bailba explained leisurely, taking her time, allowing Aelwen to digest every morsel.

“I expected that for you, fear and pressure would be what brought out the magic in you. You are so talented and have worked yourself so high up in the ranks of the arena and now of society itself, I thought that you had forgotten the true meaning of raw fear and what it feels like to be looked down upon by a mentor. That is why I yelled at you during that first day of real training. Marliza was in on it, too.

“It turns out that I could not have been more wrong. It was absolute serenity that brought out the magic in you. Apparently, you have not been calm in a very long time. I know much about you, but not all, and that fact evaded me. Tranquility is the emotion you feel the rarest. It is the emotion that brought forth the power in you that will determine the fate of the world.”

Shivers rushed down Aelwen’s spine. It was true, all of it, and yet even she had not discovered it. How much more was hidden within her that even she could not see?

Moist breath tingled Aelwen’s ear, dragging her out of her sleep.

“Come on, I know you don’t want to waste time.”

That voice she had not heard for a few days, but she still knew it. Aelwen rolled over to face Valiran, the mage who was perhaps her most willing friend here. In the shadows and rays of sunlight of the early morning, her hair was dark orange prevalent with the occasional flecking of brilliant gold here and there.

Aelwen rubbed her eyes, clearing away the stuff clumped around them. "What?" she mumbled, the fog of sleep doing all it could to engulf her again.

"Magic training. I'm going to go with you, practicing alone is awfully boring. I've had enough of Marliza and her attitude to last me a good month. It'll be nice to spend time with someone who isn't always trying to drag me down."

The newest mage rolled out of bed and began getting dressed, past the initial shock of having others watch her do so.

"I don't think Marliza is all bad," Aelwen said. At that exact moment, the image of Marliza shaking her head as the two of them almost mentioned Zarah burned in Aelwen's brain. She shut her mouth and focused on picking out a shirt.

"I know," Valiran said with a sigh. "She means well, but the way she says everything is always so condescending. I've been to her village, Havon. Her people are normal and kind, so are her parents. I don't understand what went wrong with her."

Valiran gasped suddenly as Aelwen removed her shirt. Aelwen looked over her shoulder, Valiran's jaw was hanging open.

"I know I'm attractive, but people usually hide their surprise a little better than that." Aelwen said with a half-smile.

"Your back," Valiran stammered.

Aelwen did not need to look to know what Valiran was talking about. "That's the price you pay for some semblance of family in the arena. A place that you belong."

"You were there for years, weren't you? How have they not healed?"

The scars all over her back were crooked lines, some ran deeper than others, they were all plainly visible, indents of the torture she had endured to become what she was today. Perhaps she had not endured it at all. The girl she had been was long since dead, in her place rose a fearsome beast with a true heart beneath all of her armor.

The dark skinned mage nodded and pulled on an oxford blue shirt. "Don't you have scars that have never healed and never will?"

Aelwen knelt beside the pool in the clearing dedicated to her training and tentatively dipped her fingers in. The water was crisp with the chill of the oncoming winter. Valiran watched from beside her. The air around them was, too, hence the reason they both had fur cloaks draped around their shoulders.

Valiran peered into the pool. "Anything in there?"

"I think there are fish on the bottom, but they don't seem interested in us." Indeed, dark, oblong shapes bobbed slowly along the floor of the pool.

The redhead waved a hand and a wave of magenta magic rolled over the surface of the pristine water.

"Show off," Aelwen quipped. She stuck out a hand of her own and sent magic racing from her shoulders to her fingertips. A blast of pale blue magic came out and slithered over the top of the water.

"Come here."

Aelwen stood up and faced Valiran. "Let's begin with the most crucial of basics: summoning the type of energy you want to." Valiran sounded like a teacher all of the sudden. Her voice was deeper and broader than before.

"You are lucky," Valiran continued. "The what you want is easier than the when you want it. Some mages have the trouble that they will cast a spell but it will not happen until a long time after. What type of energy is it that you want to conjure right here, right now? Blue is broad and destructive, yellow is quick and lithe, red is sleek and effective, purple is defensive and solid, the list goes on. Pick one that you've summoned before and you know you can summon."

"Slow down, I can't remember all that."

"You don't need to, this is just a training exercise. Overall, all magic has the capability to destroy and the differences are minimal nuances that only master mages bother learning about. It's a common training exercise to have beginner mages practice summoning specific colors of magic to help them learn to focus and make sense of all of their magic."

"Okay. Red," Aelwen said with hardly a thought. Red magic resembled fire. Fire had destroyed her first life, she would make it create her second.

"Okay, good." Valiran began to stroll around, like a professor inspecting all of her students. "Red energy is like fire. So, think of fire, do your best to get everything else out of your head. Try it."

Fire, fire, fire, fire.

A streak of yellow energy erupted from Aelwen. Valiran held out a hand in a lazy motion that was almost a shrug, causing a shield of purple energy to build up and stop the fierce, rampant yellow.

"That was very powerful."

"Powerful wasn't the goal," Aelwen said. She was getting sick of people trying to tell her she had done well when it was obvious that she had not fulfilled their expectations. No one ever did that in the arena.

Valiran gave no reply to that remark. She said, "Think harder about the red magic this time. Imagine every detail of it. Envision fire."

Aelwen closed her eyes. Red and orange filled her mindsight. Vicious flames jerked about uncontrollably, casting bright embers and deep black smoke into the sky.

A burst of aqua power shot from Aelwen's hands. Valiran rid the area of them with a sweep of her own red magic that swallowed up the sea colored energy and left nothing in its place.

Valiran said nothing for a few moments, she gazed up at the gray-blue sky and tried to figure out what to have Aelwen try next. Eventually, she said, "Okay, do not think, feel. Don't just envision fire—feel it."

Aelwen did exactly as she was told. Red and orange filled her mindsight once again. She could feel the unrelenting heat of the fire, increasing every second, the light of its magnificent ferocity grew, blinding her. The scent of its smoke was acrid, searing her nostrils and making her mouth dry. Each ravenous flame reached high into the sky, on its own journey to scorch away everything to its path and create a world of ash.

Aelwen squeezed her eyes shut, internalizing the feelings.

She flung open her hand. A blast of red came out, it roared like fire and barreled through the clearing.

After extinguishing the fire-like energy with a whorl of green, the two mages whooped together and jumped up and down.

"That was fantastic!" Valiran cried. "You did it!"

Aelwen yelpled in glee herself.

"Just think, soon you'll have an even firmer grasp on your power, you'll be able to wield it with hardly any thought at all. Your magic is so powerful, I have a feeling that even Rhea will be impressed."

"If she has time to be before I blow her to smithereens." With the red power still so easily accessible, Aelwen sent an arc of flame-like magic into the air above them, casting a red glow upon the saviors of the age.

Several months passed in the time-altered world. Aelwen spent every waking moment practicing her magic. As time went by, she learned how to accept the frustration, let it roll off of her and allow the pleasant feelings of accomplishment and joy to soak in. Mastering the art of filtering emotions instead of pushing them all down deep was another skill required to be a successful mage, at least for her personally.

Now that Aelwen possessed magic, she realized how much more power it gave her. Not just physical power either, but inner confidence and drive, like the flame of what she'd felt when she met Zarah had been stoked into an inferno.

Valiran accompanied Aelwen almost all of the time, which Aelwen rather enjoyed since Valiran did not ever toss around snide remarks or insults about her past. Aelwen would not have minded the company of Bailba, and they did train together sometimes, but the company of one so much older and knowledgeable than her always put her on edge. Valiran, on the other hand, was practically a magic possessing version of Iowan. She cared but did not force insightful conversations between them. Her jokes were full of wit, and while she always tried to correct, she also did her best not to condescend. Aelwen could not have hand picked a better instructor and partner to be by her side.

Each day Aelwen uncovered a new ability or perfected an old one. She had set a simple goal for herself: never stop improving. Magic was all about detail. "Intricacy is key," Valiran had told her one day, and that was something that Aelwen would not forget. Aelwen was not going to lie, either; she was really quite good at magic.

The up and coming mage spun in a circle, blasting orange magic from her palms. Valiran tumbled out of the way and sprung to her feet, shooting a streak of blue at Aelwen, who swiftly conjured a shield of purple energy to deflect the attack. She dissolved the shield and prepared to send a flash of power at her opponent, but stopped short when Marliza appeared on the opposite side of the expansive clearing.

Her usually curly hair was straightened, so long it almost reached her hips. It shimmered ebony in the clean light that filtered in through the leaves. Her attire was plain and well-fitting as usual, the only thing out of the ordinary was the satchel she had slung across her chest. Marliza held herself straighter than usual, a tense readiness was in her stance that Aelwen had never seen before, even in all of the extreme training sessions she had looked in on. Marliza's jaw was set, giving her an expression of fear and ferocity mingled into one terrifying countenance. Her dark eyes darted from place to place around the clearing.

Valiran raced to Marliza's side. "What's happened?"

Marliza did not stop her nervous glancing as she answered, "The war."

That had Aelwen on her feet as well. "What?" Her voice was the low growl of a lioness that was now stalking towards her prey: an answer.

"The Vatre-darah suffered a horrible defeat just hours ago. Their forces are scattered everywhere, thousands wounded, hundreds dead. They need you now, Aelwen. We're out of time."

Aelwen's chest heaved with strangled breaths of terror. She took Marliza's hand, Valiran took the other. Even Marliza's hands were rigid. That was all Aelwen had time to process before everything disappeared from view as darkness swallowed her, Marliza's strained grip was the only thing she knew anymore. The mystifying sensation was over in a flash, the world came back into view.

The three female mages stood on the flat dirt streets of a Paruman village, the first one Aelwen had ever been in. It was quite simple, really. Houses of stone and wood with either thatched or slate roofs. People milled about, everyone with their own individual style, focused on their daily tasks. The village was just like any that could be found in any other country.

Marliza turned to Valiran, drew a stack of paper from her crossbody bag and handed it to Valiran. "Take these to the eastern council, avoid main roads, don't let anyone but the council see them. Go."

Valiran sprinted off, papers fluttering in her hands.

"Why doesn't she magic herself there?"

"She's never been there, she doesn't know what it looks like."

"Then how does she know where she is going?"

"All mages know the way."

A more ominous answer than Aelwen would have preferred, but there were more troubling issues at hand.

"Come with me." Marliza's voice was dry but the speed of her stroll suggested she felt anything but bored.

There were few people about in the village, but the ones that were present gazed at Marliza with admiration, one even sank to their knees in respect.

"This is your village?" Aelwen asked.

"Yes."

"It's…not what I expected. All of your people are mages, right?"

"Yes."

"Why do they all live in such simple houses then?"

"Magic in moderation," Marliza explained. "It is a part of our religion; the spirits gave us magic to help us on our paths in life, not to indulge and wave away the life that was given to us."

That answered her question, Aelwen guessed. It made sense, but at the same time it did not. Rhea's turn had proved that mages were just as susceptible to emotions as humans, didn't they ever give into greed?

The walk felt unnaturally short even though they travelled at a brisk pace. Aelwen wondered if Marliza's magic had something to do with it. A dark grey lake expanded before them, miles into the distance, so far that neither of them could see its end. It seemed that they had made the journey all the way to Marliza's village only to walk from it to nature.

Marliza strode up a rock that jutted out above the water. It was positioned so precariously that it seemed as if one ounce too much would make it fall. She sat near its tilted tip, drawing her legs up to her chest and placing her hands on the rough surface to keep from sliding.

"Come," beckoned Marliza, her voice suddenly calm.

Aelwen walked up the rock to take a seat beside her. She took small, slow steps. It was not her balance she doubted but the stability of this chosen sitting place.

Once Aelwen had taken a seat, Marliza looked at her. Aelwen knew that look, it was the one someone used when they were examining a person.. Marliza's eyes looked over Aelwen's face intently, never drifting below her neck. She and Marliza had fought many times, sized each other up plenty, she had not a clue why Marliza was so interested in her now.

"My people will join you in the war." Her voice was still calm. She brushed a wispy lock of raven hair out of her face.

Aelwen took a deep breath. "Thank you. How— you said you would not take sides."

"That was before what happened today. Rhea is too far beyond reason, her conscience is lost. I will not let her bring the fate she dealt to your people to mine, not without a fight."

"Marliza, I cannot thank you enough." Tears pricked Aelwen's eyes, tears of elation on this day of dread.

The blessed mage seemed unfazed as Aelwen heaped thanks upon her. "Do you know what makes you so powerful?"

Aelwen blinked, partly to get rid of her tears, partly in confusion. "What?"

"The fact that you do not need anyone. Every mage I know draws their strength from someone, something. A place, a relative, a friend, a teacher. Never have I seen someone like you. You rely on no one, you draw your power and strength from within yourself." Marliza smiled. "I do not know where you get such inner strength from, but it has always been there, I can assure you of that. From the moment you were born you were flooding with potential, it has only ever increased since then."

Aelwen hadn't the slightest clue how Marliza knew any of that, but she did not bother asking. She didn't much care, either. Her people were dying out there, all she could focus on was getting to them. She turned her gaze to the cold rock she was sitting on, flicked a loose pebble and asked, "Do you really think I can do it?"

"I will not fill you with false hope or false doubt. You have only ever depended upon you. You are the only factor that determines how this will end."

"When are we going to battle?"

"I will muster the army, then we shall set out."

Marliza stood up, the precarious angle at which she stood not bothering her at all. She reached out a hand, "Ready to go and meet them now?"

Aelwen took Marliza's hand and stood as well, grateful for the anchor of Marlia's hand as the angle threatened to topple her. "Very much so."

The walk back to the center of the town was just as short as the walk to the lonely lake had been. Across a small stretch of grass, through a row of trees, a few minutes on a backroad and then there they were.

"The military barracks aren't far, I can magic us there if you'd like."

Aelwen couldn't help but smile as Marliza used the word she despised. A symbol of their union in this war, that was how Aelwen interpreted it. She nodded and then was choked off from the universe again, only to appear standing outside a great fortress of tightly packed stone slabs with sharpened logs pointing out between the end of the wall and the beginning of the slightly inclined roof.

Winter had fully arrived here in the normal part of Paruma that was not kept under Bailba's time-altering spell. A layer of snow a good two inches thick covered the ground. Still more drifted down peacefully from the pale grey sky. A banner of azure flapped wildly in the freezing air.

"Is that Paruma's color?" Aelwen asked.

"Yes."

"Why do the Hakmarres use purple? Don't they want to represent their whole country?"

"You'd have to ask Rhea that question." Marliza conjured herself a suit of scale armor, complete with a pair of swords crossed at her back. Aelwen replicated the action, creating herself silver plated armor and a light mail undershirt that fitted themselves perfectly over the smooth leather fighting suit she wore. She too added weapons, much more than Marliza, though. An entire belt filled with three different daggers, a sword and an axe appeared fitted around her waist perfectly and a large shield was slung across her back. Finally, a simple helmet fashioned in the same style as her armor rested atop her head, fitting perfectly. The weight may have been a hindrance had she not become accustomed to being so well equipped from experience from her training as an Arenian and the time she had spent in the war, both fighting and training.

Just for effect, Aelwen drew out a bit of her favorite shade of magic and let the red power intertwine between her slender fingers. Marliza pushed open the gigantic doors to the military headquarters and stepped in, a showful swagger in her step. Aelwen followed, moving in a similar fashion and holding her magic surrounded hand up to show off for all of the mage warriors to see.

All around the stone floored hall, as wide as twenty of the long dinner tables the mages ate at every night, warriors of every variety faced off, armed with all sorts of extravagant weapons, dressed in armor of scales like Marliza, flinging their magic at one another.

A young warrior girl, mace in hand, put up the visor of her helmet and dashed to Marliza. She bowed swiftly, "How can I help you, m'lady?" The girl smiled, revealing her a chipped front tooth. Many armies began training children at such a young age, but Aelwen had to wonder, did Paruma let children fight, too? She knew little about this culture, next to nothing about its military.

"Get General Sira," Marliza commanded.

The girl nodded and dashed away as quickly as she had come, racing down a corridor. While they waited for the general to appear, Aelwen passed the time by examining the trainees. When Marliza and Aelwen had entered, the practicing warriors had all cast a few looks at the newcomers, but now they had turned all of their attention back to their training.

A ferocity burned in the eyes of every warrior, every motion they made had their heart and soul behind it. They fought with true intent and a plan in mind.

A tall man swept down the center aisle of the room, making his way briskly toward the newest arrivals. He was thin but well muscled, with long limbs, a protruding clavicle, sharp jawline, dark eyes filled with a momentarily contained savagery and black hair cut in a style Aelwen had seen a few times before. It was popular amongst Arenians who wanted to add an extra dramatic flair of appearance to their work. The hair was shaved on the sides and the middle section was combed over. An uppercut, she believed it was called.

The man wore a form-fitting black leather fighting suit with a design of sparkling white, he had only a single longsword hanging at his side. He stopped before Marliza and dropped into a swift, graceful bow. This must be the general Marliza had sent for.

"Havon will join the war on the side of the Vatre-darah." Marliza's voice was cold, like a practiced politician. It was the way she had been taught to speak to people of such high positions even though they answered to her. Aelwen recalled the exact same lesson back at Arkada, when her only concern was one single country.

General Sira replied, "I had a feeling I would be told that." His voice was not at all what Aelwen had expected. Every general she had met had a particularly deep voice. Sira not so much, his was even a bit above average for the tone of a man's. Truthfully, nothing about him screamed, 'military member', let alone 'general'.

The strange general continued, "Fortunately, I have extended training within the last week. The incoming reports of the war gave me the feeling this decision might be made. The legions can be prepared within an hour. We stand prepared to serve at the pleasure of the ruling family." He swept into another graceful bow. Straightening again, he added, "Though, I did not think the inquiring family member would be you. Your mother usually handles military matters. What brought you here in her stead?"

"She said the decision was mine to make. My parents are not young. I will be the one ruling Havon, dealing with the consequences of whatever the choice was, whether to join the war or not, so mother allowed me to be the one to make it."

General Sira nodded. He glanced at Aelwen out of the corner of his eye.

"Who is this?" he asked.

Marliza extended a hand of introduction to her companion. "This is Aelwen. She is a Corovan who came to learn magic to fight for her people."

Sira nodded, smiling. "This is her. Many rumors have been spread about you, Aelwen. I am very intrigued to find out which ones are true."

Aelwen smiled, her heart wasn't in it and she had a feeling that it showed.

General Sira shook his head. "How stupid of me. I am Sira, Chief General of Havon."

Aelwen let her eyes dart to Marliza who quickly jumped in to explain, "The village I am heir to—Havon."

Aelwen held out a hand, letting the magic dissipate. Sira shook it.

"Alongside them," he tilted his head ever so slightly in Aelwen's direction, face towards Marliza, "I do believe we have a chance."

Marliza grinned. "General, would it trouble you to show Aelwen the stables? She has never seen our creatures, and I have not been with them for some time. It will be good to refresh my memory before we throw ourselves into this."

"Of course, follow me."

The stables were just as wide as the main hall, if not more so. The vast area was heated from a source Aelwen could not detect. The stable walls were built of great slabs of stone, not the wood paneling she was used to. Once Aelwen caught a glimpse of what each stall contained, the design made sense.

Inside of each wide stone-walled stall with an iron barred, chain locked gate stood a wildcat a bit taller than her waistline. The cats had sleek fur the color of a starless night. Their fur and flesh fit to their skin so well that the shifting of their muscles was visible. The eyes of the cats gleamed aurous, seeming to observe the very depths of Aelwen's soul.

She did her best to not let her admiration for the creatures show, lest she look foolish before Sira. "Are these your war mounts?"

"Yes." The general used his magic to widen the space between the metal bars of one of the stall doors so his hand could fit in. The wildcat on the other side nuzzled the general's scarred hand, the first sign of battle wear that Aelwen had seen on the man. "They are some of the best war beasts an army could wish for. Have you ever heard of the Noclovak?"

"No."

"Marliza, have you not informed her?"

Marliza looked suddenly ashamed. She dropped her gaze, not that the general was looking at her, his gaze was pinned on the cat he was stroking. "I have not had the time."

Sira withdrew his hand from the beast. "I see." He crossed the room and drew a hunk of bloody raw meat from a pail in the corner. He returned to the cat and held the meat out to it, once again widening the bars. The cat dug in, ripping the meat to shreds, the whole thing downed in no time. The beast even licked Sira's hand clean of blood. Aelwen noticed that the voracious animal had not so much as nicked the general's skin. He patted the cat on the head and turned back to the women. The bars went back to normal. "They strike where they wish with immense force. Always remember: a fosc never misses."

"A fosc? Is that what these are?"

"Indeed. All of these loyal, intrepid beings are foscs."

The general began to stroll down the aisle, an elegant sway to his hips. He stroked the foscs as he passed them, not one backed away from his touch.

"What was it that you mentioned, general? Noclovak?" Aelwen asked.

"They are the night hunters, a certain brigade of this military, the very finest soldiers with the most audacious foscs. The term 'night hunters' became a popular name for the mages all those years ago, the people without magic used it as a term of insult. When we dared to retaliate we did it under cover of night to avoid persecution. So, we turned it into a name of our own, the title of the supreme sector of our military, the ones who can be trusted with any task, no matter how arduous. They dress all in black to honor their title and their history. You may have heard them referred to as 'black riders' or something of the like."

Aelwen shook her head. "No, I have never heard the term."

General Sira came to a stop before a single pair of large doors. "It is an ancient tradition for the ruling family to lead their military into battle. Rulers used to fight side by side with their people, not keep themselves holed up in their castles."

It took all of Aelwen's self restraint to keep from going on a rant about how all rulers were not like the Corovan one. There were still trustworthy politicians out there and one of the finest happened to be ruling and fighting with his people at this very moment. If he had not perished yet.

"The ruling family members never ride the same mounts as the soldiers, they do keep some sign of their higher station, even in war when such things should not matter. The Havon family has ridden inyanga for generations."

Aelwen was about to voice the most obvious question when General Sira swung open another pair of doors, leading to another section of stables. These were a bit larger than the fosc stalls and resembled the corrals used for horses in the rest of the world.

A tall stag, the same color as the snow that coated the ground outside, stood in the first enclosure, a moonglow aura like those that surrounded the Ihashi emanating from it. The stag had a rack of antlers that stretched on for ten feet at least, many pearly points glistened on every antler extension. What those prongs could do to the enemy in war. Aelwen took in the rest of the brilliant animal's body— nimble legs, lean build, twitching nose, no tail. Just how well could this creature, this inyanga, be able to last in the midst of raging war?

Aelwen's face must have betrayed her thoughts because Sira answered her question. "They can hold their own in battle. Inyanga feel an immense loyalty to the family they are raised to serve, they take their duty just as seriously as any of the soldiers in the hall. Their antlers and hooves are really their only built in weapons, they do not have the claws and jaws of the foscs, but inayangas are fabulous at maneuvering. Their speed is tremendous, an asset that makes them even more valuable in the war. You cannot kill something you cannot catch."

The three mages walked to the end of the stables. Aelwen took a good look at all of the inyanga, she even gave one a quick pat on the neck. At the end of the stalls, the general faced the two women.

Sira gave the heir a look of admiration, "I eagerly await the day you rule."

Marliza inclined her head in thanks.

He turned his focus to Aelwen. "I believe that with you the cause will be revitalized, even with everything that has happened." He stepped back, splitting his attention between the two of them. "I can have the troops rallied within the hour. Meet you in the north yard."

Marliza bobbed a swift nod. "We shall await you." General Sira turned on his heel, heading back to the training quarters. Aelwen followed Marliza through a side door, around the building and to a vast clearing. Mere minutes passed before the first of the Havon troops, fully armored astride their foscs, began pouring into the space and assembling themselves.

"What about Valiran?" Aelwen asked Marliza. "We left her behind."

Marliza did not look at Aelwen to answer, instead she sized up the force gathering around them. Her force. "There's no way she reached the council yet. She has much business there, we will not see her again before we leave."

"Will she meet us on the road?"

"Perhaps." In the crowd of Noclovak, ordinary soldiers and foscs, a white brilliance appeared that towered over them all. The inyanga's movements were graceful and precise. General Sira led the creature to Marliza, who stroked its snout before climbing upon its back. Beside General Sira, Marliza made her way to the head of the gathering. Aelwen trotted after them.

At the front of the force, Aelwen took in the power that had joined the ranks of the Vatre-darah. They were all sitting atop their own beasts. All of them were armor clad and weapon bearing. They had formed neat lines and divided themselves into sections, creating a grid pattern. The entire clearing was packed full of mages. Havon's military was not large, but it was clear that the army of mages would be more valuable than any army any of the other countries could offer, with the exception of Zarah's army of dragons.

Feeling too small amongst the crowd being the only one without a mount, Aelwen released a shrill whistle and prayed she was close enough to be heard.

The soldiers kept stock still at her back. Beside her, Sira and Marliza were leaned close to one another, discussing strategies in low tones.

Doubt was just beginning to creep into Aelwen's mind when a shadow passed over the clearing. She raised her head to the clouded sky, scanning for the one she sought. Through the clouds to the north, a dark shape was visible. Moment by moment it grew, coming nearer and nearer to them. The soldiers couldn't help but gasp in shock at the sight. A queen of obsidian and gold, a beast of reptilian savagery and grace, alighted at the edge of the clearing.

Aelwen was upon the dragon's back in an instant. From her perch behind one of Zarah's spines, Aelwen looked down at Marliza. To keep the words from getting stuck in her throat, she got them out as quickly as possible. "This is it."

Marliza inclined her head stoically. "It is."

Aelwen smiled at her friend. Months ago, she had looked at Marliza for the first time and thought about what an irritating training partner she would make. She turned and stared at the blinding morning sun. "I'll meet you at the border."

"We shall see you there." Marliza was gazing off into the distance too.

On her rider's command, Zarah flew off in the direction of the Paruma-Marchia border. Aelwen forced herself not to look back over her shoulder to the country that she had hardly gotten to know and that had still become a home.

~~~~

Bailba's magic picked up on the tension and anticipation growing in the people she watched. Perched on the ledge of a cliff, she watched as the war procession made their way to their fate.
~~~~

An untouched coating of snow decorated corpses of trees. The sun was breaking over the horizon, bathing the snow in golden light. A marvelous winter sunrise. All in all, a perfect scene. The perfection of nature was interrupted by a mass of tightly clustered, marching humans covered in silver armor. The warriors rode stark black foscs, led by a dark skinned woman astride a white inyanga and a thin, dark-haired man on a fosc who rode beside her. The woman was in armor that matched the soldiers marching behind her, save a billowing cloak of azure with a silver hummingbird, an addition that would be cut away within the first seconds of real battle. The thin man wore an azure bandolier, marking him as the leading general.

Bailba watched from a cliff ledge until the army was naught but a series of specks in the distance. Then, in a whoosh of emptiness that hardly daunted her any more, Bailba stood in the high snow at the border between Paruma and Marchia. Before her waited a thousand mages ready for war, an heir and general at their head with a savior riding the queen of dragons adjacent to them.

The crone mage bowed simply. "I have trained you both."

She scanned Aelwen and Marliza the same way she had when they had each first appeared before her, taking in what techniques would work best for them and trying to figure out how to extract their magic.

"You as well." She turned the same look to Sira, who smiled. There was hidden pain in it.

Then Bailba looked over the whole of the waiting army, their foscs shifting in anticipation. "I cannot see all of your faces, but I bet I have trained a good lot of you. I am proud of all of you. I trust you all and I wish you the best of luck. I do hope to see some of you again." Bailba smiled, her wrinkles folding upwards. She blinked in contentment and with a sigh, she was gone.

Instead of magicking herself up several flights of spiral stairs inside her enormous tree home, Bailba walked. By the time she reached the fifth floor, an ache filled her bones, a pain that she knew was not from age. Her whole body brimmed with exhaustion. With nothing better to do, no students to train, nothing to concoct, Bailba decided to take a nap. Hopefully a bit of rest would dull the pain.

She sat on the edge of her bed. She had lived in the same home for decades and yet she still let her eyes drift over her room, making sure that everything was in place here while the rest of the world was rocking uncontrollably.

All was well. The lamps, tapestries and pillows in place.

Bailba was about to lay down when a golden picture frame on her nightstand caught her eye. It was one of those objects that had been there for so long that she hardly noticed it anymore. She closed her gnarled fingers around the cool metal frame, her fingers sliding into the floral engravings.

It was the only picture of herself she owned. A portrait by a skilled but poor artist. It showed a woman with deep tan skin. It was not visible in the picture, but she remembered well; her fingers had been stained with soot from helping a blacksmith earlier that day. She was wearing a close-fitting one-shouldered shirt and skirt, the colors of both made her look like the living incarnation of a sunrise.

Beside the woman, holding her hand, stood a short man. He had dusty hair with a funny cut in the front from when his hairdresser's scissors had slipped. The man was

CHAPTER TWENTY-FIVE

The scenery could not have been more flawless. A foot or so of snow lay unmarred for the first many miles of the journey. The destruction Aelwen had seen months ago from the back of Zarah was gone. No husks of buildings or decaying bodies, just pristine whiteness, a sheet of gray sky and snow covered palm trees. She had to wonder where it had all gone. When she had seen that sight, snow had begun to fall sparingly. Based on the weather conditions now, no more than a month or two had passed. A body did not decompose in such time, building remnants did not break down either. Where had it gone?

The swarm of soldiers astride their black foscs, the magical heir upon her moonglow inyanga and Aelwen herself were all travelling blindly, Zarah's sharp senses their only guide. General Sira and Marliza kept combining their power and casting out a net to feel where the Vatre-darah were. So far, neither of them had felt anything. All of the villages and towns Aelwen had passed by on her way to Paruma were gone. It was as if they had never been there at all.

The rest schedule of the legion was short. Just long enough for the mages to recover themselves, eat, sleep for nothing more than four hours at a time, usually closer to two, and for the mounts to rest themselves. Then they were off again. The journey took them two days short of a week.

From the ground, on the back of her nimble inyanga, Marliza magnified her voice. Filtered through the expanding magic, her gravelly voice became even deeper.

"Aelwen, my power has sensed something. To the west."

Aelwen amplified her voice as well. "How far?"

"Two miles at the most."

Zarah was already circling down towards Marliza like a vulture to its prey. The dragon, her scales pale silver and her antlers and spikes ice blue, set her spear-like claws into the snow. Marliza climbed up onto the dragon, not needing a vocal invitation.

Zarah rose back into the air, wheeling and swooping to the west. As the dragon soared, Marliza could not figure out how to position herself without a spine in her thigh or a wing joint in her back. Seeing the heir's struggle, Aelwen moved. "Marliza, here," She twisted to face the mage. "Sit between the spines. There's plenty of room for you to fit. Hold on to the spine in front of you and lean forward a little bit so the other one isn't stabbing you in the back."

The elder mage situated herself, her knuckles tightened around the icy back spine.

"Ease up a bit," Aelwen advised, spreading her arms and basking in the frigidness. Normally, a coldness like this would have her bent over shivering, but the fear, dread and anticipation building within her made her unnaturally hot.

"Where do I put my feet?" Marliza complained. "There aren't any stirrups!"

"Dangle them, your inyanga doesn't have any stirrups."

"He isn't a hundred feet off the ground!"

Aelwen laughed. "Try three hundred."

Zarah few onward. took Aelwen's mental command, and right after the rider finished her sentence, Zarah dove.

Marliza gasped in fright and dug her fingers into Aelwen's shoulder, desperate for purchase. Aelwen didn't feel it, she only felt the immense freedom crashing around her in wild waves. It was long since she had gotten over the fear of Zarah flying, she had never trusted any human more surely than she trusted the dragon. All she felt now was greatness and pride, her feelings were her unconscious attempt to drown out the terror that swelled in her, growing greater with every passing moment.

Marliza's magic led them to a place that did not look any different from the vast expanse of whiteness they had been travelling through for the last several days, with one exception. People milled about, nothing more than small, dark shapes from the altitude at which she and Aelwen sat. Zarah changed her scales to match her surroundings perfectly, then, heeding Aelwen's direction, swooped down, so close to the ground that her massive wings caused a miniature snowstorm.

The army was behind them, but not too close. It would be easier for Aelwen and Marliza to explain themselves before they had an entire army of powerful, magical warriors standing at their backs.

Aelwen dismounted quickly, giving Zarah a quick pat on the neck, sending silent thanks through the bond they shared. The dragon queen remained camouflaged. Aelwen wanted to speak to the people before showing them a dragon. The same sort of species the leader of the enemy rode, no less. Marliza dismounted as well. Aelwen extended her hand, pausing Marliza. "These are my people," she said calmly. "Let me be the one to meet them."

Marliza nodded in understanding. She hurried around Zarah and crouched behind the dragon, awaiting the right moment to reveal herself.

The people, it was now clear there were six of them, had formed a circle. Not one of them wore clothes without holes, and they were all too thin to survive much longer on their own out in the cold. They chattered and pointed to the newcomers.

"That's her, I swear."

"No it ain't."

"You never seen her."

"She had long hair!"

"Must have cut it."

"That's her face, I know."

"Probably an imposter."

"We'd better hope she ain't magic, then."

"I may have a broken arm, but I'll still go down swinging."

"I am Aelwen." She made her voice tumble like the wild wind across the tundra. "I have returned."

Unable to resist this perfect opportunity for showmanship, Aelwen transformed her basic armor into something grand. Her magic took hold of the metal she wore that it had created and dug into it, creating beautiful engravings, elongating the metal plates at her shoulders and fitting more tightly to the form of her body, leaving Aelwen in an engraved, glistening metallic masterpiece, a swoosh of ultramarine fabric billowing behind her. She even added a diamond encrusted longsword with a dragon head hilt.

One of the people, an older man with a grizzly beard, stepped out of the circle and stared Aelwen in the eyes. She held his glare, not twitching once. Finally, the man blinked and took a step back. "You don't look like her."

One of the other people, a skin and bones young man said, "I knew it was you! I fought aside you in battle, I could ne'er forget your face."

Aelwen's magic could feel it, only half of them believed her, and one of the believers was skeptical. "Does this help?" she asked, immediately making her regal garb disappear, leaving her only in the plain leather fighting suit, complete with hidden pockets to conceal knives.

"Prove it!" demanded a middle aged woman, a mace at the ready in her hand.

She had not thought of how to do that. Keeping her voice level despite her growing annoyance was not easy. "How would you like me to do that?"

"Fight me!" the woman replied, voice booming. "No magic. Them mages can't really fight, they rely on their magic. Without it they're useless."

"Look at you. I could best you in seconds." The woman looked down at herself, a scrap of meat compared to Aelwen's muscularity and poised power. The woman dropped her eyes. "Listen, I don't have time for this. I need to find the rest of the army. You can either come with me or freeze to death. The choice is yours."

The young man who had first vouched for her spoke to the others. "If she was the enemy she woulda killed us by now. And what good would it do her to come after us? A bunch of half starved nobodies? It don't matter if we live or die."

The young man's final words resounded in her ears. She stood before him and lowered herself a bit, her dark eyes meeting his mossy ones. "Do not ever say that. Every soldier matters. Who can say what the Hakmarres you have slain would have gone on to do if you had not vanquished them? Your every motion matters. You are the fate of this country. I may be the 'savior', but what would I be able to come and save if you had let it fall in my absence?"

He was smiling now, confidently. His soul shone like the sun. A sun that would light up the world and drive away the night. Hope still lived in the poor souls. Aelwen hoped she could extract it from more than a single soldier. She rose to her full height, turning her gaze on the whole of them. "Will you come with me?"

The Vatre-darah soldiers shared a few more glances. The woman who'd wanted to fight her said, "I'd rather give you a shot than die out here knowing I threw away a chance to live."

The others murmured in agreement. Aelwen led them in the direction of Zarah.

"How did you come to be here, friends? Where is the rest of the army?"

One of the people explained, "There was a battle here not three days ago. The rest 'er the army fled. The Hakmarres took us prisoner, but they was stupid, they put us all together. We managed to escape by workin' together. The battle was in an awful blizzard, none of us know where the rest of 'em went, and we don't want to head in any one direction and never find 'em. So we been here since then, stayin' together and hopin' to the gods that someone'll come along 'en find us or we pick up a sign."

All of the people had similar accents, she noticed. Had they been a part of a local militia, not the whole army?

"Come with me. We'll find them," Aelwen said, sending a command to Zarah through their bond.

"What the hell is that?" grumbled one of the Vatre-darah.

Aelwen turned to see Zarah had turned her scales from white and gray that matched the landscape to black and gold. "It looks like the thing that Rhea rides, a dragon or somethin'."

Marliza stepped out from behind Zarah.

"And who's that? I never seen 'er before."

"You're right, that is indeed a dragon. She is on my side, I promise, as is that woman. She is heir to a village of mages who have agreed to join our side, she brings her army with her."

As if on cue, the Havon army became visible over the snow-covered ridge.

"How do we know we can trust 'em all? The Hakmarres broke their promise. They're liars, all of 'em."

"Do you want proof," snarled a voice of steel and ice from behind them. Marliza was storming toward them, her cloak flapping in the wind. She faced Aelwen, gesturing for the two of them to speak in private for a moment. Aelwen complied, the two mages turned their backs on the curious, frightened people.

Marliza said, low and briskly, "We don't have time for this. We don't know where the army is, if there is a battle raging right now. Cut your hand open and press it to mine, I'll do the same."

"Why?" Aelwen whispered in response.

"We will tell them it is a bond that joins us and cannot be broken. They will fall for it, I promise. Knowing what they think they do about mages, they won't have any trouble believing the ruse."

With that, Marliza turned back to the people and ripped a curved dagger out of her belt and dragged it across her palm. She held her bloody palm up, displaying the cut for all to see. Her blood trickled into the snow, staining the white with crimson.

Aelwen followed her lead, drawing a knife and slitting open her own hand.

"We make a blood promise. With this gesture our blood will combine, joining us in a promise that cannot be broken. If it is, the oath breaker will suffer a terrible death."

The two mages joined hands, their blood mixed and a few drops slipped to the ground. On Marliza's mark, a subtle nod, a simple signal that the others did not pick up on, their hands parted.

"Come with us," Aelwen said, her voice taking on that practiced, official tone she had perfected in her time as a politician. "We are your only hope."

The shivering, scarred warriors nodded their heads in agreement. They may have been skeptical, but none of them were stupid. It was trust or death, and only a fool would choose the latter.

After little more than another hour of travel, signs of civilization came into view. Many people, definitely no less than a thousand, milled about slowly, most of them with their backs bent. They shuffled through the snow in worn leather boots and wrapped in poorly fashioned fur coats. Those who were not walking were lying on makeshift cots with blankets draped over their thin bodies. Aelwen never would have guessed who all of the people were if she had not been looking for them. Down below, struggling in the harsh winter climate, was the dignified Vatre-darah army, made up primarily of the glorious Marchian military, the largest and most feared in the world.

At one point.

Now, the group withering beneath her resembled a starving town of fishermen more than a magnificent army.

Once again, not throwing away her shot at a dramatic entrance, something she had come to love since her time in the arena, Aelwen sent a mental signal to Zarah who let out a roar more treacherous than the sea. All of the Vatre-darah down below, none of them having noticed the dragon or her rider due to the fact that Zarah had camouflaged herself to the sky, turned their heads in near perfect unison. In the fraction of a second it took them to snap their heads up after hearing the roar, Zarah's scales had changed from pale sky grey to navy blue and silver.

Amplifying her voice, Aelwen proclaimed, "I am Aelwen and I have returned with the queen of dragons and an army of mages at my service. Where is President Tecsequaih Mayolan? I demand council with him immediately!"

She was well aware of how unforgiving her voice sounded. Fayette had taught her well, these times required no kindness.

Zarah swooped down in her savored spiral pattern until her claws sank into the snow. Aelwen hardly had enough room to dismount with all of the people swarming at the dragon's feet, groping for Aelwen, every one of them yearning to thank her for her arrival, to hug her, to know her, just for a moment.

Her entrance had the desired effect. The faces of the people, before ashen with sunken eyes, were bright with glee. Aelwen wanted to lean into them, to tell them encouraging things, but she knew too well that she could not. Only the survivors of this perilous war would ever get the chance to meet her, that was if she made it out alive and sane as well.

Pushing her way through the crowd, a woman reached out and grabbed her shoulder. Aelwen was about to wretch her shoulder out of the desperate grip when her magic picked up on something about the touch. This woman was not like the other fanatics, simply seeking to touch and thank. She had something more valuable to offer.

"The president is wounded, m'lady. He lays in the twelfth cot down."

Aelwen nodded graciously. "Show me."

On the heels of her escort, she made her way as quickly as possible to the cot. It was up to Marliza to explain everything, to introduce herself and her army. Aelwen would handle the more pressing matters.

Tecsequaih Mayolan's hair was more gray than black. The lines of his face were deeper and more plentiful than when she had last seen him. His eyelids fluttered, he was doing his best to open them to see her, but his fatigue was weighing them down. Aelwen dropped to her knees in the snow, not caring as the moisture seeped into her pants.

"What happened?" Her voice was soft like summer cotton to staunch his wounds.

"They lacerated my abdomen. My intestines are a wreck," he explained, somehow managing to maintain his stately air even on the doorstep of death.

The mage's hand was out in an instant, reaching for the wounded area. The president saw her intent and grabbed her hand with his feeble one. The touch sent a shock of pain and deep rooted sorrow through her. This man, who had been so great, who had welcomed the refugees and granted them so much more than asylum... and now his touch, once strong, inspiring and commanding, was frail and tender.

"Don't." The word came out like glass that could shatter at any moment. His hand withdrew as if even touching her took too much effort. "When my time comes, I will accept it. You should not fight something that is meant to be."

Aelwen was frantic now. Without help he could be gone within days. "What about the Hakmarres?" she asked breathlessly. "What about them? What if they were meant to be, should we not have fought them because they were 'meant to be'?"

Tecsequaih shook his old head slowly. "That is different."

"We can't lose you," she clasped his bony hand in hers. "We can't."

The old man leaned back until his head rested on a pile of flat pillows. In war, the ruler was no better off than any of his warriors.

"Please, at least let me make you more comfortable."

"Save your magic," Tecsequaih was a moment in answering. "The world needs it more than I do."

Aelwen felt tears begin to prick her eyes. "Don't worry, I have enough." She swayed her hand over Tecsequaih like a calm wave. Her magic reached to him, a bond grew between his energy of existence, his life force, and her magic. Mages couldn't heal and nothing she could think to conjure would be of any use to him. So, she settled for what she did know. Connection. Strength. She thought of all the greatness he had exerted, the power she had felt rolling off of him the first time she'd met him, and sent it through the bond between them, funnelling it into him, hoping it would accomplish something.

"What has happened?" she asked, changing from a kneeling position to sitting.

"I have no doubt you know already, the Hakmarres broke their promise." Perhaps it was only her desperation that made her notice it, but Aelwen thought his voice sounded stronger than it had before.

She nodded. "Why did they make it in the first place?"

"They wanted to make us think they had morals, that they were willing to give us a fair chance. I should say 'Rhea' instead of 'they'. Every battle it becomes more obvious that she has a chain around their minds."

"How long ago did they break their promise? Exactly how long have I been gone?"

"They started using magic about a month ago, I think. If it had been any longer there would only be hundreds of us left. As for you, it has been two months and eight days."

Gods. In that time-altered world, it had been around nine months.

Tecsequaih added, "You probably thought that was a stupid thing to say. I know, we hardly look like a fighting force anymore. There are more of us than are here, I am sure of it. Our forces have been scattered too often of late. The Hakmarres use their magic to erase the tracks so that those separated freeze in the cold without being able to find their way back. I don't know how many of us would have made it without what you left behind."

"What?"

"The battle plans."

Aelwen still did not comprehend it.

"A soldier found them stowed away in Wyldmor. She gave them to Fayette. The general executed them all with only minor revisions."

She remembered now. Throughout the journey to Wyldmor, bored out of her wits, she had senselessly scribbled down battle plans. Before she made her escape, to do all she could to make sure the enemy did not find the plans, she had folded them many times and slipped them into a cracked stone in Wyldmor. She had never dreamt they would be found.

"Do you know where the Hakmarres' base is?"

"No. Many scouts have been sent out to locate them. Not one has returned."

"Where were the scouts sent? If they're not returning it's clearly because they were too close for comfort."

"That's the problem. Every scout group has been sent out in a different direction, they all go different distances. None of them ever come back."

Aelwen wriggled her fingers, the magic in them crackled. Never had she been so aware of all of the life surrounding her. Though it was miserable, it was still life and her magic felt it.

"I can find it. Magic senses life and is drawn to other magic. We'll find their base and attack. It is time for this to end."

The president was shaking his head defeatedly. "We will launch no more major campaigns until the winter is over. It would be suicide to do anything else."

"We can make ourselves a stronghold just like the Hakmarres. We can conjure buildings and materials."

Tecsequaih's eyes narrowed with curiosity.

"I expected you to return with magic but not enough to care for an entire military."

"I am not alone."

The president raised an eyebrow.

The mage was suddenly aware that her body was blocking his view of the mass of people and the army of Havon. She moved to the side. Tecsequaih's mouth parted. She could almost see the way that it all sunk into his brain.

"How," he breathed slowly.

"I trained with other mages. One of them was heir to a village that had not joined with Rhea. Originally, their plan was to remain neutral. They changed their minds in the end."

"I've never known anyone to change their mind about something so important so quickly. Subjects like that take time to analyze, you must look at every possible effect, to do so in a month…"

"We lived in a different realm where time was slower. She was making her decision the whole time. Mages do not handle their ruling power any less seriously than you do. They really aren't very different at all."

Tecsequaih still did not look convinced. "We should set up a meeting between Fayette and their general. Now that we have all of this new power on our side, we will have to reevaluate every battle plan we were considering for the next bout of combat. If these mages are as ingenious as Rhea, we may have a slim chance now."

"I have someone who will give us more than a slim chance." Aelwen released a shrill whistle. In a moment, Zarah was beside Aelwen, her scales rippling red and orange.

"A beast to challenge Rhea's," the president stated.

"Not just her dragon. Her entire army." Aelwen set her hand upon Zarah's crimson neck. "This is Zarah, queen of the dragons."

Hearing her legendary title, the dragon tossed back her head and roared. She lifted herself off of the ground, beating her four bright wings and stirring up the snow.

"They are the something greater than magic that was promised to me." Aelwen turned back to the bedridden old man, beaming. "Let us waste no more time. Do you accept the aid of the Havon army and the queen of the dragons? Are you ready to begin the end?"

Tecsequaih's thin lips pulled back into a kind smile. "Yes," he said determinedly.

Aelwen leapt onto Zarah. In seconds, they were far above the crowd. Everyone had fallen silent and had their eyes pinned on the duo.

She thrust an arm into the air and declared, "Aelwen has returned!"

The Vatre-darah erupted in applause. Aelwen took their noise, their joy and tucked it away within herself, a store of power to be saved for the ideal time.

She spoke again and the applause died. "As you have all seen, I have brought new friends with me. If you trust me, you trust them. We have made a blood promise to serve alongside each other until our ends. I am terribly sorry for abandoning you all without an explanation. I am back now and stronger than ever. *We* are stronger than ever. Battle plans are being concocted as we speak. With the help of our new allies, we will secure ourselves as the Hakmarres have done. We will regain our strength and find where it is they hide from us. They hide because they are afraid. They do not want us to see their fear. We will bring fear upon them, our rage will be so strong that it will shatter their world and rock the earth! We will slay the Hakmarres! The time of the Vatre-darah has come! With the fire that fills us, we will burn down their evil and ignite the future!"

Aelwen thrust out an arm, fist blazing with magic. Moving her arm in an upward arc, the magic spread across the sky. The other mages did the same, stretching out their arms and unfurling their magic high in the air. All of the magic blended together, forming a massive bubble that surrounded the entire ramshackle camp. The strongest of the mages sent extra jolts of power into the bubble, reinforcing it. The magic spread like veins, twining together into an unbreakable shield of protection. Those who had not drained themselves forming the shield set to work improving the encapsulated land, conjuring whole buildings of stone and metal.

Aelwen was in the midst of watching with awe that never dissipated, no matter how often she saw magic performed, when a hand touched her shoulder. The grip was unsettlingly firm. The mage whirled around, one hand clasped around the person's wrist, the other drawn back, prepared to strike. The face she looked into made both her hands go slack.

Sunken, dark eyes, crudely chopped black hair, a tinge of grey upon the person's once flourishing tan skin. The dismal face she looked into belonged to none other than Lysia.

The gaunt young woman who looked nearly twice her age said, voice like cracked slate, "Iowan is gone."

The air caught in Aelwen's throat, tangled in a web of stunned sorrow deeper than any ocean cavern. For once in her life, she recognized how useless it was to even attempt to hold her tears back. She forced herself to choke out, "Gone?"

"They took her. I fought them so hard. So did she." Lysia pulled down the collar of her shirt to reveal her entire upper chest covered in one mass of ugly blue and grey, a deep white scar ran from her clavicle to her breast. "We weren't enough. They took her. *She* took her."

"But she's alive?"

"I think so."

A carnivorous darkness stalked Aelwen, crouching, preparing to swallow her whole. She cleared her throat and clapped hand reassuringly to Lysia's shoulder. "We will get her back. We did once, we can do it again."

Lysia's mouth quavered into something that tried to be a smile. Gently as to avoid hurting her, Aelwen embraced Lysia, tears already running down both their faces. "We will find her."

Rhea had the chance to kill Iowan once and had not taken it. For some reason, Rhea wanted Iowan alive. As bait to draw Aelwen to her because she knew she had learned magic? That seemed to be the greatest possibility. Rhea was erratic, clever beyond belief. There was no saying for sure why she took Iowan alive. That was all that mattered, though. Iowan was alive. The Vatre-darah would have her.

That was what Aelwen told herself every minute of every day that passed. The monster of grief and anguish tried to sink its teeth into her, but she had given the monster its time. Now it was her time. Sulking and weeping would do nothing to save Iowan, to destroy the Hakmarres. Only action would do that.

Thankfully, Aelwen had spent many of the past months learning how to channel her energy to make it into something different. She grappled with the sorrow, corralling it. She could not keep it contained for long, those seconds she had it trapped she spent morphing it into incalculable rage. Her body was on fire. Her eyes were alive with a raging inferno. *Aelwen* was an inferno. It was time to burn down the world.

The basic leather clothing she wore was replaced by magnificent armor, studded with jewels and evil points on the shoulders and forearm. She was done pretending to be ordinary. They had repeatedly shoved a pedestal to her and every time she had stepped onto it against her own will.

No more.

It was time to give them what they wanted.

With a flourish of her thick grey fur cloak, she ascended, planting both feet firmly upon the pedestal and grinning at every fiendish opposition that had glared at her for so long. She could hardly wait to see how they reacted when she unleashed her conflagration upon them.

In several vast, sweeping strides, Aelwen found herself inside a circular stone building constructed moments ago by the unfathomably powerful people whose fate and will she held in her calloused hands.

General Fayette Ekua, armored, with that unmistakable glower of hers, stood at one side of the table. Sira, dressed in sheer leather and pointing at a map sprawled out on the table with the tip of his dagger, stood at the other.

"I can send them out right now, I told you. This is a waste of time."

"No," Fayette shot back sharply. "Their senses are just as honed as yours. As soon as we locate them, they will know and they will move. We have to do it all in one shot, find them and attack."

"We don't know what kind of fortress they are hiding in," the mage replied, his frustration evident. "We don't know what weapons to use, what formations."

"You are a mage, don't you all think alike?"

"No! We're all individuals, just like you!"

Fayette sighed deeply, her way of apologizing for that cutting remark. "With your army and your powers, can't you break into whatever it is we're going to be facing off against?"

"Yes, but you cannot. My army is not strong enough by itself, just like yours is not."

"We are not two separate armies. We are one unbreakable force, the Vatre-darah." Every head in the room turned towards the rumbling voice. Aelwen stood in the doorway. "We have to work together, combine our forces into one mold. If we do it correctly, when the time comes, we will be one towering, indestructible statue."

Aelwen stood before the map. Frozen wasteland covered the world for at least fifty miles on every side. "Fayette, you are right. Rhea most definitely has Hakmarres posted all around, prepared to alert her if anyone suspicious is sensed approaching." She turned the map to the right, then put it back the way it was. "Sira, you're right too. We have to be ready for anything. The first step is to find where the Hakmarres are hiding."

"And how do you propose we do that? When we can't even see where it is they're hiding?" asked Fayette, raising a brow.

"We can see. Mages cannot make themselves invisible, general. The Hakmarres have probably done exactly as we have, formed one large shield of protection and established a stronghold within it. It's rather simple: we send out a scout to report back to us."

Fayette planted her hands firmly on the table. "We *have* sent out scouts, many, not one of them—"

Aelwne held up a hand. "I'm not talking about a human scout. I'll send Zarah, my dragon. She can camouflage herself so they won't see her."

Fayette was not convinced. "So, you're going to tell the dragon what to do and she's going to do it? Just like that?"

"Just like that," said Aelwen. She looked between the generals. "If you'll excuse me, I'll go send her off right now."

Aelwen exited the building. A labyrinth of buildings had sprung up, there were people everywhere, carrying the wounded inside. They called out at the sight of her, singing her praises, reaching for her, their one last chance, their ray of hope in this sea of darkness. She ignored them all.

Despite the chaos, Aelwen spotted a large black creature perched atop the roof of one of the buildings. She let out a high whistle and the dragon swooped down to meet her. The people crowding the space dashed away, providing ample space for Zarah to land. Aelwen reached out her hand and Zarah pressed her snout against it. They both closed their eyes. Aelwen concentrated on the orders of Zarah's mission.

Stay hidden.

Find them.

She repeated it over and over in her mind while she focused on the contact between her flesh and the dragon's scales, sending the message between them. With the message clear in her mind, Zarah pulled back from Aelwen's touch and blinked once to show she understood. The dragon unfurled her four great wings and took to the sky, the color of the clouds consuming her until she could no longer be seen.

Back in the room, standing around the table with the generals, Aelwen examined the map.

"So, now we wait," said Sira.

"No," said Aelwen, running her finger over the paper. "We begin crafting ideas. A fortress is a fortress, plain and simple. Obviously we cannot set anything in stone, but we can begin planning now."

"The mages should attack first," Fayette said. "It will take their strength to break in. Those without magic should follow as a second wave."

Sira took a moment to think, then shook his head. "Perhaps the magicless should enter first so they think it is a normal raid, then my army— the mages," he corrected himself, "will be the second wave, a surprise attack."

Both generals turned to Aelwen, seeking confirmation for one of the plans.

"The whole force should enter at the same time, as one." Aelwen rested a finger on the map, in the middle of a bleak plain. "The mages use their powers to break the barrier, the rest of the army floods in behind them."

Sira smirked. "It'll be quite the shock when they realize the Vatre-darah have magic."

"Indeed. But we can't let them know right away. Don't let the mages use their magic openly. Quick shots here and there. The forces you have brought us are our secret weapon. Once the Hakmarres realize we have mages on our side, any that held back will not. We engage the entire Hakmarres, concentrating them in one area. Small groups of the stealthiest warriors, mage and not, can break off and search the fortress, find Rhea and kill her."

General Sira asked, "Do you really think that Rhea will stay in there when her stronghold is under siege?"

"Rhea will think that her army will crush ours, as they have done countless times before. If we all manage to keep the magic secret for long enough, she won't have any reason to be concerned."

General Sira raised a brow. "That's it, then? That's the whole plan?"

"Is there something about it you dislike?"

"No. I just didn't expect it to be that easy."

"Well, that's all I can think of for now, without knowing how far we have to travel or where we're going. Fayette? Your thoughts?"

The general, who had fallen silent, took a moment to respond. "I see no reason the plan wouldn't work. We'll have to meet again once we know the location, but until then, your plan is fine."

"Very well," said Aelwen. "I'll send work to you as soon as Zarah returns."

"How long will that be?" asked Fayette.

"I have no way of knowing. She travels fast, though. A few hours, rough guess."

"Good."

"General Fayette," Sira raised his eyes to the other general's. "How many able warriors do you have under your command?"

Fayette set her jaw. "I don't know an exact number."

"An estimate will suffice."

"Even that is hard to say. With this being the final battle, I expect many who have sat out in previous battles will participate. And now that we have real shelter to keep the wounded safe from the elements, many of them will recover quickly and wish to fight."

"Okay." Sira's word was kind, but his eyes were narrowed.

"Do not doubt the strength of my warriors, Sira." Fayette's voice was tinged with a thunderous growl. "We did not survive this long by being weak."

Eyes wide in offense, Sira replied, "I would never imply such a thing. I was only wondering, that's all." He reached out a hand which the Marchian general did not take. "I wish there to be no ill-will between us, general. I will gladly put aside my differences with you so we can vanquish this evil. Will you?"

Now Fayette was the one whose eyes were narrowed. She stared unblinkingly at Sira for a moment before slowly taking his hand in hers. They shook once and split.

Turning to Aelwen, Sira swept an elegant bow. "I look forward to hearing from you."

He made for the door, but before he could open it, Aelwen said, "Will you be seeing Marliza?"

"Yes. I am going to explain our plan to her right now."

"Thank her for me."

"I will."

The mage general left, leaving Aelwen alone with Fayette. "You don't like him?" asked Aelwen.

"It's not *him*. It's what he is."

"A mage?"

"Yes."

"So, then, you don't like what I am either?"

Fayette braced herself against the table. She shook her head. "I don't. I know… I shouldn't think like that. But it's so hard not to. You've been gone, Aelwen. You've missed so much. You didn't see them break their promise. You didn't see the things they did." She sighed deeply. "I can't help but feel that now, you're a little like them. Reckless. Unforgiving. A murderer. And that all the people you've brought here, they're like that too."

"I am. And so are you. We are all reckless. We are all murderers. We have all been unforgiving. That's why we're still alive."

Fayette leaned back. "I suppose you're right." A flicker of happiness flashed across her face. "I'm glad you're back, Aelwen." She clasped the mage's shoulder and squeezed.

Aelwen returned the gesture. "So am I."

"I'll try harder. To see them as human."

"Thank you."

Night had fallen and the stars were shining bright, illuminating the snow. Aelwen leaned against the windowframe in the room she had claimed as her own. It was small and sparse, but it mattered not. She would only be spending one night in it , the larger rooms were for the soldiers to fill. She couldn't sleep. The anticipation of Zarah's return was gnawing at her, forcing her eyes open and her mind awake.

Aelwen raised her eyes to the stars. When she was a child, she'd been so mesmerized by them. Staring at them now, she felt that childish joy return. They were so simple, yet so beautiful. So hopeful. Little promises dotting the darkness.

The stars she was gazing at were suddenly blotted out by a large, inky form. Aelwen started. The form passed by, approaching the stronghold. Relief swelled up in Aelwen, and she raced out of her room and outside to throw her arms around the neck of her dragon.

"Zarah!" She nuzzled her cheek against the dragon queen's sleek scales. "You had me worried. I thought something happened to you."

Zarah grumbled in reply.

Aelwen drew back. "Tell me what you found."

Another grumble came from the dragon and she pressed her snout against Aelwen's hand. Aelwen closed her eyes and savored the feeling of the power and surety of the bond she and Zarah shared. When the message had made its way from dragon to woman and Aelwen understood completely, the two of them split apart.

Not only had Zarah found the location of the Hakmarres stronghold, she had memorized its configuration.

The image still fresh in her mind, Aelwen nodded her thanks to Zarah and raced back to her room and went to work on a battle plan.

An idea was there, lingering within her, but it was not yet fully formed. The ghost of it was striking in her mind, but she could not articulate it quite yet.

That didn't mean she wouldn't try.

Crouched over a poorly sized writing desk, cramped in her room, Aelwen scribbled out the form of the structure. Then she drew a circle to represent a Vatre-darah troop and a line to indicate their movement.

No. That would trap the Vatre-darah with no way out.

She crumpled the paper and began a new one.

Her featherless quill scrawled over the paper, outlining the movement of a troop of Vatre-darah mages. Realizing that that move would carry the Vatre-darah straight to an oncoming attack, if all went as she had planned, Aelwen pushed down on her quill so that it scratched a hole in the paper.

Rhea's specialty was in keeping secrets and coordinating her forces, but not in planning. When it came to strategy, Aelwen was the one with the upper hand. Now that ability seemed very reluctant to show itself.

The idea was so close, clear in her mind, but would not come out accurately on paper. She shredded the inky page and tossed it into the hearth, then watched with satisfaction as the tatters turned to ashes.

By the time it was impossible for the bag's beneath Aelwen's eyes to get any larger and the sun was washing the world with soft light, the plan was finished. Every movement was carefully planned, every entrance deliberate. The Vatre-darah would leave this battle one of two ways: slaughtered or victorious.

CHAPTER TWENTY-SIX

The melody was more powerful than anything she had ever heard before. Had it not been crafted by the roars of beasts, shouts of tense warriors and clanging of metal, it would have taken two full orchestras to convey. Her soul song was a booming monstrosity of sound that was something far beyond magnificence.

Aboard the gargantuan reptilian queen of ebony and aureate, the crop-haired mage warrior, armed to the teeth, guided her forces to the north.

No human, magical or not, could see anything before their cold-stung eyes but more frozen wasteland littered with snow. The land sloped gently, then rose at a steeper angle, blocking their view. The army made its way up the incline.

Zarah changed her scales to match the sky exactly. She lifted herself higher, giving she and her rider a clear view over the ridge before them.

A whole new display came into view. Far below was an enormous, brilliant palace of glass with too many turrets and spires to count. The structure was immense, covering a vast swath of land. Bridges, walkways, columns and pillars linked every section of the enormity to the others, but Aelwen inferred that was not their only purpose. The structures took up much of the available space, leaving almost no broad areas for conflict. They were structures that seemed like nothing but connectors, but could be, if not known of beforehand by an incoming enemy, the defeat of any encroaching army and the thing that saved the Hakmarres from pure desecration.

Aelwen looked down at her advancing army. They were nearing the top of the ridge. The time was now.

She mentally signalled Zarah to dive, and so she did, bringing her rider right above the first rows of Vatre-darha soldiers.

Aelwen plunged her gorgeous falchion sword into the howling, frigid air. She issued a noise so loud it made the roaring winds cower, so deep it made the snow tremble, a sound that contained no words but conveyed a meaning deeper than any known word possibly could.

Resounding in the minds of every warrior standing at the ready, intoxicating them with the wild brazenness of battle, the Vatre-darah surged forward. The first wave in a tsunami that would drown the Hakmarres forever.

The Vatre-darah were visible to their enemy.

Everything had to move in time. Every troop had to advance at the right time, every legion had to move in the right direction, every mage had to keep their power secret until the right moment.

Already, a band of Hakmarres were rushing toward the oncoming soldiers, magic flaring around their fists.

Aelwen leapt from Zarah's back and prayed the Hakmarres were still too far away to fully see her jumping from the air and landing on the ground. Like magic, Zarah was a secret weapon in this fight. Aelwen swiftly pressed her hand to the clawed foot of Zarah above her, ordering the dragon away on a mission of her own.

The Hakmarres were close now.

Aelwen thrust her weapon in the air once more, hollering a charge.

The Vatre-darah sprinted around her, colliding with the mass of mages hurtling towards them. Warriors plunged their weapons into the hearts of their enemies, crying out with the power of battle. Snarling foscs seized Hakmarres in the jaws, cracking them in two with single bites. The ebony cats threw themselves about, masses of claws and muscle and teeth filled with bloodlust. Streaks of magic flew through the air, ripping open bodies and knocking people to the ground in senseless heaps.

Aelwen threw herself into the fray.

She fought with everything she'd ever had and more. She got as close as possible to her opponents so that she could press her hand to them and strike them with her magic from so close that the act went unnoticed and the Hakmarres would drop dead.

The Vatre-darah pushed their way closer and closer to the palace until they were wending their way around and between pillars and columns of glass. Aelwen prayed they were all moving the ways her plan had entailed.

The time was nearing.

Aelwen swung her sword in an arc, bringing it down to collide with the flesh of a Hakmarres warrior who spun out of the way and shot a blast of magic at her. She dodged, ducked and came up right in front of her opponent. She jabbed her armored fist up, savoring the sound of the Hakmarres' jaw breaking. These warriors were of steel and stone, broken bones would not stop them. With her fist still jammed under the enemy's chin, Aelwen clutched her sword and plunged upward, all the way through the Hakmarres' mouth and up into their brain. Spinning to face yet another enemy, Aelwen took note as a section of Vatre-darah warriors shifted to the left, molding their formation to fit perfectly around the columns.

There it was.

Aelwen fought her way out of the chaos, keeping her hands low, but shooting out magic whenever she deemed it safe. In a much shorter time than she had expected, she found herself standing by the side of the glass monstrosity, six other of the most skilled Vatre-darah standing around her.

It was time.

One of the other members of her group drew a sword and sliced at a Hakmarres hacking viciously at another Vatre-darah. The Hakmarres, irritated by this new distraction, tossed a careless mass of magic at the distraction. The plan worked. The Vatre-darah dodged swiftly and the magic collided with the glass palace. The fortress was constructed to stand against everything but the powers of its own people.

Casting a shield of protection around the seven of them would have been too risky a maneuver, so they all leapt far back as great chunks of serrated glass plunged to the ground. Once the way was clear, the Vatre-darah cadre hurtled inside. One of them, a warrior Aelwen had never seen before, took the lead, guiding them through the twisted building with no bearings but their own instinct.

After only a few moments of being inside, the shouts outside intensified. The Vatre-darah had revealed their magic, thus drawing any Hakmarres soldiers left within the stronghold out.

Rhea had crafted this fortress with the best of her wits on the inside and out. Every stairwell, landing and hallway had odd bends in it, making the entire place a confusing labyrinth. The clearness of every wall only made the situation worse, visions of different rooms, most of which being of no purpose but to be decoys to enemies, blurred together, forming confounding images of different depths before the trespassers' eyes.

"Go up," called one of the other cadre members. "The throne will be near the top!"

Aelwen almost refuted. Surely Rhea's mind was too complex for the ordinary architectural setup. However, she had had a good long look at this place. There was no underground. Having a throne room on the first floor was too stupid for even the most dimwitted tyrants. The cadre ascended another loop of transparent stairs, their feet moving so quickly that they were practically flying.

After getting stuck in four decoy rooms and turning back down too many dead end corridors to count, the cadre stood, huffing, in the doorway of a room just like all the others, the exact same but for one aspect: a glass throne with spiked edges. There was a glistening silver chain tied around the arm of the glamourous seat. Aelwen's eyes followed the chain, it did not stretch far. The shackle end lay on the ground, closed. Crouched on the transparent floor, back bent with tremendous fatigue, a shackle around their wrist, was a person. Aelwen inched closer. The person was female, her blond hair thin, the ends terribly frayed.

Aelwen's breath caught. It could not be.

The female did not lift her head and did not move, she seemed to be in some sort of trance.

"Hello," Aelwen tried.

The person moved her head a bit, lifting it enough to see who was approaching. Her eyes widened immediately and her whole body began to tremble.

Aelwen was dead sure of it now. "Iowan," she said gently, extending her arm. "Come with me." Memories of the first time she had saved Iowan from being chained to a throne flickered in Aelwen's mind. She banished them. She could think over the bizarre similarities once the war was over.

A bit of color had returned to Iowan's cheeks, just as sallow as Lysia's were. Emotion filled her eyes, but not any form of happiness. Desperation brimmed within those windows to her sunken soul, swirled with grief and longing.

"I can't," she shook her head, "The chains are unbreakable. Rhea forged them from her dragon's flame."

Aelwen swung her sword, in an instant the chain was a pile of metallic shards scattered across the pristine floor. "Dragon's don't breathe fire." She helped Iowan to her feet. "Fear makes the mind blind to the truth."

Her friend was shaking in her grasp, her legs quavering so violently she was afraid that Iowan might collapse.

Aelwen hugged Iowan to her, pressing Iowan to her body. "We are here."

In Aelwen's firm hold, Iowan convulsed. Her fingernails dug into her holder's clothing, they probably would have drawn blood had Aelwen not been so heavily armored.

"Iowan!" She cried, holding her friend tighter. "What's happening?"

Iowan shook her head, trying to dislodge the pain. "She knows," she gasped, "She knows I'm free. She's coming, we can't make it out!"

She was in almost complete hysterics. Whatever Rhea had done to her, Iowan was in a state Aelwen had never seen her in before.

"It's okay. She won't hurt you anymore." Aelwen moved Iowan so that she was standing on her own, though her legs still shook. "I know you're afraid. I am too. We all are." She nodded to the rest of the cadre that still stood by the door. "We came to save you and destroy her." The two former Arenians locked eyes. "Take your fear, embrace it. Transform it into ferocity." Galarus had said the exact same words to them too many times to count.

Aelwen conjured a kopis, she pressed it into Iowan's cracked fingers. "You must fight. Fear is the most overwhelming of all monsters. Let it take over and it will swallow you whole."

Galarus had said that to them before, too. A bit more color came to Iowan's freckled face. She stood taller and her legs stopped shaking. Aelwen conjured a suit of magnificent armor for her. Just as she did, a roar more pretrifying than the cry of a thousand demons shattered the air.

Outside the glass fortress, a battalion of airborne, scaled beasts flapped furiously and roared with battlelust. Something greater than magic had arrived. The Hakmarres would not see the light of a new day. The queen of the dragons had come and she had brought her army with her.

The dragons dove and seized Hakmarres in their jaws, chomping them in two with single bites. They grabbed Hakmarres in their talons, lifted them high into the sky, and dropped them so their bodies broke on the frozen ground far below.

Iowan was grinning now. There was pain in it, but it was a grin. A grin for revenge, for possibility.

Aelwen stepped close to Iowan one last time, embracing her with every bit of love she had ever felt for her wonderful friend. The one who had been beside her since the beginning. "I'll see you on the other side of the war," she murmured against Iowan's cheek.

The two warriors split apart, bloodlust glowing in their eyes.

Aelwen inclined her head, "Give them hell."

Hell reached them before they had a chance to face it. Rhea's empty throne was the subject of every cadre member's gaze as a cry like wild lightning resounded all around them. The sound made Aelwen's blood run cold. She knew that sound and had grown to love it. She did not love it now. Not one of them had even a second to take action before the glass roof above them was met by meathook claws. Massive chunks of glass flew at them.

The mage's minds were swifter than the sudden assault. Their honed instincts took over, casting spherical shields of protection around all of them, surrounding their fellow humans who did not wield the strength they did. Everyone's eyes turned upward, squinting through the whorl of broken glass. Up above, astride her maya blue dragon, swathed in yards of lilac fabric that swayed gracefully in the wind, with a finely carved mask of iron upon her face, sat the living incarnation of insanity.

Rhea's war beast shrieked again, snarling at the enemies cowering beneath their bubbles of safety below.

Magic calls to magic.

Aelwen concentrated on the bond forged between she and her fellow mages that surrounded her, holding their own with all of their might against Rhea's relentlessness. She couldn't send any complete messages as she could to Zarah, only flickers of intent. Sensing Aelwen's objective, the mages nodded in agreement with her.

As one, the mages tore open their shields and shot round upon round of magic upwards. Rhea was quick to realize their goal and threw up her own shield of protection. But she was not the only target of their attacks. The magic tore through her dragon's scales and ripped its wings to shreds. Rhea wheeled her mount around, but the dragon was already too wounded to comply.

The enemy beast threw its head back and howled with a shrill cry that shook the mountains to the north and plummeted down, crashing into the frozen earth. A crack like a boulder let loose from a mountainside echoed all around as the dragon's war hardened body met its match—the pure, raw strength of the earth.

Aelwen gave Iowan one moment's more attention, nodding swiftly, a signal that the last words she had spoken to her before the unexpected assault still stood firm. Then she dashed to the edge of the broken tower, leapt over the section of jagged glass that still stood and plunged toward the ground. She landed upon the back of the queen of dragons. It was time to end this.

Soaring hundreds of feet above the ground, Zarah plunged down, swooping over a brigade of advancing Hakmarres, one of the few that had managed to survive the wrath of the dragon army thus far, dragging her claws through the faces and chests of the unsuspecting warriors, staining her talons with blood. Zarah flew up again, Aelwen sensing her intention before she did so. The rider tightened her grip on Zarah's back spine in front of her and leaned forward as she had done a hundred times before. There was a very good chance this could be the last time.

Zarah folded her wings in and dived downward, sweeping over the earth and landing gracefully. Aelwen had dismounted before all four of her dragon's great feet had touched the ground. She bound towards the cruelly twisted body of Rhea's mount.

The dragon lay in a heap of broken, contorted power that was no more. But it's master was not so. From beneath an unnaturally folded leather wing emerged the iron clad horror, the living, breathing terror that was Rhea.

Aelwen gave her mortal enemy not one second to process what was happening. She sent a blast of magic straight for her enemy's head, which was blocked with a quick motion followed by an aggressive counterattack. Aelwen fought back, forging her concentration with all of her might, commanding every bit of power that ran rampant within her.

The Hakmarres leader launched a vicious attack in retaliation, bombarding her final opponent with an array of stunning magic. A good number of the attacks hit home, denting Aelwen's armor and slitting open her exposed flesh. Still, her body moved with its practiced quickness, her mind just as agile, and she managed to deter the rest of the assault.

Seizing her chance, the little time Rhea took to readjust before barraging her again, Aelwen took on the offensive and blasted Rhea with her own magic. One wave of sheer energy, followed by another and another. The waves followed one another in such close succession that Rhea didn't have time to position herself for a counterattack before the next one overcame her. A protective shield glowed atop Rhea's flesh, just enough to protect her body from the attacks, but not her clothing. Rhea sat calmly through the onslaught even as the covetous magic devoured her dress of delicate purple silk.

Rhea's mouth was twisted into a hideous smile. Her marvelous dress had completely vanished, replaced by spiked armor more vicious than any Aelwen had ever seen, long spikes that shouted a silent war chant of their own covered her limbs and head.

It was a distraction. Just a distraction.

Aelwen fought again, hurling every variation of magic she had at the menace before her. She broke those barriers within her and reached into the wells of her soul, drawing up layers of hidden strength, keeping up her attack, ignoring the blistering pain that gnawed at every bit of her that had been weakened by Rhea's magic.

Through the bond that tied mage to mage, Aelwen could feel that Rhea's effort was no less than hers. She too had to dig deep within herself, to places she had not explored in a long time, to stand against her foe.

Aelwen felt thin and weary. Her vision blurred even as she continued to launch power at Rhea. It was as if she was being dragged underwater, her movements becoming slower, her mind growing fuzzy as she was denied access to air. But she dared not stop her assault for even a moment. To open that window of vulnerability would be to commit herself to her own death. And though she felt like she was on a downward spiral nearing it anyway, Aelwen was not quite ready to die yet.

Rhea did not fail to notice the growing fatigue of her opponent. She heightened her power, assaulting Aelwen with swath after swath of determined power, refusing to back down for even a breath.

Through her growing blearly-minded confusion of what exactly was going on, Aelwen's honed warrior instincts managed to keep up with Rhea's attacks, forging defensive shields, then tearing them down to shoot out a hopeful blast of poorly-aimed magic, then building them up again.

After a time, even that reflex wore thin. Her brain warped and weary, Aelwen wanted to know what was happening, but even more than that she wanted a break. She was too slow to lift up a wall of protective energy. Rhea's magic hit her in the shoulder. Aelwen stumbled and shook her head.

What's going on? Where am I? She didn't know the answers to those questions. All she knew was that she had to keep fighting. But she couldn't, not without a break. She let herself go slack for a second, to take a breath and remember who she was and what she was doing. The exhilarating confusion of the battle started to relent like a fierce tide finally washing back out to sea.

The breath was driven out of her. She was bowled over by a wave of magic that felt like being hit by a ton of bricks. With a groan, Aelwen summoned a small barrier of magic just large enough to cover her body. Rhea released a second blast of magic. It barreled through Aelwen's energy barrier, shattering it, and hit her. Her head smacked against the ground and she felt wetness on the back of her skull. A third blast of power slammed into her. The pressure was immense, bearing down on her, squeezing the air from her lungs. The magic relented and she sucked in for air. Guessing she was still too weak to form any protection that would be of any use, Aelwen curled up and gritted her teeth, steeling herself for the next attack. But no other attack came.

She gathered her strength, scraps here and there, until she had just enough to raise her head. Rhea was standing directly before her, still clad in that menace of iron with only her dark eyes and hideous mouth visible through slits made in her mask. Why did she feel the need to hide? She was the greatest villain in an era, what was she afraid of?

Rhea did not smile that demented way she usually did. Her mouth was a tight, thin line, her eyes like thick ice that covered up the raging sea beneath. Slowly, she crouched, her eyes examining Aelwen as if she were a piece of meat at the market. Rhea's metal spiked arm flashed out so quickly that Aelwen had no time to register what was happening before a rough iron gauntlet was clamped around her chin, the pointed nails pricking her skin. Rhea hauled Aelwen up until she was standing. Aelwen did not need to look to know when one of the nails pierced her and blood began to trickle down her filthy cheek. The armored hand tightened its grip.

Aelwen quaked. She wretched her head to the side, hoping to break Rhea's grip. Her jaw cracked. The sound of the break ricocheted through her mind, filling her head like a wail in a cavern. Still, Rhea's grip did not ease. Aelwen knew she could not escape without snapping her neck. She did not have much hope left, but she would not sacrifice herself until every drop in the well was gone.

Rhea tightened her hold. Warm, scarlet liquid dripped down Aelwen's neck. With a grunt, Aelwen lashed out a leg. She hooked it around Rhea's knees and drew it forward. It was a move she'd used many times in the arena to topple many opponents. Rhea was not just another opponent. She barely tripped, then widened her stance, breaking the grip of Aelwen's legs.

Violently, Rhea thrust Aelwen out of her hold, shoving her forward. The force with which she was released made Aelwen sway side to side before regaining her balance. Just as she found her footing, Rhea's iron booted foot shot out and met angrily with Aelwen's side. She fell over, grinding her teeth as her broken jaw crashed to the frozen ground. Her head spun with the impact. Both of her hands went to her side that Rhea had kicked, her fingers tightened around the spot as if their pressure could stop the pain streaking through her. At least one of her ribs was broken, without a doubt.

Rhea lifted her foot once more and planted it firmly on Aelwen's side, just below where Aelwen was clutching her broken ribs. Through the bond they shared, Aelwen sent a plea to Zarah to help her. The dragon answered that she could not take out Rhea without risking killing Aelwen in the process.

The Hakmarres leader turned to face all of the soldiers around her, most of whom were Vatre-darah. The few Hakmarres that remained were too close to warriors of the other side for the dragons to pick them off easily without harming the Vatre-darah they were near, just as the situation was between Zarah, Rhea and Aelwen. Almost all of the battle around them had quelled, everyone eager and able to see the fight between the leaders had stopped to watch intently.

"People," Rhea began, voice like thunder that preceded the storm of the century. "Mages, non-mages, all of you. Look how stupid you were to put your faith in this wretch. She is nothing." She landed another kick on Aelwen before planting her foot atop her again. "She is weak and has never been anything more. *Will* never be anything more. Stupidity overflows in this foul being. Stupidity that you all somehow believed. She is a child with a snake's tongue. Without strength, without purpose. She has led you to your deaths with her clever words! You fell prey to her tricks, she deceived you! Do you see now what idiots you were? What a rat she is? Well, her time has come, she cannot fake it anymore! She got tangled up in her own web of lies, she had no choice but to face me! She pales beside me, a runt pitted against the alpha! All she ever gave you was false hope! Look at where that lie got her—beneath the foot of a true leader. And look where it got you—trapped on a battlefield with nowhere to go, with only one choice left to make: will you join me? Or will you die believing that she was actually something?

"Come to me. I will not harm you. I will forgive you. I know how sweet words can twist the mind. Come to me now. I will be your true solace, a guiding light that will usher you all to a bright, glorious tomorrow."

Beneath Rhea's foot, Aelwen thrashed. Rhea pressed her boot down. For a moment, Aelwen considered continuing to struggle, then decided better of it and stilled. She refrained from making any real effort to rise. Within her, she could feel the strength of her magic growing, revitalizing itself. Aelwen closed her eyes and focused on her magic, letting it fill her up with all of that wondrous, definite power.

Above her, Rhea continued her crazed ramblings. "She had gorged too long on her own words that she said so often that even she began to take them as true. Look where it got her! She was never anything but a liar, a thief who cheated you all out of your own reason!"

"Release her," snarled a creaky voice, indefinitely amplified by magic, ringing through the half-crumbled glass fortress. Simultaneously, every head in the area turned to where the sound had come from.

Standing on a mound of broken stone from a fallen archway stood a bosvark, coated with brass armor fitted to its round body. Astride the creature, barely visible behind its pointed helmet, was a bent-backed old woman with a shawl tied around her shoulders.

Rhea started at the sight of Bailba. "Never," she hissed, digging the heel of her boot into Aelwen.

With a level of speed none would expect such an old woman to possess, in a single fluid motion, Bailba withdrew a round object from the folds of her shawl, which she hurled at the wall of the Hakmarres stronghold with one hand, while with the other she shot a burst of green power. The object hit the wall. Before gravity could drag it to earth, Bailba's magic hit the object.

A wave of white light obscured Aelwen's vision. Heat consumed her. There was nothing, no one, only white heat.

Her ears rang with the echo of the blast.

Pain filled her, her jaw and ribcage the most prominently painful locations.

She blinked several times. On the fifth, she could distinguish vague shapes.

People were screaming in the distance, it sounded like they were underwater.

She blinked again. There was flaming debris around her. Lots of broken stone. Bodies of people and animals. Blood. Her vision still hazy, but clearer than before, Aelwen deduced that she was in no immediate danger from her surroundings.

Memories began to creep their way into her foggy mind. She'd been in a battle— the final battle. Rhea had beaten her. She'd tried to escape and broken her jaw. Rhea had kicked her and stepped on her, breaking her ribs. Rhea had talked to the warriors. Bailba had shown up and thrown one of her Kula nuts at the wall. She'd struck the nut with magic. Putting those pieces together with where she was now—full of pain, hot, confused—the most sensible conclusion was that Bailba's actions had caused an explosion.

Aelwen looked around. The Hakmarres fortress no longer stood. All that remained of it were the hunks of stone that littered the ground around her. An explosion indeed.

There had been dragons. Zarah and her army—where were they? Had the explosion scared them off?

Ears still ringing, Aelwen managed to get to her feet, albeit shakily. Around her, others seemed to be regaining their senses as well, groaning, moving and rising. Far too many did not rise. Whether the explosion had taken them or they had fallen prior to it, Aelwen did not know. She raked her gaze over the crowd of discombobulated fighters, slowly making sense of it all just as she had. Warriors. Dressed in vibrant green and striking blue and the soft tones of the earth. Warriors. Drenched in blood. Chests heaving. Knuckles white. Scarred. Desperate. Terrified.

Aelwen scanned the area around her, the location of a singular mage of utmost concern to her. Blood covered the ground, pools filling indents made by combat boots. Mangled bodies littered the ground, shredded, sliced, with ghostly gray eyes, flesh tainted with ugly purple and black bruises, bodies in unsettling positions that no body should bend in, blood and bile dripping from mouths still open in screams.

She moved as quickly as she could across the blood stained ground without falling over, her balance taking its time returning to her. Aelwen froze in disbelief when she caught sight of the one body, the one amongst this sea of corpses she'd been so desperate to find. The armored, masked body she'd been looking for.

Wasting no time on hesitation, Aelwen drew her falchion from its sheath. Standing above Rhea, she aimed the tip of her sword straight for the mage's heart and drove it down. Steeling herself for the impact of her blade cutting through Rhea's armor and into her body,

Aelwen closed her eyes and would have clenched her teeth if her broken jaw could have handled it.

Before her sword made contact with anything, Aelwen went flying backwards.

Her body collided with the frozen earth, sending a new, ferocious wave of pain through her. Rhea was on her feet, fists glowing with magic.

"I hoped the explosion killed you," said Rhea.

Groaning as she dragged herself to her feet once more, Aelwen replied, "Same to you." The sharp agony of those few words from her broken jaw made her wish she hadn't said a thing.

Rhea had given a speech before the explosion. Aelwen would have very much liked to give one of her own. Now, she recognized that doing so in her condition would be impossible. All she could do now was fight.

She blasted Rhea with an onslaught of magic, hoping that such a chaotic attack would fluster her opponent.

No such luck. Rhea constructed a defensive barrier that Aelwen's crazed barrage rolled right off of. The moment Aelwen stopped, realizing that this attempt of hers was useless, Rhea tore down her protection.

Aelwen's hands flared with power, readying to respond to Rhea's attack.

Rhea did not attack. Rhea bent over, grasping her gut as if she were about to vomit. She flung her head back, face towards the sky, and released a blood-curdling, ear-piercing shriek.

Every onlooker cowered, even Aelwen, and clamped their palms over their ears, pressing so hard it felt as if her heads might burst in a desperate attempt to block out the sound.

High up in the gray clouded sky, a red-orange dragon rushed downward, roaring its arrival.

Something sparked in Aelwen's brain, a flash of recognition. She had seen that exact blend of fiery colors before, the burnt red shimmer, dark orange prevalent with the occasional flecking of brilliant gold here and there. It had not been a very long time since she had seen it. When she had seen it, it had not been in such great quantity, only a part of something more, but a distinguishing part, a very specific trait of something, someone...

Rhea burst out laughing maniacally, her vocal chords surprisingly undamaged by the awful noise she had just emitted. She flung out her gaunteled hands as if in celebration. "You understand, you understand," she whooped, although nearly everyone's faces were twisted in confusion. Those words were not meant for the masses. Those words were meant for the few in the crowd like Aelwen, who had gone rigid at the recollection, who stared with terror-glazed eyes into the sky.

Marliza had hushed Aelwen when she nearly mentioned Zarah in front of Valiran.

Valiran had always acted so kind, thus highlighting Marliza's crudeness.

Valiran had been sent away by Marliza when they had gone to meet with Sira.

"Yes, she has mastered shapeshifting! Valiran is upon you, she will show no mercy!" Rhea drew her gaze from the sky and pinned it on a single mage in the crowd.

"Marliza," Rhea began, eyes landing on the bleeding mage. Aelwen's eyes fell on her in the same instant and she allowed herself a breath of relief that Marliza was still alive. Her inyanga was nowhere to be seen. She was missing a hand, sliced off halfway to the elbow and the rest of her remaining arm was coated with blood covered steel, but she was alive. That had to count for something.

"You sent away my shifter, thinking that she could be deceived by a petty trick. She is not nothing!" Those words came out as a shout that was nearly a scream, a sentence that had to do with more than just Valiran.

"When she arrived at the building, your guards were there to stop her, to take her away and lock her up. She is greater than you ever knew! She killed them all and devoured the bodies, hence you never heard any more news of her! She came to me! She knew I would never betray her like you did! She knew that I would understand the power she holds like you never could!"

"You're insane!" Marliza screamed back, storming towards Rhea. "She was never on our side! Bailba knew, she knew all along! You cannot deceive her like you almost deceived me, like you deceived thousands of people and sent them marching mindlessly to their deaths!"

Rhea scoffed. "I sent them to their deaths? I did nothing but awaken them to their true condition, to ours! You are like me, Marliza. Like Valiran. Can't you see it? All of that greatness in you, I can feel it. You will never know your true self until the laws are broken, so that you can show who you are to the world. You won't have to hide anymore. No more worries. Only freedom."

"You speak nothing but lies!" shrieked Marliza, using her one remaining hand to send a blast of power at Rhea. The attack was strong, but with so much blood loss and only one hand to manipulate her power, it was sloppy. Rhea easily dodged the strike and responded with one of her own. Unblinded by fury, nearly unscathed and with all of her limbs intact, Rhea's magic hit home, slamming into Marliza's chest and knocking her to the ground.

Rhea darted forward, seizing Marliza, whose head lolled to the side. She would have been thought dead if not for the slight rise and fall of her chest. Rhea dragged the mage to her feet, leaning Marliza's failing body against hers. Marliza twitched the fingers on her remaining hand, pitiful sparks of magic leapt from them, nothing more.

"Let her go," snarled a creaky voice amplified by magic, one of the last things they had all heard before the explosion. Just as before the explosion, all heads turned to see Bailba astride Tezani, even the reptilian head of Valiran who still circled above.

Blood trickled down Bailba's temple. Tezani favored one paw. The explosion had taken its toll on its creator.

Rhea's grip loosened at the sight of Bailba, but only for a moment. She wrapped her forearm, lined with metal spikes, around Marliza's neck. Marliza's fingers twitched in a desperate attempt to summon her power, but she did not have the strength to conjure energy, let alone the steel to coat her flesh and keep her safe.

"Release her," snarled Bailba, each word ground like a knife on a chalkboard. "What do you want from me?"

"I want nothing from you, elder one. I only want equality. We will perish without it, dying off in our solitary realm, away from the world, without them ever knowing of our glory."

"You have been told plenty, this is not the way!"

"No, no. It is not *the* way, it is the *only* way. They have brought it upon themselves. They are the ones who crushed us into dust. They refused to see our power when we wielded it kindly. So now, we wield it ruthlessly."

Rhea jabbed her spiked arm inward, the spines sinking into Marliza's throat, tearing apart vital arteries, blood spewing from the wound.

Rhea pulled her arm away a second later. Marliza's body fell to the ground like a hunk of garbage. The warrior fell into a pool of her own blood as more flowed out of her, coating her lifeless body in red.

Aelwen had had it. Sword in her grip, she sprinted across the blood stained earth toward Rhea. The Hakmarres leader had been so concentrated on holding an unblinking stare with Bailba, who gaped in horror at what had just been done, that she did not register Aelwen until she was on top of her, sword in hand, stabbing without a second thought.

Rhea screamed as she was bowled to the ground. In an instant, she was deflecting Aelwen's mindless attack with carefully aimed magic. Soon, she had a conjured stiletto in her hand. She had reason firm in her mind whereas Aelwen had abandoned it completely, lashing at every open space with no thought at all. Rhea saw through the chaos and struck purposefully, one strike was all it took to dig the knife into Aelwen's upper shoulder.

Rhea drew the knife down, slicing through layers of tissue.

Aelwen drew back with a grunt, seizing Rhea's knife-bearing hand and twisting it away. Aelwen looked down at her boots, suddenly wet. Bright blood was soaking through them. She nearly vomited, knowing whose blood it was, remembering what she had just seen in every gory detail. She forced herself not to look at the body laying a few feet away from her.

Aelwen came out of her sickened stupor and prepared to rush Rhea once more, expecting the demented mage to be preparing to launch a new onslaught of magic.

But she did not.

Glaring at Aelwen as she had glared at Bailba a few minutes before, Rhea raised a fist into the air. Then she brought it down swiftly, with such force that the armor that covered her arm clattered against her body armor.

Valiran soared down, wings extended to full length, hooked claws prepared to cut open all of the small human bodies that were getting nearer to her with every wingbeat.

Several troops scattered, yelling at the top of their lungs. Others were too stupefied to move. None of them had anything to worry about. Appearing out of the clouds like mother nature herself came Zarah, her scales turning to a brilliant blue and silver, a stark contrast to Valiran's bright red and orange. The two dragons roared roars that made the heavens quake. Then they lunged at each other with every one of their weapons bared. The dragons collided in a horrific mess of claws, teeth and spikes, ripping at each other with talon and fang.

Zarah thrashed wildly as Valiran wrapped her claws around her. Zarah thrust her head forward, impaling her opponent. She had only a second of advantage, but she used it to pummel her opponent with her four spine-tipped wings. Valiran backed away from the attack, then dove at Zarah. The dragons hooked together, claws slicing armored scales, blood pouring onto the onlookers below.

Valiran moved in close to Zarah and dug her claws into the queen.

Zarah shrieked and lashed as Valiran's claws sunk in deeper, keeping a determined hold as Zarah thrashed her body, trying to dislodge those horrible talons. They were embedded right where Zarah could not reach. Valiran darted for Zarah's throat, maw agape, white teeth prepared to be showered with blood.

Something took hold of the dragon queen and her senses overcame the storm of pain that surged through her, the chaos that surrounded her. With a skillful twist, she was out of Valiran's reach.

Valiran roared in frustration and took after Zarah.

The dragon queen looped around and plowed her horned skull into the chest of Valiran, who managed to evade so that only her outer layer of scales were peeled away, no serious damage done. Zarah rushed ahead once more, pulling herself a bit higher in the air, dragging her talons along her enemy's back. The claws of ordinary dragons were nothing compared to those of their queen.

Valiran's back split open with a horrid ripping sound, and she screamed as her spine became a river of blood.

Aelwen's once-friend plummeted, dissolving into a burst of light in midair, then coming back into view as the human that she was.

Her body hit the frozen ground with a sickening crack.

Aelwen turned at the sound of someone approaching. All she saw was Rhea's metallic face before the Hakmarres' fist slammed into her jaw. Aelwen's jaw throbbed terribly at the impact. She struck back, conjuring herself her own pair of metal spiked gauntlets. Her hits were useless against Rhea's dense armor. Still, Aelwen had the upper hand when it came to physical combat. She could not defeat Rhea, but she could avoid her.

It took Rhea no more than a minute to realize that fighting Aelwen with nothing but her fists would not lead to victory on either side. Magic would be what led to the end.

Rhea charged Aelwen, leaning to her left, leaving her right side completely exposed. Aelwen, desperate to have the chance to attack, took the bait and went for the opening. The blow was potent; beneath her thick armor Rhea felt her bones rattle. She stumbled back rapidly, clutching her side and gasping.

A passionate flame roared in Aelwen's eyes, full of determination and pride. She did not peel her eyes away from Rhea for a single moment. Yet, when Rhea flung her arms up and released a storm of raging magic, Aelwen was still baffled. She let the grand wave of spiralling colors flow over her, throwing herself to the ground as the magic whirled above. An attack from the bottom was usually the most effective, she'd learned. Laying flat on the hard ground, her armor crushing against her back, Aelwen sent up a striking spider web of power. Her magic cut through Rhea's and continued upward until it hit the clouds, lighting them so astonishingly it was as if the gods themselves had ignited a hearth in their heavenly realm.

A few moments passed before the magic dissipated, fading into the sky it had illuminated.

Aelwen resisted the natural urge to send another attack at Rhea, who stood defiantly but did not relatiliate. A common method, she had seen it dozens of times in the arena. Aelwen lowered her hands and turned her blazing glare to Rhea, daring her to make the next move.

Rhea did. She shoved her arms forward, sending a storm of swirling golden power at Aelwen. As soon as it reached her, her senses were clogged. Seconds later, it was as if her senses had been wiped from her like chalk from a blackboard. Aelwen tried to move her body but, unable to connect to her sense of motion, she had not a clue what she was doing. The very things she had relied on her whole life, what she had been wholly dependent on when Galarus took her in and shaped her to her new life, were so suddenly gone.

Panic seized her, dragging her to its murky depths. She refused to be drowned. Aelwen found her head once more.

There was strength within her that Rhea could not take.

Aelwen dove into her soul and clutched tight to her magic. She breathed it in and concentrated on the sensation of it filling every part of her being.

The earth became solid beneath her feet. She felt her fingers curl and brush the cool steel of her armor. A severe rush overcame her as the sense of her location in time and space came flooding back to her. She heard a menacing roar, like a pride of lions bellowing as one. Her sight returned, her eyes thrust from blackness to a self-created brilliance like nothing she had seen before. Nothing she had made before.

A swirling tempest of intoxicating, mesmerizing color. Of power.

Graciousness hit her in relentless waves. Never before had she felt so incredibly blessed as when her senses returned. There was no time to roll in the gratitude or fully realize what she had just undergone, for around her churned the greatest storm of magic ever seen.

Through the surging waves of magic, Aelwen caught sight of Rhea.

Still covered in iron from head to foot, the malevolent mage had encased herself in a dome of protective magic. A dome that was shrinking back as Aelwen's magic slammed against it.

Rhea's eyes were wild, but not with the hysterical, psychotic confidence of destruction as they had been earlier. No. Her eyes were wide and wild, darting about, desperate. Afraid.

Rhea sent streaks of power from her hands to reinforce the barrier. Even that was not enough. The magic was slicing its way in, reaching for Rhea.

The magic storm was reflecting in Aelwen's dark eyes and even more so in her soul.

Whatever bonds she had kept her feelings within had been snapped. No restraints could be put upon her now, even had she wished it so. Her soul itself had burst from her body. There was no containing it now.

It had a will of its own and yet was hers simultaneously. It could have expanded and turned the world to ash had it wished. However, it only had one goal. One final goal, one last care. The end could come then, the most violent end that one had ever known, and she would not fear it.

Purpose filled Aelwen, overflowing so harshly that had it been unchained as her soul was, it could have drowned everything in this universe and a hundred others. Never had she felt so sure of anything in her life and never would she again. She had not been aware that it was possible to feel so meant to be.

In a flash of effulgence that was akin to the explosion of the sun, the cyclone of power retreated back into Aelwen's body. The rush had her on her knees immediately, drawing in long breaths as her soul resettled itself.

Aelwen rose once more. Her knees quaked violently, as if they had never born a weight such as hers before. Perhaps that was true, for even she herself had never known what lay within her. That sense of purpose kept her going, although her legs as well as the rest of her body wailed for her to stop. It was not such a typhoon any more, but a raging river nonetheless.

As she made her way to her target, Aelwen took in her own condition. Her armor was terribly cracked, where it was not cracked, it was dented. Her face was a bloody mess, as was any exposed part of her flesh she could see.

The worn warrior stood before what she had trekked twenty perilous steps to reach: the body of Rhea, encapsulated in iron. Aelwen bent over, her shredded fingers brushed the armor. It was smooth, speckled with dirt and blood, cracked and dented even worse than Aelwen's.

Were it not for Rhea's heaving chest, she would have been proclaimed unquestionably dead.

Aelwen's magic reached out to Rhea's, sensing gingerly. The Hakmarres leader was too near death to offer any threat. Her eyes were rolling behind her mask, her chest heaved spasmodically. She made no indication that she had any knowledge of Aelwen's presence before her. Every bit of power she still held onto, she was trying to force it to heal her. It could not. Her magic knew, though she refused to believe.

Aelwen knelt beside Rhea. The shiny iron mask covered all of Rhea's face except her eyes and mouth. There were swirls carved into the thick metal. At the juncture of two or more swirls there was an intricate orchid flower, the symbol of Rhea's bloodline. Aelwen drew a knife from her weapons belt. Carefully, she slid the thin blade behind Rhea's head. It fit perfectly between the Hakmarres' skull and the many-times knotted leather straps of her mask. Aelwen twisted the knife, slicing the tethers. The leather bands dropped away, the frayed ends resting on the frozen earth.

Aelwen plucked the intricate mask off of Rhea, revealing her face for all to see for the first and last time. The mask was lighter than Aelwen had expected, but her eyes did not focus on the well crafted metal in her hand, for they were too preoccupied soaking in every detail of Rhea's face. It was not very unlike hers. The skin was slightly paler because of how long it had been hidden from all light. Rhea's cheeks were healthily round, and she had a mole nestled beside her nose.

Once Aelwen was beyond positive that she would never forget the face that had taken so much from her, from the world, she moved the knife to her other hand, leaned forward and slipped it down Rhea's gorget. She angled the blade and swiped it. All motion ceased in Rhea's body. Her eyes rolled back, only the veined whites visible. Aelwen could feel the warm stickiness of blood coating her fingers. She drew the knife out, wiped it on her pant leg, stuck it back in its sheath and fainted.

CHAPTER TWENTY-SEVEN

By some miracle, the house still stood.

A smile broke on Lysia's face at the sight. "Ready to go home?"

Iowan squeezed Lysia's hand in affirmation. She didn't think of Marchia as her home, but if that's what this white stone house in the middle of a reclaimed city was to Lysia, she wasn't going to argue.

Lysia released Iowan's hand to open the door. It creaked on its hinges when she pushed it open.

The parlor was just as they had left it, albeit dustier than when last they'd seen it.

Lysia stepped into the house. Iowan followed.

They weaved through the first floor of the house, taken aback by how in-place everything was. After all the death, the blood and the loss and the fear, this little white stone house was the same—unwashed dishes in the sink, coat rack with so many coats upon it it was surprising that it was still upright, cards upon the table that they hadn't picked up after their last game.

Iowan picked up one of the cards, twirling it in her fingers. "We just…go back to living now?"

"I guess so," said Lysia, running her hand over the smooth wood of the kitchen table.

The upstairs was exactly the same, everything where it had been left all those months ago. The flames of war had taken much, but they hadn't touched this little white house in the middle of the city.

They settled themselves on Lysia's bed. They stared at the opposite wall. Neither spoke. Iowan was at a loss for words, she assumed Lysia felt the same. What was there to say? After such wanton death, what words could heal the scars they all bore? How could they pick up their old lives where they left off after so much bad had happened?

"How do we do it?" asked Iowan, fidgeting with a fold in the sheets. She knew Lysia couldn't have an answer, but she needed to voice the question nonetheless to help make this absurdity a reality.

"I don't know. We'll figure it out together." Lysia laid her head on Iowan's shoulder. The small gesture sparked comfort in Iowan. Even if this place never felt like home to her, Lysia would be there and that was enough.

"I hope so."

"We always do."

~~~~

Tecsequaih stared at the white stone ceiling above him. The war was over, hence the reason he laid on a bed in the newly renovated Arkada. He enjoyed being back in Firhad, back in the building he knew so well. He was the first to reinhabit Arkada, the rest of the council members were still redecorating their offices and doing their best to recreate all of the important files that had been lost in the fire. Tecsequaih couldn't help with any of it, all he could do was lay on his bed and watch as the future of Marchia unfurled around him.

He'd been clinging to the doorstep of death for nearly a month now. After receiving his wound, Tecsequaih had thought he wouldn't last more than a few days, if he was lucky. But, although the fighting forces of the Vatre-daah had been severely depleted, they still had many good healers, the work of whom had managed to prolong the president's life.

Despite the healing of his wound, the pain of it was still there. A big, ugly scar remained in its place. He couldn't walk and, depending on the day, sometimes it hurt to move at all.

Age had caught up with and surpassed him. When he looked in the mirror, he hardly recognized the man staring back. His hair was nearly all gray and his face was wrinkled and drawn.

After the war between Marchia and Ave, he'd heard tell of the toll war took on people's appearances. They went in looking one way and came out another. Back then, he'd noticed no significant difference in himself. He was young then, and old now. He was an old man who'd had the blessing of looking younger than his years until an enemy rose from the past and reared its ugly head, intent on revenge, seeking to take everything from him.

Tecsequiah had been considering letting go, fading from this realm to the next, until Aelwen and her army of mages had arrived. The mere sight of her had been enough to make him want to live again. He teetered on the edge of death, but Aelwen was so full of life. So much potential thrived in her, she was young, with a brilliant future ahead of her. One he wanted to be there for so desperately that he relinquished his wish for death to take him. He had forced strength from the well of his being, stubbornly surviving day by day in the stone buildings constructed by the Vatre-darah mages, catching what snippets he could of whispered conversation to glean what was going on.

The final battle had been fought, Rhea had been destroyed. Stolen lands had been reclaimed. The world was moving on.

A group of Marchian healers had helped transport him from the Vatre-darah stronghold to Arkada. He had not been back to his home. He doubted he ever would. With his settlement in Arkada came a new wave of understanding. The world was moving on, repairing itself and licking its wounds. The world was becoming something other than it had been before. And he was not meant to see it. It was not his place nor duty to preside over this next chapter of existence. That was the job of those who were younger and stronger than he, those who had fought and would keep fighting for a better world until their dying breaths. He had fought. For many, many years he had fought. He didn't want to
~~~~

fight anymore. He was ready for it all to be over. To find what lay beyond the curtain of death, whatever it may be.

His time was all but spent. There was one last thing he had to do.

He was alone in the room that had become his own. A quill, parchment and inkwell sat on the table next to his bed, lest he have anything worthwhile to write down. For days, the items had laid there untouched. No more.

Groaning at the distress of the motion, Tecsequaih pushed himself onto his elbows and turned to retrieve the writing utensil. After dipping the quill in the ink, he wrote on the parchment one single, solitary sentence.

Fayette Ekua is my choice.

It was a question he had been pondering much since the war began. For a long time, he had been constantly torn. Everyone on the list was promising, how was he supposed to choose? What if he made the wrong choice?

Then Aelwen had passed out on the battlefield after exploding into a sphere of glowing power. He had received reports of her well being everyday since then. She had not awoken. No one knew if she ever would. As much as he loved her, Tecsequiah did not dare risk the fate of his country on someone who might die at any moment. Besides, if she did recover, she still had her own goals to chase, no doubt.

There were other promising candidates on the list, but one stood out among all the others. A single woman, with rich dark skin and a near permanent scowl. The general without whom the Vatre-darah never would have stood a chance; who had proven herself as invaluable again and again throughout all her years at his side, on his council.

The sentence written, Tecsequaih laid back down with a sigh. Death had been taunting him for a long time. It was time he gave in.

Soldan appeared before him.

He was not fully formed of flesh and blood, he was like a human made of mist and smoke.

Every detail of Soldan's beautiful face was exactly as Tecsequaih remembered. The world around him morphed from a white room to the soft gray void of another realm.

Tecsequaih reached out a hand to him. Soldan took it, wrapping his cool fingers around Tecsequaih's. Their eyes met.

It was time.

Without taking his eyes off of Soldan's, Tecsequaih nodded once. His final assent.

The world would go on without him.

His time here was ended.

~~~~

"They council is back working at Arkada, did you hear?" asked Iowan, sliding a plate into the cupboard.

Lysia looked up from the dagger she was sharpening. Since the war, she hadn't been able to go without the sure weight of a weapon on her at all times. "No. Finally got the place cleaned up, did they?"

"Yeah."
~~~~

"Is Aelwen there?"

"Yeah. They moved her in today." Iowan put away the last of the dishes and took a seat beside Lysia at the kitchen table.

"Why not keep her with the healer? Won't moving her make her injuries worse?"

"Fayette told me the whole process was controlled and safe. I was hoping the move might wake her up, but it didn't."

Lysia set down her honing steel, her eyes meeting Iowan's. "I'm sorry." She extended a hand to Iowan, who placed her hand in it. Lysia wrapped her fingers around Iowan's scarred hand.

All she could think to say was, 'she'll be okay'. She kept her mouth shut. She didn't know if Aelwen would survive, let alone be okay if she did. She would not give Iowan false hope, she knew the damage it could do.

Her silence didn't seem to disturb Iowan. She was staring down at the table, lost in her own head. When she lifted it, her eyes were rimmed with red, of which Lysia said nothing.

Iowan nodded to the dagger Lysia held. "A new one?"

Vaguely taken aback by the change of subject, but recognizing its necessity, Lysia held the narrow blade up to the light. "Yeah. Like it?"

"I do. What's on the hilt?"

Lysia turned the dagger so the carved hilt was facing Iowan. "A dragon. It's supposed to be Zarah, but it doesn't look much like her."

Iowan laughed, drawing her hand from Lysia's to hold the knife herself to get a better look. "You're right, it really doesn't." She gave the dagger a twirl. "It's weightend nice, though." She handed it back to Lysia.

"Indeed," said Lysia, sheathing her dagger. "That wasn't the only thing they had with Zarah on it, there was all sorts of stuff. Quivers, swords, shields."

"Yesterday at the store I saw a cape with a dragon on the back. It looked like Zarah, now that we're talking about it."

"Who knew she would be such a popular seller?"

Iowan breathed a laugh. "I'm surprised they're not selling stuff with Ae on it."

Lysia tried to hide her surprise that Iowan was able to speak so lightly of her friend she had been crying for her mere minutes ago. It was good that Iowan could bring Aelwen up in conversation without losing it. She was making progress. For the first few days, any reference to Aelwen was enough to send Iowan to the pits of despair.

Lysia laughed, but stopped short.

"What?" asked Iowan.

Lysia shook her head rapidly, amazed by how long it had taken her to realize it. "You said the council is back at Arkada."

"They are."

"All of them?"

"I—I'm assuming since they brought Ae there. I don't think they'd put her there until everyone else was there. Fayette didn't specify—why?"

"There's something I have to do." Lysia shot to her feet.

"What—"

Lysia was sprinting up the stairs before Iowan could finish her question. She raced to her room, going straight to her desk and yanking open the top drawer. Like everything else, they were right where she'd left them.

Envelopes in hand, Lysia hurried back downstairs. Iowan was still sitting at the kitchen table, looking wholly confused. At Lysia's reappearance, she sprang to her feet.

"What are you doing?" Iowan demanded.

Lysia plucked a cloak from the coat rack and fastened it around her shoulders, tucking the envelopes inside. She made for the door. Iowan grabbed her arm, forcing Lysia to face her.

"What are you doing?"

"Something I have to take care of." She shrugged out of Iowan's grasp. "I won't be gone long, I promise." She gave Iowan a quick kiss. "I love you."

Out on the streets of Firhad, Lysia waved down a carriage.

"Two blocks south of Arkada," she ordered.

The driver gave a nod and got them moving.

Through the window of the carriage, Lysia was struck with admiration by how well Firhad was rebuilding. The streets were nearly clear of debris, practically every building they passed was either fully repaired or close to being so.

Not nearly as many people were out and about as they had been before the war, but still, the amount of Marchians going about their daily business was significant.

The carriage rolled to a stop. Lysia paid the driver and got out. On the street, she pulled up the hood of her cloak and made her way for Arkada, head bowed the whole way there. Most likely, she would have been fine riding straight to Arkada, but just to be safe, she'd decided to walk two blocks to reduce the likelihood of anyone taking note of her.

In minutes, she stood before Arkada, its white walls freshly polished in celebration of the council returning. The damage—other than the roof where the bell had been knocked off—had mostly been to the interior. The Hakmarres had set the building aflame to send a message. If they'd wanted to destroy it, they could have used their magic, but they chose fire so the smoke could be seen from a distance and the interior would be ruined but still existent, enabling the mages to take up Arkada as their primary residence, if only for a time.

Head still down, hood up, Lysia approached one of the soldiers standing guard at the entrance to Arkada. She pulled the small stack of envelopes from her cloak and extended it to the soldier.

Lowering her voice, she said, "See that they find their way to Lin Akachi."

The soldier examined the envelopes, touching them, sniffing them, searching for a threat. Finding none, they said, "I will. Is there a name I should give him from whom this gift comes?"

"No."

Lysia turned on her heel and walked away from Arkada, not lowering her hood for several blocks. She walked home rather than paying for a second carriage ride. She felt relieved and good with every step she took.

~~~
~~~

The side of her face throbbed with a dull ache. Her arms felt too numb to touch the injury. She did not need to feel it to know, it was an injury she was familiar enough with. A large bruise definitely marred her right cheek. Aelwen expected her eyes to refuse to open, but to her surprise her lids slid back without resistance.

"Ae!"

Before she had a chance to process what was happening, two thin arms were clasped tight around her, nearly suffocating. Aelwen's first instinct was to fight, she was gracious that her senses stepped in before she could act on that initial impulse.

She knew the hold of those arms. The harvest, golden-brown hair of the head of the person who held her so tightly. The person's build and the way they held themself.

"Iowan?"

Sure as daylight, it was Iowan's large blue eyes that met Aelwen's as she pulled back to look her friend in the eye. Iowan's freckled cheeks, still sullen, but fuller than when Aelwen had last seen her, were covered in tears. Iowan tried to say something, but the words got tangled in her throat and her lips only trembled.

Aelwen found it impossible to restrain her own emotions. Tears flooded down her scarred face and sobs of joy were the only sounds he was capable of making. She threw herself at Iowan, ignoring the pain that seared through her at the motion. She folded her arms tight behind Iowan, drawing her close, breathing her in, praying that she would never lose her again.

Their waves of elation subsided and reason returned to their minds. They broke away from each other, but kept a tight hold on each other's hands, refusing to let go just yet. Face still streaked with tears, Aelwen examined the atmosphere.

White stone surrounded them. There was a bowl and cloth on a table beside them, as well as a potted plant. The door, a good twenty feet away, was of carved, dark wood with a bright brass knob. The wall beside Aelwen was lined with windows and a tapestry depicting a tropical coastline hung from the opposite wall.

She looked down. Beneath her was a simple cot covered with a squishy mattress. Fluffy pillows in silk cases supported her head and she was draped in vivid embroidered blankets of a cloudsoft material.

"Where are we?" Aelwen's voice still trembled with the remnants of her tears. She was quite sure she knew where they were. No place in Corova of wealth such as this was decorated so minimally. The air didn't set her nerves alive as the air of Paruma did.

"Marchia."

"That's what I thought. Arkada?" She didn't realize until after she'd said it that Arkada had been destroyed in the war.

Iowan's eyes took on a mischievous glint. "Yes."

Aelwen started. "What?"

"Yes, we're in Arkada."

"The Hakmarres—they burned it."

Iowan nodded. "It has been remade."

Aelwen reexamined the room. The walls were pristine white, there was no sign of damage anywhere on them. "How…how long was I asleep?"

"A little over a month."

Her jaw dropped. "They rebuilt Arkada in a month?"

"More or less. So much of it was stone that did not burn. They cleaned it and added more. New items were made to fill it, and here we are. I thought you'd be more concerned that you slept for a month."

"I am." Aelwen looked down to where she held Iowan's hands. They both bore scars. "But it was the price I had to pay."

"For what?"

The mage continued staring at her hands. She felt no prick, no tingle of power itching to be released within them, no confidence of what she possessed within her heart. Whatever she had done to Rhea on the battlefield with that storm of power had been something that her own body did not understand and, although it had felt beyond ecstasy in the moment, there was a deep pain in her soul that reminded her of how much she had spent.

"Ae, what happened to you out there?"

Aelwen lifted her head. "You saw?"

"*Everyone* saw."

A deep sigh escaped her. "I'm not sure, but I think it was an enervation. It's when a mage uses up their power, like a burnout. Bailba never mentioned it causing a coma, though."

Iowan started this time. "Bailba?"

Aelwen smiled sheepishly. She'd forgotten just how much explaining she had to do. "Bailba. Old Bailba. The Dark Philosophess. Turns out, she's a mage—a master mage, to be exact. She's the one who trained me. Didn't you see her at the battle? She was riding a bosvark?"

Iowan's mouth was hanging open, her eyes were even wider than before. "A big spiky thing in bronze armor?"

"That would be it."

"That was her? Bailba? Riding that thing?"

"It was indeed," Aelwen said with a laugh.

This time, it was Iowan who dropped her eyes to her hands that clenched Aelwen's. She gave a gentle squeeze. Her voice was heavy as she said, "There's something I need to tell you?"

Aelwen shifted and winced at the pain. "Then tell me." Her words were stone. She was already building a barrier against whatever ill news Iowan was about to share with her.

Iowan raised her head, and her face was once again streaked with tears, her eyes growing red. Her lips did not quiver as she said, "Tecsequaih is dead."

Something in Aelwen broke loose. In the depths of her being, she'd known. But that did not make the pain any more bearable. Her vision clouded, she swayed on the cot. Iowan released one of her hands and clamped Aelwen's shoulder to steady her.

Through the haze of grief, she heard Iowan saying, "Ae? Are you alright?"

Every possible sound caught in Aelwen's throat, tangled in a web of stunned sorrow deeper than any cavern. The world was fractured, she was falling. The room before her became nothing but a blur, a blot in a realm of loss. Somewhere in the distance, she could hear herself sobbing. The light faded, leaving her in darkness. Where was she supposed to go now? What was she supposed to do?

A faint sound.

The slate of her mind was wiped clean. She focused every bit of her strength on what she had just heard.

Muffled as if underwater, but sure as death, a voice in the darkness. It grew clearer with every breath and as it did, the darkness rescinded. The world around her changed from a black nothingness to a soft gray void.

The voice grew louder.

Out of the grayness, a shape began to form.

Human. Tall.

The form grew in detail.

Familiar. Regal.

Her heart stung as she took in every detail of that beautiful face. Not as she had last seen it—weak, frail, fading. But as she knew it in her heart. Strong. Admirable. Gentle. Righteous.

He was not fully formed of flesh and blood, he was like a human made of mist and smoke. He reached out a hand to her. She reached back. Her hand passed through his flesh like passing through fog. She shivered at the sensation. He did not cringe. His eyes met hers. Even in this state, his eyes contained so much. But none of the things that had plagued him for so long. Fear. Loss. Insecurity. Only the things that made him great. Love. Passion. Confidence. Determination. She saw her eyes reflected in his own and soon she could not tell where his smokey eyes ended and the reflection of her dark ones began. And she understood.

He was gone.

The world could not go on without people like him.

She knew what she had to do.

He gave a single nod.

Resolution?

No.

Acceptance.

Peace. Tranquility. Rest.

He smiled. Light and true and full of hope.

Then he vanished. Back into the gray.

Slowly, the shades of gray began to change, to take on shapes.

She blinked.

A room in Arkada.

Iowan before her.

A tapestry on the wall.

It was all coming back into view.

Iowan waved a hand in front of Aelwen's face.

"Aelwen? Hello? Can you hear me?"

Aelwen blinked one more time, clearing the final bits of haze from her view.

"Yes," she said. "Yes, I can hear you."

"Are you okay? You went blank, I thought you were going to pass out."

"No, I'm fine." She used her sleeve to clear the wet residue of her sorrow from her face.

"What happened?"

There was no reason to lie. "I saw Tecsequaih. He came to me."

Iowan raised a brow, her mouth formed a thin line. "Really?"

"I know it sounds crazy. You don't have to believe me. I'm not sure I would. I know what I saw."

"Well… that's good. What did he say?"

"Nothing. He made me feel."

"Okay then, what did he make you feel?"

Aelwen took Iowan's hands in hers. "Sure."

"Sure?"

"Sure of what must be done. Sure of what I can do."

Iowan still didn't look convinced. "The Aelwen I know was never unsure of what she could do."

Aelwen shifted. "It wasn't that I wasn't sure I could do it. He reminded me how far I've come, that if I've done so much, surely I am capable of more. He told me to be like him."

"Did he? I thought he didn't say anything."

She paused before answering. "Now that you say that… I'm not so sure. He never said a word. He just— he made me feel what it felt like to be in his presence again. I want people to feel like that in my presence."

Iowan scoffed. "You're a warrior mage who rides the queen of dragons. I don't think you need to worry about how people feel in your presence."

"It's…I'm not saying this right. I don't want people to respect me, I know they do. He just…reminded me how many people can respect someone even when they don't feel grand at all."

"Do you feel grand right now?"

"No."

"So, then, Tecsequaih came to you to remind you that you're revered?"

"Yes, I think so."

Iowan's face was softening. Whether it was because she understood what Aelwen was trying to say or because she thought her friend had finally gone off the edge, Aelwen wasn't sure.

The mage stared out one of the large windows beside her bed. The city was not as full of life as it had once been, and there were fewer buildings than before. Still, the streets were crowded and the shops were bright. A thin layer of snow dusted the roofs.

"They rebuilt so quickly," she said.

Iowan followed Aelwen's gaze out the window, though it kept darting around to other things—the blankets, the door, the tapestry. "Yeah. The mages who fought with us in the war and some of those who turned against Rhea in the end helped create new buildings, fix the roads, that sort of stuff. It made the rebuilding way faster, but there's still some work left to be done. Only minor things, though. Diplomatic issues are the biggest concern right now. The mages would have stayed longer to keep helping, but they were being attacked by the commoners who blamed them for the deaths of their family and friends."

Aelwen shook her head in disappointment, though she was not surprised. In a way, such a reaction from the people without magic was inevitable. "The mages returned to Paruma?"

"Yes. As we speak there is a Marchian envoy meeting with a group of mages, trying to arrange something."

"Is Bailba involved in the discussions?"

"I don't know."

Aelwen pulled back the blankets and swung her legs over the edge of the cot. She let out a hissing breath as the pain sparked through her.

Iowan moved back, allowing Aelwen space to rise. "Where are you going?"

Remaining perched on the cot, Aelwen said, "I'm not quite sure yet, but I can't just lay here useless."

"You're clearly still in pain, you still need time to heal. There's no shame in resting."

Aelwen could feel the fire of determination in her again. "There is when you know you could be making progress doing something else."

Iowan rolled her eyes. "Doing what?"

"I don't know. I just know that I'm not supposed to be resting anymore." She rose and willed herself not to double over in pain at the movement.

It was clear that Iowan could see her friend's difficulty. Knowing she could not stop her, Iowan offered an arm for support, which Aelwen graciously leaned upon. Arm in arm, they approached the door.

Aelwen stopped abruptly.

Iowan halted with a tilt, thrown off by the pause. Before she could ask if Aelwen was okay, Aelwen said steadily, eyes pinned on the door in front of them, "Fayette Ekua is president now, isn't she?"

Iowan's eyes fell to the floor. "Yes." She swallowed. "She isn't Tecsequaih, but she served beside him for years and she's turning forty soon. Her time as Chief General was coming to an end anyway."

Aelwen nodded stoically. "I know." She let out a breath. "I know."

She took another step toward the door. Right before her fingers brushed the brass knob, Iowan said, "There's one more thing I want to tell you before you get involved in everything again." This time, her head was not bowed and her face was not sad. Her eyes shone, but not with sorrow. With glee.

To her surprise, Aelwen felt a smile tugging at the corners of her mouth. "Go on."

"Lysia and I are getting married!"

Aelwen staggered, but not from pain this time. Her mouth ran dry in disbelief. "You're *what*?"

Iowan squeezed Aelwen's arm. "That's right. We haven't set a date, we're still working through the preparations—"

"Lysia? And you? You? And Lysia? Married?"

"Yes!"

"I never—you never—"

Iowan laughed bawdily at Aelwen's shock. "Turns out you missed a lot while you were gone, too."

"Clearly. When…when did you two…start liking each other?" It felt so strange to say. She never would have guessed that this would happen.

Iowan thought for a moment, then shrugged. "I can't pinpoint an exact moment. I think I felt something for her from the first time we met, but I didn't know if it was admiration, intimidation, attraction or what. Obviously, I didn't have much of a chance to get to know her before…" She trailed off. They both knew what happened next. "But then, when I came back, I was able to see her again and we got to know each other a little better. Then after you left, she was the closest friend I had and I was the closest friend she had. Things really just went uphill from there."

"Iowan…not to be the cynic…but, you really haven't known each other for that long. Are you sure marriage is the right choice?"

Iowan's eyes brightened. "Definitely. I don't know if you've ever been in love, if you've ever fought side by side in a war with someone you love, but if you have, then you know how it makes you feel."

Aelwen shook her head. "No, I haven't. I don't know. Will you tell me?"

"It makes you realize the depth of your feeling. You figure out what you're willing to do to save that person's life. And I know with every fiber of my being that I would do anything, *anything* to keep Lysia alive. I did a lot in the war. Took a lot of lives. I suffered a lot, and when I forgot why I was fighting, what I was protecting, she was always there to remind me."

"Iowan…" Aelwen wasn't sure if what she was about to ask was a good idea or not, but she decided she would rather ask and have an answer and risk offending Iowan than never know. "Did you end up with Rhea the second time because you were protecting Lysia?"

Iowan's eyes widened. Her mouth opened and closed a few times before she said, "I did." She released a shuddering breath.

"It's okay." Aelwen placed a hand on Iowan's shoulder. "You don't have to tell me the details. I just wanted to know."

Iowan expressed her thanks and understanding with a single nod. Iowan's face would never be the same. Her eyes would always hold a special light of their own, but they would never glow as they used to. She would continue to smile, but it would never be as carefree as it once had been. She would always be Iowan, but there was a new depth to her, wrought of torment and struggle and intense feeling that had forever changed who she was.

Aelwen smiled faintly. "Congratulations, Iowan. I am glad you've found your happiness."

Iowan's eyes glistened with tears that Aelwen did not fully comprehend. Iowan took Aelwen in her arms for one final embrace before they opened the door and stepped out into the halls of Arkada, arm in arm, friend leaning on friend.

Aelwen knew Arkada well enough to find her way to the President's office. Though she'd been steeling herself for the sight, her heart still twisted at the sight of Fayette in the chair, at the desk she had only ever considered to be Tecsequaih's.

President Fayette rose and swept a deep bow. "Aelwen, I see you have recovered."

"I have indeed. Though, Iowan told me it was not a fast process."

"You took the time you needed to regain your strength and step once more into your power. There is no shame in that."

At the mention of power, Aelwen was suddenly aware that she could not feel her magic. No energy buzzing beneath her skin, eager to be released, no sense that a part of the earth's being existed within her.

Fayette took a step forward. "Are you alright?"

Realizing that her confusion must have shown on her face, Aelwen schooled her face into cool neutrality. "I'm fine, it's just odd that…that he's not here." The truth of the words stung.

Fayette seemed to feel them, too. "He was a great man," was all she said before resuming her seat at the desk. "Is there something you'd like to ask me?"

Aelwen withdrew her hand from Iowan's arm. If she could not stand on her own, how could she expect to accomplish the goal that had kickstarted the journey that had brought her to this very place for the first time?

She straightened. "There is. Will you help me rebuild Corova?"

Expecting a resounding yes, her heart stumbled as Fayette dropped her gaze. The president stared at a paper on her desk. She pushed a quill around with the tip of her finger.

Iowan's hand found Aelwen's once more. Aelwen clenched Iowan's hand in hers as if by doing so she could hold on to hope.

President Fayette let out a long breath. She did not raise her eyes to either of the Corovans. "There are many reasons why I should say no. Firhad is not done rebuilding, to say nothing of the smaller cities and towns that haven't received any federal aid. The Marchian military is not what it once was. Ave suffered damages in the war and they seek our aid as well. Then there is the issue of mages returning to non-magical society. I have far too much on my plate to consider helping an entire broken nation repair itself."

Fayette raised her eyes to Aelwen's. "But I will say yes. For the memory of the man who sat at this desk before I did. I know he would have said yes, and so shall I."

It was not the type of 'yes' they wanted, but it was a yes nonetheless.

Aelwen released Iowan's hand and sighed in relief. Iowan was smiling, broad and full of hope. Seeing such faith, Aelwen couldn't help but smile a bit herself.

Fayette did not smile or show any sign of joy. "What do you need?"

Aelwen may have paused to think had she not gone over every detail of how Corova would be fixed from the day she'd set sail aboard *Mist Wing*.

"As many workers as you can spare: carpenters, pavers, roofers. And government workers. Not too many, I don't want to intimidate my people, but I need Marchians who know how to run things and keep people under control. There are bound to be angry mobs because we're changing things—I need to keep the Corovans controlled without violence. I need people who know how to fix broken things without angering people. People with good organizational skills that can keep their heads in stressful situations, people who know how to make the best decisions without causing too much disruption."

President Fayette nodded, impressed by Aelwen's analysis. "Okay. I'll assemble a team for you."

"We'll need military strength as well. I know your forces are depleted and you cannot spare many—"

Iowan jumped into the conversation. "We won't need any soldiers."

"What, you think Halmar is just going to—"

"Halmar's dead."

Halmar. Dead.

A smile even broader than Iowan's spread over Aelwen's face. And she laughed. With glorious relief, she laughed. She doubled over with hysterical joy, clenching her stomach. Tears rolled down her cheeks and splattered on the floor. For the first time in a long time, they were not tears of anguish.

She sucked in several deep breaths, savoring the crisp, clean air, untainted by Halmar's existence far to the east, and righted herself.

"I guess we won't be needing any soldiers, then," said Aelwen, wiping away her tears.

Fayette was smirking. "No, you will not. Is that all you require? Craftsman and people with governing experience?"

"If all goes as planned, yes."

"Very well. Give me until tomorrow evening to have them ready."

Aelwen was still smiling. She didn't know if she would ever stop. "Good. I'll come here to meet them all tomorrow night, and the next morning we will go to Corova."

The president nodded. "As you wish." She rose and swept another bow. "Until tomorrow evening, Aelwen."

Aelwen bowed in return. "Until tomorrow evening, Madame President."

With that, Aelwen turned on her heel and left, Iowan close behind.

Iowan and Aelwen were walking down the streets of Firhad before Aelwen thought to ask, "Our house. Does it still stand?"

"Yes, it does."

"And that's where you and Lysia live?"

"It is," Iowan said.

"Speaking of Lysia, where is she?"

They sidestepped to avoid a fast-paced carriage.

"Slow down!" shouted someone who had to leap out of the way to avoid being trampled. In doing so, they tripped over a tall lady in a suit, who grunted, "Watch it" before continuing on her way.

Aelwen's grin, which had still not left her, grew. It felt good to see normal life again. No blood or steel or death. Just people, living their lives.

Iowan replied, "She's home. She thinks I spent too much time with you, so she would always stay home to make me come back to her. I can't wait to see the look on her face when you walk in the door, she's never going to believe it."

"How much time *did* you spend with me?" Aelwen asked, caught up in that bit of information.

"As much as I could. For the first two weeks, I never left you. I slept on the floor, I ate in there, I talked to you, begged you to be okay. I only left to use the bathroom down the hall."

"You slept on the floor? No one gave you a chair?"

Iowan chuckled. "No, everyone was too concerned with rebuilding and Tecsequaih's death to think about me. Anyway, Lysia stayed with you, too, for the first week, then she said it was time that she and I start rebuilding our own lives. She said there was a chance you'd never wake up and that, even if it hurt, we'd both have to move on. So I moved back to the house. I still saw you as much as I could, and Lysia came to visit sometimes, but she didn't like seeing you like that. She said that if you didn't ever wake up, she didn't want to remember you as a weak, lifeless body, she wanted to remember you as you were—strong, passionate, always fighting."

There was a lump in Aelwen's throat that she failed to swallow.

They turned a corner and headed down the street their house was on. The building came into view. It'd been so long since Aelwen had seen it, but she recognized it instantly. Small, of white stone, a house that had become a home. She and Iowan made their way up the steps and Iowan rapped on the door.

"Come on in!" Lysia hollered from somewhere in the house.

"I never knock," Iowan whispered to Aelwen. "She won't think it's me."

Iowan knocked again.

Footsteps could be heard approaching the door. It opened, revealing Lysia. Her hair was shorter and she had a scar running over her right eye, but other than that, she looked the same as Aelwen remembered. That one rebel lock out of place, round face smiling, angular eyes wide in astonishment.

Lysia's mouth fell open. She tried to speak but failed. To make up for her loss of words, Lysia threw herself at Aelwen, squeezing her almost as tightly as Iowan had.

"You're alive!" Lysia gasped, pulling back, looking Aelwen over from head to toe. "You're alive!"

"To everyone's delight, yes, I am," Aelwen said with a laugh.

Lysia stepped aside, ushering them in. Once Aelwen had entered, Lysia took Iowan's face in her hands and kissed her. Aelwen turned away. Seeing Iowan and Lysia together like this was going to take some getting used to.

The layout of the house was exactly the same as she remembered it. Aelwen went straight to the living room and sat on the sofa, cherishing the large softness of it.

Iowan and Lysia followed Aelwen's lead and sat themselves at the other end of the sofa. Aelwen didn't fail to notice how they held each other's hands, how they leaned into one another.

"So," Aelwen asked, focusing on Lysia and trying to ignore the growing feeling that she had lost Iowan, at least a part of her, to Lysia. "Where do you want me to start?"

"With what the hell that last trick you pulled was. When the power…leapt from you."

So Aelwen explained. The enervation, President Fayette's agreement, the plan to retake Corova. She told them a little bit about her training as a mage, how she'd known the woman Rhea killed with her armor and the fiery dragon who had been the kindest of the mages she'd trained with. Then, she told them what she feared.

"Bailba told me she'd had an enervation, but she didn't lose her power. I can't feel mine, though." To prove her point, she held up a hand, attempting to conjure up some magic as she had been trained to. Nothing happened.

She could not feel the rush of possibility within her or the sparking determination of her magic waiting to be released. Only gray tiredness and pale exhaustion that she did not understand. She'd slept for a month, why did she feel so weary?

"There's nothing there. I feel…empty. Like a part of me's gone. And I don't think it's coming back."

It hurt to say those words. Aelwen hadn't had her magic for long, but once she had discovered it, it had become such a part of her, like her limbs or her heart. It felt so wrong to be without it.

Lysia and Iowan glanced at one another, each hoping the other would speak first. They didn't know magic, they didn't understand it. How could they?

After a moment of awkward silence, Iowan said, "Well, at least you don't really need your magic anymore, right? I mean, you got it so you could destroy Rhea. And you did."

"I hate to admit it, but you've got a point," Aelwen said. "I have no use for magic now. All I learned was combat magic anyway and there are no more enemies."

"Don't speak too soon," said Lysia.

"Good point. The war is over, but that doesn't mean our problems are."

That evening, the three women sat down for dinner at the kitchen table as if life were perfectly normal. They exchanged stories and cleaned their entree plates and proceeded to dessert. Aelwen was halfway through her slice of chocolate cake when the bizarre normalcy of the evening came to a halt with a knock on the door. Whoever it was at the door, it made the most sense that they would be there to see her. With an irritated sigh, she said, "I'll get it."

Aelwen opened the door to see the wrinkled, brown face of Bailba, patterned cloak draped over her shoulders, cane in hand, a leather satchel draped across her chest.

"Bailba, hello!" A million questions drifted to the forefront of her mind, questions about her magic and the future of mages and the rest of the continent. Aelwen cleared her throat, reining in her surprise. "It's good to see you. I wasn't sure if you made it out of the battle. What're you doing here now?" She peered over Bailba's hunched shoulders, seeing no mount that had borne her here. "Where's Tezani? Did you walk here?"

Bailba whacked Aelwen's knees with her cane. "For gods' sakes, girl, shut up and let me in."

Before Aelwen had the chance to step aside, the old woman was shoving her way past into the parlor and on to the kitchen. Aelwen yanked the door shut and followed behind Bailba, clenching her jaw when the mage waddled into view of Iowan and Lysia. They both set down their forks, staring open-mouthed at Bailba. Lysia was nothing but confused, Iowan was a mixture of confusion, recognition and awe.

"Old—Old Bailba," stammered Iowan. She was about to say more, but Bailba interrupted.

"Hello, Iowan. You're doing well, I see. And you," she said, turning her eyes to Lysia. "I don't know you, but hello. Now, if you'll excuse us, Aelwen and I have some things we must discuss." She peered at Aelwen's abandoned, half-eaten cake. "Enjoy your cake. It would be very kind to offer an old woman some, you know. It could be just what she needs after a long conversation. Especially after she travelled so far." After staring at Iowan and Lysia just long enough to make them uncomfortable, Bailba said, without looking behind her at Aelwen, "Aelwen, where's a good spot for us to talk?"

"Uh, the living room. It's that way," explained Aelwen, pointing down the hall.

"Wonderful. Come with me."

Bailba made her way to the living room, where she lowered herself onto the sofa, resting her cane against the armrest.

Aelwen took a seat beside her, keeping enough distance between them so she didn't overstep any bounds. Bailba had become a major player in her life story, someone without whom things would have gone much differently, and Aelwen had come to feel comfortable in her presence during her time in Paruma. But now, Aelwen did not feel that motherly familiarity or deep running teacher-student bond. Time had gone by, Bailba had been living her life while Aelwen healed, ignorant to the goings on of the world. They had become two different people in that time, the connection they'd forged when they lived together for months, constantly training and talking and just being together, had dwindled into something other than it had been before.

Paying virtually no heed to Aelwen, Bailba opened the leather satchel she wore and extracted from it a pair of knitting needles, a ball of gray wool and some of the gray wool that had already been knitted into something, though Aelwen hadn't the slightest clue what it was. Bailba situated her belongings and began to knit, continuing whatever the object was she was working on. Her needles clacked together rhythmically, she didn't look up from her work.

"I can't feel my magic," said Aelwen. It was abrupt and awkward, but she didn't know how else to fit it into conversation. The gods knew when she'd see Bailba again and she was the only one Aelwen was close enough to that she felt comfortable discussing her situation.

Bailba was silent, her attention focused on her stitching.

Aelwen continued. "I think it might be gone. I've tried using it to no avail. Can that happen, can a mage use up their magic?"

The old woman knitted several more rows before finally breaking the swelling silence. "Don't fret, lass. You still have your magic."

A surge of glee rose up in Aelwen. "How do you know?" she asked, though the answer didn't matter that much. Bailba said she still had her magic and that was all that mattered. Buried deep, inaccessible, the force of nature lived on within her.

"I can feel it. I have much more experience with these things than you, don't forget."

With a deep sigh of relief, Aelwen leaned back against the sofa. "Thank the gods. I thought I'd lost it."

"A mage cannot lose their magic. They can bury it and ignore it and not use it. They can never get rid of it. An enervation was all you suffered, quite a big one, too."

"Good. I thought it was an enervation, but then when I couldn't use my magic I was afraid it was something else." She leaned forward, hands on her knees. "How do you know it was just an enervation?"

"It felt the same as when I had my enervation. When it happened, I reached my magic out to yours. Not to interfere, to understand precisely what was happening to you. Your enervation was much larger, much stronger, but at its core, it felt the same as mine."

"Thank the gods," Aelwen said again. "How long do you think it'll be until I can use my magic again?"

Bailba laughed mockingly. "You'll have to be able to feel it before you can use it. My guess is that you'll regain feeling in about a month. Usage?" She paused in consideration. "Maybe a month after that. Maybe more."

Aelwen stared at her fingers, flexing them, searching for some sensation that the power within her was still there. She felt like a normal human. Nothing more. The waiting was not something she looked forward to. At least her magic was still there. That was a blaze of joy in itself.

Bailba went back to work on her sewing. The silence between them did not feel natural after their short conversation, it felt wrong. To break it, Aelwen said, "What will you do now?"

"Go on living as I've always done."

"Bailba, the world is safe for mages now. Well, maybe not completely, but it's on its way. You don't have to live alone in your tree anymore, you can make a life for yourself."

"I won't be alone, I'll have a new batch of trainees soon enough. There's nothing in the world for me."

"There used to be. What changed?"

"Time took its toll and my interests changed. I'm not an adventurous young thing like you, spry and able."

Aelwen laughed lightly. "You don't have to go having grand adventures. I think we've all had enough of those."

Bailba smirked at that.

"You could live in a community, though. Find your child."

The crone's wrinkled bronze face was overtaken by a shadow of emotion. "No. My child has spent their life without me. What good would I be, reappearing after years of hardship? I would earn their scorn for not being there when I ought to have been. Who's to say they'd even want to know me, being a mage and all? And at this age. What kindness would it be to make my grand entrance just to die a few days later?"

Aelwen dropped her gaze. She didn't have an answer to that. Bailba was right. Who was to say Bailba's child would want her in their life if she was normal, after being absent for so long? And her being a mage on top of that. Progress was being made toward mages becoming apart of society once more, but prejudices still ran high.

To change the subject before the discomfort took over again, Aelwen said, "You said you wanted to talk to me? All I've done is ask you questions. What do you want to ask me?"

"I want to ask you," said Bailba, pausing to start a new row, "When you are ruler of Corova, how do you plan to deal with the mage problem?"

Aelwen breathed out through her nose. She hadn't got to thinking about that yet. "I'll make a proclamation that mages are welcome in Corova," she said, making up her plan as she went. "I'll pass laws against hate crimes against mages."

"What if the non mages refuse to comply with the laws, hm? If the people riot against you for being supportive of mages, for being one yourself, what will you do?"

"I have Zarah," Aelwen said, struck for the first time by the realization that she had not seen the queen of dragons and, without her magic, she could not feel her connection to her. "I don't want to use fear as a leadership tactic, but if that's what I must do to make Corova safe for everyone, I will."

Bailba had lifted her eyes from her needlework and was focused on Aelwen, eyes narrow in judgement. "Okay. May we hope your plan is effective."

"Indeed." Aelwen paused, her mind taken up by questions about Zarah. Bailba, sensing the young woman's inquisitiveness, did not turn her attention back to her knitting. Realizing this, Aelwen said, "What of Zarah? I haven't seen her since I woke up. Do you know anything about what happened to her after the battle?"

"I saw her fly back towards Paruma. I've had no encounter with her since."

Aelwen dropped her head.

"Don't fret," chided Bailba. "She's a queen with a kingdom that needs running. She lost subjects in the final battle. She has duties just as we do. When your magic returns, contact her, meet her if you can."

"What if she doesn't want to see me again? What if she only allied with me to help destroy Rhea because she knew she was evil and now she doesn't want to be with me anymore?"

"Well," Bailba said slowly. "If that happens, I suppose there's nothing you can do about it. You'll have to come to terms with it and move on."

Aelwen didn't know what sort of answer she'd been expecting, but that wasn't it. "True," she said, knowing that nothing Bailba had said was a lie.

The old woman began putting her knitting items back into the satchel she wore.

"Are you leaving?" asked Aelwen. Bailba had only just started her knitting and now she was packing up.

"I am. Unless you have any more questions for me."

Aelwen searched for something else she had to ask the mage, but came up with nothing. "I don't. It's just, I thought you came here because you had things to ask me or tell me."

"I did. I asked you my question and answered quite a few of yours."

"That's all you came here for?"

"Yes. I figured I ought to pay you a visit once you awoke and now I have done that. I thought it would be helpful of me to answer your questions, assuming you would have a few after what happened to you. I was right. I've done what I set out to do. So, unless you have more questions for me, I'll be on my way."

"Actually, I do have one more question."

"Yes?"

"What were you knitting?"

"A scarf." Bailba rose. "Anything else?"

"No."

"Good." Taking hold of her cane, Bailba made her way to the kitchen, Aelwen close behind her.

"Old Bailba," said Iowan as soon as she caught sight of the crone. "There's a piece of cake for you on the counter."

"Ah! Wonderful," exclaimed Bailba, picking up the plate holding the cake. She made her way straight to the door and out into the street.

Before she could magic herself away, Aelwen cried from the doorway, "Bailba, wait!" She hurried to catch up with the mage. "Is this goodbye?" she asked.

Bailba screwed up her face, thinking. After a moment, she replied, "Yes…I believe our time together has come to an end."

Aelwen's mind was void of thoughts. After everything Bailba had done for her, what was there to say? What words could convey her immense gratitude, here at their final meeting? She took hold of Bailba's hand that did not hold the cake. She met the old mage's dark eyes. "Thank you," she said firmly, hoping Bailba realized the depth of those simple words. "Thank you."

Bailba smiled, squeezing Aelwen's hand in turn. "You're welcome, lass. The world is done with me, I do believe. But not with you. Not by a long shot. Do me proud."

The women split hands and, in a flash, Bailba was gone. Aelwen exhaled. Another chapter of her life, come to an end. She turned and went back inside to finish dinner with Iowan and Lysia.

CHAPTER TWENTY-EIGHT

The blood red cloak Aelwen wore snapped behind her in the fierce wind.

"You better hold onto your cloak or it's gonna blow off," Iowan called from behind.

Aelwen replied, "We're almost there, I think it'll hold."

"Why didn't we just get a carriage?" asked Lysia, who walked beside her fiance.

"Carriages cost money, which we don't have much of."

Lysia swept her hair out of her face, but it was only an instant before the wind whipped it back. "You don't think someone would give you a ride for free? You're only the most famous Corovan in Marchia."

Aelwen's face split into a smile at that. There were no people clamoring in the streets for her attention or showing up on their doorstep for her signature, but she supposed what Lysia said was true. She had vanquished the Hakmarres in the final battle, hundreds of soldiers had watched her soul burst from her on the battlefield. Surely stories had been told and her name venerated.

She slowed, falling into step with Iowan and Lysia. "We ought to keep ourselves humble."

Lysia scoffed. "You're an Arenian. I hardly think humility is second nature."

Iowan and Aelwen both chucked at that.

"You're absolutely right," Aelwen conceded. The white stone of Arkada loomed before them, and they sprang up the steps and into the building, desperate to be out of the wind.

President Fayette Ekua was awaiting them in the entry hall. She had not adopted Tecsequaih's eccentric style, preferring her military regalia.

"Welcome, my friends. Your assistants await you. Right this way."

The three women followed the president through Arkada to a room that Aelwen knew used to be dedicated to cartography, but now seemed to serve as more of a leisure room. There was a curved sofa against the far wall, a packed bookshelf and a fading hearth. A group of people stood gathered in the back corner.

That was all Aelwen was able to take in before she noticed who was standing before her, holding out his hand for her to shake.

"Lin," she blinked, trying to focus.

"Aelwen," he said. "I couldn't be more proud to lead this team of yours."

"You're—" Aelwen cleared her throat. "Certainly, I couldn't be more proud to have you on my team."

Her eyes darted to Fayette, but the president's face was blank. Lin and Aelwen shook hands. His grip was steady, not tight enough to denote a threat. Perhaps he really had left their pre-war feud behind him. The real question was, had she?

Aelwen said, "I must admit, I'm surprised. Are you not busy with your duties as financial advisor?"

"I no longer hold that position," he said without a hint of remorse in his voice. "When Fayette assumed the presidency, she chose her own council and I was not apart of it, for which a part of me is grateful. I'm looking forward to stepping back from government and spending time on other things, things that make me happy."

"Then I'm not sure this is the best job for you to take." She added a smile, but she knew he could tell her heart wasn't in it.

President Fayette approached them and put in, "Lin is the highest ranking and most experienced Marchian who does not currently hold an office and who can be spared to help you. He is the best choice."

Lin only grinned and shrugged before shaking the hands of Iowan and Lysia as well, then he gestured to the people crowded behind him.

"The team," he said.

He introduced them one by one—leaders of groups of diligent, skilled workers, former employees of the Marchian government and aspiring ones, all people who had proven themselves as trustworthy, efficient and cool-tempered. Aelwen did not doubt any of them. The one she doubted was Lin. Why him? Fayette had to know that Aelwen and Lin had never gotten along well. Aelwen remembered the shouting match she'd overheard Lin having with Tecsequaih all that time ago. Had Fayette never experienced one of his outbursts? Had he fooled her into believing he had changed his ways? Or had he really changed? Only time would tell.

Aelwen took a seat on the sofa, Lysia and Iowan following her lead. Everyone else in the room formed a circle around them, except for the president, who made her way to the door.

"This team is yours, Aelwen. Make good with them."

"I will, Madame President."

President Fayette smiled. She knew the strength it took Aelwen to say that.

"Thank you for all you've done," Fayette said.

"Thank you for all *you've* done," Aelwen replied.

With that, President Fayette exited, leaving Aelwen in the room with her two best friends and a group of people to do her bidding.

In the courtyard behind Arkada, a group of people astride impatient horses awaited the arrival of their leader. The sun had only just risen, bathing the people and their horses in a hazy, golden glow. The ground was blanketed in soft white snow that gave the sight a romantic air.

The people, bundled in furs, had their heads bowed and their hands stuffed in their pockets, trying to avoid the biting cold of the winter morning as best they could. The horses nickered and shifted beneath them, eager to be on their way, their breath and their riders' creating puffs of white against the gray sky.

Almost as one, the riders raised their heads at the sound of hooves nearing them.

Three horses, each a different color, each bearing a young Corovan woman, rounded the corner and trotted into the courtyard.

"Sorry we're late!" hollered Iowan. She and Lysia wheeled their horses round, preparing to head in the direction they had just come, though this time with a much larger company.

The troop did the same, angling their mounts so they were ready to set off as soon as their leader gave the order. Aelwen did not turn her horse and neither did Lin. When she was beside him, the two of them out of sight of the rest, Aelwen said, "There's something I need to do. It won't take long. Lead them on without me, I'll catch up."

To her relief, Lin did not look suspicious or disapproving of her. He only nodded and led his horse to the head of the troop. He swept a hand through the air and with that, they were off. Headed to the east to fix a broken kingdom.

Aelwen led her horse in the opposite direction, to the other end of the courtyard and onward, to the cemetery where the presidents of Marchia were laid to rest.

She dismounted and tethered her horse to the gate. It did not take long for her to find the headstone she sought. It was the one with the most gifts surrounding it. Flowers, artwork, objects of significance she did not understand.

There was no grand monument, no ornate statue. Only a simple rectangle of polished marble.

She pressed her hand against the headstone. Cold and unforgiving. So unlike the man whose name was etched into it.

President Tecsequaih Mayolan of Marchia.

That was all it said. No dates, no reverent words. Just his name, his final occupation and the land he reigned.

Hand still on the stone, she said, "I don't know if you can hear me. I hope you can. I want you to know that you'll never be forgotten. Never. I'll keep your memory alive while I'm here, but even after I'm long gone from this earth, I know that people will remember your name. You were too great to forget.

"But I know greatness isn't what you cared about. The pomp and pretty things, you never cared for them. You cared for people. You *loved* people. The people loved you, too. I hope you know that."

She breathed in the chill air.

"There's a lot of work to do. You didn't leave your country in a very good state," a broken smile formed for an instant, then vanished. "But it's already nearly fixed, don't worry. Fayette's doing a good job. They all are. And now it's time for me to go back home and finish what I came here to do."

She pulled her hand off the stone and turned, preparing to depart. Something didn't feel right. There were too many words she'd left unsaid. She turned back, staring at the perfectly carved letters of his name.

"Thank you. Thank you for everything you did. For me, for Marchia. Thank you for believing in me, thank you for teaching me. Thank you for helping me become who I am today because I could not be prouder of the person I've become… and I know I wouldn't be this person if I'd never known you. Thank you, Tecsequaih. I hope you are at peace. I hope you've found Soldan. I hope you've found happiness."

Green banners bearing a golden elephant's head thrashed in the wind. They were promises of the vibrant, plentiful seasons to come amidst the dead grays and blacks of winter. They were promises of the vibrant, plentiful future to come to the dead gray and black of this country.

Riding through the streets of Corova, banners held high, the troop encountered no resistance. People watched from their windows and doorways, but no one came near them.

Understandable. The last time such a cadre had traversed these lands, war had broke out soon after.

It all seemed to have decayed in the wake of Halmar's death. Everything seemed sadder than it had before. Skin and bones people in rags stood on corners, holding out their gnarled hands to every passerby. The most coins she saw one beggar with was twelve, enough to feed one person for two days if they ate frugally. People sat on the ground, pouring alcohol down their throats, rather than causing raucous chaos inside taverns while drinking themselves to death. Not one of the prostitutes that dotted the road was seen with a customer. The prostitutes themselves, who usually appeared in bright, revealing clothing, themselves spilling out of it, wore stained, drab rags and were hardly more than skin and bones.

At the doors of Orodel, no Guildsmen formed shields with their swords or told them not to enter, for no Guildsmen were there.

Aelwen exchanged a glance with Iowan. Iowan raised her eyes to the peak of the palace and nodded.

Iowan and Aelwen dismounted. Side by side, they approached the great doors and heaved them open.

Emptiness greeted them.

Quiet. Cold. Dusted with cobwebs.

Gold trim, smooth white marble floor, stone walls with tiny details carved into them. Shiny wooden stands held porcelain vases decorated with floral designs held the corpses of rotten flowers. A massive glass chandelier with diamonds hanging from pale silver chains hung in the center of the room. To the left was a spiraling obsidian staircase.

A shuddering breath escaped Iowan.

"Are you alright?" Aelwen asked.

A tear slid down Iowan's freckled cheek. "No." She took Aelwen's hand in hers and squeezed gently. "But I will be."

With her free hand, Aelwen waved the others to come in. They dismounted and some tethered their horses while others exhibited enough trust to leave their mounts unbound.

Lysia jogged in. Iowan pulled her hand from Aelwen's to enfold Lysia in her arms.

Lin took his place next to Aelwen. "There's no one here?" His eyes ran over the details of the place.

"I don't think so. Without my magic, I can't tell, but I don't think so." She approached the midnight staircase. "Stay on your guard in case I'm wrong."

Weapons in hand, the four ascended the staircase. There was no sound other than their footsteps. No voices other than their own.

At the top, Iowan asked, "Ae, do you feel anything?"

"Nothing."

They made their way down the hall.

"It's so strange," said Lysia softly. "No one made themselves leader after Halmar died?"

Lin peered around a corner. "All clear." He waved them forward. "Do they even know he's dead?"

"Does who know?" Aekwen asked, eyes roving over an open door to an empty room.

"The people. Corovans. If Halmar was as removed from public life as you said, how would they even notice he was dead?"

Lysia asked, "If the people didn't know, how did we?"

"Don't underestimate the power of the government. Just because we entered this city in force with banners flying doesn't mean we can't send a single, well-trained spy if we wish."

"The Marchian government has spies?" asked Iowan, eyes on Aelwen rather than Lin.

Still, it was Lin who answered. "A government can hardly exist without spies."

"I never met any of these spies," said Aelwen, glancing round a corner before beckoning them onward. "Tecsequaih never said anything about them."

"Believe it or not, there are things that you don't know about."

They traversed the rest of the level in silence, then continued up a second staircase. After that, they explored the next floor and the next. They opened doors and searched for hidden places. The few they found were unoccupied. Once they had made their way to the top, they worked back down and searched even more thoroughly. Eventually, they found themselves back in the grand marble-floored entry room. There was no more room for doubt. Orodel was empty.

"What now?" asked Iowan. Her weapon was sheathed and her fingers were intertwined with Lysia's.

Aelwen met Iowan's eyes. Of all the people she could look to when she said these words, Iowan felt like the one who needed to hear them most. "We get to work."

Lin ushered in the rest of the Marchians. "There's no one here," he explained. "It's completely empty." He whispered to Aelwen, "When will we hold our first meeting?"

"Tomorrow morning."

Voice raised so the Marchians could hear him once more, Lin declared, "There will be a meeting tomorrow morning."

Aelwen cleared her throat and made her own announcement. "For now, get some rest. Take whatever rooms you like, make yourselves comfortable. It has been a long day for all of us."

One Month Later

Through the streets of Corova on horseback, side by side, surrounded by Guildsmen for their own protection, rode Iowan and Aelwen. They were the only two on horses; their protectors traveled on foot. The streets still stunk of alcohol and sweat, but the scent was not as potent as it once had been.

Iowan wore everyday garb, Aelwen did as well, with the addition of a flowing cape of fuschia and gold, the colors of Corova. Colors she had grown to despise with her very being for more than a decade of her life. She did not hate them anymore. It was Aelwen who sat upon the monarch's throne now, she who bore the weight of the crown and the future of the people, and thus, she to whom the colors of the land belonged. She wore them with pride, their presence a constant reminder of all she yearned to achieve for her homeland, how far she'd come and how far she still had to go.

Crews of laborers were out repairing buildings and relaying stone in bits of road that had been torn up because they were damaged beyond repair. Plenty of unstable structures still stood and plenty of beggars still stood on the streets. There was a long way to go yet, but progress was being made, slowly but surely.

Normally, Aelwen and Iowan were out with the laborers, working with them, but today, they had something to do first.

Lysia had not come with them for this trip, she recognized that this mission was best faced by the two people in power whom it had done the most harm.

The travelling group came to a halt before a decrepit building of wooden planks with a slate roof that was in slightly better condition than nearly all of the other identical buildings that surrounded it. Above the door frame was a sign with no words, only a depiction of two crossed swords. The Guildsmen parted, leaving a clear path for the riders to reach the door. Aelwen and Iowan dismounted. As she headed for the door, Aelwen had to remind herself not to cast wary glances at the Guildsmen. Like the colors of fuschia and gold, for so long she had thought only of the Guildsmen as symbols of evil. Now, as Aelwen was the ruler of Corova, for however short a time she would hold that post, it was to her that the Guildsmen swore their allegiance. They were duty bound to protect her and carry out her orders, meaning she had no reason to fear them anymore.

Aelwen stepped aside as she and Iowan came to the door. "Would you like to do the honor?" she asked.

Iowan smiled mischievously. "I'd love to." Excitement radiated from her as she raised a pale fist and rapped on the door.

A girl opened it. Aelwen looked over the girl's shoulder, to the sand pit she knew so well. The pit was ringed with planks of wood that served as a barrier. Outside the pit, on the far side, wasa rack of freshly polished weapons. The sand white in some places, but mostly it was a dirty brown. A color that came from being stained with blood. Nothing about it seemed changed. Aelwen looked back to the girl before her. Her black hair was tied into tight braids, she had several knives at her hip and a dao sword strapped to her back. Her eyes landed first on Iowan and she was nothing but confused. Then she saw Aelwen, with her fuschia and gold cape, and her mouth went slack. The girl clenched and unclenched her fists, her eyes wide with worry.

Aelwen cleared her throat. "We're here to speak with Galarus, Arena Master. Could you fetch him for us, please?"

The girl stuttered for a few seconds before managing, "Yes—yes, one moment." She turned and sprinted away, vaulting over the wall of the arena, running through the sand, jumping over the other side and racing down the hall that led to the chambers of the Arenians. And Galarus.

Iowan asked, "Do you think he'll come?"

"Yes. Galarus has never been a coward before. Think he would become one in his last moments?"

"I don't know. We've changed. Maybe he has too."

A shadow appeared in the hallway, making its way toward them. As the person approached, their features came into view. Square shoulders, a proud walk, chin high, muscular, unbending.

Aelwen was struck by the familiarity of the person after all their time apart. "Or not," she said, sticking her hand in her pocket to extract a piece of parchment.

Galarus was fully visible now. He was tall and stoic as ever, all hard lines, even his scars were linear. He walked around the arena rather than through it at the Arenian who's opened the door had. He took his time, seemingly unperturbed by the two women at the door. He came to a halt just in front of them, crossing his thick arms, his soiree jaw jutting as if he couldn't be bothered with whatever antics they brought him.

"Iowan. Aelwen," he said, looking them up and down. "Didn't think I'd ever see you two again."

Neither of the ex-Arenians said a word. Aelwen handed Galarus the piece of parchment. He unfolded his arms to take it. His eyes narrowed with focus as he read what was written upon it. When Galarus raised his eyes to his former students, they were boiling with poorly restrained rage. "You cannot do this," he growled. "You cannot." The last words fell flat as if he recognized their uselessness. The order was signed. Nothing he said could undo the current ruler of Corova's signature on that federal order.

Iowan and Aelwen both kept their mouths shut, watching the Master. He sputtered, "I gave decent lives to so many children. To you. You would have starved to death in the streets if I hadn't saved you. I gave you a way to survive in this treacherous country. I gave you a *family*. What do you do to repay everything I did for you, for so many like you? You order the arena to close?"

The ex-Arenians traded a look to decide on who would speak. Iowan said, "You did help many children. We lived horrible lives under your authority, but we would have been worse off on our own, which is why the order does not include your death."

"Wh—what? If you know I acted in the best interests of all of you—"

Iowan cut him off. "You are a cruel man. You had us thrown in prison wagons and brought to you in chains. You beat us as children so we would fight for you. You abused us, you forced us to be violent, you took half our pay and we could only leave the arena with your express permission. You never cared for us as children, you never loved us. You saw the opportunity for profit and you pursued it, at the expense of our well being. You made rules that tied us to this place so we could not have lives that were our own because that would've deprived you of your profit making."

"I will not have it!" Galarus shouted, tearing the order in two, then four, ripping it until nothing but shreds remained.

Aelwen sighed. "I thought you might do that." She reached into her pocket and withdrew a second piece of parchment identical to the first. The same ink, the same words, the same signature.

Galarus seized it from her, glaring at it frantically. He was evidently trying to come up with a way out of this, but he would not find one.

Aelwen said, "There is a troop of Guildsmen outside. If you do not immediately begin to shut down this establishment, I will call them in and they will begin the work themselves."

The Master crumpled the order in his fist but did not shred it. His face bunched, his nerves protruded from beneath his skin. Aelwen could nearly feel the anger rolling off him and she relished it. He stared at her for a long moment before he said, "The order says I must have the arena shut down by tonight. What of the Arenians? Do I kick them out into the streets to fend for themselves?"

"Several new apartment buildings have been constructed two blocks west of Orodel," Aelwen explained. "They are a refuge for those with nowhere else to go who need a safe place to live while the rest of Corova is repaired. Tell them to go there."

Galarus' frown deepened. "Fine. Will you leave so I can get to work? It's a lot to be done in eight hours."

Aelwen nodded. "We'll be on our way." She turned to open the door. Before she opened it, she looked over her shoulder and said, "Oh, and Galarus? Those safe buildings? You're not welcome there."

"Where am I supposed to go, then?"

This time, it was Iowan who replied. "We don't care. Now that the Arenians aren't under your control, I assume there are quite a few who would be out for revenge. I'd recommend getting as far away from here as possible." With that, she turned away as well and together she and Aelwen walked out the arena for the final time.

"That felt good," remarked Iowan, climbing up onto her horse.

"It really did," said Aelwen, mounting and smoothing out her cape behind her. The Guildsmen moved into position, the riders got their horses moving, and they all headed in the direction of Orodel.

Iowan said, "I still don't see why we couldn't kill him, though."

Aelwen chuckled. The whole time they'd been planning out their return to the arena Iowan had pleaded that she and Aelwen be the ones to put an end to Galarus' life. "We've had plenty of our own adventures, we've destroyed lots of our own enemies. I figure we'll give someone else a chance to take their revenge. I'll be surprised if Galarus makes it through the night alive."

Indeed, Aelwen's theory proved correct. Night had barely settled in, she was sitting in a room in Orodel with Lysia and Iowan. They had started out discussing foreign policy and since that day, like every other day, had been devoted to politics, they'd decided they deserved a bit of leisure time and had started up a card game. Iowan and Aelwen were both losing sorely to Lysia when a servant arrived, bearing news. A body had been found in a river with multiple stab wounds and their throat slit. A large male with scars indicating a past life of combat, but no scars or wounds other than those previously mentioned to indicate his current life frequently brought him in contact with violence. A bit of research had been done and the victim had been identified as a man named Galarus who, according to all who had been canvassed, worked in the heart of the capital city.

The servant finished by saying, "Would you like investigative forces deployed to get to the bottom of this, sire?"

Iowan and Aelwen traded smirks and knowing glances. Lysia clearly understood as well, though her satisfaction was nowhere deep as the other two.

"No," Aelwen said. "Don't bother. We need to focus on reconstruction, not petty murders."

The servant seemed taken aback by the order but did not voice their disapproval. "Yes, sire," they said, leaving the room swiftly as they had come.

Aelwen scrutinized her hand of cards and laid one down. "I told you."

Iowan grinned broadly. "You did."

~~~

Corova had been reclaimed, the war won by the Vatre-darah and Rhea killed. That was what Taran was able to glean from gossip in the taverns of Corova. Aelwen was the name of the person who had taken up the mantle as temporary ruler until the country was stable enough to hold its own. That fact did bring a smile to Taran's face, though each day he listened keenly for a second name. He never heard it. No one ever mentioned Lysia, so he had no way of knowing whether she was alive or dead. They may have officially parted ways, but a part of Taran remained attached to her.

Taran kept his hood up and his ears open on the rare occasions when he did venture into the city for provisions. The city may have been making its way toward betterment, but there were still plenty of pickpockets and cutthroats lurking about. It was best for him to keep his head covered and his words brisk. The trips were his way of gaining news and things he needed.

Living alone with Lysia, it had been sufficient to craft what they needed from nature. With Eoren, things were different. He didn't want her to have passable items carved out of wood and stone, he wanted her to have real belongings.

Taran pulled his hood down, letting his fiery hair hang freely about his shoulders. He was deep enough into the woods that his skin did not crawl the way it did in the city. The snow was all but gone, the forest held the fresh scent of spring, trees bore bright green buds and the streams babbled cheerfully. Taran crossed one such stream, made his way up a little hill and found himself at the homely cottage.
~~~

Eoren was in the yard reading a book. A rush of relief overcame him at the sight of her, whole and well. He didn't like leaving her alone. Everytime he took one of his journeys to the city, dread gnawed at him that something would happen to Eoren in his absence. Everytime he came home, she was there, perfectly fine. He refused to bring her to the city with him. He knew what that place did to children. He would not allow her anywhere near it. In the future, if everything was made better as the word of'th beggar on the street claimed it would be, then perhaps he would leave behind this cottage in the woods once and for all to live in the heart of a healthy city with Eoren, where she could grow up experiencing culture and be educated and have friends her age. Until then, deep in the forests was where they stayed.

At the sight of him, Eoren's round face lit up. She sprang to her feet with an ease Taran had doubted he'd ever see her possess, racing to him on her wooden leg as if it were all she'd ever known.

"What'd you get me today?" she asked inquisitively, peering at the bag Taran had slung over his shoulder.

He unslung the bag and tossed it to Eoren, who made quick work of dumping the contents on the ground. She sorted through them one by one. A brown leather bridle, a matching halter and two bristle brushes. The child looked up at the man, mouth open, brimming with joy. She raced to Taran and flung her arms around his waist, holding tight.

"Thank you! Thank you! Thank you!"

Taran chuckled. "Want to go see how they fit?"

"Yes!" cried Eoren, scooping up the halter and brush and hurrying around to the back of the house. Taran picked up the bridle and followed her.

At the backside of the house, a new extension greeted them. Taran had finished it two weeks ago and the sight of it still filled him with pride. He had not constructed something of such a scale in sometime and was glad to find he still possesed the skill.

A peaked roof extended from the main roof. The steep sides of the roof came down to form two linear sides, the back side doubled as the outer wall of the cottage and the front was a door on a hinge the height of Taran's waist. It was all made of wood, which was the most abundant building material in the area. Cut near perfectly, smoothed and put together to form a single stable stall.

Taran swung open the door. A bay mare with kind eyes awaited them. StarQueen was the name Eoren had given the horse. Outside the taverns Taran visited for news of the world, a single stablehand was employed to watch and care for the mounts of those who visited the tavern. One such stablehand had had a bit too much to drink and had passed out on the job. Taran had taken advantage of the opportunity to steal the creature. She was a fine specimen, well built and well trained, Whoever she had belonged to would be missing her. Some time had gone by since Taran had stolen something and for his first theft in a long while to be a horse was initially an idea that set his teeth on edge. All hand gone as planned and the sheer glee on Eoren's face when he brought her home a horse swept all residue of doubt and discomfort from his mind.

StarQueen's previous owner must have been one with the skill to ride bareback, for the horse bore no tack when Taran had taken her. Since then, he'd managed to get a saddle, which Eoren rode decently with. Today, he had acquired the bridle and halter to make it easier for Eoren to steer and the brush as a nice little accessory.

Taran fastened the bridle about StarQueen, who kept almost completely still while he worked, narrating the process to Eoren. When he was finished, he led the gentle mare out of her stall and to the front yard where there was the most open space for riding.

Following a quick explanation of how to use the reins, Taran passed them to Eoren. She mounted with no difficulty at all, swinging her false leg over and into the stirrup as if it were of flesh and blood. He stayed close, a hand on StarQueen's flank as Eoren led her in a circle, then in a zigzag pattern. Now and then Taran tossed out tips about using the reins, but overall, Eoren had the situation under control.

Taran stepped back into the shade of the house, watching attentively as the child rode about.

Eoren drew StarQueen to a halt after riding in repetitive circles for half an hour. She looked at Taran with wide, excited eyes. "Can I run her?"

"I—uh—" Taran stuttered. He hadn't entertained the possibility that Eoren would want to run StarQueen so soon. She'd been riding with only the saddle for a bit, she had only just started using the reins but seemed to have the hang of them. StarQueen was a kind creature who had proven as gentle with Eoren as Eoren was with her. Taran didn't think the mare would ever hurt the child, especially not intentionally. The yard wasn't all that big, they wouldn't be able to build up much momentum before they had to stop to turn around. "Sure," said Taran.

Astride StarQueen, Eoren galloped through the clearing. The short run was smooth, steady, safe. Eoren rode back in the other direction. She was a fine rider, there was no doubt about it. Back and forth she rode, again and again, golden hair caught in the breeze, smiling wide. Taran loved seeing her like that. Pure happiness. The weight of flame and death and war gone from her. Only happy. Seeing her in such a state filled him with warmth and golden light. A broad smile spread across his face, an expression he did not hasten to hide with a scowl. His days of brooding in the shadows were done. His future was that bright warmth of Eoren's joy. Through her elation he had found his happiness. No matter what happened, if they stayed in this secluded cottage in the woods until Taran was a wrinkled old man and Eoren was a grown woman or if the city was made safe and they made a life there among the masses, so long as Eoren smiled that smile of pure happiness and that golden warmth filled him, Taran knew all would be well.

<p style="text-align:center">~~~~</p>

"The West Road?" asked Iowan. She stood on one side of a glass table, examining a map of the major roads of Corova. She glanced out the window. From up here, in the north wing of Orodel, everything looked small.

"No, I think the east," replied Aelwen. She nodded to a desk against the far wall. "The crew reports say the bridge on the east road is broken, so I think that should be repaired before we start work on the west."

"Okay." Iowan slung a brown leather bag over her shoulder. It was the same sort all of the workers wore—not too bulky and able to hold a good amount of tools. She adjusted

389

the collar of her drab brown shirt, made of the same uncomfortable material as her pants. Not her favorite thing she'd ever worn, but practical for the outdoor work she was doing.

Lysia popped her head in. "Ready to go?" Like Iowan, she wore a workers bag as well as roughspun clothing, commonly donned by the construction workers. Her hair was tied back, but that one rebel lock lay strewn across her forehead.

"You go on ahead," said Aelwen. "I'll meet you there."

Iowan and Lysia nodded and dashed off. Aelwen didn't miss the affectionate glance they shared before they left, or the way their hands brushed as they jogged away. She still wasn't used to their gestures of love, small or large.

Aelwen began sorting through a stack of papers. Old government records, most of which were useless to her. While she did, her mind strayed once more to her best friend in the arms of Lysia. Every time she saw them holding hands, kissing, leaning on one another, something deep inside her ached. It wasn't that she had a problem with Iowan and Lysia being together, it wasn't that she wished Iowan had chosen her instead of Lysia. It was… something else. A jealousy of sorts, but not a thwarted lover's rage. It was gentler than that. Softer. Not an anger, but a fact that was hard to swallow.

She straightened one of the piles of paper. Her fingers froze at the sound of approaching footsteps. All of the crews were out working on repairs. All of the government officials from Marchia who didn't want to get their hands dirty with construction work were in their respective offices on the other side of the palace.

Knuckles rapped against the doorframe.

"Come in," Aelwen said, hand instinctively drifting to the blade concealed at her waist.

Lin entered. He wore glistening plum robes, not unlike those worn by the president's council of Marchia. "Aelwen, hello. Sorry if I'm intruding, I thought you'd gone to help with the construction. I just need to grab the Rilkben records, then I'll be on my way."

"You can work in here if you want. I'm just sorting these, then I'm heading out."

"Thank you." He crossed the room and ran his fingers over bound volumes of historical data. "I saw Lysia and Iowan on their way out. Don't they have a wedding they should be planning instead of crawling in the dirt to fix old roads?"

Aelwen chuckled. "They're going to hold off until everything's fixed up a bit more."

"They could just do it in Marchia."

"They're not in a hurry. Besides, they want to be married in Corova. Symbolism."

Lin pulled a volume off the shelf and began thumbing through it. "I see. Do they know where they're going to live?"

"I'm not sure." Aelwen slid one of the piles of paper into a drawer in the desk. "They haven't said much about it."

"Ah. And you?" He put the volume back and took out another.

"Me?"

"Where are you going to live?"

She put away the other stack of papers. "I'm working on plans for a place a few blocks away. I won't bother having it built until everything else is repaired."

"You could just stay in Orodel, you know? No one would deny your right to rule."

"I know that. But no. I don't want to rule."

"You're ruling right now."

"This is different. Temporary. Once everything's alright, I'll move out and a real ruler will live in here."

Lin shelved the records he held and withdrew a thicker one. "Then what?"

"Then I'll live in a house and have a normal life. No more training or battles or planning, just me in a house, being a civilian."

"That doesn't seem like your style."

"It wasn't for a long time. But it is now."

He offered no response. After flipping through a few pages of the volume he held, he tucked it under his arm. "I read over your draft for the Paruman assimilation process. It's very thorough. I think it will work quite well."

"I hope so." Aelwen removed a strap of leather tied around her wrist and tied her hair back. There wasn't much to work with, but just enough to hang in her face and be a nuisance.

"Uh, speaking of Parumans, how is your magic? When we got here, you said you couldn't feel it and since then you haven't—"

"I can feel it now. I've been able to for a few days. I haven't tried to use it. I don't feel ready. To be honest, I don't know if I ever will. I suppose it doesn't matter. What use do I have for magic now that the war's over?"

Lin didn't bother answering. "And, uh, your dragon? Zarah, was it? I haven't seen her at all."

"Zarah and I have parted ways. It's not time for dragons to live in the world of men, we both understood that. She has her people to lead and I have mine." Aelwen removed her embroidered scarlet jacket.

"Will you see her again?"

"I don't know." She sat on the glass table and peeled off her polished black shoes. "Maybe."

Lin crossed the room. Before the doorway, he paused. "Do you know why President Fayette sent me to help you?"

"She told me why. You—"

"No. That was further justification, but not the reason."

Without looking at Lin, Aelwen retrieved a pair of worn brown boots from beneath the desk, took a seat and began putting them on. "Are you going to tell me why?"

He turned to face her, though she did not look at him. "I volunteered. I told Fayette that if you needed any kind of help, I wanted to be a part of it."

"Why? You hated me."

"I never hated you. Just… strongly disliked you." His shoulders sagged. "I volunteered because I know how much Tecsequaih cared about you. He really wanted you to succeed, Aelwen. A lot."

Aelwen lifted her head from lacing her boots. His eyes were not those of a liar.

Lin continued. His words were a tumble of rocks let loose from a cliff. "It wasn't until after Tecsequaih died that I realized how much he meant to me. Our relationship was never a steady one, and I don't know if it's right to say that I loved him, but for all that I cursed him and argued with him, in a way, he was the one who took the place of the father I lost, and I knew that, on some level, that's what my father would have wanted."

He paused for breath. "I felt so…so guilty after Tecsequaih died. So, to make it up to him, if he really is up there somewhere, watching me, I decided I would pledge my life to your service to help you become the person you want to be. That he wanted you to be."

Lin strode to Aelwen and fell to his knees. "I pledge my life to you. All I am capable of, I dedicate to you. I will serve, protect, create, whatever you demand, I shall carry out in your name."

Aelwen froze. Of all the things she'd been expecting, this had not been one of them. She stood up. In her dusty boots and common garb, she did not feel like the magnificent warrior or the marvelous ruler or the valiant rebel. Yet there was a man in shining purple robes grovelling at her feet.

She cleared her throat. "Stand up."

Lin obeyed.

"I reject your offer. I do not want your fealty, Lin Akachi. Especially not when you are promising it to me to make yourself feel better. You will not heal your wounds this way. Go out into the world, make a life for yourself, one you are proud of. Then your wounds will be healed and you will know happiness."

At first, Lin's expression was one of shock, but as she spoke, her words seemed to strike a chord within him and he softened.

Lin inclined his head. "I believe what you say is true. Thank you, Aelwen." He turned to go.

He stood upon the threshold to the room.

"Lin," Aelwen sucked in a breath. *Tell him.* A too-long moment passed. Her mind whirled with possibilities. Did she dare tell him?

"Yes?"

Did she dare tell him what she'd stolen from his office all that time ago? In the end, though she had slain countless enemies and befriended the queen of the dragons, she was not strong enough to put this one truth into words.

"Thank you," said Aelwen.

A smile flashed across Lin's face. He reached out with his hand that did not clutch the volume. Aelwen accepted it and they shook.

"You did not accept my offer, but that does not mean that none have sworn themselves to you. There are many who revere you. Make them proud."

With that, Lin left.

Aelwen left her embroidered jacket and fancy shoes in the room, she would retrieve them later. Dressed like a common working man, she made her way to the front doors of Orodel and stepped outside. The air was warming with the oncoming spring.

On her way to the east road where she would work beside builders much more skilled than herself to repair that broken bridge, people shouted her name as she passed them. They clapped and hollered praise and reached for her. She smiled at them and kept on moving until she reached the worksite. There, she picked up a pickaxe and went to work.

The sky turned a deep purple. Lysia and Iowan had departed a while ago. Only Aelwen and a few other workers remained. It was too dark to work anymore. They packed up their satchels and tools and bid each other goodnight.

Covered in dirt and grime and sweat and even a bit of blood where she had nicked herself on a sharp rock, Aelwen made her way back to Orodel. Just as when she had made the trip earlier that morning, people called her name. They leaned out of their windows, arms outstretched to her. They gathered in their doorways to watch her go by and whooped when she did.

This time, she did not smile at them. Her body ached from the day's toil, and her soft bed seemed too far away. A scowl adorned her filthy face as she walked with hunched shoulders, a posture to fit her mood.

Still, the people sang her praises all around her, though everyday she was getting better at drowning them out.

She was not a person anymore. Not in the eyes of the masses. A person was judged based on their clothing, on their demeanor. She was judged on the stories told of her, of her great deeds marked down in history books. She was not a person anymore. She was a legend.

Two Years Later

The sun shone bright up in the clear blue sky. Winter was long gone, replaced by the sweet warmth of spring. The force of nature was at Aelwen's fingertips once again, easily accessible and full of power. Her use of magic had been scant, though it did have its moments of great use. Chief amongst them was the building she walked toward now, on her way home from Orodel for the final time. A large construct of dark gray stone, an homage to Wyldmor. It's thick walls were dotted with windows and turrets jutted out here and there. A vast black door with elaborate gold leaf engravings in the shape of dragons welcomed her. Inside the castle there were a number of fine things—chandeliers, tapestries, paintings and a plentiful amount of potted plants. Mostly ferns, in honor of Arkada, but also orchids, anthuriums and hibiscus as a nod to the three major magical bloodlines that she had worked tirelessly to help welcome back to Corova in spite of the frequent grumblings and occasional riots of the people. The items inside had been purchased or received as gifts, but the structure itself was the product of Aelwen's magic. She'd never constructed a building before, much less one of such scale. The effort had left her tired and weak, but only for a day or so, and the result was well worth the strife. She shared the castle home with Lysia and Iowan, who together had done most of the decorating, being that Aelwen spent most of her time at Orodel, sometimes working so late she slept there rather than bother coming home only to return to Orodel in a few hours.

Aelwen's time as ruler of Corova had been a turbulent one, rife with difficulties and drawbacks and also with praise and joy. In her months as ruler, Aelwen had managed to lead Corova out of the final lap of its days of despair and, through hours of hard labor beside her people and frustrating meetings with the aides sent by President Fayette, to a time of stability, wealth and respect.

Things were far from perfect. The scars of poverty were still healing; there were laws protecting mages and, overall, they lived amongst the nonmages, but vandalism and hate crimes against the magical did happen. Aelwen herself had received threats for being a mage. Luckily, none of them had ever come to fruition. Corova still needed work, but now, it was not Aelwen's work to do. A monarch had been chosen and now it was they who bore the burden of Corova.

Aelwen had never been overly fond of ruling. There had been moments where she downright despised it. She would have been lying if she told anyone she was not glad her term as ruler was ended.

The Marchians who had proved invaluable during her tenure as ruler had all returned to their home country. The crown sat upon a worthy head once more. Aelwen had a home of her own as well as possessions and friends who were like family. She felt safe and happy free from worry in her homeland. A new chapter was beginning and she could hardly wait to start it.

She was reaching to push open the doors and enter her home when she froze at the sound of a resounding roar.

Aelwen turned her gaze upward, marveling at Zarah, Queen of Dragons. She soared high above, her scales their natural iridescent color, shimmering in the midday sun. She swooped through the air in arcs and loops, radiating majesty and grace.

With Zarah being in Paruma, it had been much more difficult for her and Aelwen to successfully communicate, but they had managed it a few times since Aelwen had regained her magic. Each time, Aelwen had told Zarah she wanted to see her and Zarah had always responded cryptically. Now, she had finally decided to make her appearance.

Through the bond they shared, Aelwen asked Zarah to land. She obliged, alighting in front of Aelwen, who threw her arms around the dragon's neck and hugged her close. Feeling surged through their bond, a feeling Aelwen was not familiar with coming from Zarah. She had felt it before, though, in different circumstances. She pulled back from Zarah, searching the dragon queen's face for clarity. After a moment of racking her brain, Aelwen recalled what the feeling was. Finality. Completeness.

"This is it for us, isn't it?" asked Aelwen, rubbing Zarah's snout, forcing away the lump she could feel crawling up her throat.

The dragon gurgled in reply and Aelwen knew it was affirmation.

"We did what we set out to do," Aelwen said, looking to her castle home and the city beyond. Corova, a respectable region once more. "The world is accepting mages, slowly but surely. I'm not sure they're ready for dragons, though." She breathed a laugh despite there being nothing funny about the situation. Dragons lived separate from humans because humans were cruel and careless. If they weren't, Zarah wouldn't have to leave. They could go on living together, flying over the world, reveling in their success. But that was not the way the world worked. Aelwen and Zarah had come together to vanquish the evil of the Hakmarres. Rhea had gained her mount by capturing and enslaving it, but Zarah had chosen to forge a bond with Aelwen. While they had been products of the relationship, the purpose of the bond itself had never been love or trust, it had been for Aelwen and Zarah to work together to defeat a common enemy. That goal had been accomplished.

Aelwen wondered why Zarah had waited until now to bid farewell to her. Did the dragon know today was Aelwen's last day as ruler of Orodel? Was that why she'd chosen today? Had she prolonged saying goodbye because she didn't want to anymore than Aelwen did, but recognized that it was time for both of them to move on? Aelwen sent her questions to Zarah through their bond, but the dragon queen did not answer. The reason didn't matter, Aelwen supposed. Zarah was here now, to say goodbye.

The lump in Aelwen's throat has grown. She didn't trust herself to say anything without her voice breaking, so she sent all of her praise and joy to Zarah through their bond, hoping they were enough for Zarah to understand how much she meant to her.

Aelwen was physically jolted as a rush of power came to her through the bond. She seized Zarah for balance, wondering what on earth the dragon had just done. They'd shared this bond for quite a while and she'd never felt anything like that before. The sensation was too much for Aelwen to decipher, so she stopped trying and let it sink into her naturally. It was almost identical to what she had sent to Zarah, just on a much larger, dragon-sized scale. From Zarah came waves of thanks and mountains of praise, claims of her love for Aelwen and how she would always cherish their time together. Processing it all, Aelwen met the dragon queen's eyes, her own flooding with tears. She hugged Zarah one last time, internalizing the press of Zarah's snout against her shoulder and the cool sleekness of her beautiful pearlescent scales.

They split apart, Zarah's eyes clouded with sadness, Aelwen trembling with sobs and drenched in tears. The Queen of Dragons blinked several times, the sorrow wiped from her gaze. She squared her shoulders and raised her head, the sun glinting off her antlers. Their bond not severed, Aelwen knew that Zarah wanted Aelwen's last memory of her to be a good one, of Zarah in all her proud, queenly magnificence. Aelwen took in every bit of the image before her, full of its spectacle and splendor, and stored it in her heart and mind so she might never forget.

Zarah nodded once. She tucked in her four great wings and took off. She did not spare so much as a glance back at Aelwen. Aelwen stood there, her tears drying, watching Zarah, Queen of Dragons, fly away for the last time, a gorgeous creature of resplendent glory. When the dragon was gone from sight, Aelwen turned to go inside. Her bond with Zarah was not severed, but dulled. If she tried, she could feel Zarah's presence far away at the other end of the bond, but to do so took effort and she could not sense the dragon's exact thoughts of precise emotions, only shadows of what she felt.

Aelwen let out a breath. She was glad that her tie to Zarah had not been clean cut as she'd feared, ending her tether to her forever. This dulled bond seemed much more appropriate. Each would continue on their path in life separate from the other, woman and dragon, yet no matter what they went on to face, they would always be a part of each others' stories, defining moments in their critical chapters.

Aelwen drew her sleeve across her face, clearing away any remnants of her tears, and entered the home she shared with her two greatest friends.

CHAPTER TWENTY NINE

White petals drifted through the air. The aisle was dusted with them.
Two women stood at the head of the aisle, upon a dais, their hands clasped as they made lifelong promises to one another. One blonde, one raven-haired. One who had forged a deep friendship only to be left behind. One who had made a home for herself in the wild rather than face the atrocities of civilian life.

A petal landed in Iowan's hair. Lysia brushed it away.

They slid golden bands onto each other's fingers and kissed, relishing the sweetness of their love.

The crowd erupted, clapping and cheering.

In the front row, nearly at the feet of her two friends, was Aelwen.

She had shirked her everyday attire for a blue gown that brushed the floor. It had been tailored specifically for her, as the elegant dresses the brides wore had been. She had helped both of them choose their dresses, this location, which decorations to use and which foods to serve. She sat the closest to them because she *was* the closest to them. She was the only maid of honor at this wedding. The only one they held in such high regard in their hearts.

Aelwen was taken aback when she felt tears pricking at her eyes. Tears of joy? Tears of regret? Tears of relief? She did not know. But she let them fall. She was done refusing to feel.

The wedding party moved to a different space, a ballroom. The guests formed a circle around the brides. The band struck up a tune. Lysia and Iowan began to dance. The song quickened. More people started to dance. Aelwen joined in. Iowan and Lysia were at the head of the room, separate from all of their guests, including their maid of honor.

It was strange. To have fun but not with the two people she loved the most. To occupy a room with them but not to *be* with them. Her heart ached a bit. The frame of the door that led out of the ballroom seemed to hold a new appeal.

I could leave now. I doubt they'd notice. I could leave and stop feeling these feelings.

Aelwen took a step towards the exit. Then a step back away from it. Why leave? Leaving wouldn't make the feelings leave, no matter how much she wanted them to. *The feelings might be with me forever. I might never understand.* Leaving wouldn't stop them.

She would stay. She would stay and dance and smile and laugh. This wedding was not the end of her relationship with her best friends. This marriage did not destroy the love between the three of them. Undoubtedly, it changed it into something new that she did not understand. But she would not let that stop her. She would continue to love. To be happy. With or without them, she would continue to find her way in the world.

The celebration lasted long into the night. By the time it was over, Aelwen's feet ached from dancing and her mind was foggy. For the first time, she took a carriage that she did not share with Iowan and Lysia.

The ride home was quiet. The snow had long melted, and the stone Corovan streets that had been filthy for so long were scrubbed clean and laid evenly. Even though it was dark, neat little displays were visible in shop windows—windows that were whole and clear. The streets were lit by lamps that seemed to burn brighter than they had the night she'd fled from the arena. A couple walked down the street, leaning on one another, smiling. They were not glancing around in fear or brandishing crooked knives. They were just living.

The carriage rolled to a smooth halt at the entry to Aelwen's home. Aelwen's home. Just hers now. Only hers. It was a rather large place made of stormcloud stone. Some might even call it a small castle with its many windows and turrets.

Aelwen tipped the driver and stepped out of the carriage. She sighed and pressed her hand to the ornate black door. Her fingers caressed one of the many golden dragon shapes that adorned the door.

For the first time, she was entering this home that she did not share with Iowan and Lysia.

She opened the door. The grand front hall, with its geometric carpet and two overflowing potted plants, welcomed her. The home did not feel too vast. It did not feel lonely. It felt…right.

A thin stack of letters sat on the desk in the welcome room, each of them emblazoned with a blue anchor. The symbol the crew of *Mist Wing* had adopted as their own. Each of the letters was from Gavnas, most of them were short, but there were a few exceptions. The first had arrived nine months ago and since then others had come at irregular intervals.

Out on the wild seas, Gavnas had steadily increased his own prestige since he'd last seen Aelwen. In the letters, he said he'd received word of the Vatre-darah victory and of Aelwen's mostly successful efforts to restore Corova and make her country one that was safe for everyone, mages and non-mages alike. He informed her that he had visited three continents and twelve countries and in each one had met people who had become a part of his crew because they shared his belief that if a perfect world was out there, they would find it and if not, they would die trying. The increase of his crew made it necessary for Gavnas to acquire more boats, for there wasn't enough space on *Mist Wing*. The captain had a small fleet under his charge, the ships were all different styles since few of them came from the same lands. To mark the assortment of vessels as a single force, the sails of each were adorned with a navy blue anchor, hence the symbol on each of the envelopes and the words that, according to Gavnas, were 'the names we hear whispered on the shores that we walk, the title the people have given my mismatched fleet—Anchors of Hope. A pretentious name in my opinion, but what can I do? I have no say in the will of the people'.

Aelwen smiled at the letters. Gavnas was a changed man, there was no denying that. But from his letters, she had been able to discern that he was not as crazy as she'd thought that day in the Great Library of Arkada. She and Gavnas were two different people, alike in many ways yet different in many others. They were both determined to achieve goals of their own and had gone their separate ways to do that. But that didn't mean severing the bond between them, the letters proved that.

Aelwen had not seen Gavnas in person for years, but his statuesque image, his commanding tone and the way he looked so right when he was out on the sea, remained firmly in her mind. Sometimes she wondered if he recalled her the same way, or if her facade had faded to a blurred memory in his mind. Though it was not the recollection of appearances that mattered—it was the fact that after so much had happened and they were worlds apart, by ink and quill, their words still found each other.

She drew her gaze away from the letters and made her way up the marble staircase and into her bedroom to change into something more comfortable.

The room was rather lavish and decorated with more fancy baubles than she'd ever owned before. The same could be said for the house in its entirety. Tapestries hung on the walls and on her nightstand alone were several figurines, a small jade mirror and a painted vase that held sweet-smelling cerulean flowers. Her bed was vast and soft, laying in it was like settling into a pool of clouds. Her big down-stuffed pillows were navy embroidered with gold and over the four posts of her bed was draped a swath of teal fabric.

Nothing felt strange here, which was precisely why she felt strange.

This home felt like hers. It felt…right.

Sitting on her canopy bed, Aelwen plucked a little figurine of gold in the shape of a dragon from her nightstand. It didn't resemble Zarah very much, but she kept it nonetheless. A Corovan goldsmith had given it to her as a thank you gift for all she'd done. In fact, most of what she owned she had acquired as gifts. The tapestry of snow covered mountains hanging on the back of her door had been crafted by a Corovan man, the vase on her nightstand was handmade by a Corovan artist, and a little boy had handed her the flowers that occupied it.

Aelwen turned the figurine over in her hand and set it back in its place. She made her way to one of the many windows. From here, she could see the heart of the capital city. In the day, the streets were packed with people. Now, in the quiet deep of night, there were few people to see out and about. There were no market stalls set up or shops with their lights on. None of those absences detracted from the glorious life of Corova. Even in this dark hour, when the streetlights were dim and all was silent, the greatness of Corova remained.

Through the arms of the darkness and the clouds above, the stars were visible. Stars. In their multitudes. Far above it all. The stars remained, cold and bright. A symbol of everlasting peace. A goal she had spent years of her life chasing. A goal she had finally reached.

In the center of the square that would be packed full of merchants hawking their wares in just a few hours, stood an immense statue. The mages who had chosen to leave Paruma and build lives for themselves in Corova with non mages had constructed the statue with their magic in honor of Aelwen, as a thank you for all she had done for them. Aelwen had been smart enough to realize that although Rhea was evil, not all mages were and that magic did not make one inherently bad.

Like the figure Aelwen had held a moment ago, the statue was of solid gold. Though, this one was a much more accurate depiction of whom it represented. The statue had shoulder-length hair, the same length as Aelwen's had been when she'd returned from her training as a mage. It had a sharp jawline and an intense gaze. It was a statue of a woman with a sword in each hand who wore intricate armor and a cape that flowed dramatically from her shoulders. Her chin was tilted to a haughty angle and her mouth was a thin, serious line.

All her life, Aelwen had never been one to spend time gawking over her appearance or waste hours in front of a mirror. But since that statue of her had been completed, it had become rather difficult to avoid staring out her window to see that massive version of herself, as the people saw her—glorious, great, victorious. A hero.

Years passed. The sun rose in its fiery glory hundreds of times, then burned its brightest as it sank to the horizon, making room in the sky for the marvelous silver disc that followed its descent. Trees quivered in the winds that shook the leaves from their branches before the winds calmed. The rain thawed and the time of regrowth began. Rivers halted in their churning tracks as bitter cold commandeered them. Shadows grew long and short throughout the days that passed in unity, times none the same knit together by threads of gold and silver.

Long-reigning empires were forced to choose: join or fall. Others who had fought for their place in the world held onto it with powerful grasps using hands of acceptance. One had mounted a single stair years ago and now was nearing its zenith. Old powers that had come to be despised were gradually making their return. Every step counted for something.

Where ramshackle messes had stood for decades, structures of sturdy wood and stone had risen in their place. Palaces had surged up in masterful magnificence, markets had revived along broad cobblestone streets that had taken effort and the skill to restore.

In this time, one object showed the world that this country, as insignificant in the affairs of others for decades as a speck of dirt, had returned to its former state of power. The country's greatest accomplishment, a five story statue of pure, solid gold that rivaled the sun in terms of splendor, was erected in the center of the capital city, displaying to all who raised their heads for miles the one person who was responsible for this condition they lived in, old and new at the same time. An age of prosperity once again for the people who had weathered storms beyond imagining, who had come out on the other side of the tumult of despair to see the blazing luminescence of a new era.

Two castles stood in the plentiful terrain of Corova. A massive palace of marble with polished iron gates and grand black doors. A second, much smaller, for it had only one inhabitant. It was a many turreted creation of gray stone with a large door adorned with golden dragons. The inhabitant of this abode was someone who had hardly reached middle age yet lived more of a life than many ever would. Someone who had befriended a monster, and though eternally bound to it by friendship and love, had let it go. Someone who had dove to the depths of her soul to find a power buried there.

She had loved and lost and learned.

There was Aelwen. A survivor of countless battles.

There was her castle. She had earned every bit of stone she sat upon.

She was a queen without subjects. Ruling was not to her liking. However, victory was in her blood.

THE END

ABOUT THE AUTHOR

Autumn Fleming is a high school student and avid fangirl from a small town in Upstate New York who loves all things fantasy and musical theatre. She began channeling her passion for writing into *Virago* when she was just twelve years old, finishing the first draft at fifteen, dead set on making a name for herself in the world of literature and determined to publish before graduating high school. The first of many, she has multiple projects in the works waiting to be shared with the world. Follow her on social media for updates and all things fandom!

Twitter: @Fandoms_Rise
Website: queenofwar42.wixsite/risingfandoms
Instagram: @rising_fandoms
Email: Queenofwar42@gmail.com